His eyes settled on me, a
handsome I found him. The dark, brooding ...
intrigued me more than I cared to admit. I was
forgetting myself.

He shrugged. "I feel it my moral duty to look out
for you. You are naïve about the way of life here. It is
far different than anything you've experienced. This
country changes people. Most of us are not who others
think we are. Herr Schmitt is no exception."

"If that's true, then who are you, Nick?"

His gaze still held mine, and the atmosphere
between us suddenly felt charged with tension. His
expression softened momentarily, and his eyes were
silver in the gaslight. I could almost hear him think as
his countenance underwent a myriad of subtle changes.
Was he choosing how honest he was prepared to be
with me? Could he remove that solid barrier forcing
people away?

Then the mask slipped back into place, and the
moment was gone.

The Secret of Jacaranda

by

Jude Bayton

The Secret of Jacaranda

Contact Information: author@judebayton.com

Cover Art by *Diana Carlile*

Print ISBN 978-1-955441-09-4
Digital ISBN 978-1-955441-10-0

Published by redbus llc

Dedication

To my beloved parents, Dennis and Barbara Bayton. I wish you were both still here to see me achieve my dream of becoming an author.
You gave me an extraordinary childhood, filled with sights of stunning pink flamingoes on
Lake Naivasha, charging elephants, and herds of wildebeest, antelope and zebra on the plains
of Africa. As parents, you instilled in me, by your example, a love of my planet, the animal kingdom, and my fellow man—no matter their origin.
The impressions from my childhood have remained constant in my thoughts, all because of you two. One day, I hope I can become as honourable, and as notable as you both.
Nakupenda, Dad and Mutti

Acknowledgements

To my in-laws – Rachel FitzSimons, Steve & Holly Kreidler, Gerald & Kay Janssen, Mark & Colleen Kreidler, John & Annette Rosell and Bob & Sonya FitzSimons—thank you for your continued support and encouragement on my writing journey. It means so much to me.
To Alicia Dean and Diana Carlile, thank you for all the hard work you do with my books, and the more arduous task of putting up with me.

And, as always, to my dear readers. It is YOU who give me the inspiration to keep my fingers on the keyboard.
Thank you.

Chapter One

Off the coast of Mombasa, East Africa, 1901

SEEING THE BRIGHT SUN ONCE AGAIN was glorious. Having spent the previous day below deck, my stomach roiling as violently as the waves beneath the steamer, I hungrily gulped in the fresh salty air as though starving. I turned my face towards the azure sky where birds wheeled high above the ship—a sign we were close to land.

"Miss Rossington? Ah, there you are at last."

I cringed at the trill female voice. Forcing a smile on my face, I turned to greet Mrs Clitheroe, an aging Scottish widow, who had attached herself to me like a barnacle when she'd embarked at Port Said. A dear lady, but one with the irritating habit of talking incessantly, and an annoying propensity for gossip.

"Good morning, Mrs Clitheroe."

"Are you feeling better, dear?" Her empathetic brown eyes studied my face for signs of illness.

I opened my mouth to answer, but she continued. "I did inform Captain Hayden of your terrible seasickness. 'Twas such a shame you were ill, for you missed a fabulous dinner party last night once the storm abated. Such wonderful food. It's been years since I ate prawns, and the filet of sole was delicious." The lady's enthusiasm to speak of all things edible, along with her generous girth, attested to the woman's enjoyment of frequent and bountiful meals.

I touched her arm, eager to escape. "Mrs Clitheroe, I beg you excuse me. I have forgotten something in my cabin."

"Oh." Her plump face registered disappointment. Then she caught a glimpse of someone over my shoulder. "Mrs Deacon?" she called. "What did you think about last evening's repartee?"

I quickly stepped aside so she might claim her next victim.

I left the women to talk and took myself to the bow of the ship where I looked out across the sea. The Indian Ocean sparkled like a cache of sapphires and emeralds, and far in the distance, I could make out the dark smudge of land.

"Africa." I spoke the name, and its sound rolling off my tongue made my heart beat faster. A few weeks ago, I would never have conceived of my travelling to such a foreign and most exotic continent. But each step of the long journey had made this notion more absolute. From Southampton, to Marseilles, then onto Palma, and finally Egypt, my ultimate destination to Africa still seemed far-reaching. Yet here I was. We would make port by nightfall.

I grasped the deck railing and took another deep breath. Was I prepared for this new chapter of my life? I closed my eyes, willing away the whisper of fear lying under my skin, threatening to run rampant and diminish the courage so recently mustered. My fingers squeezed the handrail tighter. I must be strong. I had to make a success of it here. If not—I was doomed.

THAT NIGHT I SLEPT LIKE the dead. On dry land once again, I'd welcomed the absence of waves shifting beneath me, comfortable in a sparse, yet adequate hotel room.

My new employer, Mr Nicholas Fleming, had reserved it for me. Per his written instruction, he would arrive after breakfast that morning, and expect me to be ready to leave by ten o'clock sharp.

The dining room buzzed with activity. Morning sun blazed into the spacious, high-ceilinged room through open windows, as large as doors. I was shown to a small corner table by a pristine young African, resplendent in starched white livery. His bright smile dazzled against the rich colour of his smooth, dark skin.

"*Memsahib* like pineapple juice?" he asked politely as I took my seat.

"That would be wonderful. Thank you," I said, my mouth watering in anticipation.

He returned shortly bearing a tray laden with a glass of fruit juice, a pot of hot tea, and a basket of tropical fruits. I thanked him once again and ordered my breakfast from the menu.

The Mombasa Hotel was surprisingly modern. I don't know what I'd expected, and in truth, had paid scant attention to the place when I checked in the night before. Then, I cared only for a hot bath and a clean, cool bed—both of which I had found. But refreshed from my rest, now I absorbed my surroundings with avid interest. I most certainly was not in England anymore.

The hotel's décor, colours and textures were cool and light—marble floors, white painted walls, no fabrics or ornaments strewn about, just pots filled with large palms and baskets of blood-red geraniums.

Other guests were enjoying breakfast. They were predominantly European—but different ethnicities too. I noticed a group of turbaned Indian fellows, sitting with two African gentlemen. The latter, resplendent in their bright jackets, a welcome splash of colour against the rest of us who were insipid in our colonial white cotton.

I spotted a somewhat familiar face and recognised an elderly gentleman from the steamship. We nodded at one another in greeting, and he returned his attention to a newspaper strewn open on his table.

It was already warm, and I relished the refreshing moistness of cool melon in my mouth. By the time my main course arrived, an un-African fare of fried eggs and bacon, it seemed rather incongruous being so British in this tropical setting. My presence disturbed the canvas of the culture.

At length, and sated from my meal, I thanked my waiter, leaving a small tip upon the table—uncertain if that was the correct protocol. I returned to my room, gathered my belongings and then waited for the porter to assist me downstairs with my luggage.

A broad canopy covered the wide verandah outside the hotel, where several wooden chairs were placed for guests to comfortably await their transportation. And here I sat, my trunk by my feet, waiting to begin the next chapter of my life.

The street lay but a short distance away and appeared to be a main thoroughfare of the port town, judging by the volume of traffic. Carts passed in both directions, dodging an assortment of pedestrians meandering along the street. My senses soaked in new sounds and unfamiliar scents, and the wonder of it all seemed surreal.

Not two months hence, I had lived in Chessington, Surrey—an unremarkable suburb of London. Sitting here surrounded by Africans, watching oxen-drawn carts pass without a carriage nor a tram in sight, I might as well be on another planet entirely.

Everywhere I looked, I saw red dirt, or *murram* as Mrs Clitheroe referred to it. As each vehicle traversed the driveway to the hotel entrance, dust scattered from their wheels like confetti.

Several carts came and went while I waited patiently. After the first few, I stopped paying attention to the traffic and found my thoughts lost in the hotel's scenic gardens, which were a riot of colour. So when the voice came, it gave me quite a start.

"Miss Rossington?" It was a deep, rich tone.

"Oh," I said, flustered, immediately getting to my feet.

The man before me appeared irritable. He sounded British, but there all similarities to my country ended. The hair underneath his broad-brimmed hat was jet black, wavy and not at all well-groomed. I could not tell if his complexion was dark from exposure to the sun or simply dirty from travel. Black stubble graced his chin, and, above a strong nose, I saw his eyes were a light grey, in stark contrast to the swarthy colour of his skin. I found myself staring. His right brow arched, and I noticed a small gap in his eyebrow where a thin scar interrupted its contour.

"Well—are you Miss Rossington, or not?" He sounded impatient.

"Yes. And you must be—"

"Is this it?" He threw a glance at my battered trunk. At my nod, he picked it up as though it weighed little more than a box of chocolates and carried it to a cart tethered close to the verandah. I followed behind, clutching my small carpetbag to my breast as though it contained the crown jewels.

A massive dog sat on its haunches in the back of the cart, alongside a pallet of what looked like tins and packages of food. The animal looked at me with an expression of disinterest then turned its head away. Mr Fleming set my trunk into the cart. He flashed me a quick glance. "If that is everything, we can get going."

"Yes, it is." I was unsure what to do next.

He paced around the back of the cart and swung himself up into the driver's seat. Then, as an afterthought, turned to look at me with a frown. "Are you coming, Miss Rossington?"

I felt idiotic. I recovered myself and went to the cart. The step was high, and I cursed the restriction of my skirt. I grabbed the seat and endeavoured to pull myself up, but I needed two hands. I placed my bag on the seat and tried again. He did not speak nor offer assistance, but stared directly ahead, across the bony backs of four large oxen.

After another try, I succeeded in my climb, and as soon as my derrière touched the seat next to him, my new employer snapped the reins, and we pulled away.

Mr Fleming navigated the hotel driveway and turned onto the busy street where we joined the flow of vehicles. He remained quiet, so I occupied myself easily. I had seen little of the town, other than the short ride from the port, though I had read some of its history before leaving England.

I knew Mombasa had a mixed heritage, derived from a variety of cultures, among them Arab, Persian, and Portuguese. This was quite evident from the differences in the architecture of the buildings, not to mention the presence of churches in close proximity to mosques.

The Arab influence dominated, likely from the city's relationship with Zanzibar, long an ally with the British. Though Mombasa was considered to be the founding place of the roots of British colonisation, I found that difficult to believe. For the stamp of Europe seemed conspicuously absent.

As Mr Fleming navigated the cart through a maze of roads, I sat entranced by the tapestry of culture—such a contrast to anything I had known in my short life. Everywhere I looked were a sea of dark faces—vivid costumes in vibrant colours. Women carried babies strapped onto their backs and secured with scarves, while balancing clay pots or other items precariously atop their headdresses.

The cart moved slowly through the crowd, who barely allowed us passage. We passed several marketplaces, their stalls bursting with fruits I had never seen before, bolts of bright cloth, even caged, colourful birds. My senses were overloaded with sight, smells, and sounds. My head fairly spun.

Eventually we reached the outskirts of town, and we approached a small dock where the road trailed down to the water and a wooden ramp. Though it had a significant international port, Mombasa itself was situated on a small island. We would need to cross a short distance of water to access the mainland.

Although subject to seasickness, I had it from Mrs

Clitheroe—my apparent resource for all things African—that this crossing lasted but a few minutes on the boat. I hoped this to be accurate, for when Mr Fleming drove the cart onto the rickety, wooden ferry I eyed the vessel dubiously, finding it appeared a better candidate for firewood than transportation. He must have seen my look of consternation, for he finally spoke to me with the assurance that the boat was sound.

There were no other carts for the crossing, though there was room for at least one other. It appeared the majority of the ferry's business came from pedestrians, and several accompanied us now. I chose to stay seated in the cart for the duration of our brief voyage while Mr Fleming conversed in fluent Swahili with the ferryman.

Mrs Clitheroe was correct in her information. Within fifteen minutes, we were driving on the mainland heading west. I much preferred the feel of solid ground under the cart's wheels.

While my companion had little to say, I busied my mind looking out across the sea as the dirt road we traversed ran parallel to the coastline. In the blue distance, sailed dhows bobbing in the shimmering water as fisherman threw their nets down into the depths. The sun grew fierce, and I was glad of my straw bonnet which protected me from the dazzling light.

After some time, we turned inland, leaving the turquoise Indian Ocean behind us and Mr Fleming finally spoke. He said we would travel at least another hour before reaching his farm. He explained that oxen were far slower than horses, but reliable and better able to tolerate the heat.

My eyes were used to pastoral views of England—tapestries of green fields divided by hedgerows and rock walls. In stark contrast, here, the vast land stretched before me as far as my eye could see. Out on the horizon, I could make out the silhouettes of tiny shadows moving in the distance.

I pointed in that direction. "Mr Fleming, Is that a herd of something over there?"

"Yes," he answered. "Wildebeest. They are at least a good mile away. But their numbers are so great we can see them en masse."

I contemplated his words.

A moment passed, and he spoke again. "I trust your accommodation at the hotel was satisfactory?"

"Yes, thank you," I replied without looking his way. Though I thought it a strange question now we were already gone from Mombasa.

"Good." He paused, and I realised he was trying to initiate conversation. "Look, Miss Rossington, I suppose this is as good a time as any to discuss your duties. I take it you read the letters from the agency?"

"Yes." When I answered the advertisement in *The Times*, I had eventually been required to attend an interview with a very formidable matron by the name of Mrs Turnbull, who acted on behalf of Mr Fleming. Once she offered me the position, I'd received several pages of correspondence with the job description, and minimal information regarding the location.

I sensed his eyes on me and turned to meet his scrutiny. Nicholas Fleming was undoubtedly a very handsome man. His bearing defined masculinity, from the strong jaw to his straight Roman nose. The scar interrupting the flow of his right eyebrow disrupted his features and gave him a dangerous edge. I realised I was staring and quickly averted my gaze.

"If you have any questions, Miss Rossington, now would be a good time to ask."

"As far as my duties are concerned your letters were well explained. I am sure I will have things to ask you once we arrive at your home and I meet Nalah. For now, I am more curious about other matters." I glanced at him. He wore a frown, but there was a softness about his mouth. "I should like to know more about your farm. Not much was mentioned in the paperwork, and knowing so little of Africa, it would be interesting to understand what it is you do here?"

He nodded. "The farm—Jacaranda, has been in my family for thirty-seven years. My father brought my mother here from his home in Cornwall. We grow sugar cane, along with other rotated crops, and raise cattle and goats. Next year I will plant tea for the first time."

"Well, it sounds far more exotic than growing potatoes and cabbage. I know little of agriculture, but I would assume you need many workers for such a venture?"

His eyes found mine and held, as though assessing me. Did he think my questions impertinent? They were not. I was genuinely interested. The moment passed, and his gaze swung back to the road.

"Your assumption is correct. I employ a great many people. Thirty-two Kikuyu, and from time to time a handful of Maasai tribesmen—along with my farm manager, Derek Walker—he's from Lincolnshire. Then there are the house staff, Wilson is my cook, Malaika takes care of running the house, Juba is my houseboy and there are others too. You shall meet them all once we arrive."

"How often do you travel into Mombasa?" I knew

it to be the nearest town.

"At least once a week. Usually I send one of the boys to pick up supplies and any post—things of that nature. But for social visits, it is far quicker to ride on horseback. These blasted oxen are the best transport, but they are bloody slow."

"Are there other children besides Nalah?" I had no details about my charge, other than she was a baby, close to four months old now.

"Thank God, no. Nalah is the only one." He glanced at me. "Nalah is not my child, Miss Rossington. She is my niece."

"Oh." That had not been mentioned.

"Her mother died in childbirth, and her father, my brother Martin, was killed in a hunting accident not a week later. The baby has been cared for by one of the local women who has several children and was Nalah's wet nurse, but I want my niece to have an English nanny—at least for her formative years."

"But I thought it customary to have native women care for European children in the colonies? I have friends who grew up in India—all of them had 'ayah's'."

His tone changed. "This is not India, Miss Rossington. Any illusions you may have should be dispensed with at once. There is nothing romantic about this continent."

"I did not mean to imply—"

"Africa is a wild, hungry land. One that devours the weak and tests the strong. As far as its people are concerned, the alliance between the British and the natives is still in its infancy. There is no loyalty here. The symbiotic relationship between me and my workers is based completely upon their getting paid. They would abandon me in a moment otherwise. Therefore, I require someone of my own culture to care for a member of my family. And that is all there is to it, Miss Rossington."

Unsure what to say to that I fell silent and reflected upon his words. Mr Fleming was assuredly a stern individual. His manner was gruff and his conversation stilted. Had I been a more sensitive type, I should have found his demeanour intimidating and worrisome. Fortunately, I was not of that ilk. I had encountered people far worse than this man.

"I look forward to meeting my charge. She bears an unusual name. Is it Swahili?"

"Yes," he sighed. "Her name means 'furious as a lioness'. My brother chose it because he thought she would have to be strong, growing up without her mother."

I was moved. "No doubt. I think it beautiful. She will be the only young English girl with that name."

He chuckled, and I was so surprised by this I turned my head to look at his face. He stared back into mine, and though his lips curved in a smile, his eyes were hard.

"I do not think you understand, Miss Rossington," he said harshly. "Nalah's mother was Maasai."

Chapter Two

"I BEG YOUR PARDON?"

The smile became more sardonic. "My niece is half African. There—you have the truth. Are you shocked?"

That was an understatement. "Yes, of course I am. It was not mentioned to me in the interview."

"No. The agency was never told. I made that decision based upon my inability to find anyone here. The British are quick enough to take what they want from their colonies, but God forbid anyone actually mates with a native." His tone was harsh, and I did not like it.

"Spare me your opinion," I remonstrated as bravely as I could. "I am shocked because of the omission, not the child's heritage."

That stopped him. His face showed incredulity. "I am amazed, Miss Rossington. A prim and proper young Englishwoman would normally be aghast and need her smelling salts at news such as this. A position as nanny to a wild charge should be terrifying. Will you not demand I take you back to Mombasa, post haste?"

"Do not mock me, Mr Fleming, for you don't know me at all. I maintain the right to be annoyed at your omission of Nalah's parentage. Not because I would think less of the child, an innocent, but rather because I should be aware of any obstacles I might have to

13

surmount based upon that parentage." He made to speak, but this time I was the stronger. "I do not know the custom here, but I know it well at home. Any child of mixed race is undeservedly blamed for their parents' union. It is a misplaced dislike, based upon the individual's inadequacies, not the child's. Yet it exists, and your niece will have a time of it with the European community. But what of her mother's people? What is their custom to a child of mixed blood?"

His expression became solemn, almost sad. "They will have nothing to do with the baby. Her mother's family are gone. They are a nomadic tribe with no interest in Nalah. The Kikuyu also do not want her. She is not of their tribe and tainted by white blood."

"I see." I did, though I would never understand how human beings could be so cold. "I take it you were unable to secure a nanny within the British community?"

He gave a wry laugh, "What do you think?"

I mulled over the situation. I harnessed no contention for the orphaned baby without control of its parentage. But I was annoyed to find myself 'tricked' into coming. Yet I had wanted nothing more than to be gone from England, and Africa offered a location far enough away from my homeland that I'd feel safe for the first time in a long while. This thought cooled my indignation.

I considered my options. "Though I disapprove of your method, Mr Fleming, my concern is for your niece. I shall honour our agreement, but I ask you not withhold any other information from me in the future. I would prefer an honest relationship with you. It's the best foot forward."

He nodded, and for the first time, he gave me a legitimate smile. The contours of his face softened, and his grey eyes flashed silver. He held out one gloved hand and took mine in a firm handshake. "It is a deal, Miss Rossington. I believe we shall get along very well indeed."

THERE FOLLOWED MUCH CONVERSATION about other subjects. I kept my eyes peeled for sightings of wildlife, but apart from seeing an occasional vulture, I was disappointed. Mr Fleming told me of his neighbours as we passed certain landmarks. Once we reached the outskirts of Jacaranda, he pointed out items of interest. Finally, he turned the cart away from the road and, as the brush parted into a clearing, I gasped. The wildness of the land suddenly fell away, and before my eyes I saw what looked like heaven.

On either side of the long dirt driveway, rows of trees stood sentry one beside another. Yet I had never seen their like before. Every branch on every tree boasted clusters of flowers in shades of blue and lilac.

"Oh, my goodness," I gasped. "How absolutely beautiful." And I meant it. I had seen beauty in a landscape before, yet never anything so lovely as this. The rich colours saturated my vision, so intense as we rode through a sea of falling petals, fluttering down like purple butterflies.

"Planted by my mother," Mr Fleming said. "And she named the house after them. They are wonderful shade trees but are particularly pretty this time of the year."

"I have never seen anything like them." I could not pull my gaze away from the sight, and then I realised we were fast approaching the house.

My expectations of what I would find here were non-existent. However, I was delighted to see a whitewashed bungalow of some size with a brightly tiled orange roof. The courtyard in the front boasted flowerbeds snaking the edge of the lawn, teeming with red Geraniums and vivid pink Bougainvillea, to name just two. As we neared, the cart slowed, and two scantily clad young men paused from their work to wave.

The driveway forked, and Mr Fleming turned away from the house and past the side of the building in the direction of several small huts. Beyond them stood a large barn and other structures. A boy raced to the cart as it came to a halt.

"*Jambo, Bwana,*" the young African greeted Mr Fleming as my new employer jumped down to the ground, quickly followed by the large dog. The boy leapt into the vacated seat beside me. "*Jambo, Memsahib,*" he said with a broad smile. His voluminous eyes were dark as treacle.

"*Jambo,*" I said, and then realised I had better alight before he took the cart away and me with it. I grabbed my bag and got out of the conveyance, then walked around to the rear of the cart. Mr Fleming strode back the way he had come, and then abruptly stopped.

"This way, Miss Rossington. One of the boys will bring your trunk. I will show you to the house. Malaika is expecting us. Come along."

I caught up with him, and we walked around to the front of the bungalow. My step faltered as I saw a group of perhaps twenty people waiting in the courtyard to greet us. There were several men, no doubt workers, as some of them held farm implements. As my eyes settled on the women, embarrassment warmed my face. I was not yet used to seeing people in the state of undress considered normal by Africans. The women's breasts were bare, only the lower halves of their bodies modestly covered up. Children ranging from infant to teen stared boldly at me as I drew closer. Their inquisitive faces ogling a stranger, a new face, and it was understandable that they were curious.

Other than a brief moment when I disembarked from the steamer, this was my first experience of being around people like this, true Africans, living in the bush within their own culture. I found it both intimidating and fascinating. As we reached the group, they parted to allow us a way through. We approached the open front door, and Mr Fleming stopped to speak to them. I do not know what he said, because he spoke in Swahili. But their interested eyes settled upon me, and there were nods and smiles of welcome. The women stared at my hair, which had started out in a chignon but had spilled from its bindings. My light brown curls were unremarkable, yet from their perspective I understood their interest, for I looked nothing like them.

There were many comments of "*Jambo*," as Mr Fleming finished his speech. I was struck by the friendly countenance of these people and surrounded by a sea of beaming smiles. I nodded and smiled back—unsure of myself—and then followed Mr Fleming and his dog into the house.

I crossed the threshold, where a small group of individuals stood to attention in a line against the wall. The house staff. Of course, introductions would need to be made.

"Miss Rossington, this is Wilson. He is our cook." A bearded man in his forties nodded at me and smiled. His eyes were warm and friendly. We shook hands. Next to him stood a much younger man, barely out of boyhood.

"This is Juba," said Mr Fleming. "He helps Wilson in the kitchen and generally does all manner of things to keep the house running." Juba stepped forward and grasped my hand enthusiastically, a radiant grin on his face. I could not help but return the smile. Then we moved on to a girl who could not have been more than fourteen who stared at her feet.

"...And Leta, one of the maids, and finally..."

A slender young woman stepped forward, but she did not hold out her hand. She was stunning, her skin a lighter brown, eyes liquid, mouth full. Her thick hair stood up from her scalp like a halo over her head. In each of her ears dangled what looked to me like a lion's claw set in silver.

"This is Malaika. She is responsible for the running of the house. I would be lost without her." The young woman's eyes settled on her employer, shining with emotion. And then they regarded me, and the warmth drained away. So that was how it would be. I was not welcome here.

"It is a pleasure to meet you," I said with more confidence than I felt. "I look forward to working with you."

"*Memsahib*," she replied while the others nodded.

"Let me show you to your quarters," said Mr Fleming. "There will be plenty of time for you to get to know everyone. And you need to meet Nalah." He ushered me past the line of servants. The hallway opened up to several rooms. We passed a large living area, a dining room and a study, before veering off in another direction to a corridor with many doors. The sound of a baby crying came from the end of the hall. My instinct overtook the anxiety I felt in arriving, and my step quickened.

Inside the nursery, I hurried to a crib to find my charge. As though the sudden sight of me had startled her, Nalah immediately stopped crying and simply stared up at me with clear hazel eyes. The baby, at four months old looked tiny and undernourished. Without another thought, I set down my bag and reached in to lift her from her bed. It was as though I lifted a doll, so slight was she. I held Nalah against me while we studied one another.

What a beauty. Her thick thatch of black hair was more European than African in texture, and her skin the colour of creamy caramel. Nalah's light eyes contemplated me. I was utterly captivated.

"Where is her nurse?" I asked Mr Fleming who had remained in the doorway.

"I believe she tends her other children."

"This child is hungry," I said. "Can you please show me to the kitchen, and I will prepare a bottle for her."

He nodded. "Follow me."

The kitchen lay at the opposite end of the house, away from the bedrooms. Wilson turned in surprise as we walked into his domain. He'd been busy putting away the items Mr Fleming had brought from Mombasa.

"Wilson, *maziwa ya mtoto yuko wapi?*" Mr

Fleming asked, and I assumed he asked about the milk.

The older man went to a door and opened it to reveal a large pantry. He pulled a tin from the shelf. "*Hapa ndio*," he replied and came over to hand me the tin.

I turned to Mr Fleming and, before he could protest, I placed the child in his arms and took the tin from the cook. Yes, as I thought—evaporated milk. "Do you know what else Nalah is fed?" I asked her uncle, who stood so rigid he might have been holding a cobra.

"Just the milk, I think." He rattled off another question to Wilson, who gave a quick response.

"Yes, she is fed only milk."

"That explains her size," I said with great disdain. "Wilson, do you have bread?"

The older man hesitated. I had no idea if he understood English.

"*Ndio, Bibi.*" He went back into the pantry and pulled out a large metal box. I joined him and motioned I wanted to cut a slice.

"If you need a sandwich, Miss Rossington, Wilson will prepare it for you."

I stopped to look at Mr Fleming, whose expression was not pleasant. "Mr Fleming, your niece is undernourished and underweight. At her age, she should be eating some solids as well as taking her milk. Therefore, I intend to remedy that." I looked directly at his face, "unless you would rather I did not?"

He gave a curt nod and, before long, Wilson had assisted me in the preparation of a small bowl of bread soaked in warm milk. Mr Fleming happily surrendered the baby to me, and I positioned her and put a small

spoonful of the mixture to her lips. She devoured it—
her body wriggled, and her lips parted for more just like
a baby bird. I fed her half the mixture and then asked
Mr Fleming to instruct Wilson in showing me where
the bottles were kept. He obliged, and once one was
ready, I left the kitchen with Nalah and made for the
nursery.

We settled down in a rocking chair together, me
and the doll-like baby. As she drank from her bottle,
our eyes locked, and we took in the measure of each
other. Though I had been nervous about taking on the
responsibility of someone else's child, her urgent need
of care surpassed any misgivings I felt. We were but
new acquaintances, yet by providing her nourishment, I
had already created our bond. And as I stared into those
innocent eyes, I remembered how it had felt to hold my
own child close, and I wanted to cry.

MY ROOM WAS CONNECTED BY an inside door to the
nursery. This I discovered once I had changed Nalah
and put her back in her crib to sleep. The little mite had
barely kept her eyes open while I dressed her. I closed
the curtains in the nursery and quietly left.

My things were already waiting for me in my
room. The door to the hallway stood open, and I closed
it and then took in my new surroundings. A large bed,
complete with mosquito netting, a stern chest of
drawers, and a cupboard, which looked as though it
dated back to the crusades. No decoration, no pictures,
not even a vase of flowers, but there was a mirror and a
small writing desk in one corner.

I pulled open the curtains, watching in pleasure as
the sunlight flooded the room. I unlatched the windows

and pushed them back, and though the air outside was warm, I relished the breeze. I set about unpacking my meagre belongings, which did not take very long. Then I poured water into the washbowl and refreshed myself, scooping up my untidy hair and fastening it into a clasp.

My tasks completed, I was at a loss of what I should do next when a knock sounded on my door. It was Malaika.

"Does *Memsahib* have need of anything?" Her tone was polite but her expression indignant.

"Yes, I should like some tea, Malaika. Tell me, am I at liberty to make it myself?"

"*Hapana.* This, the boy, Juba, he must do. *Memsahib*, stay out of kitchen."

"Then I should like to have tea, please."

The young woman regarded me with evident dislike. Youthful, her body in bloom, lithe and strong, I put her age at seventeen or eighteen. I did not blame her for being unhappy with my coming. This was her territory, not mine.

"Malaika," I said. "I think you are displeased I am here."

She regarded me, stoned-faced.

I continued. "I want you to understand I am only here to care for the baby. I shall respect your position in the house, but I ask you grant me the same courtesy. We both work for Mr Fleming."

She remained silent, and the moment grew uncomfortable. Our eyes met and held.

"I will send Juba with tea," she said in a monotone voice and, before I could respond, she walked away.

Chapter Three

ONCE I'D FINISHED DRINKING MY TEA, my eyes became heavy, and my body sagged. The sun had climbed high in the sky, and with it, the temperature. My skin glistened and I longed to cool off. Peeking through the adjoining door, I checked Nalah. The silence told me she was sound asleep—no doubt her full little belly had something to do with that.

I went back to my room, leaving the nursery door open in case the baby woke. I slipped off my dress and, clad in my undergarments, I lay down on top of my bed under the white mosquito netting and promptly fell into a dreamless sleep.

MY EYES FLICKERED OPEN. WHERE was I? After a moment, my head cleared, and I remembered I had come to Jacaranda. I listened intently for Nalah but heard nothing. So, I indulged myself and stayed exactly where I was, staring up at the ceiling through the white mesh of netting, watching a tiny lizard dart across the paint, defying gravity. How strange it was, lying under a silky tent observing a creature so foreign to my eyes.

I thought of my small room at home in Chessington. The heavy, drab furnishings, the gloomy clouds full of rain. A tiny flat with a fire so inadequate it would not heat a matchbox. How far I had ventured.

Why, in a few short weeks, my virgin eyes had beheld more wonders than I knew how to comprehend. I had been in the company of many ethnicities of people. Spanish, Arabic, French and a host of others. Such a far cry from riding the musty tram into London and being ignored by the person seated beside me.

How could I ever forget hearing the Muslim call to prayer echo hauntingly down the streets of Port Said, or sailing down the famous Suez Canal, the antithesis of my beloved River Thames. I'd exchanged graceful swans and green Weeping Willows for menacing crocodiles, and the exotic fragrance of tropical flowers and spices—so many vast and wonderful experiences for my mind to absorb at once.

What a journey I had already been on. Physically, I knew I was fatigued. But I could rest and recover. But my mind? My hands moved to my abdomen of their own volition, yearning to soothe, to find a memory long passed. The image of a golden-haired precious baby, the feel of tiny fingers grasping my own. My eyes filled with tears, and I dashed them away. This would not do.

As though she had known my thoughts, Nalah gave a small whimper. I chased the past from my mind, rose from the bed and dressed. Then I went into the nursery to begin my duties at Jacaranda.

AFTER FEEDING AND CHANGING THE baby, I carried her on my hip and explored the bungalow. Other than in the kitchen, I saw no one about, so I felt comfortable looking through various rooms and acquainting myself with the layout of the place.

The living room was quite British in design, the furniture upholstered in a floral pattern reminiscent of a country garden. There was a generous fireplace, the mantel covered in framed pictures of who I assumed were members of the Fleming family, over a grate that had been swept scrupulously clean. A large painting of a beautiful woman hung over the fireplace, her hair so pale it looked silver, her eyes large and limpid. She appeared ethereal, not of this world, a fey. I wondered if it might be Mr Fleming's mother? There were other pictures hung around the room, British in origin by their subject—cottages, castles, countrysides and seascapes.

In stark contradiction, animal hides were draped upon the floor in lieu of carpets and rugs. These varied from zebra to most likely cowhides. A set of French windows opened out to the front verandah, and I stepped outside.

The house was positioned so the Jacaranda trees were clearly visible and presented a wonderful view. The bricked courtyard, the lovely flowerbeds, the driveway sentried with blue-purple blooms, and beyond that, the African bush. I imagined it would be comfortable to sit here in the evening and feel the breeze coming in from the sea, a few miles away.

Each room connected to the next by double glass-paned doors as well as being accessible from the hallway. I wandered from the living room into the adjoining dining room. Here stood a table which could easily accommodate ten people, complete with ornately carved chairs, the upholstered seats a European design. I assumed Mr Fleming's mother must have brought a considerable amount of furniture with her from England. I spotted a tall Welsh Dresser filled with a very pretty china service, and in one corner, a drinks table holding crystal glass decanters.

I passed through the next set of double doors and was on familiar territory in the kitchen. Wilson stood at a sink, peeling potatoes, while Juba sat at the table chopping carrots. Having already spoken to them while preparing Nalah's bottle, I gave them a nod, this time leaving through the door which led back out to the hallway.

I surmised the next room must be Mr Fleming's study as the doors were closed. I had no business going in there, so I returned to the fork in the corridor back towards the nursery. It appeared there were six bedrooms, three on either side of the corridor, with a bathroom at the end of the hall. Nalah and I were in two of the rooms on the backside of the house. The other stood empty with no furniture at all.

On the opposing side of the hall, all doors were wide open except the last. The first bedroom had everything in its place and must be reserved for guests. The second room was masculine in appearance, obviously Mr Fleming's, so I did not venture inside. But when I reached the room at the end of the hall, across from the nursery, my curiosity got the better of me. I turned the knob, opened the door, and stepped inside.

It took me a moment to adjust to the darkness as the curtains were closed, and only a little light penetrated the thick fabric. The rich scent of jasmine hung on the air, pleasant and sweet. A four-poster bed with tall side tables dominated the space. It was too dark to see much detail, but judging by the elaborate shaping of the furniture, I guessed it to be French by design.

The generous vanity still boasted personal items a

woman would use every day along with a collection of glass perfume bottles. This room had its own fireplace, but the mantel held not pictures, but small figures of women in the Greek style. A chaise-longue positioned in front of the French windows appeared to have items of clothing draped across its back, as though someone had just dropped them there.

"What are you doing in here?"

I whirled around. Malaika stood in the open doorway, a silhouette with the light behind her.

"I was looking around the house to get my bearings," I replied as casually as I could while walking to the door where she waited. She moved to allow me across the threshold, and as soon as I stepped into the hallway, she hastily closed the bedroom door behind us.

"You must not go in this room," she said, her tone sharp in her stilted accented English. "This is Mrs Fleming's room, and no one must ever go in here. *Unaelewa*—do you understand?"

"Of course," I said. Then Nalah gurgled, and we both looked at the baby and it seemed to break the tension. I glanced back to the lovely young woman. "I am sorry Mrs Fleming died. It is tragic for Nalah to have lost her mother."

Malaika's black eyes locked upon mine, her brow furrowed in a frown. "This room not the room of Barika. This the room of Memsahib Amelia Fleming."

"Amelia Fleming? Mr Fleming's mother?"

"*Hapana*—no, *Memsahib*. Mr Fleming's wife—my mistress."

I was startled. "Mr Fleming is married?"

"*Hapana*. He is married no longer. My mistress, she is dead." With that, Malaika turned and walked away. I stood still, momentarily taken aback by her statement. I had assumed, incorrectly, that Nicholas Fleming was unmarried. Although why I felt surprised learning he was a widower, I do not know. The man must be close to thirty, many men of that age already had several children. I crossed the hallway and went into the nursery. My new employer had an aloofness about him which made me think he'd been alone for a long time. I wondered that he had not mentioned his dead wife. Perhaps it was too painful for him?

I spent some time playing with the baby, and then placed Nalah in her crib, my heart warming as she smiled at me. Her little arms and legs waved as though she was going somewhere, and she kicked away her cover. I stroked her hair gently and watched as her lids grew heavy, and then left her to rest.

While the baby slept, I decided to venture outside and familiarise myself with my new surroundings. I left through the open front door and stepped out into the warm sun. Thank goodness for the breeze. Though it must be close to six o'clock, the heat was relentless. With October being considered part of the cool season, I wondered how it would be come December when the tropical weather arrived?

I crossed the courtyard onto the stubby grass. The farm employed many people, but currently, I saw no other. I followed the flowerbeds, stopping periodically to examine some of the plants which I had never seen before and presumed were indigenous to the country. I walked out to the driveway and then paused to stand underneath one of the blue jacarandas, staring up at the blossoms in wonder.

I became aware of another presence, and I realised

Mr Fleming's large dog had joined me though I had not heard it approach. The beast sat back on its haunches studying me intently. I did not recognise the breed, for it seemed as big as a Great Dane, but with the blocky head and colouring of a Mastiff.

"His name is *Mzuka*," said Mr Fleming. "In English that means ghost. He's a Boerbel—bred for farming, good with people, but not with predators. He won't hurt you. He's a gentle giant."

I squatted down and reached out a hand. The animal regarded me momentarily, and then sloped over, rubbing its massive face against my dress. His fur was smooth and the soft hue of sand, his eyes topaz and bright with intelligence. I patted his head and then straightened.

"I am fascinated with the colour of these Jacaranda trees, Mr Fleming. I think them the most beautiful blossoms I have ever seen."

"They are pretty. Jacarandas are native to South America," said Mr Fleming. "But they do quite well here. Depending on where you stand, they can appear purple or blue."

"The colours remind me a great deal of the bluest hydrangeas, and forget-me-nots, too."

"My mother was an avid gardener. She worked hard to cultivate her favourite flowers, despite fighting the climate at times."

"She did an admirable job. Your home is quite lovely, Mr Fleming." I thought of the painting. "Your mother had an eye for beauty, I think. She was, herself very lovely."

He frowned as though I had spoken nonsense. Then his face showed comprehension. "Oh, you are speaking of the portrait in the living room. That is not my mother—it is Amelia, my wife."

A chill ran through me though I did not know why.

"Then your wife was a lovely woman, Mr Fleming."

His light eyes landed on me. "Look, may we dispense with titles? I'd prefer to call you by your name and for you to do the same with me."

"Of course."

"Then I shall call you Julia, and you can call me Nick. Now, walk with me, and I will show you around." It did not sound like a request. I joined step with him.

At the back of the house, we passed the pod of small huts with their red clay walls and thatched straw roofs until we reached a large building, which I took to be a barn.

"We keep our smaller livestock in here overnight," Nick explained. "It is safer as there are many animals who hunt in the dark."

"What about your cattle? How do you protect them?" I could imagine they were easy targets out in the wild.

"Cattle are kept in an enclosure called a bomas – this is a way of making a fence using what is already at hand in the bush and also easy to move. We gather thorny bushes and stack them up in such a way that the cattle cannot escape but neither can anything get in. Even the big cats cannot get through or over the branches. It's a practice the Maasai have used for years, and it is an efficient system." He pointed to another building, this one far smaller. "That is the chicken house. Wilson has an endless supply of meat and eggs, and we distribute what we don't need to the workers.

They have a weekly ration of goods from the farm as well as their wage." We walked past both buildings and Nick pointed. "There are the stables, and the other large barn is where the farm equipment is kept."

"Where do your workers stay?" I asked as we passed two young women, who looked at me and then giggled.

"The house servants have their own huts—those over there." He pointed to the group of huts we had already passed. "The others walk here from their villages."

"It is quite the undertaking, Mr Flem...Nick."

"Yes, it is. That is why I have a farm manager. Derek spends most of his time out in the fields. I couldn't do this without his help."

"Where does he live?"

"I'll show you." He took me along the back of the house where a pathway led away from the building. The grounds were not tended here, and the bushes were thick either side of the walkway. But we had not gone far when an opening revealed a small, neat, brick house.

"This is the manager's quarters," he said. "You'll meet Derek this evening. He usually dines at the house if he is finished for the day. Speaking of dinner, we eat at seven, and we don't dress for it or any of that nonsense." He whistled to *Mzuka,* "Come along. I'll walk you back."

As we walked, I looked around. "Do any of the wild animals ever come close to the house? I imagined I'd see zebras and deer everywhere. Yet I haven't seen much at all since I arrived in Africa."

"Well, you have only been here a day, Julia." Was that a hint of a smile?

"True," I conceded, but other than the distant herd we saw on the drive to Jacaranda, the only wildlife I've seen is your dog."

He chuckled at that. "Don't be disappointed. There's never much to see in the middle of the day—it's too hot. Usually, early morning and dusk are the best times. We do get a lot of monkeys near the house. They're resourceful and always on the look-out for something to steal and eat.

But once you get to open country, that's where you'll see all the grazers—herds of zebra, antelope, and wildebeest. We sometimes have the occasional nosy giraffe, and of course, the elephants are never far away."

"What about lions?" I asked nervously. "Should I be concerned about my safety?" It was something I fretted about. I was, after all, a girl from London and no native. I knew very little about life in the African bush.

"Generally, lions stay away from here because their prey is elsewhere. But it is always best to be aware. Do not walk alone at night, and if you have to, make sure you have a torch—they don't like fire. It is the leopards you have to be careful about."

I raised my brows. "Leopards? Why?"

"They are night hunters, and far more ferocious than lions. Leopards are loners. They move soundlessly and even hide up in the trees. Recently, we have had several sightings of a black leopard—which is unusual as they are extremely rare. This fellow has eaten a few goats on our neighbour's property. So, for the time being it would be better if you stayed inside at night."

We had reached the house. "I shall see you at dinner," he said, dismissing me.

NALAH WAS SUCH A GOOD baby. I suppose my feeding her solid food had really settled her down. Before dinner, I bathed and fed her, and then laid her on a thick mat on the floor with a few of her toys. I examined her belongings folded neatly in the nursery cupboard, pleased to see she seemed to have what most four-month-old babies would need.

She was a dear little thing. Pretty, too, with a thick swathe of jet-black hair and eyes which sparkled like gems. Her mouth constantly moved, as though she had much to say, and she emitted an ongoing lecture of gurgles and cooing. Would she sleep through the night? I hoped so, especially on my first evening here. It had been a long day, and I was already tired. The heat contributed to my lethargy, although I tolerated it better now I'd been in hot weather since the ship left Egypt.

I picked up the baby, nestled her in the crook of my arm and sat down in the large wooden rocking chair. As I rocked her, I recounted the tale of Cinderella. I had not got far when I saw her eyes grow heavy as she drifted into sleep. I continued rocking her and studied her little face, now angelic in slumber. She and I had much in common in some ways. She had lost her mother—and I had lost my son. Perhaps fate had brought the two of us together?

The distant sound of a gong roused me, and I gently carried Nalah to her crib. She did not stir as I laid her on the sheet. I drew the curtains closed and left the nursery to join Mr Fleming for dinner.

I hadn't expected Derek Walker to be an athletic, attractive man—but he was. He introduced himself as I entered the dining room, and one look at him cast him as a sportsman in my eyes. With curly reddish-blond hair, flashing blue eyes, a moustache, and a broad grin, Derek's manner put me instantly at ease in his company.

"Welcome to Jacaranda, Julia," he exclaimed enthusiastically, shaking my hand vigorously before guiding me to the table. "Have a seat. Nick will be here shortly. Let's have a sherry while we wait."

Juba materialised from nowhere, a decanter in hand, and poured the ruby liquid into a small crystal glass at my place setting. Derek sat directly across from me.

"Cheers," he toasted. "Here's to new beginnings."

"What are you talking about?" Nicholas Fleming came into the room, *Mzuka* at his heels, and joined us at the table.

"Welcoming Julia into the fold. I say, old chap, what happened to you?"

A streak of red ran across Nick's face. He had been cut.

"One of the pulleys came loose on the thresher, and I didn't move out of the way quick enough."

"Have you anything to dress it with?" I asked. "If not—"

"It is fine," he cut me off. "Malaika has put salve on it." He glanced up at the young houseboy, Juba. "You may bring dinner."

"Nick tells me you are from London," Derek said as Juba brought around the meal, placing two serving bowls and a platter in the middle of the table.

"Yes, I am. From Chessington, in Surrey."

"Gad, it's been a time since I've been back to the old country." Derek reached across, picked up a bowl of potatoes and handed them to me. "My family are from a small village called Coningsby, near Grantham in Lincolnshire. A beautiful hamlet with nought but potatoes and pigs."

"What an odd mixture," I said.

"Not really," Derek took the bowl back from me and handed me the carrots. "The land is quite flat there and ideal for growing potatoes. The fields are rotated, so they alternate between potatoes and grazing the pigs so they can eat all the remnants and roots—fertilise the soil too."

"Ingenious," Nick remarked drily and passed me a platter laden with roasted chicken.

"Nick is a snob," said Derek. "He believes himself on the cutting edge of new farming techniques. He thinks my ideas are archaic."

"Not all of them," Nick responded. "Occasionally you have some good thoughts. Enough to make you valuable enough to keep around here, at least."

"See?" Derek laughed good-naturedly. With his face freckled from the sun, there was a boyish charm about him. "Now you know how relieved I am to have you here, Julia. I'll finally have someone nice to talk to."

I did not answer but focused upon my dinner, which was rather good. Wilson obviously knew how to cook well. The men continued their banter and spoke of business matters to do with the farm, most of which I barely followed, even though I found it interesting.

"By the way, there's a party at the club this Saturday," said Derek. "Why don't we all go? It would be an excellent opportunity for Julia to meet everyone—all at the same time."

"What club is this?" I asked.

"The Mombasa Club," Derek answered. "It's in town, and where all the British people in the area meet up. They are a jolly lot, well, most of them. There's a nice bar, and a huge verandah."

"It's a watering hole for the upper crust, Julia," Nick said. "But as they are low in numbers, they allow anyone with a British accent to join. It's not as thrilling as Derek makes it out to be. He's been here so long; he's easily entertained."

Derek laughed. "Look, old boy. It might not be your cup of tea, but not everyone likes to be antisocial all the time. It does one good to get out, speak to other people, have a laugh."

They seemed at odds about their opinion of this club. Though they disagreed with one another vehemently, it was done with great humour.

"I take it you do not frequent the place yourself, Nick?" I enquired.

"I do not," he stated. "But if you have any desire to go, I am sure Derek would be an adequate chaperone."

"Thank you." I dabbed the serviette against my mouth. "Perhaps another time, Derek. It will take me a few days to settle in and get Nalah used to a routine."

"Of course." He rewarded me with a generous smile. "The invitation is open, and we can go when it is more convenient." His eyes landed upon his employer, "And Nick can stay here and babysit." He laughed at his own joke, but I noticed my employer did not.

Presently, our plates were removed, and we were served a deliciously light steamed pudding, topped with rich, warm custard.

"I am astounded how well Wilson cooks," I said. "Dinner was delicious."

"Nick does have the best cook in the area," Derek agreed, "You should taste his Tikka Masala."

"His what?"

"It's an Indian dish, Julia. A curry. Have you never heard of it?" Nick said.

"No." My cheeks were warm from the meal and accompanying wine. I did not want to appear ignorant.

"There are many Indians living in Kenya. They came to work for the Uganda Railway which has only recently started running. Their cuisine is one custom they brought along with them. Curry is an everyday meal."

"What type of dish is curry?" It sounded interesting.

Derek cut in. "It looks rather like a regular British stew. But the spices used to prepare the sauce are so hot they can make your eyes water. The meat and sauce are served with rice, which helps ease some of the flavour's heat. Apparently, there are as many different curries as there are different regions of India." He gestured to his empty bowl, "Makes our diet seem insipid."

Derek continued to expound upon the differences in Indian, African, and British food. It was all most informative, and he had certainly tasted a variety. Yet as he emptied several glasses of wine, his words became less clear, and his skin flushed.

"I'm going to sit outside and smoke. Julia, would you care to accompany me?" Nick Fleming got to his feet.

I glanced at Derek. "Are you joining us?"

"Don't think so. I've an early start tomorrow, so I'd better say goodnight."

I watched him leave the dining room, and then I

followed Mr Fleming out through the French windows and onto the verandah. At first, I found it difficult to see because the sky was so black. Yet my eyes began to adjust, and I picked out one of several chairs, and took a seat.

My employer said nothing. I saw the flash of a small flame as he first lit his cigar and then put the match to an oil lamp before sitting down. *Mzuka* lay at his feet. The temperature out here was significantly cooler than inside the house, I noted with relief. Unfortunately, my attire was far more suited to the British climate, not African, and I would have to remedy that.

"How did you fare on your first day at Jacaranda?" Nick asked. Though his face remained somewhat in the shadows, I could see the burning tip of his cigar.

"It went well, I think. Your niece is a good baby, and we seemed to have taken to one another."

"Good."

"I had expected to meet the woman who looked after her, yet she did not come up to the house?"

"I can assure you that Winda was only too happy relinquishing her charge to you, Julia. As I told you, the Kikuyu do not cherish those of mixed blood. My brother's lust has left a difficult legacy for Nalah. She will be a pariah to all society."

"Surely not." I reasoned. "She is of British blood too, and therefore must be acknowledged. In time perhaps they will come around."

"Then you know little of the world if you believe that. The British love Africa for its majesty, its wilderness, adventure, and its many riches. But do not be mistaken, Julia. They care nothing for its people.

Only what they can take from them."

"That is a harsh generalisation," I said. "I understand Britain's desire to increase the wealth of the Empire, its desire to strengthen their world position."

"And does your understanding condone the rape of a country? Of its treasures, its wildlife?"

"Of its land?" I said without thinking.

"Touché, Julia. You are correct, I am a hypocrite am I not?"

I was flustered as I'd insulted the man. But I meant what I said.

"Then I am as guilty as the next Englishman, by your account. Although I have a defence, albeit a poor one."

"What is that?"

"I was born here, Julia. And therefore, part of me is tied to this land. Though my father claimed Jacaranda as his, with the might of the Empire behind him, I see this farm as a temporary possession. That I have by sheer good fortune, inherited both a home and a living. A living which allows me to employ many people who might otherwise not fare so well. But I am no tyrannical ruler—my workers are paid well and are free to leave whenever they wish. So, should I stop, Julia? Let the workers leave, allow the crops to rot in the field while I go back to some pretty village in Cornwall and tend my garden there, all because of a guilty conscience?"

"That is not what I meant," I stammered. "It was not my intention to insult you. I know little of this country other than what I have learned on a ship full of Europeans, and that is in Africa, there is land for the taking, regardless of one's intent. Western civilisations always dominate less fortunate countries. It is much the same with people."

"To the victor goes the spoils," he said with heavy sarcasm.

"That does not make it right."

"Indeed." I saw he looked directly at me. "Then what would you have us do, Julia?

"That is an impossible question to ask," I said. "If I knew the answer to that, I should be a diplomat. Please do not misunderstand me, Nick. I love my country and my nationality. The British arm has reached far across the world, affording those like me, many opportunities. My discomfort is that while being in foreign countries, we have elevated ourselves into believing we are a better people, a smarter culture, and used our lessons from history to control."

"But there must always be a leader. That is a hierarchy which is human by design. The strong must always lead the weak."

"Yet the strong often abuse their power," I knew this from my own experience.

"That is often true."

We fell silent, and the moment grew awkward. Then, by good fortune, I heard the thin wail of a baby. Nalah had woken. I rose from my chair.

"Please excuse me. I must see to the baby."

"Goodnight," he said quietly, and I left him to his cigar.

Later, as I lay in my bed listening to Nalah's rhythmic breathing through the open door, I thought about Amelia Fleming. Odd that Nick had not mentioned his deceased wife, other than the portrait. And it would have seemed rude for me to ask about her. But I couldn't help the bud of curiosity I felt.

Amelia's room had aroused my interest. That everything was still in its place, waiting for her as though she had just left and would be back shortly, seemed strange. Malaika's stern reprimand had been surprising. Perhaps I could ask Derek Walker? He seemed a friendly sort and would no doubt be more than willing to answer my questions.

Chapter Four

I AWOKE TO A BRIGHT ROOM as I had left the curtains open, and I could hear the murmur of voices coming from outside. I listened for the baby, but she was quiet. Nalah had stayed up later than expected, therefore I anticipated having plenty of time to wash and dress before she needed my attention.

I picked out my thinnest dress and fastened my hair high above my neck. I checked on the baby, but she still slept. Her little arms were flung back, and her tiny mouth pursed as though she was giving a kiss. I crept away and wandered down to the dining room. The clock on the mantel showed five minutes past seven.

"*Bibi* would like chai?" asked Juba, entering the room from the kitchen. He had obviously heard me approach.

"Yes, please." I took a seat at the table, where he joined me moments later.

"*Bibi* want *mayai*—eggs for breaking her fast? Wilson can make."

"That would be wonderful. Thank you, Juba."

The French windows were flung open to allow the cool early breeze. From my seat, I had a view of a stretch of garden and a splash of blue-purple from the driveway. There were men already working in the garden—their bright coloured clothing caught my eye as they went about their tasks. Others passed the house, perhaps on their way to the barn and buildings in the back.

The sound of hoofbeats punctuated the air, and then footsteps. Nick Fleming came through the open windows and into the house, bringing with him the scent of horseflesh.

"Good morning, Julia. I hope you slept well?"

He must have been up for a while. I saw traces of dust on his face, and when he removed his hat, his hair was dishevelled.

"I slept like a log," I answered. "For some reason, sleeping underneath the tent of a mosquito net is rather relaxing. Have you already been working?"

He took a seat at the head of the table, and Juba must have heard him because he materialised from nowhere with a cup of steaming chai.

"Yes. I get up at dawn as it is imperative to beat the heat. We've a large herd about two miles from here, and I check on them every morning in case there have been problems."

"What kind of problems?"

"Predators, poachers, or anything like that."

Juba came in with a tray. He placed a plate in front of me, laden with fresh yellow eggs, two slices of bacon and a piece of toast. I thanked him. He did the same for his master.

"Are you familiar with the *Maasai* beyond knowing the name?"

"No, not at all."

"They are a nomadic tribe, who place cattle above all other creatures. Their herds are their most valuable assets, and they are totally dependent upon them. These people wander through the plains and valleys, taking their herds with them, and are often caught taking cattle from the farms hereabouts. They are a fierce tribe, renowned for their warriors, and a fearless people. They do not mix with the Kikuyu, but often will work with the British if it pays well enough."

"Do you have Maasai working here?"

"Malaika is Maasai. Apart from her, there is another named, Migali. He came here as a boy, so we grew up together. You'll meet him in a few days when he returns from seeing his family." He picked up his fork and started to eat.

I did the same—but stole glances his way. Nick Fleming had been a courteous host, especially to a person like me, just another member of his household staff. But there was an aloofness he carried with him, a buffer that kept a person from becoming too comfortable with him. I wondered what he was really like—whether he had a good sense of humour, or if he ever laughed.

"You grow quiet, Julia. I trust the food is to your liking."

"Sorry," I stammered. "I'm miles away. Yes, Wilson's cooking is very good. I seem to be eating far more than I did at home."

"Chessington, wasn't it?"

I nodded.

"I'm unfamiliar with England. Though I was educated there, I spent little time exploring. I attended the University of St Andrews in Scotland. It was too far to venture anywhere else during the holidays. Though I did visit the family seat in Cornwall before returning to Jacaranda."

"Do you have a large family?"

"Not really. Father was a younger brother, and there are cousins, most whom I have never met. Our world has always been here. My father had a life-long love affair with Africa." His expression grew pensive, "Sometimes he loved it too much."

"*Jambo, Bwana*," said Malaika as she came into the room. Dressed in a brightly patterned native dress. Both her arms were bare, the fabric tied in a sash on her shoulder, with a matching piece of material twisted and knotted into a type of turban, giving the young woman the appearance of being taller than usual.

She turned her lovely face to me. "*Memsahib*, Nalah cries."

"Oh, thank you for telling me. I did not hear her." I put down my fork and got to my feet. "Please excuse me." I went into the hall, leaving Nick and his housekeeper alone. They immediately began conversing in Swahili, and I did not understand a word.

Nalah's crying stopped the instant she saw me, and her little face lit up. She wriggled like a fish, and I lifted her into my arms.

"Hello, sweet girl," I crooned, delighted by her smiles, already feeling the bond established between us. Though my arms still ached for a different baby, my baby, it did not make me love this child any less. I had been here such a short time, but time was inconsequential to a baby. For Nalah, my being her source of sustenance and care meant I had become her entire universe. Her unconditional acceptance of me was Nature's way for her to thrive. She was a darling little girl, and I was grateful we had connected so well.

I changed her nappy, dressed her, and then carried

45

her into the kitchen to prepare a bottle.

"*Jambo, Bibi.*" Wilson greeted me with a broad grin. How happy people seemed in this country. Whether they truly were or not, I had no idea. But these Africans had a ready smile for all, their sincerity radiating from their dark eyes.

"These eggs I make you, *Bibi.* You like how Wilson cooks them?"

"Oh yes, I do like your eggs. They were delicious. Thank you so much. You are spoiling me."

The cook grinned, baring yellowed teeth inside the frame of his beard, while his face beamed in pleasure at my compliment. I attempted to pour the evaporated milk into the bottle, ready to add water, but Nalah would not keep still.

"Here." I thrust the baby at the cook, who gasped in surprise and automatically took hold of her, else she fall to the floor. I continued preparing her bottle. Kikuyu, white or Maasai, I did not care about cultures and prejudices. Nalah was an innocent baby, and she deserved to be loved no matter her skin colour or tribe. While the bottle cooled, I rummaged through the pantry.

"What *Bibi* looking for?" Wilson asked helpfully.

I was moving things about. "Nalah needs some type of grain I can feed her instead of bread." I turned to face him. Wilson sat up to the kitchen table, bouncing a content Nalah upon his knee.

"Wilson, would I be able to have cow's milk each day for the baby? This tinned milk is good, but too rich for her stomach if she has it for every meal. Who should I ask about this?"

"*Leta.*" Malaika stood in the doorway, her bearing

too regal for a servant. She joined us and flashed a disapproving glare at Wilson, who made silly faces at the baby, while she responded with gooey smiles.

"I will see it is brought to the kitchen each morning, *Memsahib,*" she stated. "Is there anything else you require for this child?"

"Actually, yes. I should like to speak with the woman who cared for her before I arrived. Can you tell me her name?"

Malaika's beautiful face frowned. "Why you want this, *Memsahib?*"

"I wish to ask questions regarding the baby, and her habits." I met her stare. "Is this a problem? Should I ask Mr Fleming for permission?" I casually brought my employer into the conversation because I suspected Malaika was being intentionally difficult. Part of me understood she felt threatened by the appearance of another woman in a house where she outranked the others. I had no desire to usurp her position, but I also had no intention of allowing her to oversee my actions. My ploy worked.

"I will take you to Winda when you are ready. You will find me in the laundry." She announced, and then without another word, turned and left the kitchen.

I felt Wilson's eyes on me. He studied my face with a mixture of pleasure and respect in his expression. I surmised he harboured no great love for Malaika.

I FOUND MALAIKA IN A SMALL HUT with a wet stone floor, bent over a large wooden tub, her arms immersed to the elbows in soapy water. She vigorously rubbed a stone against the fabric of a shirt.

She did not stop immediately but finished her task

and then pulled the clothing from the tub, wrung it out and dropped it into a bucket.

It would be easier if the two of us could get along. "That looks like hard work," I said companionably.

"These clothings, they are dirty from the soil. I soak them all night." She wiped her hands on her dress. "You are ready to see Winda?"

"Yes, please."

She gave a curt nod and then proceeded to leave the hut. I followed closely, Nalah on my hip as I walked.

Malaika led me away from the house, but not down the driveway. Instead, we walked past Derek's quarters until it looked as though we were in the wild. There was no path, but many feet travelled in this direction as the grass was worn down.

I did not speak but stayed a few steps behind the young woman as she navigated our way. It seemed we walked for at least five minutes or more, surrounded by vegetation and trees, and I wondered where on earth we were going. But then I saw a group of mud huts in a clearing ahead. As we neared, a few children, mostly naked, stopped playing and gathered in a group to watch our arrival. Their faces were curious.

"*Jambo. Nenda ukamchukue Winda*," Malaika commanded, and the tallest of the children disappeared into one of the huts, re-emerging moments later with a woman at his side.

"This woman, she is Adai, *Memsahib*," said Malaika, pointing to the hut. I did a double-take— surely not. For this person had a lined face, her body thin and gaunt, her breasts pendulous against her skin. She was old enough to be a grandmother.

"*Jambo, Winda*," I said, my tongue uncomfortable with these strange words.

"*Jambo, Memsahib.*" Her eyes were small, like black buttons on boots. They shifted from my face to the baby I held.

"Please ask Winda if there is anything I should know about Nalah, Malaika."

"Unaweza kumwambia nini Bibi kuhusu, Nalah?"

Winda nodded, and then stepped from the hut and came towards us. When she drew close, I noticed she had a scent about her, like clay. Her face was even older than I had realised, and when she opened her mouth, it was full of strong teeth, yellowed with age.

"*Mtoto huyo anapenda kulala chali. Hatalala vizuri.*"

"What is she saying?"

Malaika shrugged. "She says this baby will not sleep and is very bad."

I frowned. Nalah had slept well since I arrived. "Please ask Winda if she fed Nalah anything besides milk."

Malaika posed what I assumed was my question. The older woman shook her head.

"Yeye ni mtoto mchanga. Maziwa tu."

"Winda says no—because this is a baby."

I turned to Malaika. "How do I say thank you?"

"*Asante*," she replied.

I smiled at Winda. "*Asante, Winda.*"

She gave a nod, and then stared at the baby. Nalah stared back. Winda did not reach out to her, greet her, or even touch the baby's hand. She showed very little interest at all.

"Do all these children belong to Winda?" I asked,

noting at least ten of varying ages. They were still as they had been when I arrived, staring at me, especially my hair. I determined it was both the light brown colour, and also the texture which they found interesting. I completely understood their curiosity, for I was as fascinated by their appearance as they were mine.

"No, only five of these children, *Memsahib*. Three more, they are working in the fields."

"Blimey," I muttered. "No wonder she looks tired."

LUNCH WAS A SIMPLE AFFAIR, and one I took by myself. Wilson served a small salad with a slice of freshly baked bread out on the verandah. From my vantage point, I watched the thrum of activity on the canvas before me.

My goodness, but it was such a different view to that of my small flat in Chessington. There, my window overlooked a well-traversed road and the railway station. Here, my eyes were filled with a sea of blue blossoms, a wide swath of green grass, punctuated only by a splash of coloured clothing from the workers, and beyond that, the wilderness.

Wilson brought me a plate of scones, and as I reached to take one, there was a flash of motion, the plate suddenly spun on the table as something brushed against my face.

"Oh!" I exclaimed, simultaneously leaping to my feet in distress. What was it? A bird? And then I heard a strange noise, a sort of high-pitched grunt. I scoured the area as Juba came out to see what was amiss. I told him what had happened, but instead of being concerned he laughed.

"You have met *Mwizi*," he said.

"Who?"

"*Mwizi*—he is a monkey." He grinned. "A very naughty monkey." The boy pointed to a thick branch touching the roof of the verandah. It was connected to a large shade tree.

"Look in this tree, *Bibi* and you will see *Mwizi* hiding up there while he eats your lunch." Juba's voice sounded merry. He was delighted by this event. I followed his gaze and studied the tree. A slight movement caught my eye, and I saw a small grey creature nestled safely in the leaves.

"I can see him, Juba. He is enjoying my scone immensely." We both laughed and watched as the primate tore off pieces and tucked them into his mouth. He finished his food and then began to walk along the branch.

"What is that?" I asked, noting that the monkey looked misshapen. Something hung from its underbelly.

Juba chuckled. "It is *mtoto*, a baby, *Bibi*. This monkey, he is not a man, he is a woman."

It was fascinating. The little creature hung on for dear life as its mother casually walked deftly along thin branches and climbed higher into the tree. Within moments, she had disappeared. I returned to my seat to finish my drink. Juba picked up the empty plates and turned to leave, but I stopped him with a question.

"Tell me, Juba," I said. "How long have you worked here?"

The young man set the plates down on the table. He squinted in thought. "I come when I am very young. Perhaps five years old, *Bibi*. *Bwana*, he finds me alone out there." He pointed to the wilderness. "My people were gone, and my father and mother were dead from sickness. *Bwana* brought me to Jacaranda, and I live with Wilson until I am twelve years old. Then I am given great honour of this job I do for you now. *Bwana* says I am a butler, and this is very important job in England. Is this true, *Bibi*?" Juba's face wore such innocence and a sincere willingness to please.

I nodded earnestly. "Yes, Juba. In England, there are big houses which have butlers. The butler has the most important job because it is he who ensures the house runs efficiently. He is the person who allows visitors in the house and sometimes is in charge of many other servants."

He nodded. "This is not true for me, *Bibi*. Here, Malaika is boss in this house."

"Yes," I concurred, "but you are still young, Juba. As you grow older, you will become more experienced and wiser. Even if Malaika is in charge, it does not make you less important, for your duties are yours and yours alone. Without you, who would bring the food to Mr Fleming when he is tired from working all day? Who would help Wilson? Who would teach me about the house and the animals? You see, Juba. You are very important. I shall count on you for help now I am also working here."

Juba's beaming smile made my heart feel good. His eyes shone with pleasure and purpose. He picked up my plates and went into the house. I sat momentarily and reflected upon the young man and his story. I would ask Nick about him later.

In the afternoon, I sorted through Nalah's room to familiarise myself with her possessions and take account of her needs. Juba informed me that in two days the cart would go to Mombasa, and supplies would be purchased. I was to give him a list of anything I wanted.

There were many things already written down. I sorted through clothing which appeared too small while Nalah lay on a blanket on the floor. I had put her down on her tummy and spread several toys in front of her. She was trying her best to reach for them and not having much luck. I moved a rattle where she could grab at it.

"*Memsahib*, there is a visitor here."

I had not heard Malaika come into the nursery. I stopped what I was doing. "A visitor for Mr Fleming?"

"*Hapana*—no, this lady she is coming to see you." With that, she departed, leaving me none the wiser. I scooped up the baby. Who could possibly want to see me? I knew no one here. Mrs Clitheroe's face loomed into view, and I inadvertently shuddered. Surely not? The woman lived the other side of Mombasa.

Curious, with Nalah perched on my hip, I went to the living room, and upon entering, saw the back of a woman silhouetted in the open verandah doors. She heard my approach, for she turned in one fluid movement, and I watched as her pale eyes fastened quickly on my face, then travelled over me, pausing to stare at Nalah. Her expression underwent a subtle change at the sight of the baby, and my body responded instinctively—holding the child closer to me and standing my ground.

"Can I help you?" I stated with more confidence than I felt. I watched as she tore her eyes from the baby, back to me.

"Are you the new nanny?" Her tone was that of a

class above my own, one of money, good breeding, and arrogance.

"I am. And you are…?"

She stepped away from the door. She was dressed for riding, her khaki jodhpurs fit snuggly, her blouse shone crisp and white underneath an open jacket. She wore no hat, and her fine blonde hair hung neatly just below her ears. She was a beautiful woman, and I was aware how dowdy I must look in comparison. She came towards me with one hand extended.

"Sorry, I haven't even introduced myself. I am your neighbour, Felicity Babcock. Trevor and I live a few miles from here, at Meadowbrook."

A memory stirred of the drive here yesterday when Nick had identified landmarks and such. Now, I vaguely recalled the name. I shook her soft, small hand.

"Miss Babcock, how nice to meet you. I am Julia Rossington, and yes—I am Nalah's nanny." I gestured to the sofa, "Would you like to have a seat? I can ring for tea?"

"Gosh no, that's all right." She sank down to the sofa while I took the armchair. "I'd rather have something cold if your boy could get it." As though he had been listening, Juba came into the room carrying a small tray with two tall glasses and a jug with lemonade. He set it on the coffee table in front of me.

"Thank you, Juba." I reached forward and poured a glass for us both, careful not to let Nalah's little hands touch anything. I passed a drink to my guest, who downed the entire contents in one unladylike gulp. She helped herself to a refill.

"It would taste better with a splash of gin in it," she said, her dark eyes twinkling with mischief. "But it will do. So, Miss Rossington, how are you finding it here at Jacaranda. A bit of a change to what you are used to, I'd imagine?"

"Definitely," I said. "I'm from Chessington, near London, and—"

"I know Chessington. It's in Surrey, is it not?"

"Yes."

"I used to trot over to Epsom whenever I was there, watch the races, you know. It was always such a jolly time. How was the trip out here?"

"Good, thank you. I especially enjoyed the Suez Canal."

"Bloody ugly thing, if you ask me, nothing to look at but the desert. How long do you plan to stay?"

"I beg your pardon?"

"Well, I am sure you were not prepared for…" Her eyes slipped back to the baby. I knew her meaning only too well.

"I am here for as long as Nalah needs me," I said, looking directly at her. She was the epitome of a blue-blooded British woman. Her cool demeanour, her privileged tone, her automatic dismissal and debasement of another human being based solely upon their skin colour.

"Miss Babcock, I hope you do not mind my frankness, because I believe I can dispense with the usual formalities as we are thousands of miles away from home. Nalah is my charge, and though still an infant, nevertheless, she is a person. She did not choose her parents, but she was created from their love and as a result, is here. Her birth is no different to your own, just in the details. I'm here to care for her, to ensure she's healthy and thrives. Hopefully, I can teach and guide her, so that as she grows up, her future prospects will not be impeded by the opinions of judgemental people like yourself."

Had I gone too far? I did not care. I noticed two spots of colour on the woman's fair complexion, but much to my astonishment, she burst out laughing.

"Well, well. You do have some spirit, don't you gal?"

"A wonderful trait, isn't it, Felicity?" Nick Fleming stepped into the room, and I gasped. Had he heard my outburst?

Chapter Five

"DARLING NICK," FELICITY CROONED in greeting as he joined us, seemingly oblivious of the scowl on his face. He flashed her a look of annoyance as he walked over to where the woman had stood moments earlier.

"Felicity, I am only going to say this to you once, so please pay attention. If you find my niece so distasteful, then I would thank you to stop calling at Jacaranda. This is Nalah's home, and I will not have her treated any differently than if she was a blonde, blue-eyed, English child."

"Nick. Don't be a—"

"I mean it, Felicity. I shan't stand for it." His eyes were gunmetal silver, his jaw clenched.

I should not want to get on the wrong side of my employer. There was something quite menacing about the man. The capacity to be ruthless lay just beneath his skin.

"Oh, all right," Felicity pouted. "I'll be better." She looked at me with an innocent smile that did not reach her brown eyes. "The truth is, Julia—may I call you Julia? I really don't like any babies. Too noisy and far too much of a responsibility, in my opinion."

Nalah started to squirm and whimper.

"See," Felicity said.

I got to my feet. "I had better go and change her.

Please excuse me." I left them alone, relieved to get back to the nursery.

The remainder of my day was uneventful. I busied myself mending some of the babies clothing and then gave her a cool bath which she enjoyed immensely.

I was alone for dinner that evening, which suited me perfectly. Juba stayed close at hand, and I chatted amiably with him as I dined. He informed me that Felicity, her brother, and her father would be joining us for Sunday lunch the next day. This surprised me, for I thought my employer annoyed with the pretty blonde neighbour. He must have relented.

Later, I took a bath myself, though in shallow water as I did not want to bother Juba, and Malaika was not in the house. It was still wonderful to soak for a time, and once ready for bed, I turned in early with my book.

SUNDAY MORNING, IT RAINED, and the temperature dropped enough that a cool breeze rolled in through the open windows and doors. I sat on the verandah, sheltered from the rain, watching the grey clouds sulking on the sky, while Nalah lay on her blanket by my feet.

Nick and Derek rode down the driveway. Derek waved as they made their way to the back of the house towards the stables. And then I noticed something moving in their wake. The shape was tall and slender, running at a steady gait, yet on two legs, not four. As the figure came closer, I realised it was a man. Though not like any man I had seen before.

He slowed as he neared the house but stopped before reaching the front door. Though I could not see his features clearly, I knew he looked right at me. Who was this person? Then Derek and Nick appeared from the back, and at once, the tall African's face split into a wide grin. He clasped Nick's upper arm in greeting, and I heard the rumble of a deep, throaty voice.

This must be the man Nick had spoken about, the Maasai. I knew little about the tribe other than what I had gleaned from Juba and Nick. But it seemed they were known for their intimidating height and were ferocious warriors. Malaika was also Maasai, which explained her graceful, tall, and slender figure. I wondered if the two were related.

All three men went into the house, and I heard noises coming from behind me, which indicated they were in the living room. Malaika must have joined them, no doubt getting them refreshment after their working outside in the rain.

"Hello there, Julia." Derek joined me outside.

"Hello."

Derek took a seat and leaned down to look at the baby, who wriggled like a little eel. Raindrops dripped from the brim of his battered hat, and he swiped it off and laid it on the ground. "Nalah is growing quickly," he said. "I would swear she's grown bigger just since you got here."

"Gosh, that would be a miracle, seeing as I just arrived. But I have been feeding her some solids because she was a bit underweight. In a few weeks Nalah will look even healthier than she does now."

"Yes," he agreed. "You've been good for her. You know, I'm awfully glad you came. Have you been homesick yet?"

"No!" I said it too harshly, and Derek raised one

brow in alarm.

"I'm sorry, Derek. That was rude of me. I haven't thought much of England as I'm still fascinated by all the newness of Africa. I cannot wait to see more of the country beyond the boundaries of the farm."

"I shall see to it that you do. I will take you on an excursion."

"That would be wonderful. Thank you, Derek."

"What would be wonderful?" Nick came out of the house, the tall Maasai behind him and *Mzuka* following along.

"I'm going to take Julia to see some of the local sights. She's been at Jacaranda a couple of days already, and hasn't seen much beyond the walls of the house."

Nick's eyes shifted from his manager to mine. What was he thinking? He then turned to the man standing quietly at his side.

"Julia, this is Migali, my good friend. He has just returned from a long journey."

The man stepped closer, and I stared unabashedly, never having seen his like before. He towered above me, his frame as lean and straight as a wooden board. Even his arms seemed extraordinarily long.

Migali was wrapped in bright red cloth, with muscular shoulders bare. Around his neck he wore a thick cord strung with multiple rows of blue, red, green, and yellow beads. The same design was duplicated in what looked to be the size of bracelets, yet these were threaded through both earlobes. Migali was handsome, his face clean-shaven, the contours of him smooth and dark as the soil in England. His thick hair was intricately braided and bound with small beads. It looked as though it had been dyed red with henna.

The African's dark eyes registered no emotion as he looked at me. He did not smile but gave me a curt nod. "*Jambo.*"

"*Jambo, Migali.* It is a pleasure to meet you." My words sounded ridiculous. I was hardly taking afternoon tea with a country gentleman but speaking to an African warrior. My cheeks warmed, and I was unsure how to continue.

"Sit with us, Migali." Nick took command.

The young man did not use any of the chairs, but folded himself down onto the ground, close to the baby who had not taken her eyes from him. He leaned over her and then poked her gently in the stomach. She grabbed hold of his stick-like finger and gurgled.

"This baby, she grows," he stated and looked across to me. Even though he sat on the ground and I in a chair, our eyes were level.

"She is a healthy child," I agreed, "and a happy one as well."

There came the clink of china as Malaika came through the open door carrying a tea tray. I was surprised to see her, usually Juba had this lowly task. But as the beautiful housekeeper came closer, I understood why. Her gaze locked upon the handsome Maasai man, who ignored her and continued to play with Nalah. So, that was it—Malaika was attracted to Migali.

I poured the tea and was quite amused at the sight of this tribal warrior holding a china teacup in his enormous hand. But Migali drank with us and even tasted a piece of Wilson's shortbread.

"Where have you journeyed?" I asked.

He contemplated the question for a moment. "To see my grandfather. He is an old man, and he is very sick. I have been with him so he can die."

"Oh, I am so sorry."

Migali looked at me with a puzzled expression. "Not to be sorry. He is with the other elders now." This was stated without emotion.

Once again, Nick came to my rescue. "Migali's tribe are nomadic, and he has been all the way to Lake Naivasha to see his family. His grandfather was an important elder, and this position has now passed down to Migali's father, and one day will pass down to him,"

The culture was fascinating. Entirely foreign to anything I knew. I promised myself that I should enquire if Nick had any reading on African culture. I knew there were books in his study, but I had not been in the room to see what they were.

"Well I for one am glad you're back," Derek said amiably. "I don't think I could put up with Nick much longer."

Migali's face split into a broad smile, and I was taken aback at the transformation. "This man, he is much work," he said, indicating Nick. "He should pay us more money." The men laughed good-naturedly, and then there ensued a conversation about the farm and specifics on certain crops and livestock. Nalah started making little noises, and I knew she was working up to a cry. I picked her up, excusing myself to the men as I left them outside talking.

When I went to make up the baby's bottle, I saw Malaika in the kitchen helping both Wilson and Juba with the lunch preparation as there were visitors coming today. I perched Nalah on my hip and prepared her milk with learned dexterity of using one hand. I felt the housekeeper's eyes on me and met her gaze.

"Do you want me to help you with lunch?" I asked, wondering if she resented me for having no household responsibilities—I was an employee just as she was herself.

"*Hapana,*" she declined.

I retrieved the jug of cow's milk and poured it into the bottle. I thought about she and Migali both being Maasai. "This Migali, is he a friend to you?"

Both Wilson and Juba instantly stopped what they were doing. Had I said the wrong thing? I swung a look in her direction. Malaika's face was stone.

"This Maasai, he is friend to no one," she said flatly.

I finished making Nalah's bottle and hurried down to the nursery.

NALAH WAS FAST ASLEEP when I heard the Babcock's arrive for luncheon. I waited a few minutes and then left my room. The heady scent of roast meat wafted through the house and my mouth watered.

The chink of glasses and murmur of conversation was coming from the living room, so I made my way in there to join the others.

"Here she is. Hello, Julia." Felicity Babcock raised her glass to me as though we were old friends. I smiled and then realised the others were all staring at me. I went to stand near the fireplace—suddenly out of my depth. I glanced up at the portrait of Amelia. Her knowing eyes watched over the room.

"Julia, dear," Felicity continued. "Do come over here and meet Pops, oh, and Trevor too."

Reluctantly, I allowed her to lead me to where two men stood in conversation with Nick. The tallest of the two had a regal bearing, reminiscent of the nobility I had met in England, and I at once felt uncomfortable. I guessed the man to be somewhere in his sixties, lean in build with a large bushy moustache that was grey as the thick swatch of hair on his head. He wore a white suit, the apparent uniform of colonial Englishmen, and he turned as we approached. His face bore the marks of a lifetime spent under a tropical sun.

"Pops," said Felicity. "Here is the new nanny I told you about. This is Julia Rossington, and she hails all the way from Surrey."

"Well, I'll be dashed," said the gentleman. "I have fond recollections of Wimbledon, never missed a tournament until I moved from Blighty to this damned country." He smiled, and I saw his teeth bore the dirty stain of tobacco.

"It is a pleasure to meet you, sir."

"Don't be ridiculous," laughed Felicity. "You just call him Pops. That's what everybody does, even the servants."

"I see," I said. "Then I shouldn't like to be any different."

"And this is my darling brother, Trevor." Trevor, ensconced in conversation with Nick, broke off speaking at her light touch on his upper arm. He paused to look at me.

Trevor was a little older than his sister and close in age to our host. He was shorter than his father yet had completely different bone structure than either the old man or his sister. Trevor's face was round, and his eyes an arresting bright green. I thought him a handsome fellow, yet suspected he was well aware of it. He gave me a disarming smile.

"Hello, Julia. Nick's just been telling me what a boon you've been with the baby. It's damned difficult finding good help in this country, especially from a fellow Briton. I do hope you're settling in and will be as happy as the rest of us living in Kenya."

"Thank you, Trevor. I'm pleased to be here. Every day has been interesting so far. There's much to learn about this beautiful country and its interesting culture."

"I hope the baby doesn't keep you up all hours. They can be pesky little blighters when they're tiny. Although Nick says she's quite well behaved, and all that."

"Nalah is very good and she's already sleeping through the night, which is something I am more than grateful for."

"Excellent. Tell me, what do you think about Jacaranda? It's a fine place, isn't it?" Trevor Babcock had a certain charm about him which made even the most mundane question sound interesting. I answered his question but couldn't help notice when his eyes suddenly strayed away from me to settle elsewhere. His expression changed, and I glimpsed something fleeting in his face, a look I had seen before. That of a predator. I continued talking but followed his gaze to see where it landed.

Malaika stood in the doorway waiting politely to speak. I watched her eyes travel across the room and fall upon Trevor. At once her demeanour altered. Her stoic, harsh posture seemed to wilt, just a fraction. No one would notice unless they had themselves been a victim of unwanted attention. She saw me watching and quickly looked away.

"Lunch is served, *Bwana* Fleming," Malaika announced. We obediently left the room and went in to dine.

Wilson had outdone himself today, for the spread looked delicious. He had mastered a traditional English roast beef dinner, complete with boiled potatoes, crispy roast potatoes, green peas, cauliflower, and Yorkshire pudding. If I had shut my eyes, I could have been sitting in any English dining room, not on the coast of Eastern Africa.

As we ate, the conversation was general, but sometimes difficult for me to follow as it concerned matters unfamiliar to me. At length though, the topic of the Mombasa Club arose, and Derek eagerly joined the exchange.

"I say," he said. "The annual party's next month, according to the newspaper."

"That's right," said Trevor. "Hard to believe it's already time for the birthday bash. This year they're going to celebrate the commissioner's birthday at the same time. Typical of Sir Charles, wanting a fuss and a party—at someone else's expense. Sly devil."

"Do you plan to attend?" asked Derek.

"We are certainly not going to miss it," Felicity piped up. "There's precious little opportunity for fun around here as it is. So, when something comes along, you have to jump at it." She glanced over at Nick, who was concentrating on cutting a slice of beef. "Nick, I think you should come with us for a change and bring Julia along for some dancing. The poor girl hasn't met anyone except us boring old fogies, and it would be the ideal opportunity for her to be introduced to the English community all at once. Don't you agree, Trevor?"

"That's a super idea," he said. "Perhaps we could all travel there together?"

Nick interrupted. "I'm not sure that's plausible. First of all, I doubt I'll attend, and you should not assume Julia wants to, either."

"Don't be silly. Of course, she does," Felicity said in astonishment. "Why on earth wouldn't a young, attractive gal like Julia want to be around her fellow countrymen for a jolly evening of music and dancing?"

"Spot on, darling. I think that's the very thing," said her father in agreement.

"There are some interesting characters that frequent the club," Trevor added. "It would do you good to chat to others and get a sense of what you've let yourself in for." He gave a short laugh.

"Don't say that, Babcock. You'll scare the lady away, and she hasn't even been here a week yet." Derek admonished.

I listened to their continued banter. They had forgotten I sat among them, so absorbed in the debate were they. No one had yet to ask my opinion, though I was the subject of their conversation.

"I should certainly like to go to the Mombasa Club," I said, and the others immediately fell silent. "But as a newcomer, I'd prefer to discuss this with Nick at some other time that's more agreeable. There are things to consider as I'm here to take care of my charge. Her welfare is my primary focus. But I do appreciate your desire to make me welcome. Thank you. You are all most kind."

No one spoke for a moment, but I felt Nick's eyes on me. I looked up to see what I considered to be an expression of gratitude. I had correctly assumed my employer had no love for the social life of Mombasa.

Although young and healthy, Nick was also alone. I considered that must be by choice, for he was an attractive man who could easily find himself the object of a woman's desire. Part of me was surprised he'd such little interest in socialising. However, it was impossible to make any real assumption because I didn't know the man at all.

The remainder of the meal passed without incident. We were served a wonderfully tart apple pie, swimming in rich custard. After dinner the men stepped out onto the veranda to smoke their cigars while Felicity and I stayed in the living room, sipping cold drinks. I had a glass of lemonade, slightly flavoured with ginger. Felicity was drinking gin.

"Julia, I really must insist you make every effort to come with us next weekend. There are so many people I would like you to meet. I believe it's imperative you mix with others when you're stuck out in the middle of nowhere and in the sole company of men—I should know."

"But I don't feel that way. There are plenty of women here. There is Malaika and other women on the property I can speak with." It occurred to me to ask about Amelia Fleming.

Felicity laughed, "Don't be ridiculous. I'm talking about English women. You have nothing in common with the Africans, for goodness sake. I've lived here most of my life, and I'm not friends with any of our workers. So I hardly think it likely that someone who's been here five minutes is going to feel at home with them. Besides, what would you talk about?"

I shrugged. "I'd ask questions. I know so little about this place that many things come to mind. I've yet to see wildlife, unless you count a herd of wildebeest in the distance and a scone-snatching monkey. I know nothing of the different tribes, the language, even the history. I tried to learn as much as I could on the journey here, but I didn't get far."

Felicity sipped her drink. "You are funny," she said. "You don't act like anyone I know. But you are interesting. I'd like us to be friends. After all, I don't have many, especially living this far from town. I get terribly bored at Meadowbrook. Especially since Amelia died."

I harboured no genuine sympathy for the woman. I was sure she had been educated back in England and enjoyed a very full life compared to most. With her background, Felicity could probably live wherever she wanted. My reason for being in Kenya slept in the nursery down the hall. I was not here to make friends and socialise.

"Has my sister talked you into it yet?" said Trevor, joining us from the verandah.

"No," complained Felicity. "She is far too sensible and loyal to her job."

"Don't worry, old gal. If anyone can corrupt her, it's you," Derek said, coming through the door. "I'll work on her before Saturday gets here. After a few more days of putting up with me and Nick, Julia will be ready to go anywhere to get away from us."

"Have you heard our resident German has secured yet another contract with the Kikuyu?" Nick asked Pops Babcock as they came in from outside.

"No—dashed wily fellow. Schmitt seems to be

able to worm his way into all the deals the British can't get. And no one seems to know much about him, other than his living here a while. I've chatted with Sir Charles about him, but the commissioner doesn't seem too interested. I thought Schmitt was in the textile business, jute, or something like that. Apparently, he's made several contracts with suppliers of raw material. But someone at the club told me he made his fortune in the Kimberley Mines."

"Is that Klaus Schmitt you're talking about?" Derek asked. He had refreshed Felicity's drink and now took Trevor's to do the same.

"Yes," said Pops. "Do you know anything about him?"

"Only what you've already heard."

"What do you think keeps him in Mombasa? After all, you wouldn't think he'd want to be among the British when there are plenty of German settlements in Uganda," added Nick.

"That sounds rather prejudiced," said Trevor. "Surely the fellow can stay wherever he wants as long as he's doing no harm. It sounds as though you have a grudge against the Germans, Nick?" said Trevor. "Don't you like 'em?"

"Not particularly. Especially when you consider what's going on in the South."

"Ah, that blasted war." Pops Babcock handed Derek his empty glass to fill. "Nasty business that— glad we're not mixed up in that fiasco. Bloody mess if you ask me. Ridiculous waste of life. Whoever is running the campaign should have his backside kicked from here to the Suez," he grumbled.

"Pops believes the British should allow the

Germans and Dutch to take whatever land they want," Trevor said. "I think that would be a massive error. Why would we stand back and let anyone control that part of the continent?"

"Especially when the land actually belongs to the Africans," came Nick's dry retort. "We fight over something we do not even own to begin with."

"That's rather hypocritical coming from someone who owns land himself," Trevor stated.

I looked at Nick, expecting to see anger, but was surprised at the passive expression he wore.

"I suppose you could say that, Trevor, and you would be right. The only difference is that as you well know, Father leased this property from the Maasai many years ago. Luckily for us, their elders have allowed us to renew this lease over time at some cost to my family. We exist harmoniously because up until this point, it has been a mutually beneficial arrangement. I farm, employ some of their tribe when they need work, they occasionally steal my cattle, and the monies paid annually helps feed their villages. So, you may call me a hypocrite if you will, Trevor, but I certainly find I can sleep at night. I wonder if the same could be said for some other Englishmen."

I was impressed by his statement. It certainly shut Trevor Babcock up. I was also glad to hear that Jacaranda had not been taken from the Africans but borrowed. In truth, as much as I admired my country's long and strong reach across the world, I was also sympathetic to the indigenous people within the British Empire. I am sure I would not like to be a native of a conquered land. Yet that in itself was hypocrisy because I had enjoyed the spoils of that empire my entire life.

"My goodness, how boring you all are," Felicity whined. "Honestly, if you want to talk about politics, can you not do it elsewhere? I'd rather talk about something fun, or even have a game of cards. What about that, Nick? Do you have any cards?"

"Oh God, not that," complained her brother. "I am so sick of gin rummy I think I would rather plough a field than sit and play another game with my sister."

"I've heard they're moving more of the British East Africa offices to Nairobi," said Nick.

"Yes. I believe it's a foregone conclusion that it will happen." Pops Babcock sipped his drink and then shook his head at the prospect.

"What will that mean to all of us, Pops?" asked Felicity.

"Well, my dear," said her father. "It means all of the resources from the British government that we are used to here will not be accessible in Mombasa anymore, but in Nairobi. This will impact some families, and those who are not farming will most likely move closer to Nairobi. The rest of us will remain here as always."

"But that's awful," she complained. "It means half of the English community will be gone."

"No great loss, in my opinion," Nick commented.

"At least we have the railway now, so Nairobi is far easier to get to than it used to be," added Derek.

"Yes, but the train takes forever." Felicity was definitely upset. "How shall I stand it if everybody moves away?"

"We shall worry about it when it happens," said her brother.

"Did you hear there's a polo match in town on Sunday?" announced Derek, bringing a welcome change of subject.

Trevor's eyes glittered. "Really? Are you playing?"

"Just try and stop me," Derek said eagerly. "Although I am a bit rusty, but I have a new pony to try out. I've worked with her a little, but I have yet to see how she'll do in a real game."

The conversation steered into more comfortable topics. I waited for another ten minutes before politely excusing myself to attend to the baby. I had no idea if she had awakened, but frankly, I was exhausted from their company.

That said, my curiosity had been aroused. I should like to meet the other English people in the community—part of me even nursed a desire to go to the Mombasa Club—see who everybody was and what they did. But only after speaking with my employer. I would wait and have that discussion with Nick Fleming later in the week. For now, there were other things to think about.

Tomorrow was Monday, and Juba would go into Mombasa for supplies. I had submitted a list with requests, but part of me wished I might go along with him and enjoy being somewhere other than inside the house.

Chapter Six

JUBA FELL ILL WITH A BAD stomach in the night, so it was determined Derek would go to Mombasa in his stead. Apparently, there were items needed which could not wait another day. I was delighted when the farm manager came into the nursery and asked if I should like to accompany him into town.

"We'll take the large cart with more oxen, which makes the journey a little faster. It will give you a chance to look around a bit. Would you like to go?"

"Yes." I glanced down at the baby, who hungrily sucked on her bottle. "But I do not like to leave Nalah. There is no one else to watch her, Derek, and though I've only been here a few days, she is used to me and might fret if I'm gone."

"Then bring her along," he said, his kind eyes smiling. "It'll do the little mite a world of good to get some fresh air. We can make a little bed in the cart, and you can bring a bottle along with you in case she gets fussy. We'll be back right after lunch, so we shan't be away for long."

I was thrilled with the prospect and extremely grateful for his thoughtfulness. Derek left the nursery to get Nick's approval, and I prepared myself and the baby for our morning out.

By the time the cart rolled down the driveway, the

temperature had already climbed. Derek had procured a large wooden box, and in it, we placed a thick layer of straw, a cushion from the sofa and then Nalah's pillow and a blanket. This sat between us on the bench seat, and the baby lay content inside, staring up at the bright azure sky. I had brought along a large umbrella to use for shade, should it grow to uncomfortable for the baby.

"I hope we see some wildlife today, Derek," I commented. "When Nick brought me to Jacaranda, it was in the middle of the day, and he said all the animals were sleeping and staying out of the sun."

"He was right. But it's early yet. At the very least, I'll bet we see a few antelope." The cart trundled along the road, pulled by six massive horned oxen as big as bulls. We had not gone far and had just rounded a corner when Derek nudged me. I gasped audibly.

In a nest of bush and Acacia trees, not thirty feet away, stood two of the most beautiful creatures I had ever seen. Giraffes. One looked young, for it did not have near the height of its partner. They both turned their heads at our approach. Their huge brown eyes studied us while they chewed on leaves.

"Oh, my. Are they not lovely?" I murmured, noting how similar their faces were to the camels I had seen in Egypt. They were so graceful, and I was taken aback at their height. As we drew nearer, both animals must have sensed we were no threat, and they returned to selecting leaves from the top of the tree using their long purple tongues. When we passed them, I was again struck by their gargantuan size.

"Are they dangerous?" I asked nervously. It was one thing seeing an occasional deer at Richmond Park, but I'd never been close to anything of this magnitude.

"Not usually, if they don't feel threatened. Most of the grazing animals are used to seeing us in our carts. They're always watchful. But if you don't make sudden noises and scare them, it's generally safe. Don't ever approach one though. One swipe of that neck, and your bones would be snapped in half."

A ripple of something ran down my spine, but not of fear, more the adventure of it, the sensation that I was somewhere dangerous—in tune with Nature, but at her mercy. I was invigorated.

We trundled along, and true to Derek's forecast, we did indeed see many antelope on our journey. He pointed out the different varieties, from the smaller Thompson Gazelles, with their twitching tails, who ran as though they had springs in their hooves, to the Impala, with their strangely shaped antlers, that reminded me of something pagan. Once we were well into the journey, I finally saw my very first zebras and was almost moved to tears. I had never seen anything like this before in my life, and at once felt totally inadequate in the vast beauty that was Africa.

"I'll take you down to a watering hole sometime in the next few days," Derek promised, seeing my reaction to the wildlife. "If we go at dusk, you'll get to see all manner of creatures, perhaps even one of the big cats."

"That would be spectacular," I said. "Nick told me there has been a leopard taking some of the goats. Is it still around, do you think?"

"Oh yes." Derek chuckled. "That little devil has plagued us for weeks now. A few of the men have seen it. Black leopards are extremely rare. I'd rather not shoot the pest because of that. But we shall have to if it keeps attacking the herds."

I glanced down at Nalah, who lay fast asleep. "It sounds like something out of a book when I hear you speak, Derek. Talk of leopards and antelope is far removed from being in England and discussing the weather."

He laughed at that, and again I considered what a nice fellow he really was. His freckled face gave him such a boyish charm.

"How do you like Jacaranda so far, Julia? Any regrets leaving home for a place this far away?" His eyes were bright with interest.

"I think it is marvellous here," I gushed. "I have no regrets whatsoever. Why settle for an ordinary life when one can do something like this? Tell me, how long have you lived here?"

"Let me see," he thought for a moment. "Fifteen years—give or take. I came over when I was nineteen. I knew Martin Fleming at Oxford. He was a good chap. He invited me over, and I never went back—well, except to see my family, of course."

"Do you have a large family?"

"Gad, yes. That's why my parents were happy to see the back of me. Four sons, and I'm the youngest. All the others are married with their own families now. What about you? Any family back there in Chessington?"

I shook my head. "No. I lost both my parents to smallpox when I was very young. An elderly aunt cared for me. She died six years ago." I did not elaborate further. We fell silent, and then I thought of Amelia Fleming. I grew bold.

"Who is Amelia?" I asked.

Derek kept his eyes on the road ahead. He did not

seem perturbed by the question. "Nick's wife. Well, before she died. Why do you ask?"

"I went in her room the other day and got chastised by Malaika for doing so. I had no idea Nick had ever been married, let alone widowed."

Derek shrugged. "He doesn't talk about Amelia often—it's a difficult subject for him."

"Why?"

"Because she was murdered."

"What?" I was astounded.

"They found her body in a ravine a mile outside of Mombasa. It was a nasty business."

"Oh no—that's horrific. What happened?"

Derek sighed. "Amelia was a great one for socialising. She and Felicity always knocked about together. They'd been at the Mombasa Club for the evening. Apparently, Felicity fell ill and left early for home. Amelia planned to stay the night in town with a friend, so she remained at the club. She never arrived at her friend's that night. Her body was found later the next day. I will not tell you what the poor woman endured. Suffice to say, it was not pleasant."

"Dear God." It was a shocking story.

"As for Malaika, well, she worshipped her mistress and was devastated by her death. She's always been extremely protective of both Nick and Amelia. So don't take anything she says or does personally. It was a rotten time, let me tell you. Amelia's murder caused quite the scandal."

We rounded a bend and joined a larger arterial road. I could see the outskirts of Mombasa in the distance and more traffic headed both in and out of the city. We were getting closer to the small ferry that would take us the rest of the way.

"Did they ever find the killer?"

Derek shook his head. "No. But not for the lack of trying. Poor Nick went through hell for months while the investigation went on. It was bad enough he had lost his wife in such a brutal way, but then the post-mortem found Amelia had been pregnant."

"That is so sad." I knew that loss from personal experience. My heart went out to Nick Fleming.

"And then, to cap it all, the poor chap was accused of being her killer. I think it almost finished him off."

I gasped.

Derek turned to me, nodding. "Yes, Nick was a suspect for several months. It was devastating. The man would never have made it through such a mess had it not been for his brother, Martin."

"Why would anyone think Nick capable of such a heinous deed?"

Derek shrugged. "The husband is always the first suspect—a crime of passion, I suppose. You see, Amelia ran with a racy set at the club and was what you might call promiscuous. In light of her behaviour, known throughout the community, it was considered plausible that Nick had lost his head with jealousy."

"My goodness," I said. "I had no idea about any of this." I suddenly felt ill.

Derek noticed my pallor. "Are you all right, Julia? Look, I am sorry, I shouldn't have blurted it all out to you. It's a shocking story, especially when you have come all this way to live in Amelia's house." He gripped my hand, which lay on the baby's box. "Nick would never harm a fly. He was a good husband. Most men would have throttled their wives for constant infidelity. But not Nick. He didn't lay a hand on Amelia and was ultimately found innocent. I'd never have stayed on at Jacaranda had I thought any differently."

Derek's words appeased me, though they did not disperse the seed of anxiety I felt hearing the story. As the cart approached the rickety ferry to cross over into Mombasa, I began to wonder if I had made a terrible mistake coming to Kenya after all?

AS WE MADE OUR WAY INTO the city, I recollected some of the places I had seen a few days earlier. Unlike Nick, Derek was a guide who seemed happy to identify some of the landmarks. Up on a rise, he pointed out a massive building of two storeys, colonial in design, white, with massive pillars on the ground floor and verandahs on both levels.

"The infamous Mombasa Club," he announced as we passed the foot of the hill. Then we moved on through a busy street, teeming with shops and shoppers. Derek showed me the direction of the brand-new railway station, which connected the coastal population to inland cities such as Nairobi and Kampala. I enjoyed seeing the hodgepodge of architecture, from Portuguese influences courtesy of Vasco de Gama, and the imperial stamp of the British, to the indigenous buildings of the Africans themselves. As with my last time here, I was enthralled by the scenery and sounds, vastly different to home.

We traversed through the streets, occasionally drawing the attention of those we passed. Many women walked with their babies harnessed on their backs, leaving their hands free to carry their goods and wares. I thought it an excellent idea and stored it in my mind to revisit later.

At last, Derek steered the oxen into a wide-open square, full of colourful stalls laden with all manner of wares. He tethered the oxen at a nearby hitch. I lifted Nalah from her sanctuary and passed her down to Derek before alighting myself.

"Would you like to have a look around while I conduct some business?" he asked.

"Yes," I said earnestly. "Where are you going?"

He gestured to a nearby building. "In there. Most of our farm supplies are further in town. But this would be a good place to purchase anything you need for the baby." Derek passed me some money. He told me I would be safe in this area, and we agreed to meet back in the same spot in thirty minutes. I held onto the baby tightly and strolled away.

I drew much attention as I shopped. Seeing a white woman might not be unusual here in a Mombasa marketplace, but a white woman carrying a child of mixed blood apparently was. The glances were mainly curious, but I did encounter several Europeans, who glared at me with open hostility. I cared not. I was far more interested in looking at everything there was to behold.

The fruit and vegetable stalls offered foods I had never laid eyes upon before. No Cox's Pippin apples here, but large, strange-shaped objects, perhaps some type of melon or mango? As I stopped to peruse, the stall owners would stare first at me, and then the baby, who was enthralled and looking at everything.

"*Memsahib, njoo ununue kutoka kwangu,*" said this stall owner. Of course, I hadn't the faintest idea what he said, likely an enticement for me to buy something. I smiled and nodded, feeling ridiculous for not understanding. I must make an effort to learn the language if I planned to stay.

I found a stall selling children's items and purchased two toys for Nalah. A crudely carved wooden monkey, and a woven circle, with tiny bells sewn into it so it made a tinkling sound. The baby loved this and grabbed onto it, clenching it in her tiny fists. After a few tries, I finally managed to understand how much I owed for the purchase, and counted out my money carefully. The seller was tall, but unlike the Maasai, he had more Arabic facial features. I guessed he must be Somali, as I knew from my studies, there was a large North African presence here.

I enjoyed myself, mixing with ordinary people who I assumed went about their usual business. Periodically, I felt the eyes of someone linger on me longer than was comfortable. But I really could not expect it to be any different, being a foreigner in their land.

Whenever I passed a food stall, the amazing scents tantalised my nose. I stopped to look at one, which had a large pot bubbling over a small fire. I peered in to see what it was and, by the smell, judged it to be some type of fish stew. In a port town, I would expect nothing less. I watched a customer buy a bowl of the stew. He then helped himself to something which resembled a ball of mashed potatoes, only firmer. He used it to mop up the stew as if it were an eating utensil. It looked delicious.

"Ugali," said a voice beside me and I turned to see a well-groomed gentleman. He wore no hat upon his blond hair, and unlike many of the whites here, was rather fair complected, with a neatly trimmed beard threaded with grey. Wearing khaki trousers and a loose shirt, he was dressed in the typical European style.

"I beg your pardon?" I asked, hoisting Nalah higher on my hip. She paid no mind to the stranger, still entranced with her new toy.

"The man eats fish stew with a ball of ugali. It is a starch made with maize. Here it is a staple, as popular as bread in your country." His English was stilted. He sounded German.

Seeing my curiosity, he extended a hand. "*Entschuldigen Sie mich.* Excuse me. My name is Klaus Schmitt."

I shook it. So, this was the man Nick had discussed with Pops Babcock. "Good day, I am Julia Rossington. I work for Mr Fleming, at Jacaranda."

"I suspected as much when I saw *das kleines Mädchen*...the little girl." His pale eyes landed on the baby. His accent was very subtle. "Welcome to Kenya. How do you find it? It is very different from England, is it not?"

"Most definitely," I said.

The gentleman seemed pleasant enough. His attention remained fixed upon me as a hint of a smile played around his mouth. I guessed him to be close to forty. "I think its difference is precisely what makes Kenya so very fascinating," I continued answering his question. "In those contrasts lies such beauty."

"Eloquently said, *Fraülein* Rossington. I see Africa has already worked her charms upon you."

"Hello, Schmitt," it was Derek. He joined us, and there was a shift in the German man's countenance.

"*Guten tag*, Derek. I have introduced myself to the lovely *fraülein*. And now I must go on my way." He gave a curt nod directed to me and then left before either one of us could respond.

"Was he bothering you?" Derek said as soon as the man was gone.

"No," I frowned. "Why would you think that? He just introduced himself and we chatted about the food." Derek watched the man walking away. His expression grim.

"You don't like him, do you?"

"Cannot stand the fellow. First off, he's a Hun, and I don't trust them. Second, he's a dirty polo player." He stopped as a frantic jingle interrupted his words. Derek looked down to see Nalah waving her new toy. We both laughed.

We got back into the cart and went on to our next location. This was a gigantic warehouse situated at the port. I had been here just a few days earlier, and yet it seemed like another lifetime as my eyes now saw it so differently.

The harbour was a hive of activity, with workers bustling about. I counted three steamers that must have recently arrived. According to Derek, this was evident by the number of wares available for sale—some, still being unloaded from the ships. This pleased him immensely, and he looked forward to buying several newspapers, which though outdated, would still be fresh reading here.

Our timing really was perfect, for once we were inside the building, there were many items available, if the full wooden pallets were anything to go by. Derek directed me towards a cordoned off area in one corner of the warehouse which had been set up rather like a shop. I would do my shopping while he attended to

Jacaranda's business.

A young Indian gentleman stood behind a laden counter, and he greeted me politely as I approached. I was delighted to find a number of things on my list. Pear's soap, some tea, a few edible items, and bath salts. I also bought enough cotton material for two dresses. These were parcelled up and then taken outside and put in the cart, while Derek supervised the loading of Jacaranda's many supplies.

With the baby perched upon my hip, I strolled away to gaze at the water. I loved the sea, just not sailing upon it. But was there anything more soothing than looking out to the horizon and imagining all the amazing places beyond? Perhaps growing up on a small island gave the British a connection to water, unlike someone living in the middle of a vast continent. Even now I still couldn't believe I had crossed such a boundless ocean. England was a world away.

Nalah began squirming. She'd been good, but it was getting rather hot, and though she weighed little, I had carried her for a long while. We were both warm, and our clothing damp to the touch.

I walked back to the cart looking for Derek and discovered him signing a paper. He shook the hand of a burly white man, who looked better suited to a boxing ring than a portside warehouse.

"Ready to get going?" Derek asked as we approached. At my nod, he took the baby from me so that I could get into the cart. Handing Nalah back, I placed her in her little box where she would be more comfortable than on my lap. I gave her a drink from her bottle, which she gulped.

"I have one more stop to make, but it is on the way

out of town, Julia," Derek explained. "There, we can take refreshment and get something to take with us for lunch."

I had not realised how thirsty I was until he said this. Now my mouth felt full of wool.

We reached our destination not ten minutes later, and I gratefully accepted the cup of cool well water Derek brought me. He left the cart under a large shade tree and loaded numerous items. While he did this, I gave Nalah the rest of her bottle. The poor mite was both hungry and thirsty. Her little face glistened with sweat, and her soft black hair stuck to her head. After she'd emptied the bottle, I removed her clothes, leaving her wearing a nappy and nothing else. I hoped once we were moving, she would cool off.

No sooner had I laid her down than she fell asleep. It had already been a long day for a baby used to far less activity. I envied her nakedness and chuckled to myself, imagining what would happen were I to remove my clothing.

"What's so funny?" Derek asked after he had loaded a box into the back and clambered up into the cart. He handed me a bag.

"Nothing," I said sheepishly as he pulled away.

After Derek navigated the other traffic on the street, it was not long before we were headed away from the town. The ferry crossing was quick, and once we had left the boat, the oxen settled into a rhythmic step.

Derek indicated the package I held. "There are sandwiches in there," he said. "Take one for yourself, and please hand the other to me."

I did as he asked but was surprised to have such

normal fare. "This is not local food," I stated.

"It would be if you were in Twickenham," he remarked.

I laughed, liking Derek more all the time. "I would hazard a guess that a ham sandwich is hardly a Kenyan delicacy. But the bread is fresh, and this ham is delicious!"

"The shop's owned by Josiah Mead and his wife, Milly. They're from Ipswich, and Milly's bread baking is famous. Josiah keeps a pig farm not far from here, and he butchers and cures his own meat. I just bought a hock of ham and some sausages."

I considered this and then had a frightening thought. "Will the wild animals smell the meat as we drive back?" I had a sudden vision of a pride of lions attacking us.

"Oh, they'll smell it all right. But the scent of us will be stronger, and unless they are starving, we'll not be bothered." He looked up at the sky. "Anyway, it's unlikely any predator will be looking to eat as this is their quiet time. But there's nothing to worry about, Julia." He gestured to a space behind our seat, which I had not noticed. Down in the crevice lay a menacing looking rifle, as big as a broom. "We prepare for charging elephants and hope for gazelle." Derek grinned, and I could not help but laugh. He looked so impish and young.

"Eat your sandwich," he commanded, and I obeyed.

On our return, I fixed the umbrella, so it gave Nalah shelter. While she slept, I enjoyed the scenery, seeing more herding animals, though none were close. Derek said the noise we made travelling would keep them at bay. But there were birds aplenty, and at one point, I spied my first herd of ostriches. They were massive, almost the size of half a horse. Their long necks craned up to look at us as we rumbled along, though they seemed nonplussed at our being there. How fascinating to see these unfamiliar creatures. It was like flicking through the pages of a book, all against the backdrop of endless African plains. Derek told me facts about the many species of mammals, the terrain, and vegetation. I was utterly engrossed. By the time we turned into the driveway at Jacaranda, I had learned much.

Nalah had woken earlier but fortunately not made a fuss. Once the cart came to a halt behind the house, I wanted to get her inside. I carried her straight into the nursery and peeled off her nappy. She would feel better after a cooling bath. I planned to have one myself once the baby was settled. Nalah was still tired, even after sleeping most of the journey home. But she had been on an adventure—out of her usual routine. How odd that in so short a time, we already had a routine.

An hour passed before I had put the baby into her crib, splashed myself with cold water and changed. Then I remembered my purchases—I had left them in the cart. I would find Derek and collect them, then perhaps stop to find out how Juba felt. I hoped he had improved.

I left the house and walked around the back, uncertain where to start. I knew Juba lived in one of the small mud huts which were grouped close to the outbuildings. But to be certain, I stopped in the kitchen and asked Wilson as Malaika was nowhere to be seen.

"Juba, he very, very, sick today, Memsahib,"

Wilson shook his head. "This boy, he rests. I take him water this morning. Malaika tends him now."

The older man's concern worried me. I asked where I could find Juba's hut, and quickly went in search of it.

The huts looked identical, circular in shape, constructed with mud. The roofs were conical, thatched with local grasses. As I neared them, I was surprised by how large they appeared and how sturdy. I'd read something of them on my journey from England and knew these dwellings were temporary, as rains and weather would ultimately erode the buildings.

I passed the first hut and then stopped at the second one, which Wilson had identified as Juba's. The door to the hut was a real wooden door, although crude in design, and it lay open, so I passed through, calling out as I entered.

The air was thick, with the scent of something unpleasant. It took a moment for my eyes to adjust to the darkness after the bright sunlight.

The hut consisted of a sparsely furnished room. There was a chair, and a small cot where I could see a figure lying motionless. The air felt warmer than it was outside, and no breeze was coming in.

"Juba?" I said, approaching the bed. "It is Julia. I have come to see how you are feeling?"

When I reached him, I leaned over to look at him. He stared up at me. His face shiny with sweat. Heat radiated from his body.

"*Jambo, Bibi*," he said, but his voice cracked. Had this boy been lying here unaided all afternoon? I looked about for evidence to the contrary. I could see nothing but an empty tin cup. With a promise to return, I spun on my heel and went back to the house. I marched into the kitchen. Wilson turned with a smile, which faded when he saw my face. I was livid.

"Wilson, did you tell me Malaika was tending Juba?"

"*Ndio, Memsahib.*"

"Where is she?" I demanded as I gathered a water jug and cup.

"She washes clothes, Bibi."

I went back to Juba's hut, and administered to the boy as best I could, though feeling inadequate being unfamiliar with illness in this country. What could be ailing him?

Once he seemed settled, I left him to seek out Malaika. I was familiar with the laundry, and I stormed down the path. I discovered the housekeeper wringing out clothing. There was another woman who assisted her in this task, though she looked barely more than a child.

"Malaika, I wish to speak with you," I demanded.

She did not pause from her work or look up. "Yes, *Memsahib*, what is it?"

"Juba," I said. "Who tends to the boy this afternoon? Who has taken him food and refreshment?"

She stopped working and looked at me as though I had said something ridiculous.

"He is very ill," I went on. "I have been to check on him. Juba has been alone and without water all afternoon. Why have you not helped him?"

"I am busy." She shrugged complacently. "Juba did not ask for help."

Her lack of compassion infuriated me. "He is sick. We must call for the doctor."

She tutted disapprovingly. "This I cannot do."

"Why not?" The woman infuriated me. Her lack of concern for the young houseboy was disturbing.

"This, only *Bwana* can do." She went back to wringing clothes—apparently, our conversation had come to an end as far as Malaika was concerned.

My temper spiked and my blood boiled. Furious, I marched over to the barn, ignoring the greetings and curious stares from the few workers I passed. I went into the building to find Derek; he was not there. I walked over to the stables, paying no mind to where I was, or who was there. I covered the length of the building, looking in each stall until I saw a figure bent over, examining the underneath of a horse's shoe.

"There you are, Derek," I said, my breath short from the exertion of my search and my temper. He let go of the horse's leg and straightened up. It was not Derek, but Nick Fleming.

"Is something wrong?" He frowned, and then his eyes filled with concern. "Is it the baby?"

"Nalah is fine," I said. "But the same cannot be said for Juba. He has been ill since last night, and I have been to check on him just now only to discover no one has tended the boy. I saw no evidence of food or drink, and I believe he is fevered. He needs a doctor."

Nick was already walking towards the door, and I followed close behind. He strode straight for Juba's hut, and I had trouble keeping up with him. When we entered, I hung back to allow Nick his own examination. Juba made no sound. Nick spent a moment with him and then ushered me back outside.

"Well?" I asked nervously.

"You were right to find me," he said heading back

to the stables. "Juba is fevered and must be taken immediately to Mombasa Hospital where the nuns can tend him. I'll send Migali to find Derek. When you see him, tell him I've taken the small cart, and the oxen, but also my horse. I'll leave the cart in Mombasa, and ride back tonight as it will be much faster."

With that, Nick rushed away, leaving me standing there. I watched him go and then made my way to the house. I did not like the worry on Nick's face—would Juba be all right? All I could see in my mind was the boy's cheery face, his friendly smile. I knew nothing of tropical illnesses. Was the boy going to die?

DINNER SEEMED STRANGE WITH JUST Derek and me at the table. My appetite was poor. A day travelling to Mombasa and back, and now worrying about Juba, robbed my desire for food. Therefore, when Derek suggested we go out to sit on the verandah, I was happy to oblige.

We watched the sun sink lower on the soft, pink horizon, while I nestled a small glass of sherry in my hands. "Do you think they will have arrived at the hospital by now?" I asked. I could not stop thinking about Juba.

"Yes. In fact, Nick should be on his way back. He'll make good time on horseback. Julia, you mustn't worry. The nuns at Mombasa Hospital are well trained. If anyone can heal the boy, it's them."

"What do you think is wrong with Juba?"

"Most likely, malaria. It's one of the drawbacks of a tropical climate, unfortunately. But they have made many advances in medicine. If Juba's got it, they'll get quinine into his system quickly. He's young and strong, so his chances will be good."

I sipped my drink, clinging to the positive in Derek's words. When, not much later, a dog barked, I realised Nick must be approaching, for Mzuka had, of course, accompanied his master on the journey. Derek and I got to our feet and walked around to the stables, where Nick had left the horse for one of the men to unsaddle. He strode in our direction, removing his leather gloves.

"How is he?" I asked impatiently.

Nick stopped walking. "It is malaria. He's resting. I believe had we waited much longer, it might have been too late. The nuns have him on quinine. Juba is bathed, comfortable and in good hands. They will send word if anything changes."

I let out a sigh of relief. "Oh, thank goodness. The poor boy."

"He has you to thank for it," Nick continued. "Had you not looked in on him, Juba might be dead."

I did not know how to respond. I was still livid with Malaika for neglecting the boy, so I said nothing.

The two men began walking back to the house, but I knew I wouldn't rest until I'd spoken to the housekeeper. I told Nick I wanted to stop in and see Malaika, and that I would follow them in shortly. Then I made my way to the servants' huts.

As I neared them, a woman tended a pot hung over a small fire. Not speaking the language, I simply said Malaika's name, and she pointed to one of the mud buildings. With daylight fading, I picked up my pace. I wanted to get back to the house before dark.

Hers was the last in one of the two rows. As I drew closer, the door opened. Instinctively, I stepped between Malaika's hut and the one next to it, remaining hidden. I wanted to surprise the woman when she walked past. But the person who came out of the hut was not Malaika. It was Trevor Babcock.

Chapter Seven

TREVOR DID NOT SEE ME CONCEALED between the huts and walked briskly in the opposite direction, away from the main house. What on earth was he doing here? And why was he sneaking around without going up to the house? A fleeting memory came back to me, one of us at Sunday lunch, and how Malaika had bristled under Trevor's stare.

I knocked on the door of the hut but did not wait to be told to enter. Boldly, I marched inside. Candles burned, and Malaika had her back to the door. She spun around and almost cried out when she saw me. I took in her dishevelled state in one glance. Her turban lay on the ground unravelled, and her garment was ripped down to her waist. She'd been crying. Her face was streaked with tears, and with alarm, I saw what looked like blood in the corner of her mouth. My heart sank. I knew that look. I knew that fear shining in her eyes. For once, not so long ago, it had shone in mine.

I stepped forward, and without another thought, I pulled the young woman into my arms. Her entire body stiffened, but I did not let her go. It was only moments before the fight went out of her and she became supple, though she trembled like a scared bird.

"Ssh," I soothed, stroking back her hair. She shuddered against me, and I held her tighter still. We stood like that for what seemed minutes, and as she quietened, I slackened my hold and finally let her go. I did not speak until I led her to the bed, where I sat down, pulling her along with me.

"Has he done this before?"

She paused, then whispered. "Ndio-yes."

"Have you told anyone?"

"Hapana." Her eyes widened. "You cannot tell *Bwana Fleming. Bwana Babcock* very bad man. He will punish me."

I turned to look at her lovely face, "Malaika, it makes no difference that he is a *Bwana* and you a servant. Trevor has no right to do this to you, no right at all." Anger raged deep inside me. I wanted nothing more than to run to Nick and tell him what a bastard his privileged friend was. What gave him the right to touch this woman? I was sickened and consumed with fury.

"You must not tell *Bwana, Memsahib,*" Malaika begged. "If you do, I say you lie."

"But Trevor will come back and do this to you again if we remain silent, don't you see?" I knew the bitter truth of that statement only too well.

Malaika paused, and for a moment, I hoped she'd changed her mind. I was deflated when she shook her head. "This my story, *Memsahib*, you cannot speak of it to anyone. I must think about these words you say, and I will see."

It was the best I would get from her. I said nothing but squeezed her hand, my heart breaking for the young woman.

"Please tell me if there is anything I can do to help." Our eyes met. She raised her chin and fought to regain her dignity, and I said no more. I got up from the bed and went to the door. As I closed it behind me, I could not help but notice there wasn't even a lock on it.

I walked briskly to the house, oblivious of my path. I thought nothing of it being almost dark, or that there might be something ferocious lurking in the shadows. Seething, I dared not go near the living room where the distinctive mumble of conversation filtered through open windows into the night. I went straight to my room and splashed cold water on my face in an effort to regain my composure.

Dear God, that poor girl. Trevor Babcock's face filled my thoughts, his handsome smile which cleverly concealed the evil flowing through him. The sheer audacity of believing he had the right to take what he wanted from a woman incensed me. For a man had done that to me and it had almost been my undoing—I had wanted to die. There was no champion to defend me, no one with whom I could confide my fears or seek advice. I would not let it be that way for Malaika.

I looked at my reflection in the cloudy mirror of my dressing table. I made a silent vow I would do anything within my power to punish Trevor Babcock and stop him from touching Malaika again.

AT BREAKFAST, MALAIKA LOOKED much improved, but she would not meet my eye. With Juba gone, her duty was to step into his role, so she could not avoid me. Nick was back from the fields and already eating. He had a newspaper spread out on the table before him.

"Good morning," he said, with a cursory glance in my direction as I took a seat.

"Morning," I poured myself tea. Malaika placed a warm plate of bacon and eggs in front of me. "Thank you," I said, but she'd already retreated to the kitchen.

I had not slept well. Nightmares of the past had haunted me, and my unsettled state must have been sensed by Nalah, for she'd woken several times in the night. I'd been up before dawn and quietly made her a bottle. She was now fast asleep.

Nick folded the paper back together and then placed it on an empty seat. *Mzuka* lay on the floor next to him, and he reached down to give him a piece of bacon left on his plate. The huge hound chomped it down.

"You're quiet this morning, Julia. Is something amiss?" He posed the question as Malaika came into the room with a plate of toast. She stopped in her tracks—her eyes growing wide. I glanced at her and then Nick.

"No, nothing. Nalah was restless. I'm weary, that's all."

"The girl has healthy lungs," he commented. "I heard her a time or two." He took a sip of tea and watched Malaika place a plate of toast on the table and then leave the room.

"You didn't join us last night after you came in."

"Sorry. Yesterday was such a long day, and I'm still growing used to the heat. You must have been tired yourself, after taking Juba to the hospital?"

"I was fine. I spend most of my day in the saddle anyway, so I'm used to it. But thank you for your concern."

I turned my attention back to my breakfast and then remembered the conversation about Amelia Fleming with Derek yesterday. That had slipped my mind after all that had transpired last night.

"Nick, I hope you don't mind me saying this, but Derek told me what happened to your wife, Amelia, and I wanted to express how sorry I am."

He did not respond. Had I said something wrong? Then abruptly, he pushed his chair out and got to his feet. He leaned forward and placed his hands on the table for support. His face was taut and his eyes dark as pewter.

"Miss Rossington. Although there are many subjects I am happy to discuss with you, Amelia Fleming is not one of them. Can we be clear about that?"

Astounded, all I could do was nod in assent and watch as he stormed from the room. I sat, momentarily stunned. What had I done wrong? I leaned back in my chair, at odds with my feelings. How unlike Nick to be so curt with me. Much had happened in the past twenty-four hours, and perhaps he was just worried about Juba. I didn't like how his sharpness affected me. My situation felt tenuous. What was I doing in a place like this, where I had no one? But I knew the answer to that.

THE WEEK DRAGGED. I DID NOT see much of Nick, but he usually left the house early before it got hot. I surmised he must be taking his breakfast with him as he was absent from the dining room every morning.

Malaika went about the house like a ghost, hiding from me whenever possible and never meeting my glances. I desperately wanted to speak with her about what had happened that night. Yet I understood only too well the desire to be left alone and not be forced to recount something you would rather forget. I had to respect that.

The only person I interacted with as the days passed was Derek. Thank goodness his countenance remained pleasant, though he too felt the tension within the walls of the house, for it was palpable.

I became stifled staying put all day long, and had paid another visit to Winda, Nalah's old nanny. Tired of carrying the baby on my hip as it was uncomfortable for us both, I envied how the African women transported their babies with ease. Winda was surprised to see me, but somehow understood my needs. She helped fashion the fabric I brought with me to attach Nalah on my back in a sort of sling.

Oh, it was liberating! Now I could move around freely and take the baby along with me. I enjoyed my newfound freedom and planned to do much exploring. By the end of the week, Nalah and I had looked about the property close to the house. We had found Wilson's large vegetable and herb garden and had spent quite some time in the stables, where the baby seemed fascinated by the horses.

It was while on these short expeditions that I did my best thinking. I was still rattled by the angry reaction Nick had at my mention of his dead wife. What did it mean? I understood he wanted no reminder of a time when he'd suffered such loss and been suspected of a foul deed. But how could I stop my curiosity when I was reminded daily of Amelia as she looked down from the portrait over the fireplace?

Derek was hardly the best fountain of knowledge— but Felicity Babcock would be if I could talk to her. But I couldn't see Felicity without risking an encounter with her wicked brother, and I did not trust how I might react to the beastly man.

On Thursday, Nalah and I wandered a little further than usual in pursuit of a bright red butterfly. Somehow I lost my bearings. Usually, I kept sight of the house's rooftop in my field of vision as my landmark to get home. But after chasing the butterfly, I'd spotted a small, pig-like animal foraging in the bushes and followed it out of curiosity. Now the clever thing had disappeared into a dense patch of bushes, and I was unsure of my way back.

I did not panic, for I couldn't have gone very far. But my giddy excitement at our adventure slowly dissipated at the knowledge that I was unarmed, lost, and therefore vulnerable.

I turned back in the direction I thought we had come, but we had not ventured far when I heard a strange noise. The hair on my neck bristled, and I froze. The sound was unusual, unlike any I had ever heard. It came again…a deep rumble, primal, frightening. I was no expert, but instinctively knew it was a predator.

My heart pounded, my stomach fluttered, and my arm reached back to touch Nalah and reassure myself she was safe. What should I do? Run? Somewhere in my addled thoughts that sounded wrong, for then it might chase me. Then what? I remembered Derek saying the animals did not like humans, that they would avoid them at all cost—so what lurked in the bushes? Had this creature picked me for its next meal? I was utterly terrified, and more so, with the baby's fate in my hands as well as my own.

I made myself calm down. I must get a grip before hysteria set in. I would carry myself as though unafraid. I could make a great deal of noise as I walked back, hopefully in the right direction. Perhaps a wild beast would be confused and frightened by unusual sounds? I started to move, and then began singing. Hearing my voice break the silence of the bush sounded foreign and out of place, even to my ears. Birds fluttered away as the noise penetrated the sound of the wind and carried through the trees. I sang at the top of my lungs. A terrible version of *The Boy I love is up in the Gallery*. It would surely frighten any living creature away.

"*Bibi*, come this way." The voice startled me into silence. And as I saw the tall shape of Migali materialise ahead of me, spear in hand, tears of relief filled my eyes. I have never in my life been so glad to see another living soul.

Migali did not move but watched me approach, his eyes trained over my shoulder. I knew why. I kept going, and when I reached him, he pushed me behind him. I peeked around his side but saw nothing. Then at once, there came a rustling of leaves and a grunt followed by an almighty high-pitched shriek of pain. My muscles clenched and I gasped in fright. I felt ill hearing what sounded like a life being extinguished.

"*Bibi, njoo nami*...come," Migali said and turned into the bushes. I did not hesitate, but as he led me back to safety, I feared I would never forget that awful scream.

I WAS RELUCTANT TO GO TO dinner. Still shaken, I imagined Migali would have told Nick of my experience. What would he say? I settled the baby, washed up and reluctantly went to the dining room. Nick was already there—Derek too. The latter looked up at me with an expression warning me that I was in trouble. I took a seat.

"Nick, before you—" I began.

He cut me off. "Julia, I can assure you there is nothing you can say to garner any favour with me." He stopped as Malaika brought in a tray, placing a bowl of soup before us. For the first time in days, she looked at me with something akin to pity. I took a deep breath. So be it. If Nick Fleming wanted me gone, there was nothing I could do about it. I would find work elsewhere.

"What the hell were you thinking?" His tone was menacing. "Traipsing about like you were taking a walk in Regent's Park? This is Africa, not London. Dear God, Julia. You not only put yourself in jeopardy, but the life of the baby too. Had you but asked, a servant would have accompanied you. I cannot believe you were so foolish."

I glanced over at Derek, who suddenly took a deep interest in his minestrone soup. Apparently, he was not going to take sides.

"Mr Fleming," I refused to be familiar. "I do not argue that I made a grave decision by wandering so far away. But in my defence, I don't recall being advised any differently during daylight hours."

"She's right." Derek finally chimed in. "We have both neglected our duties when it comes to that. Julia should have been given specific instructions for where she may go and where she may not. We should probably teach her how to use a firearm as well."

"What?" I said in alarm. I had no desire to do such a thing. I was a nanny, not a cowboy.

"Nick," Derek continued. "You're more angry with yourself because you're scared something could have happened."

I threw Derek a look of gratitude and watched Nick' face soften.

"Fair point, Derek." He glanced in my direction. "I'm sorry I was harsh, Julia. He's right. It's my fault for not having prepared you."

"I'm sorry as well," I acquiesced. "But surely you understand that I cannot stay housebound every single day. I shall go mad. If you teach me what I need to learn so I have the freedom to leave the house, then I will follow your instructions. I owe a great deal to Migali for rescuing me."

"Yes, he is a good man. Fortuitously, he was tracking the black leopard—it seems both the big cat and you were stalking the same warthog."

I shuddered at the thought of the animal's screaming death-throes. Then I frowned. "Warthog? I thought it was a little pig."

"No," Derek chuckled. "Though they are related to pigs, you'll get no bacon from one of 'em, Julia. Warthogs are ugly fellows. They've large warts on their hairy heads and sharp tusks. They're clever buggers too. I'd guess the one you spotted was an adolescent by your description of its size. If it were a piglet, the mother would have been close by. Warthogs get quite big." He gestured to Mzuka who lay sleeping by the window. "Not as tall as that old boy, but a mature warthog would easily outweigh him."

"Goodness," was all I could think to say.

"They are also vicious," added Nick. "Like a European wild boar. Don't ever approach one, for if threatened, they will attack, and you don't want to be on the receiving end of those tusks."

Nick finished his soup and pushed away the empty

bowl. "You will have to learn how to protect yourself, Julia. That is, if you want to be able to roam about."

I did not relish the thought. "What do other women do? I cannot imagine Felicity with a rifle."

Nick nodded. "She has one strapped to her saddle. Everyone here carries a weapon."

"You mean every white person," I said drily. "How do African women protect themselves?"

"They travel together and don't go wandering off into the bush," snapped Nick, as Malaika collected his bowl. His eyes met mine. "There's nothing for it. I'll teach you how to fire a weapon. We'll begin first thing Saturday morning." Before I could respond he gave an unexpected grin, "Because if you keep singing songs like that in the bush, you'll frighten *all* the animals away."

NICK WAS GOOD TO HIS word. Saturday, once the baby settled down for her morning sleep, I met Nick in his study as he'd requested. He told Mzuka to stay, instructed Malaika to keep an ear out for Nalah should she wake, and then led me to the back of the house. We walked further into the bush, away from everyone at the farm, so there would be less chance of anyone getting hurt should my shooting aim be poor.

After a while, the bush thinned, and we were out in the open. The beautiful carpet of green plains rolled out before us like velvet. The sky was radiant blue, solitary clouds floated by, and in the distance, I saw the smudge of shadows as herds of undistinguishable animals roamed.

Nick had collected several empty tins from the refuse. I watched thoughtfully as he walked several yards away and placed them on different rocks protruding from the ground. He then returned to where I stood and took the rifle from where it was slung across his back. He handed the weapon to me.

"First rule, Julia. Unless you are ready to fire, you must never point a gun anywhere but towards the ground." I stared at the object in my hands. It was surprisingly heavy and utterly foreign.

"Now, this is a Lee-Enfield rifle. It's the rifle of choice for the British Military, and in my opinion a good one. It shoots a point 303 calibre bullet, which will kill a man, or animal at five hundred yards. Here, let me take the gun and show you how to hold it." He took the weapon and then held it in a position to fire, describing where I should place my head to avoid being hurt as the gun had a 'kick-back." Nick then handed it to me. I mimicked the position he had taken, feeling utterly ridiculous.

He showed me how to aim at the targets while I listened intently. Then he came up behind me, and reached around with both arms, encircling my body as he adjusted the placement of my hands on the rifle. Nick grasped my elbows, raised my arms, and as I brought the rifle level with my shoulder, he leaned forward, and his face brushed the side of mine.

At first, there was something comforting about his nearness. The rough touch of his unshaven cheek, the warmth of his breath in my ear, the fresh, wild scent of the outdoors emanating from his body. I swallowed, seeking composure. But suddenly my emotions turned upon me, conflicted in a battle because of his proximity to me, and I struggled with the desire to wrench myself away. Rivulets of sweat trickled down my spine, and my breath quickened. I did not want him this close.

"Let me try it," I said sharply, eager to get some distance between us.

Nick's arms dropped away instantly as though I had slapped them aside. He took a step back but continued his directions. Under his guidance, I followed his instructions and pulled the trigger.

The deafening roar of the shot rang in my ears and ricocheted across the plains. Squawking birds evacuated their trees, and the serenity of the area splintered. I had missed the target.

"Try again."

Finally, on my third attempt, the tin went soaring into the air, and for some strange reason, I was elated.

I do not know how many times I shot the rifle, but by the time we walked back towards Jacaranda, my arms ached from both holding the gun and from the force of it firing. Now I carried it across my back as Nick insisted that is what I would do were I stranded alone in the wilderness. Though his method seemed odd, it was a sound idea. When we arrived back at the house, my body sagged with exhaustion, and my head spun with the multitude of information and instruction from my teacher.

After lunch, my lesson continued. Nick and I sat on the verandah while Nalah laid on her blanket. He moved the tea tray from the low table and spread out a piece of oilskin. He then began to disassemble the rifle in preparation for cleaning.

"Julia, if you are going to carry a weapon, it is crucial that you understand the working parts of it and learn how to clean it as well. A dirty gun with residue can cause nasty accidents to the person firing it. I would not want you to lose your hand because of being lazy."

It was all extremely confusing. Never mechanically minded, I had to concentrate on comprehending not only the tasks, but the terminology.

"Don't worry," Nick assured me. "With practice, you will eventually hold a rifle as comfortably as you hold your hairbrush. I know it seems very strange. Especially when the only object you are used to carrying around with you in England is an umbrella. But with a weapon, you will have your liberty." He frowned. "I never asked. Do you ride?"

I nodded. "I'm no expert, but my grandparents had a small farm, and I spent much time there as a child. It has been many years, but yes, I ride."

"Good," he said. "I shall pick out one of the horses for you to use."

I felt myself blush. "Nick, I don't have the type of wardrobe to ride. I have clothing suitable for my role as nanny, and I..."

He waved a hand, "It's of no consequence." He paused from his work to study me, his eyes roaming boldly over my body. "Other than being taller, I think you are similar in size to...Amelia. You may look through her clothes. There should be plenty of things you can use until we get you your own."

"How did the lesson go?" Derek came out to join us from inside the house. He dropped into one of the wicker chairs with a long sigh.

"She's rather good for never having held a firearm before." Nick surprised me with his praise. He had said little about my prowess earlier.

"Good for you, Julia. I remember reading once that women are often better shots than men. It's because their aim is better due to their lower centre of gravity...or something like that." He pulled a cigarette case from his jacket pocket. "Don't forget we're going to the Babcocks' tonight for dinner."

Nick carried on cleaning the gun. "I'd rather we didn't."

"Oh, come on, man. Stop being such a bore. It's all right for you moping around here day in and day out, but I need a break from the monotony." I heard the tense note in Derek's voice. He did sound pent-up. My thoughts ran quickly to Malaika and Trevor Babcock.

"Julia should come along as well," Derek said.

"No!" It burst from me before I had time to stop it.

"Goodness," said Nick. "That was a strong objection." He grinned at Derek. "Apparently, Julia has better taste than I thought. She also finds the notion repulsive."

"Well, that is rotten of you both," said Derek. "They are expecting the three of us, and it won't go over well if we don't show. I'd stay on Pops's good side if I were you, Nick. Especially if you want to use his bull for stud. Remember how cross he was with Johnny Reid when he skipped his birthday celebration?"

"Fine," Nick grumbled. "You've made your point. I'll be there." I felt Nick's eyes on my face, and I met his stare. "You're coming too," he stated flatly. "We will bring the baby along as well. That should give us an excuse to leave early."

"I don't think that's a good idea," I argued weakly. "Nalah is better off keeping to her routine. I can stay here with her, and then you will not have to worry..."

"I believe I made myself clear, Julia. I want both of

you with us when we go. See that you are ready to leave at five o'clock." He snapped the rifle back together. "Do not be late."

Nick got to his feet and collected the rifle. "Tomorrow, we'll sort out your horse, and then I'll show you where the guns are kept. Now, if you will both excuse me?" He left us and disappeared back into the house.

"I didn't know you rode?" said Derek.

"It's been ages since I sat atop a horse. Hopefully, it is one of those things you never forget."

He nodded. "It is." His eyes narrowed. "Julia, why don't you want to go to the Babcocks' this evening? I thought you and Felicity got along well enough, and I'm sure you'd enjoy some female company after being stuck with us every day."

What should I say? That Felicity's brother was a rapist and should be strung up and beaten? "Felicity is nice enough, but Derek, in case it has escaped you, I'm not from the same background as any of you. I feel a little self-conscious." I wasn't lying, for I was more than aware of the difference in our upbringing and place in society. I came from a working-class family. Though I'd been lucky to get an education, that was all I had.

"But surely you've noticed that is not so important here in Mombasa. People accept you for who you are. The Babcocks are nice, and there will be other people for you to meet too. It will be jolly. Now," he got to his feet. "I am going home for a quick forty winks and a bath. See you later."

I sat still for a while—my mind in a quandary. How could I face Trevor Babcock and not say anything about his despicable actions? Why should he be allowed to treat Malaika as if she were of no value—his to do with as he pleased? I knew if I said something to Nick, he would immediately take action—Malaika knew it as well. She had remained silent. Was it my right to take that choice away from her?

Later, while I fed the baby, I still mulled it over. Nalah picked up on my mood. She fussed at the bottle, squirmed, and wriggled. I hoped this was not an indication of how she would behave for the remainder of the day.

Our neighbours lived closer to Jacaranda than I realised. By cart, which was always slower than horseback, it took less than thirty minutes. With Nick behind the reins, Derek chatted amiably on the journey.

"Babcock's been here about ten years. He's a transplant from Dar es Salaam, in Tanzania. His background is in cattle, like Jacaranda. But unlike Nick, Pops does not farm crops, other than for their own needs. He is well thought of in the community, and Felicity's into all sorts of things at the Mombasa Club."

As he spoke, I noticed his face softened at the mention of her name. So that is how it was, then? I felt a pang of concern for Derek. He was a good person, and I suspected Felicity Babcock was a powder keg, ready to go off.

Meadowbrook, the Babcock residence, did not impress me. I don't know what my expectations were, but no driveway, no flowerbeds, indeed no ornamentation of any description did little for the eye. However, the bungalow was large, and as we were shown inside, I liked the openness of the interior, filled completely with English furnishings. The African servants who attended us on our arrival looked out of place among the décor. Rather than being in the middle of the Kenyan bush, we'd stepped into a living room in Putney.

Nick had fashioned a seat for the baby, using a small box and placing a cushion in a way that supported her little back. He placed this next to the sofa, and Nalah seemed content as she looked around her new surroundings.

When the family joined us, I steeled myself. Pops was all politeness itself, in evening dress, a cigar in hand. Felicity sailed into the room in a lovely figure-hugging dress in a warm shade of russet brown. The neckline formed a deep 'V', trimmed with a band of gold stitching. The colour accentuated the bobbed blonde hair and reflected in her brown eyes.

"Oh, splendid. You are all here." She made a beeline for me.

"Julia, I'm so pleased you came along. I'm positively *starved* for female companionship. I haven't even been to town in a week." She joined me on the sofa, where I sat, keeping an eye on the baby. Felicity gave Nalah a fleeting glance and then turned her attention back to me.

"I hear your boy is sick with malaria. I hope you are taking the appropriate precautions. Nick, you have told Julia what she should be doing to stay well?"

"Good grief, Felicity, you do go on." It was her brother, and my body tensed hearing Trevor's voice. I cautiously lifted my gaze to look at him and forced a placid expression on my face.

"I'm sure Julia has been sufficiently briefed on the perils of African living. Right, Nick?" he asked.

"Of course," Nick agreed, though I noticed he did not look me in the eye—he must be thinking about my close encounter with the big cat.

Trevor took a glass of sherry from a tray on the table. I studied the man from a safe distance. People's appearances were certainly deceiving. On the surface, his looks were quite attractive. Trevor's colouring, so like his sister's, complemented his inherited features. Of average build, yet still in his prime, he cut a fine figure. But behind that façade lay a monster. For any man who abused those more vulnerable could be called nothing less.

"Is that not right, Julia?" Felicity's voice penetrated my fog of thought.

"I beg your pardon," I stammered. "I was miles away."

I don't know what question she referred to, but I was spared as footsteps sounded in the hall and another couple entered the room. Felicity got to her feet and went to greet them.

The woman looked of an age with her hostess, but her features were harsh. Dark headed, her hair was swept up in a knot, emphasising her slender neck, where rested a thick strand of pearls. I admired her dark red dress, and felt a twinge of envy, for both women were dressed beautifully. I wore my only frock, which was dark green and had seen better days.

"Julia do come and meet the Briggs," Felicity demanded. I joined her near the door.

"Billy and Davina Briggs, this is Julia Rossington, the new nanny at Jacaranda." Billy Briggs had a jolly face, big cheeks and deep-set eyes of an indistinguishable colour. His light brown hair was lank and resembled a piece of cloth draped over his scalp. His chubby face gave him a youthful look, along with skin dappled with freckles. He looked like an overgrown and overweight schoolboy.

"Good to meet you, Julia. Welcome to God's country!" He gave me a broad smile. "Would you excuse me?" Billy moved away, obviously anxious to escape female chatter and join the men standing next to the drinks table.

"How are you faring with the heat?" Davina Briggs' silky voice was almost tactile. In direct contrast to her face, it was soft, pliable.

"Not too badly, thank you. But I understand the worst is yet to come."

"Yes, it is. Can't escape it here by the coast. I'd rather be in Nairobi any day. At least the elevation makes it a little cooler, and there are fewer damned mosquitos."

"From what Pops says," interjected Felicity, "It is likely Nairobi will end up being the capital of the country instead of Mombasa. There is a lot of interest from some very influential people in London, well, according to Pops." She gestured to her father, who sported a cigar underneath his bushy moustache.

"Whereabouts do you live?" I asked, genuinely curious.

"Five miles from here, on Bonner Hill Farm. You would have passed the property on the road from Mombasa."

I had a vague recollection of the name when Nick had talked about other farms on my first day. "There are far more British people living here than I would have ever imagined. We don't hear much about East

Africa back in England. All everyone talks about is the war." I referred to the Boer War, still raging in South Africa. I followed its progress in the Mombasa paper.

Davina Briggs raised a brow. "In my opinion, we should let the Germans have the bloody lot and go home. The older my Ann and David are, the more I wish we lived in England. Honestly, if it were not for Felicity and our other British neighbours, I would have already left."

The clanging of a gong announced dinner, and we filed out to the dining room, Nick carrying the baby's box. I followed Derek as I did not know where to go. Felicity had assigned everyone to a particular spot and directed us all to our seats at the table. I was horrified to find myself sitting next to Trevor, and it must have shown on my face, because Nick, sitting directly opposite gave me a questioning stare. Fortunately, Billy Briggs sat to my right, and so it was to him I paid attention.

The food arrived, and as the dishes were brought in, I inhaled a range of strange, exotic spices which pervaded the room.

"Have you ever eaten curry, Julia?" Trevor asked.

I turned to him reluctantly. "No, I have not. But Derek described it to me just the other day."

"Then you are in for a treat." His dark eyes were smiling, but the way he looked at me held a hint of menace. Or was it my imagination now I had seen him for what he really was. His gaze slid down to my mouth and stayed there momentarily. I felt naked under his casual perusal. Instinctively I wanted to get far away from this man.

"Damned good Tikka Masala," Pops boasted from

the head of the table. "My cook is Indian, you know. Comes from Delhi. Makes the best chutney you have ever tasted."

The Babcocks' houseboy went around the table, first with a large dish of rice and then the pot of curry. I watched the others spoon the rice onto their plates, and then they made a 'well' in the centre, where the curry would go. When it was my turn, I copied the others and then examined my plate.

The dish did indeed resemble stew, only the aroma and was far stronger than any English meal I had eaten. There were thick chunks of tender beef, smooth potatoes, onions and other vegetables. Again, I felt Nick's eyes on me. He gave a slight nod at the various small bowls in front of me, filled with small pieces of different fruits. I realised he was telling me what to do. Apparently, it was customary for the women to help themselves first. I hesitated, and then saw Davina take a spoon from one of the bowls and sprinkle pineapple onto the top of her food. I did the same.

When I took my first bite of curry, I was completely unprepared for the wonderful flavours which assaulted my palate. I had never tasted anything quite like this. Rich, salty, sweet, hot, and spicy—all at once. The seasoned gravy was like tiny fireworks in my mouth, delivering unexpected explosions of flavour.

"Good stuff," muttered Billy Briggs, who, judging by the looks of him, had eaten more than a few curries in his time. "Can't beat it." I watched him chomp away, and my eyes slid across the table to where Felicity and Davina chatted amicably. Nick caught my eye, and I saw a glimmer of sympathy. Perhaps he regretted making me come along, after all.

"...And now as well as the Kaiser bagging all the ivory, we must contend with them smuggling diamonds, raping the mines and sending all that wealth to the Huns to finance their armies. If General Kitchener had been doing his job properly, the bloody war would be over by now, and there wouldn't be such a mess down there!" Pops Babcock's annoyed tone caught everyone's attention. He addressed Derek. "What is the point of a Commander-in-Chief if he does not get things done? This blasted war will just keep going if you ask me. The Boers are not going to take what is on the table. They want to self-govern, and there's an end to it."

I did not hear Derek's reply, but whatever it was, Pops did not like it. I turned back to my food. All I knew about the current political situation in South Africa was what I had seen in the papers. Better to stay out of that conversation.

I tried ignoring Trevor, but he insisted on continually making conversation.

"Now you've been here a few days, you must think you have come to a strange part of the world. How are you coping with culture shock? Jacaranda and Mombasa must seem rather primitive after London."

"Primitive?"

"Yes. Not exactly Mayfair or Pall Mall here."

I nodded, fighting the dislike which threatened to burn from my eyes. I forced my tone to sound friendly. "I do not consider it primitive here at all, Trevor. Granted, the buildings and roads are quite different, and there are no trams. But as far as the people, all the Africans I have encountered have such a propensity for good manners. They make us British folk seem obtuse."

Trevor frowned. "That is an interesting observation. So, you believe it possible for a native people to eclipse their white master with the very principle they have been taught by that master?"

"Yes."

"Then I believe you have been duped. For there are no people more polite than the British, eh, Julia?"

"I suppose it depends on how you classify polite. Manners cover a broad spectrum, do they not? From greetings, requests, to general conversation," I said. "They are free for all to learn and are best practised and not preached. But of course, you know this. If you are considered a 'master' then you are tasked with setting the best of examples to all. It would be imperative to impress upon your workers the superiority of our race. Through your behaviour, the native African learns the true meaning of our culture, one we choose to have them adopt."

I stopped to take a sip of my drink. What on earth was I doing? This was no time to fence with Trevor Babcock. But he represented all I hated in men and people with power. How dare he use his position to force Malaika to do his will? It sickened me, and suddenly I could no longer stand being in the room with him.

"Excuse me," I got to my feet so quickly that everyone stopped eating and stared at me. I left the room in search of a door to the outside. The French windows in the lounge were open, and I stepped out into the night.

"Julia? Is something wrong?" Nick came up behind me.

"I am fine," I said, glad of the dark as he joined

me, searching my face.

"Do you feel ill, should I take you home?"

"No," I said quickly. "Please, I don't want to make a fuss. I just grew warm in there. Perhaps it was a combination of meeting new people, eating spicy food..."

Nick reached out and placed a hand on my shoulder. I flinched. He removed it. "We should leave." It was a command, not a question. "Derek can stay on, and Briggs will drop him on their way back. I shall make our excuses and get the baby." Before I could answer, he had gone back inside the house.

Felicity accompanied Nick when he re-joined me. She made a great deal of fuss and offered the use of her room so I might rest. But Nick was adamant we were going home. I thanked Felicity and asked that she make my excuses. I was never more relieved than when Nick helped me into the cart and settled Nalah in her box between us.

It grew late, and the moon hung bright and low. The sounds of night were around us, distant animal calls, and the chirping of millions of insects. The oxen trundled along, seemingly sure-footed as they took us back towards Jacaranda. I supposed the trail must be familiar to them.

"What happened back there?" Nick asked eventually, as I knew he would. I wanted to tell him the truth—but was so conflicted.

"Nothing. I simply felt unwell."

"I don't believe you, Julia. I sat right across from you and saw your every gesture. Did Trevor say something inappropriate to you?"

"Why do you say that?" I tried desperately to keep

myself calm.

"Because he's famous for it. If you must know, the man has an eye for the ladies. More specifically, the hunt. I couldn't hear everything you were saying because I was listening to Pops espousing his opinions."

"It really was nothing." I busied myself with tucking Nalah's sheet around her. She had fallen asleep almost immediately. The conflict raged within. I wanted desperately to confide in Nick, because Malaika needed a champion. Yet I was more than aware of the consequences the young woman would face if she accused a white man of rape. It was unfair. The law protected Trevor because of his colour and his gender.

"I don't believe you." Nick's voice sounded stern. "And what's more, if you don't tell me what's going on, I shall turn this cart around, go back to Meadowbrook and confront the man myself." He pulled at the reins and the oxen slowed. I began to feel panicked. What should I do?

"I am waiting, Julia."

"It is not my story to tell, Nick," I began. "You put me in a difficult position, for I cannot betray a confidence. I have been asked to remain silent, but now you want me to break my word?"

"Dammit, Julia. I knew something was going on because you acted strangely when I told you we would be dining with the Babcocks. At dinner, you were as jumpy as a cricket. I need not remind you, that while you are at Jacaranda, you are under my protection. I am responsible for any harm that comes your way, or anyone else who works for me for that matter."

And at that very moment, I knew I must tell him.

Chapter Eight

I RECOUNTED WHAT I HAD SEEN and the gist of my conversation with Malaika.

"Bastard." Nick's voice was low and menacing. "I'll kill him."

"No!" I said it so loudly, the baby jerked herself awake and began to cry. I reached into the box, scooped her up and held her close. Nick loosened the reins, and the cart began to move once again.

"Before you do or say anything to another soul, you must speak with Malaika first, Nick. She must be allowed to tell you her story, her wishes. She will be humiliated that you know what happened to her and angry with me for telling you."

"I've never liked Babcock, but knowing this, he is nothing but scum in my eyes." Nick turned to look at me, and I met his gaze. "He will pay for this, Julia. I'll make sure of it."

I shuddered with dread. The threat in Nick's voice was disturbing, but he was understandably outraged. "Nick, it is imperative you handle this situation sensibly. There are laws to abide by, especially if you want Trevor punished. If you do anything rash, you will only give him ammunition to use against you, and then Malaika will not be avenged." I grabbed Nick's arm. "Please. You must listen to me. Do not make me regret putting my faith in you and telling you the truth." His arm relaxed somewhat as the heat of rage calmed. Thank God.

The remainder of the journey passed in silence, though I could feel Nick's pent-up fury. When we arrived back at the house, he stopped in the front to let me out with a very tired baby, while he continued around to the back. I went into the kitchen to make Nalah her bottle while forcing my stomach to settle as uncertainty clutched me tight. Had I done the right thing in telling Nick? There were so many ways to think about it. But I had to remind myself that at the very least, Trevor Babcock would not be able to touch the young woman ever again.

When Nalah was fed, changed, and put to bed, I looked around the house to see if Nick had come in yet. He had not. He must have gone to speak with Malaika. Much as I wanted to know, I could not leave the baby alone. Wilson would already have gone to his hut, and with Juba away, there was no one else in the house.

I passed by the portrait in the living room and my eyes travelled to that ghostly face as they were wont to do whenever I went in there. I opened the doors to the verandah and stepped out into the night. The moon shone enough to give up some of the shadows, so I could see the outline of the trees on the driveway. I sank into one of the chairs and allowed my exhaustion to take over. It had been an emotionally draining day, one way or another. I closed my eyes.

WHAT WAS THAT? MY EYES flew open, and my heart sped. I listened intently and then got to my feet, quickly stepping back into the living room where the gas lamp burned. Though I stood by an open doorway, I still felt less threatened. I listened again. There was no noise. Even the sound of crickets had quietened.

When it came again, the hair on my neck bristled. I recognised the same distinctive primal rumble I had heard when Migali rescued Nalah and I. It was the big cat.

I closed the doors to the night, but stood by the glass peering out, although I did not know what I looked for. Could it be a lion? Or was it the black leopard? Dear God, had I sat there alone in the dark, sleeping, while that predator lurked close by? The thought made my stomach clench in fear.

I pressed my face against the glass but saw nothing out in the open. And then, at once, I caught something in my periphery—a sudden movement in an otherwise still canvas. Quickly, I opened the door just wide enough to poke out my head. There it was. A flash of something. I stared harder, and then realised it was two shadowy figures. Nick, together with a tall thin native. They ran stealthily down the driveway, away from the house and into the night.

WHEN I WOKE THE NEXT MORNING, Nalah was so quiet, I went to check on her and found her still in deep slumber. I dressed and went to the kitchen. No one stirred in the house except Wilson, already at his post with a kettle on the hob.

"*Jambo, Bibi,*" he greeted me as I joined him.

"*Jambo, Wilson,*" I replied. I helped myself to a cup and saucer from the crockery cupboard and waited for the kettle to come to a boil. It did not take long, and soon I wandered into the dining room, teacup in hand.

Wilson had already opened everything up, so an early morning breeze floated into the house. I stood for a moment, transfixed by the beautiful trees, their deep blue blooms radiant against the backdrop of clear sky.

Had it already been ten days since I first laid eyes on Jacaranda? How quickly the days had passed—how much had changed in my world. I sipped my tea, and stood there, watching the first stirrings of the day.

I heard the distinctive click of Mzuka's claws upon the tile. "You are up early," said Nick, joining me in the room.

I turned away from the door. "Yes, the baby is still fast asleep, so I thought I'd have a cup of tea while it was still quiet. How are you this morning?"

He looked tired. But then it had been late when he had gone off with Migali, and the events of the evening had not been easy for him.

"Did you speak with Malaika?" I had to know. I was worried sick about her. But Nick did not answer, as the clink of china announced Wilson's entry into the room. The cook placed a tea tray on the sideboard, and Nick immediately poured himself a cup, thanking the cook as Wilson returned to the kitchen. I waited until Nick came to stand beside me at the door.

"Yes, I talked to her at length."

"And?" I was relieved he was involved, yet deep down, I worried Malaika would be angry with me.

"At first, she denied everything. But I lied to her. I told her Trevor had let something slip in conversation, and it didn't take too much convincing before she admitted the truth." He turned his grey eyes on me. "She does not know you said anything. If she suspects, she certainly did not show it. I thought it better if I kept you out of it. I hope you agree."

"Yes. Thank you for that. I want Malaika to trust me and she would never confide in me again if she knew I'd betrayed that trust."

Nick's expression was contemplative as he studied me. "Your word is important, is it not, Julia?"

"It is all I have." I walked over to the sideboard and refilled my teacup. The scent of bacon frying wafted into the room, and my stomach growled. "How did you leave things with her?"

Nick took a seat at the table. "I told her to take a few days and visit her family. Better to have her away while we sort out what to do. She leaves this morning. Migali will take her home. They are from the same village."

That was a good idea. I told him as much.

He chuckled. "You might not think so when you realise we will be down to only one house servant. With Juba already gone, it will put a lot of responsibility on Wilson."

"I am happy to help in any way I can," I said. "In truth, Nalah is an easy baby. She is still young enough that she needs lots of sleep, so I have time on my hands."

"Thank you," Nick replied, looking up as Wilson brought in a tray bearing two plates of breakfast. He set them down in front of us, and we thanked him.

"Wilson, Malaika will be away for a few days on family business. With Juba gone, Julia will help you with household tasks for the time being. Also, if you have a family member close by, you must ask them to come and work here with you for the next month."

"*Hiyo ni nzuri, Bwana.*" Wilson nodded. He looked

pleased at the prospect.

"Wilson, please let me know what I can do to help," I reiterated. I liked the cook. He was a pleasant, hardworking man. I sincerely wanted to make it easier on him.

"*Asante, Bibi.*" He grinned and then left us to our breakfast.

Although it was Sunday, Nick planned to go into Mombasa later that morning. "I am going to speak with the commissioner first, and then I plan to stop in at the hospital and check on Juba."

"I do hope he is doing well," I missed the young man's exuberant smile, his friendliness.

"He is recovering nicely, according to the last message I received from Mombasa. But Malaria is a fickle fellow. Juba will need rest for a while, even after he returns to Jacaranda."

"Poor Juba. It will be good to see him again." I ate a bite of my food. "I forgot to ask. Did you catch him last night?"

Nick's head snapped up to look at me, "I beg your pardon?"

"The leopard. I saw you and Migali running down the driveway late last night, just after I heard the leopard."

There was a subtle change in Nick's posture as he seemed to relax. "No, he was far too wily for either one of us. We'll probably have to bait him with a goat, and then wait it out."

"Oh." His answer sounded empty, devoid of sincerity. It was unsettling somehow.

"Today would be a good time for you to have a look through Amelia's things, Julia. I've a horse in mind for you, and once you have the right clothing you can try her out."

"Thank you. I will do that." The idea of riding appealed to me. The prospect of going through his dead wife's wardrobe did not.

"*Bibi, mtoto analia.*" Wilson's head dipped into the room. Even with my limited use of Swahili, I understood that the baby was crying. I excused myself from the table.

I WAS UNAWARE WHEN NICK departed for Mombasa. Nalah fussed and played around with her bottle. I hoped she wasn't coming down with something. I had enough experience with babies to spot the signs. I gave her a cool bath, played with her for some time until she grew sleepy, then I put her in the crib. I closed the nursery door and crossed the hall into Amelia's room.

Now I had permission to be there, I pulled open the heavy curtains, opened the windows and refreshed the stale air. Looking around, I found it unsettling seeing everything left this way, as though Nick's wife would return at any moment. I shrugged the feeling away. Who was I to judge, after all?

Amelia's gigantic wardrobe was at least three times larger than any piece of furniture I had seen before. It must have been custom-made, with a strong oriental flavour. The craftsmanship of the piece was beautiful. Made from mahogany, it boasted two pairs of elaborately carved doors. I pulled them open and then stood back in appreciation.

One side held a rail for hanging clothes, completely full, packed with all manner of dresses and gowns. The other was segmented into multiple shelves, in which were footwear, handbags and hats. I assumed Amelia's personal items of undergarments and stockings would be in the matching chest of drawers.

I began sifting through her things, and eventually, after stopping to admire countless outfits, I found a riding outfit. The jodhpurs looked as though they should fit, though I wouldn't know without trying them on. I slipped the jacket on over my clothes. It would work, but my chest must be fuller, for I could not make the buttons reach. Still, I could wear a blouse underneath, and that would suffice.

Footwear, however, would be an issue. I had no riding boots, and judging by the shoes in the wardrobe, my feet were larger than Amelia's. I'd use my work boots for the time being until I could purchase a pair on the next trip to Mombasa. Perhaps I might look at one of the catalogues that Derek used frequently.

I had not seen him this morning. No doubt he was still sleeping off the effects of the night before. I hoped he'd enjoyed himself and not minded us leaving him behind at the Babcocks'.

When Nalah woke, I decided to sit out on the verandah. The baby seemed to enjoy laying on her little blanket with a few toys strewn about her. I think the sounds of the outdoors piqued her interest, and while she wriggled and played, I usually read or sewed.

The grounds were peaceful. Sunday was a day off for the workers, except for the household staff who rotated. Of course, this currently did not apply as Wilson was the only one home.

Before coming outside, I'd stopped to check with the cook and ask if he needed help with anything. He said yes and brought a pan of potatoes for me to peel and place in a bowl of clean water, in preparation for dinner. This I did while keeping an eye on the baby.

There was chatter up in the trees this morning. I was now familiar with seeing the small grey monkeys who frequented the branches of the shade trees close to the house. I understood they were opportunists, always on the lookout to snatch a morsel wherever they could. I wondered if they ate potato peel? I threw a piece onto the ground a few feet away from where I sat and then waited. Sure enough, after a minute or two, a little figure scurried down the tree trunk, darted over to where the peel lay and grabbed it, rushing back up into the safety of the tree. I laughed and repeated the action. Before long, there were several monkeys eyeing me, waiting their turn for a piece of peel.

When Wilson came out to collect the potatoes, he looked at the second bowl lying empty and raised an eyebrow.

"*Nyani*," I said, triumphant that I remembered the word for monkey.

"*Nyani ni mnene*," he responded with a grin, using his hand to emulate a fat stomach. We both laughed. I scooped up Nalah and followed Wilson into the kitchen, where against his protestation, I made us both a sandwich—he had enough to do, cooking dinner. He was loath to sit at the kitchen table with me to eat. But I made him do so, and I enjoyed our stilted conversation. Afterwards, I put the baby down for her sleep and then I went into each room to tidy and straighten things up as Malaika was not there to do it.

I hoped she was home with her family by now. It was the best course of action. The young woman needed time to clear her head and not worry about anyone but herself. It's what I'd needed as well. But back then, I'd not had anywhere or anyone to go to.

It was late afternoon when the baby woke from her nap. Wilson had been showing me the laundry hut so I could familiarise myself should I need to wash our clothes. I changed Nalah and wandered into the kitchen to make her bottle, carrying her slung on my hip, when I heard the approach of a horse. It came at quite a pace, judging by the sound.

I finished what I was doing, and as I went into the hallway, Derek came bursting through the front door. His face was red, covered in sweat, and he looked as though he had been up all night.

"Where is Nick?" he said sharply. His eyes were bloodshot and wide with alarm.

"He went to Mombasa," I answered. "Derek, is something wrong? What has happened?" He looked dreadful.

He pushed past me and went straight into the living room, opened the whisky decanter and poured a measure into a glass. He tipped back his head and swallowed it in a gulp.

I had followed him into the room, but I said nothing. Derek took a couple of deep breaths. "I have just come from Meadowbrook," he said. "I stayed there overnight as I was too drunk to ride home. This morning, they found Trevor Babcock in one of the huts. His throat had been cut."

Chapter Nine

"No!" I RECOILED IN SHOCK.

Derek poured another drink and knocked it back. "All hell has broken loose over there. His father is beside himself—the servants have run away, terrified they will be blamed, and that a demon has come to Meadowbrook."

I went and sat down in one of the armchairs while my mind sought to comprehend what Derek had said. Trevor dead? At once, I was deluged with the many conversations that had taken place since I saw him leave Malaika's hut. Her desperation, Nick's anger when I told him. And then I remembered last night when I saw Nick and Migali leaving Jacaranda. I recalled his face earlier this morning when I asked him where they had gone. Something was not quite right. Dear God, had Nick killed the man? And if so, was it my fault?

"Look, I have to go and clean up, and then I'm going back to Meadowbrook. So, you will need to tell Nick when he returns. I am sure he'll want to help in any way he can."

I nodded, dumbly.

"Julia, I know I could have handled telling you more kindly, but if you want to know the truth, I'm a bit rattled. When anything like this occurs, one remembers we are but a small community in a foreign land and vastly outnumbered. Any unrest is extremely dangerous. Will you be all right if I leave you here?"

"Of course. You must go back to Meadowbrook. The Babcocks need all the support they can get. Has someone alerted the authorities?"

"Yes, I stopped in at the Briggs' farm. Billy is on his way to Mombasa to speak to the commissioner's office." He ran his fingers through his wavy hair. "I had better get a move on, Julia. Please remain in the house for your safety until Nick gets back." With that, Derek rushed out of the house to his bungalow while I stayed where I was, still in shock.

AT DUSK, NICK ARRIVED back at Jacaranda. I was in the nursery, feeding the baby, and heard his footsteps coming down the hall. He knocked lightly on the door.

"Come in."

He stepped into the room and then paused as though unprepared for the sight of me with Nalah, sitting on the rocking chair while she drank her bottle.

"Have you heard?" I asked.

He nodded. "I saw Briggs at the Commissioner's office. The news is all over Mombasa. Where's Derek?"

"At Meadowbrook. He stayed there last night and was at the house when they found Trevor's body."

Nick came into the room and went to stand by the window. His face was turned away from me, and I wondered what he was thinking.

"This is bad, Julia. When a white man is killed in Kenya, it doesn't bode well for both the settlers and the natives."

"That's what Derek said." Nalah finished drinking her milk. I got to my feet and lifted her up against my shoulder, patting her back as I paced around the room. "Nick?"

He turned to face me. He looked as dreadful as Derek had appeared. I searched his expression. I know I looked for guilt. It was too coincidental, surely? Trevor Babcock had been alive until I opened my mouth. Nick stared at me as though he interpreted where my thoughts were going. He came closer to where I stood with the baby.

"You think this has something to do with me. Don't you?"

I glanced away. But he was insistent.

"You do. I can see it in your eyes. What are you thinking, Julia? That I killed Derek because of Malaika? Is that what you believe?"

I did not answer, but I know he knew my feelings by reading my face.

His brow furrowed, and his eyes grew dark as he stared at me in disgust. "Let me tell you this, Julia." He scowled. "Trevor Babcock was evil, he preyed upon weak people, and I never liked the man. But I did not take his life. Though, God help me, I wanted to when I heard what he'd done to Malaika, and no doubt countless others. I wanted Trevor to suffer the humiliation of being outed. For the world to know what kind of person he really was. For him to endure a trial, and ultimately time in prison for his misdeeds." He sighed. "I'm disappointed you would think me capable of murder, Julia. I thought you better than that."

Something in the way he looked at me then, the sadness in his eyes perhaps, moved me. Then his face hardened, and his jaw clenched.

"Whoever killed Trevor gave him the easy way out." He was angry.

I wanted to respond and attempt to diffuse the atmosphere between us, But, before I could even take a breath, Nick brushed past me and walked out of the nursery, leaving me even more confused than I had been when he walked in.

I WAS ALONE IN THE DINING ROOM for dinner. Wilson brought me a plate of shepherd's pie which I barely tasted. But I made the effort as he had worked hard. When he served me a cup of tea after the meal was finished, much to his surprise, I took it and followed him back into the kitchen.

"What is wrong, *Bibi*?" he asked, his face wrought with concern. "Why you come in kitchen?"

"I don't want to be alone," I said honestly. "But I won't get in the way. Can I help you with the washing up?"

His expression was mortified at my offer. Had I accidentally insulted the man? Blasted cultures, I did not understand them.

"No, *Bibi*. You may not. But Wilson not mind for you to sit and talk with him. This very good." He started washing the plates in a bowl full of heated soapy water while I sat at the table feeling idle for not helping. I searched for a topic of conversation and found it.

"Did *Bwana* Fleming speak to you about Juba?" I had not asked Nick about his trip. It seemed inconsequential in light of what had happened. But I was interested in Juba's health.

"*Ndio, Bibi*. Juba is very well. The medicine, she is

working. Juba will be home in seven days."

"That is wonderful news," I said. "Juba is a good boy."

"He is my boy," Wilson flung over his shoulder.

"Your son?" I vaguely remembered Nick mentioning something about that.

"*Ndio*. Juba my, how you say…adopted child, I have very many, *Bibi*." Wilson smiled, his teeth bright against his dark complexion. I admired these people and their constant ability to remain so pleasant. I should take a leaf out of their book.

"How many children do you have?"

"*Watoto kumi na tatu*," he replied, and then grinned once more. "Thirteen children."

"Goodness," I blurted. How on earth did these African women do it? My time was monopolised with only one child. The resilience of females astounded me.

"Your wife, she is a busy woman," I said.

"*Wake wengi*," said Wilson, "Many wives."

"Oh." Was he Muslim then? For I knew they took more than one spouse.

Wilson returned his concentration to the task at hand. I stayed quiet, and then, after a while, I had an idea. Perhaps Wilson could tell me more about Jacaranda. His English was actually quite good, and he enjoyed conversation.

"Wilson, were you here with Memsahib Amelia?"

"*Ndio*. I cooked for her, *Bibi*."

"Did she like your food?"

"*Hapana. Memsahib Fleming*, she always saying food not tasty or not cooked British." He shrugged. "*Bwana* tell me not to worry."

"What about *Bwana Martin*?"

Wilson paused and stared out of the kitchen window. *"Bwana Martin* a kind man, like *Bwana Nick.* He very sad man when Barika died. *Ndugu*—brothers, dead wives."

He was right. The Fleming brothers had both endured tragic losses. In addition, Nick had dealt with his brother dying too. I thought about Amelia's death and how Derek alluded it to be a violent one. I considered the news about Trevor Babcock. Two murders, two whites.

"When did Mrs Fleming die, Wilson?"

"Many months since, *Bibi,*" he considered for a moment. *"Kumi na tisa*—nineteen."

Not so long ago, yet no one ever mentioned the woman. How strange. I recalled Derek's words about Amelia and Felicity, and their interest in the Mombasa Club. The longer I was in Africa, the more I realised how narrow my world had been. I thought of Amelia Fleming and her unborn child. How she had died brutally by another's hands. She was a victim, just as I had been myself. And while I sat at the kitchen table watching Wilson drying dishes, I made a decision. I would find out what happened to Amelia Fleming. She was unable to fight her battle…but I could.

I HAD SEEN LITTLE OF BOTH DEREK and Nick most of the week. There had been a visit from a policeman which had set the servants chatting, with furtive looks passing between them. I wondered about Malaika and if they would interview her? She was still away visiting her village as far as I knew. The uniformed fellow had been ensconced in Nick's office for a time but had not wished to speak to me. Thank goodness. I was happy with that, though were I the one making enquiries, I should have spoken to everyone possible.

One morning, Derek met me at breakfast with instructions from Nick to select a suitable horse for me to ride. In the stables, he introduced me to a mature mare named *Subira*, or Patience as it translated to English. Derek offered to watch Nalah for a spell and told me to change, take *Subira* out for a short ride and see if I liked her. I needed little encouragement. The baby slept, so the timing was perfect. I hastened into the house and tugged on Amelia's old habit.

A most capable young Kikuyu, Kijani, saddled *Subira*, then helped me mount as my limbs refused to be as nimble as they had been years ago when last I rode. I did not plan to go far because I was out of practice. I knew my muscles would take a pounding. I trotted around the perimeters of Jacaranda, and even managed a slow gallop up and down the driveway a few times. The mare was placid and responsive to my commands. She would definitely be the right horse for me.

I led her back to the stables and gave her an apple as a treat. I was helping Kijani take off her saddle and harness when Derek came out to join me, carrying Nalah in his arms. Her little hands excitedly reached for the horse and giggled in delight when she touched its coat. I thanked Kijani for his help and left him to rub the mare down. Derek handed me the baby and departed for the fields, while I went into the house feeling revitalised from my ride.

ON THE MORNING OF TREVOR'S FUNERAL, both men were present for breakfast. I planned to attend, leaving

Nalah at Jacaranda. This I could do because I'd engaged a helper for the nursery three days earlier.

After having a stilted conversation with Nick, our first since the day of Trevor's murder, I'd boldly asked permission to hire someone to help watch Nalah for the times when I needed to be elsewhere or go riding. Nick had readily agreed. We were short-handed, after all. He'd given me an amount he was prepared to pay and left me to take care of it.

I'd visited Nalah's nurse, Winda, once more. Although I wasn't fond of the woman, she had so many children, and I imagined it was difficult keeping everyone fed. I'd taken Wilson along with me to translate, and after some discussion it was agreed Winda's fifteen-year-old daughter, Akina, would be the one for the job.

The next day, Akina had reported to the house and then spent every morning with us, so both she and the baby could grow used to one another. So far, it had all gone according to plan. Akina was Kikuyu. Though she lacked the height and grace of Malaika, a Maasai, Akina had a pretty face, round-cheeked with bright, intelligent eyes. I liked her very much.

Therefore, after breakfast, Derek, Nick, and I set off for the Babcock's residence, leaving Nalah held in Akina's arms, with Mzuka at her feet.

We were silent for a while. I considered that they, like me, were contemplative—thinking about mortality. Funerals always seemed to initiate those thoughts.

I sat between Nick and Derek—their bodies as stiff as bookends.

"This is a bad business," Derek eventually muttered.

"Is there any more news about what happened to Trevor?" I asked.

"No, nothing," he replied. "I suspect they think it one of the Africans. Trevor wasn't known for his kindness. It is entirely possible he crossed the wrong fellow."

My memory conjured up the image of Nick running down the driveway that night, Migali at his side.

Derek added. "They may never find him. Anyone can disappear in a place like this. There simply aren't enough resources for the police to track a person down. I am sure the felon is long gone."

"But what if he wasn't African, but European?" I asked, feeling Nick tense beside me. I ignored it. "They cannot disappear quite so easily."

My words hung between us, yet neither man picked up the thread. The remainder of our journey was quiet, other than Derek identifying some of the vegetation for me.

I was shocked by the throng of people already at the Babcock residence. I stopped counting at fifty, having no idea there were so many whites living in the vicinity. I guessed several people had likely ridden in from Mombasa. But as Derek introduced me to different families, I learned they were mostly neighbours.

I recognised the Briggs family who had been at the Babcocks' house the night Trevor was killed. They were friendly enough but looked drawn and concerned, as did everyone else. I stood off to one side, a little self-conscious because I was practically a stranger. But then I heard a familiar voice and looked over to see the gentleman I'd met in Mombasa when I had gone there with Derek.

I searched for the man's name in my mind and then remembered it was Klaus. He walked in my direction and caught my eye.

"Good day, *Fraülein*. It is nice to see you once again, though under such unfortunate circumstances."

His face, all sharp angles, had a harshness that somehow negated the sincerity of his words. His pale eyes showed little compassion—he looked more Nordic than he did Germanic.

"Yes, it is tragic. I am sure this type of thing must be rare in places like this. No wonder it is so very unsettling.

"I am afraid not as rare as you think, *Fraülein* Rossington. Unfortunately, this is not the first time something like this has occurred. You must be aware not more than a year ago, the very same thing happened to Amelia Fleming."

The comment took me aback. The implication was she had died in a similar manner and that thought was grotesque. "Surely the authorities will do their best to discover who did this?"

"You would think so. But these British polizei, they are used to chasing people stealing fruit from the marketplace, not catching murderers. I have little faith in them. I would advise anyone living outside of Mombasa to be cautious for the time being."

"You think this will happen again?" before he could answer me, Derek approached to say it was time to join the mourners and walk to the Babcock Cemetery. We followed the long procession, and I stood with him and Nick for the duration of the service.

A vicar had come from Mombasa, and after a sermon he delivered a brief eulogy.

Pops Babcock looked completely stricken, and poor Felicity had her face covered by a veil, but the trembling of her shoulders betrayed the fact she was sobbing. When the last handful of soil had been thrown into the open grave, we followed the family back to the house, where refreshments were laid out for the mourners.

I often thought our culture had many odd customs, and a wake was included in that observation. I understood etiquette demanded the feeding of guests when they travelled distances to pay their last respects, but I'd always considered this custom rather uncouth. The irony that while living, a person could be ignored yet upon their death be surrounded by friendship, seemed cruel indeed.

I kept my distance from the Babcock family. I considered myself still a relative newcomer to the area. Their time should be spent with older acquaintances. When Klaus Schmitt gravitated towards me again, I wondered at his interest in speaking with me.

"Are you settled at Jacaranda? How do you like working for Herr Fleming?"

"I like it very well, thank you. Nick is a good employer. I have an easy job with Nalah, as she is a happy little girl."

"*Das ist gut.* I have seen Jacaranda, and it is a good farm. Have you seen much of the area?"

"Not yet. But I learn something new about this country every day. This land has an undeniable beauty, far different from anything I have seen before. I do not believe you could find the antithesis of England anywhere else. The majesty of Africa, the wildlife, the rawness of the place—it takes my breath away."

"I see *Afrika* has made her way into your heart," he said, smiling. "I feel much the same way. Although I miss my Homeland and my family, there is something here keeping me anchored. I can never quite walk away."

"How long have you lived here, Herr Schmitt?"

"In Mombasa, two years. But before coming here, I was in Dar es Salaam. There is a large German community there. Business brought me further east."

"Do you intend to stay in Mombasa?"

"*Nein.* Now the railway is finished, I may go back to Dar es Salaam. I am working on finalising my business before I can make any changes."

I nodded. "How long since you were in Germany? Where does your family come from?"

"My family are from *Rinteln,* a small town in Lower Saxony. I left there nine years ago."

Across the room, I saw Nick standing with Billy and Davina Briggs. His face was difficult to read, but he looked solemn. As Klaus continued talking about Germany, I studied my employer. Who was he really? What short time I had spent with Nick revealed very little. He was a private person. One who withheld rather than be bold. Yet my instinct had never warned me away from him or sounded an alarm. His treatment of the African workers was respectful and courteous. Indeed, his treatment of me had been exemplary. Then what made me suspicious of the man?

Had Derek's comments influenced my opinion of him? Would I feel the same way were Amelia Fleming still alive? I knew the answer to that.

Herr Schmitt asked a question, and I missed it. "I beg your pardon, what did you say?"

"I asked if you had heard about the black leopard?"

"Yes, I had a close encounter with it, although I did not see the beast."

"*Roho ya kimya*," he muttered.

"What?"

"It means silent spirit. That is what the natives are calling the big cat. They are rare creatures and highly respected. As long as the leopard has not tasted human blood, they will not kill it."

"I doubt Nick or Derek will be quite so honourable. It's been picking off the goats at the surrounding farms."

"The perils of farming, *Fraülein*."

"Yes, it seems that way," I agreed. I decided to be brave and change the subject. "Herr Schmitt, as a relatively new arrival, I do not like to ask too many questions. But with this terrible murder, I find I am curious about Amelia Fleming. After all, I live in her house, and yet I know so little about the woman. Did you know her?"

I watched his expression change and his eyes soften. "*Ja*, I knew Amelia. She was a bright flame, and we were all moths drawn to her captivating beauty." He nodded, "She looked like *ein Engel*, an angel—but in her heart, she was *eine Verführerin*...how you say? Ah, a seductress."

That was not what I'd expected to hear. "How do you mean?"

Herr Schmitt frowned. "I do not like to offend you, so perhaps I should leave it there. This is not the place to continue the discussion."

I was thoroughly disappointed. "Oh, I should value hearing your opinion."

He looked at me as though an idea struck him. "*Fraülein* Rossington, may I be bold? Do you ride?"

"Yes. Why?"

"Might I call on you? Perhaps we could ride out and see something of the area? I am often this way visiting friends and am most familiar with the place. Are you allowed a few hours away from your charge?"

Up until this week, I had been with Nalah every waking moment. But now I had the help of young Akina, and surely Nick would not begrudge my taking a little time off. If I really wanted to discover what had happened to Amelia, then I had to start somewhere.

"When were you thinking of doing this?" I asked.

"What about tomorrow? I am staying with my friends, The Paderborns, until Monday. I could call for you at three o'clock?"

"Yes," I said eagerly. "That would be wonderful."

He smiled at my response, and I looked at him properly for the first time. He was the kind of person who could look so harsh, so serious. But when he smiled, his features softened, and his piercing blue eyes twinkled. For an older man, he was still quite handsome.

"Then tomorrow it is, *Fraülein*."

Chapter Ten

DEREK REMAINED AT THE BABCOCKS after the funeral and would return later in the day. I admired his kindness with the bereaved family, especially the attention he paid to Pops. On the way back to Jacaranda with Nick, I broached the subject of some time off.

"With Akina helping me," I added, after my initial request. "My being gone for a few hours shouldn't inconvenience you or the other staff, as Akina would be watching Nalah."

"Of course," Nick responded quickly. "It was thoughtless of me not to think of this myself. I suppose I've been so relieved having you here, it hasn't dawned on me to give you time for yourself, and not be at the beck and call of a baby. Do you want to have a set day every week? Would that suit?"

"No. I think I'd rather take part of the day as I need it, based on my plans, and how Nalah is. There are times when she is difficult, and I'd rather be the one taking care of her then. Would it be all right if I just informed you when I planned to be gone?"

"That's fine."

"Good. Then I should tell you I'd like to take a few hours tomorrow afternoon. Akina will stay with the baby."

Nick glanced at me with some surprise. "You don't

waste any time. Would it be rude of me to ask what your plans are?"

With annoyance, I felt my cheeks warm. "Actually, Herr Schmitt has invited me to ride out with him and show me around."

"What?" His voice was so loud, it gave me a start.

"He's staying with the Paderborns, and has offered to take me sightseeing. I'd like to see more of the area, so I accepted."

Nick frowned. "You should have said. I would have been happy to take you," he chided.

We'd been on an unsteady footing for days now, but I refused to be intimidated by his tone. There had been plenty of time for Nick to take me out riding, but he had not offered.

I looked away. "You're always so busy, and I did not like to ask. Besides, it's good that I get to know other people in your circle."

"I would not refer to Schmitt as a person in my circle, Julia. I don't particularly like the man."

I glared at him. "Why is that?" I retorted. "Because he's German? That would be rather prejudiced of you, Nick."

"It's got nothing to do with his nationality, although I will say it doesn't endear him to me. But it isn't that. I simply don't trust him. There's always been something shifty about the fellow which keeps me on my guard." His eyes moved away from the road and onto me. "I'm not telling you to stay away from him—I have no right. But go careful with the man."

Before I could respond, there came a bellow so loud, I gasped. The oxen slowed and began to make nervous grunts. Nick pulled them to a stop and leapt down from the cart. He grabbed the reins and led the team over to a clump of trees and out from the middle of the dirt road.

I wanted to ask what was wrong, but instinct told me I should remain quiet. Nick climbed back up and leaned over behind the seat, and I knew what he sought. He grabbed the hunting rifle and then got back down off the cart.

I felt the ground vibrate, and then there was a rush of noise as several massive creatures emerged from the bush onto the dirt road.

Elephants. In all my life, I had never seen any creature so gargantuan, so intimidating, and beautiful. There were five of them, one as large as a house, three smaller and a young calf.

"Keep very still, Julia," said Nick, as they moved along the road and fortunately away from where we sat under the trees in the cart. But as they continued, the largest, a giant fellow with colossal ivory tusks, abruptly whirled around and stopped. His mammoth ears flapped back and forth, and he lifted one front leg and stomped the ground, blowing air through his trunk in a blatant act of aggression.

"Stay quiet," Nick whispered. "He's just letting us know he's the boss. He's showing off in front of the ladies."

I really did not care why he was doing it. But I imagined being crushed underfoot or impaled on his tusks. My heart raced. My body broke into a sweat—I had never been so frightened in my life! Thank God the baby was safe at home.

The big bull elephant took a few steps in our direction, and I heard Nick cock the gun. How could a bullet stop a beast as magnificent as this? We were but tiny ants in comparison. The elephant backed away once again, and then repeated the gesture, this time, coming a little closer. It was all I could do not to cry out in fear. When it happened a third time, Nick muttered something which sounded like a curse, and then he pointed the gun into the air and fired.

The explosion of sound ricocheted through the air. Birds scattered from the trees, and the branches rustled at their departure. The small herd had broken into a run yet were still quite close. But not the bull. He had not even flinched.

"Damn," said Nick, and I heard him cock the rifle again.

"Please, don't shoot him," I begged, mesmerised by the vision of this amazing creature. "We are trespassing, and he is only protecting his family. The same as you would do."

I felt Nick's eyes on me, but I did not look. I could not tear my gaze from the elephant. I stared at its face. A moment passed. And then without fanfare, he simply turned and moved slowly away to join the others.

We waited for what seemed like an eternity. When they were far enough away that the oxen were no longer as scared, Nick led the team by the reins back to the road, walking alongside them to calm their nerves until the elephants were completely out of our range of vision. Then he leapt back up into the cart.

"Welcome to Africa, Julia," he said.

I WAS PLEASED WITH AKINA. Nalah reached out her chubby little arms to me as soon as she saw me, but she looked content. It was such a relief knowing there was someone besides myself to care for the baby. I was impressed a girl as young as fourteen could be so responsible. Akina had multiple siblings she had undoubtedly cared for throughout her short life.

It was a strange afternoon, no doubt due to both our exciting encounter with elephants, and the sombre funeral. Solemn occasions always cast such a shadow. They brought deep introspection of life.

The baby went to sleep early, and I wasn't surprised. Akina had played with Nalah and likely worn her out.

Before dinner, I checked with Wilson to see if he needed any help. There was a young boy named Francis who assisted him, one of Wilson's children. After introductions were made, I wandered into the lounge. The doors were flung open to the verandah, and Mzuka lay sleeping on the threshold, where the evening breeze stirred the gently swaying curtains. I found myself standing before the fireplace, staring up at the portrait hung there. I stood in reflection, gazing at the image of the mysterious Amelia.

She sat in a white chair, with the blurred image of the Jacaranda trees behind her. Her posture was regal, both arms laying on the arms of the chair while she stared straight ahead. Yet something in her eyes drew your attention. What was it? A wicked glint? The promise of mischief? Amelia's thick blonde hair parted on the side and hung loose, dropping down across her shoulders and almost to her waist. I contemplated being a woman with her looks. They were the type men found compelling—dangerous. Who was Amelia Fleming, really? And who had taken her life?

"I often think about taking that damn painting

down." Nick's voice roused me from thought.

"You shouldn't. It is beautiful. Your wife was truly lovely."

"Yes, so I am frequently told by all and sundry." He stood next to me, gazing upward. "Yet I believe human beauty to be superficial. We have no hand in how we are predisposed to look. Real beauty is that bull elephant we encountered today. Or the perfect shade of blue on those Jacaranda trees you like so much."

"Yes, you are right. But a person's being attractive is still something to admire. We have within us the ability to recognise what makes us happy. Surely appreciation is simply that, another elixir to bring us a moment of pleasure."

"And that is all Amelia ever craved—pleasure." He moved away to the drinks table and poured us both a sherry. "Let's go outside, shall we?"

I followed Nick onto the verandah, glad he was more convivial. I took a seat. "It feels warmer tonight."

"There's rain coming. You can almost taste it."

I sat quietly for a moment. The night was tranquil, a calm before the storm perhaps? "Do you ever wish you lived nearer Mombasa? Does the remoteness ever get to you?"

"Never. I find the company of people tedious at the best of times, other than Migali. The herd mentality is not for me. Though I derive enjoyment from conversation, such as we are having."

"Then you are like that elusive leopard. Seeking solitude whenever possible. You could never live in England. You would think it overrun with people."

"I sound like a dull bore," he said. "But I cannot understand the desire to spend all your time in the company of others, discussing fashion and gossiping about other people's misfortunes."

"It is not that simple," I remonstrated. "There is an innate need for humans to interact that was established long before the British implemented afternoon tea. We are creatures of habit, and just as the wildebeest and zebra flock together for safety and companionship, so do we."

"That may be true," Nick agreed. "Then tell me, why are you here, Julia? You are a human such as you described. Yet you sought a solitary path away from society and companionship. From Chessington to the wilds of Mombasa is hardly like a day out at Selfridges."

"And there you have me, Nick," I acknowledged defeat. "I am a hypocrite of the worst standing. I do not practise what I preach."

"Commendable in my book."

Mzuka's large head rose from slumber as Wilson appeared. "Dinner, she is ready, *Bwana*."

With Derek away, we enjoyed a quiet dinner. Wilson's steak and kidney pie was delicious. He had mastered British cuisine completely. I should have to be careful, for my clothes would become snug if I carried on eating as well as this.

As we dined, our talk was inconsequential. I learned about the condition of the crops in the fields, some of the dilemmas faced when breeding cattle, and ongoing disputes between the Kikuyu and Maasai over land rights. I enjoyed hearing about subjects so entirely foreign.

"Julia, might I be impudent and ask a question?" Nick said as Wilson collected our dinner plates.

The sherry had relaxed me. It emboldened me, and without thinking, I said, "Absolutely, as long as I can ask you one as well?"

The hint of a smile tugged at Nick's mouth. Then his eyes narrowed. "Your arrangement with Herr Schmitt, tomorrow, is there more to it than a sightseeing trip?"

The question took me off guard. "What's that supposed to mean?"

"Do you have any...personal inclinations towards the fellow. Of a romantic nature?" His face was grim.

I laughed. "Don't look so concerned. Of course not. Why, does it worry you?"

His eyes settled on me, and I was struck by how handsome I found him. The dark, brooding manner intrigued me more than I cared to admit. I was forgetting myself.

He shrugged. "I feel it my moral duty to look out for you. You are naïve about the way of life here. It is far different than anything you've experienced. This country changes people. Most of us are not who others think we are. Herr Schmitt is no exception."

"If that's true, then who are you, Nick?"

His gaze still held mine, and the atmosphere between us suddenly felt charged with tension. His expression relaxed momentarily; his eyes turning liquid silver in the gaslight. I could almost hear Nick think as his countenance underwent a myriad of subtle changes. I knew he was deciding how open to be with me. Whether or not to let me penetrate the thick wall he'd built around his emotions.

The struggle was brief, and the mask slipped quickly and efficiently back into place—the moment lost. Disappointed, I was not to be thwarted.

"Now it's my turn to ask a question."

"You just did."

"It doesn't count as it was relative to your statement. Anyway, you didn't answer it." I insisted and noticed the hint of a smile return to his face.

I took a breath. "I want to know about Amelia."

His demeanour underwent a rapid change. "You have a short memory. That subject is off-limits," he said flatly.

"That's unfair," I said bravely. "I live in her home. I feel at a loss not understanding who Amelia was, not necessarily to you, but to everyone else. Why so much secrecy? If you wish her memory forgotten, why put the portrait where everyone can see it?"

Nick seemed to weigh my words, and then he looked across the table through the open door to the living room. He stared at the painting. "There is no great secret, Julia. It's just hard to talk about that time. It was awful." He reached forward for the decanter and refilled his sherry glass. He took a sip.

"Amelia was a free-spirited, lovely woman who did not belong in Kenya. She was the antithesis of everything I stood for. She was like a butterfly—delicate, beautiful, but always ready to fly away. I suppose that was part of the appeal. The challenge of capturing the butterfly and keeping it for myself." He took another sip.

"We were happy, to begin with. Until she grew bored. That's when she started spending a great deal of time at the Mombasa Club, and everything began to go wrong." Nick's eyes moved from the painting to look at me. "My wife was unfaithful, Julia. She hungered for admirers and attention, and she shared herself with so many, I could not name them all."

I gasped at his bluntness. This I had not expected.

"Of course, I was devastated, embarrassed and damned mortified. My brother Martin urged me to divorce Amelia—send her away—but I could not. For as provocative and outgoing as she might act, I knew the frightened soul hiding behind the façade. We fought frequently because of her infidelity, and she eventually spent more time in Mombasa than she did here. But though I loathed her behaviour, the way she looked at me, spoke to me—I never wished her dead."

"Yet you were accused?" I asked.

"The husband is always the first suspect. Yes, they questioned me repeatedly, but I did not kill her. Why would I? It would have been easy enough to dissolve our marriage, pay her money and pack her off to England. Although Amelia might have liked that, which was another reason not to do it."

"Did the police suspect anyone else?"

"Yes, all her lovers were interviewed—well, those they identified."

Nick must have been completely humiliated having his private life spread wide for the community to see. No wonder he preferred isolation. I would as well.

"Did you have your own suspicions?" I asked.

"Not really. Though I never believed it to be a stranger. I always suspected it was someone she'd had a relationship with. Amelia could be cruel when she wanted to be. Though never enough to deserve a death such as hers."

"You've had much to contend with recently," I said compassionately. "Loss is difficult, and more so when it is someone we love. To lose a wife and then your brother and his wife too? I admire your strength, Nick. I don't know if I could have coped as well as you seem to have done."

"And what of your loss?" he asked.

I blinked. He was getting too close. "What do you mean?" I said glibly, averting my eyes from his face.

"If this is the time for telling tales, then what is your story, Julia? For I can see you have one of your own to tell."

"Nonsense," I replied a little too quickly.

Nick studied my face as though deliberating what he would say next, then seemed to think better of it. "Shall I ask Wilson to bring the coffee outside?"

"Yes, that would be pleasant."

Nick rose from the table and went towards the kitchen. I swallowed the remainder of my sherry and contemplated how easy it would have been to tell Nick the truth.

Chapter Eleven

IT WAS INCREDIBLY LIBERATING RIDING across the plains, feeling hot wind blow through my hair and warming my face. Subira galloped with ease as though she was reminded that her forebears were once wild.

Herr Schmitt and I had left Jacaranda at a sedate pace, but now in the open grasses, I felt the horse's pent-up energy and wanted to let her run.

At some point, he overtook me, and I realised he wanted me to follow. So, I complied, and Herr Schmitt led me under the shade of a tall Acacia tree—its flattened canopy resembling a crude umbrella.

We tethered the horses, and my escort detached a water bag which he offered to both animals. I watched, considering there was something surreal about riding out with an eligible bachelor in the African bush. I harboured no romantic interest in Herr Schmitt, yet I wasn't certain of his intention with me. He was a source of information, however. For now, that was enough. Surely with his abode being in Mombasa, he could fill in some of the gaps of what I did not know about Amelia Fleming.

Dressed in khaki trousers and white shirt, he wore a wide-brimmed hat to block the sun. But his bearing, his posture still gave him the appearance of formality.

I wore Amelia's jodhpurs and jacket, which though

protective, were surprisingly cool. My hair had loosened from its pins under my own sun hat, but I could not be bothered fiddling with it.

I watched Herr Schmitt retrieve a leather pack attached to his saddle. He walked back to where I leaned against the trunk of the tree.

"I hope you do not mind, but I have brought a picnic for us to enjoy?" Herr Schmitt gestured to the bag. I was not hungry but appreciated the thought.

"That will be nice, thank you."

"There is a grassy spot there. Shall we sit?"

I followed him to a small green thatch near the edge of the shade and sat down on the ground cross-legged, feeling a little like a native. He unpacked a few items and then unwrapped a cloth to offer me a sandwich.

"Did you tell me it was the Paderborns you are staying with?"

"*Ja*, Josef *und* Hilary are old friends. Josef lived in Dar es Salem for a time before coming here to farm. They are good people—you should meet them."

"I am sure I will. I have only met the Babcocks and the Briggs thus far. How often do you visit them?"

"Not often. I am kept busy in Mombasa."

I found I could not remember his occupation. "What is it that you do in Mombasa? If you told me, it has slipped my mind."

"I do not believe we spoke of it. I am a merchant, for want of a better word. I supply raw materials to different companies in my homeland. Africa is rich in cocoa, sugar cane and many other crops which Europe does not grow. I expect before too long I shall expand, as there will be many coffee plantations here once more

Europeans arrive."

"Do you see that happening?"

"*Ja*. Especially from your country. The British have a long reach when it comes to Africa."

"As do your countrymen," I replied.

"*Touché, Fraülein*. There, you have me. Perhaps, we should avoid talking of politics and war?"

"Yes," I agreed. "Instead, you can regale me with information of Mombasa, or at least, your impression of it. I saw little of the town when I arrived, and other than the day I met you, those are my only trips there. Mind you, I have only been here two weeks." I accepted a small flask he passed to me. It contained water, and I took a sip.

"Mombasa *ist eine alte Stadt*—an old city with a colourful past. So many cultures have left their stamp there."

"Yes," I said. "I noticed that immediately. And now it is the turn of the British to make their mark, is it not?"

"*Ja*. Although I do not think the Mombasa Club is much to be proud of. You have not been?"

"No. But I saw the building up on the hill. I keep hearing about the place, and it has me curious. Tell me, are you a member?"

"Not exactly." He took a drink from his own flask, and I wondered if it was water? "Though I am allowed entry as a visitor, memberships are only available for the British. I frequent the place because I like to stay up with the events within the European Community, and it is the best way to do it. They host plenty of parties and the occasional game of polo too."

"Derek mentioned a polo game just the other day.

He was trying to encourage both Nick and I to go along. My employer did not seem keen on the idea."

"Little wonder. That place holds no good memories for Herr Fleming. Amelia made him look a fool with all her...how do you say? Her antics."

"It is unfortunate her legacy is always connected to that. But what was she really like, as a person? Did you know her very well?"

"*Nein*. I had only been here a short time when she died. We had met at the Club and once or twice sat together at a polo match. Amelia was very entertaining. She talked a lot and laughed often. I found her intelligence unsuited to a life in *Afrika*. Not because she did not have..." He struggled to find the word. "Der mut...courage. Amelia had plenty, but she was a lost soul here. She could not find enough to occupy her thoughts, her ambitions."

He took another sip of his drink, and I found myself thinking that for a man who did not know Amelia Fleming very well, he certainly had a strong opinion of her psyche. But I did not remark upon it.

"Tell me about your life in England, *Fraülein*?"

"Please, call me Julia. There isn't much to tell, really. I'm from a small town near London. My parents are both gone, and I have no close family. I'd always wondered what it would be like to travel the world, so when I saw this position posted, I applied for the job, and here I am."

His face was full of admiration. "That was brave of you. Most young women would not embark upon such an arduous trip without the company of a husband or family. To undertake the journey alone was something."

From the compliment bestowed, and the interest he displayed, I became more than aware that the two of us were alone in the middle of nowhere. Stirrings of the past took away my indulgent pleasure, and I sat up a little straighter.

"I assure you, Herr Schmitt, I've suffered more adversity riding the local bus to Hammersmith on a Saturday morning." My joke was lost on him of course, for he was not British. I continued anyway.

"I suppose had I ridden with a camel train through a blistering desert I would agree with you. But the truth is, I had a delightful experience, thanks to the marvellous steamships of the P&O Line. I met fellow British passengers on the voyage out, made several ports of call in such interesting places. So, all in all, I can say it was a very pleasant journey, other than fighting off the occasional bout of sea-sickness in bad weather."

He nodded. "*Das ist gut.* And now you are here, learning all about this wonderful land. I shall be interested hearing more of your thoughts when you have been on the continent a little longer. *Afrika* has a way of capturing your soul so that you either cannot leave—or wish you had never stepped foot on its shores. I hope you come to love it as I do." His face grew wistful.

The horses whickered and he snapped out of his thoughts. "*Kommen.* We should continue our ride. The horses grow restless, and I am sure we shall have baboons on our trail when they smell our sandwiches!"

WHEN HERR SCHMITT TOOK HIS LEAVE, I walked Subira around the back to the stables, took off her saddle and made her comfortable. Kijani joined me and offered to rub her down. I happily accepted, ready to wash the dirt and dust from my skin.

I heard Nalah's crying as soon as I entered the house, and my step quickened. I rushed into the nursery, then stopped in surprise to see Malaika sitting in the rocking chair, the baby squirming in her arms. I had no idea she had returned from being with her family.

"Where is Akina?"

"She have me to watch baby, as she needed at home, Memsahib." The lovely young woman got to her feet and unceremoniously deposited the angry child into my arms. "This baby, she will not stop shouting. I do not know what is wrong." With that, she walked out of the room.

"Well," I muttered to myself. Then I realised Nalah had stopped wailing. Her tear-filled hazel eyes stared up at me in utter adoration, and a rush of love swelled in my breast for this child who was not of my body, but was now of my heart.

I WAS GLAD TO HAVE MALAIKA back in the house, even though she still avoided speaking to me and tended to leave a room if I entered. After a few days, I got used to her behaviour and stopped noticing it.

Early in June, Nick went to Mombasa to collect Juba and brought him home. The young man had lost weight, but he was recovered and very happy to be back. I'd asked Wilson to bake something special.

We celebrated Juba's return which pleased the young man immensely. Though Nick and Derek had given me a strange look when I invited them to join us for cake, they reluctantly agreed and made Juba very happy.

Today, I had company. Felicity Babcock looked better than she had for the past few weeks. Her face was not riddled with despair, and neither were her eyes red from crying. I was pleased to see the improvement, for I understood how the suffering of loss diminished a person.

Felicity sat holding Nalah on her lap. The baby was fascinated by the shiny buttons on the woman's riding jacket and attempted to pull them off.

"Julia, you simply have to go," Felicity pleaded. "There's no one else I can ask. All the women in the area are married and practically matrons. And God knows I haven't had anything to be happy about in weeks. Is it such a huge sacrifice to make? Derek will take us. I just can't go with him on my own as Pops won't allow it."

I groaned inwardly and set my tea-cup down in the saucer. Felicity was going to make it impossible for me to say no.

"Hello, there." Derek strode into the room, bringing the smell of dust from outside. "What are you gals up to? Sounds as though there's scheming and plotting afoot."

Malaika glided into the room behind him and placed a fresh pot of tea on the tray before quietly withdrawing.

"I'm trying to persuade Julia to accompany us this weekend to the Club," Felicity complained while Derek poured himself a cup of tea.

"Ah, the birthday bash." He settled himself on the sofa next to Felicity. "You really should tag along,

Julia. You have been here for weeks and haven't gone anywhere. Stop being such a stick in the mud. Besides, it's high time you met some of the Mombasa Brits."

He was right. The time had flown since I'd first arrived, yet the only place I had ventured to was Meadowbrook, to see Felicity. Unlikely as it was, the two of us had become friends. We visited one another at least three times each week.

I glanced at the lovely blonde woman bouncing the baby on her knee. Felicity had been very responsible since the death of Trevor, bearing the weight of her father's racking grief as well as her own. She deserved some fun.

"Oh, all right." I relented.

Felicity's face lit up with excitement. "Really? That's smashing, Julia! Thank you. We shall have such a gay time of it!"

"My goodness," said Nick, striding into the room with Mzuka at his heels. "What's all this fuss about?" He stopped abruptly, seeing Nalah perched on Felicity's lap, then recovered and went to pour himself tea.

"I've been bullied," I complained, as Nick went to stand by the fireplace and leaned back against the mantel, drinking his tea in one swallow. He placed the cup on the mantelpiece, and his eyes settled on my face.

"Felicity has nagged me until I have agreed to go with her and Derek to the party this Saturday," I explained.

Nick's expression underwent a swift change. "At the Mombasa Club?"

"Yes, of course, silly," piped Felicity. 'It's the annual birthday party, and I never miss it." Her face beamed. "Nick, why don't you come along with us. It would be so much fun for us all to go together! It's been years since you went, and it won't be the same now without Trev. What do you say? Come on, Nick!"

He looked appalled. "No, Felicity. I have no desire to step foot in that building ever again, if possible. All it harbours for me are bad memories and people I would rather not see or talk to. There's nothing appealing about the prospect—other than cheering you up. But please, Felicity, do not ask this of me. You know how I feel."

Felicity had the grace to look a little guilty and was kind enough to drop the subject.

Nick continued. "But do take Julia with you. She has had little excitement or social interaction." He glanced at me. "Julia, do you want to go?"

I looked from him to Felicity's radiant face, then at Derek, who sat grinning at the entire performance. I could not bring myself to renege on my promise, although I was tempted to back out and show support for Nick.

"Yes. But only if it is all right with you. Will you be able to watch the baby, or shall I ask Akina to come?"

His gaze flickered to his niece, busy chewing on her fist. "I'll watch Nalah for part of the time, but it's probably a good idea if the girl comes, at least for the evening. Perhaps Malaika can assist as well."

It was settled. I would go to a party in two days' time.

I HAD NEVER OWNED MANY clothes. My father was a teacher, with a meagre income which barely kept us fed. When I left home to become a nanny, what little income I earned I sent to my parents to supplement their living. After they both died, there was no money, for their home had been part of the school property.

I did not consider myself attractive. I had a good head of wavy hair, and the colour of my eyes was often remarked upon, for they were a very deep blue, like my mother's. But I considered my lips too full, my nose too straight instead of snubbed. Fortunately, I seldom used a mirror. So as long as I was clean and tidy, that sufficed.

This, however, was not my frame of mind today. In three hours, I would be leaving for a party in Mombasa, and I had no inkling what I could wear.

I was still going through my options when there came a knock at my bedroom door. It was Malaika.

"*Memsahib*, *Bwana Fleming* asks I tell you to choose something from *Memsahib's* wardrobe for party." The young woman kept her eyes down-cast, as she was wont to do whenever we encountered one another.

I understood her feelings of shame only too well. Had she realised I'd betrayed her secret about Trevor Babcock's despicable actions? I doubted it, for Nick's concocted explanation had saved my being blamed. Therefore, her continued dislike of me stemmed from her loyalty and love for Amelia Fleming.

But this was no time to address any of it. I needed something to wear, and I was running out of time.

"Did your *Memsahib* have a dress which could fit me?" I asked the young Maasai. She gave a curt nod.

I had an idea. "Malaika. Will you please help me?" She looked up quickly, her face puzzled.

"I am to go to Mombasa and meet others from my

country for the very first time. I do not want to shame Jacaranda by looking too poor to be there. Do you understand?"

She shook her head.

I tried again.

"Malaika. I am white, but still a servant here. I sleep in the house because I care for the child. But I am paid wages, like you and the others. This money, it does not buy pretty dresses. I want to borrow something from *Memsahib* Fleming, but I need you to choose what I can wear. Will you help me?"

Her lovely face registered surprise at my request, and she did not answer immediately. And then, much to my relief, she nodded.

"*Memsahib* not make fool of *Bwana* by dressing as servant." Her black eyes flashed. "Come."

The young woman might never dress in western clothing, but she certainly had a canny eye for design. With Malaika's help, I was nicely turned out in a dress of sapphire blue silk. The style simple, with a plunging neckline rescued by a frill of intricate lace for modesty. The bodice was lined with embroidered stars of dark blue, which were repeated along the cuffs of the half-length sleeves and again three quarters way down the skirt.

The fabric was so rich and luxuriant yet also cool against my skin. After I had put it on, Malaika had gestured for me to take a seat in front of a small mirror.

"I arrange hair for you?" she asked. I looked at her hair which was so thick and curly it added several inches to her height. She caught me staring.

"My hair very different, *Memsahib*. But I have helped *Memsahib* Fleming, so Malaika knows how."

I sat very still as she brushed my hair and then pulled it up in the back to fasten into a loose bun. She kept the front full to softly frame my face, and when she was finished, I was thrilled.

The next thing was a hat, and this was borrowed from Amelia's collection also. A wide-brimmed dark blue affair trimmed with beading and a feather in the same colour.

"There, Memsahib. You are ready."

She had transformed me. I did not look like a baby's nanny. I looked like a woman.

"*Asante sana*, Malaika. You are kind to have helped me."

Her dark eyes met mine in the mirror. "*Kama vile ulinisaidia pia, Memsahib* - As you helped me too."

With a last word to Akina regarding the baby, who lay cooing on her blanket on the floor, I waited in the living room for Derek. He was not there yet, but Nick sat in the armchair reading a paper. He glanced up as I came into the room, and his gaze settled on me.

"My goodness," he said. "You look quite lovely this evening, Julia. The dress was a good choice for you. I don't believe I've ever seen it before. That shade of blue matches your eyes perfectly."

I took a seat across from him and tried not to blush at the compliment.

"Thank you, Nick. It is good of you to lend me something to wear. Malaika chose this and also did my hair. I do appreciate it."

"Well, I am glad we have a use for the clothes. To be honest, I should have got rid of them long ago. But it has been easier to close Amelia's room and forget about it all for now."

"Forget about what?" Derek sauntered into the room and stopped when he saw me. "Dash it, Julia. You look stunning!" Quickly I got to my feet. I did not enjoy both of their scrutiny. The sooner we departed, the better.

"Are you ready to go?" Derek asked.

"Yes." I turned to Nick. "Akina knows what to do with the baby. But should there be any problems, call on Malaika and she can help. If Nalah will not settle, then you must sit with her in the rocking chair. She—"

"Will be fine," Nick said, finishing off my sentence. "Julia, I'll make sure the baby is well taken care of. Now off you go and enjoy your evening."

His words sounded hollow, and when I looked at Nick, his eyes burned with something I could not read.

"Right then, old fellow," said Derek. "I wouldn't wait up for us as I'm sure we'll be awfully late back." He gave a grin in anticipation of the night's festivities and slapped Nick on the shoulder. "We'll see you at breakfast."

With that, I followed Derek out of the house.

Chapter Twelve

WE MADE A JOLLY TRIO AS we journeyed to Mombasa. The hour flew past as we chatted and laughed. Derek and Felicity were quite entertaining with their tales and parodies of some of the people I would meet at the party. I confess I don't know whether I was more excited or terrified at the prospect. I was, after all, not of their class. Though respectable enough, I held no title nor breeding.

As we drove, the backdrop of scenery grew more spectacular. The sun sank low on the horizon and painted the landscape in reds and bright oranges, filling the vast skies with a captivating palette. In the far distance, tiny silhouettes danced across the backdrop of colour as the herds made their way across the broad plains.

Felicity was in fine fettle. She wore a lovely gown of silver, which made her blonde tresses appear golden. The style of the dress was modern and extremely feminine. The silky fabric accentuated her tiny waist and pert bosom, with a neckline far deeper than I would be comfortable wearing. But Felicity Babcock was a woman who could carry it off. On me, the outfit would have looked dreadful. I noticed Derek's eyes settle on her figure frequently. Was there something between them?

The ferry crossing was fast, and before long, I saw the Mombasa Club building lit up high on the hill. The anticipation was thrilling. I was about to meet new people and walk in the footsteps of Amelia Fleming. Who knew what I might learn about her by the end of the evening?

As the cart pulled up outside of the building and we got out, there were attendants to take the oxen by their yokes and lead them to an area where they would be tethered and given water.

We stepped onto the verandah, and the hundreds of candles lighting the entire width of it made it seem as though we had entered a fairyland.

"Come along, Julia," said Felicity. "Don't dawdle." I must have slowed my gait trying to absorb it all. I walked faster so I would not lose sight of my escorts.

The foyer and the interior of the building put me in mind of the Mombasa Hotel, with its cool white marble flooring, high ceilings and countless windows flung open to the night air. In the main salon, there were a multitude of tables dotted about and a long bar at one end of the room, with well-turned-out gentlemen clamouring for drinks like flies on rotten food. At the opposite end of the room near the open doors was a dance floor, currently well occupied as a small jazz band played a popular tune.

Derek found us an empty table, and once we were seated, he disappeared to battle his way to the bar promising cold drinks upon his return. Felicity glowed like a firefly. Her eyes glittered with excitement as they scoured the room. She waved her hand periodically as she encountered certain friends, exclaiming, "Oh, look, it's the Peabody's. There, I see the Smythe's," and so on. I paid no attention to the names, but smiled at her, pleased to see her so happy.

Derek returned with three glasses of sparkling champagne. I had only ever tasted it once before, so I giggled as the bubbles tickled my nose.

Felicity burst out laughing. "Really, Julia. You are such an innocent."

Little did she know.

"A toast!" Derek declared. "Here's to our first night of fun in many months! May we have a fabulous time and dance until dawn." We clinked our glasses together and drank.

FELICITY HAD BEEN ON THE DANCE FLOOR for ages. I had accepted one dance with a young man named Nigel Jenkins but had declined further offers as the champagne was making me lightheaded.

I was far from being bored with so much to watch. This was apparently a big night for the club. Out of the corner of my eye I saw a lady who appeared to be making her way over to where I sat. *Oh dear*. Hermione Clitheroe, the lady I had met on the voyage here. It was too late to escape.

"It *is* you!" she exclaimed, arriving at my table huffing and puffing, her face pink with exertion. Mrs Clitheroe dropped into Derek's vacant seat. Dressed in bright red chiffon, the shade emphasised the same colour in her complexion, so the woman resembled a large tomato. Her chubby hand grasped mine, gave it a sweaty squeeze and then let go.

"How are you, my dear?" she said kindly. "It looks as though Kenya quite agrees with you. My, how well you look!"

"Thank you, Mrs Clitheroe. I could say the same to you. How is your family?"

"They are well," she said. "I am here with my son Tommy and his wife." She pointed to the bar. "He's over there somewhere. How do you like living at Jacaranda? Is it what you expected?" I recognised the gleam in her eye and understood immediately she had heard my charge was of mixed race.

"It is even better!" I replied with extra enthusiasm for her benefit. "Mr Fleming is a wonderful host, and I adore the baby. There are so many nice people living in the area, and I have made great friends." I watched disappointment flicker across her face. She had hoped I was unhappy and would tell her my complaints. Of course, I would never do such a thing.

"I did hear about that awful murder. Tommy said the Babcocks are neighbours of yours? I saw you are sitting with the daughter. My, what a to do! According to my Tommy, this sort of thing never happens here. Have they found anything out about who might have killed the man?"

"No," I replied drily. "Not as far as I'm aware."

"Well, it strikes me that's rather odd. If it is one of the blasted natives, I think something should be done about it and fast. Otherwise, we'll all end up slaughtered in our beds. Ooh," she shuddered, and her chins wagged. "That is a scary thought indeed. Well just so long as they don't kill me before I go back to Brighton, then I shan't mind."

"And who might this be?" Derek arrived at the table with fresh drinks. He set them down and then stood up straight for an introduction.

"Derek, this is Mrs Clitheroe. We were shipmates

on the way over here." I flashed him a quick look, indicating I was trying to get rid of the woman who had her eyes pinned on Derek.

"Any relation to Tommy?" Derek asked.

"Yes, indeed. He is my son. I'm here visiting him from Brighton."

"I do hope you are having a jolly time of it in Mombasa. Tommy's a good chap. Is he showing you all the sights?"

"He is. I've been to Nairobi, Malindi, and out on a coral beach. I've never seen such places in my life. But I don't think I could ever live here. I like my British weather too much, not to mention a good paper that isn't over two weeks old."

It did not look like Mrs Clitheroe planned on leaving our table anytime soon. I looked at Derek with what I hoped was an appealing glance. It took him a moment to get the gist of what I was trying to imply, but smart fellow that he was, he finally got the point.

"Mrs Clitheroe, I hope you don't mind, but I came over to see if I could get Julia to have a dance. Would you think us awfully rude if we abandoned you so we can kick up our heels? It's not often we get out, as you know. I want to make the most of having a band to dance to. It's such a treat."

"Oh," she said without even trying to hide her disappointment. "Of course. I should not want to spoil your fun, Julia. I hope I shall see you again before I leave. I've only two weeks left before returning to Brighton."

"Hopefully," I lied. "But if for some reason I don't run into you again, have a safe trip home."

"Come along, Julia," said Derek as a new tune

began. "This is one of my favourites!" And though I was reluctant to dance again, I found it preferable to the entrapment of such a gossipy lady.

Moments later, we literally bumped into Klaus Schmitt on the dance floor. His partner was a heavyset lady who was both taller and larger than Klaus. They both nodded in greeting while Derek apologised for running into them before steering us out of their way.

After the dance, Derek abandoned me to find Felicity, and I realised I should probably eat something. Although I had only drunk two glasses of champagne, I was so unused to alcohol I felt slightly lightheaded. I wandered over to the tables put alongside one of the walls bearing platters and bowls of finger food. I found a plate and made my way along with some other guests, helping myself to items I could take back to the table and eat.

Instead of returning to where I'd sat before, I decided to find somewhere less obvious, in order to avoid Mrs Clitheroe. Unfortunately, most of the tables were occupied, or appeared that way, judging by possessions abandoned while people danced and mingled. But I noticed there were a couple of chairs not being used over in one of the far corners. I tentatively made my way through crowds of people and reached the quiet spot with some relief. Although I had no table, I at least had privacy.

The food tasted wonderful, although I think anything would have because I was ravenous. There were sausage rolls, cucumber sandwiches, and odd little triangular shape envelopes of pastry, containing spiced meat and vegetables. The flavour was reminiscent of the delicious curry I had eaten at Meadowbrook.

Once I had finished, my hands were sticky, and I went in search of the ladies lavatory to wash them. I asked directions from one of the dining attendants who sent me up to the second floor.

A continuous line of people came up and down the stairs like a long caterpillar. I arrived on the next landing and followed women threading their way down the hall. There were so many of us, I wondered how long it would take for me to get a turn. But I was pleasantly surprised to find a huge room dedicated to the fairer sex. There were lavatories either side of the room divided by a row of mirrored vanities down the centre aisle.

After I washed my hands, I found a vacant spot and sat down on a little velvet-covered stool and reached into my bag to find my handkerchief and small vial of rose water. As I freshened up my face, I found the incessant chatter somewhat deafening. I suppose living away from town, I had become used to quiet.

Above all the voices, there seemed one in particular that stood out above the others—a haughty tone with an acerbic edge.

"Of course, he'd never show his face here again," the person said. "How could he after what happened to Amelia. But I am amazed Felicity is already out dancing and drinking, with her brother not five minutes in the grave. Bloody shocking if you ask me."

I stiffened. My instinct told me to leave and not listen to malicious gossip. But curiosity got the better of me. Who was this woman?

"Can you believe Felicity brought the nanny with her tonight?" asked another.

"Such poor taste," the acerbic one answered. "I

suppose when one is friendless, one must bring a paid servant rather than attend alone." There was a slight titter among her audience at this.

But she was not finished. "I am amazed the new gal looks halfway decent. I dare say she must be in bad financial straits to come all the way from England to care for a native brat."

And that was the final straw. I did not mind their assault on me and Felicity, but Nalah was another matter entirely.

I snapped my bag shut, got to my feet and followed the voice. I marched up to where she sat and stopped right behind her.

Her heavily made-up face saw my reflection in her mirror, and she slowly turned around. The woman was easily in her fifties, perhaps even older. The lavish amount of face powder emphasised the deep wrinkles on her forehead and around her thin mouth. I saw recognition in her eyes, but her expression did not falter.

"Can I help you?" she asked, with all the authority of too much money and a title.

"No," I said sharply. "But I can help you. First, an introduction. My name is Julia Rossington, and I am the Fleming's nanny. My beautiful girl is being raised to be a lady, and not an evil pariah who denounces others to make themselves feel important. I'm also good friends with Felicity Babcock, who has been very depressed after the death of her brother, and exhausted from trying to keep her father's spirits up. She has come out tonight to enjoy the emotional support of her so-called 'friends'. Fellow British women, from whom one would expect kindness and warmth while she mourns.

Not persecution and nasty gossip."

The woman rose to her feet, and I was suddenly aware of others who had stopped their ablutions to witness our exchange.

"How dare you speak to me like that!" Her pale eyes were bright with anger, and two red spots blazed on her cheeks.

"I can speak any way I choose," I replied. "You might have a title and wealth, but you do not have ownership of my thoughts and opinions. Perhaps you should consider using your enviable social position to influence people in a good way, and not just as a passport to say hurtful untruths."

With that, I spun on my heel and walked through the sea of gawping women out of the room and back down to the main floor. As I reached the bottom of the stairs, instead of joining the party, I went outside.

I felt flushed, and my heart raced from my outburst. There were guests standing along the length of the verandah, talking in small groups, so I kept walking away from the main doors until I reached the corner. I stepped around it, just out of sight and leaned against the building, sucking in the cool night air as though my life depended on it.

After a few moments, my breathing slowed. I replayed the scene in my mind and wondered if I had made a mistake confronting the woman—whoever she might be. Yet the truth of it was she deserved far worse than my words. People like her sickened me.

Well, it was too late to worry about it now. At least I didn't have to come to Mombasa often and I might never see her again.

I turned to retrace my footsteps and realised I stood

by a closed window. Peering in, I saw it was not part of the main room as I expected, but a smaller space sporting a billiard table. There were several men inside. Some with their jackets removed and cravats loosened. They appeared to be playing, holding their cues while waiting for a turn.

I caught sight of Derek. He was not participating, but observing, drink in hand. Something was being said which must have been funny, because he laughed, though I couldn't hear anything above the noise from the party inside and the loud crickets in the grass.

They were teasing a man bent over the table, taking a shot at one of the billiard balls. He must have pocketed the ball because I did hear a sudden cheer. The man straightened, and then turned to say something to one of the others. I caught a glimpse of his profile and blinked in astonishment. Surely not! No, it couldn't be…I looked again. My stomach churned.

Lord Jeremy Ratcliffe. Dear God, let me be wrong. This time, despite the knot of fear which squeezed in my belly I stared though the glass. There was no mistaking the aquiline nose, the sharp chin, that arrogant tilt to the head. Suddenly my breathing became laboured. I rushed to the edge of the balcony and was violently sick.

I lost track of the time after that. I could not go back into the club for fear I would see the man. Instead, I picked a chair on the verandah, farthest from the door and stayed put. If I could have run back to Jacaranda, I would have. Unfortunately, I had no choice but to wait for Derek and Felicity, who I knew would be in no hurry to leave.

"Miss, are you unwell?" I looked up with a start to

see the woman who had been dancing with Klaus earlier. Before I could respond, she pulled out a chair and sat down opposite me. I was in no mood for company, but I didn't know what to say.

"You're a little flushed." She said with a hint of an accent to her words.

"I grew too warm in there. I needed some fresh air."

"It is crowded. Tell me, are you Miss Rossington, from Jacaranda?"

"Yes." I imagined Klaus must have told her.

She smiled, and her expression was kind. "I am Hilary Paderborn, a friend of Klaus Schmitt and also one of your neighbours."

"It's nice to meet you," I replied, still wishing to be alone. My mind was scrambled, in a panic, and in no mood for idle chit-chat.

She must have read my thoughts. "If I am disturbing you, miss, please tell me, and I'll leave you in peace. You just looked so forlorn, and I wanted to help."

"I'm sorry," I said guiltily. "I don't mean to be rude. I felt unwell. I'm a newcomer, and to be honest, I'm out of my depth tonight. I am a nanny and unused to events like this. A few minutes ago, I had a slight altercation with another lady and spoke my mind bluntly. I'm afraid it spoiled the party for me, and now I'd rather go home."

Her dark eyes twinkled with merriment. "That was you?" she said. "The woman you spoke to was Lady Arabella Sharpe. A fussy old baggage if you ask me. You are to be congratulated! There is talk of it already, but secretly everyone will applaud you. Most of us have been on the receiving end of her wicked tongue."

That was a relief. "She said some cruel things about the Fleming family, and me."

"It doesn't surprise me at all. Pay her no mind whatsoever. Now tell me, how are you settling in at Jacaranda? I have meant to call, but there hasn't been an opportune time. We are renovating our home and it has turned into quite a fiasco. My husband, Josef, is too busy with the crop just now to help. So, I'm sorry not to have introduced myself before."

"Please, there is no need to apologise. I could have come and seen you, but I have not. Living away from Mombasa doesn't really allow for a social life, does it? I suppose everyone must depend on their neighbours for that, and hope they get along well enough." I decided to be bold. "Were you friends with Amelia Fleming?"

The women's broad face underwent a swift change—one of distaste. "No. I would not say that. I had little in common with her as we were cut from quite different cloths. Amelia was never anything but polite to me, at least to my face." A flicker of hurt flashed in her eyes. I understood, having just experienced that myself.

"It's strange living in her house and knowing so little about her. Had she simply gone back to England, her presence would be less felt. But somehow with her being killed, it's as if she's still around. It must have been terribly unsettling for the women in the area when she was murdered," I stated. "Living so remotely, it does make a person feel more vulnerable."

"Yes," Hilary agreed. "And now with what has happened to Trevor Babcock, I wonder why we remain here instead of returning home to Geilenkirchen to farm there."

"Hilary?" A man called her name, and she turned to wave at a figure near the entrance.

"Over here, Josef." He headed towards us, and I was taken aback by the size of him—he was as big as a grizzly bear.

"I have looked everywhere for you. It grows late and I've a mind to return home if you are ready."

"I am," she said. "But first, Josef, this is Miss Rossington, the English lady who is friends with Klaus and staying at Jacaranda."

The bear turned his attention to me. Josef Paderborn had a thick shock of black hair, bushy eyebrows, and a dense beard that hung below his chin. His body was too big for the suit he wore, and he looked as though he was more than ready to rip it off.

"Good evening, Miss Rossington. It is nice to meet you. I hope you don't mind if I drag my wife away. I hate these affairs and have suffered enough for one evening." His smile softened his wild appearance.

"I understand," I agreed. "I feel the same. Only my cohorts will be the last to leave, I fear."

Hilary reached across the table and touched my arm. "If you are ready to go home, you are welcome to ride back with us." She glanced up at her husband. "Josef, we have room, do we not?"

"Of course," he said without hesitation. "We pass Jacaranda on our way home."

Relief flooded through me. "Are you sure? I don't want to put you to any trouble, but I should like it very much. But I must speak to Derek and Felicity first. Can you wait a few minutes? I hate to delay you."

Josef pulled up a chair and lowered himself into it

slowly. "It is not a problem. We will wait for you here."

I quickly made my way back into the building, keeping watch in case I saw Jeremy Ratcliffe. But he was nowhere in sight, and I made no attempt to find Derek, who might be with him.

Felicity was sitting with a group of men and women who were quite merry with drink. I pulled her to one side and told her I planned to leave with the Paderborns. She started to protest, but her raucous group began laughing at some tale or other, and she relented, anxious to get back to the party. I knew Felicity was unconcerned about being alone with Derek on the ride back to Meadowbrook, for Pops would be none the wiser as he'd already be abed. I asked her to tell Derek I had gone on. With that, I left the party, as eager as a criminal escaping a prison cell.

The Paderborns drove a cart not dissimilar to the one Derek had driven. I sat in the back of the cart, with Hilary to keep me company, as both she and her husband were built well, and there was not enough space for the three of us up in the front. We were comfortable enough, sitting upon sacking filled with hay, and leaning back against the side of the cart enjoying the cool night air.

Now on first name terms, Hilary was telling me about her children, eleven-year-old twin boys, Karl and Kurt. They were being cared for tonight by their nanny, a Kikuyu woman named Grace. Hilary regaled me with stories of their antics, and I was thoroughly entertained the entire drive home.

It was strange travelling this late, even with the light of Josef's lantern. The full moon offered some respite from being in total darkness, but as we drew further away from Mombasa, and became engulfed in the night, an eerie silence descended, broken only by the distant call of an animal. I wondered if the black leopard would be stalking the grounds of Jacaranda tonight?

We arrived at the house quickly, no doubt due to our constant conversation en-route. I found I liked this couple very well. No wonder Klaus Schmitt visited them often. I thanked them and climbed down from the cart, promising Hilary I would pay her a visit in the next few days. I wanted to meet her children and see their farm.

As their cart pulled away, I let myself in through the front door. The house lay in darkness, and all was quiet. Even Mzuka didn't bark. I tiptoed down the hall going straight into the nursery, half-expecting to find Akina asleep in the rocking chair. She was not there, and much to my concern, neither was the baby.

I went back down the hall into the living room. A gas light still burned low, no doubt left on for my coming home, but the room was empty. I tried to staunch the fear flooding my mind. I told myself that Nick would be certain to watch over his niece and no harm could have befallen Nalah.

Where was Nick? I went back down the hall once again, and this time I realised his bedroom door stood ajar. Quietly I stole inside. The curtains were not drawn, and moonlight shone through the window enough for me to see my way. I heard a little sound, and at once knew relief recognising Nalah, making her little sleep noises. I went over to the bed, my foot touching the flank of Mzuka, who gave a small grunt. Then I stood for a moment to enjoy the tranquil tableau before me.

Nick lay upon his back, one arm flung over his head, while the other held Nalah in the crook of his elbow. They were both sound asleep. My eyes fastened on Nick's face, the strong cheekbones, thick brows, and the scar splitting his eyebrow into two parts. Even in slumber, he looked so serious, in stark contrast to the honey skinned child next to him.

I walked around to the other side of the bed and gently lifted Nalah into my arms. I stepped slowly out of the room, took her into the nursery and put her into her crib. She did not even stir. Then I went into my room, stripped off my clothes and climbed into bed.

But sleep evaded me, for every time I closed my eyes, the leering face of Jeremy Ratcliffe's cousin Charles loomed before me. I had travelled across the world to escape the man who had single-handedly destroyed my life, and now his despicable cousin was here. Was I never to be free of the past?

Chapter Thirteen

NALAH WAS HAPPY TO see me when I lifted her from her crib. It was still early, and I had barely slept a wink. I headed into the kitchen finding Wilson already there preparing breakfast, while Juba unpacked eggs he must have just collected from the hen house.

"*Salamu, Memsahib*," Juba greeted me.

"*Jambo*, Juba," I replied as I went to Wilson, who already had his arms reaching out for Nalah. This was our morning routine. The cook would hold the baby while I prepared her bottle with milk Wilson brought in from the dairy on his way to work each day. Nalah loved him. He made silly faces, and she giggled in delight. No wonder Wilson had so many children, blood and adopted. He obviously had a way with them.

"Did *Memsahib* have much dancing at the party in Mombasa?" Juba asked.

I poured milk into a bottle. "Only two dances, Juba. And that was plenty." I went to collect Nalah, who started whimpering when she spotted her bottle in my hands. I took a seat at the kitchen table and settled her on my lap. She grabbed the bottle and pulled it towards her face, missing her mouth and instead hitting her nose. She immediately began making little huffs of irritation. I slid the teat of the bottle into her mouth, and she instantly went limp in my arms.

Juba began whisking eggs in a bowl, and I watched him, enjoying that he looked so well now he'd recovered from malaria. He would always be susceptible to flare-ups, and we would need to keep an eye on him.

How odd that sitting here in the kitchen with these two African men was such a normal start to my day. Catching a tram into town or popping into the newsagents to buy a paper seemed a lifetime ago. The thought took me back to England, and the memory of Charles Ratcliffe bled into my mind. I would not, *could* not think about him.

Nalah finished her milk, and I picked her up and put her over my shoulder to make sure she burped. She did, almost immediately, and both servants laughed at her unladylike manners. I excused myself, and took her back to the nursery, changed her nappy, and then grabbed her blanket and headed to the dining room.

I put the baby down on the floor, spreading her blanket out and placing toys for her to look at, then I helped myself to a cup of tea from the pot on the table and sat down. Juba brought in a plate of eggs and toast. I thanked him for it and started eating.

"Good morning, Julia." Nick joined me. As usual, he had already been out working. He pulled off his hat, hung it on the back of his chair and took a seat. I watched him pour himself a drink.

"I didn't hear you come in last night," he stated. "You must have crept about like a ghost."

I smiled. "I didn't want to wake you or the baby. But I thought it best to put her in her crib in case you rolled over and squashed her."

The look of panic on his face made me smile. I

knew he had not considered the possibilities when he put her on the bed next to him.

Juba arrived with a plate of food. Nick thanked him. "I'm sorry, Julia. Nalah cried when I put her to bed, so I thought I'd stay with her until she fell asleep and then carry her into the nursery."

"And once she fell asleep, you waited to make sure she was away with the fairies and fell asleep yourself."

He nodded fervently.

"We have all done it, Nick. Babies are hard work. You should have kept Akina here to take care of her."

"She was here earlier in the evening. But I wanted her to go home before dark." He took a bite of his eggs. "Well, are you going to tell me about the party? Did you have a nice time? Is Derek sleeping off being drunk?"

"Too many questions. Let me see. The party was not my cup of tea, although I met a few nice people." I hesitated.

"And?"

"I'm afraid I was very rude to a Lady Arabella Sharpe. I might not be welcomed back."

Nick's eyes widened in surprise. "She's an old battle axe. What on earth did you say?"

I told Nick the gist of the conversation. That we had all been insulted. I also repeated what I could remember of my comments. He threw his head back and laughed.

"I would have paid good money to see her face!" he said. "Well done, Julia. Well done indeed!"

"After that, I really wanted to come home, and once I had spent time talking to the Paderborns, I accepted their offer of a ride back here. I told Felicity I was coming home early. So, I have no idea if Derek is hungover or not, though he seemed to be having rather a jolly time of it."

"That sounds like Derek. Some people enjoy the company of others." He looked pensive. "I suppose I was like that once too. But life can throw much at you, and it changes everything."

I knew exactly what he meant. After all, there had been a time when I still had stars in my eyes and hopes for a future where I could do anything I wanted—and look what had happened to me.

"Clever girl, Nalah," Nick said abruptly. I turned to see that the baby had rolled from her tummy onto her back for the first time. She lay like an upended crab. Her little legs and arms wriggled, and she omitted shrieks of delight.

Nick stared at his niece. "She really is a joy."

My heart went out to him because in his voice was the sadness of loss. A brother and his wife, Amelia, and the unborn child he would never see. But at least Nick had this tiny girl. And as I sat in reflection, I watched her handsome uncle go and sit on the carpet, Mzuka lying close by. Smiling, I watched Nick tickle Nalah's tummy until she began to giggle. Her laughter sounded like the peal of a clear bell, and I found myself laughing as well. Nick looked up at me, his grey eyes shining with pleasure, and as our eyes met, something between us shifted. Our gaze held. Then the sound of someone coming into the room broke the moment, and I quickly looked away.

"*Bwana*, there is a man to see you about some seed. He waits at the barn."

Nick got to his feet. "Ah, yes. I was expecting him.

Thank you, Malaika." Nick gave me a farewell nod and left the room.

I could feel the housekeeper's eyes on me. Hesitantly, I met them. Malaika made no attempt to hide her thoughts. She stared at me with instinctive comprehension, then she came closer so she could speak quietly.

"*Memsahib* not want to be owned by a man. But Malaika sees the light in your eyes when you look at *Bwana*."

"That is ridiculous," I snapped, stepping aside to go and pick up the baby. I scooped Nalah into my arms and strode from the room still feeling Malaika eyes on me as I walked away.

WHILE NALAH TOOK HER NAP EARLY that afternoon, I asked Wilson to watch her while I took Subira for a ride. I'd only ridden the horse close to the farm up until now, but for some reason, today I had the sudden urge to venture further afield. I went to the gun cabinet and took the rifle Nick had shown me how to use. Gripping it in my hands, I felt like a member of a wild west show. Nick had been totally correct saying I was only used to carrying an umbrella.

The weapon felt awkward, but I was determined to follow the rules. The memory of my close call with the black leopard lingered in my mind—I would not be caught defenceless again. Kijani helped me saddle up the horse, who whickered when she saw me, anticipating being out of her stall. Before long, we galloped down the driveway under what remained of the blossoms and headed out to the dirt road. I was determined to get a taste of the country by myself.

Somewhat unfamiliar with my surroundings, I had a general idea of what lay in each direction after living at Jacaranda these past weeks. We trotted down the road until the first clearing, and then I steered Subira out towards the plains. As the scraps of bush finally cleared, I stopped the horse and sat for a few moments to stare at the landscape which spread out as far as my eye could see.

An ocean of grass stretched before me, punctuated by solitary Acacia trees and smatterings of rocky outcrops here and there. The blazing sun on the horizon was massive and looked as though it almost touched the ground. Its vibrant rays swept across the plains, dusting them in sunlight and creating silhouettes of everything it touched.

I felt Subira's muscles twitch beneath me, and I knew the mare itched to run. I dug my heels against her flank, and she took off like a bullet from a gun.

Though it was the horse who ate up the ground as we galloped across the plains, I felt as though I was running in the wind. My hair came loose, my eyes stung, and I felt alive! This was Africa. No buildings, no people, just me, the horse and the wind. I let Subira have her head, and she galloped for a while longer until the heat took its toll, and she began to slow.

I wheeled her around, so we might travel back the way we had come, but at a slow trot. My eyes scanned the area. Were there any animals close by? Now we were not kicking up dust or making noise, I saw groups of zebras milling around a small thatch of trees, seeking out the shadows. They grazed, unperturbed by our presence. It was ironic comparing the striped mammals to my mount, a descendant of their breed. There were

Impala and Thompson gazelles interspersed with the zebra, seemingly comfortable with one another. How different to the pastoral fields of England with their sheep and cows.

When we reached the dirt road, I turned Subira away from the house and in the direction of the crop fields. I had only seen the farm's fields from the cart when we travelled to Meadowbrook, and I was curious to see them at close range. I told myself the interest stemmed purely from a desire to learn, not from the desire to see my employer.

We ambled along until I heard voices in the distance, and I left the road. Here the land flattened and was full of healthy crops, although I did not recognise what kind. Workers stood dotted throughout the fields, and some of them waved as I passed them. There were several large fields, all adjoining one another, and over near the tree line stood a roughly built hut, with two horses tethered outside in the shade. I recognised Nick's horse and went in that direction. I dismounted and tied Subira next to his mount, a large roan who muzzled his stablemate in welcome. I pulled off my gloves and went into the open hut.

It was much darker inside and cooler. The space was not large, but it held a table and two wooden chairs, and in them sat Felicity Babcock and Nick. They seemed surprised to see me, though they had likely heard my approach. Nick hurriedly got to his feet. I had interrupted something because the atmosphere felt tense. I did not feel welcome.

"Oh, I'm sorry. I shouldn't have barged in—"

"Don't be ridiculous," Nick retorted too quickly. "You just surprised me. Come in and have some refreshment."

"Hello, Julia." Felicity said, her voice laced with what I took for irritation. I wondered at the two of them being holed up in here, away from seeing eyes. What was going on?

"Hello. Did you enjoy the rest of your evening at the Club?" I asked, accepting a cup of water from Nick. I had not realised my mouth was so dry.

Felicity rolled her eyes. "I did until I got lambasted by Lady Arabella Sharpe. She was quite put out with you. I also had Klaus Schmitt pestering me about where you had gone and with whom. Honestly, you would think I was your keeper." Her tone had softened as though she found the idea amusing. "Actually, I found it rather a dud if you want to know the truth. The days of fun and games at the Mombasa Club are long over, I fear." Her eyes landed on Nick's face as she uttered the last sentence.

Was Felicity reminding Nick that she and his deceased wife had once been the life and soul of the place? If so, it was cruel. I finished my water and set the cup onto the table.

"Thank you, Nick. Well, I am off. I was out riding, and on a whim decided to come and see the fields I hear so much about. I'll let you two get back to it. Felicity, are you returning home or coming to Jacaranda when you are finished here?" I sounded impertinent but did not care.

"No, I shall go home. I'm still tired from last night."

I nodded. Before Nick could say anything, I bid them both farewell and left the hut. Nick followed me out.

"Julia, why not stay, and I can show you around?"

I mounted Subira and looked down at him. His face looked drawn, tired. Whatever I had interrupted had not been anything he was enjoying.

"I'll come back another time. Thank you, Nick. I should get back to the baby anyway. I've been gone long enough. I'll see you at dinner." I turned the horse and then nudged her into a trot. Once I reached the road, Subira broke into a gallop. As we raced back to Jacaranda, I could not help but wonder what I'd interrupted between Nick and Felicity.

DINNER THAT EVENING WAS A QUIET AFFAIR. Derek had not surfaced from his house, no doubt still the worse for wear after his evening in Mombasa. Nick and I sat at the table, with little conversation between us. He seemed distracted. His mind elsewhere.

Tonight, Wilson had cooked a chicken casserole, and it was as tasty as anything I had eaten before. As I ate, I looked at my employer.

"Is everything all right, Nick? You seem rather withdrawn this evening."

He glanced up, and our eyes met. "Sorry. I've been mulling over a problem with one of the crops. It's dominating my thoughts. I don't mean to be rude."

"You're not rude. I was just concerned." I took another bite and swallowed. "Does Felicity visit you much while you are working?"

"What? No, not really. Only when she wants to be a nuisance."

"She must miss her brother. Perhaps she's lonely?"

"I doubt it. Felicity spends a great deal of time coming and going to Mombasa. She is quite preoccupied with having fun. She stopped by today because she wanted to discuss something personal about her father."

"I see." I did not. Something about the comment rang false.

"I imagine she misses your wife a great deal." Nick's eyes snapped up to lock with mine, and what I saw there made me lament having said that.

"Sorry," I mumbled. "That was insensitive of me. I meant nothing by the remark."

He surprised me with a shrug of his broad shoulders. "It's all right, Julia. No harm done. You're quite right in your assessment, though. Felicity has been lost without Amelia. The two were halves of one whole. Inseparable, silly, and always ready to have fun. I'm sure it's been hard on Felicity, and now with Trevor's murder."

"Is there any news on that?" I had heard little since the day after it occurred.

"No." Nick averted his gaze. What was he hiding? Again, the image of he and Migali sprinting down the driveway revisited my thoughts.

"It surprises me no more is being done to discover who did it. Especially as they might strike again."

"I believe the consensus is it was probably someone in transit as Trevor's wallet was gone. Most of the Africans living here would not be bold enough to commit a murder and then stay. None of Babcock's workers, or ours, have left. So, the theory of it being a stranger, still stands."

"Or a European," I said, watching Nick's eyes narrow to a frown.

"You think that likely?" he asked.

"Anything is possible. Especially when the murderer would know fingers would point first towards one of the natives."

He contemplated this for a few seconds. "Perhaps. Anyway, I will not miss the man, especially after learning of his deeds. But his killer needs to be found. Pops will not rest until justice has been done. The man is completely distraught over his son's death."

I understood. For I felt the same about my own son. We fell silent. Juba came in and collected our empty plates.

"I'm riding out tomorrow afternoon to see Don White, a good friend of mine who farms west of here. If you'd like to accompany me, you could bring Nalah, and have some time away and a change of scenery?"

I did not hesitate. "That would be marvellous. As long as we won't get in the way?"

"No. I would enjoy the company." He sounded sincere. Yet Nick's mind was preoccupied. And though I hated to contemplate the thought, I wondered if Felicity Babcock had something to do with it?

Chapter Fourteen

THE SUN SHONE FIERCELY AS we trundled along in the cart. Nick had erected a makeshift canopy covering where we sat, so that Nalah was shaded, and it really helped. Mzuka lay in the back of the cart.

The wind was down and the air quite still. There seemed to be a lot more flies buzzing around, and I had brought a piece of mosquito netting which I laid on top of the box where Nalah lay. I wished I could wrap myself in it too. The flies were so annoying. I commented as much to Nick.

"One of the downfalls of living in Africa, I am afraid," he said. "In time, you get used to them."

I doubted I would. I changed the subject and asked him about the man we were going to see.

"Donald White is an old friend. We were in the same regiment many years ago. He is from Aldershot, in Hampshire, but fell in love with Africa and decided to remain here. He has a farm near Maweni, two hours away, give or take. Don has two children, Steven, and Lindsey. They are eleven and twelve years old at last count. You'll like his wife, Janet. She's a terrific cook."

Nick told me a few stories from his days in the military with Don, and then changed the subject after I spotted a group of vultures above us, indicating a kill close by. It was not long before he pointed out a group of hyenas attacking the carcass of a dead animal, in a frenzy of hunger. They were far enough away to ignore us passing, but Mzuka was on point, watching and ready to protect us. I was grateful we were not close enough to see any detail of the poor victim's remains.

Nick pointed out different vegetation and talked about the various wildlife we encountered. We drew the attention of a group of baboons, who eyed us curiously. Nick advised me to never feed them, as they would converge upon us, and could be vicious.

We continued on, passing a small lake which looked most inviting in the blistering heat. Nick promised we would stop there on our return.

The White's residence was a sprawling bungalow, similar in appearance to Jacaranda. As we drove down the driveway, there came the sound of barking. Mzuka leapt out of the cart and bounded ahead of us, where he was greeted by two dogs, who looked to be the same breed.

"His sisters," said Nick as he brought the cart to a stop. "They are littermates." He climbed down and walked around to take the baby. The front door swung open and a petite, black-haired woman came out to welcome us. She was very pretty, her eyes dark-blue and warm with welcome.

"Nick! You are a sight for sore eyes!" There came the scramble of feet, and a boy and girl burst from the house. They ran to Nick and wrapped their arms around him.

"Uncle Nick," said the boy. "I've got a new rifle."

"I haven't," his sister complained.

"Children!" said their mother. "Please give Nick a chance to get inside the house." She watched as I passed the baby into his arms.

"Oh, look at Nalah. She has grown so much since I saw her last."

I climbed down from the cart. Nick turned to me.

"Janet, this is Julia. She is the nanny I told you about. She has been a godsend."

Janet reached out to take the baby from Nick's arms. She gave me a friendly smile. "Hello, Julia. It's lovely to meet you. You are obviously taking good care of Nalah. Look at her, she's thriving. Come on inside and let us have tea." She glanced at Nick. "The children will take you to see Don. He's over in the cane field." With that, Janet bade me follow her into her house.

The interior boasted a British feel to it, as it seemed all the colonial houses did. But this house felt like a real home. The focus was on comfort, not appearance. Janet led me into her kitchen. She explained she did not have a cook, as she set a kettle on the hob to boil, motioning to a seat at the table.

"Here, why don't you hold her while I make the tea." She handed me the baby, and I took a seat, watching Janet get out cups and saucers and put some biscuits onto a plate.

"I am so pleased to finally meet you, Julia," she said, setting a bowl of sugar cubes and a small jug of milk onto the table. "It makes me happy knowing Nick has you there to help him. It's been a rotten couple of years for him." her compassion warmed me to her immediately.

"Yes, so I've learned. I was unaware of his losses when I took the job. He's certainly had more than his fair share."

Janet shook her head. "Undoubtedly. Nick's a fine

man, and he was a good husband. I was sorry Amelia couldn't settle down and have a family. Still," she tucked an errant lock of hair behind one ear. "I suppose not everyone wants the same things in life." She studied me. "Have you met all your neighbours yet?"

I bounced Nalah on my knee. "Some of them. The Babcocks, the Briggs and the Paderborns. Everyone has been very welcoming."

"Shocking news about Trevor Babcock," Janet said. "It's rare incidences like that occur here."

"Yet it happened to Amelia Fleming," I said without thinking.

She paused, and our eyes met. "Yes, it did. And I only wish they could catch whoever is responsible for both murders. Donald constantly frets about our safety, especially when he's gone working in the fields."

The kettle whistled, and Janet set about making a pot of tea. When the cups were full, she sat down across from me. "Your accent sounds as though you are from the south of England. Whereabouts, if you don't mind me asking?"

"Chessington, in Surrey," I replied.

"I know it!" she said, eyes bright with pleasure. "I'm a neighbour! I grew up in Richmond-Upon-Thames, not ten miles from you, on the other side of Kingston."

"And yet here we meet in the wilds of Africa," I said with a chuckle. "Fate is a strange bedfellow." I took a sip of tea and then set it back down as there came a noise from outside. The sound of men's voices and children squabbling broke the quiet. Janet quickly got to her feet. "I'd better make more tea," she said and went back to the hob.

I got up as well and put Nalah on my hip. "What can I do to help?"

"If you go into the pantry, there's a cake tin in there on the bottom shelf. Would you fetch it, and I'll slice up the Victoria Sponge for everyone."

Janet's children burst into the kitchen, still at odds about something. Her daughter's hair was so blonde it was practically white, and her eyes were as pale as the sky. She looked nothing like her mother, yet the boy, Steven, had Janet's black hair and pretty eyes.

"Would you two take the baby for me?" I asked. "If you can go in the living room, she loves to lie on her tummy and roll over." I passed her to Lindsey, who happily accepted Nalah, holding on to her tightly while the baby smiled at the girl with a gummy grin. They took her out of the kitchen. Janet seemed pleased that I'd included her children.

"Can you go ahead and slice the cake?" she asked. "I'll finish the tea and we'll take the tray into the living room."

A few minutes later I was being introduced to Donald White. He was close in age to Nick. Now I saw where Lindsey got her colouring. Donald was as blond as Nick was dark headed—shorter, but every bit as well-built. He smiled warmly at me.

We sat down with our tea and cake while the children were totally engrossed with Nalah—a seemingly mutual admiration. Through the open glass doors from the living room, I could see Mzuka and his siblings lying out on the verandah, panting after their boisterous play.

Nick and Don were discussing crop prices. Harvest would be in three months and with the war in the south, prices were apparently very unstable. Janet listened to the conversation with interest, and then told them to stop talking about business and have better manners.

"Yes, dear," Donald said sweetly while pretending to look terrified of his tiny wife. "What would you like to talk about instead?" he enquired politely, though he was grinning.

Janet rolled her eyes. "Anything but sugar cane." She turned her head to Nick. "Can you stay for dinner this evening? We'd love to have you."

Nick glanced at me to see my reaction. I had no issue with spending time with this nice family. I had brought a change of clothes for the baby and her bottle. I nodded.

"That sounds wonderful," he said. "But we can't stay late. I prefer not to travel after dark with the baby in tow."

"Of course," said Janet. She looked pleased as punch, and I considered she must get lonely, just as I did. I looked forward to being in her company for a while.

WE ATE RELATIVELY EARLY, AND I was grateful for that. Janet made a salad fresh from her vegetable garden, sliced a loaf of bread straight from the oven, and served thick slices of salty smoked ham. It was a wonderful meal. We ate out on the shaded verandah and sipped glasses of cool lemonade.

My afternoon had been lovely. The men had returned to the fields with the children in tow. I put Nalah down to sleep in Janet's bedroom, and she had slept for almost two hours. It allowed me some time to relax in the comfort of Janet's living room while we got to know each other.

Of all the people I had met so far, this kind lady was someone I could envisage as my friend. We each told something of our pasts to one another, although I left out a large part of mine and did not share the reason why I had come to Africa. Janet confided that she had dreamt of becoming a nurse but abandoned the dream after meeting Donald.

After dinner, I helped tidy up, leaving Nalah bouncing on Nick's knees as he sat outside talking to Donald. As I dried the dishes Janet washed, she paused to look at me.

"I hope you don't think me strange saying this, Julia. But I have really enjoyed my day with you. There are so few women to befriend out here, and most I meet are foreign, reclusive, or like Felicity Babcock. Hilary Paderborn is probably the only one I have anything in common with, but she has so much on her hands at their farm." Janet's dark eyes softened. "I should like us to be friends. By that, I mean I want to know you better. Will you come and visit again, and perhaps I can come to Jacaranda too? I know it sounds silly asking, but it's not as though we'll run into each other at the greengrocer's, is it?"

I laughed, delighted with her request. "Oh, Janet. I'm thrilled you feel the same as me. I've made no real friends at all, well unless you count Nick and Derek. I would be delighted to see you and your family again. Sooner rather than later."

She was pleased with that. As we finished cleaning up, we agreed to meet again within the next two weeks. Janet would send word and then bring the children to Jacaranda.

With that, when we finally parted for home, the farewell was cheery as there were already plans made. The entire family waved us off as Nick steered the oxen back down the driveway.

We spent the first part of our journey chatting about the afternoon. Nick seemed thoroughly pleased with my remarks about Janet. I told him she planned to visit the following Saturday.

"You could not do better than counting Janet White as a friend," he said. "She's a wonderful woman. It will be good for you both to have each other to talk to."

"Yes," I said, noticing Nalah's eyes blinking heavily. I laid her down in her cushioned box between Nick and myself. "I think I can learn a lot from her about living remotely, too. But mostly, I like her mind. She is an intelligent woman. Did you know she went to college?"

Nick looked astounded. "No?"

"Indeed. She was interested in medicine—still is, as a matter of fact."

"I knew she was good with healing, but I had no idea…" He trailed off and then looked at me. "You have known Janet for four hours or less. I have known her since before her children were born. How the hell did you learn so much?"

I grinned. "Now that would be telling."

We both fell quiet, lost in our thoughts while Nalah fell fast asleep under the rhythmic rocking of the cart.

After a time, I saw we were approaching the lake we had passed earlier in the day. The sun was slowly sinking in the sky.

Much to my surprise, as we drew closer, Nick turned the cart off the road. He jumped down, took hold of the oxen's harnesses, and led them over to a small clump of trees. He tethered the reins and the beasts immediately set about grazing where they stood.

"Come and join me," he said. "I'll carry the baby in her box so she can stay sleeping."

I climbed down from the cart and walked around to where he stood. Nick set the box down and retrieved the rifle, slinging it across his back before picking up the box again.

"We'll go over this small hill, and then you can get the best view. You can't see much from the road." He set off, and I quickly followed.

There was a strange noise coming from somewhere in the distance, though I could not determine its source. The gradient slope was slight and made for an easy walk. As we crested the top, I stopped, and the breath caught in my throat.

We faced the west. The dark orange sun hung so low on the horizon it looked as though it floated upon the surface of the shimmering lake. In the few minutes since we had arrived there, the sky had changed into a palette of pinks, oranges and yellows, and the clouds looked as though they had been dabbed by a heavenly paintbrush. But the scene was like nothing else I had ever been privileged to witness, because dotted through the water, as far as my eyes could see, were hundreds of pink flamingos.

They looked as though they had been scattered across the water like confetti. Their strange croquet necks, their one-legged postures, filled my range of vision until everything looked magical and surreal. Here then, was the source of the strange sound, for bird chatter filled the air.

I was speechless. My mind tried to process how an image this beautiful could be right in front of me, yet somehow could not. I was almost moved to tears.

Nick came to stand beside me.

"What do you think, Julia?" His voice was soft, though it carried the joy of seeing this scene.

"I have never seen a sight this lovely in all my life," I whispered.

He set Nalah's box down in front of us and rested his hands on his hips. "It's one of my favourite places to come when I need to think. I just wish it was a little closer to home."

I turned to look at his face. He was peaceful, reflective.

"If it was too easy to get to, it would lose its magic, I think." I said reverently, as though speaking loudly would break the spell.

"For a newcomer, you really have an understanding of what it is to be here, Julia." He moved in front of me, and his silver eyes searched mine. His hand came up and gently, he ran the back of it across my cheek, stroking my skin. "You are so lovely in the light of an African sunset. You look as though you've always belonged here." He took a step closer, and I swallowed. Before I had time to consider what he was about, Nick cupped my chin in his hand, tilted his head and leaned towards me.

His lips touched mine, and before another thought passed through me, I automatically opened my mouth to receive the kiss. He tasted delicious, like the wild outdoors, his lips warm, hungry, urgent. His arms lowered to take me into an embrace, while mine rose to wrap around his neck. My hands roamed into his thick hair, and my fingers buried themselves in the strands.

Then my mind snapped. My body remembered rough, invasive hands, grabbing at me and laughing at my attempts to pull free. Another's delight rang in my ears, spurring the monster along. Suddenly I gasped as though choking, and with all my might, I pushed Nick away from me as hard as I could.

He stumbled, completely taken by surprise at my response, hurried to right himself, then stared at me, confusion written on his face. We were both breathing fast, our lungs racing for air.

My hands wiped my lips. "I'm sorry," I muttered. Blood rushed into my face, and I turned away so he would not see it.

Behind me, I heard him pick up Nalah's box. Without saying a word, he began to walk down the hill to the cart. Mindlessly I followed. My brain numbed by the disgust of a memory so foul, I dare not allow it in.

I clambered back into the cart. Nalah slept on, ignorant of my changed mood, my fear. Nick untethered the oxen and walked them back to the road, and soon we were on our way.

After a few minutes he finally spoke.

"I'm sorry, Julia. I should not have presumed you wanted me to kiss you."

I did not reply. I didn't know what to say.

He took my silence as reproach. "I apologise."

I turned to face him, tears stinging my eyes. I dare not speak lest I cry with my shame. I know he saw my state, I know he thought himself the culprit. I could not tell him different. Quickly I looked away.

"It will never happen again," he said.

We did not speak at all for the remainder of the

drive to Jacaranda. And when we arrived, it was to find the housekeeper waiting upon our return.

As I got down from the cart, her eyes me mine, and I felt as though Malaika looked into my soul.

Chapter Fifteen

I DID NOT SLEEP WELL. MY dreams were dark, fitful and frightening. When I dressed that morning, I stayed in my room and waited for the baby to wake. I sat on the bed, my mind thick with the webbing of my past and confusion for my present. My fingers touched my lips where not so long ago, Nick's mouth had been. I closed my eyes. The initial memory of his kiss brought pleasure, the sensation of his embrace comfort. So, what had changed that feeling into terror?

I could not sit still. I went to stand by the open window. The sky was blue, the breeze carrying a touch of cool air coming from the sea. Wretched, I stared out and willed my mind to quiet. It would not. What did I expect? It had been two years since I'd been touched by a man, and then it had been violently. Was it any wonder that the first time I was touched again, I'd panicked?

I was no psychologist. Yet something dark had come over me last night in Nick's arms. Something instinctively fearful. I had pushed Nick away and not said anything when he had apologised. What must he think? Did I care? Yes. Though I had been mortified at his attentions, deep down, I knew Nick to be a good and proper man. I had not intentionally meant to confuse him with my behaviour. But it was too personal to talk about, least of all to him.

What should I do? He was my employer. We must rectify the situation. But how to do that without telling him the truth? I began to pace, my mind furiously thinking. Perhaps I could just speak with him calmly and not address what had taken place, rather how we should proceed forward? Surely then, we could both be spared the embarrassment of revisiting last night. Nalah whimpered in her crib, and I went straight into the nursery to get her up. Yes, I would talk to Nick, and we'd put the matter behind us.

I did not see him until dinner time, and then we were not alone, for Derek joined us. I greeted them both casually and kept my eyes averted from Nick while Derek talked nonstop. He was still full of excitement about the party in Mombasa, and after he had gently chided me for leaving early, he regaled Nick with stories about his evening.

"I got slaughtered at billiards," he said when Nick asked if he had played that night. Apparently, Derek loved the game. "Bad enough Klaus Schmitt beat me, but then I got a sound thrashing from an old acquaintance of mine. Jeremy Ratcliffe. Do you know him?"

My fork clattered to my plate, the peas rolling off the tines. I felt both men's eyes on me. I did not look up—just picked it up and carried on eating.

"No, I don't believe I do."

"Comes from a large family. Jeremy and I met in school. He's over here scouting out something or other. Was a bit cagey when I asked him about it. Anyway, he'll be in Mombasa another three weeks before he heads south."

Thank goodness. But three weeks seemed an eternity. The saving grace was our paths need not cross, as long as I stayed away from Mombasa. That should be easy. I seldom had need of anything that Juba could not pick up for me. Relieved, I finished my meal. After dessert had been consumed, Derek surprised me by leaving immediately. Usually, he stayed around for an after-dinner drink with Nick. Though this was an opportunity to speak with my employer, part of me wanted to escape back to my room and avoid being alone with him.

"Please don't go yet, Julia," said Nick after Derek departed. "Will you sit outside with me for a few minutes, before you retire?"

I nodded, and reluctantly followed him from the room. He brought a small glass of whiskey with him, and I sat wringing my hands with nerves.

"Julia, I know this is awkward, but we should talk about what happened at the lake."

"I disagree," I burst out. "I mean, I should rather not. Can't we just pretend it didn't happen?" I was glad the light was low. I knew my face must be flaming with embarrassment.

"Not if we're to continue living under the same roof. We have to clear the air." Nick took a sip of his drink and then set it down on the small side table. "I do not make a habit of kissing members of my household. I truly cannot explain what came over me, though it doesn't excuse my actions. All I can tell you is I enjoy your company. We'd had a pleasant afternoon with dear friends, and I was more relaxed than I have been in a very long time. Again, no excuse, but I hope you'll consider that while staring at a beautiful sunset I became swept away." Nick picked up his glass and took another sip. I could tell he was uncomfortable.

He continued. "Julia, you have changed the dynamics of my home. Before you arrived, the house was lonely, no atmosphere other than that of sadness. Now you're here, everything seems brighter. The baby has thrived under your care and attention, and that seems to have spread to the rest of us as well. The very last thing I want to do is destroy that. You may call it madness which prompted my action, or even loneliness. But it was a mistake on my part. I do hope you will forgive me, and, more importantly, trust me, when I say it will never happen again. Of course, if this apology and explanation comes too late, then I understand. But the truth is Jacaranda would not be the same with your leaving. "

I sat, momentarily struck dumb by the honesty of his declaration. I respected he owned his actions and was not trying to underplay the impact it could potentially have on our working relationship. I could not help but feel flattered by his kind words—how could I not? His sincerity was real.

"Perhaps it was all you just stated which resulted in our actions, Nick," I said finally. "I do lay the majority of blame on your shoulders. But I should take my share as well. I could have pushed you away immediately, told you a resounding 'no' before it had even gone that far. And you're right, the beauty of the evening, the romantic setting, all things could have contributed to that interlude. The truth is, I really want to stay on at Jacaranda. I have found a home with your family here. It would sadden me to leave, and it would break my heart to be parted with Nalah now we have become so close. If you can keep your distance, other than as a platonic friend and my employer, I will take you at your word. Perhaps we can erase what happened in our minds and pretend it did not occur. I will if you will."

Nick let out a heavy sigh. "Thank you, Julia. You are being gracious and forgiving. It is no wonder I respect our friendship because you are unlike any other woman I've ever met." Even though it was now quite dark I could see when he raised his glass.

"A toast to you, Julia Rossington. Thank you for being a decent person. I look forward to our ongoing friendship."

WEDNESDAY, ANOTHER GOAT WAS FOUND half-eaten. There had been no livestock attacked for a few weeks, and so it seemed the ghost leopard had returned. Mindful, this morning I loaded the rifle into the cart and climbed up into it. Juba was driving. He would take me to the Paderborn's farm and drop me off on his way to Mombasa. I looked forward to a day out, and Nalah seemed to pick up on my mood, for she was in great spirits.

Hilary was delighted to see us pull up. She ushered us into the house and called out for her children to come and be introduced. Within moments, two identical boys ran into the living room, barely stopping in time before crashing into the furniture.

"Boys!" Their mother cried in alarm. "Please stop running!" Hilary looked over to me. "Julia, this is Karl and Kurt, my sons."

If I remembered correctly, the boys were eleven years old. But the twins, with their riot of light blond hair, tanned skin and clear brown eyes, took after their father—their size belying their age. They stood still long enough to say hello to me. With an awkward greeting to the baby, they scampered off as soon as they were given permission.

A tea tray was brought in by Hilary's housekeeper, a man of some age, with yellowed eyes. I settled a sleepy Nalah on the sofa and enjoyed a fresh cup of tea.

"I am so glad you are here today," Hilary began, her eyes warm and friendly. "I hope you don't mind, but we have another guest. Klaus has come to visit. He is out in the fields with Josef but knows you will be here."

"It will be nice to see him," I said sincerely. I'd barely spoken to him at the party in Mombasa, though it had not been intentional. "Klaus was kind enough to show me around not so long ago. I found his company enjoyable, and his knowledge of the country vast."

"Yes, he has spent much time travelling around the continent. I don't think he ever wants to go back to Germany, but he must."

"Why is that?"

Hilary looked at me with a puzzled expression creasing her brow. "Because his wife is still there."

I know my face betrayed my surprise.

"Let me guess, he did not mention Marta? That does not surprise me. Klaus's wife is an invalid. She lives in a sanatorium where she is well cared for. They have two adult children who have families of their own. Klaus works here because it is the best way for him to make money. His export company helps him pay for the expenses incurred by Marta's illness."

"My goodness," I exclaimed. "I had absolutely no idea he was even married."

Hillary paused from sipping her tea. She looked at me quizzically as though debating whether to ask me a question or not. She decided to go ahead.

"It may be rude for me to ask you this, Julia. I have not known you very long. But do you have a romantic interest in Klaus?"

"Absolutely not," I said quickly. "I have enjoyed his company on more than one occasion but in friendship only." I did not add that his behaviour had been slightly more flirtatious. It was not appropriate to say, nor was it important.

"I am glad. He and Josef will be back here for lunch. So, we have a little time to ourselves to enjoy each other's company."

We spent the remainder of the morning chatting and getting to know one another. I was not quite so relaxed with Hilary as I had been with Janet White, but I did enjoy her company. She was someone I had more in common with than Felicity Babcock, and we found lots of topics to talk about.

The men arrived promptly at noon. I gave Klaus the baby to hold while I helped Hilary in the kitchen as she prepared lunch. We made thick sandwiches with some type of German sausage I had never heard of before, which was called *wurst*. Klaus was delighted to see me, and I, glad to reacquaint myself, once I apologised for not taking the time to talk to him at the party.

"You know," he said, bouncing the baby on one knee. "I heard about your conversation with Lady Arabella." He grinned. "I have to tell you that you have my compliments. Very few people have the...*mut*...how you say?"

"Courage," interjected Hilary.

"Ahem, yes. The courage to stand up to women like that. My only disappointment was that you left early because of her, and I did not get to have one dance with you the entire evening. Perhaps that will be remedied another time?"

I felt self-conscious at that remark. Especially having just been told the man was married. But I also recognised he would not openly flirt with me in front of his friends who knew his marital status. "I'm unsure how soon I will be back in Mombasa," I said, with Jeremy Ratcliffe at the forefront of my mind. "But perhaps there might be a party here at one of the farms, and then I will definitely repay you that dance."

We took our sandwiches out onto the verandah while the twins took our place in the kitchen and were fed by Hilary's cook. Hilary brought a thick blanket to lay on the floor by my feet so that Nalah could lay on her tummy and play. We ate our sandwiches and drank strong coffee even though the day was warm. The food was delicious.

"How long are you staying?" Josef asked as he finished the last of his sandwich.

"Juba will collect me on his return from Mombasa. I think he will be here close to three o'clock."

"Excellent," Josef replied. "We have plenty of time, then!"

AS PROMISED, JUBA ARRIVED mid-afternoon. We had not left the shade of the veranda since going out there for lunch. The four of us had fallen into an easy camaraderie as we chatted about various topics from the price of grain, the political climate, the availability of

English goods in Mombasa, and whether Nairobi would ultimately become the largest British settlement in Kenya.

But it was time to go. I thanked my hosts and wished them goodbye, allowing Klaus to escort me to the cart. He held the baby until I got settled, and then passed her up to me. I liked the German, but his feelings towards me felt more than platonic, though he gave no indication of pressing further attention my way. I did not want his affection. His loyalty to a wife, albeit in another country, was important to me. I would like Klaus and respect him more for being a good husband.

Juba chatted like a bird the entire way home. When we reached Jacaranda's driveway, I noticed how green the trees had become now the blossom had fallen. I still missed seeing the lovely blue petals scattered on the ground which had mesmerised me on my first day here. Yet the bright green leaves were still pretty, just not as ethereal.

Nalah slept most of the journey home, but now she sensed we were arriving, she stirred and began to squirm. I picked her up and sat her on my lap. Juba stopped the cart before he continued around the back to the barn. He held the baby while I jumped out, and I thanked him for chauffeuring me. I reminded him what a pleasant day out it had been for me, and it was all down to him. He beamed with pride.

As I reached the door to the bungalow, it opened before I touched it. Malaika stood on the threshold her face taut with worry.

"*Memsahib*, I am glad you are back."

I was immediately concerned. "What is the matter, Malaika? has something happened?"

She ushered me into the kitchen, where Wilson sat at the table, his head cradled in his hands.

"What is wrong?" I said, beginning to worry. "Has something happened to Nick, or Derek? Are they hurt?"

Wilson uncovered his eyes and shook his head. He looked up at me with a sorrowful expression. "It is worse, *Bibi*. *Bwana* Derek, he has invited someone for dinner, and we do not know what to do?"

I gave a sigh. It was no emergency, after all. I asked Wilson to wait one moment and took Nalah into the nursery to change her. Then I re-joined them in the kitchen, prepared her bottle, and took a seat at the table.

"Now," I said as Nalah gulped her milk. "Please tell me. What is the problem?"

From Wilson's explanation, it seemed there would be a guest for dinner along with Pops and Felicity Babcock. Again, I did not understand why this had upset the cook to this degree. Wilson was used to cooking for many guests who were invited to Jacaranda. Why was he suddenly so concerned?

"This guest like a British king," Wilson moaned. "What do British kings eat?" he lamented.

I was confused. What on earth was he talking about. I glanced at the housekeeper. She looked every bit as worried as the cook.

"Wilson, there is no British King, only a British Queen. This queen, she would not come to Jacaranda, even for your wonderful cooking." I smiled at him, but he was not having it.

"This man, *Bibi*, he is royal. *Bwana* Derek tell me he live in castle—like king."

A knot of something uncomfortable seeded in the pit of my stomach. "Did Derek say the man is nobility,

217

not royalty?"

"*Ndio!*" Malaika joined the conversation. She turned to the cook. "*Mtu huyu sio mfalme Rafiki, lakini mzee mwenye nguvu.*"

I watched the fear drain from his eyes as Wilson's face relaxed. Even Malaika smiled with relief. I however, felt no such emotion. I knew of two noble people in Kenya. One I had insulted, the other was evil.

Footsteps sounded in the hall, and we all looked up as Nick came into the kitchen followed by his shadow, Mzuka.

"Damn Derek," he muttered, going to the sink to pour himself water from a large jug. Nick tipped back the glass and drained it. Then he seemed to realise he was the object of our scrutiny. "What?" he asked. "Is something wrong?"

"Wilson's worried about cooking this evening. He tells me we are to expect company for dinner?"

"Yes," grumbled Nick. "Thanks to Derek. That's why I am back early. I had planned to work late on the accounts. Only now we have company coming, he has set me back another day."

"Who is coming?" I asked, lifting the baby to my shoulder. I patted her back, but I wanted to hug her tightly as I suddenly felt vulnerable.

"The Babcocks have a guest staying, and they want to bring him over. Some aristocrat from England. Bamfield, or some such name. He's a Lord, apparently, from some place near Newcastle, I believe."

The words came out of my mouth like I spat out rotten food. "Is it Lord Ratcliffe by any chance?"

"Yes, that's him," Nick said, pouring himself another glass. "He's passing through Mombasa on his way south. How do you know the name?" One eyebrow arched.

I tried to stop the waver in my voice as I replied. "He was at the Mombasa Club party."

"Well, that explains Felicity's interest in the fellow. Well, I'd better get going if I am to finish in time." With that, Nick went to leave. But as he reached the doorway where Malaika stepped aside, he stopped.

"Is everything all right? You look rather pale, Julia."

"I'm fine," I lied, and watched him walk away. But as my eyes met Malaika's, her expression told me she had not believed my words as easily as Nick Fleming. I got to my feet. The room seemed to be closing in on me, and at once my head felt light. Nalah squirmed in my arms. I rushed to the door and thrust her at Malaika, who could do no more than grab her. Then I pushed past her and ran down the hallway to the bathroom, and there I was as sick as a dog.

Chapter Sixteen

I TOLD MALAIKA I WOULD NOT BE at dinner. That I was unwell and would stay in the nursery with Nalah and that she should pass along this information to Nick. She nodded at the instruction, but I could tell she did not believe me. Her voluminous dark brown eyes studied me intently, and I turned my attention to folding some of Nalah's clothing so I could look away.

As the sun set, I heard the familiar sounds of pots and pans being used in the kitchen. and Juba and Wilson sang a song together as they worked side by side preparing dinner. The baby had fallen asleep, and I sat in the rocking chair, unable to relax, unable to do anything but think.

It was ludicrous. I had travelled thousands of miles away to the continent of Africa to escape a past I could not live with. And now, one of the two men responsible for my misery would be in the same house as me for dinner? How was that possible? My mind flipped through the pages of my life, though I never wanted to revisit that awful year.

"Julia?" A voice whispered at the door. I quickly got to my feet, not wanting the baby to wake. It was Nick. I joined him in the hallway, closing the nursery door softly behind me. I had anticipated his coming once Malika told him I would be absent for dinner. We walked to the living room.

"Malaika says you are unwell and will be staying in your room this evening." His gaze raked over me as though he sought an apparent cause. Though I did not condone lying, the guilt was bearable in comparison to facing Jeremy Ratcliffe.

"Yes. I have a headache and would prefer my own company. I hope that's all right?"

I knew Nick could not argue it. My job at Jacaranda was to care for Nalah. I bore no responsibility as a social companion. He could not force me to come to dinner.

"I'm sorry to hear it." His eyes searched my face, and I looked away quickly else he see my guilt.

"You will be missed this evening." He walked over to the sherry decanter and poured himself a small glass. He gestured to see if I would join him, but I shook my head. I could tell by his expression he did not believe my lie. But Nick was measuring whether to confront me or not.

"I have grown used to your company, Julia, especially at these blasted social events, which I find a bore. This evening will be torture. Much as I like my neighbours, it will be excruciating watching Felicity strut like a peacock in front of a man born with a title and done little to earn it."

I dissected his words. Was Nick jealous? I remembered seeing Felicity with him just this past Sunday. The thought sat uncomfortably, though I did not want to know why.

"Look on the bright side," I said. "At least with Felicity there, you'll have little responsibility to carry a conversation. She will take care of that."

The corner of Nick's mouth turned up in a smile. He studied me a moment longer. "Are you sure you won't change your mind, Julia?"

"No. I'm sorry. Now, I had better check on Nalah." I gave him a curt nod and escaped back to the nursery.

IT WAS DARK OUTSIDE. THE chatter coming from the dining room was loud, as it spilled out across the verandah and into the night. I had my windows open as usual and found it an odd mix, conversation, and the chorus of crickets.

I lay on my bed, still in my work dress, though I had let my hair loose. The pins I used struggled to keep it tidy, but by the end of the day, my scalp ached from the pressure. My eyes were closed, and I was trying not to think about Jeremy Ratcliffe being in the same building as myself. Occasionally, I thought I could detect his voice among the others. Mostly I heard Felicity and Derek.

When a loud crash sounded, I sat bolt upright, then got to my feet. What on earth was that? I listened intently and heard a commotion, a rush of voices all speaking at once. Moments later, there came a knock upon my door. It was Nick.

"Julia, we have need of you. Please help." He did not wait for an answer but spun on his heel back towards the living room. I did not hesitate but ran after him. When I reached the room, I saw someone laying on the carpet. It was Felicity.

"What happened?" I asked, my eyes focused upon her. She looked white as a ghost. There was a film of cold sweat glistening upon her brow. I felt for her pulse. It was light but steady. I looked up to meet her father's worried face. He had lost a son, and now looked frightened he might lose a daughter as well.

"It's all right, Mr Babcock. Felicity has fainted. Put a cushion underneath her head and make her comfortable. She'll be right as rain in a minute." I saw the instant relief on his face. I looked up at Nick. "Have Wilson make her a cup of tea with plenty of sugar and milk." I picked up Felicity's hand and rubbed it between both of mine.

"Wake up, Felicity. You are fine. Open your eyes for me." At this, the painted lids fluttered, and then opened wide, the brown orbs questioning what she was doing on the floor.

"You are all right," I said. "You fainted. How are you feeling?"

She blinked. "A bit dizzy. But I want to sit up."

"Let me help." As his voice found my ears, my body froze. Jeremy Ratcliffe stood not a foot away from me, reaching down to gather Felicity into his arms. I did not look up. I moved back out of the way while he lifted the woman and carried her to the sofa, closely attended by both Derek and Pops Babcock. They placed cushions behind her neck, and while preoccupied, I left the room to find Nick. He was making the tea himself. He turned as he heard me approach.

"How is she?"

"Already feeling better. She is on the couch resting. A cup of sweet tea should set her to rights, though. The men are tending to her, so I should like to go back to my room now." I did not mention what was in my thoughts, that Jeremy had not had long enough to recognise me. After all, he would not expect to see someone like me in a foreign country. As long as I got out of the way now, I'd be safe.

Nick watched me closely.

"What is it?" I asked.

His eyes were fastened upon my face. His expression unfathomable. "Your hair is beautiful," he said softly.

I'd forgotten it was loose. "Oh." I said, momentarily lost for words. I wanted to get to my room, but something about the way he looked at me made me hesitate. The kettle began to boil, and Nick snapped his gaze from me.

"I must go," I mumbled, and left him in the kitchen.

Closing my door, I finally took a deep breath. Had I managed to stay inconspicuous? Ratcliffe had not seen me properly—I was sure of it. For all I knew, he might not remember me anyway. I climbed into bed, and as I lay quietly under the mosquito netting, sleep evaded me.

THE NEXT MORNING, WILSON asked to feed Nalah. The two of them had become great pals from our little routine at breakfast. I left him to it and stepped out on the verandah, holding a cup of tea in my hands. A slight mist floated in the air partially hiding the trees and driveway. I imagined I stood in a mystical land.

"Wilson is utterly smitten," said Nick, joining me.

I turned. He had a clean scent about him, most likely from his shaving soap. His face looked fresh, and I knew a sudden urge to reach out and feel his skin. I quickly looked away. I must be mad. "Wilson has a natural way with babies. Nalah adores him. Children always sense who to trust, don't they?"

"Mmm," Nick's attention had already moved along.

"How was Felicity when she left last night?"

"Recovered enough to talk incessantly." Nick's grey eyes rested on my face. "Is everything all right, Julia? You were not yourself last night. I know you felt unwell, but I've never seen you so jumpy."

"I'm fine," I said, "You are imagining things." I turned back to go inside, but his arm shot out and his fingers lightly held my forearm. I stopped in surprise, both at his touching me and the sensation it gave—pleasure? I looked directly into his face and saw concern in his eyes. I tugged my arm from his grip.

"Nick, I was unwell, that is all." With that, I left him alone on the verandah before he could see the lie on my face.

WHILE THE BABY SLEPT, I helped Malaika sort through the linen cupboard. Although the young woman was still distant, she did not appear to carry the resentment I had felt when first arriving at Jacaranda. We emptied everything from the shelves onto the bed in the guest room. Now we unfolded each item, looking for moth holes, or anything which might render the fabric unusable.

"I have seen little of Migali," I said, making sure I did not look at her face as she would be scowling. I had not seen the Maasai warrior for some time. I understood from Derek that the man came and went, with little fanfare. Migali was like a ghost.

"He goes to our village," Malaika said flatly. "Migali is son of elder. He has much to learn."

"I see." I opened up a blanket and spotted three

holes in the middle. I put it in the pile which would be given to the workers. "Will you stay here at Jacaranda forever, Malaika?" I was curious. The girl had her entire life before her. It seemed a shame to spend it as a housekeeper. I thought her intelligent.

"That is what my family want." Her voice trailed off, and I looked at her, noting the wistful look in her eyes.

"What about you? What do you want?"

She considered my question for a long moment, and then looked directly at me. "To be a teacher," she said, and then began to work again as though her admission was foolish.

"You do?" I said in surprise. "Have you been to school yourself?" I was embarrassed to admit I knew so little of the woman.

"*Ndio*. The sisters taught the children in my village."

"Teaching is a noble profession, Malaika. Is there somewhere close where you can train to become a teacher?"

"*Ndio*, in Nairobi there is a college." Her narrow shoulders sagged. "But it costs much money, and though I want to go, my money goes to my family." She fell quiet, and I began to think. Both Migali and Malaika had much to offer. They were young, strong, and determined. Migali obviously had a clear path as a leader in his community. But what of Malaika? Did she not deserve an opportunity to become all she could? Was there anything I could do to help? I made a mental note to talk to Nick about it later, but I did not say anything to the young woman.

THE NEXT DAY, NICK CAME HOME at lunch, with the unwelcome message we were all expected at the Babcocks for an impromptu gathering that very night. Apparently, it was Jeremy Ratcliffe's last evening with them, and though he wanted no fuss, Felicity had decided to surprise him by inviting a few guests for cocktails. She hoped it might also cheer her father seeing his neighbours because the old man still struggled with his son's passing.

"I would rather not attend," I said when Nick finished speaking. Derek took little notice as he ploughed through his food, but Nick immediately challenged me.

"Why ever not? You can bring the baby, as it will not be a long affair. Felicity wants to wish Ratcliffe a *bon voyage*, eat a slice of cake, and that is all. It would be rude of you not to come, Julia. Especially as you did not join in when they were here Wednesday night."

There was irritation in his tone. Though I enjoyed being treated as an equal under Nick's employ, I resented being expected to socialise whenever he chose to mix with neighbours.

"I'm sorry if that angers you, but I am here to be Nalah's nanny. Surely that does not require my attending engagements whenever they arise for you." I could not help it. I had no desire to go to the Babcocks. Especially as Ratcliffe was there. Just the thought of it set my heart racing.

Nick stared at me. I saw the muscle in his cheek tighten. "Julia, it is in the capacity of Nalah's nanny that I require your attendance. I wish to have my niece with me this evening. As she is your charge, it necessitates you accompany her." Before I could remark, Nick got to his feet and left the dining room.

"What was that all about?" asked Derek, coming up for air from eating his soup.

"This evening. I really don't want to go, but Nick insists I do."

"What's the problem? I thought you liked Felicity?"

"I do. But Derek, I'm unused to attending social engagements. The families I have worked for in the past did not include me in their activities. Here it isn't the same. Nick's expectations are for me to go wherever he goes. I'm out of my depth."

"What nonsense, Julia." He dabbed his mouth with the serviette. "You're no different than the rest of us in Kenya. The only criteria separating us is how much money we have in the bank." He smiled kindly. "Nick likes and respects you. I know he enjoys your friendship a great deal. The man has lost most of his family. He's got no one else to ask except for you and me." Derek pushed his chair from the table and stood. "Stop worrying. It will be a nice evening, you'll see."

I sat there long after he had gone. How on earth was I supposed to do this? Dear God, I was to spend an evening in the company of a man who had idly stood by and watched while his cousin brutally raped me.

Chapter Seventeen

WE ARRIVED AT MEADOWBROOK to see the front doors flung open to the night, allowing music from the gramophone to spill out into the evening. It was cooler than usual, the humidity promised rain.

I got out of the cart, my heart pounding so loudly I was certain the others would hear it. The baby fussed— she sensed something was wrong with me. Nick ushered us into the house. I had avoided speaking with him, choosing to ride in the back of the cart as we had brought Akina along with us. Nick wanted to ensure I had help this evening if needed. I was relieved to sit away from him. It had taken all my resolve not to leap out of the cart and run back to Jacaranda, leopard or no. I'd rather take my chances with a ferocious wild cat than a calculating snake in the guise of a nobleman.

Felicity looked stunning tonight in a shimmering gold silk dress. The fabric caught the light as she moved, and I noticed Derek's eyes follow her as she made her way over to welcome us. As usual, her gaze flickered over my attire, which was lacking, as always. Tonight, I wore a dowdy black dress and no ornamentation. I'd scooped my hair into a French knot, planning to remain as inconspicuous as possible. There was every chance Jeremy Ratcliffe would not notice recognise me at all, never mind recognise me.

In the living room, I handed Nalah to Akina. I sipped sherry and made polite conversation with Davina Briggs, who I had met previously. But my eyes stayed on the lookout for Ratcliffe.

I sensed when he entered the room, my body stiffened. I could hear him speaking. His nasal, upper-crust voice drowned out all the others in the room.

"You haven't met my friend, Julia," said Felicity, who suddenly appeared at my side. Before I could react, I found myself staring into the face of a man whose very existence made me sick. His aristocratic features were unchanged other than his skin being darker from his time under the sun.

"My pleasure," he said with a nod and an insincere smile while his eyes raked over me. I saw no recognition in his face—thank God.

"And mine," I responded, immediately looking away while Davina Briggs was also introduced. Felicity began to explain where the Briggs farmed, and I knew it would be only moments until she told Ratcliffe I worked as a nanny for Nick. If she told him my occupation, it might trigger a memory, and I could not risk it. I quickly excused myself and went across the room and out onto the verandah, as far away as possible. The evening air wrapped around me and cooled the heat of my fear.

"Julia?" I turned to see Nick come out behind me. "Is everything all right? You seemed in a hurry to get out of the room,"

I turned to face him. "I am not comfortable being here. I wish you had not forced me to do this."

He frowned, his eyes searching my face. "I don't understand. You've been here with me on many other occasions and enjoyed yourself. So why the sudden change of heart?"

What could I say? I was in an impossible dilemma. Oh, why had he insisted I come tonight? "Nick, there are times when a woman should not have to explain herself. When her wishes should be respected without explanation or justification. Like you, sometimes I have my own reasons which I prefer not to share."

He considered my words. I thought he would badger me to say more. But instead, he gave a deep sigh. "I'm sorry, Julia. My intentions were not bad. I wanted you to come, and I thought you were being obstinate. I should have known you were not. As soon as it is polite, I'll take you back to Jacaranda."

"Thank you." I sat down in one of the chairs. I would remain out here where Ratcliffe would not find me. There came a shout from inside as someone called Nick's name. He frowned.

"I had better go before they come out here looking for me." He gave a curt nod and stepped back into the house.

But I was in no mood to sit. I was like one of the gazelles out on the plains, constantly moving to avoid being a target for predators. I got to my feet and paced the length of the long verandah. As I reached its end, I paused, staring out into the night.

"Nothing remotely similar to Newcastle, is it?"

I whirled at the sound of the aristocratic voice. Jeremy Ratcliffe stood bathed in the light streaming from inside of the house. He struck a match and lifted it to light the tip of his cigar, the flame momentarily illuminating his wicked face. He inhaled, then blew the smoke out of his thin mouth and into the night. He walked towards me, and I took an involuntary step backwards.

"I thought you looked familiar the other night, though you were only in the room a few minutes. But there was something about that hair of yours which bothered me." He inhaled again and took another step. "How long has it been? Two years? Three? You know, Charles was rather smitten with you for a time. I cannot see why as you are not at all pretty. But I suppose it was the child. He's never been able to father one, you know, not in the marriage bed, nor out of it. When he saw your swollen belly, he was over the moon. No wonder he wouldn't rest until he found you. You cannot imagine how much money he spent on private investigators looking for you and his brat. You are clever though, you got away. Though Charles still bears the mark you put on his face." He looked around. "Africa? What a jolly good place to hide." He laughed. "Well, it was until I turned up."

I gasped for breath as my worst fears unfolded. Though this man had not taken my innocence, he had enjoyed the spectacle of it more than once, and in some way that made him crueller than his cousin, Charles. I contemplated denying I was who he thought. But it was pointless.

"I have nothing to say to you or your despicable cousin."

He chuckled at that, and even in the poor light, I could see the malevolence in his eyes. What was it about wealth and rank which caused one human to suppose he had ownership over another? Though my feet itched to flee, I boldly took a step towards him. I had been so frightened of the Ratcliffes then. A penniless young woman, innocent and trusting. But no more. That person had disappeared the night my son died in my arms.

"As you recall, I was employed by your cousin and his family. Back then, I was manipulated by a bully who used his position and authority against me to fulfil his perverse tastes." I stared hard at the eyes, so like those of his despicable relative. "But no more. Yes, I may have run to Africa, but I can tell you, Lord Ratcliffe, you are no longer in Newcastle. You are on my territory. I am not employed by your family, and you do not have the upper hand. So, I ask you to leave me be."

He stared for a moment as though he had not quite comprehended my words, and then he gave a derisive chuckle.

"My, my. The maid speaks with such conviction." He stepped closer to me, but I held my ground. I would not let him see how he bothered me.

"You are correct in that you are no longer under any obligation from me or my family." His eyes gleamed in the dark as they raked over me from head to toe. "But it seems I know a great deal about your past, Miss Rossington, a past I am sure you would prefer to keep secret."

Instantly shame saturated my thoughts as I was transported back to another time, a frightening place. I shook my head to cast those thoughts aside. I could not endure this anymore. I rallied.

"My past is none of your business, and neither is my present. Do you not have better things to think about than the murky history of you and your demented relative? The people here have busy lives. Unlike the

British aristocracy you hide behind, where your boredom and inactivity lead you to inflict your depraved desires on others less fortunate."

"How dare you." His voice was low and threatening. I had gone too far, but I cared not. The days of my being terrified by people of his kind were over. Is that not why I started this new life? Come this far? He moved closer, and I stepped back. He suddenly threw away the remainder of his tobacco and then grabbed me roughly by the shoulders and shook me violently.

"You will do my bidding," he hissed. "Or everyone will hear of your time in my cousin's bed. How you played his whore for a sixpence."

"Take your damn hands off her."

Relieved and horrified, I watched Nick stride from the open doors in my direction. He was like a wild beast, his body primed for attack, taut as a spring. Ratcliffe instantly let go of me, and I ran from him, desperate to put distance between us.

He faced Nick and slid a smile onto his face. "There you are, Fleming. Your nanny was feeling faint. I was trying to steady her before she fell down."

Nick said nothing but took one look at my face, read my expression and carried on past me. Then, before I could say a word, he threw a punch and hit Ratcliffe square in the nose.

"Stop!" I shouted as he pulled back to land another strike. Nick's arm faltered and then dropped to his side. His eyes narrowed, and then fastened upon Ratcliffe, who had not moved an inch but was trying to staunch the blood flowing from his nose.

"Touch her again, and I'll kill you," he said in a

low menacing voice. I felt my flesh run cold as he came to me, and I saw the rage in his eyes.

"Are you harmed?"

I shook my head unconvincingly. "Please take me inside," I whispered. "I would like a glass of water." I watched him hesitate, and my breathing became shallow. I could see Nick trying to decide which road he wanted to choose.

He threw a malevolent glare at Jeremy Ratcliffe, then he grasped my arm and led me back inside the house. Nick said nothing as we went into the kitchen where a startled servant brought me a drink. I gulped it down.

"Stay here," he commanded, leaving me there. My head thumped. I was so hot, my hands were clammy, and I had started shaking. Was I in shock? Ratcliffe's face swam before me and the wicked intent of his words. Yet I could not let it get to me. Thank God the man would be leaving tomorrow anyway. He could do me no harm. But that was untrue. Jeremy Ratcliffe could ruin my reputation wherever he was. Word travelled fast within the British community, and if Nick found out about my past, would he want me anywhere near his niece? I wrung my hands. What was I to do? I could not return to England. If I did, I would be taken straight from the ship and thrown into the gaol.

WHEN NICK COLLECTED ME, I sat bent over the table, my head laying in my arms, too heavy to hold upright. He did not speak but pulled me to my feet, and with Akina holding the sleeping baby in her travel box, led me out of the back door and to our cart. I was now under the full onslaught of a migraine, and it pained me even to open my eyes. Nick assisted me into the back of the cart, saw me settled, and then he and the young African climbed into their respective seats.

I was never so glad to be home. Akina took Nalah into the nursery and prepared her for bed. I undressed and slipped under the cool sheets and fell into a welcome sleep, half hoping I would never wake again.

BIRD SONG FILTERED THROUGH MY dreams, and slowly my eyes opened. Sunlight poured into the room. I lay still, as though I had fallen asleep only to wake in foreign surroundings. I took a few deep breaths and then recognised the tell-tale dull ache—the aftermath of a dreadful headache. Echoes of the previous night teased the fringes of my mind, but I shrugged them aside. I could not think about it—not yet.

Nalah! At once, I remembered I had not put her to bed. The last I had seen of my charge was in the arms of Akina. I sat bolt upright, swung my legs to the ground and headed directly to the nursery without even covering my night attire. Her bed was empty. Panic ensued.

Heedless, I burst from her room and charged down the hallway. Rounding the corner, I rushed into the kitchen and stopped abruptly at the odd tableau presented there. Seated at the table with their breakfasts in front of them sat Wilson and Juba, who looked up at me with surprise painted upon their faces. At the table's head sat Nick, a half-eaten plate of food in front of him and a happy baby laying in his arms, sucking hungrily on her bottle.

"Oh," I said. "There she is."

Nick's eyes locked with mine, and then he seemed

to realise I was inappropriately dressed. He cleared his throat.

"Good morning, Julia. I trust your headache is improved?"

"Yes, thank you," I mumbled.

"Excellent. Why do you not dress and then join us in here for breakfast?" He raised his eyebrows and then gestured to the men with a quick nod of his head. I understood and fled down the hall to my room, my cheeks warm with embarrassment.

By the time I returned, Wilson had made me a plate of toast, and I thanked him and sat down at the table. Nalah lay on her blanket by Nick's feet, her little hands reaching out to Mzuka, who lay just out of reach staring at her. Juba had disappeared, and Wilson was washing the breakfast dishes.

I ate half of my toast and guzzled down the hot cup of sweet tea. Instantly I began to feel more human as the brew nourished my blood.

"Thank you for seeing to Nalah, Nick."

"No need for thanks." He searched my face. "How are you really feeling this morning?"

"I am much improved, thank you."

"That was a nasty migraine you had last night. Do you get them often?"

"A few times a year."

"Do you know the cause?"

I shrugged. "It can be many things. Weather, health, worry—I never know when they will hit me until it is too late." I took another bite of my toast.

"You must have been extremely upset last night. No wonder you felt ill." His grey eyes looked directly into mine, and I knew he waited for me to tell him what had actually transpired out on the verandah with Ratcliffe and why. Much as I had felt about revealing Malaika's secret to him, I now struggled with the decision to tell him the absolute truth about my past. I put down my toast and levelled my gaze with his.

"If you have something you wish to ask, Nick, please don't play games with me and try to entrap me into an answer."

One black eyebrow raised in admission of my accusation. He took a sip of his tea. "I'm sorry. You are of course, correct. I want to know what was wrong with you at the Babcocks and ultimately what that bastard did to you." His eyes narrowed, and the scar cutting through his brow paled. "Julia, I bear you no threat. But you live under my roof, and therefore under my protection. If I see you troubled or upset, I need to know why, so I might remedy the situation." He paused as Wilson put dried cutlery into a drawer with a loud clatter. The cook quickly darted a look at Nick and then nodded before leaving the kitchen.

I waited until Wilson had closed the door behind him. "I understand, and I do appreciate your concern. But you cannot protect me from my own history—from my past."

He frowned. My response was not what he had expected.

"I'm in a predicament." I declared, setting down my toast. I pushed the plate aside. "I do not care for secrets, but there are times in a woman's life when certain events happen which can decimate her. These issues, though usually not of her doing, can still have a catastrophic influence on her life and wellbeing." I knew I spoke in riddles but did not care.

He gave a derisive laugh. "What, do you not think we all have our secrets? Secrets we know could destroy us if ever revealed?"

I studied Nick's handsome face. What was his? The image of him hitting Ratcliffe the night before and the look of anger on his face entered my mind. And what of Trevor Babcock and Nick's possible role in his demise? I frowned.

"But our gender plays a role, do you not agree? What might be acceptable behaviour in a man is not always considered the same for a woman. And what if by telling you my secret, I forever regret its disclosure? You might find me so despicable that you cast me out."

Nick's face softened. "Am I that bad of a person you can readily think so little of me? I pride myself on at least being fair—knowing there are two sides to every story."

Again, the visage of Trevor flashed before me. Oh, why did everything have to be so complicated? My past weighed heavily on my shoulders as I watched my employer's serious countenance. He studied me intently, yet his demeanour was non-threatening, his posture reposed. I had never shared my secret with another living soul, nor had I been tempted to. But for the first time, I was.

"Can it be that bad, Julia?"

I blinked, and a tear unexpectedly rolled down my cheek. I brushed it away, appalled I was so emotional.

Nick leaned forward from his seat. "My intent is to help you, not punish you. I cannot stand idly by and see you thus. What has happened, Julia? You must tell me."

The dam retaining all my fears and my ugliest memories began to crack as his kindness chipped through my resolve. In a moment of utter weakness, I started to talk. And once I had begun, it was as though I could not stop. Like a vast flock of birds fleeing their cage and captivity, so did my story spill from my tongue.

I spoke of a brutal rape at the hands of Charles Ratcliffe. How his cousin, Jeremy, had gleefully watched on more than one occasion. That I had been held against my will and subsequently forced to remain quiet—and threatened with physical harm, being forever shamed and cast out as a fallen woman should I tell a soul. I told Nick of my desperate escape to London, and of my pregnancy. The birth of my darling James and his short time upon earth. How I had hidden from the Ratcliffe family who hunted me as they did the foxes upon their estate in search of my child, a child Charles Ratcliffe never thought to father.

And then I stopped speaking to wipe away the tears streaming down my face as I thought of my baby, my precious son.

Once I had composed myself, Nick spoke. "And that is why you came to Kenya? To get away from them?"

I nodded. "When I ran from the Ratcliffes, I had no money. I stole a ring from Charles's room because I was desperate to get away. It was a stupid thing to do because I broke the law, therefore giving him something to hold over my head forever. After I lost my son, leaving England seemed the best option for me. I foolishly thought I could start again, finally escape the ugly memories and be safe once more."

"Until Jeremy Ratcliffe arrived in Mombasa."

"Yes. I saw him the night of the party at the

Mombasa Club, and I could not believe my eyes. I was unaware of his interest in Africa. When he came to Jacaranda, I stayed in my room to avoid seeing him and prayed he would not recognise me when you summoned me to attend Felicity after she fainted."

"Dear God," Nick said. "And I forced you to come to the Babcocks and put you in harm's way." His eyes bored into mine. "Oh, Julia. Had I known any of this, I would have called the bastard out and never subjected you to his attentions. I am so very sorry."

I shook my head. "You were not supposed to know. Perhaps I should have told you the truth straight away when I saw Ratcliffe in Mombasa. But I didn't think he would recognise me, and besides, it's not a tale to be bandied about. It is an experience I am deeply ashamed of and shall never forget." Suddenly I was deflated by the telling. The weight of my secret and the heartache from its revelation sapped all my energy. Nick's eyes still stared at my face, and though I tried to avoid meeting them, it was useless.

"What can I do to help you?" he asked quietly. "Name it, and it is done."

A list of requests instantly fell into my mind, none of them good and all of them involving Jeremy Ratcliffe. But it would solve nothing. The damage had been inflicted years earlier, and at least the villainous man would soon be leaving. "Nothing. Though I thank you for the offer, Nick. I would only ask you not welcome him at Jacaranda, and that I do not have to see him ever again."

"That goes without saying," he said quickly. "I have a good mind to ride over to the Babcocks and finish what I started last night."

"No!" The word burst from my lips. "You must stay away from him. Promise me, Nick." I searched his face for reassurance.

"I promise." His eyes were bright with anger. I realised that although Nick Fleming was my employer, he had also become my friend somewhere along the way.

The baby whimpered. I'd forgotten she was even there. Mortified, I went to the blanket and scooped Nalah into my arms. Nick got to his feet and came to stand beside me. He bent his head to place a gentle kiss on his niece's forehead, and then placed a hand upon my shoulder. His face was so close to mine, I could see dark flecks in his grey eyes. I waited for him to speak, yet nothing happened. He gently squeezed my shoulder as he stared at me.

"Well, there you are," Derek announced as he walked into the kitchen. "I thought you were all abed as no one was in the dining room. Why are we not eating in there?"

"No reason," Nick replied, pulling his hand away.

I moved to where Derek stood by the door. "I must see to the baby," I muttered, leaving the kitchen before Derek could say another word.

I took Nalah straight into the nursery, all the while wondering if I had just made a terrible mistake. After what I had just told Nick, he had every right to send me away with a moment's notice. Yet something told me he would not. That the sadness in his face as I relayed my story was sincere. Perhaps for the first time in my life I really had found someone who wanted the best for me.

Chapter Eighteen

I SLEPT WHILE THE BABY TOOK HER nap, and by the time we both woke, it was close to lunchtime. I changed Nalah, freshened myself up, and then took the baby into the kitchen to prepare her bottle. Malaika was there with Wilson, and they both smiled in greeting. I passed the baby to Wilson as usual and went to make a bottle.

A sudden commotion outside drew us all to the back door, where a lone rider dismounted and handed the reins to one of the stable boys.

"*Bwana* Frederick!" Malaika hastened her steps as she went to greet the man, who though dressed in an army uniform, had what looked like a cowboy hat on his head. He clasped Malaika in a brief embrace and then caught sight of me standing with Wilson.

"Wilson! *Weka kettle na tengeneza chai*!"

The cook beamed and handed the baby to me before returning inside the kitchen. I assumed he had instructed Wilson to put on the kettle. Now the man approached me with Malaika at his side.

"Howdy," he said, reaching out his hand to shake mine. "Don't tell me Fleming's gone off and gotten married?" He grinned at me, his smile disarming under blond moustache and his teeth even and white. The man looked every inch an American, from his cleft chin to his startlingly blue eyes. He looked to be in his forties and was a handsome devil.

"No, he has not!" I laughed. "I am Julia Rossington. Mr Fleming hired me to care for his niece, Nalah." I gestured to the baby, who was fixated on the man's hat. He reached out to chuck her under the chin, and she giggled.

"Nick does not expect me," he said as we turned to go inside the house. "I guess it will have to be a surprise."

Malaika led us into the living room, where she opened the verandah doors to let in the fresh air. The man removed his hat and laid it on a chair while I put the baby down on her blanket.

"It seems we should introduce ourselves," he said. "My name is Captain Frederick Burnham, an old friend of Nick's family. I'm on my way to Mombasa, bound there to meet a ship from Southampton tomorrow afternoon."

"I see."

He settled himself in one of the armchairs. "I'm an American, but I currently serve in Her Majesty's British army and have been in the south fighting the Boers. I was wounded, and so while I recuperate, I've been sent north to rendezvous with one of their new managers and escort him south."

"I am so sorry to hear you were wounded. I know it has been a bloody war."

"Indeed, it has, ma'am. Here's hopin' it'll be over with soon." His voice trailed off as Malaika carried in a tea tray and placed it on a small table. She poured him a cup and passed it over. She then went to stand near the door.

"Tell me, are you a newcomer to Kenya, Miss

Rossington?"

"I am. Please call me Julia. I arrived from England almost two months ago."

"This place is a far cry from Kensington, don't you think?" He laughed easily, and I found I liked his cheeriness.

"Yes, though I find the Africans a far more civilised nation than the English."

Burnham laughed out aloud. "Never was a truer word spoken. You British are an odd sort, never quite know where you are with the lot o' them!"

Before I could respond, the sound of pounding hooves coming at a fast pace down the driveway, and a dog barking filled the air. We leapt to our feet at the same time and rushed out onto the verandah. I immediately recognised Nick's dog and his riderless horse. Burnham quickly ran over to the horse and grasped its reins, shouting to anyone within earshot to bring him his horse. I followed him, leaving Malaika to watch the baby, and as I reached the American, he looked at me, his face concerned.

"Ma'am, you should go back inside and lock the doors. If you have a weapon, keep it close and make sure it is loaded."

I frowned. "I don't understand?" What on earth was going on?

"No need to understand anything. But something has happened to Nick, and until I find him, we must assume we are in danger. Now please, go into the house and do as I ask."

MALAIKA FETCHED WILSON AND Juba from their huts and sent them into the house. She also instructed all the other workers to go to their homes and wait there. We closed and locked all the doors and windows, and I took out a gun from the cabinet and made sure it was loaded. The baby lay in her crib, but she was restless, no doubt because of the atmosphere inside the house.

I could not rest. I spent my time walking from room to room, looking from one window to the next. One, then two hours passed. Wilson made lunch for us to eat together in the kitchen, but it was a half-hearted affair. We were all worried about Nick.

What if something terrible had happened to him? I could not bear it if Nick didn't come back to Jacaranda. That thought settled in my mind, and as I paced the length of the house, I examined my feelings.

That Nick Fleming was a good man, I had no doubt. He displayed it in his care of the workers, his family loyalty and his kindness. But what of Trevor Babcock and the night I saw Nick steal away with Migali? I shrugged it away.

Then what were these feelings I had for the man? Our friendship had quietly come about through our common love of Nalah. I enjoyed his company immensely and found him interesting and intelligent. Yet something had changed since the evening he kissed me at the lake. Before my violent memories had intervened, I had lost myself in Nick's strong embrace—surrendered my body to meld against his, so intoxicating was the touch of his lips upon mine.

Was that love? Or was it lust? My views on the latter were biased by the bastard who had relentlessly used my body at his every whim. Not only had Charles Ratcliffe stolen my innocence, he'd stolen my faith in the hope of ever finding happiness with a man.

"*Memsahib*, they come!" shouted Juba, and I hurried to the front of the house. Several Kikuyu, along with Migali and Captain Burnham carried a large blanket that sank down under its occupant's weight. I set down the rifle inside the door and took off at a run towards the men.

"He lives," barked Burnham. "But he's lost a lot of blood. Boil water, put a sheet upon the kitchen table and find as many dressings as you can."

I sped back to the house, and by the time the group came into the kitchen, we were ready for him. The men lifted him gently onto the table and then stepped back. Captain Burnham pulled out a knife and sliced through Nick's clothing quickly.

"He's been shot, Julia," he explained. "The bullet has passed through him, but it has caused a lot of bleeding. We must clean, stitch and then dress both wounds before we move him again." He looked at Malaika. "Tell me, where are the medical supplies kept?"

"*Bwana's* study," she replied.

"Malaika, take Julia and show her where they are. We are looking for chloroform, carbolic acid, dressings and a needle to stitch him up with."

Thank goodness the house was so organised. I had no trouble finding everything Burnham needed. When we returned to the kitchen, most of the men had been shooed away, other than Migali. Wilson attended the stove where the water was boiling and another set to heat up. Nick lay completely still, his face drawn and grey. Blood still oozed from a nasty wound in his shoulder.

"Right," began the captain. "I will clean the wound

first. If he wakes, we shall give him a little chloroform to keep him still. Migali can come and hold him steady." The tall Maasai came forward and stood at the head of the table. Burnham prepared the solution of carbolic with warm water and gently cleaned the area. Blood still seeped onto his skin, but I knew the stitches would put a stop to that.

He worked quickly and with purpose, obviously no stranger to this type of wound. I stayed by his side and assisted wherever I could. After he completed the front stitches, he frowned.

"What is it?" I asked, worry knotting in my stomach.

"He still bleeds, even with the sutures. If it will not stop, I shall have to cauterise the wound. But for now, we can move him onto his side and deal with the exit wound."

Migali moved Nick carefully onto his side. He was still unconscious, but he groaned in pain.

"This wound is less serious," Burnham said with some relief. And it appeared he was right because this time he was finished quickly. He placed a thick dressing over the stitches. This would protect them as Nick would need to lay on his back due to the severity of the damage to the front of his shoulder. Once he was in position the captain examined the stitches once more.

"Do you think the bullet has hit a blood vessel?" I asked. I knew little of medicine, but I had studied biology and anatomy many years earlier.

"I did originally," he replied. "But there has been less bleeding, and now it begins to clot." He pointed, "See?"

I nodded.

"Therefore, I think cauterising will stop any more blood loss and allow him to stabilise. I shall give you this rag to place over his mouth and nose if he stirs when I apply the heat." He waited until he was ready to apply the hot iron to Nick's flesh. Burnham nodded to Migali to keep Nick still, handed me the cloth which reeked of the chemical, and then leant forward and held the metal against Nick's puckered skin.

Immediately Nick's eyes flew open, and his mouth widened into a scream.

"Now!" Burnham shouted. Migali held Nick down while I put the rag against his face, and within seconds, he stilled. The putrid stench of burned flesh filled the room and it gagged my throat. Though the place looked nasty on Nick's shoulder, it was reassuring to see no blood escaping now.

Malaika readied Nick's bed. She piled extra pillows to support his wounded shoulder and then fussed over the men who carried Nick into his room. I stayed in the kitchen with Frederick and with Juba's help, we cleaned away the mess we had made. Then, while Captain Burnham went to check on his patient, I looked in on Nalah, who slept soundly, thank goodness. I freshened myself up and then roused the baby, changed her, and carried her out to the kitchen. Leaving her in Wilson's capable hands, I went to look in on Nick.

His room was dark. The curtains drawn shut, and he was little more than a shadow lying in the bed. Migali sat in a chair next to the bed, looking so out of place among the western furnishings in the room, garbed in his tribal clothing. I did not speak but leant over the bed and placed my hand on Nick's cheek. He was rather warm, and I knew his next hurdle would be a fever. I moved back and looked at the warrior at Nick's side.

"Will you be staying?" I asked quietly.

"I guard my brother," he stated.

I left the bedroom and returned to the kitchen. Nalah was still drinking her bottle, and so I went along to the living room where I found Captain Burnham sat in a chair, nursing a snifter of brandy. As he watched, I helped myself to a drink as well. I sat across from him and then raised my glass.

"A toast to you, Captain, and your neat stitching. You could not have arrived more fortuitously. Thank goodness you were here."

We toasted one another and sipped our drinks. The brandy burned as it warmed my mouth and my throat. "Do you think Nick will be all right?"

He raised his brows. "As long as a fever doesn't do him in. He lost a good deal of blood, and he'll need rest and nourishment to get his strength back. If we can keep fluids in him, that will help combat the fever. By the way," he looked puzzled. "Where is Derek Walker? I thought he usually went with Nick out to the fields."

Until that moment, I had not given Derek a thought. "Perhaps he's at the Babcock's? I really don't know." I took another sip of brandy. "Captain, the fact Nick was shot is very worrying. Do you think it could possibly be an accident?"

"No." His answer came quickly. "Accidents happen when there are people around who are not experienced with weapons. This is Kenya. First of all, Migali says they were alone, and even if there were others in the vicinity, guns are handled with extreme care."

"Then you think it intentional?" I could barely get the words out.

"I do. Look, ma'am, can I be honest with you after what we have been through this afternoon?" He sounded earnest.

"Of course."

"I'm not here meetin' anyone off a ship tomorrow. It's a cover for my real reason for bein' in this part of the country. I'm afraid I cannot say more yet."

"Oh," I mumbled. What was this about, then? It was rather cloak and dagger. Perhaps it had something to do with the war? "Are you implying that what happened today is a result of your being here?"

"No," he said quickly. "Not at all. Although I think the *reason* I have come *and* what just happened to Nick might be."

It was a riddle to me. If an attempt on Nick's life was due to some unknown situation, why would it be kept a secret if lives were at stake? I thought I would ask Frederick Burnham that question, but Derek stormed into the room before I could speak.

"I just heard about Nick. Burnham, lucky you were here. What the hell is going on?"

I stood up and rushed over to him. "Derek! I am so glad you have come. Poor Nick, he's been wounded. And if it were not for the good captain here, would likely have died."

Captain Burnham also got to his feet and went to shake hands with Derek, whose face was racked with concern.

"I should have been there," he said angrily. "I was tied up escorting Ratcliffe on his way, and then Felicity insisted I come back to Meadowbrook for luncheon. How is Nick?"

"Holdin' his own for the moment, but he's got a slight fever, so we're not out of the woods yet."

Derek gave a grim nod and then left to go and check on his friend. Captain Burnham refilled our drinks and poured one for the farm manager, who was not gone long.

"Nick's sleeping soundly, but as you say, he does feel a little warm." Derek sat next to me on the sofa and knocked back his drink in one gulp. "Migali has the windows open and is trying to keep him as cool as possible."

"I'll keep an eye on him overnight, Derek. Now," he set down his glass and gave a sigh. "I would like your input about what could have happened to Nick?"

Derek glanced at the uniformed American. "It's all rather unsettling, Fred. First Trevor, now Nick. I have never known unrest like this. For the life of me, I cannot imagine who would want to harm either one of them. If the workers have issues, we usually hear about them. They do not usually resort to murder."

"Couldn't agree more, Walker. The Africans are a peaceful people. If they have any problems with the whites, they like to handle it their way, not with a white man's weapon."

"Then do you suspect one of the British?" I asked, hearing the tremor in my voice.

Derek appeared shocked by my question. "Hardly, Julia. You have met all the people who live in this area. Did any of them strike you as a killer?"

His tone sounded harsh, but he was upset, having just seen his good friend critically ill.

"It may not be anyone you're familiar with," said Burnham. "Perhaps it's a person who came specifically to commit the deed?"

"They would still have a motive," I added. "That is where the focus should be. If someone wanted Nick dead, why? The same could be said for Trevor Babcock as well."

"Excellent point, Julia," the captain said. He got to his feet. "I shall go and check on our patient. Juba is headed to Mombasa to alert the authorities." A shrill wail found its way to our ears. The captain grinned. "And if I'm not mistaken, that sure sounds like a baby who needs her diaper changed."

THE EVENING PASSED QUIETLY. MALAIKA made up a cot in Nick's room so the captain could keep an eye on him. I desperately wanted to help, but Burnham told me to focus on the baby. He said there was no point in us both staying awake through the night. He promised I could do more once Nick's fever broke.

But I could not sleep. Every time my eyes closed I travelled back to the evening at the lake and Nick's passionate kiss. I remembered his arms around me when he taught me how to use the rifle. The gentleness in his eyes whenever he looked at his niece. No matter how I tried, I could not get him out of my thoughts. What was wrong with me?

A little voice whispered a word that I had never used to anyone other than my sweet baby boy.

Love.

Chapter Nineteen

I WAITED UNTIL FIVE-THIRTY IN the morning before going to Nick's room. I was desperate to see how he fared. I crept down the hallway and saw the door to his room was ajar, so I quietly pushed it open and peered around.

Migali lay stretched out on the floor at the foot of the bed, with the dog at his side. While Burnham was fast asleep in a small cot close by. I squinted in the semi-darkness and saw Nick's outline on the bed. All four slept soundly, each omitting odd noises in their slumber. Reluctant to disturb them, I slowly backed away and went on to the kitchen.

I was surprised to see Malaika at the table so early in the morning. Wilson had yet to appear, but the young Maasai woman held a cup between her hands and looked up as I entered the room.

"*Memsahib* awake early?"

"I could say the same about you," I retorted as I took a seat across from her. "Is something wrong, Malaika?"

"*Hapana.* I am thinking about many things this day." Her lovely face was creased with concern.

"And what are these thoughts about?"

"They are about my life, *Memsahib*. I must make choices which are *ngumu*…difficult."

"Tell me what they are so I might be able to help you."

Her large eyes, black as coal, surveyed me as she considered her options. "*Memsahib* is woman also. Can help Malaika." And then she did something so unexpected it caught me completely off-guard—she smiled.

I returned the gesture. "First, you must stop calling me *Memsahib*. Please call me Julia."

She seemed taken aback by this request, and I hoped I had not breached some type of cultural etiquette. But we were equals, both employed by the same man. The only difference between Malaika and myself was our culture and our work at Jacaranda.

"Jewwleeah," she said slowly. Then she repeated it several times until she was able to pronounce it.

"That is better," I said. "Now, please tell me what is on your mind, and we can sort it out together." I had a feeling it might have something to do with the sleeping warrior in Nick's room.

"I want Migali for husband, but not allowed. I not want be servant here forever."

"Why are you not allowed?"

"Migali will become elder. His family must choose wife. Will not choose me. My family not having enough cattle."

I studied her beautiful face. There was no emotion there. She hid her feelings very well.

"If you cannot be Migali's wife, you should pursue your dream of becoming a teacher."

She lifted her gaze to look at my face, and there it was, a raw emotion—a hunger.

"I no give up this idea. I want to teach children

many things so they can stay, or go away whenever no longer children."

I sat back in my chair dumbfounded. This young woman had been a victim. She was also unable to take the man she cared for as her husband. Yet, she was not defeated. Within her still burned another flame, that of an educator. My heart swelled with such respect for Malaika, and I realised I would do anything in my power to help her.

CAPTAIN BURNHAM MUST HAVE SMELLED THE sausages frying in the kitchen under Wilson's steady hand. He joined me in the dining room, where I had just set Nalah down to play with her toys while I ate breakfast.

"Good morning, Captain Burnham. How is Nick doing? May I go and see him?"

"Mornin', Julia. Our patient did not burn up with a fever at all. I think the chloroform must have done a good job on him because he slept all night and has just woken up demandin' a cup of chai."

I pushed away my plate and got to my feet. "I shall take him some," I stated. "Will you keep an eye on the baby?" I gestured to where she lay in the middle of the room with her favourite playthings. He nodded assent, and I left him to eat breakfast alone.

When I went into Nick's room, Migali was gone. I took the cup of chai and set it down on the night table, then I went to the windows and opened the curtains halfway to allow in some light.

"If that's you, Fred, you better have brought me a hot drink." Nick's voice was dry and raspy.

"It isn't Fred, but I have brought you chai," I responded and went back to retrieve the cup.

Nick half sat, half lay, his back padded with pillows to keep the pressure off his wound. He still looked terrible. His skin was grey, and there were dark shadows beneath his eyes. He needed a shave, and his black hair was tousled from sleep. But I thought he looked simply wonderful because he was alive.

"Julia," he mumbled. "I feel bloody awful."

"You look it too. I can't understand why?" I replied sarcastically, holding the cup to his lips so he could sip his drink. He took some of the chai slowly, pausing between each attempt and savouring each taste of the warm liquid.

At length, he pulled his face back, and I returned the cup to its saucer, then took the chair Migali had sat in the night before.

"Thank goodness Captain Burnham had come to Jacaranda. He saved your life, Nick."

"Fred's a good chap. He wrote a while ago and mentioned he might be travelling through on his way to Mombasa, but I'd forgotten all about it." He grimaced.

"Are you in a lot of pain?"

He grinned. "About as much as if I'd been impaled through the shoulder by a rhino."

"I am so sorry."

"Not as sorry as the bastard who did this to me is going to be," he said angrily. "I will not rest until I know who it is."

"Do you remember any of what happened?"

"Some. Migali and I were in the north field. The shot came out of nowhere. I felt the bullet go through me and it knocked me off my horse. Nuru took off at a gallop, and I blacked out."

"Do you know what direction the shot came

from?"

"Not really as it was all so damned sudden. But there was no one around the area. We had just finished inspecting the field. The workers were tilling the southern area, not that I would suspect them."

"Do you think it could have been accidental?"

He did not hesitate. "Absolutely not."

A shudder of concern passed through me. If someone was intent on killing Nick, then surely they would try again? He must have known what I was thinking.

"Whoever did this will not be happy when they find out I survived. I intend to find out who they are before they have another chance."

"If it was intentional, Nick, then who would hate you enough to want to kill you? Have you wronged anyone in any way?"

His eyes met mine, and I saw the depth of pain and fatigue in his expression. "Not that I'm aware of," he said quietly. "But I'll give this all a great deal of thought."

I got up and encouraged him to finish his drink. "Now," I said, "the best thing you can do is rest. You lost a lot of blood, and we need to get you stronger so you can worry about all of this later." I set the cup back down. As I reached over to pull his covers higher, he lifted his hand to grasp mine. I did not pull away but paused to look down at him.

"Julia," he said softly. "I will rest easier knowing you are here." He gave my hand a little squeeze, and before I could respond, his eyes closed, and he fell fast asleep.

Chapter Twenty

NICK MADE A SWIFT RECOVERY. AFTER the fourth day, he was up and walking about, albeit slowly. Captain Burnham had asked Wilson to make beef broth and feed the patient as often as possible. He was to have several eggs a day and as much meat as he could tolerate. The captain insisted it would help to replenish the iron in Nick's blood. I wondered at the man's extensive medical knowledge, but Nick had told me several stories about the fellow, and they were all vastly impressive.

A family friend, Captain Frederick Burnham was something of a legend in America, England and now Africa. He was a fearless fighter and an invaluable scout to the British Army. Nick regaled me with specific adventures, which had the makings of a fabulous story for boys with all the fighting, even cowboys and Indians. Yet, I still saw the man as a hero for other reasons. He had saved Nick's life.

Derek was running the farm, and although Burnham had not left for Mombasa he still spent some time away from Jacaranda, although what he did, I had no idea. He would return late each afternoon and would closet himself with Nick until dinner. I often wondered what they spoke of but assumed it was likely to do with whoever had tried to kill Nick.

My days had been busy. Nalah grew more demanding as she entered her sixth month. She was still a good baby but slept less, and while awake, demanded more of my attention. Akina came often, and with that I would escape for an hour here and there. I'd stay near the house, for none of us were safe to travel far while a gunman still roamed.

I spent a great deal of my time reading. I borrowed books from Nick's study, and even discovered a cupboard full of Amelia's old magazines, which I devoured.

Sometimes I would find myself alone in the living room in the late afternoon. I would sip a cool glass of lemonade and stare at the portrait hanging over the fireplace. Amelia's lovely eyes stared back, a hint of boredom in her expression. I'd been so preoccupied with the shock of Ratcliffe being in Africa, and Nick's situation, that I'd forgotten my quest to discover what had really happened to the poor woman.

Today was no different. I had checked on Nick and the baby, as they were both sleeping, and then gone to sit outside while I read an old newspaper Captain Burnham had acquired from somewhere.

"There you are!"

Felicity joined me on the verandah. She wore her riding clothes and looked rather untidy in comparison to her normal self.

"Hello there. I wasn't expecting to see you. Have you ridden over here all alone?"

She slumped down into a chair and groaned. "Do not start lecturing me. I am sick and tired of hiding in the house from this unknown assailant. Another day locked up with Pops, and I shall go crazy." She suddenly stood up, disappeared into the living room and returned with a glass of sherry. She settled back into her chair.

"God, it's been eons since I saw you, Julia. Not since the debacle at Meadowbrook with Nick and Ratcliffe." Felicity was never the diplomat. "That was almost a week ago."

"I suppose it was. Time has been rather inconsequential since Nick was hurt."

"Unbelievable, if you ask me. Though after what happened to Trevor…" Her voice wobbled, and she took a sip of her drink. It seemed to right her. "My money is on Ratcliffe," she stated.

"What are you talking about?"

"For who shot Nick. The man was headed for Mombasa the day of the shooting. He could easily have been the one who did it, especially after Nick humiliated him at the party."

"I hardly think a punch on the nose constitutes murder," I said drily. "You've been reading too many Penny Dreadfuls, Felicity."

"Rubbish," she snapped. "You know what men are like when it comes to their pride. And the British nobility are the worst offenders." Her eyes narrowed into slits. "What was it all about, anyway? Why on earth would Nick bloody Ratcliffe's nose?"

I would not tell her the truth. It was none of her business. I deferred the question elsewhere. "You had better ask Nick. After all, it was his fist that did the deed."

She was not mollified by that answer. "I shall ask him, Julia." She wagged a finger in my direction. "I know you are keeping something from me."

"Good grief, what is all the racket?" Nick came out to join us. He moved slowly, using a carved walking stick Migali had given him so he would not fall and reopen his wound.

"Oh, Nick, it is good to see you." Felicity beamed with pleasure. "I have been terribly worried since we heard the news. How are you? Does it hurt awfully?"

"I'm doing well under the ministrations of Nurse Rossington and the good captain. And yes, it hurts like the bloody dickens, but every day it improves. How are you keeping at Meadowbrook?"

"Pops is a bear and refuses to stay put, yet he makes me stay home. I wish they would hurry up and find whoever did this to you. I was telling Julia it was most likely Ratcliffe."

I shuddered at the sound of his name.

Nick had just taken a seat. "What? Are you serious?"

"As stone. He is the obvious choice. After you left the party last week, he was absolutely mortified. He drank several glasses of Pop's good whiskey, and when he left for Mombasa, he still looked murderous."

"That may be, Felicity, but it is highly doubtful."

"Why do you say that?"

Nick glanced across first at me and then his neighbour. "They found the bullet. It's from an army issue revolver. I don't think his Lordship would have such a weapon, and whoever shot that gun was in close range for it to hit me."

The excitement drained from Felicity's face. "Oh."

I sat bolt upright. "Close range? Then that would imply it was no error. Surely Mzuka would have heard anyone close to you and barked?"

"Yes, my thoughts exactly," Nick answered. I looked at the expression on his face, and comprehension dawned as I read the same conclusion that was going through my head.

"Unless the dog knew them," I spoke quietly as the ominous meaning took hold.

Nick nodded, his grey eyes the colour of ice. "Indeed."

THE THOUGHT OF NICK'S ATTACKER BEING someone who was known to us muted our moods the rest of the day. Felicity, so pleased to be elsewhere than Meadowbrook, stayed on. She was surprisingly good company once she stopped talking about frivolities and fashion. She played with Nalah, who seemed to delight in the attention, and even helped me bathe the baby. We talked a great deal, and when I broached the subject of Captain Burnham, she told me she thought very highly of him and that it was a shame he was married.

Nick had gone to rest late in the afternoon when Derek strode into the house and stopped in surprise seeing Felicity, whose horse was in the barn.

"This is a nice surprise." His boyish grin showed his evident delight, and again I thought he had feelings for the beautiful woman.

"I simply had to get out," she said. "I am starved of youthful company, and Julia has made me most welcome and allowed me to get in her way all day."

I chuckled. "Nonsense, you have been a great help to me. You can come anytime you want."

"Well, don't get used to it," Felicity responded quickly. "It's not every day I feel so domestic."

"Are you dining with us?" Derek asked. "If so, I

can ride back to Meadowbrook with you."

"Is that safe?" I asked.

"Most likely," he said. "If we go at dark, we're less of a target. But I'm also worried about that damned leopard. He's less likely to be a concern if there are two of us."

I quickly agreed with him. In the worry of the last few days, I had all but forgotten about the big cat.

Felicity was nonplussed. "I should love to stay. Besides, I have yet to see Freddy since he got here." She was at once the coquette, and I caught the sudden cloud chase away Derek's smile. So, I had the right of it then. He was in love with Felicity. I wondered if she knew, or if she felt the same way about him?

AFTER THE SERIOUSNESS OF THE PAST FEW days, dinner was delightful. With five of us seated around the table, the conversation stayed buoyant and jolly. Felicity was an unabashed flirt with all the men. Yet she did it with such honesty she was thoroughly entertaining.

And then there was Nick. I found his eyes resting upon me several times. I would look up and meet his gaze. He did not smile, nor did he do anything, but his expression seemed thoughtful. I wondered what he thought about and cringed at the idea he was contemplating what he knew of my past.

The captain was fascinating. He told us wild stories of his times panning for gold in Alaska, his antics growing up in Sioux territory in Minnesota, and other tales which made the rest of us seem quite dull. Felicity hung on his every word, and I felt a twinge of empathy for Derek as he sat in the shadow of such an accomplished man.

Eventually, the talk turned serious. Captain Burnham brought up Trevor Babcock's name when he informed us that a new police officer would be coming to Jacaranda within a week. With the murder of Trevor, and now an attempt on Nick's life, the commissioner had sent a telegram to London requesting help. There was concern these acts were the start of a potential uprising.

"Well, that explains Pop's mood," Felicity said. "He's been very out of sorts for days, though he wouldn't say why. Still," she took a sip of her sherry. "I'm glad of it. It's about time they caught the man. Then we'll all sleep better in our beds at night." Her eyes glistened, and I knew she still mourned her brother deeply, though she would never let anyone know it.

"Speaking of sleep," piped up Derek. "We had better be off, Felicity."

"But the night is still young, Derek," she whined. "And I'm having a wonderful time."

But Derek had already got up from the table. "You collect your things while I get the horses."

With that, he left the dining room, and we all rose to see her out.

After Felicity had gone, the captain, Nick and I settled in the lounge.

"Captain Burnham, do you think this new policeman will be able to shed any light on what happened to Nick and Trevor after so much time has elapsed?"

He pursed his lips. "Well, that will depend on how clever the fellow is. It's my understanding these boys go through rigorous training nowadays, learn tricks that the likes o' you an' me can't fathom. It will be interestin' to see what he has to say."

I looked from one man to the other. "That you believe the killer is someone you know is disturbing. Do you have a suspect?" The thought I could be friends with a murderer was terrifying.

The men glanced at one another. If they knew anything, they weren't about to tell me.

"In an investigation, one must always refuse to show their hand. In making our true suspicions public, the villain would lay low, and his guard would be up. Much better he believes we're on a wild goose chase and worryin' about an uprisin'. He won't be so inclined to be as careful. And trust me, we are watchin'."

"That makes sense," I commented. "Yet I wonder at this person's intent, their real motive in singling out these specific two men." I looked at Nick. "Is there anything you and Trevor were involved in together that might make you a target? A business deal or something of that nature?"

"I am impressed with your powers of deduction, Julia." Captain Burnham said. "You do yourself credit, ma'am."

"Oh, thank you," I said and then turned to look at Nick once more. "No one else has been attacked so far, which begs the question why Trevor and now you. Why not the other way around?"

"Opportunity," Nick answered. "And to your question, no. Farming business has always been conducted between me and Pops Babcock, never his son. I saw little of Trevor after Amelia died. Prior to that, he was a regular visitor to Jacaranda."

This piqued my interest greatly. I wondered at the

relationship between Nick's wife and Babcock? Perhaps I could ask Malaika?

"Anyway," Captain Burnham said. "I do believe we will learn more once the new detective has done some diggin'."

"He cannot get here soon enough," I stated.

Nick gave me a wicked grin. "As far as everyone around here is aware, he arrives in Africa within the week. But the truth is, he's been here for several days already, makin' very subtle enquiries in Mombasa as we speak."

GOOD AS HIS WORD, the detective arrived later that week. I was astonished to learn upon introduction, that not only was Mr Allen Edge an agent with Pinkerton's, but an associate and compatriot to Captain Burnham.

Mr Edge came from a small town he called Marble Falls, somewhere in the heart of Texas, and it sounded extremely fascinating and just about as wild as Kenya. The man was not the type of person one would want to cross. He was well-built and used to hard work. His skin was leathery and sun-darkened, but it was his eyes which caught your attention, for they were as bright a blue as the Indian Ocean. He wore a silver-grey cowboy hat, much in the style of Captain Burnham, and thick boots, which he said were made from the skin of an alligator.

The Africans were unsure what to make of him and kept a polite distance, but Mzuka and Nalah were completely besotted with the man after one introduction. Babies and animals always had the best instincts, in my opinion, so based upon their reaction to him, I decided I would like him very well.

Mr Edge, the captain, and Nick spent the first afternoon in Nick's study, not emerging until dinner that evening. Wilson had cooked meatloaf in honour of the two Americans at the table. This was a strange concoction to me, minced beef with onions, shaped into a loaf and served with a tomato sauce. But it was quite enjoyable, and both men ate a second helping, which made the cook beam with pleasure.

Nick, Derek and I sat at the table with the Americans. I did little talking while we ate, being far more interested in the men's conversation. They discussed a terrible mining disaster which had happened several weeks earlier in South Wales. Apparently, coal dust had been ignited by a blasting shot which had subsequently caused a massive explosion. This, resulting in eighty-two souls perishing. The men discussed the mining methods used in Europe in comparison to those used in South Africa.

But when their subject turned to the mining of diamonds, I was fascinated. Captain Burnham was discussing the monopoly of the ownership of many mines in Southern Africa.

"Now take this Cecil Rhodes," he began, "Fella's a smart man if you ask me. See, he knew the rarer the diamond, the higher the price. An' he did not want to compete with any other."

"How did he control that?" I piped up.

The captain wagged a finger at me. "He devised a clever plan. Over the course of many years, he slowly bought up land, piece by piece, so he and his partners could run the whole shootin' match. An' it worked."

"Damned greedy if you ask me." Grumbled Derek. "How do they expect fair trade and healthy competition? Sounds like the British East India Company all over again."

"God forbid," said Nick. "The region is a mess. Internment camps that starve the civilian women and children while their men are off fighting the British. Men, I might add, who have no reason to care who wins, British or Boer, as both will treat them abysmally. The Afrikaans are better suited to fight in their terrain, but they are vastly outnumbered. I believe they will fall in a very short matter of time."

"You have the right of it there, Nick." Burnham agreed. "Though I threw my hat in with Lord Kitchener, I don't always agree with his policies. The camps are a terrible idea. The politicians are in an uproar over them in England."

"And in the midst of this mayhem," Nick added. "The only people profiting are the bootleggers."

This caught my attention. "Do you mean smugglers?"

"I do. With the war in full swing, it has created the perfect opportunity for diamonds to be smuggled out of the country, dodging the excisemen. A fortune has been made." Nick turned to look directly at me. "Think about it. A small handful of gems can be so easily hidden and taken out of the country—a country in such turmoil the left-hand does not know the antics of the right hand. Many opportunists are getting filthy rich since the war began."

This had not occurred to me. "Where do they take the diamonds?" I asked naively.

"Europe and the United States," chimed in Mr Edge, who had been silent to this point. "I'm unfamiliar with the logistics in Africa as I'm new to the continent, ma'am. But I've worked on smugglin' cases once they reach Britain and my own country. Those stones are sold for a premium, and it is a damnable cut-throat business, I can tell you."

The room fell quiet as we all contemplated his words. I had never considered this side of affairs. Since coming to Africa, my world had shrunk to the size of Jacaranda. Seldom did I ever see a newspaper. If I did, they were several weeks old.

"It's all overblown in my opinion," Derek said disdainfully. "I have no doubt smugglers are taking all the chances they may with the officials so thinly spread in the region, but I always believed the mines were kept rather secure."

"Then it has been some time since you've been south," said Burnham, his tone accusatory. Was the captain putting Derek in his place? I was uncertain, but something lurked there. If Derek noticed, he did not show it.

"You are correct, Burnham. It has been a while. And like most places, they do have a tendency to change when you are absent, just not in your mind's recollection." Derek tipped back his drink, then got to his feet. "And now I must deprive myself of your esteemed company, gentleman. I have several tasks awaiting me back at my house."

We all said goodnight as Derek left through the verandah doors. After he was gone, the Americans ventured outside to smoke. "Will you come with us, Julia?" asked Nick getting ready to follow their lead as he placed his serviette upon the table.

"Perhaps not. I think I'll leave you three to your discussion, and devour a few pages of my book if you don't mind?"

His eyes settled upon mine. Tonight, they were molten silver. His colour had returned, no doubt, from the combined efforts of the entire household. I thought he was going to speak, but he remained quiet. The moment grew longer.

"Is something amiss?" I asked.

He seemed to snap out of his thoughts. "No, of course not. I'm sorry. I was just thinking about when you first arrived here. It has been, what…two months or thereabouts? Yet I can barely remember a time when you were not a part of Jacaranda."

It was as though Amelia's eyes bored into my back from her portrait hanging in the adjoining room. For an instance I considered a rebuke for Nick's flattery. But then I recalled the sight of his bleeding body being carried into the kitchen less than a week hence, and I changed my mind. Instead, I rose from my chair and bade him goodnight.

But later, as I settled down with my book, *The Tenant of Wildfell Hall*, it was not the main character, Helen Graham who captivated my imagination, but a dark-haired, handsome man with a scar running through his brow.

Chapter Twenty-One

THE NEXT MORNING NICK ANNOUNCED HE HAD INVITED several people to Jacaranda the following day. This surprised me more than if he'd told me he planned to attend a party at the Mombasa Club.

"Are you absolutely sure you should do this?" I was incredulous. "You are barely able to get through an entire day without rest. How do you plan to be a host?"

Nick drank coffee in the kitchen while I gave the baby her bottle. Nalah was hungry and grunted in contentment as she devoured her milk. The captain and Mr Edge had departed earlier for an undisclosed destination.

"Of course, I'm sure." I saw him look around the room. "Look, after you put the baby down for her nap, would you be willing to take a brief walk with me so I can explain? But first, I must meet with Juba as he leaves for Mombasa this morning to fetch supplies. After that I'll be in my study."

IT TOOK A WHILE TO SETTLE THE BABY. Our routine changed each week as she grew and became more demanding of my time. But it was no hardship playing with Nalah. She was a dear little girl, and I could already see she held the promise of beauty. I loved to hear her laughter, and I melted every time she turned those bewitching hazel eyes to my face and smiled.

Although she often fussed when I put her in the crib to sleep, I would not pick her up and rock her to sleep. I wanted her to be able to go to sleep by herself, though there were many times I cuddled her in the rocking chair just to be close. Now, I waited by the nursery door to see if she would protest, but after a minute, she was quiet, and I went in search of Nick.

The study door was open, but I knocked anyway.

"Julia," he said, looking up at me from his desk. "Ready?"

I nodded. "I must let Malaika, or Wilson know to keep an ear out for the baby."

"Malaika went with Juba to town, so you will have to ask Wilson." It did not take a moment to find the cook, and he agreed obligingly.

Nick and I left through the kitchen door, with Mzuka at our heels.

"Let's not go far," I stated as we started walking up the driveway. "You mustn't tire, and I don't want anyone taking another shot at you."

"Goodness," Nick said. "Is it possible you like me after all?"

I flashed him an exasperated look, but he laughed, completely unfazed. We reached the end of the driveway, and I stopped.

"What is it?" Nick asked.

"I don't want to go any further. Can we not just walk around closer to the house? I really don't feel safe."

"Of course." He complied, and instead of turning onto the dirt road, we retraced our steps back towards the house and then detoured in the direction of Derek's bungalow.

"What is it you wished to speak to me about?" I said. "Is it the party tomorrow?"

A muscle worked in his jaw, and I saw he had not shaved today for there was stubble on his chin. "In a way. Look, Julia. I have great respect for you, and I think you eminently trustworthy, so there are some things I need to tell you."

What was this? One glance at his face told me he was serious. I did not speak but kept walking.

"First of all, I should tell you that Captain Burnham's arrival was no coincidence…I sent for him."

I stopped in my tracks. "What?"

Nick held up his arms in surrender. "You can scold me when I am finished. But for now, please listen while we have the privacy to speak openly."

"I'll remain quiet," I promised.

"Freddy Burnham is an old friend of mine. He's been working with the British army for some time now, but due to an injury, he is released from official duties at the moment." I already knew this but held my tongue.

"Freddy and I correspond, have done since we met. Nothing regular, you understand, just periodic notes. When Trevor was killed, I wrote and told Freddy about it. His initial concern was native unrest and the fear it might escalate into something beyond the murder of a white farmer, into something far more gruesome. But he was himself working, trailing smugglers who were headed up the coast to Mombasa. Much to his surprise, he discovered a link between the men he followed and a man we both know, Klaus Schmitt."

"You cannot be serious?" I gasped.

"I am deadly serious. The connection is vague but can still be tied to Klaus's export business. It was enough to get Freddy more involved, with the additional backing of the British Commissioner."

"But why would the captain follow them to this area if they were headed to the port?"

Nick shrugged. "To see them hand over their cargo for the next leg of the journey."

"I am not sure I follow," I said.

"It's simple, Julia. The diamonds were removed and then passed along through a network of people, each being responsible for their leg of the journey to the ports. Freddy thinks the final handoff occurs away from a large town where the eyes of many might be watching. From here, the diamonds will end up in Mombasa and shipped off abroad. After some nosing around into Schmitt's financial affairs, there was enough to make the authorities suspicious. Schmitt had a prosperous business in Dar es Salaam, further down the coast from Mombasa. But the port there is strictly governed, and he'd already been fined for non-payment of excise taxes. He was having serious financial problems. But all that has dissipated since his arrival in Mombasa. We suspect he is earning money by this smuggling operation."

"That sounds unbelievable, Nick. But even if it were true, where does Trevor fit into the picture?"

"Well, that's where it gets a little sketchy. It's not official, but one of the workers at Meadowbrook saw Trevor meet with Klaus on more than one occasion. If you remember, Trevor even defended Klaus at the Babcock's when his father spoke derogatorily about the man. So, it seems likely they may have met without

Pops or anyone else knowing."

It was much to absorb. To cast a man from the role of friend and businessman to that of a smuggler seemed ridiculous. But this was not a game. A man had died and another had come close.

"And where does Mr Edge come into it?"

Nick grinned. "He is a fine fellow, is he not? Allen is an old friend of Freddy's. He is a very shrewd investigator with the Pinkertons in America. He has been tracking the illegal smuggling of precious gems into New York for quite some time now. He is paid by the Diamond cooperatives in South Africa. They have incurred great losses from this racket."

"Why are you telling me this, Nick?"

"Because it's the reason we are having the party tomorrow. Freddy wants to get everyone here in one place so that he and Mr Edge can talk to them in a social setting and see what they can glean."

"That's a good plan, but it doesn't change the fact that you're still recovering from your brush with death. You have no business overdoing it, no matter the reason."

He stared at me, and I watched as a slow smile spread across his face. "You should be careful, Julia Rossington. Or you might have me thinking that you care for me."

My instinct was to bolt, but something rooted me to the spot. I tilted up my chin and raised a brow. "And you should be careful, Nicholas Fleming. Because perhaps I do." The enormity of what I had said hit me. Feeling my face flush, I spun around and marched back towards the house.

THE DAY OF THE PARTY WAS EXTREMELY BUSY. My heart went out to Wilson, who had flown about the kitchen like a fly trapped in a jam jar. He had brought in extra help, and I stayed out of the way while he organised the food, as though we were to embark upon a military campaign. I helped Malaika with the house instead. We moved furniture up against the walls, and extra tables were brought in from the barn and dusted off.

Nalah picked up on the excitement in the air. Her eyes were bright, and she watched everything around her with glee, her legs kicking as though she wished to leap up and join in. The event would begin at five o'clock, but I knew that Janet White and her family would come a little earlier as they were the farthest away.

I had not seen Nick since breakfast, which had been a hurried affair. I had managed to get through dinner the night before without too much embarrassment after flirting with him, because the two American gentlemen were there, thank goodness. The same could be said for breakfast, though I caught him staring at me on more than one occasion, a puzzled expression upon his dark brow. But there was no time to contemplate my thoughts. There was still much to do before the party began.

Akina came to help with Nalah in the middle of the afternoon. I gratefully passed the responsibility over to the young Kikuyu and allowed myself the luxury of getting ready for the evening. I went into Amelia's old room and opened the now-familiar wardrobe to see what I might borrow. I felt no guilt doing this. After all, Amelia Fleming had loved fashion, and part of me hoped she would be happy to know her things were not locked away.

I took my time going through the wardrobe, digging further in the corners, which I had not done before. And then I saw a particular gown and sighed in pleasure. I lifted it out and laid it gently on the bed.

The sea-green silk had a wide band of gold crusted tulle running around the hem of the dress. The bodice, which dipped into a 'v' both in the front and back, was also crusted tulle, but in turquoise. It complemented the gown, giving it the ethereal appearance in my imagination of a mermaid. It was beautiful, and though I was not normally concerned about clothing, I desperately wanted to wear this beautiful dress.

I turned the key in the door, stripped off my work clothes and carefully put on the gown. I could not fasten the back of it without help but felt it would work. My chest was fuller than Amelia's, but I had lost weight since being in Africa, I supposed from leading such an active life, and that helped the fit. I went to stand before the full-length mirror and gasped in astonishment. I did not consider myself attractive, far from it, in fact, but there was such a quality to this gown that it could make an ostrich look pretty. The soft hue of the fabric reflected in my eyes, turning them aqua in colour, while my hair seemed a warmer shade of brown.

I would wear this dress tonight, and for the first time in recent years, push away the shame of my degradation at the hands of Charles Ratcliffe. Tonight, I wanted to be a desirable woman for one man…Nick Fleming.

JANET WHITE GASPED WHEN SHE came in through the front door and saw me dressed for the evening.

"Julia, you look absolutely beautiful," she said wistfully as she gazed at the gown. Malaika had scooped up my hair into a loose bun and pulled a few strands to frame my face. She'd fastened aquamarine earrings to my ears, and I wore a matching pendant which nestled in my decolletage. Tonight, I was bold, for I also had a dab of rouge on my lips and cheeks, and smudges of kohl around my eyes which made my blue eyes brighter. I had rubbed a touch of sandalwood oil on my neck, behind my ears and my wrists, and for once, I felt attractive.

"You are kind," I said gratefully. "This is a dress of Amelia's, and I wanted to feel pretty for a change. She had a wonderful sense of fashion." I smiled at my friend. "But look at you. The pink of your gown is perfect with your gorgeous black hair. You look lovely." And she did. Janet had the type of beauty which triumphed no matter what she might wear. The woman would be pretty garbed in sacking.

We chatted for a few minutes until we heard the men coming in to join us. Donald and Nick looked dapper in dark suits and starched white shirts. I greeted Donald with a hearty welcome and then swung my glance to his companion. Nick's eyes slaked over my body without any effort to conceal his interest. I felt each second that his stare slowly travelled from my hem line, up my body until finally settling upon my face. As his eyes met mine, my breath quickened, and my mouth went dry. I wetted my lips, and his gaze dropped instantly to my mouth. He did not smile at me as the others had. Instead, he devoured me, and my senses became charged with an energy that reached out to him, willing him closer. As if responding to the call, he moved away from Donald White until he stood right before me. Slowly, he deliberately bent his head and moved to whisper in my ear.

"You are perfection," he said softly, his breath tickling my skin and moving a curl of my hair. "And God help me, I cannot keep my eyes from you." He pulled back and hesitated, our faces close together. Tension hung in the space between us, and I knew a raw hunger and it startled me. If, in that moment, he kissed me as before, I would never let him stop.

"Hello, everyone!" Felicity's voice pierced the air, and both Nick and I snapped back into our roles as he greeted the newcomers, while I showed Janet and Donald into the lounge where Malaika and Juba waited with trays of drinks.

THE GATHERING WAS WELL ATTENDED. People filled the lounge with chatter, and the verandah doors were open so that others could venture outside into the evening air. I recognised several of the guests. The Babcocks, Briggs and then I spotted the Paderborns, who arrived with Klaus Schmitt in tow. I'd not had a chance to see Derek and assumed he and Nick mingled with everyone, as did Juba and Malaika with the cocktails and sherry. Wilson and his helpers scurried in and out of the kitchen, laying a feast of meats, relishes, pastries and sweets in the dining room. The only people who seemed to be missing were the Americans.

"*Fraülein* Rossington. *Guten Abend*." The German materialised before me, looking handsome and well-groomed.

"Herr Schmitt, what a pleasure it is to see you. Are you well?"

"Indeed, I am, and I must say you look magnificent in this lovely gown you are wearing. The colour, it brings out the radiance of your eyes." He grasped my hand and pressed it to his lips.

My cheeks grew warm. "Thank you." I pulled my hand away a little abruptly. "You are kind to say so."

"Good God," blurted Derek, suddenly appearing at the German's side. "Julia, I almost did not recognise you. You look stunning!" He smiled at me, but it did not reach his eyes. That was very unlike Derek.

"Schmitt, old boy," he said to the German gentleman. "Mind if I tear you away from our lovely Julia for a minute?"

Klaus shrugged his shoulders. "Of course, Derek. But not for long as I would much rather be in the company of a beautiful *fraülein* than you." He clicked his heels together, gave me a curt nod, and the two of them walked away.

I sauntered off into the kitchen to check on Wilson. As always, he was in good spirits, even though he was up to his elbows in dishes. Then I went down the hall to check on Akina and the baby. In the half-light, the young African girl lay fast asleep on a cot while the baby slept soundly. I turned to leave the room but paused as I heard voices coming from outside the open nursery window. Curious, I moved closer. The thin curtains were drawn to keep out insects, but I could hear one of the people speaking.

"I did not know he was coming here." It was barely audible, but the German accent was hard to miss.

"What have you done?" This voice was not as

familiar, though I knew I had heard it before.

"Do not worry," said Klaus. "This has nothing to do with you."

"But it does," the other man hissed. "You have brought this on me."

The baby stirred, and my attention was broken. She did not wake. But the men had moved on, and it was quiet once again. I left the nursery, but my mind worked furiously. What was Klaus talking about, and with whom?

I returned to the party and moved between our guests looking for Nick. He stood near the verandah door, drink in hand, speaking with Mr Edge and Captain Burnham, who must have arrived in my absence.

"Nick, may I speak with you?" I blurted immediately, interrupting their conversation.

"Go ahead, Nick," the captain said. "Me an' Edge will venture outside for a smoke." He gave me a nod. "Don't mind me sayin', but you look real pretty in that dress, ma'am."

I thanked him as he and his compatriot stepped out into the night.

"What's wrong, Julia?" Nick asked as soon as they were gone.

I recounted what I had just heard. "Klaus is in trouble, but what of the other man he was with? I did not know his voice, though I have heard it before."

"We must tell the captain. He's the person who needs to know. Come." Nick clasped my hand in his, and having done so, seemed to realise his faux pas. He looked searchingly at my face to see my response. I gave him a weak smile and followed him out into the night, leaving the buzz of conversation behind us.

"He knows we're onto him," said Burnham when I quickly shared my story. He threw his cheroot down and ground out the embers with his heel. He told us to return to the party, and then along with the Pinkerton agent, he headed around to the front of the house in search of Klaus.

"What's going on?" Derek came up to us immediately.

"It's Klaus," muttered Nick so that no one else might hear. "Mr Edge and the captain are going to have words with him."

"What the devil for?" Derek's face showed surprise.

"He might be mixed up in a smuggling ring. They've been watching him for several days now."

"Good God, are you sure?"

"I'm positive," Nick said. "I'll keep you informed as I learn more."

I remained quiet at their exchange, but I noticed Derek's colour was up. He'd probably already drunk too much, which most likely had something to do with Felicity Babcock. I was convinced he was in love with her but unsure if Felicity felt the same. I hoped so, for they were actually quite well suited.

"Julia?" It was Janet. As she approached, I left the two men to talk privately.

"I've been looking everywhere for you," she said. "We haven't had a moment to talk since I arrived."

"I'm so sorry. Although everything was planned, everyone seemed to get here at the same time. Are you enjoying yourself?"

"Absolutely." She grinned. "Any time away from a

house full of children and animals is almost a holiday." She glanced over at Nick and Derek, and her eyes narrowed. "Tell me," she whispered. "Is there something going on between you and the handsome Mr Fleming?"

"Why do you ask?"

"Several reasons, really. First, the way he looked at you when he saw you tonight, then he said something privately to you. And because the two of you cannot seem to keep your eyes off one another."

My first instinct was to deny her statements as nonsense. But Janet was a dear person and the closest I had to a friend. "Nothing is actually going on," I replied, "but I think we are both intrigued with the idea that it might someday."

Janet grinned and reached out to grab my hand. "I think you would make a wonderful couple," she gushed. "You complement one another. Look how well you rubbed along at my house that day. And if I am honest, I've never seen Nick look this happy since I first met him."

I looked over to the subject of our conversation just as Derek walked away. Nick caught me staring and came over to join us.

"Are you ladies enjoying yourselves?" he asked politely.

"We are," Janet replied. "I was just telling Julia I thought you looked extremely well."

"I am most definitely on the mend, due in part to the care of your friend here." He gestured to me.

"Nonsense. All credit has to go to Captain Burnham and Wilson, the cook. Between the two of them, they have made all the difference and sped up his recovery. If I ever—"

Suddenly there was the loud report of a gunshot. Nick pushed both of us towards the door to the house. "Get inside! Quickly!"

Janet and I hurried into the house with him following close behind. Everyone in the lounge looked as though they were unsure what they had heard.

"Be quiet!" Nick shouted over the hum of conversation. "I just heard gunfire. Please stay in here until we find out what is going on." With that, he left the room and went towards the front of the house.

I left Janet and quickly followed Nick. I was not about to let him risk his life or take any chances. He got to the open front door and peered outside. Then he took off at a slow run. Where was he going? Increasing my pace, I crossed the threshold then stopped in my tracks.

Klaus lay on the ground in a pool of blood. Captain Burnham knelt beside him as Mr Edge ripped away a sleeve from Klaus's shirt. He quickly tied the fabric around the German's upper arm, where I could see blood pumping like a tiny volcano spewing lava. The tourniquet was pulled tightly, and then the captain and Mr Edge lifted Klaus up and carried him to the house. Several guests had wandered outside to see the spectacle. Nick now shooed them away to create a path for the Americans to take the injured man inside.

I followed behind and then pushed my way into the kitchen, where it was a déjà vu of when Nick had been shot just days earlier. This time, the captain said the bullet was lodged in Klaus's arm, and he would need to extract it.

Janet White materialised beside me. "I can help him, Julia."

I remembered her desire to pursue nursing. "I think you should. I'll go and find Nick." I left her in the kitchen and closed the door behind me.

Nick was outside speaking with Mr Edge. He turned at my approach. "Can you help me send everyone home?"

"Yes. Of course." I replied.

BY TEN-THIRTY THAT EVENING, all the guests had departed. Captain Burnham managed to remove the bullet from Klaus's arm and staunch the bleeding of the artery, but he planned to take Klaus to Mombasa at first light to be seen by a surgeon. The patient was now officially a prisoner who was put in the spare room, with Mr Edge remaining by his side on guard.

Nick had just poured Captain Burnham a whisky when I joined them in the lounge. I had been with Wilson, clearing up the kitchen from both the party and it being a makeshift surgery.

"Would you like a dram, Julia?" Nick asked as I came in.

I shook my head. "No, thank you. But I will take a sherry please." I accepted the small glass and went to sit on the sofa next to the captain.

"Regarding our conversation," Nick told the American. "You can discuss anything in front of Julia. She has my complete trust."

I looked at Nick in surprise, flattered by his words. He smiled at me.

"Good, then we must get down to business. I have to tell you I don't like this, not one little bit. Whoever is doin' this has the upper hand. He could pick us off one at a time before it's said and done."

"Wait," I interrupted. "I thought you or Mr Edge shot Klaus. That he was trying to get away?"

"Partly true, ma'am," said Burnham. "He was makin' a run for it, but someone in the bush shot him. Furthermore, I'll bet you a dollar the bullet is from the same gun as the one used on Nick."

"Migali will get to Mombasa tonight with my letter to the commissioner," Nick said. "By morning, we should have the guards here, and perhaps Klaus will have come around and we can question him. We also need to speak with Josef Paderborn."

As soon as Nick spoke the name, something clicked. "That's it!" I exclaimed.

"What?" Burnham asked.

"The second voice I heard outside the window with Klaus. It was Josef. I knew I had heard it before."

"Remind me what you heard him say," Nick instructed.

I recounted the conversation to the best of my ability.

The captain rubbed his chin. "The fellow may not be involved in this after all. Well, ain't that a turn-up. Maybe the German was using him as a front?"

I felt instantly relieved, for I liked the Paderborns and wished them no ill. They had been so kind to me that night at the Mombasa Club.

The captain drained his glass and set it on a side table. "I'm all done in, folks. I have to relieve Edge in a few hours, so I guess I'd better go get some rest. All right if I use the sofa in your study, Nick?"

"Please do, Freddy. Malaika left a pillow and blanket in there for you."

"Mighty kind. Thank you." He nodded to us both.

"I'll wish you a good evenin' and see you in the mornin'."

The room fell quiet as the older man left. I finished what was left of my sherry and sighed. "You know what? There has not been a dull moment since I arrived here."

Nick chuckled. "Ironic, really. Are you always a catalyst for disaster, Julia?" He looked exhausted, but there was still a glint of mischief in Nick's slate eyes as he gave me a lazy smile.

"Apparently. Well, at least on this continent anyway." I set down my glass. "It's hard to fathom that this sleepy area of Kenya could be harbouring a smuggling ring. Especially as everyone living around here seems so normal, just hardworking folk."

"There's the rub of it," Nick said. "The hard work, I mean. The land is as wild and unyielding as the animals living here. Every crop takes a toll on you, financially, physically and emotionally. Sometimes people cannot make ends meet. It drives them to do things they would not normally consider doing."

"Like Klaus, you mean?"

"Yes. I have never been fond of the man, but perhaps I am biased with us fighting the Boers. Yet he isn't an evil man, quite the opposite." He stared hard at me. "You liked him well, I recall."

He was jealous, and somewhere inside I felt a spark of pleasure seeing it in his expression. "Klaus was nice to me when I first arrived, and I appreciated it. Did you know about his wife?"

"No, didn't know the man had one?" He looked surprised.

"He does, and children too. His wife is an invalid

and lives in a sanitorium back in Germany—a very costly one, according to Hilary Paderborn. Perhaps there lies his motive to become a smuggler." I got to my feet.

"Motive, yes. But not an excuse. Smuggling is a nasty operation. Somewhere along the line, there are always people hurt, sometimes killed." He stood up and faced me. If I reached out my hand, I was close enough to touch him. I remained still.

"Julia," he began. "Once this situation is resolved, the smugglers captured, and when my life is no longer in danger, I would like the chance to talk to you about a few matters." His eyes sought mine, and I knew he waited to see my response to his words and the implication of what he said.

"I think that would be a good thing," I said softly.

He smiled at my answer, and my heart warmed a little more towards this gruff, solitary man, whose kindness belied his harsh exterior. Then he reached out to take my hand and raised it to his mouth. As his warm lips gently touched my skin, his eyes blazed into mine, and everything around me seemed to fade away. There was nothing in that moment but the two of us, his fingers clasping my hand, and our eyes communicating that which we were not yet ready to say.

Chapter Twenty-Two

I DO NOT THINK ANYONE SLEPT WELL, least of all Herr Schmitt. Nalah was in a fussy mood, and after I had fed the baby, Akina kindly stayed to play with her. This freed my time, for I was preoccupied with the arrival of several constables from Mombasa who had been placed around the perimeter of the property. No one was allowed out, and no one in. I was unsure why.

Other than the house staff, there were no other workers to be seen inside or outside. But Derek came into the kitchen as I asked Wilson to prepare extra food as the constables would be at Jacaranda for lunch. I had not seen the farm manager since the previous night, prior to Klaus being shot. He looked as tired as the rest of us. There was a sheen of sweat on his brow, and his red hair looked unruly.

"Are you unwell, Derek?" I asked, noticing his eyes seemed glazed.

"Hungover," he mumbled. "Just poked my head in to check on our prisoner. Burnham says Klaus is still unconscious."

"Yes, he wants to get him to Mombasa as quickly as he can. I think they are almost ready to leave." I gestured to a cart being readied by Mr Edge outside the kitchen window.

"I have offered to take him," Derek said.

"Burnham wants to stay here and supervise whatever it is the constables are going to do."

That concerned me. "But the captain is the person with medical experience. Surely he should be the one going, in case Klaus gets worse."

"He's unconscious, Julia. That is unlikely to change because he is in a cart." Derek poured himself coffee from a large tin pot on the stove. Wilson continued washing vegetables in the sink. But I was not happy with this plan. I excused myself and went along to the spare room, where I found both Mr Edge and Captain Burnham preparing Klaus for his journey.

"Good mornin', ma'am," they said in unison as I went into the room.

"Good morning, gentlemen. I am sorry to interrupt, but Derek tells me you have asked him to accompany the patient to Mombasa?"

Burnham finished tying a binding around Klaus and the improvised stretcher which had been assembled. "Indeed I have. Well, he offered to do it as I have much to oversee here. That damned commissioner of yours only sent half the men he promised, so I'm short-handed as it is. With Schmitt being comatose, there's little he needs in the way of attention. Fever is the enemy now, and the quicker he is in the hospital, the better." He frowned. "Are you worried about him, ma'am?"

"Yes," I said, flustered. "What if he should worsen? Without you there to tend him, he could die. Does he not hold the key to much information? His knowledge could prove invaluable."

"Indeed," the captain answered. "But we have matters here which also require my presence and are every bit as vital." He paused. "Would you feel better accompanying the patient? I saw your nursin' skills when Nick was wounded. You are more than capable to care for him in his current state. If you do, I will not have to spare another. It would be helpful."

He had a point. Klaus would likely sleep the entire journey. But if he should wake, at least he would see someone familiar and friendly towards him.

"Then I shall go along too. That way, Derek can concentrate on driving, and I will tend Klaus should he come around."

We were to leave within the half-hour, so I made arrangements for Akina to stay until my return and asked Malaika to pass my whereabouts along to Nick when he returned from the fields with Migali.

The men loaded Klaus into the back of the cart usually used for hay. The captain had already explained to me that the sides were built higher, therefore providing a defence from animals and any errant bullets. There was also a canopy draped across a metal frame which would provide plenty of shade. They carefully placed the patient into the back of the cart, and with the captain's assistance, I climbed in after the stretcher was secured. Burnham handed me a small bag with medical supplies in case they were needed, and then a large canteen of water was set beside me before they secured the back board. I stood up to watch as one of the constables climbed up to sit at the front of the cart while Derek stood surveying the scene.

"What is this?" he asked. "I thought I was to have an escort?"

"No, sir, there's been a change of plans. Miss Julia has kindly offered to accompany you to Mombasa, and free up my men. Klaus poses no real threat in his current condition, and I have faith in this young lady's nursin' skills. That isn't a problem, is it, Derek?"

"Not at all," he said, though I did not feel his sincerity. "I will enjoy the company of Julia far more than I would another." His smile was weak, and I wondered what bothered him. Perhaps he would feel safer with more constables by his side.

Derek continued. "But, Freddy, are you not concerned for mine or Julia's welfare with a killer on the loose? What if they come back to finish off Klaus?"

The captain's face darkened. "I would never endanger this woman's life," he said angrily. "Julia is protected in the back there, safe from animals or bullets. Besides, we do not foresee trouble as we took the liberty of announcing that Herr Schmitt died last night."

"What?" Derek sounded incredulous.

"You heard me correctly, Derek. We felt it wise to put that about and draw attention away from Jacaranda. Since the attack, no one has been permitted to come or go from the property other than Nick. The only people to witness Klaus being alive are those you see before you now. Therefore, I believe your journey will be quite safe."

The captain had explained this to me on our way to the cart. I didn't feel as though I were in any danger. Besides, both men carried weapons, and I was safe inside the cart. But I wondered why Nick had left considering what was happening?

At length, we set off at a steady pace. I knew it would be some time until we got to the town, but only a matter of a few hours, surely Klaus could hold on that long. I moved so that my back rested against the board where Derek and the constable were seated. I was under cover, but the opening of the canopy was in the front to allow the cooler air in. I could converse easily enough with them both.

The young constable was named Cyril. He hailed originally from Cardiff, in Wales and was a quiet young man, barely twenty if I had to guess, and new to the continent. He was reluctant to engage in conversation, and after making several attempts I gave up.

"How is our patient?" asked Derek, after we had been going along for a while.

"He hasn't moved an inch," I replied. Sitting under the canopy provided plenty of shade, but it did not allow the passage of much fresh air. I felt Klaus's forehead. It did not seem any warmer than when we had set out, which was encouraging. Still, I opened the canteen of water and poured some into a bowl where it sloshed about from the motion of the cart. When I reached out to dampen my cloth, I noticed two large canvas bags in the corner of the cart. Perhaps they were left from a previous trip with the vehicle.

I wetted the cloth and sponged Klaus's face, neck and hands, then I wiped the sweat from my brow and threw the water out through a gap between the wooden sides of the cart and the canopy. The wheel hit a large rut in the road, and I fell to one side.

"Sorry," Derek said. "I didn't see that one."

"It's fine," I replied. Then I noticed one of the bags had fallen over, and the bulk of its contents had loosened the rope tying it closed. Some items had spilled out, so I reached across and pulled it toward me. But as I studied the bag, I realised it was stuffed with clothing, men's clothing. I peered a little closer and then slipped my hand inside to see what filled it so full.

I explored the contents of the bag by touch while listening to Derek as he began discussing the Mombasa Club with the young constable. My fingers came into contact with a book. Curious and being nosy, I pulled it out of the bag. The book title was in another language, perhaps German? I opened it up and almost exclaimed out aloud. The book was hollow and filled with a thick wad of banknotes. I quickly looked over my shoulder— the men were now chatting about cricket. I lifted out the bills and saw a small velvet pouch nestled at the back. Carefully I opened it, though I already knew what I would find.

Diamonds.

Chapter Twenty-Three

MY HEART WAS STILL RACING when Derek slowed the wagon down.

"Why are we stopping?" I asked.

"One of the oxen is acting lame," Derek said, hopping down. "I want to check his hoof." He walked over to the lead ox, a massive white creature.

"Are you certain, sir?" asked Cyril. "I never noticed a problem?" His accent was distinctly one from the Welsh mountains.

"Yes. It won't take a moment to look. Hmm, there is something here," Derek muttered. "Damn, but I can't quite get at it." He glanced up. "Cyril, my man, can you give me a hand? If you can dig it out, I'll hold his leg steady."

The constable set down his rifle on the seat and climbed down. I watched from my position in the back of the cart, though I could only see the oxen. I was unsure what to do or think. Who did the bags belong to? I had not seen them put into the cart at Jacaranda. Were they Klaus's possessions? If so, wouldn't Burnham have already gone through them?

There was the sound of a thud. "What is it, Derek?" I called. I could only see his shoulders and head as he stood up.

"It's Cyril." Derek called. "The blasted ox only

clocked him with his hoof, and the fellow's knocked out."

At that, I went to the back of the cart and undid the ties of the canopy to get out. I grabbed the medical bag and walked around the side of the cart, only to stop in my tracks.

Derek pointed the revolver at me as he covered the distance between us. "I want you to believe me when I say it's a shame it has to be like this, Julia. I rather liked you." He drew alongside the cart until he was only a few feet away.

"Derek? What are you doing?" I could hear the faint promise of hysteria in my voice as I stared at the freckled face in disbelief.

"Getting away," he said. "At least, I was until I saw you rummaging about in my bags."

"*Your* bags?"

"Well, they're not Cyril's." He grinned, gesturing his head towards the young man lying in a heap on the ground.

"What did you do to him?" I gasped.

"Cold cocked him. He'll be all right in an hour or so, other than a headache. Which is what you have now become, dear Julia." His eyes shifted from my face to look over my shoulder. I heard the sound of hooves approaching, but was too frightened to take my eyes off Derek and the barrel of the gun. My hopes leapt that it would be Nick, or someone who could help me, but as I watched Derek's face I knew I was wrong.

A horse passed me with another tethered behind it. The rider came to a halt and dismounted. I was stunned into utter silence.

"Jesus, Derek. Put that bloody gun away!" Felicity

barked at him. "You're taking this a little too far."

"She knows," he said.

"Oh." Felicity looked at me and shook her head. "Honestly, Julia. I thought you were different, but like most of the help, you have a propensity for sticking your nose in the wrong places."

"I don't understand. Felicity, what on earth is going on? What has Derek made you do?"

She roared with laughter. "Derek? Good God, woman. Is it any wonder our sex never amounts to much. There's always the assumption that the man is in charge. But in this case, dear girl, it is quite the reverse. Derek reports to me." She glowered at him. "I thought it was just going to be you and a couple of guards?"

"It was. But it got changed at the last minute. I had to improvise." He waved the gun towards the prostrate form of Cyril. "I haven't taken care of Klaus, yet."

It was clear what his intentions were. What should I do…what could I do? My mind raced, but fear robbed my thoughts, my instincts. How could Felicity Babcock be responsible for a smuggling operation? What else was she capable of doing? "Felicity," I said, forcing my voice to sound calm. "Why are you doing this? You have to stop, before it's too late."

Her brown eyes flickered across my face. "You're such an innocent; do you know that? You took one look at me and immediately drew the same opinion as everybody else. Amelia's sidekick, her plain little shadow." She gave a heavy sigh. "Everyone underestimates me, Julia. Amelia, Pops, Trevor, Nick and now you." Felicity stepped closer. I didn't move as Derek still had the gun levelled on me.

"I suppose that's been a good thing, though—made

it easier to get the diamonds in and out, right under their pompous noses, well, at least until they started causing trouble." She sighed. "But that is all in the past. This time we're travelling with our shipment, and I will finally be free of this godforsaken country. I just wish Amelia had been here to see me succeed. That would have put her nose out of joint."

I looked at her face, and then at Derek, and suddenly it all became shockingly clear. They were the killers. Something had happened which threatened their plans, and they had silenced their victims.

"You killed Amelia." It was not an accusation.

"My, aren't you clever," she almost purred with pride. It sickened me, but I continued anyway. "And your own brother too?"

She laughed. "Brother? Trevor was a damned pervert. Do you think the servants were the only women he took liberties with?" I could see the brightness of her eyes as they threatened tears. "I should have done it years ago. The rotten bastard deserved it."

"And Amelia? Did she deserve it? I thought you were her best friend?"

"I was," she snapped. "Until she overheard Derek and me at the Mombasa Club. She threatened to blackmail us both unless we brought her in on our little arrangement. I wasn't going to have that. She'd held herself above me for far too long."

"But why did you shoot Nick?" I said. "He'd done nothing to hurt you."

"Oh, that was me," said Derek. "He was starting to pry, and we were close to our last shipment. I couldn't let him ruin all our hard work.

"I always liked Nick," Felicity said in a tone as

though we discussed the weather. "Until he let his brother rut with that African bitch. That's when everything had to change."

"You mean Martin Fleming?" I was confused. "What did Nick's brother have to do with any of this?"

Felicity's eyes narrowed. "I loved Martin my entire life. Did you know that our parents always planned for the two of us to be married, and join Jacaranda and Meadowbrook together. But I caught him rutting with that dirty Maasai, and that was the end of my dream."

"Did you kill Martin?" Now my voice shook. Felicity was an absolute madwoman.

"Not exactly," she said with a hint of a smile. "But I might have done something to his rifle, so it didn't fire correctly." She gave a sudden frown. "Enough of your questions, Julia. We don't have time for this. Derek?" She gestured to the cart. "Take care of that while I do something with her."

Felicity reached out and grabbed the back of my hair so tightly I cried out in pain. As my eyes watered, my mind clouded, and an image dropped into my thoughts. It was a man, laughing while he pulled my head back by my hair as he assaulted my naked body. A wave of anger suffused my senses, and I roared out loud as I twisted away, my arms rising up to knock Felicity away. She shouted in surprise and then rushed back at me, but I was ready, meeting her head on as we clashed against one another. Both of us grappled to grasp a handful of hair or flesh.

"Derek!" she shouted at the top of her voice. But he was already in the cart. She threw a punch to my face, but my skin was wet with sweat, and her knuckles slid off without harming me. I moved my foot behind her ankle and then kicked her as hard as I could. Felicity's leg gave way. She lost her balance and fell awkwardly to the ground just as the sound of a gun blasted. I froze where I was. She stayed on the ground and started laughing.

"Well done, Julia. Aren't you the scrapper? Pity that won't help you now. This is one problem you can't charm your way out of." She beamed with confidence, but I watched it drain away as Felicity's expression changed to one of alarm when she realised the identity of the person holding the gun.

"It appears that you're the one with the problem now, Felicity," Nick said.

Chapter Twenty-Four

CYRIL HAD A ROTTEN HEADACHE, but fortunately for him, that was the worst of his injuries. By the time Captain Burnham arrived, the scene was in order.

Mr Edge, who'd accompanied Nick, though out of our range of vision, had apparently snuck into the cart. There he'd waited, and accosted Derek as soon as he'd climbed into the cart to finish off Klaus. His actions were camouflaged by my fighting with Felicity. Once Derek's weapon was secured, Nick had shown himself.

I had so many questions to ask, but Nick assured me we'd discuss everything once we were back at Jacaranda. For now, I waited while a second cart brought by Captain Burnham was driven forward. Felicity and Derek were handcuffed and placed under arrest, and then along with Derek's bags, put in the cart with several constables who were to guard them, one being Cyril, who wanted the satisfaction of seeing Derek taken to the gaol.

As they prepared to leave, I suddenly remembered what I had hidden in my pocket. "Captain Burnham!" I called out and ran to his horse.

He steered the mount in my direction. "What is it, ma'am?"

I reached up and handed him the small velvet pouch. "I think you might be looking for these. I found them in Derek's bag. There's a hollowed-out book in there too, filled with money."

"I'll be damned," he said with a hoot. "Well done, well done indeed!"

With a wave, he whirled his horse and caught up with Mr Edge to ride alongside the cart. Two other constables had already departed in Nick's cart with Klaus Schmitt and left for Mombasa at a fast pace.

By silent agreement, we did not speak on the ride home. Nick was tired as he was still recovering from his accident, and I was exhausted from all the anguish and shock of my experience. We rode at a canter, Mzuka following behind, and arrived back at the house relatively quickly.

I slid off my horse and did not protest when Kijani took the reins from me and led the horse away. Nick dismounted, and as Malaika ran out of the front door, he asked her to help me inside and to draw me a bath. Wilson appeared from the kitchen and promised to bring me a cup of tea. Within the hour, I had been bathed and dressed by Malaika, brought a hot sweet tea by Wilson, and sat contented on the verandah watching Akina play with the baby on her little rug. Juba brought me a slice of Battenburg cake, and I shared it with Akina, and I finally felt myself relax.

Before she left, I gave Akina one of my bracelets as a thank-you for taking such good care of Nalah. It was a cheap charm bracelet I had purchased years ago in a small shop in Newcastle. It had a small horse, a dog, a cat and a bird as charms, and by the young girl's reaction, you would have thought I had given her gold. She was so happy that she hugged me, and her eyes were wide with elation. I told her to keep it close, and as she left for home, I hoped no one in the village would take it away from her.

I spent the rest of my afternoon with Nalah, and it seemed I had not seen the baby in days, though in reality, it was since the party the previous evening. We played, and then I fed and bathed her before putting her down for the night.

Malaika came to my room and informed me that the American gentlemen were staying overnight in Mombasa and that it would be just Nick and myself at dinner. She then asked if I would help her compose a letter to a mission school near Nairobi, where she might be able to gain a position to train as a teacher. I was delighted and told her I would be glad to help.

When she had gone, I left my room and crossed the hall to Amelia's bedroom. Knowing what I now knew about her, I felt comfortable being amongst her possessions. Nick's wife had been the type of person I would never have befriended, for she seemed to have more in common with Felicity than me. But that she was killed so brutally made me sympathetic and sorry she'd been so badly betrayed. Considering what was known about how she died, Felicity and Derek had been barbaric.

I opened her cupboard as I had countless times now, and as I examined the dresses, I saw a plain gown in a beautiful hue similar to the blossoms of the Jacaranda trees that had made such an impact upon me when I first arrived. It was perfect. I would wear it tonight.

As soon as I walked into the living room, I could tell by one look at his face that Nick approved of my dress choice. He passed me a sherry. "You look lovely in that shade of blue. It brings out the spectacular colour of your eyes."

"Thank you. It is, of course, one of Amelia's. She had excellent taste in clothing."

"I'll say," he chuckled. "And expensive."

"Dinner, she is served." Announced Juba from the open doors to the dining room, and we both walked towards the houseboy.

Wilson had prepared roast lamb, roast potatoes, peas, and carrots. The food smelled delicious, and at once I was suddenly starved as though I had not eaten in weeks.

"Did you manage to rest at all today?" Nick asked as I passed the mint sauce to put on his lamb.

"Not really. Though I had a nice afternoon with the girls. How are you? You are the one convalescing."

"I will not lie. I was rather exhausted. I fell asleep and did not wake until an hour ago."

I wondered how he must feel, knowing two people he called friends had been responsible for the death of his wife and an attempt on his as well. I watched as he ate his meal. There were still dark shadows underneath his eyes, and his skin had a pallor to it showing he was not quite back to his normal state of health.

I sighed. "It was a very eventful, not to mention shocking day. Have you had a chance to absorb it all yet?"

"No," he said plainly. "And I am not sure I ever will." He took a sip of his drink. "I really feel for Pops Babcock. A double blow for him. The man has no one left."

I did not respond to that, nor did I mention what Felicity had told me about her brother. That could wait for another day. "Tell me. What made you and Mr Edge come after us? If you had not, I might be dead."

Nick set down his knife and fork and pushed his empty plate to one side. "It's all down to Freddy. The man has such a sharp mind. He already suspected Derek of being up to no good—apparently, he'd been watching him for several days. I think the handgun was a clue, and there were some other behaviours that aroused his suspicion. In truth, Klaus was out of the woods last night. He told Freddy everything he knew about Derek's involvement, but could not identify the other person, Felicity as it turned out.

Freddy knew Klaus was going to make it and wasn't concerned the journey to Mombasa would harm him. But he slipped him a sleeping draft to keep him knocked out so that Derek would believe he was in a coma.

When you decided to go along with Derek, it changed the plan. Although you posed less of a threat to Derek, which could help keep his guard down. Migali would be on your trail, and Edge and I would be right behind him, though we stayed off the road which slowed us down.

Once we caught up with you, Edge slipped into the cart, and I had my gun trained on Derek the entire time. I knew he wouldn't do anything until the other person arrived. I just never imagined it would be Felicity."

"It was still risky," I said. "Both Cyril and I could have been shot."

"Yes, you are correct. I wasn't there when you decided you were going to escort Klaus to Mombasa. When I found out you were with Derek I was livid with Freddy for allowing you to go. I'm so sorry you were put in harm's way."

"It was rather frightening," I agreed. "But it turned out for the best in the end. It's all so sad, though. Many have lost their lives because of the greed of one unhappy, dissatisfied woman. Were you aware Felicity loved your brother?"

He nodded as Juba claimed our empty plates. "Yes. Martin liked her well enough, but not romantically. I don't think he ever encouraged her affections."

"Felicity didn't need him to, from what I can tell. Once she decided she wanted him, that was that."

"Yes. That wicked woman single-handedly took away my wife, my unborn child, and my brother." Nick said quietly. "If Nalah's mother, Barika, had lived, Lord knows what Felicity would have done to her as well." He thanked Juba as he placed a bowl of rice pudding before him, then continued. "Thank God it's all over. Of course, there will be a hell of a trial, and everything will get raked up again. The newspapers will have a field day."

"At least you'll be exonerated once and for all. The nasty gossips will be silenced, and you can get on with your life."

His silver eyes swung up to look directly into my face. "Yes. And that is something."

After our meal, I encouraged Nick to turn in. Though it would have been pleasant to sit outside and continue our discussion, he needed rest. There would be time for talking tomorrow.

Later, as I lay in my bed under the white mosquito netting, I watched a tiny lizard race across the ceiling, while my mind replayed a kaleidoscope of the day's horrific events.

And then slowly, very slowly, my thoughts wandered to a different scene. When Nick Fleming had held my hand in his and kissed it tenderly.

Now that all the secrets were finally out in the open, I wondered what the future would bring.

Chapter Twenty-Five

I AWOKE TO HEAR THE BABY CHATTERING in the nursery. The sun shone bright outside my curtains, and I realised the hour was late. In the kitchen, Wilson greeted me with my morning cup of chai, and as usual, took the baby from my arms to give her a bottle. I had already missed breakfast.

"*Bwana* say he back for luncheon, Will see *Memsahib* then." He pulled funny faces at the baby, who giggled as she downed her milk. I ate some toast and then changed the baby once more before going in search of Malaika.

WE SPENT MOST OF THE morning sitting out on the verandah working on Malaika's application letter to send to the Nyondo Missionary School in Rabai, a small town north of Mombasa. I enjoyed spending time with the young woman and felt great pride in her efforts to better her education and give back to her village. Nalah fell asleep on her play mat, and rather than disturb her, I settled back into my chair while Malaika read back through her letter once again.

I started when Migali appeared in the doorway. The man was so tall and muscular, yet he moved with the agility and quietness of a cat. Malaika saw him and tensed.

"Malaika. You should take Migali into the kitchen and prepare him something to eat. He has been working very hard these past few days." I had no idea of his tasks, but I wanted them to spend some time together, regardless of their situation. The beautiful African woman set down her papers, gave me a tiny smile and went inside the house. I stared at the peaceful, sleeping baby, and took pleasure that there was finally a calm.

BY THE MIDDLE OF THE AFTERNOON, everything had changed. Nick had not come home for lunch but sent one of the workers to pick up a sandwich for him as he could not get away. I was back outside again, enlisting the help of the bright sunlight to see my stitching while I sewed.

The peace was broken at the sound of Captain Burnham galloping down the driveway with Mr Edge close behind. I wondered if American men were always quite so loud, boisterous and in a hurry.

"Hello there, Miss Julia!" Burnham said as he bounded up the verandah steps.

"Captain, it is good to see you. Let me get you a cool drink, and you can tell me all about Mombasa."

"That would be mighty fine," he said agreeably and took a seat. "Mr Edge will join us presently," he added.

I came back with a tray bearing three glasses of lemonade. The captain took one and practically drained the entire thing, then he set the glass down and gave a large sigh of pleasure.

"That was sorely needed, I can tell you. Now, first things first. I'll fill you in on all that's happened since yesterday." He leaned back in the chair, made himself comfortable, then removed his wide-brimmed hat and laid it on his knee. "Schmitt is recovering well. No infection, and he should be out of the hospital in a week or so."

"He will be in a great deal of trouble, will he not?"

"Yes, it is likely. Mr Edge and I will put in a good word for him as his information was critical in apprehendin' the real villains. Also, he does not appear to have any involvement with any of the murders. As for Derek Walker and Felicity Babcock, well, there ain't no other way than to speak plainly. They'll both hang, unless they are found insane, in which case it will be the madhouse, Bedlam, most likely."

I thought of Felicity and how friendly she had been, how she had played with the baby. Derek, and his jolly laugh, his welcome to me when I first arrived—all of it a sham. It was depressing. And though they had been evil and caused such sorrow, I still could not take any pleasure in their fates.

When Mr Edge joined us, he told us he had telegrammed his employers, who were delighted with the results of the situation. They would also encourage some leniency towards Klaus Schmitt due to his helpful information. "And you, ma'am, you are to get a reward."

"I beg your pardon?"

"There has been a reward posted for information leading to the capture of the diamond thieves. If you hadn't overheard Schmitt that night, none of this would have happened."

I wasn't sure I liked this. Granted, I was doing my duty, but I did not want responsibility for the punishment all three would receive.

"Now, don't you go worryin' yourself and feelin'

guilty," the captain said. "Those folks brought it on themselves. It was their choice to break the law, and there's no justifyin' murder, not under any circumstance."

He had a point. I nodded glumly.

"Like I was sayin', ma'am," Mr Edge continued. "The de Graaff Company will need you to open a bank account in Mombasa, and then they will transfer three hundred of your British pounds for your pleasure."

I gasped. It was a small fortune for someone like me—several years wages at least. "Are you certain? That seems a large amount of money..." I stammered.

"A drop in the ocean to those folks," said Burnham. "Besides, what you went through because of my poor judgement, you earned every cent of it."

DINNER WOULD BE SERVED LATE THAT EVENING. The American gentlemen were preparing for their permanent departure the next morning, and Nick was delayed. A strange mood had taken me. Perhaps due to the past weeks being so unusual, the events too wild to imagine, not to mention my close call with death. I felt saddened, and I suppose, in retrospect, it was about loss. In these past years, I had lost my parents, my livelihood, my innocence, my child, and to some degree, my country. In my new life here in Africa, I had sought a new beginning. But it, too, had been blighted by death, the ghost of Amelia, the murder of Trevor, the shock of betrayal.

I sat in the rocking chair with Nalah in my arms, lost in thought, until I realised she was sound asleep. Normally I tried not to fuss over her at bedtime, but tonight I needed to feel her warm little body close to mine—I was restless and out of sorts. I continued rocking her a while, and then gently set her in her bed and quietly stole away.

It would be another hour until dinner was served. I could hear voices coming from the living room and imagined Mr Edge and Captain Burnham having a predinner drink. But I did not want their company. I wanted fresh air.

I told Juba I was going to go for a quick walk, and then left out of the back door. The day was ending, and I greeted one or two Kikuyu who were on their way home. I passed the huts but did not stop to speak to Malaika. How she had disliked me in the beginning. It was good to be on a better footing with her. I wished her the very best in both of her worlds, that of becoming a teacher and perhaps becoming Migali's wife.

As I walked, I felt a cool shift in the air. I looked up seeing the perfect blue palette of the day, painted with clouds that floated like graceful dancers in the sky. I pressed on.

When I reached Derek's bungalow, I stopped walking and stood in front of the empty place, thinking. I pictured his smiling freckled face, ruddy hair, his ready smile and then the angry, twisted expression of a crazed man holding a gun. It was all too much. I had seen so much anger, so much hatred in the quarter-century I had been alive. I did not want any part of it. I turned away and walked a little farther, following a well-trodden path I hadn't been down before.

It was strange to think that now I had money. Tomorrow, Nick would take me to Mombasa, and I would open a bank account for the very first time in my life. Three hundred pounds was a small fortune, enough that I could leave Kenya and go anywhere I wanted. But I could never go back to England—the Ratcliffes had seen to that. I would be arrested for thieving, and who knows what would happen to me?

It was so unfair. The bud of self-pity threatened to bloom as it did periodically, but then Amelia's face came into my mind, and I realised how very lucky I was to still be alive.

How ironic that my promise to discover her fate had come to a conclusion. Indirectly, of course, but there was now no mystery. Amelia's death had been the beginning of a series of losses which Nick, like me, had endured. How similar our paths were. Nick had Nalah but no other, and I was alone in the world too. Both of us had almost been killed by the same man we considered a friend, and Nick had also dealt with Felicity's deadly duplicity.

I continued walking, completely absorbed in thinking about the journey that had led me from Chessington to Jacaranda...and Nick.

A noise jolted me from my contemplation. It was a gazelle, a mother, with her youngster alongside. She saw me and froze. I stopped moving, and after a moment, she perceived me as no threat and they both leapt away.

Where was I? I looked about me and realised I had wandered much farther away than I'd intended. The path had led me to the base of a steep grassy rise, almost a hill. Several Acacia trees were dotted in front of me, but it looked as though the ground dropped away beyond them.

I'd never been here before. Curious, I moved

forward and then saw the land did indeed slope down, and at the bottom was a muddy pool of water.

It wasn't much larger than the pond at Ham Common, where my mother had taken me frequently to watch the boys sail their little boats. But this pond had no toys sailing the waters, but wildlife. There were at least a dozen antelope and zebra drinking at the shoreline.

Momentarily I was lost in the beauty the sight presented, until I remembered I had no weapon to defend myself should I need it. I turned to go and started in surprise as Nick approached.

"Julia Rossington, will you never learn? What is the first rule of being out alone," he said softly, without reprimand.

"Take a rifle," I replied quietly. "But in my defence, I had not intended walking so far. I was lost in my thoughts. Nick, I had no idea this place was even here." I gestured to the pool below.

"This is the watering hole I told you about," his voice was muted. I surmised it was intentional so he would not frighten away the wildlife. "Here, let us sit for a while and see who comes along. No, not there," he said hurriedly, pointing to a moving black line as wide as my finger which moved across the grass.

"What's that?" I asked, leaning over for a closer look.

"Those are Soldier Ants, though I believe the correct term is *Siafu*. They're huge ants that move about in thick columns when searching for food. See how uniform their ranks are?"

"Are they harmful?"

"Not to humans, though they've a nasty bite as

they have strong jaws. They'll march straight through anything in their path and can devour insects and rodents in minutes. Come, let's move over here and out of their way." He walked a few steps further along, and I followed.

Once we were seated, Nick lay down the rifle and leaned back on his elbows. He winced immediately and sat bolt upright again. "I keep forgetting my damn shoulder isn't quite back to normal."

"Not only your shoulder, but it also feels like everything is upside down at the moment."

"Yes, you're right. I'll be glad to return to some semblance of normalcy, though I'm not sure anything will ever be the same again. I need my full strength back so I can pick up where I left off with the plans for our tea crop. There may even be more land available now the British are moving their headquarters to Nairobi. I'm sure some of the farmers will go there and try their hand growing coffee."

I turned to look at his profile, his strong nose, the scar through his eyebrow. "What about you? Will you move inland as well?"

"No," he said firmly and looked my way. "Jacaranda will stay in my family as long as I can work it. I could never leave the place, the people." He pointed to the water below us, where a family of warthogs had arrived. "I would never have this in my own back garden. There is nothing better than being here."

He fell silent, and we watched for a while as the activity seemed to grow more intense. A lone giraffe arrived and spread his legs out wide to dip his long neck low enough to take a drink.

I looked out to the horizon, at the sun sinking low, a ball of flaming orange as it fell from the sky. The land below it turned from green to black shadows while the silhouettes of trees were like giants walking the earth.

When the silence suddenly came, it was palpable. The animals backed away from the pool, and beside me Nick's body stiffened. He reached slowly to pick up his rifle, laid it upon his lap, then turned to me with his finger on his lips. The light was growing dim, but the pool was still illuminated by the sun's orange glow.

When I first saw him, I caught my breath. He had materialised from the darkness like a spectre. His lithe, sleek body moved stealthily towards the water. The black leopard, or *roho,* Spirit, as the Africans called him. Reaching the pond, he drank thirstily, frequently pausing, turning his head from side to side, staying vigilant.

"He's beautiful," I whispered.

The leopard stopped drinking and his head snapped up sharply. He lifted his nose in the air and tried to find our scent. I could hear Nick's breath as he rested his hand on the rifle.

I knew the instant the leopard caught our scent. He backed out of the water and stared in our direction. Then he moved around the pool towards the base of the slope.

"Don't move," whispered Nick, and his right-hand pressed on my leg emphasising the point.

We watched, mesmerised as the leopard advanced up the slope. My heart beat furiously as instinct prepared me to flee. Yet, I was totally absorbed in watching the marvellous cat, hypnotised by his purposeful steady advance.

When he reached the crest, he was but thirty yards away from where we sat, captivated. He stopped, he stared, and his long tail twitched. He was taking our measure.

Nick lifted the rifle.

"No," I said softly. "Please."

The cat did not move. He continued to look at us. And then, with almost a perceptible shrug, he slowly turned around and went back the way he had come, disappearing into the night as easily as he had arrived.

I let out the breath I had been holding. "Oh my," was all I could say.

Nick got to his feet and held out his good arm to pull me up. "Come on, we should get back to the house. It will be completely dark in ten minutes, and that fellow might not be as friendly next time our paths cross." I took his hand and stood.

"Thank you for not shooting him, Nick," I said as we made our way back towards the path leading to Jacaranda.

"Animals aren't here for us to kill, Julia. I am fully aware I'm in their territory and not the other way around. Yet even in the wild, it is the survival of the fittest, and man has the upper hand." As we walked, he slung the rifle on his back and then grasped my hand. "Hold onto me as it's hard to see where you step."

His grip was firm, his skin rough and calloused from hard work. I liked how it felt touching him, liked how just the feel of his hand gave me safety, protection. When we reached Derek's bungalow, the chatter of creatures was louder, therefore the predator was no longer close. But still Nick kept hold of my hand, and I didn't protest.

A little further along, Nick abruptly stopped walking. The hand that held mine tugged so that I turned, and we were face to face. His eyes were dark as pewter in the oncoming evening, but I was close enough to see him plainly. Nervously, I wetted my lips. What was he going to do?

His eyes flicked to my mouth, and his own parted. "Julia," he said softly. "I very much want to kiss you." His fingers tightened on my hand and lifted it to his lips. I felt the graze of his stubble against my skin.

I swallowed. The air was thick with something wild and primitive that engulfed the land and burned between us. What was this bond I felt with Nick? How could he have such magnetism that drew me to him regardless of me fighting my desire?

"What troubles you?" His eyes narrowed as he searched my face. "Do you want me to go?"

I shook my head, seeking the words which hid from my tongue. "No, please don't. I'm conflicted, confused by what I feel for you, Nick. Part of me wants to abandon all my thoughts and run into your arms, while the other voice in my head warns me to run away."

He nodded and took a step closer. His free hand cupped my chin, and he tilted it upwards and looked deep into my eyes. "Julia," he said softly. "You've had such sorrow in your past. It's only natural for you not to trust anyone with your heart." The hand which held mine pressed it against his chest. "I'm not perfect. I'm flawed and broken. But though I'm scared to let you have it, I give you my heart to keep or discard." He pulled me closer until our bodies touched, and his eyes were bright with emotion.

"I love you, Julia. Though I have fought it, you have got into my blood as deeply as this land. Your being here has made Jacaranda a real home once again, and I cannot bear to think of you being anywhere but here, with me." He bent down, and his mouth claimed mine.

My eyes closed, my head fell back as my arms found him and wrapped tight about his waist and then moved to lock around his neck. He plundered my lips, his kiss so fierce, so hungry, it took away my breath. And yet I clung on, my fingers climbing through his hair, digging into his scalp. I wanted to step inside his skin, and only then would I be close enough to this wonderful, passionate man.

Nick broke the kiss yet kept his face close to mine as we panted like wild beasts preparing to fight. "Will you be mine, Julia?"

"I already am," I whispered.

Epilogue

THE HOUSE SEEMED QUIET WITHOUT THE rambunctious American gentlemen. They had been gone the better part of two months now, and slowly Jacaranda returned to normal.

Nick stayed out in the fields longer each day as he trained Migali as the new farm manager. This was only possible with the permission of Migali's father, who, as an elder, carried the right to deny his son. The promise of a regular payment sweetened the arrangement. Migali would retain many duties required by his village. But as his father was still young, it was likely to be many years before Migali inherited his important position within the tribe.

Yesterday, I had travelled to Mombasa with Malaika, and we visited the National Bank of India, where I had my new account. There, I opened another account in Malaika's name, and transferred fifteen pounds into it. This would cover her schooling costs with the missionaries at Rabai and purchase any items she needed once she arrived. She also had both Nick's and my promise to purchase as many heads of cattle as needed so that she could marry Migali. It was wonderful to help these two young people, and Jacaranda would benefit from their hard work.

Pops Babcock had decided to leave the area and

head inland to Nairobi with many other colonists. Meadowbrook held no good memories, and he was too old to run the farm alone. He sold his lease to Nick, who planned to use the land for the new tea crop. The Babcock house would be remodelled into a small school, with living quarters for Malaika when she returned. She and I had grand plans to not only teach the children, but their parents too.

Juba was promoted to run the house with Malaika now gone, and I hired Akina to take Juba's place, which pleased her greatly. She now had her own hut, and her independence—a more loyal friend I could not find.

Wilson was given a catalogue to order new pans and dishes for the kitchen. He was fascinated by the photographs in the book. When he wasn't working, he could not be separated from burying his nose in the pages.

My little Nalah was growing like a weed. I imagined she would be like her Maasai mother, tall and graceful, with the svelte body of a warrior. Though I thought of my darling James often, I still loved this baby as though I had carried her in my own womb.

It was dusk. My favourite part of the day. Akina fed the baby while I sat out on the verandah, staring up at the trees and seeing if I could spy any of the monkeys who were often on the lookout for food.

"There you are." Nick came out and took the seat next to me on the small rattan sofa. His hand reached over to take mine.

"How was it today?" I asked.

"Good," he said. "Migali hired another ten labourers to plough over at Meadowbrook, so that should help tremendously."

"He is turning into an exceptional farmer, is he not?"

"Indeed," Nick chuckled. "He'll give himself a bad name among the Maasai if he's not careful."

Juba appeared with a tall glass of lemonade and handed it to Nick.

"*Assante*," he said, taking the drink. When the young man left us, Nick draped his arm across the back of my seat and my shoulders. His fingers stroked my neck.

"How was your day, Mrs Fleming?" He called me that often, as though he still could not believe he had a wife.

I smiled. "It was most productive. Janet and the children called this morning."

"How is dear Janet? I really need to ride over and talk to Don. I have a question I need to ask him about his fertiliser."

"Fascinating," I said, "you men do cover some interesting topics."

Nick turned towards me and leaned over, so he faced me. His skin was sun-darkened and dusty from a day at work. I wrinkled my nose.

"I think you might need a bath, Mr Fleming. You smell rather like a turnip."

He raised his eyebrows and then kissed me quick and hard. "Your wish is my command."

WE HAD MARRIED AT JACARANDA, OUTSIDE and in front of friends and all the workers. A vicar had been brought in from Mombasa, and we held a giant picnic on the grounds in celebration. Though some thought it strange, the picnic was for everyone regardless of position or creed.

Hilary Paderborn had sewn my dress and done a marvellous job of it too. I had chosen Jacaranda blue for the fabric's colour, in tribute to Nick's mother and the place she had made a home. Malaika was my bridesmaid, and though it was an unorthodox ceremony, it was a wonderful day.

As a surprise to us, Migali invited some fellow warrior friends from his village to dance in our honour. These Maasai men towered above everyone, with their braided hennaed hair and ruddy coloured garments covering their torsos.

They lined up and began to sing in low tones, every few beats uttering a kind of grunt together, which sounded very intimidating. They moved in a snake-like line while they sang, still repeating the guttural sound, and then separated and spread out next to one another. The singing continued, as one by one, each jumped straight up vertically from a standing position to a great height indeed. As their feet touched the ground, there was a loud rattle, for affixed to their ankles were metal boxes filled with stones. Eventually, with loud whoops and cries, they jumped as one, each time landing with the loud rattle in unison. It was a spectacular sight, and we felt incredibly privileged to be gifted by their presence. It was a day I would never forget.

Nick had hired a man to take a special photograph of us after the ceremony, standing outside the house. This was a cherished possession of mine now. I had the framed picture on the dressing table in our bedroom.

It was there I waited now, while my husband finished with his bath down the hall. I lay back on our bed, closing my eyes until I heard the soft pad of Nick's feet on the rug when he came into the room, shutting the door behind him. I opened my eyes to see him drop his towel, standing naked before me. I raised up on one elbow and gave him my full appraisal.

"You're not bashful, are you?" I said, laughing.

"The body is a beautiful thing," he said, and added with a grin, "especially yours." Nick moved to get onto the bed, and I made room for him. He lay down, his wet hair on the pillows, and he pulled me over to him so that my head rested on his shoulder, which had finally healed.

We lay still for a moment, the top of my head touching his chin, his arm wrapped around me.

"Nick?"

"Hmm?" He was sleepy.

"There was a reason Janet came today."

"Was there?" I could tell he wasn't really listening.

"I needed her medical advice."

Nothing. Then he moved abruptly, and my head fell to the pillow. His face was suddenly inches away from mine, and his eyes alert. "What? What is wrong? Tell me at once!"

I chuckled. "Calm down. It's nothing to worry about." I grasped his hand, brought it to my mouth and kissed it, and then I took it, flattened his palm, and rested it against my stomach.

Nick frowned. I pressed his hand once again.

He did not speak, but much to my amazement I saw moisture well in his lovely silver eyes. He blinked it away.

"It won't be the baby you lost when Amelia died," I whispered. "Nor will it be my James. But whoever this little person is, it'll be ours."

Nick kissed me then. A long, loving kiss which told me more than he could ever say in words. And as he took me into his arms, I felt the warmth of his skin, and became wrapped in the heat of his love.

Later, much later, when we lay sated in the rumpled sheets of our bed, I listened to the steady breathing of my sleeping husband by my side. And far off in the distance, I heard the low, sultry call of a black leopard.

The Secret of Jacaranda

About the Author

Jude Bayton is a Londoner, who currently resides in the American Midwest. An avid photographer and traveller, Jude enjoys writing about places close to her heart. To keep up with her latest releases and her monthly blog, subscribe to at judebayton.com

Find Jude Bayton at:
judebayton.com
Facebook: Jude Bayton
Twitter: @judebayton
Email: author@judebayton.com

Other Books

By Jude Bayton
The Secret of Mowbray Manor
The Secret of Hollyfield House
The Secret of Pendragon Island
The Secret of Lorelei Lodge

Printed in Great Britain
by Amazon

45247359R00185

Daniel Glattauer

GESCHENKT

Roman

Deuticke

Als *Wunder von Braunschweig* wird eine Serie zahlreicher anonymer Bargeld-Spenden in Braunschweig an soziale und karitative Einrichtungen sowie unverschuldet in Not geratene Einzelpersonen bezeichnet, die im November 2011 begann.

1 2 3 4 5   18 17 16 15 14

ISBN 978-3-552-06257-3
Alle Rechte vorbehalten
© Deuticke im Paul Zsolnay Verlag Wien 2014
Satz: Eva Kaltenbrunner-Dorfinger, Wien
Druck und Bindung: CPI – Ebner & Spiegel, Ulm
Printed in Germany

MIX
Papier aus verantwortungs-
vollen Quellen
FSC® C006701

GESCHENKT

KAPITEL EINS

Manuel

Meinen Sohn hätte ich mir anders vorgestellt. Ich blickte
manchmal vom Bildschirm auf und tat so, als würde ich nachdenken. Eigentlich beobachtete ich aber Manuel – nämlich
dabei, wie er sich unbeobachtet fühlte, und er sah gar nicht
souverän dabei aus. Ich hielt es offen gestanden für eine Zumutung, dass er Manuel hieß, eine Zumutung ihm und mir
gegenüber. Warum hatte man mich nicht gefragt? Ich hätte
Manuel nicht zugelassen, ich hätte Manuel verhindert, Manuel, den Namen, jedenfalls. Manuel, den Menschen ... was
soll ich sagen, das war eben höheres Schicksal. Mein Schicksal war regelmäßig eine Spur zu hoch für mich. Okay, wenn
es wenigstens jemals oben geblieben wäre. Aber nein, irgendwann kam jedes meiner höheren Schicksale zu mir herunter
und sagte »Guten Tag«. In diesem Fall in Form meines vierzehnjährigen Sohnes.

Der zehnte Tag mit Manuel an meiner Seite verlief unspek-
takulär, wie beinahe alle Montage in diesem Jahr. Dienstage
eigentlich auch. An Mittwochen nahm ich mir oft frei, und
der Rest der Woche verging irgendwie automatisch. Die Bedeutung dieses Montags erschloss sich mir erst sehr viel später,
und da habe ich durchaus Hochachtung vor meinem dreiundvierzig Jahre alten und von Alkohol empfindlich getrübten
Gedächtnis, dass es in der Lage war, im Nachhinein so viele Bilder und O-Töne zusammenzutragen, die meisten von meinem
Sohn, der bei mir im Büro saß und Schulaufgaben machte
oder zumindest so tat.

»Und, kommst du zurecht?«, fragte ich.

»Warum soll ich nicht zurechtkommen?«

Vielleicht waren alle vierzehnjährigen Vollpubertären mit Graswuchs über der Oberlippe und einer Stimmlage zwischen unsachgemäß bedienter Violine und vergammeltem Bass so abweisend, keine Ahnung, mich nervte es jedenfalls.

»Ich will nicht wissen, warum du nicht zurechtkommen sollst, ich will wissen, ob du zurechtkommst oder nicht«, erwiderte ich.

»Wer hat behauptet, dass du wissen willst, warum ich nicht zurechtkommen soll?«, fragte er.

Er fragte es deshalb, weil er wusste, dass ich mich auf so eine stumpfsinnige Diskussion sicher nicht einlassen würde und dass unser Dialog damit beendet war. Eines der Probleme in meiner noch ziemlich neuen Beziehung zu meinem Sohn war nämlich, dass mich Manuel nicht ausstehen konnte. Das erklärte auch all die trüben, leeren und über der Gähngrenze gelangweilten Blicke, mit denen er mich nun schon die zweite Woche bedachte. Sie spiegelten nur wider, was er sah: mich. Hätte er gewusst, dass ich sein Vater war, hätte er mich zwar wahrscheinlich auch nicht gemocht, aber er wäre vielleicht gnädiger zu mir gewesen.

Nein, er wusste es nicht. Und ich wusste es offen gestanden auch erst seit wenigen Wochen.

Alice

Im Frühsommer hatte mich Alice angerufen und bedauert, dass wir überhaupt keinen Kontakt mehr hatten. Ob wir uns nicht wieder mal treffen wollten, sie hätte jede Menge Neuigkeiten. Mit Alice hatte ich eigentlich nicht mehr gerechnet. Mit Tanja, mit Kathi, mit Brigitte, vielleicht mit Corinna, ja eventuell sogar mit Sonja, aber nicht mit Alice. Ich hätte auch niemals gedacht, dass es ihr noch in diesem Leben leid tun könnte, keinen Kontakt mehr zu mir zu haben, nach ihrem damaligen Abgang, aber so konnte man sich in den Menschen täuschen, in den Frauen sowieso, da war ich gewissermaßen ein Naturtalent.

»Ja, sicher, treffen wir uns, gerne. Wo?«, fragte ich.

»Am besten bei mir«, sagte sie.

Am besten bei mir. Diese Worte übten eine ziemliche Faszination auf mich aus, und wenn Männer es schaffen, hier nicht in eine ganz bestimmte Richtung zu denken, noch dazu im Frühsommer, in dem sie überdies gerade ungebunden sind, dann herzlichen Glückwunsch. Ich schaffte es jedenfalls nicht. Um die drei Tage bis zu der Verabredung zu überbrücken, kramte ich die alten Fotos von Alice hervor, von unserem Wochenende in Hamburg, und ich hoffte, dass sie nicht mehr als ein halbes Kilo pro Jahr zugenommen hatte. Mit siebeneinhalb Kilo mehr könnte ich leben.

Wir hatten übrigens nur dieses einzige Hamburg-Wochenende gemeinsam verbracht, denn ich war damals noch mit Gudrun verheiratet gewesen, und Gudrun war im ungefähr siebenten Monat schwanger mit Florentina, was Alice beim Rückflug aus Hamburg zu meinem Leidwesen spitzgekriegt hatte, weil ich immer dann, wenn ich Angst habe, sozusagen ein offenes Buch bin. Und ich habe beträchtliche Flugangst. Ich kann niemandem verübeln, falls er jetzt denkt, dass ich ein Riesenarschloch war oder sogar noch bin, aber es ist eben nicht immer alles so, wie es aussieht, selbst wenn es verdammt danach aussieht. Doch zurück zum Wiedersehen mit Alice.

Eigentlich genügten mir die paar Sekunden an der Türschwelle, um zu erkennen, dass ich mich umsonst rasiert hatte. Ich brauche jetzt also gar nicht groß zu schildern, wie phantastisch man fünfzehn Jahre später noch immer aussehen konnte und wie gut es einem zu Gesicht stand, wenn man schnurgerade seinen Weg gegangen war, weil das im Fall Alice für mich leider überhaupt keine Rolle mehr spielte, da ich keine Rolle mehr für sie spielte. Sie hatte Medizin fertig studiert und arbeitete bei so was wie Ärzte ohne Grenzen, nur insofern dann doch begrenzt, als die ausschließlich Projekte in Afrika betreuten. Und Alice war gerade auf dem Sprung nach Somalia, wo sie ab September ein halbes Jahr lang einen neuen Stützpunkt aufbauen sollte. Das musste sie ausgerechnet mir, den sie nach einer Wochenend-Affäre vor fünfzehn Jahren zum Teufel geschickt hatte, ganz dringend berichten. Ich wusste nur noch nicht, warum.

»Und, Geri, was machst du so?«, fragte sie.

Das war doppelt beleidigend. *Geri* hieß, dass ich in ihren Augen für Gerold noch immer nicht reif genug war. Und *was machst du so* klang ganz danach, dass sie mir nicht zutraute, etwas mehr als nur *so* zu machen, *so* ins Blaue, *so* aus dem Ärmel, *so* nebenbei. Vermutlich sah man es mir an.

»Ich bin noch immer Journalist, aber nicht mehr bei der *Rundschau*, sondern bei einer kleineren ... äh ... Gratiszeitung, die wirst du nicht kennen. Ich betreue dort das Ressort Soziales.«

»Soziales? Das finde ich wunderbar«, sagte sie.

»Ja, wunderbar.«

»Und wo habt ihr eure Redaktion?«, fragte sie.

»In der Neustiftgasse.«

»Und hast du da ein eigenes Büro?«

Ich fand mein Leben ja auch nicht gerade spektakulär, aber eine etwas spannendere Nachfrage zum Thema *Fünfzehn Jahre Gerold Plassek* hatte ich schon verdient, fand ich.

»Ja, ich hab einen kleinen Büroraum.«

Beides war maßlos übertrieben, sowohl Büro als auch Raum, nur klein war richtig.

»Sehr fein«, sagte sie.

Dann druckste sie ein bisschen herum. Und schließlich erzählte sie mir von ihrem prächtigen Kind, das sie ganz allein großgezogen hatte. Es war ein Bub. Ein bereits großer Bub. Er war vierzehn Jahre alt. Er war ein Musterschüler, ging ins Gymnasium, hatte dort viele, viele, viele, ja unzählige Freunde, die dafür sorgten, dass er so fest verwurzelt war, dass er sich praktisch nicht mehr vom Fleck rühren konnte. An ein halbes Jahr Somalia war für ihn nicht im Traum zu denken. Er musste in Wien bleiben. Er konnte bei ihrer Schwester Julia wohnen und war weitgehend versorgt, bis auf ...

»Du hast einen vierzehnjährigen Sohn?«, fragte ich.

»Ja, genau.«

»Ich hab eine fünfzehnjährige Tochter.«

»Ja, ich weiß, ich kann rechnen«, sagte sie beziehungsweise fauchte sie wie Leslie, die Siamkatze meiner Exfrau, wenn man ihr zu nahe kam.

Ihr Bub war also weitgehend versorgt, fuhr sie fast schon übertrieben freundlich fort, bis auf die Nachmittage, die Zeit zwischen Schule und Julia sozusagen. Ihre Schwester Julia war nämlich Tanz- oder Fitnesstrainerin oder beides, und nachmittags gab sie daheim immer ihre Musikgymnastikstunden. Und da dachte Alice interessanterweise an mich, konkret an mich und meinen Büroraum.

»Manuel kann dort seine Hausaufgaben machen«, sagte sie.

Manuel? Nein, das konnte er nicht. Das ging nicht. Das war unmöglich. Das ließ der Chef nicht zu. Und würde er es zulassen, dann würde ich nicht zulassen, dass er es zuließ. Ich und ein vierzehnjähriger Bub namens Manuel, den ich weder kannte noch kennenlernen wollte, zu zweit in dieser tristen Kammer, das ging einfach nicht. Schon der Gedanke an einen Gedanken daran war denkunmöglich.

»Du hast doch sicher hundert Freunde, warum kommst du da ausgerechnet zu mir?«, fragte ich.

»Ich dachte, du und Manuel, das passt vielleicht.«

»Ich und ein fremder Vierzehnjähriger? Kannst du mir einen einzigen Grund nennen, warum das passen sollte?

»Einen einzigen?«

»Ja, nur einen einzigen«, wiederholte ich.

»Weil du Manuels Vater bist.«

»Was?«

»Weil du Manuels Vater bist.«

»Sag das noch mal.«

»Weil DU Manuels Vater bist.«

Das war tatsächlich ein Grund. Er löste bei mir eine dieser tiefen traumatischen Krisen aus, von denen es heißt, dass man dabei in einen Schockzustand verfällt und die Fakten aus Selbstschutz von sich wegschiebt, bis sie sich irgendwann nicht mehr wegschieben lassen und in die für Katastrophen zuständigen Gehirnzellen einsickern. (Die waren bei mir zum Glück in ständiger Bereitschaft.) Ich saß einige Stunden bei Alice, und wir tranken ein Glas Cognac – also es waren ein Glas und eine halbe Flasche, und Alice mochte keinen Cognac.

Sie saß kerzengerade auf der Sofakante und erklärte mir ausführlich, warum es besser war, dass sie mir meinen Sohn vierzehn Jahre lang verschwiegen hatte. Aber man konnte es auch auf eine kurze Formel bringen: Sie und Manuel hatten von mir als Vater eben in jeder Hinsicht nichts beziehungsweise in keiner Hinsicht irgendetwas zu erwarten gehabt. Das machte mich gleichzeitig wütend und traurig. Wütend deshalb, weil man sich so etwas nicht unbedingt sagen lassen musste als frischgebackener Vater. Und traurig deshalb, weil es wahrscheinlich stimmte.

Diesmal erwarteten sie aber etwas von mir, und da schaffte ich es einfach nicht, nein zu sagen. Es ging aber ohnehin nur um zwei, drei Stunden pro Tag, und das über lächerliche zwanzig Wochen. Und ich war ja auch irgendwie neugierig auf meinen Sohn.

»Weiß er, dass ich sein Vater bin?«, fragte ich.

»Noch nicht.«

»Mir wäre es nämlich lieber …«

»Ja, das dachte ich mir«, sagte sie.

Sie hatte ihren Sohn bereits auf einen »guten Freund aus alten Zeiten« vorbereitet.

»Sehr gut«, sagte ich.

Ein erstaunliches Geschenk

Es war also der zehnte Arbeitstag mit Manuel im Blickwinkel, und meine Neugierde auf einen eigenen Sohn war bereits sattsam gestillt. Ich konnte mir nicht vorstellen, dass wir beide es hier noch Tage, Wochen oder gar Monate miteinander aushalten würden, und wenn ich mir sein Gesicht ansah, konnte ich mir erst recht nicht vorstellen, dass er es sich vorstellen konnte. Das Schlimmste war, dass er einfach nicht bereit war, in menschenwürdiger Weise mit mir zu kommunizieren, egal welches Thema ich wählte.

»Beatles oder Stones?«, fragte ich zum Beispiel. Das war doch *die* Frage für einen Vierzehnjährigen! Ein einziges Wort hätte mir genügt, ich hätte sofort das Popgeschichte-Album eines halben Jahrhunderts für ihn aufgeblättert.

»Wie meinst du Beatles oder Stones?«, erwiderte er.

»Welche Musik gefällt dir besser, die von den Beatles oder die von den Rolling Stones?« Schon für diese Langversion, die klang, als würde man einem Alzheimer-Kranken einen Witz erklären, verachtete ich mich selbst.

»Muss ich darauf antworten?«, demütigte er mich weiter.

»Nein, du musst nicht antworten, aber es hätte mich einfach interessiert«, erwiderte ich.

»Also gut, mir gefällt beides nicht besonders.«

»Was für eine Musik gefällt dir denn besonders?«, setzte ich nach.

»Das kommt darauf an.« Ein Hoffnungsschimmer.

»Worauf kommt es an?«, fragte ich.

»Es kommt darauf an, welche Musik gerade gespielt wird.«

»Ja, darauf kommt es im Grunde immer an«, erwiderte ich. Damit war das Thema beendet. Und ich schwor mir, nie mehr das Wort an Manuel zu richten. Und wenn er mich weiter ächtete, würde ich ihn luftdicht verpacken und per Luftpost zu seiner Mama nach Somalia schicken.

Nun aber geschah etwas Außergewöhnliches, das diesen Tag für mich so nachhaltig besonders machen sollte: Norbert Kunz, mein Chef, rief mich in sein Büro. Es ging um einen Artikel in der Donnerstagsausgabe von *Tag für Tag*, der von mir stammte. An dieser Stelle muss ich ein bisschen ausholen, um meine Daseinsberechtigung und meine Aufgabengebiete bei der vom Großhandelskonzern Plus herausgegebenen Gratis-Tageszeitung *Tag für Tag* zu erläutern.

Nach meinem Absprung von der *Rundschau* – okay, es war eher ein Absturz als ein Absprung – holte mich Norbert Kunz zu *Tag für Tag*. Er hatte meine journalistische Arbeit immer sehr geschätzt, außerdem waren sein Vater und der Papa meiner Exfrau Gudrun enge Freunde, die noch dazu gemeinsam Golf spielten. Man sagt ja immer, Blut sei dicker als Wasser, aber so dick wie Golf ist nicht einmal Blut.

Am liebsten hätte ich in der Kultur-Abteilung gearbeitet, aber erstens gab es keine, weil *Tag für Tag* ein weitgehend kulturloses Blatt für ein weitgehend kulturloses Publikum war, und zweitens konnte ich es mir ohnehin nicht aussuchen. Ich war für die *bunten Meldungen zum Tag* zuständig und betreute die Leserbriefspalte. Wenn Sie sich fragen, was es bei Leserbriefen zu betreuen gab, dann sollten Sie einmal sehen, wozu Leser von *Tag für Tag* fähig waren. Mein drittes Aufgabengebiet war schließlich *Soziales*. Das nannte ich immer, wenn mich wer fragte, was ich so tat und worüber ich schrieb. Es klang freilich sozialer und vor allem aufwendiger, als es war. Denn abgesehen von einem Seebeben mit zehntausend Toten – darunter aber bitte mindestens fünf Österreicher – war *Tag für Tag* kein Elend elendig genug, um etwa einer Werbeeinschaltung für Gartenlaubenheizgeräte den Platz wegzunehmen. Das Problem beim *Sozialen* war, dass niemand dafür inserierte und dass es also kein Geld abwarf. Denn vom Leid der Armen und Schwachen konnte sich keiner etwas abschneiden, nicht einmal die Halsabschneider vom Großhandelskonzern Plus. Deshalb wurden Sozialthemen in Dreizeiler verpackt und irgendwo zwischen den *bunten Meldungen zum Tag* versteckt.

Umso mehr war ich überrascht, als mich Norbert Kunz nun extra zu sich bestellte, um mich auf so eine Kurznotiz anzusprechen. In der Donnerstagsausgabe hatte ich, weil mir noch eine *bunte Meldung zum Tag* gefehlt hatte, eine überfüllte Obdachlosen-Schlafstätte in Wien-Floridsdorf erwähnt, der die Subventionen gekürzt worden waren und deren ehrenamtliche Betreiber die Hälfte der Obdachlosen nun wieder auf die Straße würden setzen müssen. Norbert Kunz hatte diese Meldung mit Leuchtstift orange angestrichen und tippte mit dem Finger darauf, was nichts Gutes bedeutete. Ich erwartete, dass er mich wieder einmal darauf aufmerksam machen wollte, dass so etwas bei uns nicht ging, dass wir ein wirtschaftlich geführtes Unternehmen waren und die Finger von den Randgruppen lassen sollten, für die es eigene Zeitungen gab, von der Caritas, vom Roten Kreuz, von der Heilsarmee, von der Gruft, weiß der Teufel von wem. Aber es kam anders.

»Macht Ihnen Ihre Arbeit eigentlich noch manchmal Spaß,

Herr Plassek?«, fragte er. Kunz war zwar nicht gerade der Herzensmensch, dem das Wohlbefinden seiner Mitarbeiter ein Anliegen war oder auch nur einen Gedanken wert, aber ein Zyniker war er auch nicht, dazu fehlte ihm der Humor.

»Ehrlich gestanden arbeite ich hier nicht, um Spaß zu haben«, erwiderte ich.

»Ich auch nicht.«

»Das beruhigt mich«, sagte ich.

»Aber es gibt Momente, da weiß man plötzlich wieder, warum man es tut«, sagte er.

»Ach ja, gibt es die?«, fragte ich.

»Ja, die gibt es. So einen Moment habe ich gerade erlebt.«

»Fein, das freut mich für Sie. Wenn ich einmal so einen Moment erlebe, melde ich mich bei Ihnen. Kann aber sein, dass Sie da schon im Ruhestand sind. Dann melde ich mich bei Ihrem Nachfolger«, sagte ich. Wenn einer von uns beiden ein Zyniker war, dann nämlich ich.

Kunz rang sich ein gequältes Lächeln ab und erzählte mir, dass ihn soeben der Leiter der Obdachlosen-Schlafstätte in Floridsdorf angerufen hatte, und zwar völlig aufgelöst und so außer sich vor Freude, dass er kaum sprechen hatte können, weil nämlich etwas Wunderbares geschehen sei.

»Er hat mit der Post ein dickes Kuvert bekommen. Von einem anonymen Absender. Und in dem Umschlag war Geld. Bargeld. Sehr viel Bargeld. Raten Sie mal, wie viel, Herr Plassek.«

»Keine Ahnung.« Ich war da kein Experte. Mir hatte noch nie jemand Geld geschickt, weder anonym noch nicht anonym.

»Zehntausend Euro.«

»Wow.« Da musste ich schlucken. Das waren fünf Monatsgehälter bei *Tag für Tag*, zumindest für mich.

»Damit können die einen zweiten Raum mit Betten ausstatten und müssen über den Winter keinen einzigen Obdachlosen hinauswerfen«, sagte Kunz.

»Das ist schön, das ist wirklich schön«, erwiderte ich. Und ich meinte es ernst. Mich konnten positive Nachrichten sehr anrühren. Vermutlich deshalb, weil es so selten echte positive Nachrichten gab. Was uns üblicherweise als positive Nachricht verkauft wurde und was wir Journalisten munter weiterverkauften, war Werbung, mithilfe derer sich irgendjemand auf Kosten anderer bereicherte, sonst nichts.

»Aber warum hat er da gerade *Sie* angerufen?«, fragte ich. Jetzt wirkte mein Herr Chefredakteur ganz schön euphorisch, so sah man ihn selten.

»Im Kuvert des anonymen Spenders befand sich ein kleiner Zeitungsausschnitt. Nichts sonst, nur das Geld und dieser beigelegte kleine Zeitungsausschnitt. Und jetzt raten Sie mal, welcher Zeitungsausschnitt das wohl war.«

Schon wieder raten, ich war schlecht im Raten. Doch Norbert Kunz gab mir Hilfestellung und tippte auf den knallorange hervorgehobenen Artikel, auf meine *bunte Meldung* vom Donnerstag.

»Ja richtig, Herr Plassek. Unsere kleine Zeitungsnotiz hat offensichtlich einen Menschen dazu veranlasst, spontan zehntausend Euro an Obdachlose zu spenden. Ist das nicht irre?«

»Ja, das ist irre«, sagte ich. Obwohl es genau genommen nicht *unsere* kleine Zeitungsnotiz, sondern *meine* kleine Zeitungsnotiz war, aber egal. Hätte ich geahnt, dass diese Meldung irgendeinem Menschen auf dieser Welt zehntausend Euro wert sein könnte, hätte ich sie jedenfalls etwas liebevoller formuliert.

»An der Geschichte bleiben wir jetzt natürlich groß dran«, sagte Kunz.

»Wie meinen Sie das, *groß dranbleiben*?«

Er sah mich an wie einen Idioten, dem man die Grund-regeln des Boulevardjournalismus erklären musste. »Aufmacherstory, Seite eins. Titel: Tag für Tag *rettet Obdachlosenprojekt*. Untertitel: *Großzügige Spende unserer Leser schafft neue Quartiere für die Ärmsten der Armen*. Oder so ähnlich. Dazu das Faksimile unserer Meldung. Und vier, fünf, sechs Seiten Fotoreportage über das Obdachlosenheim. Interview mit dem überglücklichen Heimleiter. Gespräche mit Obdachlosen. Wie stürzt man ab? Wie ist es, auf der Straße zu leben? Milieustudie. Eine Grafik der von uns finanzierten neuen Schlafstätten …«

»Die sind nicht von uns finanziert«, erlaubte ich mir, Napoleon mitten in seiner Vision der siegreichen Schlacht zu widersprechen.

»Indirekt schon, Herr Plassek, indirekt schon.«

»Und wann, dachten Sie, soll ich mit dem Interview und mit der Reportage …?«

»Nicht Sie, Herr Plassek, das übernimmt Frau Kollegin Rambuschek. Sie ist bereits über alles informiert und wird sich vor Ort …«

»Wieso Sophie Rambuschek von der Wirtschaft? Soziales ist doch an sich meine Arbeit, oder hab ich da was falsch verstanden?« Jetzt war ich selbst für meine Verhältnisse relativ irritiert.

»Schon, schon, Herr Plassek, aber wir brauchen Sie hier im Haus«, sagte er.

Ach ja, richtig, es gab ja auch noch die Leserbriefe und die *bunten Meldungen zum Tag*. Ich lächelte, und er wusste, wie ich es meinte. Zum Glück war mir das alles hier nicht so wichtig. Die Rambuschek, die war jung und hungrig, die hatte noch eine Karriere vor sich. Ich war nie hungrig gewesen, immer nur durstig. Und ich hatte niemals eine Karriere, aber die hatte ich wenigstens hinter mir.

Irgendwie verspürte ich das Bedürfnis, Manuel von dieser seltsamen anonymen Spende zu erzählen.

»Interessiert dich, was mir mein Chef gerade mitgeteilt hat?«, fragte ich.

»Warum soll's mich nicht interessieren?«, erwiderte er. Ich ging mal davon aus, es interessierte ihn, und schilderte ihm, was vorgefallen war. Er wirkte danach zwar kaum weniger weggetreten als vorher, aber er stellte zum ersten Mal, seit er als Sohn und Bürokammergefährte Einzug in mein Leben gehalten hatte, eine kluge Frage: »Haben die anderen Zeitungen auch darüber geschrieben?«

»Keine Ahnung«, sagte ich. Ich las keine anderen Zeitungen und die eigene natürlich erst recht nicht. Aber wir besorgten uns daraufhin die gesamte Palette der Donnerstagsausgaben und stellten fest, dass die Obdachlosengeschichte mit den gekürzten Subventionen sozusagen das lokale Thema des Tages gewesen war, dem einige namhafte Gazetten große Berichte gewidmet hatten.

»Dann war deine Meldung überhaupt nichts Besonderes«, befand Manuel.

»Ich habe nie behauptet, dass sie besonders war«, sagte ich.

»Und derjenige, der das Geld gespendet hat, hat wahrscheinlich nur *Tag für Tag* gelesen, sonst hätte er einen anderen Zeitungsausschnitt beigelegt«, sagte Manuel. Das entbehrte nicht einer gewissen Logik, doch es war feindselig formuliert und verächtlich intoniert, und ich musste diese Sache jetzt einmal dringend ansprechen.

»Manuel, was hab ich dir eigentlich getan?«

»Was sollst du mir getan haben?«

»Ganz genau, was soll ich dir getan haben, kannst du mir das bitte erklären?«

»Du hast mir gar nichts getan, es ist nur …«

»Was ist nur?«

»Ach, gar nichts«, murmelte er.

»Nein, es ist nicht gar nichts, es ist etwas, und ich will, dass du mir sagst, was es ist. Ich bestehe darauf! Hast du mich verstanden?« Er hatte mich verstanden. Dichte Schleier der chronischen Langeweile lösten sich auf, und seine Augen waren plötzlich doppelt so weit geöffnet wie sonst, sodass man erkennen konnte, dass sie die gleiche grün-kupfer-bernstein-gelbe Farbmischung hatten wie meine, bildete ich mir zumindest ein.

»Warum muss ich hier sein? Wo bin ich hier überhaupt? Wo bin ich da hineingeraten? Was ist das für ein Zimmer? Was ist das für eine peinliche Zeitung? Was sind das für komische Leute? Was machen die hier? Wie kann man hier arbeiten?« Er gönnte sich eine kurze Pause, um Luft für weitere Angriffe zu holen. »Und du? Was ist denn mir dir los? Dir ist ja alles egal. Du sitzt nur da, schaust in den Bildschirm und tust nichts. Okay, ich tue auch nicht viel, aber ich bin noch jung. Außerdem, was soll ich hier schon machen?« Er schaute mich verängstigt an, weil er wusste, dass er den Bogen überspannt hatte. Aber nun war ohnehin schon alles egal, da konnte er mir auch gleich die ganze Wahrheit sagen. »Du hast immer die gleiche grüne Weste an. Und deine Schuhe! So was tragen Erwachsene nicht, so was tragen auch keine Jugendlichen, ich kenne überhaupt niemanden, der so was trägt. Außerdem stinkst du nach Alkohol. Mama hat gesagt, dass du ein cooler, netter Typ bist, mit dem man bestimmt viel Spaß haben kann. Aber du bist überhaupt kein cooler Typ, nett vielleicht, ein bisschen, aber überhaupt nicht cool. Du hast kein Auto und auch kein Motorrad. Wenn du wenigstens ein Fahrrad hättest, aber du hast nicht mal ein Fahrrad. Und Spaß hatten wir noch nicht ein einziges Mal. Ich brauche eine halbe Stunde für die Hausaufgaben, die restliche Zeit sitze ich sinnlos herum und warte darauf, dass du vielleicht mal ...«

»Alkohol stinkt nicht«, sagte ich.

»Doch, Alkohol stinkt, und wie er stinkt!«

»Was du da behauptest, ist eine Frechheit. Ich würde nie etwas trinken, was stinkt!« Jetzt lachte Manuel, er konnte also lachen. Er war wahrscheinlich erleichtert, dass er mir solche Sachen sagen konnte, ohne dass ich durchdrehte. Andere Väter beziehungsweise andere alte Freunde seiner Mutter wären wahrscheinlich auf der Stelle ausgezuckt. Natürlich war es nicht lustig, sich so etwas von einem Vierzehnjährigen sagen zu lassen, aber es hatte Pfeffer, und das gefiel mir. Immerhin war ja auch ein kleines Kompliment für mich dabei, nämlich dass mich Alice ihm gegenüber als coolen, netten Typ ausgewiesen hatte. Und ehrlich gestanden war es mir wichtiger, wie Frauen, die es zu Ärztinnen ohne Grenzen gebracht hatten, über mich dachten, als so ein Halbwüchsiger, der noch glaubte, Schule und Leben hätten etwas miteinander zu tun und die Welt wäre abwechselnd cool oder scheiße.

»Ich finde es gut, dass du alles ausgesprochen hast«, sagte ich, wobei ich mir nicht sicher war, ob es wirklich schon alles war. Jetzt war er erstmals beeindruckt von mir, das konnte ich sehen, beeindruckt oder schockiert, eins von beiden.

»Nimm's nicht persönlich«, erwiderte er. Aber nein, persönlich hätte ich es niemals genommen. Bei der Verabschiedung gab er mir freiwillig die Hand.

»Grüße an Tante Julia«, rief ich ihm nach. So. Und jetzt brauchte ich dringend ein Bier. In der untersten Lade meines Schreibtisches musste noch eine Reservedose sein – lauwarm, aber egal.

Abende, bei denen ich davon ausgehen konnte, sie am jeweils nächsten Morgen zu bereuen, verbrachte ich mit meinen Kumpels in Kneipen. Als echter Wiener, der noch dazu im Arbeiterbezirk Simmering aufgewachsen war, verabscheute ich zwar die aus Deutschland importierten Wörter »Kumpels« und »Kneipen« – bei uns heißt es »Haberer« und »Beisln« –, aber wenn ich sie »Kumpels« und »Kneipen« nannte, konnte ich mich leichter davon distanzieren. Und das war notwendig. Denn in Wirklichkeit standen wir nur völlig uninspiriert herum, tranken ein Bier nach dem anderen Schnaps, erzählten uns gegenseitig, wie gemein das Leben zu uns war, nein, nicht gegenseitig – jeder erzählte sich die Gemeinheiten seines eigenen Lebens, und die anderen warteten, bis sie wieder an die Reihe kamen. Zur Belohnung dafür, dass wir einander so tapfer zuzuhören vorgaben, gab dann einer die nächste Runde aus, und dieser eine war meistens ich.

Schlimm wurde es ab zwei Uhr früh, und da konnte man die Uhr danach stellen, wenn nämlich meine Kumpels, allen voran Horst und Josi, ihre alkoholgetränkten Blicke herumschweifen ließen und von den noch anwesenden Frauen zu phantasieren begannen, die allesamt keinen Vergleich zu ihren eigenen ehemaligen oder aktuellen Partnerinnen daheim scheuen mussten. Das war dann für mich der Zeitpunkt, entweder nach Hause zu gehen oder noch eine letzte Runde zu bestellen, wobei ich der zweiten Variante meistens den Vorzug gab.

Am liebsten und alkoholisch ertragreichsten versumpfte ich in Zoltan's Bar in der Schlachthausgasse, die quasi mein verlängertes Wohnzimmer war, was zugegebenermaßen kein gutes Licht auf meine Wohnverhältnisse warf. Bei Zoltan, einem gebürtigen Ungarn, der hervorragend zuhören und nicken konnte, aber selbst kaum ein Wort sprach, hatte ich schon viele Aufs und Abs verdaut, vor allem Abs, und so was prägt einen nachhaltig und führt einen immer wieder zu dem Ort der Verdauung zurück.

Diesmal würgte ich das Paradethema *Frauen nach zwei Uhr früh* erfolgreich ab, indem ich von meinem Spenden-Erlebnis bei *Tag für Tag* zu erzählen begann und damit sogar so etwas wie eine kleine Diskussion anregte. Da es die ersten Einschätzungen waren und in der nächtlichen Trunkenheit ja die unweisesten Typen oft die größten Weisheiten von sich geben, habe ich sie mir bis heute gemerkt.

»Zehntausend Euro anonym spenden? Wer macht denn so was?«, fragte Josi, ein gelernter Konditor auf Jobsuche.

»Das muss einer sein, der selbst einmal obdachlos war und dann zu Reichtum gelangt ist«, meinte Franticek, der eher den umgekehrten Weg beschritt. Seine böhmischen Großeltern waren bedeutende Kunstschmiede gewesen, die Eltern hatten sich mit dem Betrieb noch über Wasser gehalten. Franticek leider nicht mehr, er hatte kürzlich Konkurs angemeldet, eine Leistung, deren Wertschöpfung ein baldiges Ablaufdatum hatte.

»So was macht kein Mensch ohne eigennützigen Hintergedanken«, entgegnete Arik, Berufsschullehrer und vermutlich der Hellste aus unserer Runde. »Ich bin mir sicher, dass der Spender nur auf einen günstigen Zeitpunkt wartet und sich dann zu erkennen gibt.«

»Oder das Ganze ist ein Fake, und der Typ vom Obdachlosenheim hat das selbst inszeniert, um in die Schlagzeilen zu kommen«, sagte Josi.

»Aber dann rollt der das doch über das *Tagblatt* oder über die *Rundschau* auf und nicht über so ein Schmierblatt, das ohnehin keiner liest. Du verzeihst mir, Gerold.« Das kam von Arik, und ich verzieh ihm sofort.

»Ich glaube eher, da war Schwarzgeld oder Schutzgeld oder Drogengeld oder so was im Spiel, und das musste jemand dringend loswerden«, entgegnete Horst, der sich auskannte, weil er ein Wettbüro in der Kaiser-Ebersdorfer-Straße betrieb.

Das ging dann noch bis vier so dahin, und die Theorien wurden immer kruder und verschwörerischer, ehe Zoltan, der uns geduldig zugehört hatte, die Sperrstunde einmahnte.

»Ein Getränk noch?«, fragte ich.

»Okay, meine Herren, eine allerletzte Abschlussrunde. Die geht aufs Haus«, sagte der Chef. Es gab sie also doch noch, die feinen Charaktere, die herzenswarmen Zeitgenossen, die selbstlosen Spender, die nichts im Schilde führten, die kein anderes Ziel verfolgten, als Mitmenschen glücklich zu machen, Mitmenschen wie mich. Bei mir mussten es gar keine zehntausend Euro sein, bei mir tat es auch ein geschenkter und gut eingeschenkter Gute-Nacht-Weinbrand in Zoltan's Bar um vier Uhr früh.

KAPITEL ZWEI

Ex und Florentina

Abende, bei denen ich die berechtigte Hoffnung hegte, sie am jeweils nächsten Morgen nicht zu bereuen, verbrachte ich meistens mit Frauen. Aber nicht so, wie das jetzt vielleicht klingen mag, leider nicht so – oder sagen wir, mittlerweile eher selten.

Die Einladung zum Abendessen bei meiner Exfrau Gudrun war ein Ritual. Es erinnerte an höfische Zeiten, als der Monarch der Gefolgschaft einmal im Monat die Ehre zuteilwerden ließ, ganz nah dabei zu sein und am selben Tisch zu speisen. Ich war sozusagen die Gefolgschaft, eine Art Minnesänger, der vom Singen befreit war. Der Monarch hieß Berthold Hille und war als Lobbyist in der Schwerindustrie tätig, genauer will man es nicht wissen, außer man ist Staatsanwalt. Zu seinen sympathischsten Gesten zählte, dass er meistens nicht anwesend war, wenn ich bei der Monarchin zu Gast war. Diesmal machte er leider eine Ausnahme.

Die Monarchin hieß Gudrun Hille, ehemals Plassek. Sie war meine Jugendliebe gewesen, das erste Mädchen, das ich geküsst hatte, und wenig später die erste Frau, mit der ich umschlungen im Bett gelegen und gedacht hatte, allein dafür hätte sich mein Leben bereits gelohnt. Ich möchte an dieser Stelle alle Jugendlichen eindringlich davor warnen, zu früh damit zu beginnen, an die große Liebe zu glauben, und zu lange daran festzuhalten. Ich begann mit siebzehn und schaffte es bis fünfundzwanzig, also immerhin acht Jahre. Dann bemerkte ich plötzlich, dass im Schnitt jeder zweite Mensch, der mir auf der Straße oder auf einer Party begegnete, eine Frau war und dass viele kleine Lieben in Summe mehr waren als eine große, der obendrein gerade die Luft ausging. Zu diesem Zeitpunkt begann sich Gudrun bereits für Herrn Hille zu interessieren, der schon als junger Kerl ein Herr war, sofern er überhaupt jemals jung gewesen war. Jedenfalls sah er immer schon wie einer aus, der es im Leben zu etwas bringen würde, und darin sah er mir so überhaupt nicht ähnlich, von Tag zu Tag weniger.

Weil Trennungen nicht weniger traurig waren, wenn sie aus Vernunftgründen geschahen, ließen wir uns etwas Originelleres einfallen: Wir heirateten. Die Ehe bestand aus einer nostalgischen Hochzeitsreise an die spanische Costa del Sol, Marke *Best of Plassek*, und acht weiteren Monaten Zugabe, in denen jeder bereits seinen eigenen Interessen nachging. Ich zum Beispiel interessierte mich für hochprozentige geistige Getränke. Und weil zwei Pointen am Ende einer großen Liebesbeziehung besser waren als eine, setzten am Tag unserer Scheidung bei Gudrun die Wehen ein, und einen Tag später kam unsere Tochter Florentina zur Welt. Rührenderweise schloss Herr Hille sie noch am Tag ihrer Geburt in sein Industriellenherz, und gleichzeitig mit Florentina war sozusagen eine neue Familie geboren, eine honorige, in der es für mich nur noch zum sporadischen Minnegesang reichte. Das sollte jetzt aber nicht pathetisch klingen, ich war ja selbst schuld, ich hatte meine Tochter kampflos einem vermögenden Lobbyisten überlassen.

»Und wie laufen die Geschäfte, Monsieur?«, fragte ich Berthold, der sich nach dem Essen behäbig zurückgelehnt und eine Zigarre angezündet hatte. Florentina neben mir kicherte. Es war die bisher beste Phase in der Beziehung zu meiner Tochter. Sie war fünfzehn und revoltierte gerade gegen Spießertum, Reichtum und Proporz, also gegen ihren Stiefvater. Okay, es war eine sanfte Revolution, die es für sie nicht notwendig machte, auf ihre Armani-Diesel-Grundausstattung zu verzichten. Aber so ein konsum-desorientierter, unrasierter, schlampig gekleideter, dezent versoffener Kerl wie ich, der es sich scheinbar leisten konnte, nichts zu leisten, und der noch dazu ihr leiblicher Vater war, hatte für sie etwas interessant Verwegenes und genoss einen gewissen Kultstatus. Ja, den genoss ich wirklich. Ich durfte ihr sogar ein paarmal flüchtig über die Haare streichen und sie an der Schulter nehmen. Das musste natürlich lässig wirken, Florentina durfte nicht ahnen, dass mir dabei regelmäßig fast das Herz stehenblieb und dass ich meine Tochter am liebsten an mich gedrückt und nie mehr losgelassen hätte.

Mit Gudrun, meiner Ex, war ich halbwegs im Reinen. Schlechtes Gewissen und Schuldgefühle dem jeweils anderen gegenüber waren bei jedem von uns etwa gleich groß gewesen, sodass wir uns irgendwann entschieden hatten, in beiderseitigem Einvernehmen darauf zu verzichten. Ich vertrug nur diesen mitleidigen Blick nicht, der mir mitteilen sollte, dass sie sich ernsthafte Sorgen um meine Zukunft machte – sie und alle anderen, alle außer mir, und ich sollte doch endlich auch damit beginnen. Aber ich hatte wirklich keine Lust, plötzlich an meine Zukunft zu denken, das hätte ich früher machen müssen, dafür war ich mir jetzt schon zu alt.

»Und wie laufen die Geschäfte, Monsieur?«

»Danke, danke, wir dürfen uns nicht beschweren«, sagte Berthold. Der Plural war notwendig, um zu verdeutlichen, wie sehr seine gesamte Familie, zu der auch ich mich irgendwo zählen musste, von seinen Geschäften profitierte.

»Sag, Gerold, deine Kollegin … diese Frau Rambusek …«

»Rambuschek.«

»Ja richtig, Rambuschek, die hat da eine tolle Story an Land gezogen, die Sache mit der anonymen Spende für die Obdachlosen.«

»Du weißt davon? Liest du seit neuestem *Tag für Tag*?«, fragte ich.

»Aber nein, wo denkst du hin«, sagte er und lachte schwerindustriell, das war so eine Mischung aus Hohn und Zigarrenhusten. »Die seriösen Zeitungen haben alle nachgezogen, die haben die Berichte und Interviews von der Rambuschek rauf und runter zitiert.«

»Apropos seriöse Zeitung, ich habe vor, bei *Tag für Tag* zu kündigen«, sagte ich. Das stimmte zwar nicht, der Gedanke war mir vor genau drei Sekunden gekommen, aber es war ein berauschendes Gefühl der Freiheit, diesen Satz so auszusprechen und die verdutzten Gesichter zu sehen.

»Du willst kündigen? Um Himmels willen, warum denn? Wo willst du hin?«, fragte Gudrun.

»Zur *Neuzeit*. Wir sind im Gespräch.« Das kam so schnell und überzeugend, dass ich beinahe selbst dran glaubte.

»Cool«, sagte Florentina und strahlte mich an. Schon dafür hatte sich meine Phantasieleistung gelohnt. Die *Neuzeit* war in der Medienlandschaft zwar unbedeutend, aber sie war linksliberal, anspruchsvoll und jugendlich. Eines der wenigen Printmedien, für das man sich nicht genieren musste, weder als Leser noch als Schreiber.

»Und in welcher Funktion hat man für dich dort Verwendung?«, fragte mich der Mann mit der Zigarre. Gudrun konnte einem leid tun, mit einem Mann verheiratet zu sein, dem nichts anderes als *Funktion* und *Verwendung* einfiel, wenn es um eine neue berufliche Herausforderung ging.

»Wahrscheinlich Richtung Kultur. Kunst, Musik, Literatur – mal sehen«, sagte ich.

»Jetzt bin ich wirklich überrascht«, erwiderte Gudrun. Das hieß, sie glaubte mir kein Wort. Oder traute mir zumindest nur den ersten Teil meiner Ansage zu, nämlich dass ich bei *Tag für Tag* kündigen würde. Das müsste sie dann ihrem Golf spielenden Vater beibringen. Nein, das konnte ich ihr nicht antun. Aber der Gedanke an die *Neuzeit* war wirklich schön.

Am Freitag wurde für elf Uhr überraschend eine Redaktionskonferenz einberufen. Das wirklich Überraschende daran war, dass ich daran teilnehmen durfte oder musste, je nachdem, wie man es sah. Elf Uhr früh, das war ehrlich gestanden noch nicht ganz meine Zeit, da war ich zwar scheinbar schon anwesend, doch mein Kreislauf wartete noch auf das Schwenken der Fahnen zum Start für die ersten Aufwärmtrainingsrunden. Norbert Kunz gelang es relativ rasch und eindrucksvoll, mich wachzurütteln.

»Liebe Kolleginnen, liebe Kollegen, ich habe eine erfreuliche Nachricht für uns alle. Es ist schon wieder eine anonyme Geldspende eingegangen. Diesmal in einer Kindertagesstätte. Wieder in einem weißen Briefumschlag ohne Absender oder sonstigen Hinweis. Wieder zehntausend Euro in bar. Und das Großartige daran ...« Jetzt holte er tief Luft. »Wieder befand sich neben dem hohen Geldbetrag ein Zeitungsausschnitt von *Tag für Tag* im Kuvert.« Während die Kolleginnen und Kollegen spontan zu applaudieren begannen, ohne zu wissen, wem genau sie applaudierten, genoss ich bereits so einen ganz kleinen persönlichen Triumph, weil ich wusste, dass es abermals eine meiner *bunten Meldungen zum Tag* gewesen sein musste, die einer ins Schleudern geratenen sozialen Einrichtung einen unverhofften Geldsegen beschert hatte.

Weil Kunz wohl zu Recht davon ausging, dass keiner von den Kollegen die Notiz gelesen hatte, trug er sie jetzt öffentlich vor.

Die Kindertagesstätte Kleeblatt in Wien-Meidling, eine private Elterninitiative, die derzeit 120 Kinder aus schwierigen Verhältnissen betreut, steht vor der Schließung. Zwei Sponsoren sind abgesprungen, die Hausmiete kann von dem kleinen Team aus Erziehern und ehrenamtlichen Helfern nicht mehr allein getragen werden.

Na ja, Pulitzerpreis-verdächtig hörte sich die Meldung zwar nicht an, aber Kunz hätte dennoch ruhig erwähnen können, dass ich derjenige war, der sie ausgewählt, formuliert und in die Zeitung gehoben hatte.

Er las uns dann auch die Dankes-E-Mail vor, die die Kleeblatt-Leiterin der Redaktion zukommen hatte lassen:

Sehr geehrte Mitarbeiter und Mitarbeiterinnen von Tag für Tag,

ein Wohltäter oder eine Wohltäterin, ein wunderbarer Mensch, der seinen Namen nicht nennen will, hat uns mit einer Spende von 10 000 Euro fürs Erste von unseren großen Sorgen befreit. Wir können unseren Kindern, die nicht auf der Sonnenseite des Lebens stehen, nun weiterhin etwas von dem geben, was für behütete Kinder selbstverständlich ist: ein Zuhause, Zuwendung, Zuneigung, Wärme. Der Auslöser war ein winzig kleiner Artikel in Ihrer Zeitung. Der Zeitungsausschnitt lag der großzügigen Geldspende bei. Unser Kleeblatt-Team möchte sich auf das Herzlichste bei Ihnen bedanken. Journalismus, der solche Dinge bewegen kann, der auf die Not von Menschen hinweist und zu guten Taten anspornt, ist gar nicht hoch genug einzuschätzen in unserer frostigen Zeit. Bitte machen Sie weiter so. Uns haben Sie sehr viel Glück beschert. Im Namen des vierblättrigen Kleeblatts, Ursula Hoffer.

Wenn man sich die Kollegen und Kolleginnen jetzt ansah, bemerkte man, dass jeder irgendwie verklärt dasaß und ein kleines Lächeln auf den Lippen oder in den Augen hatte, als hätten wir selbst die gute Tat vollbracht. Dabei war es nicht nur der reine Zufall, sondern sogar eine Art Groteske, dass ausgerechnet die billig gemachte Konzern-Zeitung der windigen, rechtspopulistischen Plus-Gruppe, die ständig in Korruptionsskandale verwickelt war, nun schon zum zweiten Mal positiv in Erscheinung trat. Man mochte beinahe meinen, der edle Spender machte sich einen Spaß daraus, *Tag für Tag* als Boten für seine großherzigen Taten einzusetzen. Aber natürlich wertete das die Zeitung enorm auf und ließ sie plötzlich in einem ganz anderen Licht erscheinen.

Mein Lächeln verging mir übrigens relativ rasch, als nämlich Norbert Kunz seine redaktionellen Umgestaltungspläne bekanntgab: Sophie Rambuschek sollte von nun an wöchentlich eine große Sozialreportage verfassen und in einer täglichen Kolumne über in Not geratene Menschen berichten.

»Aber bitte keine Ausländerschicksale, oder zumindest so wenige wie möglich, sonst kriegen wir Probleme mit dem Eigentümer«, schränkte Kunz ein.

Die *bunten Meldungen zum Tag* sollten ausgebaut und weiterhin von mir betreut werden, wobei Rambuschek dort nun auch die weniger aufregenden Sozialgeschichten in Kurzform unterbringen konnte. Ich sollte dafür im Wirtschaftsressort mit *Notizen zum Tag* aushelfen.

»Das mache ich nicht«, sagte ich spontan, gar nicht beleidigt, sondern durchaus realitätsnah. »Mit Wirtschaft hab ich wirklich nichts am Hut.«

»Gut, gut, Herr Plassek, darüber reden wir noch«, erwiderte Kunz. Das klang irgendwie bedrohlich. Vielleicht konnte Gudrun ja ihren Vater bitten, seinen Freund Kunz senior beim Golfspiel ein paarmal gewinnen zu lassen, damit ich meinen Job nicht schon vorher verlor – ehe ich ihn hinschmeißen konnte.

Auf dem Weg der Besserung

Am frühen Nachmittag traf mein junger Bürogefährte mit dem düsteren Blick ein und legte mir wortlos ein in *Tag-für-Tag*-Zeitungspapier gehülltes dünnes Päckchen auf den Tisch.

»Was ist das?«, fragte ich. An unserer Beziehung hatte sich

eindeutig etwas geändert, denn Manuel erwiderte nicht: »Was soll das schon sein?«, sondern er sagte: »Mach's einfach auf.«

Es handelte sich um eine CD mit einer grauen Weltkugel auf dem Cover. Die Band hieß offensichtlich Efterklang und die Scheibe *Piramida*. Ich sah ihn fragend an.

»Weil du mich mal gefragt hast, welche Musik mir gefällt«, sagte er. Das war süß von ihm.

»Efterklang? Sagt mir gar nichts, da bin ich aber neugierig. Darf ich sie mir ausborgen?«

»Du darfst sie behalten, Tante Julia hat sie bezahlt.«

»Wow, danke, das ist aber lieb von euch!« Ich war wirklich gerührt, nun schon zum zweiten Mal am gleichen Tag. Es war immerhin das erste Geschenk, das ich jemals von einem Sohn von mir bekommen hatte.

»Du musst zuerst die Nummer *Apples* hören, und dann *The Ghost*, die gehen am schnellsten ins Ohr.«

»Das werde ich machen«, versprach ich und beschloss, dass mir die Musik unbedingt gefallen würde, egal wie entsetzlich sie klingen mochte.

»Und, fällt dir was auf?«, fragte ich.

»Ja, du hast einen neuen Pullover.« Neu war er nicht, aber wenigstens dunkelblau.

»Und die Schuhe sind auch besser«, sagte Manuel. Schwarze Schuhe, hartes Leder, klassisch, konservativ, na also. Wir beide waren irgendwie auf dem richtigen Weg, und das konnte mich ganz schön aufbauen.

Während Manuel reihenweise Schulbücher aus seinem Rucksack hervorzauberte, damit diese auch einmal an die frische Luft kamen, erzählte ich ihm von der zweiten Geldspende und dass schon wieder eine von mir verfasste Meldung der Auslöser dafür gewesen war.

»Aber das weiß ja keiner, dass du das geschrieben hast«, beschwerte er sich und ließ sich auf seinen bereits gut eingefahrenen grauen Drehstuhl fallen.

»Ja leider, aber es weiß auch keiner, wer die zehntausend Euro gespendet hat.«

»Stimmt«, sagte er.

»Außerdem wird es bei *Tag für Tag* jetzt jede Woche eine große Sozialreportage geben, also eine Geschichte über Menschen, denen es schlecht geht.«

»Warum? Damit noch mal jemand zehntausend Euro spendet und die Zeitung damit angeben kann?« Eigentlich ein hochintelligentes Bürschchen, mein Sohn, dachte ich. Und die krächzende Stimme würde er auch bald verlieren.

»Und bei den großen Geschichten, steht da wenigstens dein Name drunter?«, fragte er. Das war mir jetzt ein bisschen peinlich.

»Die Reportagen wird meistens eine Kollegin von mir schreiben, ich nur manchmal, wenn ich Zeit habe«, log ich.

»Ah so«, sagte er. Es hätte schlimmer kommen können. Ich hatte schon mit »du hast doch eh immer Zeit« gerechnet.

Wir saßen dann eine Weile relativ beschaulich da und gingen unseren Tätigkeiten beziehungsweise Untätigkeiten nach. Aber irgendwann bemerkte ich, dass Manuel unruhig und zappelig war und dass ihm offenbar noch etwas auf der Zunge lag, etwas, das seine Wurzeln im Kieferbereich hatte, wie sich schließlich herausstellte.

»Ich muss am Montag zum Zahnarzt.«

»Oje, du Armer«, erwiderte ich. Mir liefen sofort hundert Ameisen mit hochhackigen Stiefeln über den Rücken. Ich hatte nämlich panische Angst vor Zahnärzten. Seit meiner Kindheit verfolgten sie mich bis in meine Träume. Ungefähr so lange war ich auch schon nicht mehr bei einem von ihnen gewesen, und sie selbst fahndeten ja zum Glück niemals nach einem Verweigerer, das war ihr einziger menschlicher Zug.

»Ich hab Angst vor Zahnärzten«, sagte Manuel.

»Äh … brauchst du nicht zu haben, die tun einem überhaupt nicht mehr weh, das ist mit der modernen Zahntechnik heute alles viel besser geworden.«

»Ich kann dort nicht allein hingehen«, sagte er bitter.

»Das kann ich verstehen«, erwiderte ich. Bei mir hatte auch immer wer mitgehen müssen, der mich auffangen und in Sicherheit bringen konnte, für den Fall, dass ich bewusstlos wurde.

»Du musst mitgehen!«, verkündete Manuel.

»Ich?« Er wusste nicht, was er da sagte.

»Ja, du. Tante Julia kann nicht, und sonst kann auch keiner, weil alle arbeiten, und da hat Tante Julia gesagt, ich soll einfach dich fragen, wen sonst, es ist ja sonst keiner da, und die Mama ist in Afrika.« Jetzt verstand ich, deshalb hatten sie mich mit der Musik-CD gefügig zu machen versucht.

»Manuel, es tut mir wirklich leid, ich hätte dich gerne begleitet, aber ich hab am Montag leider ab vierzehn Uhr durchgehend wichtige Termine«, sagte ich.

»Sehr gut, ich hab früher aus, dann hol ich dich um halb eins ab, und wir bringen das hinter uns«, erwiderte Manuel.

Die Zahnärztin

Von der Sonntagnacht noch ein wenig angeschlagen, sah ich mich genötigt, auf nüchternen Magen gleich wieder ein paar Deziliter Wodka nachzugießen, sonst hätten mich keine zehn Pferde oder unehelichen Kinder in diese Teufelspraxis in der Margaretenstraße gebracht.

Für Manuel erfüllte ich insofern den Zweck, als seine Angst

von Fremdschämen verdeckt wurde, welch ramponierte Gestalt ihn da zum Folterstuhl begleitete.

»Und der Vater kommt mit hinein?«, fragte die Ordinationsgehilfin mit berechtigter Skepsis.

»Er ist nur ein alter Bekannter meiner Mutter, aber er kommt mit rein«, erwiderte Manuel. Ich war leider nicht in der Lage zu widersprechen, sondern postierte mich neben der Tür.

Bei gewissen Filmszenen war stets mein Standpunkt gewesen: Bitte stecht mir doch gleich selbst die Augen aus, bevor ich mit ansehen muss, wie einer das wem anderen antut. So ähnlich erging es mir nun mit Manuel, dem die weiß vermummte Täterin unter Surren und Rattern und Pfeifen eine Maschine nach der anderen in seinen Kinderrachen schob und nachträglich mit dem spitzen silbernen Besteck darin herumrührte und nachbesserte, um dem Martyrium seinen letzten Feinschliff zu geben.

Irgendwann war die Sache ausgestanden. Manuel sprang auf, als wäre nichts gewesen. Ich dagegen war mehr tot als lebendig, aber nun kam die Ärztin direkt auf mich zu, befreite sich mit einer schwungvollen Bewegung von ihrem Mundschutz, lächelte mich an und sagte spöttisch oder auch nicht: »Ich habe hier selten einen so mitfühlenden Vater erlebt wie Sie.« Wie sie dabei aussah und wie sie mich dabei ansah, das wirkte auf mich so, als hätten die hundert Ameisen, die mir abermals über den Rücken liefen, nun plötzlich alle warme Filzpantoffeln angehabt. Jedenfalls stellte dieser erste Blickkontakt mit einer Frau, die überdies gerade mein eigenes Kind verarztet hatte, eine historische Ausnahmeerscheinung von herausragender Begegnungsqualität dar, und das empfand ich nicht nur so, weil ich gerade mit sicher mehr als einem Promille im Blut quasi neben mir stand. Ich war immerhin dreiundvierzig Jahre alt, und ich konnte auf Hunderte erste Blickkontakte zurückblicken.

Leider war ich nicht in der Verfassung, irgendetwas Sinnvolles zu sagen. Also sagte ich gar nichts. Und auch Manuel brachte verständlicherweise den betäubten Mund nicht auf, um zu dementieren, dass ich sein Vater war. So ging das Schlusswort an die Ordinationsgehilfin, und dieses war eindeutig an uns beide gerichtet.

»Nächste Woche bitte zur Kontrolle.«

KAPITEL DREI

Lorbeeren für Sophie

Die folgenden Tage waren davon geprägt, dass Gott und die Welt einander gegenseitig fragten, ob sich der Wohltäter zu erkennen geben würde, oder ob es vielleicht noch zu einer dritten anonymen Geldspende in so beträchtlicher Höhe kommen könnte. Alle Augen waren dabei auf die Gratiszeitung *Tag für Tag* gerichtet, und hier natürlich auf die ersten großen Sozialreportagen und Kolumnen von Sophie Rambuschek. Sie tat mir irgendwie leid, weil sie unter enormem Leistungsdruck stand, und das las man dann auch aus ihren Texten heraus, in denen sie verkrampft und allzu leicht durchschaubar um Mitleid für die jeweiligen Opfer heischte.

Meiner Meinung nach war es generell unmöglich, bei einem Leserpublikum bestimmte Gefühle zu erzeugen, die man als Schreiber nicht selbst auch in sich trug. Sophie Rambuschek, die Betriebswirtschaft studiert hatte und journalistisch sozusagen die Adoptivtochter vom Dow Jones war, beschrieb nun auf einer Doppelseite zum Beispiel das Elend einer ländlichen Gemeinde, die im Vorjahr von einem *Jahrhunderthochwasser* heimgesucht worden war und bisher vergeblich auf versprochene Hilfszahlungen aus irgendeinem Katastrophenfonds gewartet hatte. Die Geschichte enthielt zwar eine Unmenge an bis aufs letzte Komma sauber recherchierten Zahlen, aber sie vermittelte nicht den Hauch von Betroffenheit. Und zwar deshalb nicht, weil es Sophie Rambuschek persönlich vermutlich scheißegal war, ob da irgendwelche Bauern Zuschüsse kriegten oder nicht – hätten sie ihre Häuser eben nicht entlang eines Hochwasser führenden Flusses gebaut.

Ihre einzige, versteckte und geradezu flehentliche Botschaft lautete: Bitte, lieber Gönner, erbarme dich und lasse noch einmal zehntausend Euro in Kombination mit meinem Zeitungsausschnitt zu den Opfern rüberwachsen, damit ich ein Jobangebot von einer ordentlichen Wirtschaftszeitung erhalte und endlich von diesem Schmierblatt wegkomme!

Dieser Wunsch erfüllte sich vorerst leider nicht, und schon nach wenigen Tagen hieß es gerüchteweise, die Plus-Eigentümer wollten die Sozialberichterstattung bald wieder einstellen, es hätte bereits Beschwerden wichtiger Inserenten gegeben.

Angenehmerweise nahm mir die Rambuschek ein bisschen Arbeit ab, indem sie zu meinen *bunten Meldungen* täglich ein bis zwei Kurznotizen beisteuerte. Die waren freilich derart lieblos formuliert, dass ich nicht umhinkam, ein wenig daran herumzufeilen, obwohl mir die Sache im Grunde ziemlich egal war.

Am Mittwoch schickte sie mir folgenden Text:

Die 78 Jahre alte Rentnerin Anneliese S. wurde am Dienstagabend in der Nußdorfer Straße von einem maskierten, südländisch aussehenden Täter überfallen und ausgeraubt. Sie hatte es dem Räuber allerdings leichtgemacht, weil sie einem Bettler ein paar Münzen gegeben und dabei nicht auf ihre Handtasche geachtet hatte. Vorher hatte sie ihre gesamten Ersparnisse, fast 9000 Euro, von der Bank abgehoben. Das muss der Täter gesehen haben.

Also wenn ich Anneliese S. wäre, die übrigens genau so alt wie meine Mama war, und man hätte mir meine gesamten Ersparnisse geraubt, und ich müsste dann in der Zeitung lesen, dass ich es dem Räuber leichtgemacht hätte, weil ich für einen Bettler ein paar Münzen aus der Geldbörse geholt hatte, dass ich also quasi selbst schuld war und den Überfall durch meine unnötige Gabe an einen Mittellosen provoziert hatte, dann würde mir das vermutlich den Rest geben. Und was den

Täter betraf, fand ich Bemerkungen wie »südländisch ausse-
hend« mehr als entbehrlich. Ich kannte nicht wenige Südländer, die durchaus nordländisch aussahen und umgekehrt. Und
ich kannte sogar Südländer, die südländisch aussahen und
trotzdem keine Räuber waren, man mochte es nicht für möglich halten, zumindest nicht bei *Tag für Tag*.

Meine leicht korrigierte und gekürzte Version lautete also:
*Die 78 Jahre alte Rentnerin Anneliese S. wurde am Dienstagabend
in der Nußdorfer Straße Opfer eines Überfalls mit großem Schaden.
Ein bisher unbekannter Täter entwendete ihr die Handtasche, als
sie einem Bettler gerade ein paar Münzen gab. Unmittelbar davor
hatte die Frau von der Bank 9000 Euro, ihre gesamten Ersparnisse,
abgehoben.*

Exakt diese unscheinbare *bunte Meldung zum Tag* sorgte Ende
der Woche für großes öffentliches Aufsehen, für Riesenschlag-
zeilen in allen lokalen Medien und für ausführliche Berichte
und Spekulationen im Radio, im Fernsehen und im Internet.
Denn der entsprechende Zeitungsausschnitt von *Tag für Tag*
befand sich zusammen mit zehntausend Euro in einem absenderlosen weißen Kuvert, welches Anneliese S. – sie hieß Anneliese Seilcek – zwei Tage nach dem Überfall aus ihrem Brief-
kasten holte. Im ersten Augenblick glaubte sie, dass der Dieb
selbst es war, der seine Tat bereute und ihr das Geld zurück-
geschickt hatte. Aber wie wäre er zu ihrer Postadresse gekommen? Außerdem waren nicht die gestohlenen neuntausend,
sondern zehntausend Euro beigelegt. Und solche Hand-
taschendiebe würde man sich schon wünschen, die tags darauf nicht nur den Schaden wiedergutmachten, sondern auch
gleich zehn Prozent für den erlittenen Schock draufschlugen.
Logisch weitergedacht, würden diese Diebe dann der Reihe
nach bankrottgehen, und der Diebstahl als solcher wäre bald
ausgestorben.

Nun, die alte Frau ging schließlich mit dem Kuvert zur Polizei. Dort wusste man aufgrund des Zeitungsausschnitts sofort, dass es sich um den dritten nun bekannt gewordenen Fall einer anonymen barmherzigen Großtat handelte. Nach einem Obdachlosenheim und einer Kindertagesstätte wurde erstmals auch einer unverschuldet in Not geratenen Einzelperson die rettende Hand gereicht, Gott weiß woher.

Detektivisch hochinteressant war die Frage, wie der Wohltäter Name und Adresse des Opfers hatte ausfindig machen können. Die einzige Zeitung, die den Familiennamen der alten Frau, also Seilcek, ausgeschrieben hatte, war das *Tagblatt*. Hatte der Gönner also *Tagblatt* gelesen, danach die Adresse der alten Frau im Telefonbuch nachgeschlagen und schlussendlich aber den Zeitungsausschnitt von *Tag für Tag* verwendet? Wenn ja, warum? Weil die Botschaft in diesem prächtigen Gratisblatt so angenehm kurz und bündig war? Weil man auf einen Blick sehen konnte, was Sache war? Weil Sophie Rambuschek diese Notiz gestochen scharf, in der Wortwahl brillant und extrem wohltäterfreundlich formuliert hatte?

Von Letzterem war zumindest Chefredakteur Norbert Kunz überzeugt. Vor versammelter Redakteursrunde hielt er mit wässrigen Augen und bebender Stimme – beides ließ auf eine soeben erfolgte Vertragsverlängerung oder Gehaltserhöhung seitens der Eigentümer schließen – eine feurige Lobesrede auf *Tag für Tag* im Allgemeinen und auf die tüchtige Sophie Rambuschek im Besonderen.

Ich hielt mich in unmittelbarer Nähe einer feierlich geöffneten Magnum-Sektflasche auf und hatte gemischte Gefühle. Einerseits freute ich mich für Sophie, die von den sozialen Strapazen der letzten Tage bereits schwer gezeichnet war, darüber konnten auch ihr beiges Business-Kostüm und ihre frisch gestrichenen Lippen nicht hinwegtäuschen. Andererseits gingen mir die scheinheiligen Huldigungen und das gegenseitige

Schulterklopfen meiner Berufskollegen mächtig auf den Zeiger. Außerdem fühlte ich mich ehrlich gestanden schon ein bisschen an den Rand gedrängt, denn immerhin waren es zum dritten Male meine *bunten Meldungen zum Tag* gewesen, die die Geldspende begleitet hatten. Umso mehr freute es mich, dass Sophie dann doch noch auf mich zukam, ihre Hand auf meine Schulter legte und mir ein »danke« ins Ohr flüsterte. Darauf tranken wir dann noch ein, zwei Gläser Sekt.

Besuch bei Mama

Am Sonntag besuchte ich Mama. Ich brachte ihr einen Strauß bunt gesprenkelte Gladiolen mit, wie Monet sie gemalt hätte, das waren ihre Lieblingsblumen. Außerdem hatte ich zwei Ziegel Kaffee dabei. Das war eher symbolisch und sollte ihr sagen: Schau, dein Sohn favorisiert gesunden, kräftigenden, einen klaren Kopf machenden Kaffee anstelle von Wein, Wermut, Whiskey und ähnlich bösen Getränken. Komischerweise war Mama die Einzige, bei der ich so etwas wie ein schlechtes Gewissen verspürte, dass ich doch ganz schön regelmäßig größere Mengen Alkohol zu mir nahm. Natürlich kein Vergleich zu meinem Vater, der vor sieben Jahren an den Folgen einer Leberzirrhose verstorben war. Offiziell war zwar ein Virus der Auslöser gewesen, aber wer meinen Vater gekannt hatte, wusste, dass seine Nahrung in den überflüssigen Jahren nach seiner ÖBB-Frühpensionierung vorwiegend flüssig gewesen war, worunter Mama sehr gelitten hatte, ohne es sich anmerken lassen zu wollen, was das Ganze nur noch schlimmer machte. Aber sie wollte mich eben nicht zusätzlich belasten.

Ein Besuch bei meiner Mutter war immer emotional, wir hingen einfach sehr aneinander und wussten ganz genau, wie es um den jeweils anderen stand. Ich wusste, dass sie fürchtbar einsam war. Und sie wusste, dass ich es mir auf dem absteigenden Ast sozusagen bereits bequem gemacht hatte. Aber das durften wir voreinander natürlich niemals offen zugeben, was unsere Zusammenkünfte extrem anstrengend machte.

Auch diesmal übertrafen wir uns wieder gegenseitig an zweckoptimistischen Ansagen.

»Und was machen deine Blutwerte?«

»Viel besser, viel besser, sagt der Arzt. Und wie geht es der kleinen Florentina?«

»Der geht es prächtig, sie ist gar keine Kleine mehr, sie ist schon halb erwachsen. Und sag mal, Mama, kommst du wirklich noch ganz allein zurecht?«

»Ja, um mich brauchst du dir keine Sorgen zu machen, ich hab ja viele Nachbarinnen, die schauen alle auf mich. Und, Geri, was macht die Arbeit? Hast du viel zu tun?«

»Ja, ich bin momentan sehr beschäftigt, Mama. Aber ich sage immer, besser zu viel Arbeit als zu wenig.« Und so ging das die ganze Zeit. Ich holte mir vom vielen Lächeln regelmäßig einen Krampf in den Mundwinkeln, und sie vermutlich ebenfalls. Aber wir konnten einfach nicht anders, wir mussten uns ein bisschen die heile Welt vorgaukeln.

Kurz überlegte ich, ob ich ihr von Manuel erzählen sollte, aber das erschien mir dann doch etwas verfrüht, oder es kam vierzehn Jahre zu spät, je nachdem, wie man es sah. Wahrscheinlich hätte sie das auch eher belastet, nun nochmals unverhofft Oma zu werden, und wieder durfte sie die Rolle nicht ausleben, obwohl sie es sich im Stillen immer so sehr gewünscht hatte.

So kamen wir auf die Spendensache zu sprechen, die natürlich auch Mama zu Ohren gekommen war und die sie tief beeindruckte, das war klar. Ich hätte ihr ja gerne mitgeteilt, dass ich quasi an der Quelle der Wohltatenserie saß, aber dann hätte ich ihr beichten müssen, dass ich seit zwei Jahren bei *Tag für Tag* beschäftigt war und dort *bunte Meldungen* und reaktionäre bis stumpfsinnige Leserbriefe zu betreuen hatte. Mama war die Wahrheit im Prinzip zumutbar, aber eine solche hatte sie sich wirklich nicht verdient.

»Das muss ein wunderbarer Mensch sein«, sagte sie. Schon dieser Gedanke reichte aus, dass sich in ihren Augen die Wasserschleusen öffneten. Ich fand es faszinierend, dass Mama niemals aus Selbstmitleid weinte, immer nur aus Anteilnahme. Sie war ein Paradebeispiel von einem Menschen, der nie an sich, sondern nur an die anderen dachte, der stets alles gegeben und nie etwas genommen hatte. Das Problem solcher Menschen bestand darin, dass sich die Vorräte und Reserven dessen, was sie geben konnten, irgendwann erschöpften, weil sie eben einfach nichts annehmen konnten. In meiner zwar kurzen, aber vermutlich besten Zeit als Feuilletonist bei der *Rundschau* hatte ich diesem Thema, der Wechselwirkung von Geben und Nehmen, einmal eine ganze Beilage gewidmet, und wir hatten dazu sogar ein kleines Symposium veranstaltet.

»Dieser geheimnisvolle Helfer, der hat in seinem Leben wahrscheinlich viel bekommen. Und jetzt will er etwas davon zurückgeben«, sagte ich also, wobei mir schon klar war, dass ich eine Binsenweisheit von mir gab, doch ich wollte Mama irgendwie Trost spenden, weil sie ja nichts mehr hatte, was sie geben konnte.

»Ja, aber ist das nicht wunderbar, Geri, dass er es auch wirklich tut?« Sie war unverbesserlich.

»Doch, klar ist das wunderbar, Mama. Vor allem ist wunderbar, dass er es anonym tut, das ist nämlich wunderbar unüblich«, erwiderte ich.

Am Abend hörte ich endlich diese CD mit dem Titel *Piramida*. Ursprünglich wollte ich mir dazu einen Weinbrand einschenken, um die Gefühle, die nach einem Besuch bei Mama immer in mir aufstiegen, wieder hinunterzuspülen. Aber dann hatte ich plötzlich das Bedürfnis, mich zu testen, ob ich auch nein zu Alkohol sagen konnte, nur mal so aus Spaß. Nun, ich holte die Flasche aus dem Schrank, stellte sie auf den Couchtisch, sah sie an und sagte: »Nein!« ... Die Flasche war leer. Zum Glück waren noch zwei Dosen Bier im Kühlschrank.

Efterklang versetzte mich in eine seltsame Stimmung. Ich wäre von selbst nie auf die Idee gekommen, mir so eine Musik anzuhören. Da wartete man oft minutenlang, dass etwas passierte, und dann war der jeweilige Track auch schon zu Ende. Ich hörte lieber Bruce Springsteen, Neil Young, The Smiths, The Cure, Joy Division, Nick Cave, Tom Waits und solche Sachen. Das waren erstens meine musikalischen Wurzeln, und zweitens waren diese Typen ungefähr der gleiche Menschenschlag wie ich, mit dem einen Unterschied, dass sie die Songs über unerfüllte Hoffnungen und tägliche Niederlagen schrieben und spielten, und ich hörte und lebte sie eben nur.

Efterklang klang ganz anders. Ich musste auf Google nachlesen, was es damit auf sich hatte, und da bestätigte sich mein Verdacht. Diese Musiker, die aus Dänemark kamen, legten es auf Mystik, Abgeschiedenheit und Einsamkeit an. Das Album *Piramida* hatten sie in verfallenen Industrieanlagen einer ehemaligen sowjetischen Bergarbeitersiedlung aufgenommen, der Ortschaft Pyramiden auf Spitzbergen – also vom Arsch der Welt aus gesehen einfach geradeaus weiter. Auf so eine Idee musste man erst mal kommen.

Aber was mich wirklich bewegte: Wie kam ein Vierzehnjähriger dazu, sich solche todtraurigen Sachen anzuhören und als seine Lieblingsmusik zu bezeichnen? Das führte schnurstracks zu dem Gedanken, dass Manuel vielleicht insgeheim ein total unglücklicher, einsamer Bursche war, der wahnsinnig darunter litt, dass er keinen Vater hatte und dass seine Mutter ohne ihn nach Afrika gegangen war. Gleichzeitig bemerkte ich, dass es mir bei solchen Gedanken gar nicht gut ging und dass mir in dieser Situation zwei mittlerweile leere Bierdosen beim besten Willen keine moralische Stütze sein konnten.

Ich hatte plötzlich ganz enorme Sehnsucht nach einer Frau, mit der ich einfach nur eng beisammensitzen und vertraut reden oder auch vertraut nicht reden konnte, aber mir fiel außer einer gewissen Zahnärztin keine konkrete ein, und für unkonkrete Frauen war ein später Sonntagabend in meinem Alter und bei meiner Konsistenz absolut nicht mehr empfehlenswert.

Also wählte ich mein Notprogramm und rief meine Kumpels an.

»Hallo Josi, wie läuft's ... Im Pyjama? Ah, ich verstehe ...«

»Hallo Arik, wenn du jetzt gleich die Mobilbox abrufst und heute noch lustig bist, dann ruf mich zurück.«

»Hallo Franticek, was machst du? ... Ah so, ich verstehe, dann will ich nicht länger stören.«

»Hallo Horsti, wo bist du? ... Hütteldorfer Straße ... Rebusbar? Alles klar.« Die Rebusbar in Penzing war zwar eine wirklich üble Spelunke, aber immer noch weniger trist und einsam als Pyramiden auf Spitzbergen, dachte ich. »Okay, rühr dich nicht vom Fleck. In einer halben Stunde bin ich da«, sagte ich.

Es ist schon wichtig, dass man viele Freunde hat, damit man sich wenigstens auf einen davon verlassen kann.

So schwer, wie mein Kopf war, hätte ich mich am Montag normalerweise krankgemeldet, aber seit Manuels Existenz in meinem Leben kam das irgendwie nicht mehr in Frage. Außerdem musste ich mich früher oder später sowieso aufraffen, am Nachmittag waren wir zur Zahnkontrolle angemeldet. Ich hoffte, dass meine lokale Betäubung von der Vornacht bis dahin anhalten würde.

Über Efterklang verlor ich gegenüber Manuel nur einige wenige Worte. Ich sagte, dass ich es cool fand, dass er sich in seinem Alter für elektronische Musik interessierte und nicht für die billigen Popsongs aus den Charts.

»Aber sag mal, macht dich diese Musik nicht traurig?« Das wollte ich dann doch noch ansprechen.

»Warum soll sie mich traurig machen?«, erwiderte er.

»Okay, Manuel, ich stelle dir jetzt noch eine Frage. Und auf diese Frage will ich eine bestimmte Antwort *nicht* hören. Ich will von dir jetzt *nicht* hören: Warum soll ich prinzipiell traurig sein? So, hiermit weißt du auch, was ich dich fragen will, richtig? Also was will ich dich fragen?« Er lachte, das gefiel ihm.

»Du willst mich fragen, ob ich prinzipiell traurig bin.«

»Richtig.«

»Und ich darf nicht antworten: Warum soll ich prinzipiell traurig sein?«, fragte er.

»Richtig.« Jetzt musste er lange nachdenken.

»Wie kommst du auf die Idee, dass ich prinzipiell traurig sein könnte?«, fragte er. Na ja, das war schon einmal ein kleiner Fortschritt.

»Auf die Idee komme ich deshalb, weil du traurige Musik hörst und sonst auch immer sehr ruhig und ernst bist, zumindest in meiner Gegenwart.«

»Würde es dich stören, wenn ich traurig bin?«, fragte er.

46

»Ja.«

»Warum?«, fragte er. Das war eine gute Frage, auf die ich meinem Sohn keine vollkommen ehrliche Antwort geben konnte. Also probierte ich es mit einer beinahe ehrlichen.

»Weil mich traurige Menschen selbst traurig machen.«

»Du bist ja sowieso schon ein trauriger Mensch«, sagte er. Das saß. Und wie er mich dabei ansah, das war mir gar nicht angenehm.

»Wie kommst du darauf?«, fragte ich.

»Sonst würdest du nicht dauernd Alkohol trinken.« Na klar. Da zeigte sich wieder, dass die jungen Menschen absolut unzureichend über die Bedeutung und Wirkung von Alkohol aufgeklärt wurden. Alles konzentrierte sich auf die Drogenprävention, und über Alkohol wusste keiner mehr Bescheid.

»Ich trinke Alkohol, weil er mir schmeckt. Und wenn mir etwas schmeckt, dann bin ich auch nicht traurig«, sagte ich. Er nickte zwar, aber er glaubte mir kein Wort. Außerdem war er hochintelligent und rhetorisch brillant, denn mit wenigen Wendungen war es ihm gelungen, mir seine eigene Traurigkeit anzuhängen.

Auf mein Drängen hin riefen wir dann seine Mama in Somalia an, wo es wegen der Zeitverschiebung bereits zwei Stunden später war. Manuel hatte zwar beteuert, dass er beinahe jeden Abend mit ihr telefonierte, aber ich wollte auch einmal dabei sein, immerhin war ich sein Nachmittagsbetreuer – und sein Vater obendrein.

Alice war gleich am Apparat und wirkte sehr gehetzt, wahrscheinlich operierte sie gerade simultan fünf Afrikaner.

»Hallo Geri, ist alles okay bei euch?«

»Ja, alles okay, dein Sohn wollte nur ein paar Worte mit dir wechseln«, sagte ich und reichte ihm das Telefon. Das war zwar wirklich gemein von mir, und er zog eine Grimasse, aber letztlich hatte ich erfolgreich eine Mutter-Sohn-Verbindung hergestellt. Meinen Ohren waren von dem Gespräch allerdings nur Bruchstücke vergönnt.

»Hallo Mama.«

»Ja, gut.«

»Bei Gerold im Büro.« Immerhin nannte er mich Gerold und das hier Büro.

»Kalt.«

»Nein, Sonne. Sonne und Wolken.«

»Ja.«

»Mathematik.«

»Ja.«

»Ja.«

»Ja, bin ich.«

»Jaaaa, ich verspreche es dir.«

Jetzt sah er mich schräg von unten an. Sie hatte ihn wahrscheinlich aufgefordert, nett zu mir zu sein.

»Nein, noch nicht.«

»Weiß nicht.«

»Sag du's ihr.« Das war interessant. Mit »ihr« könnte Tante Julia gemeint gewesen sein.

»Heute?«

»Heute muss ich noch mal zum Zahnarzt.«

»Nein, mit Gerold.«

»Ja, er geht mit.«

»Ja, wirklich.«

»Ja, sag ich ihm.«

»Ja.«

»Tschüss.«

»Ja, mach ich.« Er reichte mir auf pubertär ruppige Weise mein Telefon.

»Was sollst du mir sagen?«, fragte ich.

»Dass es nett von dir ist, dass du mit mir zum Zahnarzt gehst.«

»Zur Zahnärztin«, korrigierte ich. »Aber deine Mama hat recht, das ist nett von mir.«

In der Höhle der schönen Löwin

Bei der Medizinerin mit den blonden kurzen Haaren und dem entzückenden – was nannte ich am besten als Erstes? – also mit dem entzückenden Achtzig-Grad-Übergang von der entzückenden Kinnkante zum entzückenden Halsansatz, bei dieser Medizinerin, die uns nach der dritten und entscheidenden Tür gastfreundlich die Hand entgegenstreckte, um uns in ihrer heimelig nach Chlorphenol duftenden Werkstatt auf das Herzlichste willkommen zu heißen, handelte es sich um Frau Rebecca Linsbach, siebenunddreißig Jahre alt, unbestimmten Familienstandes, seit sieben Jahren Vertragsärztin mit eigener Praxis, öffentlich erst ein Mal groß in Erscheinung getreten, und zwar mit einem vermutlich aufsehenerregenden Referat beim österreichischen Zahnärztekongress 2013 in Salzburg, zum volksnahen Thema *Implantatversorgungen im atrophen Kiefer; Augmentationsverfahren, Distraktionsosteogenese und Prothetikkonzepte.* Ansonsten war sie virtuell unauffällig, keine Buchveröffentlichungen bei Amazon, keine Freunde bei Facebook, keine Aktivitäten bei Twitter. Ein einziges Bild, gefertigt von der Ärztekammer, Kategorie Passfoto, Prädikat: ganz besonders sehenswert. (Quelle: Internet, diverse Suchmaschinen.)

»Und wie geht es dem tapferen Patienten?« Sie sah mich an, meinte aber wahrscheinlich Manuel. »Irgendwelche Komplikationen?«

Das war leider keine Frage, auf die man antworten konnte: Ich bin noch mal hierhergekommen, in die Höhle der Löwin, um Sie zu fragen, ob wir uns nicht vielleicht etwas näher kennenlernen können, abseits von atrophen Kiefern sozusagen.

Also sagte ich: »Nein, also soweit ich das von außen beurteilen kann, dürfte mit meinem ... dürfte mit unserem jungen Patienten alles sehr gut verlaufen sein, nicht wahr, Manuel?« Er warf mir einen relativ verächtlichen Blick zu.

Dann ging leider alles sehr rasch. Sowie Manuel auf dem weißen Stuhl lag, war Rebecca Linsbachs volle Aufmerksamkeit auf ihn gerichtet, und sein ausgeleuchtetes Mund-Innenleben wurde abwechselnd bewundert, besprüht, bewässert, betastet und beklopft, wobei ich verwundert war, wie kalt mich das diesmal ließ. Schon hieß es: »Wir sind fertig, junger Mann. Bitte eine Stunde nichts essen.« Und dann endlich doch noch an mich gerichtet: »Im Frühling möchte ich Ihren Sohn gern wiedersehen.«

»Er ist nicht mein Vater, nur ein alter Freund meiner Mutter«, sagte Manuel.

»Seine Mutter arbeitet ein halbes Jahr in Somalia, sie ist ebenfalls Ärztin, keine Zahnärztin, aber dafür Ärztin in Afrika.« Ich lächelte trotz flauer Pointe möglichst gewinnend und möglichst ohne meine Zähne herzuzeigen.

»Ah, interessant«, sagte sie im Tonfall von »Ah, uninteressant«. Aber völlig egal war ich ihr nun auch wieder nicht, man spürt so etwas als Mann. Es gibt ja auch durchaus gesunde und schöne Frauen, vielleicht sogar makellose Zahnärztinnen mit entzückenden Kinnkanten und Halsansätzen, die auf fossile Typen wie Gérard Depardieu nach fünf Jahren Wodka-Staatsbürgerschaft stehen.

Wir befanden uns dennoch leider unmittelbar vor der Verabschiedung, und ich musste unbedingt noch etwas sagen, sonst war die Chance für immer vertan.

»Frau Magister, ich hoffe, es ist nicht unverschämt, wenn ich Sie einfach so direkt frage, ob Sie vielleicht ... ob ich vielleicht ...«

»Aber selbstverständlich. Habe ich mir ohnehin schon gedacht, dass das dringend notwendig wäre. Sie können gleich draußen bei meiner Assistentin einen Termin für nächste Woche vereinbaren. Eher generell routinemäßig? Oder haben Sie Schmerzen?« Manuels völlig unnötiges blödes Gelächter brachte mich total aus dem Konzept, aber ich kriegte trotzdem einen brauchbaren Satz zusammen: »Eher generell routinemäßig. Die Schmerzen werden dann schon noch rechtzeitig dazukommen.« Jetzt sah ich sie doch noch lächeln. Und dabei wurde sie von meinem Zwischenhirn gestochen scharf fotografiert.

KAPITEL VIER

Die vierte Spende

Anfang Oktober fehlte vom Täter, also vom Wohltäter, noch immer jede Spur, obwohl die Profile der zahlreichen wie Pilze aus dem Boden geschossenen Experten der Fächer Psychologie, Spekulation und Wahrsagung täglich schärfer, facettenreicher und kunstvoller gezeichnet wurden. Die Gönnersuche entwickelte sich zum Volkssport. Die Menschen liebten dieses ungewöhnliche Sozialrätsel. Endlich einmal fahndete man nicht nach einem Räuber, sondern nach dem krassen Gegenteil davon, und jeder noch so stumpfsinnige Artikel darüber schien wohltätige Zwecke zu verfolgen und auf seine Art zur Weltverbesserung beizutragen.

Bald kam es zur vierten Spende. Sie wurde nicht nur im Wiener Raum, sondern auch weit über die Stadtgrenzen hinaus wie ein gesellschaftliches Großereignis gefeiert und versetzte *Tag für Tag* in einen wahren Glückseligkeitsrausch, der sich nun auch wirtschaftlich auswirkte. Denn immer mehr Inserenten fanden Gefallen daran, ihre Güter in der populär gewordenen Gratis-Postille zu bewerben und sozusagen als weitere Geschenke an die Menschheit zu verkaufen.

Ja, auch diesem vierten zehntausend Euro schweren Geldkuvert war ein Zeitungsausschnitt von *Tag für Tag* beigelegt, und nahezu alle Hobby-Ermittler, einschließlich meiner Kumpels aus Zoltan's Bar, waren sich über das Leseverhalten des Wohltäters oder der Wohltäterin von nun an einig: Er oder sie konzentrierte sich ausschließlich auf die *bunten Meldungen zum Tag*. Sophie Rambuschek konnte mit ihren großen Sozialreportagen und Kolumnen frisch eingefärbtes künstliches Herzblut vergießen, so viel sie wollte, dem Gönner war dafür keine Spende zu entlocken.

Er mochte es lieber schlicht und wenig ergreifend:

Bei der Wiener Sozialberatungsstelle Hilfe jetzt *werden die Mittel knapp. Die karitative Einrichtung für Menschen in Notlagen, die sich auf die Fahnen geschrieben hat, rasch und unbürokratisch zu helfen, sieht sich aufgrund ständig steigender Anfragen gezwungen, immer mehr Hilfesuchende abzuweisen.*

Sophie hatte ursprünglich geplant, diesem Thema die große Sozialstory zu widmen, hatte sich dann aber doch für die Krise der Freiwilligen Feuerwehr entschieden, der in einigen Bezirken die Ressourcen fehlten, ihrer Arbeit effizient und flächendeckend nachzugehen. So war aus den Sorgen der Sozialberatungsstelle *Hilfe jetzt* nur eine Kurzmeldung geworden, und das war offenbar ihr großes Glück.

Was aber sagte der Umstand, dass sich der anonyme Geldspender ausschließlich bei Kurznotizen von *Tag für Tag* bediente, über ihn selbst aus? Dazu lieferte die öffentliche Diskussion bereits ein breitgefächertes Angebot an Deutungsvorschlägen.

1. Offensichtlich wollte er bei der Auswahl der Bedürftigen so wenig Aufwand wie möglich betreiben.

2. Er war ja nicht einmal bereit, für die Zeitung Geld zu bezahlen, aus der er die Empfänger seiner Spenden rekrutierte.

3. Oder es ging ihm darum, keinen Zeitungsladen aufsuchen zu müssen und auch sonst nicht auf Hilfestellung angewiesen zu sein. Er fand die Gazette sozusagen auf der Straße und musste mit keinem Menschen in Kontakt treten, um seine Spendenwahl zu treffen.

4. Das Niveau und selbst die Ideologie der Zeitung, die sogenannte Blattlinie, waren ihm vollkommen egal.

5. Oder er hatte durchaus medien- und sozialpolitische Motive. Dann war es ihm vielleicht sogar ein Anliegen, die rand-

gruppenfeindliche Law-and-Order-Postille zum Sprachrohr der sozial Benachteiligten zu machen.

6. Er tendierte jedenfalls klar zu den kleinen, versteckten Hilferufen und ignorierte die groß aufgebauschten Sozialdramen.

7. Er war vielleicht ein alter Mann oder eine alte Frau, der oder die keine Lust, keine Kraft oder keine Zeit mehr hatte, sich intensiv und hintergründig mit Sozialfällen zu beschäftigen, weshalb er oder sie stereotyp zur Gratiszeitung griff und mehr oder weniger x-beliebig aus den *bunten Meldungen zum Tag* schöpfte.

8. Und doch war dem Wohltäter wichtig, die Quelle seiner Informationen anzugeben, sonst hätte er darauf verzichtet, regelmäßig den jeweiligen Zeitungsausschnitt mitzusenden. Ob er dabei so weit gedacht hatte, dass es ohne diese Ausschnitte niemals zu einer derartig großen medialen Aufmerksamkeit und Breitenwirkung in der Bevölkerung gekommen wäre, auch darüber durfte man rätseln.

Die göttliche Arbeit

Ich freute mich natürlich auch über die vierte Spende. Nicht nur weil sich der Gönner eindeutig auf die offiziell immer noch von mir verwalteten *bunten Meldungen* eingeschossen hatte, sondern weil ich schon als Kind Robin Hood geliebt hatte und weil es einfach schön war, nun relativ hautnah mitzuerleben, wie sich da jemand der Kleinsten und Schwächsten in der Gesellschaft annahm, beziehungsweise jene Menschen unterstützte, die sich aus freien Stücken und ohne öffentliches Tamtam in den Dienst einer guten Sache stellten. So weit zum Positiven.

Leider hatte ich es in meiner Redaktion mit zunehmend

manischen Persönlichkeiten zu tun, allen voran Norbert Kunz, die tatsächlich glaubten, sie wären mindestens Gott, und die enormen Druck auf mich ausübten, mich zum Glauben zu bekennen, was nichts anderes bedeutete, als dass ich für das gleiche Geld um ein Vielfaches mehr arbeiten sollte. Die Leserbriefspalte wurde aufgrund des enormen Andrangs im Umfang verdreifacht, was hieß, dass dreimal so viele Psychopathen wie bisher ihre kruden Theorien zum Besten geben durften – und ich musste mich mit diesen abstrusen Texten herumschlagen.

Noch schlimmer erging es mir mit den *bunten Meldungen zum Tag*. Sophie Rambuschek war mit ihrer tonnenschweren Sozialkiste heillos überfordert und obendrein frustriert, weil sich der Spender ihrer groß aufgezogenen Reportagen ums Verrecken nicht erbarmen wollte. Leider war es aber inzwischen unmöglich, die Sache wieder einzustellen, war doch Sophie sozusagen das journalistische Gesicht zum anonymen Geldsegen geworden. Mit ihrem hübschen Konterfei wurde auf Plakaten und in Inseraten für das neue Gutmenschentum Marke *Tag für Tag* geworben.

Und doch wusste jeder, dass es der Spender offensichtlich nur auf die Kurznotizen abgesehen hatte, die bereits zu einer von der Konkurrenz mit Argusaugen überwachten Festung ausgebaut worden waren. Die Auswahl der Sozialmeldungen war zur Chefsache mit Senatsbeschluss erklärt worden. Alle paar Stunden steckten sie in Sitzungsmarathons die Köpfe zusammen und grübelten und feilschten, wie und womit man des Gönners Herz erweichen und seine Börse um weitere zehntausend Euro erleichtern könnte.

Ich aber hockte im stillen und finsteren Kämmerlein und bearbeitete den Rest der bunten Themen – alles, was nicht sozial war, also die öden und destruktiven 99 Prozent des Weltgeschehens. Zudem müllten mir enthemmte Vertreter des verbleibenden hundertsten Prozents, nämlich die wachgerufene Zielgruppe larmoyanter bis militanter Möchtegern-Wohltäter, jetzt von früh bis spät meine Mailbox zu. Das waren Menschen, die theoretisch immer schon Gutes leisten wollten, aber praktisch noch nie die Mittel dafür hatten. Sie sahen nun die Chance, am großen Spendenkuchen mitzunaschen, und flehten für kaum durchdachte Hilfsprojekte um ein paar Zeilen Berichterstattung in den Kurzmeldungen. Ich schickte solche Mails postwendend an Sophie Rambuschek, die leitete sie mit der Frage »Was sollen wir damit machen?« an Norbert Kunz weiter, und von dort gelangten sie dann mit dem Hinweis »Herr Plassek, bitte höflich antworten!!!« wieder zu mir zurück.

Bilder von der Unerreichbaren

Das Besondere an diesen ersten Oktobertagen, und da war ich schon anders drauf als die anderen, das Besondere war Rebecca Linsbach. Den Gedanken, dass diese Frau, die ich ja überhaupt nicht kannte, im Grunde unerreichbar für mich war, schob ich mühelos zur Seite. Da musste ich erst gar nicht darüber spekulieren, in welcher Führungsetage ihr Ehemann wohl saß, welche Geländelimousine er von welcher Loft-Parkgarage zu welchem Landsitz fuhr, und wie viele goldige Linsbach-Kinder abends, nach mindestens einstündigem zeremoniellem Zähneputzen, in ihre Bettchen gebracht wurden, damit ihnen Mama und Papa im Dialog noch ihre Lieblingsgutenachtgeschichten vorlesen konnten. Und wenn die Kleinen eingeschlafen waren, wurde das Kaminfeuer im Wohnzimmer entfacht, und Mister James Linsbach rührte die Cocktails an, oder er schüttelte sie, oder man hob sie sich für später auf, je nach Dringlichkeit und Stimmung.

Daran dachte ich – nicht. Ich war ja kein Masochist. Real hatte ich nur Rebeccas Google-Porträt vom Zahnärztekongress vor mir und verglich es mit den Bildern, die mein Zwischenhirn von ihr gespeichert hatte. Diese Bilderfolge ergab einen kleinen Film, den ich mehrmals täglich abspulte, um mir zwischendurch auch etwas Schönes zu gönnen, das mich vom Üblichen ablenkte. Am liebsten spulte ich den Film nachts ab, wenn ich im Bett lag und mein Kopf untüchtig gemacht worden war, Zwischenbilanzen über den Tag oder gar über mein Leben zu ziehen. Da sah ich neuerdings Rebecca und bildete mir ein, dass alles, was vorstellbar war, auch umsetzbar sein konnte, selbst das faktisch Unmögliche.

»Bist du ein bisschen in die Zahnärztin?«, fragte mich Manuel irgendeines Nachmittags zu meiner Verblüffung. Er hatte dabei dieses schmutzige Grinsen auf der Oberlippe, das Grinsen eines halbaufgeklärten Vierzehnjährigen, bei dem die Liebesbotschaften aus den TV-Kanälen und Internet-Foren noch nicht wirklich im Kopf angekommen waren, geschweige denn im Herzen, sondern ein paar Etagen tiefer rumorten.

»Bin ich ein bisschen *was?*«, fragte ich. Jetzt konnte er mal beweisen, was er so draufhatte.

Er legte den Stift zur Seite, mit dem er sowieso noch kein Wort in das vor ihm liegende Heft geschrieben hatte, seit er ihn vor gut zwanzig Minuten in die Hand genommen hatte.

»Du weißt schon, was ich meine, verknallt, verschossen ...« Klar, die übliche Kampfsprache. Ich war ja ein Befürworter strengerer verbaler Waffengesetze, zumindest für Jugendliche.

»Verliebt, meinst du?«, fragte ich. Das Wort verursachte ihm natürlich Pein, er war eben ein Bub, und da hatte sich seit meiner eigenen Kindheit erstaunlich wenig geändert.

»Ja, sie gefällt mir, sie ist ehrlich gestanden genau mein Typ«, sagte ich.

»Aber da wirst du dich ordentlich anstrengen müssen.«

Jetzt grinste er wieder, aber nicht mehr dreckig, sondern eher verschwörerisch.

»Wieso glaubst du das?«

»Na ja, bei deinen Zähnen.«

»Die wird sie mir schon richten und polieren«, sagte ich. Jetzt lachte er laut los. Ich hielt es nicht für allzu weit hergeholt, dass er mich zunehmend witzig fand. Und ich hatte plötzlich sogar das Gefühl, dass ich in der Lage war, ihm ein echtes Vorbild zu sein, nämlich darin, wie man die Dinge subjektiv sehen konnte, wenn sie sich objektiv ganz anders darstellten. Damit konnte man gar nicht früh genug beginnen, denn das war auf Dauer wichtig, um zu überleben.

Mit Florentina in der Bierbar

Als Vater erlebte ich in dieser Woche sogar noch eine zweite kleine Sternstunde: Florentina rief mich an und wollte sich mit mir treffen, ohne Gudrun, nur wir beide. Begegnungen zu zweit mit meiner Tochter waren an den Fingern einer Hand abzuzählen. Vor unendlich vielen Jahren war ich einmal zum Ponyreiten mit ihr im Prater gewesen, ein traumatischer Sonntagnachmittag, den ich bis heute nicht vergessen konnte. Als die kleine Prinzessin auf dem Pferd saß, begann sie plötzlich zu weinen und war nicht mehr zu beruhigen. Zugegeben, auch ich als Zuschauer hatte mir von dem Pony mehr erwartet als fünf gelangweilte Schritte mit jeweils fünf Minuten Verdauungspause dazwischen. Das Problem war, dass Florentina damals glaubte, ich wäre schuld, denn schließlich hatte ich sie auf das lahme Pony gesetzt, während die anderen Kinder auf den anderen Pferden davongaloppierten. Mir blieb nichts übrig, als Gudrun zu alarmieren, damit sie das hysterisch brüllende Kind abholte. Berthold, der neue Papa, ließ es sich nicht nehmen mitzukommen. Er stellte sich demonstrativ zwischen uns und breitete seine Arme aus, als wäre er ihr Retter. Als Florentina ihn sah, rannte sie wie besessen auf ihn zu. Er hob sie hoch, wirbelte sie durch die Luft, drückte sie an sich, küsste sie. Die Tränen waren im Nu weg, und die Kleine strahlte über das ganze Gesicht. Zur Belohnung durfte sie sich ihren Mund mit rosa Zuckerwatte bekleben, Berthold wusste eben, wie man gebrochene Kinderherzen wieder kittete. Beim Abschied winkte ich ihr, aber sie winkte nicht zurück. Seit damals vermieden wir Zweierzusammenkünfte, wo es nur ging. Okay, ich war derjenige, der sie vermied. Ich hatte einfach panische Angst, meine kleine Florentina wieder auf ein falsches Pony zu setzen.

Es war also ihre Initiative und ihr Anruf und ihre Idee und ihr ausdrücklicher Wunsch, und so trafen wir uns im Treiblos, einer alternativen Bierbar im verruchten Stuwerviertel – auch das ihre Wahl –, in der Leute unter vierzig im Grunde nicht vorkamen. Da wollte sie mir offenbar mehr als nur auf halbem Weg entgegenkommen. Ich hatte vorher schon ein paar Gläser getrunken, weil ich wahnsinnig aufgeregt war. Kinder konnten einen ganz schön stressen.

Ihr Auftreten, ihre teuren Klamotten, die sich radikal verbilligten durch die Art, wie sie sie trug, ihre verwischte Schminke und das silberne Sternchen in ihrem Nasenflügel, das davon träumte, ein dreckig punkiges Piercing zu sein, sollten jeden Zweifel zerstreuen, dass hier ein Kind den Raum betreten haben könnte. Zu dem Outfit gehörte auch, dass sie an jedem x-beliebigen männlichen Gast oder Kellner, egal wie grindig er war, einen flirtenden Blick erprobte, und das tat mir richtig weh.

»Für mich ein Bier, was trinkst du, Florentina? Apfelsaft?«, fragte ich.

»Auch ein Bier«, sagte sie.

»Ehrlich?«, fragte ich. Das war mir absolut nicht recht, es war erst Nachmittag.

»Ja klar, ich trinke immer ein Bier, wenn ich fortgehe«, sagte sie und lächelte mich verschwörerisch an, weil sie tatsächlich glaubte, dass sie damit bei mir punktete. Ich war leider der Letzte, der das Recht hatte, hier ein Machtwort zu sprechen.

Ungefähr in diese Richtung entwickelte sich dann auch unser Gespräch. Florentina wollte sich bei mir über ihre spießigen »Alten« beschweren. Sie hatte genug von daheim, von Schularbeiten, von zeitlichen Limits beim Internetsurfen, von geregelten Mahl- und kontrollierten Heimkehrzeiten, von Ordnungsappellen und Aufrufen zu Disziplin, Sauberkeit und Höflichkeit, von Stil und Etikette. Außerdem zog sie ernsthaft in Erwägung, alles hinzuschmeißen und das Gymnasium abzubrechen.

»Um was zu machen?«, fragte ich.

»Keine Ahnung, irgendwelche Jobs, ich will einfach frei sein. Ich will nicht so enden wie Mama und Papa ... also Berthold«, sagte sie.

»Willst du lieber so enden wie ich?«, fragte ich. Ich hatte selten einen Satz ausgesprochen, der mir so fest an der Zunge geklebt und der sich so schmerzhaft losgelöst hatte wie dieser.

»Du lebst wenigstens dein Leben, tust, was du willst, und kümmerst dich nicht darum, was die anderen von dir denken«, sagte sie.

»Aber verwechsle das bitte nicht mit Freiheit, liebes Kind«, erwiderte ich. »Meine Freiheit besteht darin, zwischen Wein, Bier und Schnaps zu wählen, und das kann ich mir auch nur deshalb leisten, weil deine Mama mir einen Job verschafft hat, einen Job, den ich obendrein hasse. Das ist meine Freiheit!« Innerlich bebte ich vor Angst, dass Florentina jetzt wieder den Blick von damals bekommen würde, als sie auf dem Pony gesessen hatte.

»Aber du bist wenigstens echt. Du bist dir immer treu geblieben, und nur das zählt«, sagte sie. Ich schaffte es gerade noch, ihre Hand zu nehmen und fest zu drücken, dann musste ich leider sofort aufstehen und die Toilette aufsuchen.

Als ich mich wieder im Griff hatte und zum Tisch zurückgekehrt war, rückte Florentina mit der Sprache raus und erzählte mir, dass sie seit drei Monaten einen Freund hatte. Er hieß Mike und war einundzwanzig Jahre alt. »Und er ist Musiker«, sagte ich.

»Ja. Wieso weißt du das?« Sie war tatsächlich erstaunt.

»Ich kenne meine Tochter. Schlagzeug?«

»Nein, Bassgitarre.«

»Gute Bassisten braucht man immer«, log ich.

»Und was spielen die für Musik?«

»Indie und Psychedelic Rock, eher langsame Sachen.« Psychedelic – das klang gar nicht gut.

»Und habt ihr schon …?«

»Ich nicht. Er schon, aber nur Haschischzigaretten, nichts Starkes.« Ich hatte zwar etwas anderes gemeint, aber das machte mich auch ganz schön nervös.

»Willst du Mike kennenlernen?«, fragte sie mich.

»Ja, sehr gerne sogar. Unbedingt! Das finde ich toll, dass du mich das fragst.«

»Er ist süß. Er wird dir gefallen«, sagte sie. Da war ich mir nicht so sicher.

»Er erinnert mich an dich.« Das war zwar einerseits entzückend, andererseits bestätigte es meinen üblen Verdacht. »Aber kein Wort zu Mama und Berthold, das musst du mir versprechen. Die dürfen nichts von ihm wissen«, sagte sie.

»Von mir werden sie nichts erfahren, das schwöre ich.« Ich starrte mein leeres Bierglas an und spürte, dass ich ganz dringend Nachschub brauchte. Aber es ging irgendwie nicht, denn Florentinas Glas war ebenfalls leer.

»Ich möchte übrigens auch, dass du wen kennenlernst, aber es ist vielleicht noch etwas zu früh«, sagte ich.

»Hast du eine neue Liebe?« Sie riss die Augen auf und ließ ihre grün-kupfer-bernstein-gelb umrandeten Pupillen aufleuchten. Wir drei hatten praktisch die gleichen sechs Augen.

»Nein, nein, das nicht ... oder ... das heißt ... vielleicht ... aber ich meine ganz wen anderen. Es ist bloß noch zu früh«, wiederholte ich. Jetzt hatte ich sie zwar komplett verwirrt, aber wir beließen es dabei.

»So, und weißt du, was wir jetzt machen, Florentina? Wir bestellen uns einen Kaffee. Einverstanden?«, fragte ich.

»Ja, Kaffee ist gut«, erwiderte sie.

»Und dann möchte ich dir gerne noch ein paar Worte zum Thema Schule sagen.«

»Muss das sein?«

»Ich glaube schon.«

»Okay«, sagte sie.

Schlacht um die Spenden

Als für Donnerstagnachmittag kurzfristig eine große Konferenz einberufen wurde, an der alle Mitarbeiter von *Tag für Tag* teilnehmen sollten, tippten wir natürlich sofort auf eine fünfte anonyme Spende. Nun, wir behielten zwar recht, aber das war leider längst noch nicht alles.

Man konnte schon an den fahrigen Handbewegungen und am nervösen Zucken im Gesicht von Norbert Kunz erkennen, dass irgendwas nicht stimmte und dass die über Wochen künstlich aufgebaute Euphorie plötzlich zu kippen drohte. Außerdem stellten sie uns diesmal nur ein paar Karaffen Leitungswasser hin und öffneten nicht eine einzige Flasche Sekt.

Doch zunächst einmal wurde uns die gute Nachricht verkündet: Bei der Familie Wenger aus Großreinprechts in Niederösterreich war eine Spende in der Höhe von zehntausend Euro eingegangen. In dem absenderlosen weißen Kuvert befanden sich nicht nur zwanzig Fünfhunderter, sondern auch der obligate Zeitungsausschnitt von *Tag für Tag*. Das Anwesen der bäuerlichen Großfamilie mit fünf Kindern war durch einen Blitzschlag über Nacht vollkommen verwüstet, ja »dem Erdboden gleichgemacht« worden, der Landwirt und seine abermals schwangere Frau standen »vor den Trümmern ihrer Existenz«, so hieß es wörtlich im Kurztext. Man hätte beinahe Wetten darauf abschließen können, dass diese Meldung den Wohltäter zu einer Geldspende veranlassen würde. Und so war es dann auch geschehen.

Danach hielt Kunz allerdings eine seltsame Rede, mit der ich zunächst gar nichts anfangen konnte. In bitterem und aggressivem Ton mokierte er sich über die Abgründe der hiesigen Medienlandschaft, über Neid, Missgunst und Verrat. Er stellte es so dar, als wäre *Tag für Tag* quasi die leitende moralische Instanz des Landes, eine Oase der Barmherzigkeit, ein Hort christlicher Nächstenliebe, katholischer als der Katholizismus selbst, weshalb der Spender nicht umhinkam, dieses Medium für seine guten Zwecke zu gebrauchen. Aber draußen lauerte der Feind, spionierte, legte Hinterhalte, stellte Fallen und wartete auf seine Chance, die Guten zu diffamieren und in Skandale zu verwickeln.

Dann sprach er es endlich aus: Clemens Waltner, leitender Geschäftsführer von *Tag für Tag*, ferner Aufsichtsratsmitglied und führender Kopf (dem Aussehen nach zu urteilen eher Bauch) des Großhandelskonzerns Plus, war unter Verdacht geraten, hinter der anonymen Spendenserie zu stehen, sie also sozusagen selbst ins Leben gerufen und mit noch unausgeforschten Komplizen abgewickelt zu haben, um der maroden Gratiszeitung Publicity zu verschaffen und neue Inserenten anzulocken – was ihm ja tatsächlich gelungen war, wenn die Behauptung stimmte.

Aber ich konnte mir eigentlich nicht vorstellen, dass sie stimmte. Für so eine ausgeklügelte Sache, in die man noch dazu mindestens fünfzigtausend Euro hätte investieren müssen, sprach ich einem Herrn Waltner – den ich einmal bei einer Firmenweihnachtsfeier beim Gulaschessen aus der Nähe beobachten durfte, worauf ich mich fragte, wieso solche gierigen Leute immer weiße Hemden trugen – also ich sprach ihm einfach die soziale und auch jede andere Intelligenz ab.

»Diese Geschichte ist von A bis Z erstunken und erlogen«, behauptete natürlich auch Kunz unter beifälligem Gemurmel der Belegschaft. Dafür sprach freilich schon einmal der Umstand, wer diese Geschichte überhaupt erzählte, beziehungsweise wer sich anschickte, die Bombe in seiner am Freitag erscheinenden Ausgabe platzen zu lassen. Es war das Konkurrenzblatt *Leute heute*, eine voyeuristische Programmzeitung, die sich normalerweise an die Fersen und Unterhosen von C-Promis heftete und etwa die gleichen Zielgruppen bediente wie *Tag für Tag*. Angeblich waren der Redaktion Tonbandaufzeichnungen in die Hände gespielt worden, auf denen Waltner gegenüber zwei engen Freunden in einem Nachtcafé zu vorgerückter Stunde und auch gar nicht mehr extrem nüchtern damit geprahlt haben sollte, kein Geringerer als der anonyme Wohltäter zu sein. Quasi zum Beweis hätte er die Montagsausgabe von *Tag für Tag* aus seiner Tasche gezogen, auf die *bunte Meldung* über den Blitzschlag in Großreinprechts gezeigt und angekündigt, dass diese Familie demnächst in den Genuss von zehntausend Euro kommen würde. »Die haben's auch wirklich verdient«, sollte er noch hinzugefügt haben. Allein schon diesen Satz traute ich ihm niemals zu.

Daneben verfügte *Leute heute* angeblich über weiteres belastendes Material. Die Polizei, so hieß es, ermittle und führe erste Zeugenbefragungen wegen Betrugsverdachts durch, und in der Chefetage von Plus seien bereits Durchsuchungen veranlasst worden. Dies alles war einer Vorankündigung zur großen Enthüllungsstory von *Leute heute* zu entnehmen, die uns Kunz nun vorlas und die bereits über die Agenturen lief.

»Liebe Kolleginnen und Kollegen, ich kann Sie beruhigen, kein Wort davon ist wahr«, versicherte uns der Chefredakteur und wischte sich mit dem Handrücken über die schweißige Stirn. Instinktiv glaubte ich ihm, obwohl er selbst gar nicht wissen, sondern nur hoffen konnte, dass nichts davon wahr war. Immerhin waren die Medienanwälte bereits eingeschaltet und hatten eine einstweilige Verfügung erwirkt. Das bedeutete, dass *Leute heute* die Skandalgeschichte nicht oder nur auszugsweise veröffentlichen durfte. Außerdem bereiteten die Rechtsvertreter von *Tag für Tag* bereits eine Millionenklage wegen Verleumdung vor.

Und alle hatten es gewusst

Am nächsten Tag stand es natürlich groß in allen Zeitungen und lief über sämtliche Sender und durch alle Kanäle. »Objektive, seriöse Berichterstattung« bedeutete nämlich, dass man in dritter Spur an jedem Rufmord teilnehmen durfte, wenn man nur offenließ, ob es die Wahrheit oder eben Rufmord war. Man konnte so auch ausführlich alle Anschuldigungen nennen, man musste einfach nur die Gegenseite zu Wort kommen lassen, und eine dankbarere Gegenseite als Clemens Waltner konnte man gar nicht finden. Für ihn, den sonst nie wer interviewen wollte – außer ich vielleicht, ich hätte ihn gerne gefragt, warum er beim Gulaschessen weiße Hemden trug – für ihn war jede noch so negative Schlagzeile besser als keine Schlagzeile und quasi unbezahlte Werbung für den Handelsriesen Plus. Er genoss jeden einzelnen Auftritt und bestritt dabei gar nicht, dass in der Bar über die anonymen Spenden geredet worden war und dass er in einer Weinlaune auch gescherzt haben könnte, er selbst wäre der große Gönner. Vielleicht habe er sogar tatsächlich eine Ausgabe von *Tag für Tag* gezückt, wahllos auf irgendeine Meldung getippt und behauptet, dass das »seine« neue Spendenadresse wäre.

»Ja, wir hatten tatsächlich viel Spaß in der Bar, wir haben mächtig herumgeblödelt«, wurde er zitiert. »Dass die von *Leute heute* Spaß von Ernst nicht unterscheiden können, wird sie teuer zu stehen kommen, das kann ich denen versprechen«, ließ er der Programmzeitung via Medien ausrichten.

Mich selbst berührte diese Skandalgeschichte extrem unangenehm, wobei sich mein Mitleid mit Kunz und der Redaktion von *Tag für Tag* in Grenzen hielt. Die hatten selbst auch niemals eine Gelegenheit ausgelassen, die Konkurrenz in Misskredit zu bringen und deren Ruf zu schädigen. Ich fand es einfach nur wahnsinnig enttäuschend, wie schnell eine so außergewöhnlich gute Sache, die allen Schutzbedürftigen in diesem System einmal ein kleines bisschen Hoffnung geben konnte, zum genauen Gegenteil pervertierte.

Man musste sich nur anhören, was meine Kumpels dazu sagten, die zum wöchentlichen Gelage in Zoltan's Bar in der Schlachthausgasse vollständig versammelt waren und bereits ungeduldig auf mich, ihren Medienvertreter, gewartet hatten. In ihren Augen hatte ich ja tatsächlich an Bedeutung und vermutlich sogar Charisma dadurch gewonnen, dass ich beim Skandalthema des Tages sozusagen als Beobachter in der ersten Reihe fußfrei saß, während sie, die normalen Wutbürger, nur billige Stehplätze im Hintergrund hatten, von wo aus sie verschwommen mitbekamen, dass sie offenbar wieder einmal verarscht worden waren. Die einzige Chance ihrer Rehabilitation bestand nun darin, es ohnehin immer schon gewusst zu haben.

»Hab ich euch nicht von Anfang an gesagt, dass das Ganze ein Fake ist?«, eröffnete Josi, der Konditor.

»So etwas macht eben kein Mensch ohne Hintergedanken – das waren meine Worte«, sagte Arik, der frustrierte Berufsschullehrer.

»Aber Geri, du kannst uns nicht erzählen, dass ihr in der Redaktion nichts davon mitgekriegt habt. Das muss ja intern abgesprochen worden sein«, sagte Horst, der Wettbüro-Betreiber.

»Freunde, erstens hatten wir wirklich keine Ahnung davon. Und zweitens wissen wir ja noch nicht einmal, ob Plus da tatsächlich die Finger im Spiel gehabt hat. Ich glaube das nämlich nicht. Es gibt nur Anschuldigungen, aber nicht den Funken eines Beweises«, sagte ich.

»Na klar, das muss er jetzt sagen«, meinte Josi und klopfte mir dabei freundlich auf die Schulter. Für ihn konnte ich das ärgste Schlitzohr auf Gottes Erden sein, Hauptsache, ich gab bald wieder eine Runde aus.

»Irgendwas wird an der Sache schon dran sein, sonst würden nicht alle so groß darüber berichten«, sagte Horst.

»Umgekehrt, Horst, es wird deshalb so groß darüber berichtet, damit an der Sache irgendwas dran ist. So funktioniert Journalismus«, sagte ich.

»Schon ein mieses Geschäft«, sagte dazu Arik.

»Und was meinst du, Franticek?«, fragte ich. Unser böhmischer Kunstschmied hatte sich bisher auffallend ruhig verhalten und wirkte irgendwie niedergeschlagen. Er war wahrscheinlich genauso naiv wie ich gewesen und hatte an die spektakuläre Ausnahme von den Regeln unserer Gesellschaft geglaubt, nämlich an eine Serie von uneigennützigen, guten Taten.

»Stell dir vor, du bist der Leiter von so einem Obdachlosenheim, oder du kümmerst dich gratis um verwahrloste Kinder, und du kriegst diese irre Spende, und du freust dich riesig, weil da jemand an dich gedacht hat, weil dir jemand die Hand gereicht hat, weil jemand an dich glaubt und auf dich zählt und deine gute Sache mit sehr viel Geld unterstützt. Und dann stellt sich heraus, dass so ein Scheißkerl von Machtmensch wie dieser Waltner, dass der das womöglich alles nur vorgetäuscht hat, dass er irgendein Scheißschwarzgeld von irgendeinem Scheißkonto abgehoben und an irgendwelche Armen geschickt hat, die ihm in Wirklichkeit scheißegal sind, nur damit sein Scheißkonzern, der ohnehin nur Scheiße produziert, damit der diese Scheißzeitung, entschuldige, Geri, damit der diese Scheißzeitung, in der nichts als Scheiße steht …«

»Hast du dich dann bald ausgeschissen?«, fragte Horst.

»Die nächste Runde geht auf mich«, beschwichtigte Zoltan, der Chef des Hauses, dem der liebe Frieden in seinem Lokal über alles ging.

Ich verstand natürlich gut, was Franticek meinte, aber mir ging etwas ganz anderes durch den Kopf: Angenommen, der Skandal war nichts als heiße Luft, und es gab den anonymen Wohltäter wirklich, was musste der jetzt wohl denken? Würde ihm nicht das Grauen kommen angesichts solcher selbstgefälligen Gestalten wie Waltner und Konsorten, die einen Heidenspaß daran hatten, die großen Gönner zu mimen und nachzuäffen? Würde er es ertragen, dass sie jetzt auf seinem Rücken ihre Medienschlachten austrugen und ihre millionenschweren Schadenersatzprozesse führten? Angenommen, es gab den Wohltäter also wirklich, könnte er jetzt überhaupt noch einmal zu einem weißen Kuvert greifen? Ich fürchtete, dass der Zauber ein für alle Mal vorbei war.

KAPITEL FÜNF

Der Vierer war noch zu retten

Am 14. Oktober um 12.30 Uhr mitteleuropäischer Sommerzeit war ich das erste Mal in meinem Leben freiwillig und ohne Begleitung beim Zahnarzt, nein, eben nicht, sondern bei der Zahnärztin. Ich hatte mir für den Anlass bei H&M eine extrem schöne, 49,90 Euro günstige, weinrote Strickjacke gekauft. Und ich war beim Friseur gewesen und hatte mir hinten nahezu den kompletten Überhang wegschneiden lassen, sodass ich nicht mehr wie ein arbeitsloser Heavy-Metal-Tontechniker aussah, sondern wie ein arbeitsloser Klavierlehrer vom klassischen Fach. Außerdem hatte ich einen Pfefferminzkaugummi eingeworfen, einen von denen, die mir Manuel jetzt regelmäßig auf den Tisch legte, wenn er zu mir ins Büro kam.

»Wann waren Sie das letzte Mal zur Kontrolle?«, fragte die Vorzimmerdame.

»Zur Kontrolle war ich ehrlich gestanden noch nie.« Sie sah mich ungläubig an. »Ich habe kurz nach meiner Kindheit die Kontrolle über meine Zähne verloren«, sagte ich. Sie fand das aber leider nicht lustig und schickte mich zum Röntgen in die Kammer. Danach ließ sie mich im Warteraum vor einem Stapel unberührbarer Ärztemagazine mit abstoßenden, in Rosa gehaltenen Drüsen- oder Schleimhaut-Covers dunsten.

Endlich wurde ich ins Refugium von Rebecca Linsbach vorgelassen, die mir in der Tür gleich einmal schwungvoll die Hand entgegenstreckte. Rebecca war zwar ungefähr so bezaubernd wie in der Nacht davor in meinen Träumen, aber sie tat so, als würde sie mich nicht kennen, und das fand ich schade.

Vielleicht erkannte sie mich wirklich nicht, vielleicht fehlten ihr dazu Manuel oder mein Hinterhaar.

»Lachen Sie mich bitte nicht aus, wenn ich zugebe, dass ich ein bisschen Angst vor Ihnen habe«, sagte ich. Sie lächelte. Frauen mögen Männer, die nicht immer die Starken spielen müssen, und diesbezüglich hatte ich wirklich einiges zu bieten.

Dann zeigte sie mir mein Gebiss, das bereits als Poster an der Wand hing, und diagnostizierte: »Herr Plassek, das ist leider ein Desaster.«

Es stellte sich rasch heraus, dass die meisten Zähne zum Wegschmeißen waren, und die restlichen benötigten eine Brücke.

»Solange es keine Zugbrücke ist«, sagte ich. Aber irgendwie kam mein Witz diesmal nicht so richtig an.

»Oben den Vierer links können wir noch retten.« Das war quasi die frohe Botschaft des Nachmittags, für die ich mich gleich einmal auf das Innigste bedankte.

Ich hätte gerne noch ein paar private Worte untergebracht, aber Rebecca drückte leider aufs Tempo und brachte mich sofort in die horizontale Lage.

»Ich schlage vor, wir probieren es gar nicht erst ohne Lokalanästhesie. Sollten Sie trotzdem Schmerzen haben, einfach die Hand heben.« Ich hielt sie schon einmal sicherheitshalber eine Weile hoch.

Die nächste Stunde war nur mit geschlossenen Augen zu überstehen, wobei der Horror weniger darin bestand, was gerade von mir wegbrach und ob da Nerven dranhingen, die die Narkose überlebt hatten. Schlimmer noch war jeweils die Vorstellung, was in den darauffolgenden Sekunden an Gräuel und Massaker auf mich zukommen würde. Einmal tat es wirklich verdammt weh, und ich umfasste spontan Rebeccas Handgelenk, das war so ungefähr meine heftigste Gefühlsregung der vergangenen zehn oder zwanzig Jahre. Sie tat aber so, als wäre nichts. Bei ihr schien leider nahezu alles Routine zu sein, nichts kam mehr spontan, nichts berührte sie, nicht einmal, dass ich auf ihr Kommando »Bitte gründlich ausspülen« etwa drei Liter Blut spuckte.

Als sie fertig war, sagte sie dennoch einen zumindest inhaltlich wunderschönen Satz, der mich vermutlich durch den gesamten Herbst tragen würde. »Herr Plassek, Sie wissen, das war heute erst der Beginn, auf uns beide wartet eine Menge Arbeit.« Am liebsten hätte ich erwidert, dass Beziehungen eben immer auch eine Menge Arbeit waren. Aber ich beließ es dann bei einer etwas dezenteren Botschaft.

»Jedenfalls bin ich froh, mich überwunden zu haben und zu Ihnen gekommen zu sein.« Ich an ihrer Stelle hätte geantwortet: »Da haben Sie eine gute Wahl getroffen.« Aber nein, sie erwiderte nur lapidar: »Das war auch dringend notwendig.« Obwohl sie gar nicht so aussah, als müsste jeder ihrer Gedanken geradezu zwanghaft bei den Zähnen enden. Beim Händeschütteln zum Abschied riskierte ich dann doch noch ein paar persönlichere Worte.

»Ich freu mich jedenfalls, nächste Woche wieder zu Ihnen zu kommen«, sagte ich.

»Es genügt, wenn Sie kommen, Sie müssen sich ja nicht gleich freuen«, erwiderte sie.

»Darf ich mich trotzdem freuen?« Sie hob und senkte die Schultern und lächelte verlegen.

»Darf ich?«, fragte ich.

»Sie dürfen«, sagte sie.

Donnerstags kam Manuel immer erst gegen drei zu mir, weil sie vorher Basketballtraining hatten. Anfangs hatte ich seinem Hobby keine allzu große Bedeutung beigemessen, weil Basketball nicht so ganz mein Sport war, wobei eigentlich gar kein Sport so ganz mein Sport war, außer Tischfußball vielleicht, da benötigte man nur zwei flinke Handgelenke und konnte nebenbei auch einmal einen Schluck trinken.

Nach und nach hörte ich aber aus seinen Erzählungen heraus, wie wichtig ihm Basketball war und welche Spielerpersönlichkeit in ihm da bereits herangereift sein musste. Er schien so etwas wie die Schaltzentrale seiner Nachwuchsmannschaft Torpedo 15 zu sein, und der Trainer sagte ihm angeblich eine ähnliche Karriere voraus wie jene seines Vorbilds Jeffrey Lynn Green von den Boston Celtics, den man auch *Green Monster* nannte, was bei zwei Meter sechs und hundertsieben Kilo nicht wirklich übertrieben war. Warum ich das so genau wusste? Manuel hatte mir *Green Monster* mit allen wichtigen Daten als Bildschirmhintergrund in meinen Computer eingebaut, und ich hatte keine Ahnung, wie man so ein Monster wieder wegbekam.

Wenn Manuel donnerstags vom Training eintrudelte, war er meistens aufgekratzt und mitteilungsbedürftig, und da legten wir dann neuerdings immer eine Plauderstunde ein, in der ich nahezu alles über seine Mitspieler und Gegner, über Spielaufbau und Taktik erfuhr und auch die Regeln immer besser beherrschte, sodass ich demnächst hier alles hinwerfen und im zweiten Bildungsweg bei Torpedo 15 anheuern konnte, sollten die an einer Verstärkung für ihre Junkie-Geriatrie-Liga interessiert sein.

Ich hatte an diesem öden Donnerstag in der vom Spenden-
wirrwarr in Schockstarre versetzten Redaktion schon mit einer gewissen Vorfreude auf Manuels aktuelle Trainingsbe-
richte und Basketball-Fallstudien gewartet. Doch diesmal kam
er mit hängenden Schultern ins Büro geschlichen, und als er
mich sah, begann er heftig zu schluchzen und war eine Weile
überhaupt nicht zu beruhigen.

»Hey Bursche, was ist passiert? Hast du dir wehgetan?«,
fragte ich.

»Nein.«

»Hat dir wer wehgetan?«

»Nein.«

»Was dann?«

»Der Machi ist weg.«

»Wer ist der Machi?«

»Der Machmut, unser Shooting Guard.« Richtig, jetzt
wusste ich es wieder. Manuel war der Point Guard, der für den
Spielaufbau zuständig war, während der Shooting Guard auf
Würfe aus weiter Distanz spezialisiert war. Von diesem Teufelskerl Machmut hatte mir Manuel schon öfter erzählt. Wenn
irgendwo am Horizont ein Korb auftauchte, dann baute der
Bub mit Garantie jeden Ball, den er in die Hände kriegte, dort
ein.

»Was heißt, er ist weg? Von wo weg? Wo ist er hin?«

»Das weiß ich nicht. Er ist geflüchtet.«

»Wie geflüchtet? Von daheim? Vor seinen Eltern?«

»Nein, *mit* seinen Eltern. Vor der Abschiebung.« Das klang
gar nicht gut. Als sich Manuel etwas beruhigt hatte, erzählte er.

Machmut Pajew stammte aus Tschetschenien. Vor etwa
sechs Jahren waren seine Eltern mit ihm nach Österreich geflüchtet und hatten einen Antrag auf politisches Asyl gestellt. Nach einiger Zeit im Flüchtlingslager kam die Familie
Pajew in einem Ausländerwohnheim unter. Machmut ging

zur Schule, war dort angeblich einer der Gescheitesten, sprach auch schon sehr gut Deutsch, und alle mochten ihn, sogar die Mädchen, obwohl er abstehende Ohren in der Dimension von Katamaransegeln hatte. Bei Torpedo 15 war er wegen seiner weiten Würfe bereits ein kleiner Star – die Achse Manuel-Machmut war sozusagen das Herzstück der Mannschaft, die beiden Buben verstanden einander blind.

In den vergangenen Wochen hatte er mehrmals angedeutet, dass er wahrscheinlich bald nicht mehr zum Training kommen konnte, weil die Asylanträge abgelehnt worden waren. Das hatte zunächst kein Mensch verstanden: Seit wann brauchte man fürs Basketballspielen Asyl, war das nicht ein freier Sport für alle? Dann erklärte der Trainer seinen aufgeregten Schützlingen, dass die Pajews keine Aufenthaltsgenehmigung für Österreich erteilt bekommen hatten und in ihre Heimat abgeschoben werden sollten. Manuel gegenüber hatte Machmut beim letzten Training wortwörtlich gesagt: »Wenn wir wieder zurückmüssen, kann die Polizei meinen Vater gleich hier erschießen, weil daheim bringen sie ihn sowieso auf der Stelle um.«

So, und jetzt war es wirklich so weit gekommen: Machi war nicht mehr zum Training erschienen.

»Das ist schlimm. Versteh ich gut, dass dich das fertigmacht«, sagte ich in dem Wissen, dass sich der Trostfaktor dieser Worte in Grenzen hielt.

»Wir müssen was unternehmen«, erwiderte Manuel.

»Wie meinst du, wir müssen was unternehmen?«, fragte ich.

»*Du* musst was unternehmen«, konkretisierte er. Die Aussage machte mich ein bisschen ratlos, denn ich galt jetzt nicht unbedingt als der große Hervorzauberer von untergetauchten tschetschenischen Flüchtlingsfamilien.

»Du musst was darüber schreiben, damit der Machi dableiben darf«, erklärte Manuel. Das war eine Schnapsidee, fand ich.

Doch der Raubkatzenblick, mit dem er mich dabei ansah und der mich stark an seine Mutter erinnerte, gab mir zu verstehen, dass mein Spielraum, nein zu sagen – und ich musste leider nein sagen –, relativ klein war. Ich brauchte also wirklich überzeugende Argumente. Zur Auswahl standen:

1. Solche Tragödien waren keine Einzelfälle. Die ersten davon waren sogar groß durch alle Medien gegangen. Das hatte aber nichts an den Fremdengesetzen geändert. Wer einen negativen Asylbescheid hatte, musste einfach wieder zurück in die Heimat, da half nichts. Da konnten Journalisten wetteifern und Stimmung machen, so viel sie wollten. Die Welt war eben grausam, und diese Grausamkeit durfte nicht durch ungesetzliche Akte der Menschlichkeit unterbrochen werden, sonst fiel sie auf, und es entstand Unmut, und das konnte sich die Politik auf Dauer nicht leisten. So ungefähr ging dieses Argument.

2. Mir waren bei *Tag für Tag* quasi die Hände gebunden. Selbst wenn ich wollte, durfte ich gar nicht darüber schreiben. Für die Sozialreportagen war Sophie Rambuschek zuständig. Und die sozialen *bunten Meldungen zum Tag* wurden mittlerweile von den Chefs persönlich ausgesucht. Ich selbst war hier in der Redaktion nur der NvD, der Nasenbohrer vom Dienst. Dieses Argument war zwar das stichhaltigste, aber es war zeitgleich auch mein persönliches Armutszeugnis, also schied es aus.

3. Selbst wenn es mir erlaubt gewesen wäre oder ich mir einfach die Freiheit genommen hätte, darüber zu berichten, so gab es für mich eine grundsätzliche Frage, und die lautete: Worüber sollte ich eigentlich berichten? Die Familie war verschwunden, vermutlich hatte sie bei Landsleuten in Wien Unterschlupf gefunden. Würde es mir gelingen, ihr Versteck ausfindig zu machen, und würde ich darüber schreiben, wäre das geradezu kontraproduktiv, dann würde man sie dort abholen, in Schubhaft nehmen und später abschieben.

So, das waren die drei Möglichkeiten, ich entschied mich aber instinktiv für die vierte und sagte: »Solange ich nicht weiß, wo Machmut und seine Eltern stecken, kann ich nichts darüber schreiben. Ich kann ja nicht einmal schreiben, wie es ihnen geht.«

»Es geht ihnen gut«, sagte Manuel.

»Sagt wer?«

»Sagt Machi.«

»Woher weißt du das?«, fragte ich.

»Weil er's mir geschrieben hat. Er hat mir eine SMS geschickt.«

»Echt?« Jetzt war ich sozusagen baff. »Warum sagst du mir das nicht?«

»Ich hab es dir eh gerade gesagt«, erwiderte er.

»Und wo ist er?«

»Das weiß ich nicht. Das darf er niemandem verraten, sonst holen sie ihn dort ab.«

»Zeigst du mir die SMS?«

Manuel reichte mir sein Handy. Der Text lautete:

Hallo Mani, wie geht es dir? Mir geht es gut, ich bin in Sicherheit. Ich darf nicht sagen, wo ich bin. Aber dort, wo ich bin, die sind voll lieb zu uns, und es gibt sogar immer Spaghetti. Ich will aber trotzdem wieder nach Hause. Ich will nicht nach Tschetschenien, dort kenne ich niemanden. Und mein Paps muss sich dort dann die ganze Zeit verstecken, und wir haben nichts zu essen und verhungern vielleicht noch. Bitte sag deinem Onkel von der Zeitung, dass er uns helfen muss. Bitte!!! Du weißt, wir haben im November das Finalspiel gegen Union CS. Da muss ich spielen, da geht es um alles. Dein Machi.

Ich brauchte eine kurze Pause zum Durchatmen. Bei mir reichten ja oft ein paar gezielte Worte aus, um mich aus heiterem Himmel gegen die Tränen ankämpfen zu lassen, das hatte ich von meiner Mama geerbt, das hatte ich im Blut, und zwar auch in Form von Restalkohol, der mich immer ziemlich sentimental stimmte.

Jedenfalls war das gerade eben wieder eine meiner berühmten höheren Bestimmungen gewesen, die da lautete: Ich konnte zwar nichts tun, aber ich *musste* es tun. Schon allein dieses einen Wortes wegen – des *Onkels* wegen.

»Hast du ihm gesagt, dass ich dein Onkel bin?«, fragte ich.

»Warum soll ich es ihm nicht gesagt haben?«, erwiderte Manuel.

»Zum Beispiel, weil es nicht stimmt.«

»Stört es dich?«, fragte Manuel.

»Nein, im Gegenteil, ich finde, Onkel klingt sehr sympathisch.«

»Es passt zu dir«, sagte Manuel.

»Findest du?«

»Ja, du bist ein typischer Onkel«, sagte Manuel und lächelte wieder.

Das tat mir gut. Es war so, als wäre ich auf einer Skala von eins bis hundert, auf der ich bisher über zehn noch nie hinausgekommen war, plötzlich mit einem Riesensprung auf fünfzig gehechtet. Ich war sozusagen auf halber Strecke, und deshalb brauchte ich jetzt ein schnelles Bier.

Sophie muss krank werden

Ich quälte mich die Treppe hinauf ins lichtdurchflutete Büro von Sophie Rambuschek, das mir im Vergleich zu meinem eigenen wie die Suite eines Fünfsternehotels vorkam, und erzählte ihr Machmuts Geschichte.

»Tragisch«, sagte sie. Sie war im Stress und hatte nur mit einem Ohr zugehört.

»Kannst du was Größeres daraus machen?«, fragte ich.

»Du, Geri, da reden wir noch«, sagte sie, ohne von ihrem Bildschirm aufzublicken. Sie würde also nichts Größeres daraus machen und auch nichts Kleineres. Wahrscheinlich war die Story für sie gleichzeitig mit dem Wort Tschetschenien gestorben. Ich musste also noch einen Gang zulegen.

»Sophie, ich hab eine Bitte«, sagte ich. Jetzt sah sie mich zum ersten Mal, seit ich ihr Büro betreten hatte, an, damit hatte sie nicht gerechnet. Ich hatte bei *Tag für Tag* noch nie eine Bitte an irgendwen gehabt, mit Ausnahme der Bitte, dass man mich bitte möglichst großräumig in Ruhe lassen sollte.

»Gibst du mir morgen deine Reportagenseite?« Jetzt blies sie Luft durch ihre ziemlich konturenscharf nachgezeichneten Lippen.

»*Du* willst was schreiben?«, fragte sie mich tief verwundert. Stimmt, ich war hier im Haus nicht gerade bekannt dafür. »Da werden wir Norbert fragen müssen«, sagte sie. Norbert, soso. Journalistinnen konnten ja generell gar nicht jung genug sein, um von ihren Chefs, die gar nicht alt genug sein konnten, das Du angeboten zu bekommen, das sie natürlich nicht ablehnen konnten, was für die Chefs wahrscheinlich den Funken eines sexuellen Abenteuers hatte.

»Vergiss es. Wenn wir Kunz fragen, weiß ich schon jetzt, was er sagen wird«, entgegnete ich.

»Wie stellst du dir das sonst vor?«, fragte sie.

»Du bist morgen krank.« Jetzt blies sie die doppelte Portion Luft durch ihre ziemlich konturenscharf nachgezeichneten Lippen.

»Schau, Sophie, gönn dir mal einen freien Tag, ein verlängertes Wochenende, schlaf dich so richtig aus, entspann dich, geh shoppen, mach's dir daheim gemütlich, mach Yoga, nimm ein Vollbad, lies ein Buch, schau dir einen blöden Film an …«

»Ich war noch nie krank«, gestand sie.

»Dann wird es ohnehin höchste Zeit.«

»Geri, das geht nicht, das kann ich nicht machen«, sagte sie. Tja, entziehe Workaholics die Arbeit, und sie werden nicht mehr wissen, wofür sie leben.

»Sophie, ich hab dich noch nie um etwas gebeten, und ich würde dich auch heute nicht bitten, wenn es nicht so wichtig für mich wäre. Soll ich dir erklären, warum es so wichtig für mich ist?«

»Nein, das brauchst du nicht«, sagte sie. Das hatte ich, in aller Bescheidenheit, wirklich gut eingefädelt.

»Dann sei bitte morgen ausnahmsweise krank, sag einfach ja zu einem freien Tag. Den hat sich hier keine so sehr verdient wie du.« Dem Argument hatte sie natürlich nichts entgegenzusetzen. Ich wunderte mich, wie hart ich arbeitete, um den Onkelstatus ja nicht wieder zu verlieren.

»Und wann soll ich mich krankmelden?«

»Nicht vor Mittag.«

»Und was soll ich haben?«

»Migräne, Hexenschuss, Brechdurchfall, Gastritis, Blutvergiftung, Atembeschwerden, Kreislaufprobleme, Hyperventilation ...« Ich selbst hatte alles davon schon gehabt.

»Und du machst die Reportagenseite?«

»Ja.«

»Wirklich?«

»Ja, wirklich.«

»Kann ich mich drauf verlassen?«

»Du kannst dich drauf verlassen. Sophie, du bist ein Engel!«

Einer der wenigen mir bekannten Nachteile von Alkohol war, dass man nach einer Stunde geistiger Arbeit das Gefühl hatte, dass es ungefähr zwanzig Stunden gewesen sein mussten und dass man keinesfalls auch nur eine Minute weiterarbeiten konnte, weil sämtliche klaren Gedanken restlos aufgebraucht und nur noch die unklaren übrig geblieben waren, die dann zumeist auf einen Besuch in der nächsten Kneipe hinausliefen. Zum Glück wusste ich das schon vorher und hatte mein Konzept für die Reportagenseite darauf abgestimmt.

Ich selbst schrieb den Kurzkommentar. Das waren nur dreißig Zeilen, den Inhalt flüsterte mir mein gesunder Menschenverstand ein: Man konnte – Asylbescheid hin oder her – eine Familie mit einem Kind nicht sechs Jahre hierbehalten und quasi einbürgern, um sie dann von einer Minute auf die nächste in die tschetschenische Pampa zu verdammen, wo sie überdies politisch verfolgt war.

Manuels Arbeit bestand darin, alle Zahlen und Fakten zum Schicksal der Familie Pajew zusammenzutragen, also ihren Werdegang, ihre Flucht und ihr Leben in Österreich zu skizzieren. Zu diesem Zweck telefonierte er zum Beispiel fast eine Stunde mit seinem Basketballtrainer, stellte eine kluge Frage nach der anderen und machte sich professionell Notizen. Ich beobachte ihn dabei und bemerkte, wie sehr er in der Recherchetätigkeit aufging. Das war zwar einerseits bewundernswert, andererseits war er vielleicht doch nicht mein Sohn.

Wikipedia steuerte Informationen über das österreichische Asylrecht und über den Tschetschenien-Krieg und seine Flüchtlingswellen bei.

Ich sorgte hauptsächlich für eine sinnvolle Aneinanderreihung deutscher Sätze.

Die wirklich große und wichtigste Geschichte war schließlich auf Machmut zugeschnitten, der mit eigenen Worten seine Situation beschreiben und seine Ängste und Wünsche äußern sollte.

»Wie soll er das machen?«, fragte mich Manuel.

»Er soll dir eine SMS schicken, so eine ähnliche wie die vorhin, nur zehnmal so lang.«

»Und was soll da drinstehen?«

»Alles, was ihm gerade einfällt, was ihm wichtig erscheint und was von Herzen kommt.«

»Auch über Basketball?«

»Natürlich. Er soll schreiben, worauf er sich am meisten freut, falls er hierbleiben darf, welche Hobbys er hat, was er mit seinen Freunden unternehmen will, wie schön es in Österreich ist, wie schön es ist, Deutsch zu sprechen, wie schön es ist, in die Schule zu gehen, wer seine Lieblingslehrer sind, was er am liebsten isst ...«

»Spaghetti und Tiramisu«, warf Manuel ein.

»Ah so? Okay, dann sag ihm bitte, dass wir das wahrscheinlich zu Wiener Schnitzel und Kaiserschmarren ausbessern müssen.« Manuel lachte. Er hatte mich verstanden, mehr noch, er hatte im Grunde bereits den Journalismus verstanden, und das mit vierzehn Jahren.

Am Nachmittag rief mich Norbert Kunz an und teilte mir aufgeregt mit, dass Sophie Rambuschek mit Verdacht auf Lungenentzündung im Spital gelandet war.

»Da hat sie es aber ein bisschen übertrieben«, sagte ich.

»Wie bitte?«

»Sie hat sich ein bisschen zu viel zugemutet in letzter Zeit.«

»Jaja. Sie hat behauptet, dass Sie, Herr Plassek, dass Sie eventuell eine Notgeschichte für die Sozialreportagen-Seite hätten, also dass Sie eine Doppelseite produzieren könnten?«

»Sie muss sehr hohes Fieber haben«, sagte ich im Spaß.

»Wie bitte?« Mit humorlosen und obendrein gestressten Menschen erlaubte man sich besser keine Scherze. »Ja, im Ernst, ich schreibe Ihnen die Doppelseite, ich hab eine gute Story.«

»Sehr schön. Worum geht es denn?«, fragte Kunz. Das hatte ich befürchtet.

»Ein Familienschicksal, eine exklusive Geschichte, sehr tragisch, sehr berührend, sehr dramatisch, sehr... aus dem Leben gegriffen, schicksalhaft sozusagen. Und berührend. Und exklusiv.«

»Okay, Herr Plassek, machen Sie, machen Sie! Sie wissen, Redaktionsschluss ist um siebzehn Uhr.«

»Jaja, bis siebzehn Uhr krieg ich das hin.«

Give me Five

Machmuts SMS-Berichte waren wirklich nichts für labile Gemüter. Der Bub erzählte so bewegend und authentisch, dass wir gar nicht viel korrigieren mussten. Als Titel wählten wir – für *Tag für Tag* eindeutig zu subtil, aber Manuel bestand darauf: *Ich will nicht wieder flüchten müssen.* Daneben stellten wir ein großes Foto, das uns der Trainer von Torpedo 15 zur Verfügung gestellt hatte. Es zeigte den strahlenden Buben mit den abstehenden Ohren, wie er von seinen jubelnden Teamkollegen, allen voran Manuel, nach dem Sieg auf den Schultern in die Kabine getragen wurde. Wäre ich der verantwortliche Politiker gewesen und hätte diese Geschichte gelesen und dieses Bild gesehen, dann hätte es für mich nur zwei Möglichkeiten gegeben: Entweder diese Familie bleibt in Österreich, oder ich trete zurück. Allerdings wurde in der Praxis leider kein Mensch Politiker, um dann wegen eines vierzehnjährigen tschetschenischen Buben und seiner Eltern, die sich mit falschen Erwartungen in den Westen verirrt hatten, sein Amt niederzulegen.

Punkt fünf waren wir fertig, und ich pfiff aus dem letzten Loch. Solche Anstrengungen war ich einfach nicht mehr gewohnt und wollte mich ehrlich gestanden auch nicht mehr daran gewöhnen. Aber seit ich meinen Sohn kannte, hatte ich ihn noch nie so feurig und lebendig und impulsiv und lebenslustig gesehen, und allein dafür hatte sich der Aufwand schon gelohnt. Wir hatten zweifellos gerade wieder eine Sternstunde unserer Beziehung erlebt, egal was wir mit unserer Reportagenseite letztendlich bewirken würden. Da war die Enttäuschung sozusagen programmiert. Denn für Manuel war klar, dass wir seinen Freund Machi gerade gerettet hatten, dass der nun bald aus seinem Versteck kommen und sich in aller Ruhe auf das wichtige Basketballspiel in vierzehn Tagen würde vorbereiten können. Ich wusste es leider besser. Da musste schon ein kleines Wunder geschehen. Doch die Erfahrung hatte mich gelehrt, dass immer dann, wenn ein kleines Wunder geschehen musste, garantiert keines geschah.

Jedenfalls ging es beim Verabschieden diesmal ausgesprochen herzlich zu, weil Manuel tatsächlich erstmals stolz auf seinen neuen »Onkel« gewesen sein dürfte. Und ich konnte nun ein paar Gesten setzen, wie ich es immer schon so gerne getan hätte, konnte ihm zuzwinkern und dabei die Zunge gegen den Gaumen schnalzen lassen, konnte ihm meine offene Hand entgegenstrecken, um ihm Five zu geben, und er klatschte mit Begeisterung dagegen. So haben wahrscheinlich alle spät berufenen Väter einmal angefangen.

Ich befand mich bereits auf dem Weg zu Zoltan's Bar, als Norbert Kunz anrief und mich bat, in sein Büro zu kommen.

»Muss das sein, ich bin schon unterwegs«, sagte ich.

»Ja, bitte, Herr Plassek, es muss sein.«

»Können wir das nicht hier am Telefon besprechen?«

»Nein, Herr Plassek, das können wir nicht am Telefon besprechen.« Wenn er mich zweimal hintereinander mit »Herr Plassek« ansprach und dazwischen Atemgeräusche einlegte, als würde man ihm gerade ohne Narkose einen Luftröhrenschnitt verpassen, dann deutete das auf ein gravierendes Ereignis hin. Also kroch ich widerwillig in die Redaktion zurück.

»Herr Plassek, glauben Sie mir, es ist mir wirklich alles andere als angenehm, Ihnen das jetzt mitteilen zu müssen …«, sagte er, tief in sein hässliches khakigrünes Bürosofa versunken, und zog an einer Zigarette. Ich hatte gar nicht gewusst, dass er rauchte – vielleicht eben nur bei besonderen Anlässen wie diesem. »Herr Plassek, wir haben Ihre morgige Reportage leider herausnehmen müssen.«

»Wie bitte?«

»Die Reportage über die Tschetschenen kann leider nicht erscheinen. Befehl von oben.« Ich blickte instinktiv hinauf zum Luster. In diesem Moment war ich nicht einmal fähig, fassungslos zu sein.

»Das ist nicht Ihr Ernst.«

»Sie können mir glauben, ich habe alles versucht, um die Geschichte zu retten. Ich habe um Ihre Story gekämpft. Ich persönlich halte sie nämlich für eine gute, gelungene Reportage, sehr menschlich, sehr menschlich. Es ist also keine Kritik an Ihrer Arbeit, bitte fassen Sie das nicht als Kritik an Ihrer Arbeit auf. Journalistisch gesehen haben Sie alles richtig gemacht. Ich war verblüfft, wie gut Sie sich …«

»Warum?«, fragte ich. Kunz zuckte zusammen. Ich hatte die Frage relativ laut gestellt.

»Herr Plassek, wir kennen die Eigentümerverhältnisse, wir kennen unsere Anleger und Geldgeber, wir kennen unsere Inserenten und Abonnenten, wir kennen die Marktgesetze, wir kennen die wegen der Spendenaffäre angespannte Situation, wir kennen die politischen Strukturen, wir wissen, wofür die Plus-Gruppe steht.«

»Sie steht für Scheiße«, erlaubte ich mir anzumerken.

»Herr Plassek, ich verstehe Ihren Ärger, aber Sie müssen auch akzeptieren, dass wir hier Regeln zu befolgen haben. Wir haben eine klare Positionierung in der Ausländerfrage. Wir sind kein Einwanderungsland ...«

»*Sie* sind vielleicht kein Einwanderungsland, ich schon«, sagte ich.

»Wir können nicht plötzlich zum Sprachrohr für dahergelaufene illegale tschetschenische oder sonstige Flüchtlinge ohne Papiere und ohne gar nichts werden. Wenn wir da einmal ja sagen, haben wir demnächst halb Tschetschenien ...«

Mit jedem Wort dieses beschämenden Gequatsches verspürte ich das immer dringlichere Bedürfnis, den gläsernen Couchtisch ein paar Meter hochzuheben und dann fallen zu lassen.

»Das heißt, meine Reportage wird morgen nicht erscheinen?«, fragte ich.

»Ja, leider, wie gesagt ...«

»Keine Zeile davon?«

»Nein, also ... keine Zeile«, stammelte er.

»Okay, dann ist ja so weit alles klar.« Ich sprang auf, eilte zur Tür, öffnete sie und schleuderte sie mit größtmöglicher Wucht hinter mir zu, in der Hoffnung, dass durch den Aufprall die Wände beben und bröckeln würden, dass letztlich das gesamte dreistöckige Redaktionsgebäude in sich zusammenfiel und wie ein dampfender, stinkender brauner Scheißhaufen auf der Straße lag. Und die Passanten rümpften ihre Nasen und sagten: »O Gott, wie eklig, das war *Tag für Tag*.«

Doch nein, es kam nicht so weit, denn die Tür war eine Vorgesetztentür und hatte eine professionelle Federung, um harte Schläge auszutarieren. Der befreiende große Knall fand nicht statt. Ich musste also leider noch einmal kehrtmachen und ins Chefbüro zurückgehen.

»Herr Plassek?«, fragte Kunz ahnungsvoll.

»Ich kündige«, sagte ich.

»Herr Plassek, ich verstehe Ihren …«

»Ich kündige«, wiederholte ich.

»Herr Plassek, machen Sie nicht etwas, das Sie vielleicht …«

»Ich kündige, ich werde dieses Haus heute verlassen, und ich werde es nicht mehr betreten.«

KAPITEL SECHS

Das böse Erwachen

Der Tag und ich verendeten in umgekehrter Reihenfolge in Zoltan's Bar in der Schlachthausgasse. Zuerst war es noch zu früh, um an die Konsequenzen meiner Aktion zu denken. Und als der Zeitpunkt dafür beim besten Willen nicht mehr hinauszuschieben war, konnte ich zum Glück nicht mehr denken. Ich wusste im Nachhinein übrigens auch nicht, was ich in dieser Nacht so dahergeredet hatte, möglicherweise hatte ich meinen Kumpels die ganze Geschichte erzählt, inklusive Manuel und Vaterschaft. Einer von ihnen musste mich irgendwann in der Früh nach Hause gebracht haben. Samstagmittag fand ich mich jedenfalls auf meinem Bett wieder.

Es war nicht unbedingt meine dringliche Absicht, an diesem Wochenende noch einmal zur Besinnung zu kommen, aber mein Handy hörte nicht mehr auf, mich mit *Unchain My Heart* zu foltern, bis ich den Anruf schließlich entgegennahm.

»Die Geschichte über Machi ist nicht in der Zeitung«, schrillte es in hohen Beschwerde-Frequenzen in meinem Kopf.

»Ja, Manuel, ich weiß, es tut mir leid.«

»Wieso nicht?«

»Weil sie sie rausgenommen haben.«

»Wieso?«

»Weil sie ihnen nicht gepasst hat.«

»Wem?«

»Den Chefs.«

»Wieso nicht?«

»Weil das das falsche Thema für *Tag für Tag* war.«

»Was heißt, das falsche Thema?«

»Das ist kompliziert, das erkläre ich dir später mal, Manuel. Mir geht es momentan nicht so gut.«

»Und wann kommt die Geschichte?«

»Gar nicht.«

»Wie gar nicht?«, fragte er.

»Gar nicht gar nicht. Die Geschichte wird überhaupt nicht erscheinen, sie ist gestorben, sorry«, sagte ich.

»Was machen wir jetzt?«

»Was sollen wir machen?«, fragte ich.

»Das frage ich dich!«, sagte er, und er sagte es ziemlich laut.

»Keine Ahnung«, erwiderte ich wahrheitsgemäß.

»Und was soll ich Machi sagen?«

Ich versuchte nachzudenken. Es gelang mir nicht. »Keine Ahnung, Manuel. Sag ihm, dass es uns leid tut, wir haben's probiert, wir haben's wirklich probiert, mehr konnten wir nicht tun«, sagte ich.

Zuerst schwieg er, dann drückte er mich weg. Das war zwar zum Glück geräuschlos und ging schnell, aber es verursachte einen Schmerz, der länger anhalten sollte als mein Kater. Dagegen gab es nämlich keine Tabletten.

Am Nachmittag, als es mir zumindest physisch etwas besser ging, war einer meiner ersten klaren Gedanken jener, dass Manuel ab Montag nicht mehr zu mir ins Büro kommen konnte, weil es mich im Büro nicht mehr gab. Kurz überlegte ich, ob ich versuchen sollte, die Kündigung rückgängig zu machen, aber das überlegte ich wirklich nur sehr, sehr kurz. Danach stellte sich mir die Frage, wem ich die Wahrheit am einfachsten beichten konnte, entweder Manuel selbst oder seiner Mutter in Afrika oder seiner Tante in Wien. Ich entschied mich für Tante Julia, die ich nur von ein paar kurzen Begegnungen aus meiner Zeit mit Alice kannte, damals war sie vielleicht achtzehn gewesen. Ich hoffte, dass sich diese unangenehme

Sache telefonisch erledigen ließ, und ich hatte das Glück, Julia auch gleich zu erreichen.

Eine Weile redete ich so vor mich hin, zum Glück existiert ja praktisch rund um die Uhr ein Wetter, über das sich ausgiebig sinnieren lässt. Bald bemerkte ich allerdings, dass mir der Satz einfach nicht über die Lippen kommen wollte, der Satz, dass es für mich und Manuel keine gemeinsamen Bürostunden mehr gab. »Kann ich mit dir reden?«, fragte ich schließlich.

»Ja«, erwiderte Julia frostig. Zumindest die Hälfte der Geschichte kannte sie also schon. Wahrscheinlich saß Manuel seit Stunden bei ihr auf der Couch und hörte seine traurige Musik.

»Können wir uns auf einen Kaffee treffen?«

Wir vereinbarten ein Treffen im Café Aida in der Thaliastraße.

Julia vom anderen Stern

Okay, ich sah an diesem späten Nachmittag wahrscheinlich wirklich ziemlich zerstört aus, zerstörter noch als sonst. Nach meiner Erfahrung traf man im Wesentlichen auf zwei Arten von Menschen. Die einen bemühten sich, neutral zu bleiben und das äußere Erscheinungsbild ihres Gegenübers als gegeben hinzunehmen, weil eine der wenigen unumstößlichen Freiheiten des Individuums darin bestand, so auszusehen, wie man eben aussah, da sich das pure Leben darin widerspiegelte. Die anderen bestraften einen unaufhörlich mit ihren abschätzigen Blicken. Julia war leider von der zweiten Sorte. Aber das konnte man einer dreiunddreißig Jahre jungen Gewächshausorchidee von einer Frau, die auf der Sportakademie zur Fitnesstrainerin ausgebildet worden war und sich von Tofu und Früchtetee zwangsernährte, um ihrem Lebenssinn gerecht zu werden, nämlich gesund, makellos und topfit zu bleiben bis in den Tod, eigentlich gar nicht verübeln. Jedenfalls machte es mir in ihrer Gegenwart wenig Spaß, meine dringend notwendigen Biere zu bestellen, und ich trank hauptsächlich, wenn sie gerade wegsah.

Leider konnte ich mein Image mit dem Inhalt meiner Worte auch nicht gerade auf den Kopf stellen. »Julia, es gibt ein Problem. Ich habe meinen Job verloren, das heißt, ich habe gekündigt, wegen der Sache mit dem tschetschenischen Buben, Manuel wird dir sicher davon erzählt haben.«

»Du hast gekündigt?«, fragte sie. Jetzt hatte auch sie diesen Raubkatzenblick, der mir von ihrer Schwester Alice noch gut in Erinnerung war.

»Ja, gekündigt – fristlos. Und das bedeutet, dass Manuel ab Montag leider nicht mehr zu mir ins Büro ...«

»Wie stellst du dir das vor?«, unterbrach sie mich ziemlich lautstark.

»Wie bitte?« Ihre Frage irritierte mich, denn ich stellte mir eigentlich überhaupt nichts vor, es war nicht meine Absicht, mir etwas vorzustellen, die Dinge sprachen ohnehin für sich. Und exakt in diesem Punkt war Julia vollkommen anderer Meinung, worüber wir dann länger diskutierten – eigentlich war es Julia, die diskutierte, ich hörte nur zu.

Jedenfalls stellte sie im Folgenden klar, ich sei ein hochgradig fehl- oder gar nicht gesteuerter, lahmarschiger Mensch, der nur in den Tag hinein lebte. Also wenn ich in etwas hineinlebte, dann wohl eher in die Nacht, aber ich sagte lieber nichts dazu, Julia war ziemlich gereizt. Außerdem war ich in ihren Augen ein gewissenloser Mann, der nicht bereit war, auch nur die geringste Verantwortung für sein Kind zu übernehmen. Manuel sei in der Pubertät und brauche so dringend eine männliche Bezugsperson, ein Vorbild. Aber ich sei als Vater ein Totalausfall. Dabei hätte ihre Schwester Alice, gegen jede Vernunft und gegen genügend Stimmen von außen, so sehr auf mich gesetzt und mir die einmalige Chance gegeben, doch noch eine Beziehung zu meinem Buben aufzubauen. Und jetzt, da Manuel endlich Vertrauen zu mir gefasst und sogar an mir zu hängen begonnen habe, jetzt wolle ich einfach wieder abtauchen, weil das eben ganz meine Art war, weil es meinem schwachen, miesen, unsensiblen, egoistischen Charakter entsprach.

»Manuel hängt an mir?«, fragte ich.

»Ja, ich weiß auch nicht, wie du das geschafft hast, aber er mag dich«, sagte sie.

»Er ist ein großartiger Bub.«

»Ja, das ist er, ganz wie seine Mutter«, sagte sie.

»Er könnte seine Hausaufgaben bei mir in der Wohnung machen«, sagte ich. Gleichzeitig schossen mir Bilder vom Zustand meiner Wohnung durch den Kopf.

»Das halte ich für keine gute Idee«, sagte Julia. Wahrscheinlich konnte sie mir die Bilder meiner Wohnung von den Augen ablesen.

»Weißt du was, schlaf deinen Rausch aus, und wir reden morgen weiter«, schlug sie vor. »Ich muss zum Training.«

»Okay«, sagte ich. Aber wenn sie *das hier* bereits für einen Rausch hielt, dann lebte sie tatsächlich auf einem anderen Stern als ich, was die Kommunikation zwischen uns nicht unbedingt einfacher machen würde.

Die Neuzeit bricht an

Auf dem Nachhauseweg besorgte ich mir bei einer Imbissbude eine Salamipizza und ein paar Getränkedosen. Als ich bezahlte, hielt ich plötzlich einen zusammengefalteten Zettel in der Hand, der in der Geldbörse gesteckt hatte.

Daheim sah ich ihn mir genauer an. Da hatte ich mir offenbar Notizen gemacht, sofern es sich dabei überhaupt um meine eigene Schrift handelte, sie war jedenfalls gar nicht so leicht zu entziffern. Von oben nach unten gelesen stand da:

Rundschau / Benjamin Zeller

Stadtkurier / Lydia Meiselhammer

Tagblatt / Ferdinand Schmidtbauer

und, doppelt eingerahmt und mit einer *1* und drei Ausrufezeichen versehen:

Neuzeit / Clara Nemez.

Ich musste die Namen der Zeitungen und ihrer jeweiligen leitenden Redakteure in Zoltan's Bar auf das Papier gekritzelt haben. Es war aber schon seltsam, dass ich nicht den Funken einer Erinnerung daran besaß. Vielleicht hatte ich tatsächlich genau diesen einen Schnaps zu viel erwischt, der mir dann die Festplatte unter der Hirnrinde gelöscht hatte oder zumindest die nächtliche Datei.

Jedenfalls hatte ich mir zum Ausklang dieses Katastrophen-Samstags eine vergleichsweise erfüllende Beschäftigung eingehandelt, die darin bestand, den Sinn dieser Aufzeichnungen zu enträtseln, beziehungsweise die Absicht zu erkennen, die dahintergesteckt hatte.

Ob ich das Rätsel schon beim Einschlafen oder erst im Traum gelöst hatte, konnte ich nicht sagen. Als ich am Sonntag mit relativ klarem Kopf aufwachte, wusste ich jedenfalls, was zu tun war. Zunächst war ich leider gezwungen, das Gebäude von *Tag für Tag* noch ein letztes Mal zu betreten, um die fertiggestellte Reportagenseite zum Fall Machmut von meinem Computer auf einen USB-Stick zu laden. Danach suchte ich die Nummer der *Neuzeit* heraus, rief an und verlangte Chefredakteurin Clara Nemez, die ich nur von ihren satirischen Leitartikeln her kannte, die so ungefähr die scharfsinnigsten waren, die man in diesem Land lesen konnte. Frau Nemez war gerade in der Mittagskonferenz, erfuhr ich von ihrer Sekretärin.

»Ich bräuchte nämlich heute dringend einen kurzen Gesprächstermin bei ihr«, sagte ich. Da ich ohnehin wusste, was sie mich gleich fragen würde, setzte ich nach: »Ich bin ... äh ... freier Journalist. Und es geht um eine brisante Asylgeschichte.«

»Das ist heute ein bisschen ungünstig ...«

»Ich weiß, es ist Sonntag, ihr habt nur halbe Belegschaft und so weiter, aber es wäre wirklich sehr wichtig.«

»Ginge das eventuell auch nächste Woche, telefonisch? Oder noch besser, Sie schreiben uns eine E-Mail ...«

»Bitte, es ist wirklich brisant. Ich brauche nur fünf Minuten, vielleicht sechs, höchstens sieben, acht sind unwahrscheinlich, und mehr als zehn können es gar nicht sein.«

Sie seufzte. »Um vierzehn Uhr?«

»Danke!« Sie mochte mich. Oder sie wollte mich dringend loswerden.

Clara Nemez war weniger Orchidee, mehr Bambusstrauch, und auch sonst eher das Gegenteil von Tante Julia. Sie sah mich an und gab mir das Gefühl, dass mit mir eigentlich alles in Ordnung war und dass ich, dem äußeren Erscheinungsbild nach zu schließen, durchaus den richtigen oder zumindest einen gangbaren Weg beschritt. Ich befand mich aber auch in deutlich besserer Verfassung als am Vortag und trug sogar eine sakkoähnliche schwarze Jacke, das seriöseste Kleidungsstück, über das ich verfügte. Außerdem war so einer wie ich für Journalisten der *Neuzeit* nichts Besonderes. Die kamen auch mit den ganz normalen Menschen von der Straße und aus der Spelunke in Berührung, das hatten sie den meditativ-fidelen Musikgymnastikerinnen aus den Wiener Schnösel-Bezirken eindeutig voraus.

Doch das änderte leider nichts am Inhalt unseres Gesprächs. Als Frau Nemez den Schock überwunden hatte, dass da ein Exkollege von *Tag für Tag* bis in ihr Büro vorgedrungen war, um ihr eine vom Gratis-Horrorblatt abgelehnte Geschichte zu verkaufen, ging es ihr postwendend ums Prinzip. Und dieses besagte, dass es schwer genug war, alle festen Mitarbeiter zu beschäftigen, und dass deshalb generell keine Beiträge von Autoren außerhalb des Hauses veröffentlicht werden konnten, weder von der *New York Times* noch von *Tag für Tag*. Ich konnte den Inhalt meiner Story aber gerne dem zuständigen Kollegen Seibernigg anvertrauen, der würde sich der Sache ganz bestimmt wohlwollend annehmen, sofern sie relevant war. Seibernigg war leider so gar nicht mein Fall. Ich hatte ihn einmal im Anschluss an eine abendliche Pressegala bei einer Weinverkostung beobachtet. Leute, die einen Schluck nahmen und dann minutenlang herumspülten und -gluckerten und dabei ihre Stirn in Falten legten, waren mir prinzipiell suspekt. Vielleicht war ich aber auch nur neidisch, dass solche Menschen nur ein paar Degustationsschlucke benötigten, um betrunken zu sein. Jedenfalls war Seibernigg für mich de facto keine Möglichkeit.

»Dann bedanke ich mich, dass Sie sich Zeit für mich genommen haben«, sagte ich und wollte mich schon zur Tür wenden. Dabei musste ich kurz an Manuel denken, was einen heftigen Drei-Sekunden-Blues zur Folge hatte. Und genau diesen dürfte sie mir angemerkt haben, weil sie eben nur nach außen hin Bambus, aber innerlich anscheinend mindestens Zyklame war. Denn sie fragte: »Worum geht es denn in der Geschichte?« Meine über Jahre gut verborgene Wut aufs Leben fand plötzlich ein Ventil und entlud sich gegen jene Banditen, die ein System aufrechterhielten, in dem einem kleinen talentierten Basketballspieler mit Segelohren, der niemandem etwas Böses wollte, das Recht auf seine Heimat abgesprochen werden konnte.

»Lassen Sie mich einmal hineinlesen«, sagte Clara Nemez,

als ich mich wieder beruhigt hatte. Ich steckte den Stick in mein Notebook, öffnete die Datei und zeigte ihr Machmuts in der Ichform abgefassten Stimmungs- und Lagebericht. Nach wenigen Zeilen begann sie zu nicken, nickte immer heftiger, hörte gar nicht mehr auf, und ich konnte beobachten, wie aus ihren geöffneten Händen plötzlich Fäuste wurden.

Danach sah sie mich erwartungsvoll an, als müsste ich exakt noch *ein* wirklich sehr gutes Argument liefern, damit sie die Redaktions-Prinzipien auf den Kopf und die Reportage tatsächlich ins Blatt stellen würde.

Am leichtesten tat ich mich in solchen Fällen erfahrungsgemäß immer mit der Wahrheit, also sagte ich: »Wissen Sie, warum mir diese Sache persönlich so wichtig ist?«

»Sagen Sie es mir.«

»Es geht mir dabei eigentlich um meinen Sohn Manuel.« Ich brauchte nicht länger als drei Minuten, um es ihr zu erklären. Und dazwischen, ich schwöre, so etwas war mir vor Fremden noch nie passiert, dazwischen musste ich mir in den Augenwinkeln herumwischen und ordentlich schlucken, damit mir die Stimme nicht versagte. Aber wenigstens steckte ich sie damit an, denn auch sie bekam den glasigen Blick, und schon deshalb war sie vermutlich gezwungen, ein Machtwort zu sprechen, und es war genau jenes, das ich mir für Manuel so sehr gewünscht hatte.

»Okay, wir machen es, wir bringen morgen die Geschichte, aber viel können wir Ihnen dafür nicht bezahlen, unser Budget ist ...«

»Sie brauchen mir überhaupt nichts dafür zu bezahlen«, sagte ich im ersten Freudentaumel. Wenn man arbeitslos war, konnte man ja relativ unbeschwert großzügig sein.

»Papperlapapp, Sie kriegen das übliche Honorar.« Also der Typ, der in solchen Angelegenheiten stur blieb, war ich nun auch wieder nicht. Also willigte ich ein.

»Ich habe aber noch eine Bedingung«, sagte sie. An *aber-noch-eine-Bedingung* waren schon Weltfriedensverträge gescheitert. Entsprechend furchtsam blickte ich wohl drein. »Sie müssen uns für Dienstag eine Nachfolgegeschichte liefern. Wenn wir in dieser Asylsache Druck auf die Behörden machen wollen, dann müssen die anderen Medien darauf anspringen. Und das erreichen wir nur, wenn wir nachsetzen. Verstehen Sie mich?« Ja, ich verstand sehr gut. Arbeit kam auf mich zu, und ich hatte keine Ahnung, wie ich die bewältigen sollte. Aber ich sagte sicherheitshalber einmal: »Ja, klar, das ist doch selbstverständlich.«

»Schaffen Sie das selbst?«, fragte sie. Ihr Vertrauen in die Fähigkeiten eines vergammelten *Tag-für-Tag*-Exjournalisten hatte offenbar doch seine Grenzen.

»Natürlich«, sagte ich und versuchte, arrogant zu lächeln.

»Und prüfen Sie bitte, ob sich an der Situation der Flüchtlingsfamilie aktuell etwas verändert hat, nicht dass die vielleicht schon alle gemütlich daheim sitzen«, sagte sie.

»Ja, klar, mache ich.« Nun steuerte ich relativ gezielt den Ausgang an, um nicht noch weitere Bedingungen zu provozieren. »Ich bin Ihnen jedenfalls sehr dankbar, Frau Nemez, Sie haben unter anderem mein Wochenende gerettet«, sagte ich an der Türschwelle.

»Schauen wir einmal, ob wir was erreichen«, antwortete sie. »Eines noch, Herr ... Plassek, weil ich gerade Ihren Namen lese«, rief sie mir nach. »Plassek, Plassek ... Haben Sie einen Verwandten, der früher mal für die *Rundschau* geschrieben hat?« Das war eine der eher interessanter formulierten Fragen, die man in jüngerer Zeit an mich herangetragen hatte. Ich wollte lieber gar nicht genau wissen, was sie mir unterschwellig suggerierte.

»Ja, das war mein blauäugiger kleiner Bruder, der Journalist werden wollte, um die Welt zu verbessern«, erwiderte ich.

»Und was ist aus ihm geworden?«, fragte sie.

»Ich«, sagte ich.

Vaterschaftstest überflüssig

Zuerst die unangenehme Nachricht: Sie befand sich auf meiner Mobilbox und stammte von meiner Exfrau Gudrun.

Hallo Gerold, ich bin's, kannst du mich bitte dringend zurückrufen? Papa hat einen Tobsuchtsanfall bekommen. Was ist denn in dich gefahren? Der alte Kunz hat's ihm erzählt. Du kannst doch nicht gleich alles hinschmeißen, nur weil einmal was nicht so läuft, wie du dir das vorstellst. Gerold, so einen Job wirst du nicht mehr so leicht bekommen. Du weißt, wie viele Journalisten auf der Straße sitzen. Bitte denk doch auch an Florentina, sie schaut zu dir auf. Willst du ihr sagen müssen, dass du arbeitslos bist? Oder denk an deine Mama. Hat sie das verdient? Was ist mit deinem Stolz? Also bitte, versuche die Sache wieder einzurenken. Norbert Kunz ist kein Unmensch, er wird sich umstimmen lassen. Und Berthold kennt einen von den Plus-Leuten, er kann für dich ein gutes Wort einlegen, damit ...

So etwas konnte ich jetzt nicht gebrauchen. Ich musste mich auf das Wesentliche konzentrieren, auf Manuel. Als ich ihn anrief, befand er sich gerade mit Freunden auf dem Weg ins Kino. Ich berichtete ihm, dass unsere Reportage zum Fall Machmut am Montag in der *Neuzeit*, einer viel, viel besseren Zeitung, erscheinen würde. Mit seinem grellen Jubelschrei legte er kurz meinen rechten Gehörgang lahm. Ich warnte ihn aber gleich, dass nun Arbeit auf uns beide zukam und dass wir dringend die Lage besprechen mussten.

»Soll ich nach dem Kino zu dir kommen, wo du wohnst?«, fragte er. Na ja, eigentlich besser nicht, aber eine Alternative fiel mir auch nicht ein.

»Ja, gute Idee«, sagte ich. »Pizza oder Kebab?« Ich legte mir bereits die Antwort auf »Wie meinst du Pizza oder Kebab?« zurecht. Aber er überraschte mich.

»Butterbrot mit Schnittlauch, wenn du hast.«

»Klar, habe ich«, erwiderte ich.

Ich packte also in einem Laden am Westbahnhof Butter, Brot und Schnittlauch ein und Fruchtzwerge, aber die legte ich wieder zurück ins Regal, da hatte ich mich mal kurz um ein Jahrzehnt verrechnet. Mit vierzehn tranken sie wahrscheinlich literweise Red Bull, den Alkohol der Gebietskrankenkassen, aber davor grauste mir, ich konnte so eine Dose gar nicht in die Finger nehmen. Also kaufte ich Apfelsaft – und für mich das Übliche.

Als ich mein Wohnküchen-Büro-Schlafzimmer überblickte, das mit viel Phantasie als Miniloft für Minderprivilegierte durchging, verspürte ich eine hartnäckige Aufräumblockade, denn die Dinge lagen ja nicht zufällig dort, wo sie lagen, sondern hatten sich über Monate den jeweiligen Platz erkämpft. Aber die überall verstreuten Kisten und Kartons mit leeren Flaschen und Dosen waren bei näherer Betrachtung wirklich etwas störend. Ich schaffte sie alle in den Vorraum, wo sie aber leider nicht bleiben konnten, weil sich dann die Eingangstür nicht öffnen ließ. Am liebsten hätte ich sie meinen ehrenwerten Nachbarn, Herrn und vor allem Frau Engelbrecht, die mich schon einige Male grundlos wegen Lärmbelästigung angezeigt hatten, nur weil ich im Stiegenhaus gestolpert war – am liebsten hätte ich sie ihnen auf den von ihren *Straßenschuhen* militant bewachten Fußabstreifer gestellt, aber ich wollte mir nach der Kündigung nicht sofort eine Delogierung einfangen. So landeten die Kisten und Säcke vorübergehend in der Badewanne, und ich legte zur Beruhigung ein paar Handtücher darüber. Danach hatte ich noch die Kraft, zwei Gläser und zwei Teller abzuwaschen, und schob Manuels CD von Efter-klang in den Audioplayer, damit befand sich die Wohnung in einem nahezu perfekten Zustand, sie musste nur irgendwann einmal aufgeräumt und geputzt werden – und entrümpelt und generalsaniert, aber das hatte Zeit.

»Cool, meine Musik«, sagte Manuel, sah sich gar nicht groß um, steuerte direkt auf die Couch zu, ließ sich hineinfallen, und wir waren auch schon mitten im Gespräch.

»Hast du neue Nachrichten von Machmut?«, fragte ich.

»Ja, es geht ihm gut, aber er möchte endlich wieder nach Hause.«

»Wir müssen morgen noch eine Geschichte über ihn und seine Eltern abliefern«, sagte ich.

»Cool. Und hast du eine Idee?«, fragte er.

»Nein. Du?«

»Am besten, wir besuchen sie, und du schreibst was dar-über«, schlug Manuel vor.

»Tja, das wäre natürlich das Beste, aber dazu müssten wir zum Beispiel wissen, wo sie sind.«

Jetzt lächelte mich Manuel verschmitzt an, und mir kam ein relativ spektakulärer Verdacht. »Sag bloß, du weißt, wo sie stecken?« Jetzt lachte er. »Wo?«

»Das verrate ich dir unter einer Bedingung.« Schon wieder eine Bedingung, mein Leben bestand bald nur noch aus Be-dingungen von Menschen, denen ich bedingungslos ausgelie-fert war.

»Wir gehen dort morgen Vormittag gemeinsam hin«, sagte Manuel.

»Morgen Vormittag? Hast du keine Schule?«

»Doch, das ist die Bedingung«. Ah, jetzt verstand ich. »Machi geht momentan auch nicht zur Schule«, sagte Manuel. Vor einer schulpolitisch korrekten Tante Julia hätte dieses Argument garantiert nicht bestehen können, aber ich fand es eigentlich sympathisch solidarisch, also drückte ich ein Auge zu und sagte ja zum Schuleschwänzen.

»Aber nur dieses eine Mal, und der Tante sagen wir nichts.« Er nickte.

Nun erzählte er mir endlich, wo unsere Austro-Tschetschenen Unterschlupf gefunden hatten, und zwar bei einer evangelischen Pfarrersfamilie in Neustift am Walde, an die sie der Basketballtrainer von Torpedo 15 vermittelt hatte, was aber unbedingt geheim bleiben musste.

»Das ist ja großartig, dass da die Kirche im Spiel ist«, jubelte der Journalist in mir.

»Es ist keine Kirche, nur ein alter Pfarrer und seine Frau.«

»Aber die werden uns nicht die Tür aufmachen«, fiel mir da leider gerade ein.

»Doch.«

»Wieso glaubst du das?«

»Machi hat schon mit der Pfarrersfrau geredet, und die hat gesagt, dass ich mit meinem Onkel kommen darf, aber nur unter der Bedingung ...« Endlich wieder eine Bedingung. »Aber nur unter der Bedingung, dass du was darüber schreibst, und zwar wieder in der *Neuzeit*, weil die *Neuzeit* ist wirklich eine gute Zeitung, für die alle Menschen gleich wertvoll sind, egal aus welchem Land sie kommen, hat die Frau gesagt, hat der Machi gesagt«, sagte er. Die wollten mir also tatsächlich ein sogenanntes Exklusiv-Interview geben. So viele gute Nachrichten an einem einzigen Sonntag – das war mir fast ein bisschen unheimlich.

Jedenfalls war das Problem mit der Nachfolgegeschichte nun so gut wie gelöst. Und ich überwand mich, doch noch das unangenehme Thema anzuschneiden.

»Du, Manuel, ich hab bei *Tag für Tag* gekündigt und hab ab morgen leider kein Büro mehr für uns beide.«

»Ich weiß, Tante Julia hat's mir schon erzählt«, sagte er relativ entspannt.

»Und wo willst du jetzt an den Nachmittagen hingehen, um deine Aufgaben zu machen?«

»Hierher, zu dir in die Wohnung.«

»Ich weiß nicht, ob das so eine gute Idee ist.«

»Das hat Tante Julia auch gesagt.«

»Schau mal, wie's hier aussieht«, sagte ich.

»Nein«, erwiderte Manuel. Das war die perfekte Antwort, fand ich. Jetzt benötigte ich endgültig keinen Vaterschaftstest mehr.

KAPITEL SIEBEN

Die Pajews in ihrem Versteck

Am Montag, meinem ersten offiziell arbeitslosen Werktag seit vielen Jahren, holte ich Manuel noch vor Unterrichtsbeginn in der Nähe der Schule ab. Das fand zu einer Tageszeit statt, die ich bis dahin nur aus Erzählungen gekannt hatte – unter der treffenden Bezeichnung Morgengrauen. Dafür war ich in der vorhergehenden Nacht zu einer Uhrzeit schlafen gegangen, zu der ich mir sonst erst langsam zu überlegen begann, was ich mit dem Abend noch vorhatte – oder der Abend mit mir. Jedenfalls hatte das einen von Schwindelanfällen begleiteten Jetlag am Rande des Kreislaufstillstands zur Folge, und ich war hauptsächlich damit beschäftigt, meine Augenlider am Hinunterkippen zu hindern, während wir in einer Bäckerei saßen und Manuel bei Kakao und Buttersemmel mächtig stolz die aufgeschlagene Ausgabe der *Neuzeit* bewunderte, unsere Doppelseite mit dem riesigen Titel *Der Fall Machmut*. Untertitel: *Ich will nicht wieder flüchten müssen.*

Danach nötigte er mich, Fragen zu sammeln, die wir dem evangelischen Pfarrerspaar stellen konnten. Ich machte solche Dinge lieber aus dem Bauch heraus, ich hasste Vorbereitungen jeder Art. Ich empfand das Leben generell nämlich als durchgängige Serie von Vorbereitungen auf etwas Irrationales, das dann niemals stattfand, während einen die wirklich bahnbrechenden Ereignisse stets unvorbereitet trafen, wie zum Beispiel Geburt, Windpocken, Verliebtheit, Impotenz und Tod, in meinem Fall auch Vaterschaft. Vielleicht sollte ich darüber einmal mit dem Pfarrerspaar reden.

Die etwa zweistündige Geheimmission in Neustift am Walde war dann extrem aufwühlend für alle Beteiligten, mit Ausnahme der beiden Kinder, die sich sofort über Basketball unterhielten und dabei rasch die Umstände ihres Zusammentreffens vergaßen. Den Anblick der jämmerlich und auf beschämende Weise schuldbewusst wirkenden Eltern Pajew, die im hintersten Eck der Küchenbank zusammengekauert dasaßen, hätte ich mir gerne erspart. Ich neigte ja dazu, in beklemmenden Situationen die Flucht nach vorne anzutreten und blöde Scherze zu machen. In diesem Fall lag mir auf der Zunge: »Schon scheiße, wenn man zur falschen Zeit am falschen Ort zur Welt kommt.« Oder: »An so regnerischen Tagen ist es ohnehin das Beste, sich irgendwo zu verstecken.« Doch die Pajews konnten vermutlich über gar nichts mehr lachen, also zwinkerte ich ihnen wenigstens aufmunternd zu und kam mir selbst dabei ziemlich jämmerlich vor.

Der alte Pfarrer erinnerte mich vom Aussehen her an Karlheinz Böhm, den ich vor Jahren einmal für die *Rundschau* interviewt hatte. Die beiden hatten auch das gleiche Händeschütteln, das den Geschüttelten bis in die Zehenspitzen wärmte. Besonders beeindruckend fand ich die Pfarrersfrau. Sie war mindestens siebzig und investierte offenbar alle ihr verbliebenen Kräfte in das, was ihrem persönlichen Empfinden nach gerecht war, was aber schon drei Häuser weiter keinen Menschen hinterm Ofen hervorgeholt hätte. Statt in der Dominikanischen Republik in einem Liegestuhl am Pool zu liegen, einen Baileys zu schlürfen und den Ruhestand zu genießen, saß sie im kalten Oktober in Wien vor einem dicken Notizblock und zermarterte sich das Hirn, wie man eine Flüchtlingsfamilie, die sie vor drei Tagen noch nicht einmal gekannt hatte und die jetzt in ihrem Haus wohnte, vor der sicheren Abschiebung bewahren konnte. Ich kannte mich mit diesem juristischen Kram ja nicht wirklich aus, aber wenn ich das richtig verstanden hatte, dann gab es da doch noch eine kleine Chance. Die Pajews hatten dem Pfarrerspaar nämlich versichert, dass bei den ersten Asylanhörungen vor sechs Jahren kein Dolmetscher anwesend gewesen war, obwohl die Tschetschenen damals noch kaum ein Wort Deutsch gesprochen hatten. Das bedeutete, dass die Pajews ganz dringend einen guten Anwalt brauchten, dem es vielleicht gelingen konnte, das Verfahren wegen eines Formfehlers neu aufzurollen. So ein Anwalt kostete natürlich immens viel Geld, und es gab keine Instanz, an die sich das Pfarrerspaar offiziell wenden und um Hilfe ersuchen konnte, ohne damit zu verraten, wo sich die Pajews illegal aufhielten.

Zunächst einmal brauchte man also die Zusicherung der Behörden, die Abschiebung zumindest so lange hinauszuzögern, bis sich der Anwalt, der noch gar nicht gefunden war und der auch nicht bezahlt werden konnte, in den Fall eingearbeitet hatte und sagen konnte, ob hier noch ein Rechtsmittel möglich war. Das Ganze klang unheimlich kompliziert und aussichtslos. Aber ich ließ mir nichts anmerken.

Und wenn unser Besuch wenigstens einen Zweck sicher erfüllt hatte, dann war das jener, dass sich die Schicksalsgemeinschaft der Pajews um zwei Personen erweitert hatte und dass jeder seinen Beitrag leisten wollte. Das Pfarrerspaar tat es aus purer Nächstenliebe und für den Glauben an eine von Gott gewollte irdische Gerechtigkeit. Manuel tat es für seinen Freund Machmut und für Torpedo 15. Und ich tat es für Manuel, also für mich selbst.

Daheim stellten wir kurzfristig auf Bürobetrieb um und richteten es uns mehr oder eher weniger gemütlich ein. Von der Anstrengung her hatte ich Montagmittag bereits genug für die ganze Woche. Aber es gab erstaunlich positive Nachrichten, die mich für einige Stunden vergessen lassen sollten, was mir mein Job in den letzten Jahren bedeutet hatte, nämlich gar nichts.

Zum Beispiel brachten sie im Radiojournal auf Ö1 einen ausführlichen Beitrag zum Fall Machmut, der mit den Worten begann: *Wie die* Neuzeit *in ihrer heutigen Ausgabe exklusiv berichtet* ... Auch im Fernsehen wurde die Geschichte aufgegriffen, und man zeigte sogar kurz das in der Zeitung erschienene Basketball-Gruppenfoto mit Machmut, auf dem ja auch Manuel zu sehen war, der sich somit erstmals auf einem TV-Bildschirm entdecken durfte. Für viele Buben seiner Generation war es ja der erklärte Höhepunkt des Lebens, einmal von einer TV-Kamera wahrgenommen zu werden, denn wessen Gesicht im Fernsehen war, der hatte es geschafft – er hatte es nämlich geschafft, ins Fernsehen zu kommen, sonst nichts, das genügte bereits. Die Frage war nur, was mit dem Rest Lebens anzufangen war, wenn das Ziel einmal erreicht war. Aber diesbezüglich brauchte ich mir bei Manuel keine Sorgen zu machen, er war kein Kind seiner Zeit, er aß Butterbrot mit Schnittlauch und hörte Efterklang und Brasstronaut – das waren auch solche Träumer, diesmal aus Kanada, die hier sonst kein Mensch kannte.

Um mit den positiven Nachrichten fortzufahren: Das Postfach meines Laptops quoll förmlich über vor E-Mails, die sie mir von der *Neuzeit* weitergeleitet hatten und in denen sich Leser, darunter viele Studenten, über die drohende Verbannung einer Familie in den Kaukasus – und das nach sechs Jahren Asylverfahren – empörten und für den Verbleib der Pajews in Österreich starkmachten. Manuel, der für die Internet-Verkehrskontrollen zuständig war und das mustergültig erledigte, erzählte mir dann auch noch aufgeregt von eigens gegründeten Foren, in denen Unterschriften für Machmut gesammelt wurden, so auch auf der Homepage der Basketball-Jugendvereine, wo selbst der Verbandspräsident ein paar berührende Worte fand.

Und schließlich bestätigte mir auch Clara Nemez am Telefon, dass die Reportage voll eingeschlagen und viel Staub aufgewirbelt hatte und das Innenministerium um eine öffentliche Stellungnahme wohl nicht herumkommen würde. Ich erzählte ihr im Gegenzug von unseren Recherchen und von den rührigen Pfarrersleuten und ihren Rettungsideen für die Pajews. Dafür erntete ich nicht nur Komplimente, sondern prompt auch vier leere Seiten, die es in den folgenden vier Stunden zu füllen galt, also pro Stunde eine Seite. Das war für mich schlichtweg nicht zu bewältigen. Erstens war ich aus der Übung, und zweitens entwickelte sich in meinem Kopf überhaupt nichts, was in Richtung klare Gedankenstruktur ging. Außerdem brauchte ich dringend mindestens ein Bier, was aber dank Heimvorteil mein geringstes Problem war. Nur Manuel musste nicht unbedingt etwas davon mitbekommen.

Clara Nemez erkannte das Dilemma an meiner Stimme und bot mir an, die politische Seite des Falles zu übernehmen, was mir natürlich sehr recht war, weil das für mich sonst mit mühsamen Telefonrecherchen bei Behörden verbunden gewesen wäre, und ich hasste alle drei: Recherchen, Telefone und Behörden sowieso.

»Ich kann auch was schreiben«, sagte Manuel, der meinen Zustand hautnah miterlebte, und allein für diese Ansage und den Blick dazu hätte ich ihn gerne in die Arme genommen oder gleich adoptiert. »Ich kann zum Beispiel über Machi schreiben, wie er bei Torpedo 15 spielt, welche irren Körbe er schon geworfen hat und wie wichtig er für die Mannschaft ist, vor allem dann im Endspiel gegen Union CS, da geht es um den Herbstmeistertitel.«

»Hervorragende Idee«, sagte ich, und ich meinte das vollkommen ernst. Wenn uns Menschen etwas bewegte, dann waren das genau solche Geschichten, also nicht das große Gemetzel, das irgendwo weit weg an Robben veranstaltet wurde, sondern eine noch ziemlich verknautscht aussehende Babyrobbe namens Bobby, die den Schlächtern entkommen war und nun mutterlos auf einer Eisscholle hockte. So erschütterte einen auch nicht die globale Perversion der riesigen Flüchtlingsströme, der überfüllten Lager und der unüberschaubaren Massenabschiebungen. Sondern um die Menschen zu rühren und im besten Fall zum Handeln zu veranlassen, brauchte es eben einen kleinen Machi mit abstehenden Ohren, der spektakuläre Körbe werfen konnte und einem wichtigen Match entgegenfieberte. Wird er spielen dürfen, oder kommt er unverschuldet in die Hölle? Diese Frage würde die Gemüter erhitzen und vielleicht sogar Politiker in Zugzwang bringen.

Mir selbst blieb dann eigentlich nur noch ein Stimmungsbericht aus dem Versteck, das Interview mit der Pfarrersfamilie, deren Identität natürlich geschützt werden musste, und die gesetzliche Causa, also die Sache mit dem fehlenden Dolmetscher und der theoretischen Möglichkeit einer Wiederaufnahme des Asylverfahrens, wobei ich nicht unerwähnt lassen wollte, dass ein erfahrener Rechtsanwalt dringend gesucht war, der zudem Geduld mit der Bezahlung haben musste. Vielleicht würde sich ja ein solcher durch den Artikel angesprochen fühlen.

Um es kurz zu fassen: Wir erledigten unser Vier-Stunden-Programm mit Bravour. Ich war diesmal sogar ein bisschen stolz auf meine Leistung, denn ich hatte während der Arbeit einige Getränkedosen vernichtet, und normalerweise gelang mir überhaupt nichts Kreatives, wenn ich trank.

Die beste Geschichte allerdings – wir gaben ihr den Titel *Machi, wir brauchen dich* – hatte eindeutig Manuel abgeliefert. Sie war zwar einfach formuliert und artig abgefasst wie ein Schulaufsatz, und man merkte ihr das Bemühen des Schreibers um eine tadellose Abfolge von Subjekten, Prädikaten und Objekten an. Aber jeder Satz war vollgepfropft mit Leidenschaft, und das war eine Kunst, die weder eine Journalistenschule noch eine Literaturschmiede lehren konnte – aus Buchstaben gebaute Gefühle in eine Badewanne zu gießen und sein Leserpublikum dort mitten hineinzusetzen.

Auch Clara Nemetz war beeindruckt und meinte, dass diese Liebeserklärung eines Vierzehnjährigen an das Mit- und Füreinander in einem verschworenen Basketballteam genauso stark und überzeugend sein konnte wie ein rechtskräftiger Asylbescheid.

Meine Sorgen gehören mir

Am Montagabend hatte ich mit meinen Kumpels in Zoltan's Bar ein bisschen gefeiert, ich gebe es zu. Der folgende Dienstag fiel mir also erst mittags auf, als sich einerseits mein Durst zurückmeldete und nach Leitungswasser verlangte und andererseits ein Zahn rechts oben hinten quasi die Alarmglocken läuten ließ und mich an den bevorstehenden Besuch bei Rebecca Linsbach erinnerte, dem ich mit gemischten Gefühlen unterschiedlicher Art entgegensah. Na ja, so unterschiedlich waren sie eigentlich gar nicht, vom Kombipack aus Liebe und Schmerz lebte immerhin unter anderem die gesamte Literatur.

Zum Glück stand an diesem Tag sonst nichts an. Manuel

wusste ich für den Nachmittag in festen, trainierten Händen –
in jenen Tante Julias, die mit ihm eine Winterjacke kaufen
wollte. Was meine Exfrau Gudrun betraf, stand noch ein Tele-
fonat aus, sie hatte mich ja per Mailbox noch nicht ganz und
gar zur Schnecke gemacht. Ich hätte sie vielleicht am späten
Nachmittag selbst angerufen, aber sie kam mir zuvor.

»Hallo Geri, das ist ja wirklich eine Wahnsinnsgeschichte,
die du da aufgetan hast! Du bist damit in aller Munde. Ich bin
total beeindruckt, und Florentina erst. Und auch Berthold gratuliert dir, er hat mich extra aus Warschau angerufen«, sagte sie.
Sie hatte dabei diese unkontrolliert nach oben und unten aus-
scherende Stimme, wo sich chronische Desillusionierung und
punktuelle Faszination ins Gehege kamen, so wie damals, als
ich ihr den Heiratsantrag machte, zu einem Zeitpunkt, als unsere Liebesbeziehung bereits gescheitert war.

»Ja, das ist eine recht starke Geschichte«, sagte ich so beiläufig wie nur möglich. Es kam nicht oft vor, dass ich Gudrun gegenüber in aller Aufrichtigkeit falsch bescheiden sein konnte.

»Wie hast du das denn … Wo hast du die Story eigentlich
her? Und wie hast du … Die Texte sind wunderbar geschrieben … und so viele«, stotterte sie herum. »Und sag, wer ist
denn dieser … Wie kommst du zu dem entzückenden Buben,
zu diesem Manuel?«

»Wie die Jungfrau zum Kind«, sagte ich beinahe wahrheitsgemäß. »Er ist der Sohn einer sehr guten alten Bekannten.«

»Kenne ich sie?«

»Alice? Nein, das glaube ich nicht.«

»Ich hab übrigens noch mal mit Papa geredet«, sagte sie
nach einer längeren Kunstpause, in der sich ihre Stimmbänder
auf normale Lage eingependelt hatten, auf Desillusionierung.
»Und er sagte mir, dass dich Norbert Kunz wieder zurückneh-
men würde.«

»Tatsächlich?«

»Du brauchst dich nicht einmal zu entschuldigen, du brauchst nur ...«

»Liebe Gudrun«, jetzt lief ich wirklich Gefahr, böse zu werden. »Liebe Gudrun, das Thema *Tag für Tag* ist für mich ein und für alle Mal erledigt. Die haben die Geschichte über Machmut, die jetzt Wellen schlägt, aus dem Blatt geworfen, weil sie ihnen nicht in ihre miese Ideologie gepasst hat. Ich – gehe – dort – nicht – mehr – hin! Verstehst du mich so weit?«

»Und wovon willst du leben?«

»Von Beiträgen wie diesen für die *Neuzeit*«, antwortete ich.

»Aber wie viele solcher Geschichten gibt es?«

»Genügend«, sagte ich.

»Und die warten auf dich?

»Teils warten sie, teils warte ich, und manchmal werden wir uns entgegenkommen, schätze ich.« Das waren diese Sätze, die mir selbst ziemlich gut gefielen, aber mit denen Gudrun absolut nichts anfangen konnte und an denen sie letztlich gemerkt hatte, dass sie mit mir nichts mehr anfangen konnte.

»Geri, ich mache mir einfach Sorgen ...«

»Ich weiß, Gudrun, aber ich sage dir, es ist absolut sinnlos, dass du dir Sorgen machst, die ich mir nicht mache. Es sind meine Sorgen, die gehören mir. Und ich mache sie mir, wenn ich sie mir mache, und wenn ich sie mir nicht mache, dann mache ich sie mir eben nicht, und erst recht mache ich sie mir nicht, wenn du sie dir an meiner Stelle machst. Verstehst du, was ich meine?« Jetzt sagte sie nichts mehr, und wir konnten uns in weiterer Folge relativ ruhig und friedlich voneinander verabschieden.

Kaum hatte ich Gudruns Anruf samt ihrer, wie ich wusste, durchaus berechtigten Sorgen weggesteckt und wollte mir die aktuellen E-Mails zum Fall Machmut ansehen, da erhielt ich den nächsten Anruf. Es war Clara Nemez von der *Neuzeit*. Und es war offenbar der Tag der aufgeregten weiblichen Telefon-stimmen.

»Herr Plassek, ist es Ihnen möglich, dass Sie heute kurz zu mir ins Büro kommen?«

»Heute? Das ist eher schwierig«, sagte ich mit Blick auf mei-nen gestreiften Flanell-Pyjama. »Worum geht es denn?«

»Das möchte ich Ihnen nicht am Telefon sagen.«

»Ist es eine schlechte Nachricht?«

»Nein, es ist keine schlechte Nachricht, es ist eine gute Nach-richt, eine ganz besonders gute Nachricht, denke ich. Und dar-über sollten wir reden.« Okay, das war ein Argument. Ich hätte gerne noch gefragt, ob diese ganz besonders gute Nachricht vielleicht mit Arbeit für mich verbunden war. Aber ich ris-kierte es und versprach, am späten Nachmittag in der Redak-tion vorbeizukommen.

Die sechste Spende

Ich wurde ein bisschen wie ein Popstar empfangen, allerdings eher so die Marke Keith Richards oder Ozzy Osbourne, wo schon auch etwas Demut vor dem hohen Alter und seinen Spuren mitschwang, vielleicht war es auch Mitleid, denn das kleine Begrüßungskomitee war eindeutig bereits die nächste Generation von Journalisten und Journalistinnen und wirkte auffallend frisch und unverbraucht. Sie sagten alle brav ihren Namen auf, warteten den Händedruck ab und verschwanden dann wieder in ihre Büros.

»Wollen Sie vielleicht Kaffee? Oder Tee? Oder Wasser?«, fragte Clara Nemez. Sie wirkte aufgekratzt.

»Nein danke, bemühen Sie sich nicht.«

»Oder ein Bier?« Ich überlegte.

»Ja, vielleicht, ein kleines Glas«, sagte ich.

»Wir haben nur eine Flasche.«

»Okay, dann halt eine Flasche.« Ich musste sie ja nicht austrinken. Sie wartete, bis ich den ersten Schluck gemacht hatte.

»Herr Plassek, wir haben heute Mittag eine anonyme Geldspende bekommen«, sagte sie dann mehr oder weniger ansatzlos.

»Heute Mittag?«, fragte ich. Man erwischt ja bei Sensationsbotschaften nicht immer gleich auf Anhieb die Sensation.

»Ja, der Brief muss beim Empfang abgegeben worden sein. Ich habe schon nachgefragt, aber Frau Kunnert kann sich nicht daran erinnern. Jedenfalls ist der Brief bei mir in der Hauspost gelandet. Und als ich ihn öffnete … Sehen Sie selbst.« Sie reichte ihn mir. Es handelte sich um ein weißes Kuvert mit aufgeklebtem Papierstreifen, auf den »An die Chefredaktion, Clara Nemez, persönlich« gedruckt war. In dem Kuvert befanden sich ein dicker Stoß Geldscheine und ein Zeitungsausschnitt.

»Zehntausend Euro?«, fragte ich.

»Erraten!«, sagte die Nemez.

Dann sah ich mir den Artikel an, bei dem mir sofort mein Name ins Auge sprang. Es war eine der in der heutigen Ausgabe erschienenen Geschichten zum *Fall Machmut*, und zwar jene über die Chancen für eine Wiederaufnahme des Asylverfahrens wegen möglichen Formfehlers. Und hierbei waren exakt zwei Sätze mit grünem Leuchtstift markiert und mit drei Ausrufezeichen versehen. Es war das Zitat der anonymisierten Pajew-Beschützer, die sagten: »Die Familie benötigt jetzt dringend einen erfahrenen Rechtsanwalt. Dafür fehlt uns leider noch das Geld, aber wir werden versuchen, unter Freunden zu sammeln.«

»Die zehntausend Euro sind also für die Pajews bestimmt, damit sie sich einen guten Rechtsbeistand leisten können«, schloss Clara Nemez. Ich nickte. Bei mir begann gerade eine

Phase, wo mir die Dinge wegen des zu großen Ausmaßes an Unfassbarkeit über den Kopf wuchsen. So musste ich sie nun um ein weiteres Bier bitten.

»Ich schlage vor, wir trinken ein Glas Sekt, das kann ich jetzt gut vertragen«, sagte sie. Das sollte mir natürlich auch recht sein. Clara Nemez hatte ja ohnehin von Anfang an so ausgesehen, als könnte man mit ihr ganz gut feiern. »Das ist offensichtlich die Fortsetzung der großen Spendenserie«, sagte sie.

»Offensichtlich«, erwiderte ich.

»Darauf stoßen wir an.«

»Ja.«

»Der Wohltäter hat sozusagen mit Ihnen die Zeitung gewechselt. Sie sind unser Glücksbote, Herr Plassek.« Bei diesen Worten lachte sie, was bedeutete, sie ging davon aus, dass das natürlich der reine Zufall war. Ich konnte nicht sagen, warum, aber mir fiel ein Felsbrocken vom Herzen. »Das heißt aber auch, dass *Tag für Tag* zu Unrecht bezichtigt wurde, die Spendensache selbst initiiert zu haben«, schloss Clara Nemez.

»Es sei denn, die neue Spende stammt von den Plus-Leuten, um den Verdacht von sich abzuwenden«, sagte ich. Aber das war eigentlich unmöglich, denn dafür hätten sie sich niemals einen Artikel über einen Asylfall ausgesucht, den sie vorher aus politischen Gründen abgelehnt hatten.

»Wie auch immer, wir müssen entscheiden, was wir jetzt tun«, sagte sie. In einer Sache waren wir uns rasch einig. Da Manuel und ich wahrscheinlich die Einzigen waren, die wussten, wo sich die Pajews aufhielten, war es wohl an uns, ihnen, beziehungsweise dem Pfarrerspaar, die zehntausend Euro zu überbringen. In diesem Zusammenhang erhielt ich nun gleich die nächste gute Nachricht. Die auf Asylfälle spezialisierte Anwaltskanzlei Reichert hatte via *Neuzeit-Online* bereits kundgetan, das Mandat übernehmen zu wollen, notfalls sogar unentgeltlich, das hieß wahrscheinlich, sie wollten stattdessen medial abgefeiert werden. Man wartete nur noch auf die Zusicherung der Behörde, die geplante Abschiebung zu stoppen. Wegen des großen Aufsehens, das der Fall in der Öffentlichkeit erregt hatte, durfte man davon ausgehen, dass diese Zusicherung wohl erfolgen würde und die Pajews ihr Versteck bald verlassen konnten. Ich freute mich schon riesig darauf, Manuel diese frohe Botschaft zu überbringen.

»Und wie wollen wir inhaltlich mit der anonymen Spende umgehen?«, fragte Clara Nemez. Ich rechnete ihr hoch an, dass sie mich in diese Frage einbezog.

»Ich finde, man sollte kein allzu großes Tamtam darum machen«, sagte ich. Allerdings war ich der Typ, der um nichts im Leben ein großes Tamtam machen wollte, nicht einmal ein kleines Tamtam, eigentlich gar kein Tamtam, denn ich war ja im Grunde der geborene Anti-Journalist, der sich sagte: Die Dinge sind, wie sie sind, egal ob man sie in die Welt hinausposaunt oder für sich behält.

»Aber ganz verschweigen können wir die Sache auch nicht. Das sind wir schon dem Spender schuldig, damit er weiß, dass sein Geld gut angekommen ist. Außerdem killt mich sonst mein Eigentümer«, sagte sie.

»Am besten, man bringt eine kurze, fundierte, sachliche Meldung ohne Effekthascherei, nicht auf der Titelseite, sondern irgendwo im Blattinneren, aus, Schluss, basta«, sagte ich.

»Können Sie sich das vorstellen?«, fragte sie.

»Ja, das kann ich mir gut vorstellen«, erwiderte ich.

»Fein. Also Sie schreiben uns die Meldung?«

»Ich?« Das war ein kleines Missverständnis.

»Es ist Ihre Geschichte, Herr Plassek. Ihnen ist diese Spende zu verdanken«, sagte sie. Das klang seltsam. Ich war es nicht gewohnt, dass mir etwas zu verdanken war.

»Okay, vier, fünf Sätze – mehr brauche ich nicht«, sagte ich. Und sie schenkte mir noch ein Glas Sekt ein.

Am späten Abend lehnten wir an der Theke von Zoltan's Bar, und ich berichtete brühwarm von der neuen Zehntausend-Euro-Spende. Für mich war es in erster Linie ein Test, wie Außenstehende – und meine Kumpels standen eigentlich immer ziemlich weit draußen von allem – reagierten, ob ihnen vielleicht etwas auffiel, und ob es unter Umständen das Gleiche war, das mir sofort aufgefallen war und das mich doch einigermaßen verwirrte.

»Die Wohltäterin muss großes Vertrauen in die *Neuzeit* haben, dass die das Geld dort nicht einfach in ihre eigene Tasche stecken«, sagte Josi, der arbeitslose Konditor.

»Wohltäterin? Warum glaubst du, dass es eine Frau ist?«, fragte Franticek, der Kunstschmied.

»Das sagt mir mein Instinkt. Frauen sind einfach sozialer. Nein, falsch, anders – Frauen sind auch dann sozial, wenn sie nichts davon haben«, erwiderte Josi.

»Das beste Beispiel ist die Frau, die dich geheiratet hat, Josi«, fand Horst, der Wettbüro-Betreiber.

»Geh scheißen«, erwiderte Josi.

»Ich bin froh, dass es nicht der Widerling von Plus war«, sagte Franticek.

»Ich glaube, es ist ein alter Millionär, der früher *Tag für Tag* gelesen hat, und wie dann der Skandal war, hat's ihm gereicht. Und jetzt ist er zufällig in der *Neuzeit* auf Geris Geschichte über die Flüchtlinge gestoßen, und da hat er sich erbarmt und hat noch einmal einen großen Geldbrocken nachgelegt. Und das war es dann. Das glaube nämlich ich«, meinte Arik, der Berufsschullehrer.

»Ich sage euch, dass der sich nicht um die einzelnen Schicksale schert. Der hat einen Haufen Schwarzgeld und will es verschwinden lassen, und das macht er auf sehr elegante Weise, sodass ein paar Arme auch was davon haben.« Das kam von Horst.

»Jedenfalls, gratuliere, Geri! Die Geschichte ist dir wirklich gelungen. Jeder redet darüber, und jetzt kommt auch noch die Spende dazu. Dein Bub wird stolz auf dich sein. Und du pass auf, dass du uns nicht noch berühmt wirst auf deine alten Tage«, meinte Arik.

»Was sagt eigentlich unser großer Schweigefürst Zoltan dazu?«, fragte Josi.

»Ich schlage vor, das Haus gibt eine Runde auf Geri aus. Auf Geri und den Geldgeber«, erwiderte der Wirt. Der Vorschlag wurde ohne Gegenstimme angenommen.

Ich brach diesmal relativ bald auf und wälzte mich daheim stundenlang im Bett. Es war da nämlich ein extrem schlaf-störender Gedanke im Raum, den ich um jeden Preis loswer-den wollte, der sich aber einfach nicht abschütteln ließ. Auch wenn es außer mir zum Glück noch niemand bemerkt haben dürfte und ich mir das Ganze vermutlich ohnehin nur einbil-dete, so spürte ich es dennoch bis in die linke kleine Zehe – ich spürte nämlich, dass diese geheimnisvolle Spendenserie, so un-glaublich das jetzt klingen mochte, irgendwo auch mit mir zu tun hatte, ja, mit mir, nicht mit *Tag für Tag*, nicht mit der *Neu-zeit*, sondern mit mir als Person. Denn wenn alle sechs Spen-den etwas gemeinsam hatten, dann dass sämtliche beigelegten Texte von mir stammten – entweder hatte ich sie selbst ver-fasst, oder ich war zumindest verantwortlich gewesen. Oder irrte ich mich da? Die erste Spende bezog sich auf die Kurz-meldung über das Obdachlosenheim, die hatte ich geschrie-ben. Im zweiten Kuvert befand sich die Notiz über die Kin-dertagesstätte, auch die hatte ich selbst verfasst. Die dritten zehntausend Euro waren für die Rentnerin bestimmt, der die Geldbörse gestohlen worden war, den Text hatte zwar Sophie

Rambuschek beigesteuert, aber auch er war in den von mir verwalteten *bunten Meldungen* erschienen. Dies galt genauso für die in Not geratene Sozialberatungsstelle. Okay, jene skandalumwitterte Geschichte über die vom Unwetter heimgesuchte Bauernfamilie, die im fünften Geldkuvert lag, die hatte Kunz ausgesucht und vielleicht sogar selbst geschrieben, aber auch sie fand sich in meiner Rubrik der *bunten Meldungen zum Tag*. Der Wohltäter konnte jedenfalls annehmen, dass sämtliche Artikel, auf die er seine Spenden gründete, von mir ausgesucht und verfasst worden waren. Er musste nur einmal bei *Tag für Tag* angefragt haben, wer für die Kurznotizen verantwortlich war, und da würde man ihm meinen Namen genannt haben.

Gut, das alles konnte der ganz normale blanke Zufall gewesen sein. Aber die sechste Spende, die war mir nun wirklich nicht mehr geheuer: Wieso wurde ausgerechnet ein Asylfall in einer unauffälligen linksliberalen Stadtzeitung dafür auserkoren? Wer (außer mir) wechselte so radikal die Seiten, sprang von *Tag für Tag* zur *Neuzeit*, wo es doch täglich in allen großen Gazetten des Landes Dutzende prominent platzierter Sozialreportagen und Unmengen an Kurzmeldungen zu praktisch jedem Aspekt der Hilfsbedürftigkeit gab? Wieso wollte der Spender ausgerechnet einem kleinen Tschetschenenbuben unter die Arme greifen? Doch nicht vielleicht deshalb, weil eben ich es war, der diesen Artikel verfasst und mit seinem Namen unterzeichnet hatte?

Im nächsten Moment schämte ich mich beinahe für diese Gedanken. Gerold Plassek, sagte ich mir, was glaubst du eigentlich, wer du bist? Dreiundvierzig Jahre lang warst du unauffällig, hast dich zurückgehalten, hast dich nie vorgedrängt, hast immer alle anderen gewinnen lassen, nicht aus edlen Motiven, nein, zumeist aus reiner Bequemlichkeit und weil du dich eben gut kennst: Du bist nicht der Typ, der für die großen Dinge vorgesehen ist. Und was soll das jetzt, was ist das auf einmal, Gerold Plassek? Du wirst uns doch nicht plötzlich größenwahnsinnig werden? Du hast ja wohl genügend Schwächen, aber eines warst du nie: Du warst nie eingebildet genug, dir einzubilden, jemand ganz Besonderer zu sein. Bilde dir bloß nicht ein, dass du jetzt damit beginnen kannst.

KAPITEL ACHT

Schwer Verdauliches

Am Mittwoch holte ich Manuel von der Schule ab, diesmal zu einer christlichen Tageszeit, also nicht vor, sondern nach dem Unterricht. Ich hatte per SMS eine Überraschung angekündigt.

»Dein Fahrrad kannst du stehen lassen, wir gehen auf Pommes mit Majo und Ketchup«, sagte ich. Er wirkte daraufhin relativ betreten, als fürchtete er, dass das bereits die Überraschung war. Ich aß also Pommes, ich hatte nämlich noch nicht gefrühstückt, während er sich über ein in dichtes Salatgrün gewickeltes Vollwert-Bio-Grobkorn-Soja-Vitalsandwich Marke *Das findet Tante Julia richtig geil* hermachte, und das, obwohl der Bub mitten im Wachstum war. Aber egal, irgendwie wurden die Kinder wahrscheinlich auch auf diese Weise groß.

In einem dramaturgisch geeigneten Moment zog ich das Spendenkuvert heraus – ich hatte es so präpariert, dass einige Geldscheine hervorschauten – und warf es mit den Worten »das ist für Machi« extrem lässig auf den Tisch. Ich kam mir selbst dabei ein bisschen wie Jamie Foxx in *Django Unchained* von Quentin Tarantino vor, mit dem kleinen Unterschied, dass ich kein ehemals versklavter dunkelhäutiger Kopfgeldjäger in den Südstaaten war. Die Wirkung war dennoch verblüffend, Manuel machte die eindeutig größten Augen unserer bisherigen gemeinsamen Geschichte.

Ich erklärte ihm dann die näheren Umstände des Geldsegens und die erfreuliche Entwicklung im Fall Pajew. Ich hatte auch ein paar aktuelle Tageszeitungen mitgebracht, und wir überflogen gemeinsam die Artikel zu unserem Thema. Die meisten Blätter hatten der Tatsache, dass der anonyme Wohltäter offensichtlich wieder aktiv geworden war, große Aufmerksamkeit geschenkt und der Berichterstattung über die Spendenserie viel Platz eingeräumt. In einigen Artikeln wurde explizit mein Name genannt – mit dem herablassenden Hinweis versehen, dass ich ein geschasster *Tag-für-Tag*-Reporter war. Aber ich wurde zum Glück in keiner einzigen Zeile mit der Spendenserie in Zusammenhang gebracht, und auch Manuel sagte vorerst nichts dazu, er war ganz auf Machmut und die Leserbriefe konzentriert.

Tag für Tag nutzte die sechste Spende übrigens zu einem massiven Rundumschlag gegen die verleumderische Medienlandschaft und prophezeite dem Konkurrenzblatt *Leute heute* in den bevorstehenden Medienprozessen den finanziellen Ruin.

Mir gefiel es, dass sich die *Neuzeit* bezüglich der Spende komplett zurückhielt und die Fakten für sich sprechen ließ. Damit erzielte man meiner Meinung nach eine viel größere Wirkung und passte sich der Anonymität der guten Taten an.

Wir fuhren dann mit der Straßenbahn Linie 38 und dem Bus 35A zu der Pfarrersfamilie nach Neustift am Walde. Für mich war es wohltuend mit anzusehen, wie sich die Buben in die Arme fielen, wie weit Machmuts Eltern, rein nach der Optik zu urteilen, schon aus ihrem Versteck herausgekommen waren, was für entspannte Gesichtszüge sie hatten und wie vertrauensvoll sie uns diesmal zulächelten.

»Sie sind ein herzensguter Mensch«, sagt die Pfarrersfrau, als ich ihr das Geldkuvert übergab.

»Da irren Sie sich gewaltig. Ich hätte die zehntausend Euro gerne behalten, aber leider steht ja schon in allen Zeitungen, für wen sie bestimmt sind«, erwiderte ich. Ich musste so etwas sagen, weil die Tränen von meiner Augenoberfläche nicht mehr allzu weit entfernt waren. Ich hasste rührende Szenen, wenn ich selbst davon betroffen war. Man war irgendwie komplett machtlos dagegen.

Das fast noch schönere Geschenk war die Nachricht, dass die Pajews wahrscheinlich schon am nächsten Tag in ihre Wohnung zurückkehren konnten, weil dann die Frist zur neuerlichen Begutachtung ihrer Asylsituation offiziell begann. Das bedeutete, dass der kleine Machi bereits am kommenden Donnerstag beim Basketballtraining dabei sein konnte.

»In die Schule musst du übrigens auch wieder gehen«, erinnerte ich ihn, um die Euphorie ein bisschen zu bremsen.

Als kleines Dankeschön für unseren Botengang wurden wir schließlich genötigt, Manti zu essen, eine Speise, die Frau Pajew angeblich nach tschetschenischem Rezept zubereitet hatte. Das waren, dem Geschmack nach zu urteilen, Teigtaschen, die mit Teigtaschen gefüllt waren, die wiederum mit Teigtaschen gefüllt waren, so nach dem Matrjoschka-Prinzip. Jetzt verstand ich, warum die Familie um keinen Preis zurück an den Kaukasus wollte. Außerdem lagen mir noch die fetten Pommes im Magen. Aber wenigstens packte der Pfarrer nachher seinen selbst gebrannten Birnenschnaps aus.

Manuel braucht keinen Vater

Wieder daheim im Miniloft, widmeten wir uns den Themen, die der Tag offengelassen hatte. Mir zum Beispiel blieb noch eine Stunde Zeit, mich mental auf meinen nächsten Spendenbesuch vorzubereiten – nach der Geldspende nun eine kleine Zahnspende, Blutspende inkludiert. Kurzum: Rebecca Linsbach wartete auf mich, zumindest stellte ich mir vor, dass sie auf mich wartete, aber dabei verging die Zeit auch nicht schneller.

Da Manuel absolut keine Lust hatte, sich unmittelbar nach

dem schillernden Beweis, wie aufregend das Leben sein konnte, mit einer Mathe-Hausaufgabe herumzuschlagen, fing er an, mir die großen Abenteuer seiner Kindheit zu erzählen, wie er, sein Fahrrad auf den Schultern, einen reißenden, vermutlich Krokodil-verseuchten Fluss durchquert hatte, wie er bei einem Zeltlager Pest und Cholera oder zumindest eine Lungenentzündung überleben konnte, wie er im legendären Australien-Urlaub unter kilometerhohen Wellen von seinem ersten Surfbrett fast erschlagen worden war oder in freier Wildbahn eine Killer-Hornisse erdrosselt hatte – und noch anderes mehr. Die meisten Geschichten begannen mit den Worten: »Wie ich mit der Mama dort und dort war ...« Da fasste ich irgendwann den Mut und sprach es endlich einmal an.

»Du, Manuel, sag mal – dein Vater?« Ich sah aus dem Fenster, um der Frage kein allzu großes Gewicht zu geben.

»Wie, mein Vater?«, fragte er.

»Was weißt du von ihm?«

»Nichts. Wieso?«

»Hat dir die Mama nie was erzählt?«

»Nein. Sie hat gesagt, da gibt es nicht viel zu erzählen. Aber wenn ich es wissen will, dann erzählt sie es mir natürlich.«

»Und?«, fragte ich.

»Ich wollte es nicht wissen.«

»Warum nicht?«

»Weil es mich nicht interessiert.«

»Ah so«, sagte ich.

»Er interessiert sich ja auch nicht für mich«, sagte er.

»Wieso bist du dir da so sicher?«, fragte ich.

»Wenn er sich für mich interessiert hätte, dann hätte er sich irgendwann gemeldet, dann wäre er einmal da gewesen, dann hätte er mir zum Geburtstag gratuliert oder mir was geschenkt, oder wir wären mal gemeinsam Radfahren gegangen oder zu einem Match oder ins Kino oder irgendwas«, sagte er.

Mir brannte es natürlich auf der Zunge, ihm darzulegen, dass sein Vater möglicherweise vierzehn Jahre gar nicht gewusst hatte, dass er sein Vater war. Aber so was klang auch nicht gerade schmeichelhaft für einen Sohn. Außerdem hätte er unter Umständen Verdacht geschöpft, und das wollte ich auf keinen Fall riskieren, zumindest jetzt noch nicht.

»Vielleicht traut er sich einfach nicht, sich bei dir zu melden«, erwiderte ich also.

»Warum soll er sich nicht trauen?«

»Weil er vielleicht Angst hat, dass du ihn nicht magst.«

»Wie soll ich ihn nicht mögen, wenn ich ihn gar nicht kenne?«

»Stimmt.« Ich sollte wirklich langsam aufhören, blöde Fragen zu stellen.

»Aber fehlt er dir denn nicht manchmal?«, fragte ich nur noch.

»Nein.«

»Wieso nicht?«

»Weil, wenn man etwas nie gehabt hat, dann kann es einem auch nicht fehlen, weil man gar nicht weiß, was es ist, das einem fehlt.«

»Stimmt.« Das war ziemlich klug. Manchmal hatte ich den Eindruck, dass er deutlich mehr auf der Platte hatte als sein Vater.

»Und Mama braucht ihn erst recht nicht, die hat genügend andere Freunde, die sich auch um mich kümmern.« Mich zum Beispiel, dachte ich, dass er jetzt möglicherweise dachte.

»Dich zum Beispiel«, sagte er.

Von der Zahnwurzel zum Herzen

Als ich Rebecca Linsbach sah, wurde mir erst so richtig bewusst, was sich in diesen knapp anderthalb Wochen alles ereignet hatte, und wie wenig das an dem Umstand änderte, dass diese mir von Termin zu Termin anmutiger erscheinende Frau nur an einem Bruchteil meiner Person interessiert war, noch dazu an den nur mit Mördergeräten zugänglichen Bruchstellen dieses Bruchteils, und selbst dieses eher brutale Teilinteresse war höchstens beruflicher Natur, wenn nicht gar geheuchelt. Immerhin gelang es ihr nach und nach, mir die Furcht vor der Angst vor dem Schmerz zu nehmen. Und auf den desolaten Achter oder Neuner da rechts oben hinten, der die längste Zeit an meinem Schlaf genagt hatte, konnte ich wirklich gerne verzichten.

Wenn es ihr prinzipielles Ansinnen war, mit ihren Patienten nur ja kein wie auch immer geartetes Gesprächsverhältnis aufzubauen, welches den Dentalbereich überschritt, so machte sie diesmal allerdings einen schweren Fehler. Sie fragte mich nämlich, natürlich völlig beiläufig, um die Verabschiedung einzuleiten, aber das war mir egal: »Und wie geht es Ihrem Sohn?« Daraufhin sah ich sie bewusst so irritiert wie möglich an, und tatsächlich erinnerte sie sich augenblicklich an Manuels Klarstellung von damals. »Ach ja, Sie sind ja … Er ist ja … Sie sind ja … nicht der Vater, sondern nur … sondern ein guter Freund seiner Mutter, die derzeit in Afrika lebt, wenn ich mich recht erinnere.«

»Sie erinnern sich recht«, erwiderte ich. Und dann trat ich ungeniert die Flucht nach vorn in Richtung Wahrheit an. »Aber soll ich Ihnen etwas verraten?«, fragte ich. Ich gab ihr nicht den Funken einer Chance, nein zu sagen, also nickte sie anstandshalber. »Manuel ist in Wirklichkeit doch mein Sohn. Er weiß es nur nicht. Und ich weiß es auch erst seit wenigen

Monaten.« Jetzt hatte ich das erste Mal das Gefühl, dass sie an etwas anderes als an Zähne dachte, aber darin wirkte sie noch recht unbeholfen, sodass ich ihr schnell ein bisschen Last von den zarten Schultern nehmen musste. »Entschuldigen Sie bitte, dass ich Sie hier mit meinem Privatkram belästige.«

»Nein, nein, Sie belästigen mich nicht. Es ist nur eher ungewöhnlich ...«

»Ja, ungewöhnlich ist es. Ich habe mich ehrlich gestanden auch noch nicht ganz daran gewöhnt.« Jetzt lächelte sie. Doch ich ließ mich nicht ablenken. Und auch ihr war wohl klar, dass man nach so einem Vater-Outing nicht einfach kommentarlos eine Zahnarztpraxis verließ. Also erzählte ich ihr in ungefähr drei bis fünf schnellen Sätzen, wie ich zu meinem Buben gekommen war, beziehungsweise er zu mir.

»Ja, wie das Leben manchmal so spielt«, sagte sie daraufhin. Sie war wahrscheinlich weltweit der einzige Mensch, dem ich diese erschütternde Phrase noch in der gleichen Sekunde verzeihen konnte.

»Aber jetzt haben wir unser erstes gemeinsames Erfolgserlebnis, mein Bub und ich«, schloss ich temporeich an.

»Ah ja?«, sagte sie matt.

»Sein Basketballfreund Machmut sollte mit den Eltern nach Tschetschenien abgeschoben werden, nach sechs Jahren Asylverfahren. Das konnten wir zum Glück verhindern.« Ich spürte förmlich, wie sich in dem wenigen Raum ihres Gehirns, der nicht vom Zahngott kontrolliert wurde, das Räderwerk in Bewegung setzte.

»War das die große Geschichte in der Zeitung?«, fragte sie. Menschen, die nicht selbst bei einer Zeitung arbeiteten, verwendeten gerne den Singular »in der Zeitung«, als gäbe es weltweit nur eine Zeitung.

»Ja, darüber wird derzeit groß in den Medien berichtet.«

»Und Sie sind?« Das war quasi mein Durchbruch bei ihr –

das erste nicht geheuchelte zahnunabhängige Detailinteresse an meiner Person, das ich nicht ungestillt lassen konnte.

»Ich bin Journalist. Ich habe in der *Neuzeit* über den Fall berichtet.«

»Und Ihr Sohn ist der entzückende Bub, der über seinen Freund geschrieben hat?«

»Ja, das ist Manuel«, sagte ich stolz, obwohl er mir gerade wieder die Show gestohlen hatte. Jedenfalls las Rebecca nicht nur offenbar die *Neuzeit*, was unter Zahnärzten wohl eher die löbliche Ausnahme war, sie sah mich plötzlich auch mit ganz anderen Augen an. Nein, es waren im Grunde die gleichen Augen, aber sie sah mich erstmals wirklich damit an, und das verursachte ein gewisses Kribbeln in der Gegend um den Zwölffingerdarm, wie ich es von früher kannte, als schwere Verliebtheiten so häufig vorkamen wie grippale Infekte.

»Und die Familie darf in Österreich bleiben?«, fragte sie, fast schon ansatzweise leidenschaftlich.

»Ja, sie darf vorerst bleiben.«

»Das ist schön«, sagte sie.

»Ja, schön«, sagte ich. Wir machten gerade Quantensprünge in unserer Annäherung. Also brachte ich auch noch die anonyme Zehntausend-Euro-Spende unter, und wie wir sie erst vor wenigen Stunden persönlich hatten überbringen dürfen.

»Da geht einem das Herz auf, nicht wahr?«, sagte sie.

»Ja, das geht einem ganz schön auf, das Herz«, erwiderte ich und seufzte befreit. Jetzt waren wir also tatsächlich von der Zahnwurzel zum Herzen vorgestoßen. Damit war für diesen Tag nahezu alles erreicht, was ich mir hatte erhoffen dürfen, und ich konnte in Ruhe nach Hause gehen.

»Ach ja«, rief sie mir nach. Ich drehte mich um und versuchte, so gutaussehend zu lächeln, wie es die lokale Betäubung meiner Backe zuließ.

»Zwei Stunden nichts essen«, sagte sie.

Wenn ich mit mir allein war, und das war im Allgemeinen meine Lebensform, gingen mir im Gegensatz zu früher, als meine Gedanken entweder um mich oder führerlos um sich selbst kreisten, neuerdings vor allem zwei Menschen und zwei Themen durch den Kopf. Die Menschen waren Manuel und Rebecca, wobei ich mir die Zweitgenannte eher für die Abend- und Nachtstunden aufhob, während sich Manuel mehr oder weniger im ganzen Tag aufhielt.

Problematischer waren die Themen. Meine Arbeitsplatz-situation war da die Nummer eins, ich befand mich näm-lich in keiner. Im Grunde hätte ich zumindest eine Zeitlang gut damit leben können. Dachte ich jedoch in dem Zusam-menhang an gewisse Personen – und ich nenne jetzt einmal wahllos Gudrun, Florentina, Mama, natürlich Manuel und sogar Rebecca, aber auch Tante Julia und nicht zuletzt Guts-herr Berthold Hille –, so beschlich mich ein Gefühl des Un-behagens, und ich wurde den Verdacht nicht los, dass ich mich vielleicht um einen Job bemühen sollte, und zwar mög-lichst rasch. Denn es gab noch ein weiteres ziemlich stich-haltiges Argument dafür: Ich hatte keine Einkünfte mehr, nur noch Ersparnisse, aber die waren aufgebraucht, und das noch ausstehende Honorar von der *Neuzeit* würde das Kraut auch nicht fett machen, wie man hierzulande gerne sagt.

Bei mir brauchte es immer eine Weile, ehe ich das Nahe-liegende tat, das sich in diesem Fall übrigens mit dem deckte, was mir auch meine Kumpels schon dringend ans Herz gelegt hatten. Schließlich überwand ich mich, rief Clara Nemez an und fragte sie, ob ich nicht gelegentlich mit einer Geschichte für die *Neuzeit* aufwarten durfte, so als freier Mitarbeiter, also ohnehin relativ unverbindlich. Überraschenderweise sagte sie sofort ja, sie hätte bereits mit Peter Seibernigg, dem zelebrierenden Weinverkoster und Ressortleiter der Inlandredaktion, darüber gesprochen. Seibernigg selbst war es gewesen, der meine Pajew-Beiträge überschwänglich gelobt und vorgeschlagen hatte, mich mit Sozialreportagen auf Honorarbasis in die Berichterstattung einzubinden, verriet mir Clara Nemez. Seibernigg war bei näherer Betrachtung ein äußerst sympathischer Mensch, auf den ich große Stücke hielt, hatte ich das schon erwähnt?

»Sozialreportagen« – das war zugleich auch das Stichwort für Thema Nummer zwei, das mir durch den Kopf geisterte. Ich musste ständig an die anonymen Spenden denken, und ich ertappte mich dabei, langsam ein bisschen ungeduldig zu werden in meiner Neugierde, wer tatsächlich dahintersteckte. Und dann rief auch noch Sophie Rambuschek an und wollte unbedingt mit mir auf ein Bier gehen, um sich mit mir über »dieses und jenes« zu unterhalten, was mir gleich ein wenig verdächtig vorkam.

Wir trafen uns im Café Westend, und sie hatte den hintersten Tisch im letzten dunklen Eck reserviert, als sollte hier eine konspirative Sitzung abgehalten werden. Ich erzählte ihr ein paar halb private Dinge, nein, es waren ganz private Dinge, von denen ich ihr aber nur die Hälfte erzählte, weil ich bald bemerkte, dass sie nicht interessiert war. Danach startete sie eine kleine Charme-Offensive und beteuerte, wie sehr ich ihr und dem Hause *Tag für Tag* abging, wie übel man mir mitgespielt hatte, wie leid es nun allen tat, vor allem »Norbert«, der schwere Depressionen und Plassek-Entzugserscheinungen hatte, der vermutlich weder essen noch schlafen konnte und zu einem Skelett abgemagert war, welches überdies an Knochenschwund litt – so in dieser Art.

»Das heißt, du sollst mich zurückholen?«, fragte ich.

»Nein, nein, Geri, wirklich nicht, ich schwöre. Es weiß kein Mensch, dass wir uns hier treffen.«

»Und ein Mensch weiß nicht, *warum* wir uns hier treffen, und der bin ich«, sagte ich. Darauf reagierte sie einigermaßen gekränkt, als bedurfte es eines Grundes, wenn alte Freunde zusammensaßen und ein Bier tranken.

»Ich dachte immer, wir beide verstehen uns und haben ein Vertrauensverhältnis«, sagte sie.

»Okay, Sophie, dann verrate mir bitte, womit ich deinem Vertrauen dienlich sein kann«, erwiderte ich. Und dann fiel endlich das erlösende Wort: Spendenserie.

»Ich möchte einfach nur wissen, wie du … darüber denkst, Geri. Ich verspreche dir hoch und heilig, dass das unter uns bleibt«, sagte sie.

»Moment mal, heißt das, du glaubst, dass ich etwas weiß, was du nicht weißt?«, fragte ich. Jetzt ließ sie die Maske fallen, lächelte mich süffisant an und beugte sich unangenehm verschwörerisch zu mir herüber.

»Geri, komm, wir beide brauchen uns nichts vorzumachen. Die Spenden und deine Meldungen, das gehört zusammen. Versteh mich nicht falsch, Geri, ich gönne es dir. Ich finde, das ist eine super Idee … beziehungsweise eine schöne Entwicklung, die das genommen hat, zumal dabei auch wirklich noch anderen Menschen geholfen wird. Ich finde das total legitim. Und die Reportage in der *Neuzeit* war auch wirklich sehr gut geschrieben, da kann ich mir stilistisch was abschauen. Du hast es also echt verdient …«

»Was hab ich verdient?« Ich brauchte dringend noch ein Bier.

»Geri, das pfeifen doch die Spatzen von den Dächern, dass du und dieser ominöse Wohltäter, dass ihr gemeinsam …«

»Sophie, jetzt reicht es mir!« Das war laut, am Nebentisch reckten sie die Köpfe. Aber ich kam jetzt erst so richtig in Fahrt.

»Ein für alle Mal: Ich hab mit den Spenden nichts zu tun, nicht das Geringste! Ich hab keine Ahnung, wer dahintersteckt! Es ist Zufall, es kann nur der reine Zufall sein, dass es vielleicht so aussehen mag, dass quasi ich ... oder meine Artikel oder zumindest einige davon ... dass dieser Wohltäter ... Das ist Zufall, Sophie! Glaub mir das und richte es bitte auch allen anderen aus, sag's Norbert Kunz, und wenn du ein Arschloch von Plus siehst, dann sag ihm, dass ich hier leider nicht behilflich sein kann, dass es hier nämlich keinen Skandal gibt und dass sie leider einen anderen erfinden müssen. Es wird ihnen bestimmt bald einer einfallen, da mach ich mir keine Sorgen.«

»Geri, ich schwöre dir, niemand hat mich beauftragt, es ist rein privates Interesse, ehrlich. Ich wusste nicht, dass du da so ... dass dich das so aufregt, so kenne ich dich ja gar nicht«, sagte sie ziemlich kleinlaut.

»Und wenn du sagst, du weißt nichts davon, dann weißt du nichts davon, das glaube ich dir natürlich, du bist einer der wenigen, dem ich so was blind glaube«, sagte sie. Man konnte zwar jemandem blind vertrauen, doch konnte man jemandem auch blind glauben? Aber egal.

»Da bin ich erleichtert«, erwiderte ich. Wir hatten also doch noch einen halbwegs versöhnlichen Abschluss gefunden.

»Aber eines möchte ich dir schon noch sagen, Geri. Dass das Zufall ist, ich meine die Spenden und deine Artikel, dass das der reine Zufall sein soll, das kannst du gleich hier auf der Stelle vergessen.«

Ein naturtrüber Typ

Wem es an diesem Wochenende überdurchschnittlich schnell gelang, mich auf gänzlich andere Gedanken zu bringen, das war Florentina. Und zwar mit Mike, ihrem ersten und hundertprozentig sicher nicht letzten Freund, dafür wollte ich von nun an täglich beten, dafür zahlte es sich vermutlich aus, tiefreligiös zu werden. Wenn ich vorher eine Vorstellung hatte, was von einundzwanzig Jahre jungen Männern zu halten war, die weder Schüler noch Studenten noch Lehrlinge noch Praktikanten, sondern Bassisten einer Wiener Psychedelic-Rock-Band waren, die sich überdies gerade auflöste, so bestätigte sich diese Auge in Auge mit ihm eindrucksvoll. Natürlich, ein blutjunger gesellschaftlicher Quer-Aussteiger am Beginn einer ehrgeizigen Drogenkarriere und ein in die Jahre gekommener, gesettelter Langweiler mit geregelten Hopfen-und-Malz-Zeiten, das ging irgendwie nicht gut zusammen. Dabei war ich ihm wahrscheinlich gar nicht unsympathisch, das hätte ja vorausgesetzt, dass ich ihm irgendetwas war, aber dafür hätte er mich wahrnehmen müssen, und Wahrnehmung war prinzipiell nicht so seine Stärke.

Wir saßen also im Treiblos, und es war für mich absolut kein Vergnügen zu beobachten, wie Florentina diese außen bleiche und innen hohle Gestalt anhimmelte, wie sie ihm über die Haare strich, seine Wangen streichelte, ihn auf den Nacken küsste und immer neue Stellen fand, ihn wie ein Stofftier zu knuddeln und zu liebkosen, was er regungslos über sich ergehen ließ, ohne selbst auch nur eine einzige nette Geste in Richtung Florentina zu setzen.

Trotzdem, es half nichts, meine Tochter war in diesen wachkomatösen Typ nun einmal hoffnungslos vernarrt, und es gab wohl nur einen einzigen Menschen, der fähig wäre, ihn ihr auszureden, und das war sie selbst.

»Mike geht Anfang nächsten Jahres für zwei Monate nach Kuba«, berichtete Florentina.

»Gratuliere«, erwiderte ich. Der Glückwunsch galt eigentlich ihr, aber ich sah ihn dabei an, wobei ich bereits ahnte, dass das nur ein Teil der Wahrheit war.

»Soll ich dir was verraten, Papa?« Sie konnte einen wirklich extrem lieb ansehen. »Ich fliege auch nach Kuba. Ich reise ihm in den Schulferien für vierzehn Tage nach«. Das war eine eher niederschmetternde Nachricht, die ich erst einmal verdauen musste.

»Ihr habt vierzehn Tage Schulferien?«, fiel mir als Erstes ein.

»Nein, nur eine Woche, die andere Woche fehle ich halt, am Anfang vom Halbjahr versäumt man eh noch nichts«, erklärte sie mir. Ich versuchte, möglichst ganz anders zu reagieren, als praktisch jeder Vater es in so einer Situation getan hätte. Ich nickte verständnisvoll.

»Hast du denn genügend Geld für die Reise?«

»Noch nicht, aber zu Weihnachten krieg ich sicher noch was vom Opa dazu«, sagte sie.

»Und Mama und Berthold wissen von deinen Plänen?«

»Nein.«

»Kennst du sie schon, Mike?« Ich musste ihn ansprechen, sonst schlief er uns noch ein.

»Nein«, erwiderte er. Er sprach nur das Notwendigste, aber der Inhalt war solide.

»Ich will nicht, dass er sie kennenlernt – er und meine Alten, das passt überhaupt nicht zusammen«, sagte sie. Und zu ihr passte es nicht, und mir passte es nicht, wenn sie »meine Alten« sagte. Aber ich überging es.

»Wenn sie deinen Freund nicht kennen, wird es aber schwierig für dich werden, die Kubareise daheim durchzubringen, schätze ich.«

»Die muss ich daheim gar nicht durchbringen«, erwiderte sie.

»Wieso nicht?«

»Weil ich nächsten Februar eh schon fast sechzehn bin, da können sie mir nichts mehr verbieten. Sie können mir überhaupt nichts mehr verbieten.« Das gefiel Mike, jetzt drehte er sein Gesicht zu ihr, und sie durfte ihn küssen. »Außerdem werde ich ihnen sagen, dass ich bei Alena und ihren Eltern auf Mallorca bin, das werden sie mir schon erlauben«, sagte sie.

»Wer ist Alena?«

»Meine beste Freundin, auf die kann ich mich verlassen, die hält dicht.«

»Ich weiß nicht, ob das so eine gute Idee ist«, antwortete ich. Nach außen hin blieb ich ruhig, aber eigentlich machte mich die Sache von Minute zu Minute nervöser, und ich wusste nicht mehr, wie ich mich verhalten sollte. Einerseits lag es nicht in meiner Macht, Florentina die Reise zu verbieten. Andererseits konnte ich nicht einfach stillschweigend mit ansehen, wie sie ihre Mama austrickste, um diesen Zombie auf seinem Trip durch Kuba zu begleiten. Womöglich kam sie uns dann als Junkie zurück, und ich hatte ihr sozusagen den Weg dorthin geebnet, das hätte mir in meiner Biografie gerade noch gefehlt.

Am liebsten hätte ich ja auf der Stelle Gudrun angerufen und Florentinas Geheimpläne ausgeplaudert. Aber einen schlimmeren Vertrauensbruch gegenüber meiner Tochter konnte ich gar nicht begehen, und das hätte dann wohl das abrupte Ende meiner Beziehung zu ihr bedeutet, die gerade erst begonnen hatte, eine zu sein.

Ich entschuldigte mich kurz, um Zeit zu gewinnen, und nahm beim Vorbeigehen an der Bar einen Schnaps, der zwar nicht nach kubanischem Rum schmeckte, der mich aber auf einen hochinteressanten Gedanken brachte. Als ich zum Tisch zurückkehrte, saß Florentina allein da.

»Wo ist Mike?«

»Der hat schon gehen müssen«, sagte sie.

»Verabschieden ist anscheinend nicht so seine Sache.«

»Entschuldige, Papa, er meint es nicht so, er hat mir gesagt, dass er dich total okay findet. Er kann solche Dinge halt einfach nicht so zeigen. Wenn wir zu zweit sind, dann ist er ganz anders.«

»Du bist wirklich verliebt in ihn?«

»Ja, wahnsinnig. Ich liebe ihn über alles«, sagte sie.

»Und das mit Kuba, das meinst du ernst?«

»Ja, das meine ich todernst. Ich muss dorthin, unbedingt. Und ich werde es tun, davon kann mich niemand abhalten«, sagte sie. Gut, das war dann wohl geklärt, und mir blieb praktisch nur noch diese eine Möglichkeit.

»Kuba hat mich auch schon immer interessiert«, log ich.

»Ja, dort soll es ganz toll sein. Dort sind die Menschen zwar arm, aber sie singen und tanzen auf der Straße, und sie sind immer fröhlich, nicht so wie bei uns«, erwiderte sie.

»Du wirst lachen, aber ich hab schon seit längerem vor, dort einmal hinzufliegen.«

»Ja? Warum machst du's nicht?«, fragte sie.

»Weißt du, ich bin nicht der Typ, der gerne allein herumreist, und bisher hat sich noch niemand gefunden, der mit mir nach Kuba ...«

»Dann komm einfach mit mir mit, dann fliegen wir gemeinsam«, sagte sie, und das war jetzt nicht bloß eine Höflichkeitsfloskel, sondern es steckte eine ordentliche Ladung Enthusiasmus dahinter, von der ich gleich eine schöne Portion abbekam. Es tat nämlich verdammt gut, von der eigenen Tochter ins Boot geholt zu werden, und ein gewisser Berthold Hille musste einmal draußen bleiben. Dafür nahm man dann sogar in Kauf, dass das Boot an der Karibik lag und eine naturtrübe Erscheinung namens Mike an Bord herumlungerte, dass einem Mittelamerika im Prinzip gestohlen bleiben konnte, dass man Reisen generell verabscheute und Fernreisen hasste, dass man nämlich irre Flugangst hatte, und dass das Unternehmen eigentlich nicht finanzierbar war. Aber diese Dinge schob ich einmal beiseite, denn Februar war für mich ohnehin utopisch ferne Zukunft. Und im Grunde ging es hier um angewandte Pädagogik und um nichts anderes.

»Aber ich sage dir gleich, du hast mich dann immer am Hals, und ihr beide habt keine ruhige Minute für euch. Ich werde euch ordentlich auf die Nerven gehen«, warnte ich sie. Ich lachte dazu, sodass sie nicht bemerken konnte, wie ernst ich es meinte.

»Das macht nichts, Papa, du kannst einen gar nicht nerven, du lässt jeden nämlich immer so sein, wie er ist, und schränkst niemanden ein«, sagte sie. Ein zweifelhaftes Kompliment, fand ich.

»Wenn wir gemeinsam reisen, dann hat das auch den Vorteil, dass wir deiner Mama die Wahrheit sagen können«, bemerkte ich.

»Ja, stimmt eigentlich. Ich werde ihr gleich heute ...«

»Nein, nein, du sag am besten gar nichts. Ich werde mit ihr reden, da warte ich aber noch auf einen günstigeren Zeitpunkt. Und Mike lassen wir lieber komplett draußen aus der Sache.« Vielleicht war er bis dahin ja ohnehin bereits über Bord gegangen, das war zumindest mein Hintergedanke dabei.

KAPITEL NEUN

Vorzeitige Bescherung

Ich musste gar nicht an ferne finanzielle Großprojekte wie Kuba denken. Ein unmittelbarer Blick in den Kühlschrank genügte, um zu erkennen, dass die Zeit reif war, die Ärmel hochzukrempeln. Das Problem war, dass ich keine Ahnung hatte, worüber ich schreiben sollte. Weder war ich ausdauernd genug, den großen medialen Tagesthemen hinterherzulaufen, noch war es sinnvoll, mich von meiner journalistischen Neugierde leiten zu lassen, denn wie ich diese kannte, leitete sie mich über kleine Umwege relativ zielstrebig zu meinen persönlichen Angelegenheiten zurück beziehungsweise in Zoltan's Bar.

So entschied ich mich dafür, Peter Seibernigg eine Angebots-E-Mail zu senden und verfasste folgenden Text: *Lieber Herr Seibernigg, ich freue mich sehr, für Ihr Ressort gelegentlich Beiträge aus dem Bereich Soziales liefern zu dürfen. Natürlich habe ich schon Ideen, aber für den Einstand wäre es vielleicht am besten, wenn Sie mir einen Auftrag erteilen. Erstens schätze ich ihr Gespür für …* Den letzten Satz strich ich wieder, denn es war nicht notwendig, mit Mitte vierzig plötzlich Schleimspuren zu ziehen, außerdem hatte ich beim Wort Gespür Seibernigg vor mir, wie er gerade Wein verkostete. Also schrieb ich: *Sie haben den redaktionellen Überblick und wissen am besten, welche Themen größere Aufmerksamkeit verdienen und eine Reportage auf Ihren Seiten rechtfertigen. Ich freue mich auf Ihre baldige Antwort. Freundliche Grüße, Gerold Plassek.*

Seiberniggs Antwort ließ nicht lange auf sich warten: *Hallo Herr Plassek. Interessiert Sie das Thema Kost-Nix-Laden? Das gäbe*

eine schöne Reportage her. Diese Gratis-Läden schießen ja wie die
Pilze aus dem Boden, und hier geht es einmal nicht um Profit, son-
dern tatsächlich um aktive Hilfe für Bedürftige. In der Taborstraße
muss so ein Laden angeblich wegen einer Mieterhöhung zusper-
ren. Sagen Sie, ob Sie Lust haben, die Story zu schreiben. Wenn ja,
schicke ich Ihnen ein paar Links. Herzlich, Peter Seibernigg.

Wenn etwas nichts kostete, klang das in meinen Ohren
automatisch sympathisch. Ich musste also keine zehn Sekunden nachdenken, sondern nahm das Angebot gleich dankend
an.

Am frühen Nachmittag empfing ich Manuel bereits mit Ungeduld und fragte ihn sofort, ob er denn viel für die Schule
zu tun hätte. Zum Glück nicht. Abgesehen von Mathe-, Eng-
lisch- und Deutsch-Hausaufgaben und Lernen für den morgi-
gen Französischtest war er sozusagen beschäftigungslos.

Mein verlockendes Angebot, mit mir einerseits auf Recherche, andererseits sozusagen gratis shoppen zu gehen, konnte er
natürlich nicht ausschlagen.

Also machten wir uns auf den Weg in die sogenannte
Schenkzentrale in der Taborstraße.

Ich hatte mich im Netz in die Materie eingelesen, und deshalb war mir die Philosophie von Kost-Nix-Läden bereits vertraut, sie erinnerte mich stark an die klassische Weihnachtsbe-
scherung, und die gab es an diesen Plätzen quasi öffentlich und
jeden Tag, noch dazu ohne Verpackungsmüll. Da hieß es zum
Beispiel: *Du kannst bei uns nehmen, ohne geben zu müssen. Du*
kannst aber auch Sachen vorbeibringen, die du nicht mehr brauchst,
wenn sie funktionieren und sauber sind. Oder: *Wir möchten einen*
offenen Raum für alle schaffen, die sich gegenseitig beschenken wol-
len. Dinge können gebracht und mitgenommen werden, ohne dass
Geld beteiligt ist. Wir haben keinerlei Gewinnabsichten und finan-
zieren die Miete über regelmäßige Geldspenden.

Wer nun verstaubte Altwarenhandlungen oder die üblichen Flohmärkte mit Socken in allen Grautönen und Vinyl-Schallplatten von David Cassidy bis David, nein, eben nicht Bowie, sondern Hasselhoff erwartete, irrte gewaltig. Ich hätte eigentlich jeden einzelnen dieser reich bestückten, bunten, äußerst porzellanhaltigen und mit Kristalllustern dicht behängten Räume sofort gegen mein gesamtes, voll möbliertes Miniloft getauscht. Um mir die so lästige wie teure Speditionsprozedur zu ersparen, konnte ich ja aus meiner Wohnung einen Kost-Nix-Laden machen und einfach hierherziehen, dachte ich, das wäre dann Geben und Nehmen in seiner perfektionierten Form gewesen, zumindest für mich.

Bevor Manuel in den Raum mit den Sportartikeln abrauschen konnte, erhielt er von mir den Auftrag, die Augen offen zu halten und sich Notizen zu machen, welche Menschen welche Dinge ablieferten und welche Dinge einsteckten. Und wenn er mir einen wirklich großen Gefallen tun wollte, dann sollte er doch bitte unter den Besuchern eine kleine Blitzumfrage *für die Schülerzeitung* starten, was sie hierhergeführt hatte, was für Erfahrungen sie bisher sammeln konnten und was sie von den Gratis-Läden generell hielten. Das war zwar im Grunde Kinderarbeit, aber Manuel liebte solche Tätigkeiten – ganz im Gegensatz zu mir.

Ich steckte gerade zwischen Bergen von Geschirr und bestaunte ein sinnlich extrem anregendes Ein-Liter-Steingefäß, das mich an meine Kindheit erinnerte, weil mein Opa so einen ähnlichen Krug besessen hatte, als sich eine etwa dreißig Jahre junge Frau mit ordentlich Metall im Gesicht und dem Namensschild *Nina* an der Brust mir zuwandte und flüsterte: »Du kannst den Bierkrug gerne gratis mitnehmen.« So im Sinne von: Uns ist es allen schon mal nicht so gut gegangen.

Ich klärte Nina auf, dass ich in journalistischer Mission hier war und an einer Reportage für die *Neuzeit* arbeitete, was sie offenbar dermaßen beeindruckte, dass sie mich gleich wieder siezte, noch ehe ich mich über das Du von vorhin freuen konnte. Jedenfalls bekam ich in einer kleinen Extrakammer, wo wir uns ungestört unterhalten konnten, Kaffee aus der Thermosflasche, und Nina spulte die komplette Entstehungs- und Entwicklungsgeschichte dieses Secondhand-Schlaraffenlands herunter.

Das einzige traurige Kapitel betraf ausgerechnet die nahe Zukunft: Das Haus, in dem sich der Laden befand, gehörte einer Treuhandgesellschaft, die das Gebäude zu sanieren beabsichtigte und angekündigt hatte, die Miete ab Jänner um mehr als ein Drittel zu erhöhen. Somit war die Schenkzentrale über Zuwendungen von Privatpersonen de facto nicht mehr finanzierbar, man würde den Gratis-Laden leider dichtmachen und in eine billigere Gegend am Stadtrand übersiedeln müssen. Dem Eigentümer konnte das nur recht sein, denn den Gerüchten nach sollte hier nämlich schon bald ein exquisiter Feinkostladen eröffnet werden.

Ich notierte mir Namen und Telefonnummer des Vermieters, verabschiedete mich von Nina und sammelte Manuel ein, der die Recherchen bereits abgeschlossen und seine Top-Drei-Geschenkartikel ausgewählt hatte, die vermutlich für eine neue Form des modernen Dreikampfs bestimmt waren: eine Jockey-Mütze, einen Eishockeyschläger und eine Taucherbrille.

»Und du hast nichts gefunden?«, fragte er mich. Kurz dachte ich an den schönen Bierkrug, aber ich war ja gewissermaßen noch im Dienst, und deshalb erwiderte ich:

»Nein, heute nicht.«

Wir tauschten unsere Erfahrungen aus und besprachen die nächsten Schritte. Wenn es nach mir gegangen wäre, dann hätten wir den Hausbesitzer, er hieß Dietmar Steininger, gleich anschließend in seiner Treuhandkanzlei im ersten Stock besucht und zu den Gerüchten über die Mietpreiserhöhung befragt, damit die Sache für heute erledigt war, ich war nämlich schon ziemlich erschöpft.

»Das würde ich an deiner Stelle nicht tun«, sagte Manuel.

»Wieso nicht?«

»Wenn er dich sieht, weiß er gleich, was das für eine Geschichte wird.«

»Wie meinst du das?«

»Na ja, er wird nicht annehmen, dass du ein großer Fan von einem Feinkostladen bist.« Sollte ich das jetzt als Kompliment auffassen?

»Muss er auch nicht«, erwiderte ich.

»Aber dann wird er gleich wissen, dass du schlecht über ihn schreiben wirst, und darum wird er dir nichts sagen oder zumindest nicht die Wahrheit.« Ich war verblüfft. Mein hochintelligenter Bub hatte die Fähigkeit, um drei Ecken zu denken und selbst Menschen zu durchschauen, die er noch nie gesehen hatte.

»Und was würdest du vorschlagen?«, fragte ich.

»Am besten, du rufst ihn an und interessierst dich nur für den Feinkostladen und sagst, dass du das supergut findest, dass dort einer hinkommt. Und in der Zeitung schreibst du dann, dass du es superschlecht und gemein findest.«

»Manuel, dass ist zwar an sich genial gedacht, aber absolut unseriös«, sagte ich.

»Na und? Hauptsache, das Geschäft, wo es alles umsonst gibt, muss nicht zusperren«, erwiderte Manuel.

Feinkost für
Scheichs und Oligarchen

Da weder Rom an einem Tag erbaut worden noch Athen an einem Tag bankrottgegangen war, ließ ich das Reportageprojekt über Nacht ruhen – unter anderem in Zoltan's Bar – und wartete auf den versprochenen Rückruf von Hausbesitzer Dietmar Steininger, der mich Mittwochmittag im Bett erreichte. Ich nahm mir fest vor, mich zwar an den Tipp meines klugen Sohnes zu halten, dabei aber ohne eine einzige Lüge auszukommen.

»Guten Tag, Herr Doktor Steininger, mein Name ist Plassek, ich schreibe für die *Neuzeit*, und ich interessiere mich für den geplanten Feinkostladen in der Taborstraße.« Das waren so etwa meine ersten Worte.

»Werter Herr … äh …«

»Plassek.«

»Werter Herr Plassek, das ist noch etwas verfrüht. Jetzt wird zunächst einmal das Gebäude saniert, und dann werden wir weitersehen, da laufen noch Verhandlungen mit den Mietern. Dem will ich nicht vorgreifen«, erwiderte er eher kurz angebunden.

»Aber haben Sie vielleicht schon vage Vorstellungen, wie so ein Feinkostladen, oder darf ich Gourmettempel sagen, wie so ein Gourmettempel im Herzen Wiens, nur einen Steinwurf vom Stadtzentrum entfernt, also wunderbar erschlossen sozusagen, wie der aussehen könnte? Das würde mich und alle Konsumenten natürlich brennend interessieren«, sagte ich. Okay, das war jetzt nicht unbedingt die reine Wahrheit, aber der Mann musste ein bisschen auf Touren gebracht werden.

»Jaja, da haben wir schon schöne Konzepte. Mir schwebt etwas Universelles vor. Das Beste von fünf Kontinenten. Erlesene

Spezialitäten aus Europa, Amerika, Australien, Asien und ... äh ...«

»Afrika«, sagte ich.

»Richtig. Etwas Weltumfassendes, Übergreifendes, Spezifisches, Unverwechselbares. Wissen Sie, Herr ... äh ...

»Plassek.«

»Wissen Sie, Herr Plassek, wir leben in einer globalen Gesellschaft ...« Das war der Auftakt zu einem Plädoyer für das Feinste vom Feinsten und steigerte sich in eine Art Wirtschaftstreuhand-Konsumrausch der Eliteklasse. Ich unterbrach selten, und nur um ihm verbale Aufputschmittel zu verabreichen wie:

»Sie sind ein richtiger Genussmensch.« Oder: »Damit haben Sie sich aber sehr ausführlich beschäftigt.« Oder: »Da spricht der Fachmann.«

Dafür erntete ich hochkarätige Zitate wie: »In meinem Laden sollen sich der Scheich aus Saudi-Arabien und der russische Oligarch die Klinke in die Hand geben.« Oder: »Es gibt eine Käuferschicht, der ist das Geld egal, die zahlen alles, um fast nichts zu bekommen, aber das *fast nichts* muss besonders sein, und darauf kommt es heute an.« Oder, mein absoluter Lieblingsspruch: »Ich sage Ihnen, Sie werden in der Taborstraße vietnamesische Qualitätsprodukte kriegen, die es nicht einmal in Vietnam gibt.« Schließlich war seine Feinschmeckerzunge so gelockert, dass er auch das heikle Thema ansprach: »Momentan müssen wir uns leider mit einem etwas anderen Publikum herumärgern.«

»Sie meinen die Schenkzentrale?«

»Verstehen Sie mich nicht falsch, Herr ... äh ...«

»Plassek.«

»Ja, Herr Plassek, ich finde den Gratis-Gedanken an sich gut, zwar ein bisschen naiv und weltfremd, aber gut, und diese jungen Leute haben sicher noch sehr viel Idealismus. Aber die

Kehrseite ist, dass das natürlich auch Problemfälle anzieht, die wir dann hier im Haus haben, Bettler, Alkoholiker, Gestrandete, Sie wissen schon.«

»Ja, ich weiß.«

»Das hier ist einfach nicht die richtige Gegend.«

»Was wäre denn die richtige Gegend?«, fragte ich.

»Irgendwo weiter draußen, in der Peripherie.«

»Am besten über die Landesgrenze hinaus, nicht wahr«, bemerkte ich.

»Das haben *Sie* gesagt«, erwiderte er. Jetzt lachte er laut auf. Und ich bedankte mich für das interessante Gespräch.

»Eine Frage noch, Herr ... äh ...«

»Plassek.«

»Herr Plassek, richtig. Wird das Interview in der Gourmet-Beilage oder auf den Wirtschaftsseiten erscheinen?« Bisher war ich ohne nennenswerte Lüge ausgekommen, jetzt musste ich allerdings aufpassen.

»Gourmet, Wirtschaft, möglicherweise auch Stadtleben. Ich kann Ihnen das noch nicht mit Sicherheit sagen, das bestimmt letztendlich die Chefredaktion. Ich bin nur ein kleiner freier Mitarbeiter«, erwiderte ich.

Ich und Michelangelo

»Wie war der Französischtest?«, fragte ich mit schlechtem Gewissen.

»Wie soll er gewesen sein?« An Manuels Rückfrageschema hatte sich nicht viel geändert.

»Wenn es nach mir geht, soll er leicht gewesen sein. War er leicht?«, fragte ich.

»Ja, total. Wenn ich dafür gelernt hätte, würde ich mich jetzt ärgern.« Das beruhigte mich.

»Hast du Lust, mit mir die Reportagenseite zu machen?«, fragte ich.

Offensichtlich musste dabei ein flehentlicher Unterton mitgeschwungen haben, denn er sagte: »Na klar, ich kann dich doch nicht hängenlassen.« Für ihn war meine Person eben stets das jeweils übergeordnete Sozialprojekt, aber ich fand generell gut, dass die Kinder heutzutage schon frühzeitig lernten, ein bisschen Verantwortung für ihre Väter, Onkel oder auch nur die alten Freunde ihrer Mütter zu übernehmen.

Bei der journalistischen Umsetzung des Faktischen ins Sprachliche waren wir, wie sich in der Folge zeigte, bereits ein eingespieltes Team. Er las mir von seinem Notizblock die Langversionen seiner Recherchen vor, die er durch spontane Einfälle gerne ausufernd ergänzte, und ich machte daraus kurze, schnörkellose Sätze. Zum Beispiel: »Da war so eine Frau, die war schon älter, ich schätze, so zwischen fünfzig und neunzig …«

»Kannst du's vielleicht ein bisschen enger eingrenzen?«

»Okay, dann war sie halt so zwischen sechzig und achtzig, die hat so graue oder weiße kurze Haare gehabt und eine rote Brille, rund war die, also eine runde rote Brille, eigentlich rotschwarz, und die hat gesagt, dass sie selbst einmal Schmuck gemacht hat, so Ringe und Ketten, Modeschmuck, glaub ich. Sie hat mir auch eine Kette gezeigt oder ein Halsband oder eine Halskette, irgend so was, eigentlich eh schön, so grau oder silbern, mit Kreisen und Scheiben. Und diesen Schmuck hat sie früher verkauft, da hat sie sogar ein eigenes Geschäft gehabt, in der Neubaugasse, und da hat sie viel Geld damit verdient, weil die Leute haben das gerne gekauft, weil's ihnen gefallen hat und weil es nicht so teuer war wie echter Schmuck, wie Gold zum Beispiel. Aber das Geschäft hat sie dann irgendwann einmal zugesperrt, weil sie schon alt war und weil sie nicht mehr wollte. Und da ist ihr natürlich viel Schmuck übrig

geblieben. Und jetzt geht sie zweimal in der Woche, oder dreimal, das kann ich jetzt nicht lesen, ob das zwei oder drei heißt,
egal, da geht sie in die Schenkzentrale und bringt immer ein
paar Ringe und Ketten von sich mit. Und wenn sie das nächste
Mal kommt, und ihre Ringe und Ketten sind weg, weil jemand
die mitgenommen hat, dann freut sie sich, weil dann weiß sie,
dass jetzt wahrscheinlich irgendwer ihren Schmuck trägt, und
das genügt ihr, da braucht sie gar kein Geld mehr dafür.«

Von Manuels ambitionierten Schilderungen blieben dann
für die Reportage nur ein paar schlanke Sätze, in diesem Fall:
*Eine Frau um die siebzig, mit kurzen Haaren und roter Brille, lie-
fert alle paar Tage ihren selbst gefertigten Modeschmuck hier ab.
Bis vor ein paar Jahren hat sie ein florierendes Geschäft in der Neubaugasse betrieben. Heute leistet sie sich den persönlichen Luxus,
ihre Ringe und Ketten zu verschenken. »Ich freue mich immer, wenn
ich komme, und mein Schmuck ist weg. Dann weiß ich, dass den
jetzt jemand trägt, und das macht mir einfach ein gutes Gefühl«, erzählt sie.*

Nach drei Stunden waren wir mit der Reportage fertig, Manuel brach Richtung Tante Julia auf, und ich tat etwas Unge-
wöhnliches, ich arbeitete gleich weiter, als gäbe es kein Morgen oder Übermorgen. Seibernigg hatte mir Links von allen
möglichen Kost-Nix-Läden in Österreich und ähnlichen Modellen in Deutschland und der Schweiz geschickt. Das ergab
schließlich einen schön gerafften, übersichtlichen Gesamt-
überblick. Was das brisante Hauptthema der Geschichte anging, die Mietpreiserhöhung und den geplanten Feinkosttem-
pel, überlegte ich lange, in welchem Ton ich das transportieren
sollte – eher heiter-ironisch, das passte nicht, oder zynisch, das
machte ich lieber mündlich als schriftlich, oder ziemlich direkt, das lag mir fern, oder richtig frontal, das lag mir noch
ferner, oder moralisierend, das lag mir am allerfernsten –, ehe

ich entschied, überhaupt nichts dazu zu sagen und mich jeder Wertung zu enthalten. Es genügte, wenn man die Interviews mit Hausbesitzer Steininger und mit Nina vom Gratis-Laden einander gegenüberstellte und jedes für sich sprechen ließ. Einen schärferen Kontrast zwischen *Kaufen um jeden Preis* und *Schenken von Herzen* konnte man nämlich gar nicht erzielen. Und daraus sollte dann jeder seine eigenen Empfindungen schöpfen und seinen Standpunkt ableiten.

Als das erledigt war, hatte ich noch die Kraft, Seibernigg die fertiggestellten Dokumente zu mailen, dazu Titelvorschläge, Tipps für die Bebilderung und Angaben, wie ich mir die Aufteilung und Gewichtung der Beiträge vorstellte. Danach hatte ich ungefähr so ein Gefühl, wie Michelangelo es gehabt haben muss, als sein letztes Fresko für die Sixtinische Kapelle fertig und die Kirche sozusagen austapeziert war. Keine Ahnung, was er im unmittelbaren Anschluss daran gemacht hatte, vielleicht hatte er die Zahnärztin seines Herzens einmal ganz privat besucht. Davon konnte ich vorerst leider nur träumen. Also ging ich auf ein, zwei Bier. Ganz ehrlich: Viel mehr als ein, zwei wurden es diesmal wirklich nicht.

Einmal etwas ganz anderes

Am Donnerstag stand ich zeitig auf, ohne jetzt eine Uhrzeit nennen zu wollen, denn in der Zivilbevölkerung gibt es gigantische Auffassungsunterschiede, was zeitig ist und was nicht.

Seibernigg war offenbar noch früher aufgestanden, denn er hatte mir bereits eine Mail aus der Redaktion der *Neuzeit* geschickt. Es war eine äußerst angenehme Mitteilung, und ich wünschte mir, dass künftig wenigstens ein Tag in der Woche so ähnlich beginnen würde wie dieser. Er schrieb: *Lieber Herr Plassek, tolle Arbeit, gratuliere! Schöne, dichte Reportage, geht un-*

ter die Haut. Und das Interview mit Steininger ist ein echtes Gusto-
stück an Feinkost, reif fürs Kabarett! Kompliment auch von Clara
Nemez. Wir spielen die Geschichte gleich von heute auf morgen,
Fotograf für die Taborstraße ist schon bestellt, ich schicke Ihnen am
späten Nachmittag die fertigen Seiten zum Absegnen. Herzlich,
Peter Seibernigg.

Der Mann wurde mir von Minute zu Minute sympathischer, und was seine Mimik bei der Weinverkostung betraf –
das hatte er damals wahrscheinlich so übertrieben zelebrieren müssen, weil er von der Fachwelt dabei beobachtet worden
war. Wir alle machten ja die sonderbarsten Gesichter und Figu-
ren, wenn wir unter Beobachtung von Fachwelten standen, das
war zum Beispiel auch das Hauptproblem aller Politiker.

Irgendwie spürte ich, dass dies ein besonderer Tag war, nicht
nur weil es im Spätherbst noch einmal zwanzig Grad hatte
und die Sonne so richtig grellgelb schien, sondern weil ich
mich derart auffallend wohlfühlte, dass es mir schon beinahe
unheimlich war, und weil ich überdies den Drang hatte, einmal etwas ganz anderes zu tun. Etwas ganz anderes war ja sowieso schon, dass ich überhaupt den Drang hatte, etwas zu tun,
und nicht nur zuzusehen, wie die Dinge von sich aus geschahen, was an sich eher meine Stärke war.

Zuerst dachte ich, ich könnte vielleicht meine Wohnung
aufräumen und putzen, und zwar wirklich putzen, so mit
Putzmittel und Bürsten und Tüchern, also richtig professionell. Aber mein Kühlschrank hatte Priorität, ich brauchte
wenigstens die wichtigsten Grundnahrungsmittel wie Butter,
Bier, Brot, Eier, Schnittlauch und solche Dinge. Dafür benötigte ich freilich Geld, und zum Thema Geld fiel mir niemand außer Gudrun ein, was meinen Plan, einmal etwas ganz
anderes zu tun, leider wieder ein bisschen über den Haufen
warf.

Bevor ich den Canossagang zu ihr antreten wollte, machte

ich noch einen kleinen Umweg über die Filiale meiner Bank, um auch ihr eine gewisse Außenseiterchance zu bieten, mich einmal mit etwas Positivem zu überraschen. Und exakt diese Minimalchance nutzte sie – ich hatte gewusst, dass dieser Tag ein besonderer war: Auf meinem Konto waren 3211 Euro eingegangen, das Honorar der *Neuzeit* für die Pajew-Geschichten, wobei ich zuerst dachte, die hätten sich um eine Kommastelle geirrt. Aber nein, da war zunächst der Posten für die Texte, und dann tauchten weitere 2500 Euro auf, die als »einmaliges Sonderhonorar« ausgewiesen waren. Kurzum, die hatten mich wirklich reich beschenkt, und draußen schien zudem noch immer die Sonne.

Keine Frage, ich musste Manuel an meinem Honorarglück beteiligen, und da fiel mir spontan ein neues Fahrrad ein – ehe mir einfiel, dass sein aktuelles Fahrrad eigentlich erst drei Monate alt war. Und dann, endlich, ließ ich meinem außergewöhnlichen Drang zu *etwas ganz anderem* freien Lauf: Ich beschloss, mir selbst ein Fahrrad zu kaufen, um wieder Fahrrad fahren zu lernen, um später mit Manuel einen Fahrradausflug zu unternehmen, um nämlich genau das zu tun, was ein richtiger Vater mit seinem richtigen Sohn schon längst einmal getan hätte.

Früher klappte man Fahrräder zusammen

Im Sporthaus Gruber in der Schönbrunner Straße hatten sie schätzungsweise fünftausend Fahrrädern ein eigenes Stockwerk zur Verfügung gestellt. Ich hasste generell jede Art von großer Auswahl, sie gaukelte uns eine Freiheit vor, die im Grunde das genaue Gegenteil davon war. Je größer ein Angebot war, desto unübersichtlicher war es nämlich auch, und je unübersichtlicher, desto undurchschaubarer, und je undurchschaubarer, desto leichter konnten ungeübte Konsumenten wie ich verarscht und ausgenommen werden.

Deshalb blickte ich mich erst gar nicht groß um, sondern wartete, bis sich der sportlich uniformierte junge Mann, der aussah, als hätte er vor ein paar Stunden die Tour de France gewonnen – und vor der Dopingprobe war er in ein Kaufhaus geflüchtet und tarnte sich nun als Verkäufer – ich wartete also, bis er sich mir zuwandte. Dann gingen wir gleich in den Dialog.

»Guten Tag, was wünschen Sie?«

»Ein Fahrrad.«

»Was für eins?«

»Kein rotes.« Er lachte.

»An was haben Sie gedacht? BMX? Crossbike? Citybike? Cruiser? Retrobike? Mountainbike? Trekkingbike …?« Ich hatte an gar nichts gedacht.

»Haben Sie auch Klappräder?«, fragte ich. Keine Ahnung, ob so etwas heute noch produziert wurde. 1980 in Simmering war man jedenfalls nur jemand, wenn man ein Klapprad besaß.

»Klappräder?«, fragte er. Er war kein sehr guter Verkäufer, denn er verzog angewidert sein Gesicht. »Sie meinen vielleicht Falträder?«,

»Keine Ahnung. Früher konnte man Räder zusammenklappen, vielleicht faltet man sie heute«, erwiderte ich. Er lachte.

»Wofür brauchen Sie es denn?«, fragte er dann.

»Zum Fahrradfahren«, erwiderte ich. Er lachte wieder, die mussten sonst relativ wenig Spaß bei ihrer Arbeit haben. »Also es soll möglichst billig und sehr gut sein. Und leicht zu fahren. Ich bin ehrlich gestanden ziemlich aus der Übung. Ich möchte gern mit meinem Sohn ein paar kleine Radausflüge machen, auf der Donauinsel und im Überschwemmungsgebiet, natürlich nur, wenn es nicht gerade überschwemmt ist, sonst wäre ich jetzt ja in der Schlauchboot-Abteilung. Sie haben sicher auch ein eigenes Stockwerk für Schlauchboote, nehme ich an«, sagte ich. Das überhörte er, darauf war er nicht spezialisiert.

»Wie wäre es mit einem Hollandrad?«, fragte er.

»Klingt gut, kann man da während der Fahrt Tulpen pflücken?« Diesmal lachte er nicht, obwohl das wirklich einmal ein guter Gag war, fand ich. Er zeigte mir dann ein paar dieser niederländischen Exemplare. »Was ist das hier, haben die da einen Tennisschläger eingebaut?«, fragte ich.

»Das ist der charakteristische Vollkettenschutz. Am Hinterrad haben Sie die typgemäße Seitenverkleidung. Und der Sattel ist bei diesen Modellen so eingestellt, dass Sie aufrecht sitzen können. Das ist für Senioren gut geeignet, ich meine, *auch* für Senioren«, sagte er.

»Ganz ehrlich, würde mein vierzehnjähriger Sohn sagen, dass das ein cooles Rad ist?«, fragte ich. Er lachte dreckig.

»Ich kenne Ihren Sohn nicht, aber man nennt die Hollandräder auch Oma-Räder«, erwiderte er.

»Okay, dann ein anderes«, sagte ich. Es gab da eine Serie, die mir recht gut gefiel, bis ich erfuhr, dass sie auf den Familiennamen »Fitnessbikes« hörte. Danach blieben meine Blicke bei ein paar hübschen »Retro-Rädern« hängen, aber retro war ich im Grunde selbst, dafür brauchte ich kein Rad. So wurde es schließlich ein charmantes Citybike mit 21-Gang-Kettenschaltung und Multipositionslenkung, und zwar das billigste für zweihundertneunzehn Euro, weil sie ohnehin alle gleich aussahen.

»Wollen Sie eine kleine Fahrprobe machen?«

»Hier im Sportladen? Sind Sie so gut versichert?«, fragte ich. Wir beließen es schließlich bei einem kurzen Auf- und Absteigtest, der zufriedenstellend verlief. Somit war das Geschäft abgeschlossen, und wir zwei konnten unseren ersten gemeinsamen Heimweg antreten, mein neues Fahrrad und ich – nebeneinander natürlich, wie es sich für ein junges Paar ziemt.

KAPITEL ZEHN

Die siebente Spende

Am Dienstag nach Erscheinen meiner Doppelseite über die Gratis-Läden schickte mir Clara Nemez zwei E-Mails mit roten Ausrufezeichen, im Sinne von Dringlichkeit hoch. Die kürzere bezog sich auf die längere und lautete: *Lieber Herr Plassek, wenn es Ihnen möglich ist, kommen Sie bitte in der Redaktion vorbei, oder wir treffen uns auf einen Kaffee. Das müssen wir jetzt wirklich ausführlich besprechen. Ganz herzlich, Clara.*

Also nur Clara, ohne Nemez, das war sozusagen der sanfte Übergang zum Duzen.

Die zweite E-Mail sprang mir vom Bildschirm mitten ins Gesicht. Es war quasi die Bestätigung, dass eine schlimme Befürchtung eingetreten war, die mich schon tage- und vor allem nächtelang gequält hatte, wobei Befürchtung nicht ganz das richtige Wort war. Denn an sich war es ja ein irrer Glücksfall oder sogar eine Serie von Glücksfällen. Das Problem bestand aber leider darin, dass ich genau der falsche Typ für so eine Art von überraschendem Glück war.

Die E-Mail stammte von der vollmetallisierten Nina aus der Schenkzentrale in der Taborstraße, war an die *Neuzeit* gerichtet und mit dem Hinweis *Bitte an Herrn Reporter Gerold Plassek weiterleiten* versehen. Nina schrieb:

Hallo Herr Plassek, wir haben hier gerade Freudensprünge gemacht, und das haben wir nur Ihnen zu verdanken. Da hat uns jemand mit der Post zehntausend Euro geschickt, einfach so, ohne zu sagen, wer er oder sie ist, und ohne irgendwas dafür zu verlangen. Und wofür das viele Geld? – Für die Miete!!! Damit wir hier unsere Kunden weiterhin Geschenke austauschen lassen können. Damit wir nicht zusperren müssen. Wir haben schon einige Spenden bekommen, aber dreihundert Euro war bisher das Höchste. Und der oder die schicken uns zehntausend Euro!! Wahnsinn! Wahrscheinlich sind das die Gleichen, die schon mehrmals zehntausend Euro geheim wo hingeschickt haben. Und jetzt ausgerechnet zu uns! Wir fassen es noch gar nicht! Und das verdanken wir wie gesagt Ihnen. Warum? In dem Kuvert war genau Ihr Zeitungsbericht über unseren Laden. Kurz haben wir überlegt, ob wir das Geld überhaupt behalten dürfen. Aber wer soll es sonst kriegen? Es ist ja für unsere Miete bestimmt. Wir sind überglücklich.

Sie müssen unbedingt einmal zu uns kommen und mit uns feiern. Wir würden Ihnen auch gerne etwas schenken, irgendwas, was Ihnen Freude macht.

Die besten Wünsche an Sie!

Nina und das Schenkzentrale-Team.

Ich saß dann sicher noch eine halbe Stunde mehr oder weniger wie gelähmt da und versuchte mir bewusst zu machen, was da eigentlich gespielt wurde und was das für mich bedeutete. Ich kam nicht dahinter, vielleicht konnte es mir Clara Nemez ja erklären.

Bevor ich aufbrach, schrieb ich Nina noch eine kurze Antwortmail:

Hallo Nina, das freut mich außerordentlich für euch! Ich bin auch sprachlos. Zum Feiern komme ich gern einmal.

Wenn ich das Wort »feiern« höre, bin ich eigentlich immer gleich dabei. Herzliche Grüße, Gerold Plassek.

PS: Habt ihr noch den schönen großen, beigefarbenen Bierkrug? Könnt ihr ihn für mich zurücklegen? Damit hätte ich eine große Freude! Mein Opa hatte nämlich so einen ähnlichen.

Ich lotste Clara Nemez ins Café Ritter in der Ottakringer Straße, wo ich in meiner Jugend öfter gegen mich selbst Billard gespielt hatte, statt in die Schule zu gehen. Sie empfing mich mit den Worten »Ich bin die Clara« und streckte mir die Hand entgegen.

»Hallo, ich bin der Gerold, Feinde nennen mich Geri«, erwiderte ich. Danach bestellte ich ein großes Glas Weißwein gespritzt, ich wollte mir vor Clara nicht die Blöße geben, andauernd nur Bier zu trinken.

»Der Wohltäter hat sich offensichtlich auf dich eingeschossen«, sagte sie relativ bald und sehr gelassen, sie konnte ja auch leicht gelassen sein. Ich erzählte ihr dann im Detail, wie die Sache mit den Spenden bei *Tag für Tag* abgelaufen war, dass also ausnahmslos meine *bunten Meldungen zum Tag* davon betroffen gewesen waren.

»Dann gibt es für mich überhaupt keinen Zweifel mehr, dass du von Anfang an persönlich gemeint warst. Der Spender hat es auf deine Arbeit abgesehen, Gerold, auf deine und nur auf deine. Das muss dir klar sein, das muss uns allen klar sein.«

»Okay«, sagte ich. Ich bestellte mir jetzt doch ein Bier. Weißwein war für meinen Magen zu sauer und zu ätzend, zumal in Kombination mit solchen Erkenntnissen.

»Freust du dich denn gar nicht?«

»Warum soll ich mich freuen?«, fragte ich. Das hätte übrigens auch Manuel gefragt, nein, stimmt nicht, Manuel hätte »Warum soll ich mich denn gar nicht freuen?« gefragt, aber er hätte das Gleiche gemeint.

»Zum Beispiel, weil sich dein Marktwert als Journalist dadurch enorm erhöht, weil die *Neuzeit* sich dich bald gar nicht mehr leisten wird können.« Sie schmunzelte, um mir zu zeigen, dass da schon auch ein bisschen Ironie mitschwang, weil sie ja ahnte, wie unwichtig mir mein Marktwert ungefähr sein musste. »Brauchst du denn kein Geld?«, fragte sie und fixierte dabei unfairer Weise meine graue Wolljacke.

»Doch, aber eine geheime Spende vom Wohltäter wäre mir im Prinzip lieber gewesen«, erwiderte ich.

»Du wirst berühmt werden«, setzte sie nach.

»Großartig«, murmelte ich.

»Jeder wird dich kennen. Über dich wird berichtet werden. Alle werden das Spendenphänomen Plassek ergründen wollen.«

»Da gibt es kein Phänomen, ich bin alles andere als ein Phänomen«, sagte ich.

»Mit dieser Meinung wirst du aber ziemlich allein dastehen«, warnte sie mich. Danach entstand eine kleine Pause. Clara sah mich so seltsam forschend von oben nach unten und dann wieder nach oben an wie jemand, der um jeden Preis etwas aus einem herauslesen will, was aber nicht drinsteht. Schließlich überwand sie sich und fragte: »Also wie groß dürfen wir es bringen?«

»Was?«, fragte ich sicherheitshalber.

»Dich«, erwiderte sie. Ich schloss kurz die Augen und wünschte mir dabei, unsichtbar zu sein. Der Trick funktionierte aber nicht. Als ich die Augen wieder aufmachte, blickte sie mich immer noch mit der gleichen Begeisterung an.

»Muss das sein?«, fragte ich.

»Ja, es muss sein, wenn ich meinen Job behalten will. Den bin ich nämlich sofort los, wenn in einer anderen als in unserer Zeitung steht, dass der Big Spender ausschließlich auf Berichte oder Notizen von einem gewissen Herrn Plassek zurückgreift. Gerold, sowie sie von der neuen Spende erfahren, schreiben sie das, und zwar alle. Wir müssen es also bringen! Oder willst du es lieber zuerst in *Tag für Tag* lesen?« Das war natürlich ein Totschlagargument.

»Okay, wer macht es?«

»Ich«, sagte sie.

»Aber bitte so zurückhaltend wie möglich.«

»Versprochen.«

»Okay«, sagte ich, um dieses leidige Thema abzuschließen. Aber sie sah mich noch immer irgendwie erwartungsvoll an. »Ist noch was?«, fragte ich.

»Ja. Wir brauchen eine ganz, ganz winzige Biografie von dir. Würdest du mir in fünf Sätzen verraten, wer du bist, was du tust und was du willst?«

»Wer ich bin und was ich will?«

Ich seufzte. Wie sollte ich in fünf Sätzen ausdrücken können, was mir in dreiundvierzig Jahren nicht gelungen war, in Erfahrung zu bringen. Aber Clara war eine wirklich nette, aufrichtige Person, und ich wollte mich zumindest bemühen.

Wer sollte mir dankbar sein?

Auf dem Weg zu Zoltan's Bar spürte ich, dass meine Außenwelt gerade im Begriff war, sich drastisch zu verändern, und zwar in Richtung öffentlicher Wahrnehmung meiner Person. Da kam mir nämlich ein griesgrämiger alter Herr mit Krückstock entgegengehumpelt, der sofort wieder wegschaute, als er mich sah, weil es bis heute erfreulicherweise keinen Grund gab, den Blick an mir haften zu lassen. Aber morgen oder übermorgen würde er vielleicht schon stehen bleiben, die Augen aufreißen und sagen: »Herr Plassek, sind Sie es? Ich kenne Ihr Gesicht aus der Zeitung. Gratuliere! Tolle Sache mit den Spenden! Weiter so! Und denken Sie auch einmal an uns alte Herren mit Krückstöcken!«

Wenigstens bei Zoltan war alles noch beim Alten und würde es vermutlich auch bis in die Ewigkeit bleiben. Eigentlich wollte ich mich von den Ereignissen des Tages erholen und gar nicht groß darüber reden, aber die Kumpels merkten mir rasch an, dass mir meine persönlichkeitsimmanente Geruhsamkeit abhandengekommen war, und bohrten so lange, bis ich ihnen alles über die siebente Spende und mein Treffen mit Clara Nemez erzählt hatte.

»Ist ja irre«, sagte Zoltan, der Wirt, und das waren eindeutig drei Worte mehr, als ihm normalerweise über die Lippen kamen. Schon daran ließ sich die Dimension der Bedeutung der jüngsten Vorkommnisse ermessen.

»Hast du denn irgendeine Ahnung, wer es sein könnte?«, fragte Franticek, der Kunstschmied. Ich hatte nicht die blasseste Ahnung, aber mir war mit einem Schlag klar, dass das genau die Frage war, die mein Gehirn die nächsten Tage und Wochen in Geiselhaft nehmen würde.

»Eins ist klar, es muss jemand sein, der dich gut kennt, jemand aus deinem Bekanntenkreis, wahrscheinlich ein reicher Freund«, sagte Josi, der Konditor.

»Ich hab keine reichen Freunde«, erwiderte ich.

»Das glaub ich ihm, sonst würde er nicht mit uns hier rumhängen«, bemerkte Franticek.

»Es könnte aber auch jemand sein, der zwar dich kennt, aber du kennst ihn nicht«, sagte Arik, der Berufsschullehrer.

»Was hätte das für einen Sinn?«, fragte ich.

»Vielleicht will er, dass du dahinterkommst, wer er ist«, sagte Josi.

»Das könnte er billiger haben«, entgegnete ich.

»Ich sage euch, der wird sich niemals zu erkennen geben. Wenn einer sieben Mal anonym spendet, dann will er auch anonym bleiben. Er will einfach nicht, dass jemand weiß, dass er so viel Geld hat. Logisch, weil's nämlich Schwarzgeld ist, das ihm übrig geblieben ist und das er jetzt loswerden will, was ich nämlich immer schon sage. Und weil er eine soziale Ader hat,

spendet er es für wohltätige Zwecke«, meinte Horst, der Wettbüro-Betreiber.

»Was an sich ein gutes Modell ist, mit dem man die Welt retten könnte, wenn es sich unter den Reichen herumspricht«, ergänzte Arik.

»Richtig. Besser sie spenden es, als man nimmt es ihnen irgendwann weg. Genau so denkt der Typ«, sagte Horst.

»Ja, aber was hat das mit Geri zu tun?«, fragte Franticek.

»Dem ist er für irgendwas dankbar und revanchiert sich
auf diese Weise«, meinte Horst. Das hielt ich für eher unwahrscheinlich, ich hatte es meiner Umwelt nämlich seit jeher
nicht gerade leichtgemacht, mir für etwas dankbar zu sein.

»Oder er glaubt, dass Geri weiß, woher er das Geld hat. Und
indem er Geri in die Spendensache involviert, zieht er ihn
praktisch auf seine Seite«, sagte Josi.

»Super Theorie, Josi! Geri, warst du zufällig mal Zeuge bei
einem Banküberfall, den sie bis heute nicht aufgeklärt haben?«, fragte Arik, um die Sache ein bisschen ins Lächerliche
zu ziehen.

»Jedenfalls ist er ab morgen ein Star, wenn dann alle darüber berichten. Und uns wird er schon bald nicht mehr kennen«, sagte Franticek, augenzwinkernd natürlich, weil er
wusste, dass ich immer der Gleiche bleiben würde.

»Aber heute könnte er wenigstens noch eine Runde ausgeben«, sagte Josi.

»Die eine oder andere«, verbesserte Horst. Im Grunde ging
es ihnen nämlich um nichts anderes, aber so ehrliche Menschen musste man erst einmal finden.

Glückwünsche aus
Stockholm und Mogadischu

Ich hatte kurz, aber dafür schlecht geschlafen. Ich kam mir vor wie ein Molekularforscher, der verzweifelt bemüht war, keinen blassen Schimmer in hundert Einzelteile zu zerlegen, um zu prüfen, ob die Spur einer Substanz darin war, die ihm helfen konnte, dahinterzukommen, wer der anonyme Wohltäter war. Nein, leider, egal in welche Richtung ich dachte – ich dachte letztendlich immer im Kreis.

Mein Handy hatte ich auf lautlos geschaltet, weil mich ständig irgendwer anrief. Ich war aber entschlossen, nur Telefonate von mir bekannten Anrufern entgegenzunehmen, deren Nummern ich gespeichert hatte – wobei ich zugeben muss, dass ich überhaupt keine Nummern gespeichert hatte. Auf der Mobilbox waren fünf neue Nachrichten, die ich mir später anhören wollte. SMS waren es nur drei, da las ich schnell einmal drüber.

Erstens: *Lieber Gerold, vielleicht stimmt diese Nummer ja noch. Ich hab dich hier groß vor mir auf dem Bildschirm. Wow! Erinnerst du dich an mich? Lyckönskningar! Corinna. Ich lebe jetzt in Stockholm und habe drei Töchter …*

Klar erinnerte ich mich an Corinna. Sie hatte strohblondes Haar, und so war es eigentlich logisch, dass sie irgendwann im Norden landen würde. Ich hätte aber eher auf Dänemark getippt.

Zweitens: *Papa, du bist ganz groß in der Zeitung!!!! Ich bin so stolz auf dich!!! Freu mich auf Kuba! Deine Flori.*

Da stürmten meine Mundwinkel einmal so richtig weit hinauf. Leider fehlte ihnen oben der Halt. Ich war das viele Grinsen einfach nicht gewohnt.

Drittens: *Hallo Geri, ich hab schon versucht, dich zu erreichen. Im Internet lese ich ganz große Berichte über dich und die Spen-*

denserie. Ich finde es wunderbar, ich hoffe, du kommst damit klar. Manuel hat mir alles schon im Detail erzählt. Er ist glücklich und mächtig stolz auf seinen XXX. Ich finde das alles so wunderbar! Telefonieren wir! Grüße aus dem glühend heißen Mogadischu, Alice.

Hier machte ich eine kurze Denkpause und ließ es mir ein paar Sekunden einfach nur gut gehen.

Schließlich setzte ich mich vor den Computer und versuchte mir einen Überblick darüber zu verschaffen, was da mit mir gerade gemacht wurde. Im Postfach befanden sich ungefähr zwei Dutzend Mails, ein Großteil davon war mir von der *Neuzeit*-Redaktion weitergeleitet worden. Hauptsächlich waren es Komplimente und Glückwünsche von Lesern und Leserinnen, die sich entweder nur auf die Schenkzentrale oder auch auf den Fall Machmut oder auf die komplette Spendenserie bezogen. Einige Absender warfen direkt die Frage auf, ob ich denn wüsste, wer der Wohltäter war, und wann das Geheimnis nun öffentlich gelüftet werden würde.

Eine einzige Mitteilung nährte meine Hoffnung, dass sich der Spender vielleicht von sich aus an mich wenden würde, um das Rätsel zu lösen. Der Inhalt war aber eher kryptisch und lautete: *Sehr geehrter Herr Plassek, warum ausgerechnet Sie? Haben Sie viel gegeben? Haben Sie schon genug gegeben? Nehmen Sie sich doch einmal die Zeit, darüber nachzudenken. Und geben Sie weiter. Ihr treuer Leser.*

Kurz überlegte ich, ob ich gleich darauf antworten sollte. Doch mehr als »Wer sind Sie?« fiel mir dazu nicht ein. So fand ich es schlauer, vorerst gar nicht zu reagieren. Sollte diese Person Konkreteres zu sagen haben, würde sie sich schon wieder melden.

Als Manuel aus der Schule kam, war ich mit meiner Online-Presseschau bereits durch, ohne markant klüger über mich und mein Verhältnis zum Wohltäter geworden zu sein. Als äußerst gewöhnungsbedürftig empfand ich meine immer gleiche Visage, die mir aus nahezu allen Berichten über mich entgegenglotzte. Es gab da nämlich nur dieses eine Archivbild, das vor etwa zwei Jahren angefertigt worden war, als *Tag für Tag* es sich nicht hatte nehmen lassen, alle seine Mitarbeiter öffentlich herzuzeigen. Mich erinnerte es frappant an eines dieser Fahndungsfotos, denen normalerweise Texte beigefügt waren wie: *Achtung, dieser Mann ist gefährlich und schreckt nicht davor zurück, von seiner Schusswaffe Gebrauch zu machen.* Oder als Symbolbild: *Die Zahl der psychisch auffälligen Personen nimmt dramatisch zu.*

Tag für Tag hatte dieses Foto sogar auf die Titelseite geknallt: *Tag-für-Tag-Journalist Plassek im Mittelpunkt der spektakulären Spendenserie.* Im Text war ich dann nicht nur *unser langjähriger verlässlicher Mitarbeiter*, sondern auch die *Drehscheibe im großen Spendenkarussell* und *der Schlüssel zur Lösung des Rätsels um die in diesem Ausmaß einmalige wohltätige Geheimaktion.* Die meisten anderen Blätter trugen zum Glück etwas weniger dick auf. Einige zitierten die *Neuzeit* und erwähnten dabei auch, dass ich meine Stelle bei *Tag für Tag* fristlos gekündigt hatte, weil die Reportage über die geplante Abschiebung der tschetschenischen Familie Pajew nicht hatte erscheinen dürfen.

Claras Kurzporträt über mich in der *Neuzeit* war erfreulicherweise unpeinlich, wenn auch eindeutig zu schmeichelhaft, sodass sich meine Wangen verdächtig danach anfühlten, als wären sie rot angelaufen, während ich die Zeilen las. Sie beschrieb mich als *ruhigen, entspannten Kollegen mit Rückgrat und sozialem Gewissen, der sich nie in den Vordergrund spielt, der frei von journalistischer Eitelkeit ist und sich so auf angenehme Weise von der branchenüblichen Wichtigtuerei und Machtgier* abhebt. Sie zitierte, dass Journalismus *für mich ein Job wie jeder andere war*, wobei sie verschwieg, dass mir der Vergleich fehlte, weil ich eigentlich gar keinen anderen Job kannte und auch nicht kennenlernen wollte.

Und wie erklärte ich mir meine offensichtliche Schlüsselrolle in der Spendenserie? *Gar nicht. Ich glaube ja noch immer an den blanken Zufall, auch wenn dieser Glaube zugegebenermaßen gerade ziemlich auf die Probe gestellt wird*, zitierte sie mich. Das Porträt endete schließlich mit meinem Dank an den Spender selbst.

An dieser Stelle möchte ich Ihnen, geschätzter Wohltäter oder geschätzte Wohltäterin, ans Herz legen, auch Projekte zu unterstützen, die von meinen Kolleginnen und Kollegen in der Neuzeit *vorgestellt werden. Überdies hoffe ich, dass Ihnen nicht so bald das Geld ausgeht. Und im Namen aller bisher Beschenkten: einfach nur vielen Dank!*

Genau an diesen Sätzen stieß sich Manuel, was freilich nichts daran änderte, dass er sich in einem euphorischen Ausnahmezustand befand, da er in der Schule nun vom Machmut-Retter zum weltweit berühmtesten Journalisten-Neffen aufgestiegen war.

»Wieso sagst du, dass der Spender auch andere von deinen Kollegen unterstützen soll?«, fragte er.

»Weil ich unter gewaltigem Druck stehe.«

»Wie, unter gewaltigem Druck?«

»Na ja, alle schauen nur auf mich und auf meine Geschichten.«

»Das ist doch gut so!«, sagte er.

»Nein, das ist gar nicht so gut, das verstehst du nicht, Manuel.«

»Dann erkläre es mir.« Man sollte eben niemals »das verstehst du nicht« behaupten, zumindest nicht gegenüber Manuel.

»Ich kann praktisch indirekt darüber bestimmen, wer die nächsten zehntausend Euro kriegt – falls es noch welche gibt.«

»Das ist doch großartig, dann kannst du immer diejenigen aussuchen, denen du das Geld am meisten gönnst oder die es am meisten verdienen oder die es am dringendsten brauchen«, sagte er.

»Das kann ich aber nicht beurteilen, und ich *will* es auch gar nicht beurteilen, und ich will überhaupt nicht auswählen müssen. Ich bin nicht Gott.«

»Meine Mama ist auch nicht Gott, sondern nur Ärztin, aber sie muss auch manchmal auswählen, wem sie zuerst hilft, und sie hilft immer zuerst denen, wo sie glaubt, dass sie es am meisten brauchen.«

»Ich bin nicht nur nicht Gott, ich bin auch keine Ärztin«, sagte ich in einer letzten rhetorischen Zuckung, in Wirklichkeit hatte mich Manuel bereits ins Aus argumentiert. Aber er war noch nicht fertig.

»Außerdem sind deine Geschichten mehr wert als alle anderen, und du kannst mehr Geld dafür verlangen.« Einen Marxisten würde ich wohl nicht mehr aus ihm machen, fiel mir dazu ein.

»Geld bedeutet mir nicht so viel«, sagte ich zwar, fand aber gleichzeitig, dass dieser Satz irgendwie fürchterlich blöd klang.

»Wenn dir Geld nicht so viel bedeutet, aber du hast einmal viel davon, dann schenk es eben her, dann kannst du gleich selbst ein Wohltäter sein.« Das war eine dieser klassischen Manuel-Weisheiten, auf die man eigentlich nur noch anerkennend nicken konnte. »Aber vorher kauf dir bitte wenigstens eine neue Hose, eine neue Jacke, einen neuen Pulli und ein neues Hemd«, empfahl er mir.

»Die Schuhe hast du vergessen«, erwiderte ich.

»Und drei Paar neue Schuhe«, sagte er und lachte. Ich boxte ihm federleicht auf den Oberarm.

Es war gar nicht unverschämt

Was meine Mundhöhle betraf, fehlte nur noch das Ende der Chronik einer angekündigten Keramikbrücke links unten hinten. Es war also mein allerletzter Termin bei Rebecca Linsbach, und mein Besuchsziel war extrem ehrgeizig, nämlich dass es eben nicht bei diesem allerletzten Termin mit ihr bleiben sollte.

Die an sich spaßbefreite Sprechstundenhilfe hatte insofern eine Wandlung durchgemacht, als sie mich überaus freundlich empfing, mir konzentriert in die Augen sah und Wiedererkennen signalisierte, indem sie »Aaaaaaah, guten Tag, Herr Plassek« sagte, wobei sie Plassek ungefähr so betonte, als hätte sie Clooney oder Damon oder Pitt gemeint, oder wenigstens Udo Lindenberg. Hier kam ich also erstmals in den Genuss eines gewissen Neopromi-Bonus, der noch erheblich aufgestockt wurde, als sich die Flügeltür öffnete und mir Rebecca Linsbach entgegenstrahlte. Wir schüttelten uns überaus ambitioniert die Hände, wobei ich ihre Hand etwa drei Sekunden länger hielt, als es patiententechnisch dringend notwendig gewesen wäre.

»Sie sind ja über Nacht eine richtige Berühmtheit geworden«, sagte sie.

»Ja, wie das Leben manchmal so spielt«, erwiderte ich und lächelte. Sie wusste zwar nicht, warum ich lächelte, aber sie lächelte solidarisch mit. Und nach dem Auslächeln wäre dann garantiert jene Pause eingetreten, die dazu geführt hätte, dass wir uns der Sache zugewandt hätten, also der Keramikbrücke, und die wahrscheinlich vorletzte Chance auf die Ankurbelung eines Wiedersehens wäre vertan gewesen. Deshalb begann ich sofort mit jenem Schlüsselsatz, bei dem ich selbst nur die einleitenden Worte im Detail kannte. Und die lauteten: »Ich hoffe, es ist nicht allzu unverschämt, wenn ich Sie frage ...« Bis zum Wort *frage* gab sie mir nicht zwingend das Gefühl, dass es allzu unverschämt war, also fragte ich einfach weiter. »Ich hoffe, es ist nicht allzu unverschämt, wenn ich Sie frage, ob Sie mit mir vielleicht einmal auf einen Kaffee gehen würden ...« Ich hätte natürlich auch sagen können: »... wenn ich Sie frage, ob ich Sie vielleicht einmal auf einen Kaffee einladen dürfte«, aber dann hätte sie möglicherweise gedacht, dass ich etwas von ihr wollte, dass ich mir sozusagen etwas von ihr erkaufen wollte, mit einem Kaffee, und das war ja absolut nicht der Fall, oder zumindest sollte sie keinesfalls in diese Richtung denken, und Frauen neigten dazu, in diese Richtung zu denken, das wusste ich. Doch das Schwierigste stand mir ohnehin noch bevor, nämlich die Begründung. »Ich hoffe, es ist nicht allzu unverschämt, wenn ich Sie frage, ob Sie mit mir vielleicht einmal auf einen Kaffee gehen würden. Ich möchte Sie nämlich gerne etwas näher kennenlernen.« Nein, das sagte ich natürlich nicht. Das wäre einfach nicht gegangen, da hätte sie mich, um einzuwilligen, nämlich wenigstens annähernd so gerne etwas näher kennenlernen möchten müssen wie ich sie, und das traute ich ihr ehrlich gestanden nicht zu. Also brachte mich die Wahrheit hier nicht weiter, ich musste taktieren und sagte schließlich: »Ich hoffe, es ist nicht allzu unverschämt, wenn ich Sie frage, ob Sie mit mir vielleicht einmal auf einen Kaffee gehen würden. Ich möchte mich nämlich gerne ein bisschen mit Ihnen unterhalten. Konkret gibt es da einige Dinge, zu denen mich Ihre Meinung interessieren würde. Vielleicht können Sie mir sogar den einen oder anderen Tipp geben.« Ja, so sagte ich es. Und es klang hoffentlich so neutral, wie leider der Blick anmutete, den ich von ihr dafür erntete, und solche neutralen Blicke waren immens gefährlich. Dazu passten nämlich wunderbar Sätze wie *Im nächsten Halbjahr bin ich leider sehr beschäftigt.*

Aber ich hatte Glück. Rebeccas neutraler Blick ging in ein Lächeln über, und sie sagte: »Ja, können wir gerne machen! Das trifft sich sogar sehr gut. Ich habe nämlich auch eine … wie soll ich sagen, eine Frage an Sie, ganz unverbindlich, ohne Ihnen zu nahe treten zu wollen.«

»Treten Sie nur näher, ich habe Ihnen gegenüber keinerlei Berührungsängste«, erwiderte ich im ersten Begeisterungstaumel ob ihrer sensationellen Antwort, also extrem spontan. Unspontaner hätte ich eine so plumpe Anmache nämlich niemals über die Lippen gebracht.

»Ich hab Ihnen gegenüber auch keine … Berührungsängste«, sagte sie da. Kurz wurde mir ein bisschen schwindlig, aber dann tippte sie leider auf eines ihrer Zahn-Foltergeräte, und da erst verstand ich die Botschaft. Sie hatte also doch Humor, sehr schwarzen sogar, kariesschwarzen sozusagen. Ich wollte mich gerade an eine extrem vorsichtige Frage nach dem Zeitpunkt unseres in Aussicht gestellten Wiedersehens herantasten. Da sagte sie: »Ich habe heute bis achtzehn Uhr Sprechstunde. Gleich ums Eck gibt es ein nettes Café, das Margaretenstüberl, wenn Sie wollen …«

»Heute? Heute passt mir perfekt! Morgen wäre es ein bisschen schwierig gewesen, aber heute gegen achtzehn Uhr, das ist eigentlich ideal«, sagte ich.

»Fein, dann hätten wir das«, erwiderte sie.

Normalerweise rutschte man nach solchen Erfolgen in ausverkauften Stadien auf den Knien dreißig Meter in Richtung der ekstatisch jubelnden Fanzone, aber ich blieb einmal in meinem Leben nüchtern und erwiderte: »Ja, das hätten wir.«

Jedenfalls konnten wir uns entspannt der dienstlichen

Sache zuwenden. Ich nahm den mir bereits vertrauten Platz auf der Liege ein, schloss nahezu genusssüchtig die Augen und dachte, dass unser erstes Date jetzt höchstens noch durch eine schwere Katastrophe vereitelt werden konnte – zum Beispiel den dramatischen Einsturz einer Keramikbrücke mit zahlreichen verschütteten Weisheitszähnen. Aber das zu verhindern, hatte sie ja sozusagen selbst in der Hand.

Patient und Gentleman

Zwischen überlebtem Zahnarztbesuch und Zahnärztinnen-Date blieben mir gerade einmal anderthalb Stunden, um von der Patientenrolle in die Officer-and-Gentleman-Rolle zu schlüpfen, oder zumindest in eine subkulturelle Variante davon, was einen Panikeinkauf von Jeans, Weste und Schuhen notwendig machte. Geld bedeutete mir wie gesagt zwar nicht viel, aber ich war dennoch dankbar, dass ich in dieser außergewöhnlichen Situation nicht auf die Schenkzentrale angewiesen war, sondern ein Modehaus bemühen konnte. Um Zeit zu sparen, zeigte ich auf die erstbeste annehmbar gekleidete und auch preislich attraktive männliche Schaufensterpuppe und sagte: »So wie der da, nur ohne Mütze und in meiner Größe.«

»Was hast du vor?«, fragte mich Manuel etwas verängstigt, als ich mit der dicken Einkaufstasche nach Hause kam.

»Ich treffe die Zahnärztin – privat«, sagte ich.

»Du machst Witze.«

»Nein, im Ernst.«

»Sie trifft sich mit dir? Warum?«, fragte er. Das war erstens eine Frechheit, zweitens hatte ich jetzt wirklich keine Lust, ihm das Zwischenmenschliche zu erklären. »Wenn du sie triffst, kannst du sie ja gleich fragen, ob sie am übernächsten Samstag mit dir mitkommen will, du weißt schon – zu unserem Spiel gegen Union CS«, fügte er hinzu. Das war eigentlich eine phantastisch gute Idee. Oder vielleicht war es doch keine so gute Idee.

»Sie wird am Samstag keine Zeit haben, sie ist sicher glücklich verheiratet und betreut ihren Mann – oder er sie«, sagte ich.

»Ihr Mann kann auch mitkommen, je mehr Zuschauer, umso besser«. In diesem Fall war ich entschieden anderer Ansicht.

»Hallo, ich bin der Gerold, Feinde nennen mich Geri«, sagte ich, um mein Herzklopfen zu übertönen. Und sie kannte die tolle Pointe ja noch nicht.

»Rebecca, freut mich.« So aufregend sie war, so beneidenswert unaufgeregt wirkte sie, was sie gleich noch aufregender machte – und mich aufgeregter. Das war im Grunde ein Teufelskreis.

»Stört es dich, wenn ich mir ein Bier bestelle?«, fragte ich, statt es einfach mal ohne zu probieren, aber es ging nicht.

»Nein, stört mich nicht, wenn du auch gleich eins für mich mitbestellst«, erwiderte sie. Das war die erste große Überraschung.

Die zweite kam nach aufwühlenden Minuten biografischer Enthüllungen ans Tageslicht: Rebecca war ungebunden, ich buchstabiere: u, n, g, e, b, u, n, d, e, n. Sie hatte viele enge Freunde, darunter zahlreiche Männer, aber ihre dauerhaften Beziehungen waren mittlerweile alle überdauert, ohne dass jemand ernsthaft hängengeblieben wäre. »Man kann es eben nicht erzwingen«, sagte sie.

»Nein, das kann man nicht«, bestätigte ich.

»Und ich bin in dieser Hinsicht auch ziemlich anspruchsvoll.«

Klar war sie das, sonst würde sie nicht mit mir hier sitzen, machte ich mir Mut.

»Doch die innere Uhr tickt natürlich, und ich werde auch nicht jünger«, sagte sie.

»Jünger werden wir alle nicht, aber am ehesten wahrscheinlich noch du, Rebecca«, erwiderte ich. Sie lächelte. Warum konnten mir nicht öfter solche Sätze einfallen?

Sie nutzte dann leider die erstbeste sentimentale Gedankenpause, um das Thema zu wechseln und mich beim Wort zu nehmen, bei einem Wort, das ich bereits vergessen hatte. Das Wort hieß Tipp.

»Du wolltest ja einen Tipp von mir. Also sag, worum geht es denn?«, fragte sie.

Das erwischte mich komplett auf dem falschen Fuß, und ich stammelte eine Weile herum und verkrampfte mich zusehends, sodass sie sicher bereits glaubte, dass es um Leben und Tod gehen musste, so in Richtung: Wie kommt man rasch und unbürokratisch zu einer Spenderleber oder zu einem frischen Lungenflügel, denn ein runderneuertes Gebiss allein reicht auf Dauer nicht aus. Bis ich sie dann quasi mit dem Gegenteil überraschte. Ich erzählte ihr, dass ich ohne Manuels Wissen ein Fahrrad gekauft hatte und auch schon heimlich mit dem freien Training begonnen hatte, mit dem Ziel, meinen Buben zu einem Fahrradausflug einzuladen. Und da war nun die Frage … also die Frage … Okay, egal, etwas Besseres fiel mir eben nicht ein: »Wo fährt man da am besten, ich meine, vom Gelände her, ich dachte, sportlich wie du aussiehst, weißt du sicher, wo es sich in Wien gut Fahrrad fahren lässt, vor allem Mitte November.« Sie war immerhin höflich genug, mir mitzuteilen, dass sie als Salzburgerin sich in Wien nicht so gut auskannte und dass ich doch einfach ein paar dieser Ausflugsbroschüren studieren sollte, die sie einem überall dutzendfach nachwarfen.

»Ah, sehr gute Idee, danke, das werde ich machen!«, sagte ich.

Danach ging es ohne Umwege ans Eingemachte.

»Warum sagst du ihm eigentlich nicht, dass du sein Vater bist?«, fragte sie.

»Es war irgendwie noch nicht der richtige Zeitpunkt dafür da, ich warte besser noch ein bisschen«, druckste ich herum.

»Warten worauf? Dass er selbst dahinterkommt? Das würde ich nicht riskieren, das kann viel zerstören, weil er dann das Gefühl hat, dass du dich nicht zu ihm bekannt hast«, sagte sie.

»Er will gar nicht wissen, wer sein Vater ist, hat er mir mal verraten.«

»Klar. Weil er Angst hat, enttäuscht zu werden.«

»Richtig. Und ich habe Angst, dass er enttäuscht ist, wenn er erfährt, dass ich es bin.«

»Das wird er aber nicht sein, ganz im Gegenteil«, sagte sie.

»Wieso glaubst du das?«

»Weil man das weiß, wenn man euch beide sieht – und wenn man dir zuhört, wie du über ihn sprichst. Ihr passt zusammen, seid eine Einheit. Da ist große Zuneigung im Spiel. Du bist wichtig für ihn.«

»Das freut mich zu hören«, sagte ich und freute mich zu hören, dass sie so von mir sprach.

»Der Bub ist enorm wichtig für dich. Weißt du warum? Er nimmt dich in Anspruch, er weckt dein schlummerndes Verantwortungsgefühl, er rüttelt dich wach.«

Das Wort Verantwortungsgefühl hatte ich im Zusammenhang mit mir ehrlich gestanden bisher noch selten zu hören bekommen, nicht einmal schlummernd. Am liebsten hätte ich jetzt eine jener beiden zarten Hände ergriffen, die mit tippenden Fingern auf dem Tisch lagen. Aber das war irgendwie noch nicht der richtige Zeitpunkt. Zum Glück war ich der Typ, der praktisch sein Leben lang auf richtige Zeitpunkte warten konnte.

Natürlich wollte auch Rebecca wissen, ob ich denn eine Ahnung hatte, wer mich da so eindrucksvoll und publikumswirksam in seine große geheime Mission eingebunden hatte.

»Nein, keine Ahnung, aber ich bin mir sicher, dass mich diese Person nicht kennt. Oder wenn sie mich kennt, meint sie es gar nicht gut mit mir. Öffentlichkeit ist nämlich so überhaupt nicht mein Ding«, sagte ich.

»Aber das Ding dieser Person ist Öffentlichkeit offenbar auch nicht, also passt ihr ja wieder ganz gut zusammen«, erwiderte sie. Eigentlich wollte ich mit Rebecca jetzt nicht unbedingt über die Spendenserie spekulieren, das konnten wir uns ja für eines unserer hoffentlich zahlreichen Folgetreffen aufheben. Was mich viel mehr interessierte, war ihre noch offene »unverbindliche Frage«, in deren Zusammenhang sie mir angekündigt hatte, mir nicht zu nahe treten zu wollen.

Als ich sie schließlich darauf ansprach, lehnte sie sich tatsächlich relativ weit zurück und begann von ihrer Freundin, der Zahnärztin Nora, zu erzählen, die mit neun Kollegen und Kolleginnen ehrenamtlich eine außergewöhnliche Praxis betrieb, nämlich zahnärztliche Hilfe für Sozialfälle, für Wohnungslose und Bedürftige, und zwar im sogenannten Zehnerhaus in der Schleifmühlgasse.

»Ich arbeite dort auch einmal wöchentlich und möchte das noch intensiveren«, sagte sie. Mit einem Mal wurde mir klar, warum sie bei mir von Anfang an keine Berührungsängste gehabt hatte.

»Das ist eine gute Sache«, sagte ich.

»Ja, stimmt«, erwiderte sie. Es entstand eine Pause, in der sie mich so ansah, als sollte ich auf etwas kommen, aber ich sah nur, wie sie mich ansah, und das verlangte mir volle Konzentration ab.

»Wir müssen den Behandlungsraum herrichten, müssen alles auf den neuesten technischen Stand bringen, wir brauchen zum Beispiel dringend neue Lasergeräte und ein paar andere Dinge«, erklärte sie.

»Aha«, sagte ich. Langsam klingelte es.

»Und dafür fehlt uns leider das Geld.«

»Ich verstehe.«

»Und als ich Nora von dir erzählt habe, dass ich dich kenne, dass du mein Patient bist, da hat Nora gemeint, ob ich dich nicht einfach fragen kann ... denn fragen kann man ja mal, hat Nora gemeint ...«

»Fragen kann man eigentlich immer. Fragen kostet nichts«, sagte ich. Das stimmte allerdings nicht, fragen konnte mittlerweile ziemlich teuer werden, man musste nur etwa an die Psychotherapie denken, oder an Architekten oder Steuerberater, aber egal, das passte jetzt nicht hierher.

»Ob du in der *Neuzeit* eventuell ein paar Zeilen ...«

»Aber natürlich«, sagte ich. Es gab nicht so viele Momente, wo man nicht wusste, ob es einem katastrophal schlecht oder phantastisch gut ging, ob man sich auf- oder abgewertet, geehrt oder ausgenutzt vorkommen sollte. So einen Moment erlebte ich gerade, und ich beschloss instinktiv, mich so zu verhalten, als wäre es exakt die goldene Mitte davon.

»Du meinst ...«

»Eigentlich eher Nora.«

»Du meinst, dass Nora meint, dass euch vielleicht jemand zehntausend Euro spenden wird, wenn ich darüber berichte?«

»Ja, wie gesagt, Nora ...«

»Also du selbst glaubst das nicht?«

»Doch, aber verstehst du, ich wäre gar nicht auf den Gedanken gekommen ...«

»Ich verstehe, es war Noras Gedanke, aber du findest ihn schön.«

»Natürlich«, sagte sie kleinlaut. Jetzt hatte ich sie tatsächlich ordentlich in Verlegenheit gebracht, und ihre Ohren hatten die Farbe von diesen großen exotischen Früchten angenommen, die man im Supermarkt erwerben konnte, in die aber noch nie wer hineingebissen hatte, zumindest niemand, den ich kannte. Kaki hießen die, oder? Komisch, dass mir das mit dem Reinbeißen zu Rebeccas Ohren einfiel.

»Und wenn keine Spende kommt? Werdet ihr dann sehr enttäuscht sein, Nora und du?«, fragte ich.

»Nein, gar nicht, überhaupt nicht, ich würde es ja schon toll finden, wenn einmal in der Zeitung steht, dass es uns gibt und dass man zu uns kommen kann und dass wir niemanden wegschicken, auch wenn wer keine Krankenversicherung hat.«

»Natürlich mache ich das«, sagte ich. Jetzt sprangen ihre Hände mit den tippenden Fingern mit einem Satz auf meine und machten kurze wärmende und knetende Bewegungen. Das war quasi bereits die Belohnung im Voraus.

Die Situation war ungewöhnlich. Mich hatte noch nie irgendwer dafür geschätzt, dass es in meinen frisch gekneteten Händen liegen könnte, etwas Gravierendes zur Verbesserung von jemandes Lebensumständen beizutragen. Ich genoss also plötzlich das mir wenig vertraute Gefühl einer gewissen Macht. Und wenn ich mir Rebecca so ansah, wie sie mich ansah, musste ich zugeben, dass ich es mir schlimmer vorgestellt hatte, einmal für einen kurzen Augenblick ein Machtmensch zu sein.

KAPITEL ELF

Im Sterntalerland

In der folgenden Woche schrieb ich drei große Sozialreportagen für die *Neuzeit*, das waren mindestens zweieinhalb mehr, als ich mir unter normalen Umständen zugemutet hätte, aber die Umstände waren eben nicht mehr normal, und es zeichnete sich auch kein Umschwung zurück zur Normalität ab. Was meine Motivation betraf, wunderte ich mich eine Weile, woher sie gekommen war, bis ich mich mit ihr abfand und alles andere als ein schlechtes Gefühl dabei hatte. Wahrscheinlich genügte es, wenn einige Menschen, die mir wichtig waren oder mittendrin plötzlich wichtig wurden, etwas von mir erwarteten. Nein, sie erwarteten es eigentlich gar nicht, sondern sie wünschten es sich, denn Erwartungen konnte ich an sich ganz gut nicht erfüllen, bis sie schwächer wurden und man schließlich aufhörte, sie von mir zu erwarten – darin war ich durch Lebenserfahrung geschult. Aber jemandem einen Wunsch abschlagen, das fiel mir schwer, zumal diese Wünsche gar nicht aus Worten bestanden, gegen die sich gemeinhin vernünftig argumentieren ließ, sondern oft nur aus Blicken, die man mir zuwarf und die ich nicht einmal auffangen musste, weil sie nämlich automatisch an mir kleben blieben. Weltmeister im Zuwerfen von kleben bleibenden wunschgesättigten Blicken war Manuel. Er sah mich an, und ich wusste, was er von mir wollte, und vor allem, wie sehr er es wollte. Manchmal war das so eindringlich, und ich spürte seine Wünsche so stark, dass ich gar nicht mehr unterscheiden konnte, ob es tatsächlich noch seine oder bereits meine eigenen Wünsche waren.

Zum Beispiel erzählte er mir vom Sterntalerland, einem

Kinderhospiz im Burgenland, wo die Familie seines Schulfreundes Paul eine Woche verbracht hatte. Pauls neunjährige Schwester Lilli hatte eine Gehirntumor-Operation hinter sich, und obwohl sich die Familie den Aufenthalt in einem Therapiezentrum nicht leisten konnte und die Krankenkasse natürlich kaum etwas dafür zahlte, weil sich die Krankenkassen in unserem kranken System gerade selbst sanieren mussten, statt dass sie den Bedürftigen halfen, sich zu sanieren, also obwohl der Familie die Mittel fehlten, war sie im Sterntalerland aufgenommen worden, und es wurde angeblich Lillis schönster Urlaub überhaupt, vor allem wegen Estrella, die sich ausschließlich von Mostbirnen ernährte, weshalb sie auch relativ schlank geblieben war und sich so bei etwa vierhundert Kilo hielt. Estrella war ein Pferd. Und für Lilli war es wahrscheinlich der letzte Urlaub gewesen, aber sie war trotzdem glücklich, und Paul konnte jetzt wieder etwas besser schlafen, erzählte mir Manuel.

Im Anschluss an seine Ausführungen, die mich ohnehin bereits fertiggemacht hatten, weil ich schöne Geschichten mit vorhersehbarem tragischem Ende nervlich nicht aushielt, sandte mir Manuel diesen klebrigen Wunschblick zu. Und am nächsten Tag fuhren wir mit Zug und Autobus ins tiefste Burgenland, wo sich übrigens auch die Menschen vorzugsweise von Most ernährten und einen schief anschauten, wenn man ein Bier verlangte.

Wir fuhren also dorthin und machten unsere Reportage, die uns ziemlich unter die Haut ging. Ich war ganz schön erleichtert, als Manuel einmal so richtig losheulen musste und ich vorübergehend in die Rolle des Trösters schlüpfen konnte.

Den meisten schwerkranken Kindern und ihren Eltern war gar nicht anzumerken, was sie alles durchgemacht hatten und was ihnen zum Teil noch bevorstand. Im beinahe idyllischen Sterntalerland, wo einen Ruhe umgab und einem Wärme entgegenströmte, durften sie die Zeiger der Uhr anhalten, um die Zeit noch für ein paar Tage stillstehen zu lassen, um an schöne Dinge zu denken und Kraft für die Zielgerade zu sammeln. Jede Minute war hier kostbar, als wäre sie ein Konzentrat aus mehreren Jahren Weiterlebens. Daran konnte man erst ermessen, wie weit unter ihrem Wert uns die Zeit in unseren Alltagstretmühlen verkauft wurde. Oder wir selbst warfen sie achtlos weg und waren uns dessen nicht einmal bewusst. Ja, ich war wahrscheinlich auch so ein Fall, vielleicht sogar ein Paradebeispiel dafür.

Die Linke Hand im Sumpf

Bei der *Neuzeit* war inzwischen eine Sekretärin eigens dafür abgestellt worden, den Spenden-Postverkehr zu betreuen und zu koordinieren. Täglich trafen Dutzende Briefe, Anrufe und E-Mails von kleinen Hilfsorganisationen, von privaten Helfern oder von erklärten Opfern der Armut oder widriger Lebensumstände ein, die sich erhofften, den Sprung in die Zeitung und von dort direkt in die Arme des Wohltäters zu schaffen. Die meisten Bittgesuche waren *an Herrn Gerold Plassek persönlich* gerichtet. Die Sekretärin, Angelina hieß sie – ich fand es ja riskant bis fahrlässig, ein österreichisches Kind Angelina zu nennen, überhaupt wenn es mit dem Nachnamen Schröckshuber hieß, aber die Eltern werden sich schon was dabei gedacht haben – Angelina war jedenfalls bereits mehr mit mir beschäftigt als ich selbst. Immer wieder kamen Gerüchte in Umlauf, wer der Spender oder die Spenderin war, wo er oder sie beobachtet und auf frischer Wohltat ertappt worden sei. Offenbar herrschte in der Redaktion so etwas wie *Tatort*-Atmosphäre, freilich mit positiver, antikrimineller Energie. Schon zum wiederholten Male, und das war ein bemerkenswertes

Phänomen, wurden Trittbrettfahrer bekannt, die sich an den anonymen Großspenden orientierten und ihrerseits Geldgeschenke verteilten – nicht so hoch und nicht ganz so geheim, sie wollten also schon wenigstens namentlich erwähnt werden, aber immerhin.

Seibernigg erzählte mir am Telefon von der Linken Hand, einer immer größer werdenden Bürgerinitiative junger Leute, die sich im Internet organisierten und in ihrer Freizeit die professionellen Streetworker unentgeltlich bei ihrer Arbeit unterstützten. Sie mischten sich unter Kleindealer, Süchtige und Prostituierte auf dem Straßenstrich, versuchten in Gesprächen, ihr Vertrauen zu gewinnen und sie unauffällig zu begleiten, möglichst hinaus aus ihren Sümpfen und Sackgassen – auf noch unbeschrittene Wege, wo sich vielleicht einmal ein neuer Horizont auftun könnte.

Man musste mich nicht lange überreden, der Linken Hand eine Reportage zu widmen. Ich brauchte nur an Florentina zu denken und mir Mike, das Schattengewächs an ihrer Seite, sozusagen im Arbeitseinsatz vorzustellen.

Bei der Vorort-Recherche, der ich immerhin einen Nachmittag und drei Abende opferte, hatte ich optisch den Vorteil, absolut unverdächtig zu sein – die Streetworker ordneten mich eher ihrer Klientel zu, während mich die angeschlagenen Jugendlichen für eine Linke Hand auf Augenhöhe hielten, weil diese linke Hand natürlich ständig eine Bierdose umfasst hielt. Ich wollte dort so authentisch wie möglich auftreten. Außerdem bestand ja theoretisch die Chance, eine der naturtrüben Gestalten vom Heroin zum Gerstensaft zurückzuführen, also war ich bei den Recherchen diesbezüglich äußerst spendierfreudig. Manche schlossen mich gleich so ins Herz, dass sie mit mir nachts noch gern in eine Kneipe gepilgert wären. Aber das konnte ich Zoltan nicht antun, dass ich in seinem Lokal plötzlich mit dreißig verkrachten Jüngern der

Drogenszene antanzte, die fünf Wirklichkeiten gleichzeitig erlebten, nur nicht ihre echte, die sie sich weggeschluckt oder weggespritzt hatten.

Manuel hatte in dieser Umgebung meiner Meinung nach überhaupt nichts zu suchen. Aber er war leider gegenteiliger Meinung und drängte vehement darauf, mich bei den Recherchen zu begleiten. Wir einigten uns schließlich darauf, dass er am Nachmittag eine Stunde dabei sein durfte, um den Sozialarbeitern ein bisschen auf die Finger und auf die Lippen zu schauen. So konnte er sich wenigstens auch ein Bild davon machen, wie Jugendliche, die oft nur ein paar Jahre älter waren als er, bei Tageslicht aussahen, wenn sie einmal in die falschen Kreise geraten waren und der Spiralbewegung nach unten nichts entgegensetzen konnten oder niemanden hatten, der sie rechtzeitig auffing und ihnen wieder den Drall nach oben verpasste. Je weiter unten sie waren, desto schwerer kamen sie jemals wieder hinauf, da entglitt ihnen oft sogar die letzte Linke Hand, die man versuchte, ihnen entgegenzustrecken, erzählten uns die Betreuer. Und es war ein Irrtum zu glauben, dass das Kinder aus einer anderen Welt waren als jener, in der die behüteten Florentinas und Manuels ein und aus gingen.

Zehnerhaus mit Zugabe

Die nächste Recherche war für mich gewissermaßen eine reine Herzensangelegenheit, ich durfte es mir nur nicht anmerken lassen. Und eine Zahnarztpraxis für Sozialfälle im Zehnerhaus war offen gestanden auch nicht gerade der perfekte Rahmen für Herzensangelegenheiten. Wir waren zu dritt, denn Manuel hatte den Lokalaugenschein von vornherein verweigert. Ich kam mir phasenweise wie ein unbedarfter Interessent vor, der zwei im Arbeitsrausch befindlichen Immobilienmaklerinnen in die Hände gefallen war. Die überaus sympathische Nora, die mich mit ihrer Blockfrisur ein bisschen an Betty Geröllheimer von den Feuersteins erinnerte, trichterte mir bei der Führung durch die kargen Dentalräumlichkeiten einen zahntechnischen Gerätekatalog nach dem anderen ein. Rebecca konzentrierte sich mehr auf die statistischen Grundlagen der ehrenamtlichen Tätigkeit und erklärte mir, welcher Randgruppe welcher Zahnverfall zuzuordnen war, wozu Nora auch schon die Abbildung des passenden Bekämpfungsinstruments hochhielt, das dringend angeschafft werden musste.

Das herzliche Angebot, einem Akuteinsatz beizuwohnen, schlug ich höflich aus. Meine eigenen Erfahrungen waren mir noch akut genug in Erinnerung. Und auch die Gespräche mit Patienten im Warteraum wären an sich entbehrlich gewesen.

»Starke Schmerzen?«, fragte ich einen Rübezahl mit doppelter Backengröße. Das war sicher eine der blödesten jemals gestellten Interviewfragen. Er nickte. Damit war das Gespräch im Grunde auch schon beendet.

»Keine Sorge, die haben Goldhändchen. Mir haben sie beide Reihen ausgehoben und komplett neu aufgestellt, und es hat überhaupt nicht wehgetan«, log ich. Er nickte.

»In einer halben Stunde ist alles überstanden«, ergänzte ich. Er blickte noch einmal schmerzverzerrt auf.

»Vielleicht sogar schon in einer Viertelstunde«, modifizierte ich. Er nickte.

Mit dem nicht von der Hand zu weisenden Argument, noch ein paar ergänzende Fragen zu haben, gelang es mir, Rebecca für ein abschließendes »stilles Mineralwasser« ins nahe gelegene Café Arthur zu lotsen. Nora wäre gerne mitgekommen, oder auch nicht, das ließ sich schwer überprüfen, sie war jedenfalls an ihren Schichtdienst gebunden. Ich hatte mich wirklich bemüht, einen guten, soliden, kompetenten, seriösen

Eindruck bei ihr zu hinterlassen. Die Sichtweise enger Freundinnen und Kolleginnen von Angebeteten spielen in Liebesdingen nämlich eine immens wichtige Rolle, davon konnte ich einige triste Lieder singen. Mich hatten Freundinnen meiner realen oder ersehnten Geliebten selten ausstehen und niemals guten Gewissens empfehlen können, ich galt unter ihnen generell als *schlechter Umgang* oder *Mann ohne Perspektiven*, was ich besonders unfair fand, weil auch Perspektivlosigkeit immer eine Frage der Perspektive war. Aber diesmal hatte ich es eindeutig leichter, da war die Perspektive quasi vorgegeben, und deshalb war ich in Noras Gunst gleich einmal von ziemlich weit oben weg gestartet.

»Ich weiß gar nicht, wie ich dir danken soll, dass du diesen Artikel über unser Projekt machst«, sagte Rebecca. Ich schon, dachte ich.

»Ich schon«, riskierte ich dann auch. »Du würdest Manuel eine Riesenfreude machen, also mir und Manuel, wenn du am nächsten Samstag, also nicht kommenden Samstag, sondern erst den darauf...« Der Satz begann mir zu kompliziert, ich probierte es mittendrin noch einmal anders. »Hast du am nächsten Samstagnachmittag vielleicht zufällig Zeit und Lust, zu Manuels Basketballspiel mitzukommen, also mich zu begleiten? Torpedo 15 gegen Union CS. Es geht um den Herbstmeistertitel, und Manuel würde sich wie gesagt riesig freuen, Manuel und Machmut, du weißt schon, der kleine Machmut aus der Zeitung, und ... auch ich natürlich ...«

»Nächsten Samstagabend bin ich leider schon verabredet«, erwiderte sie. Das klang unangenehm bedeutungsschwanger und schrammte zudem haarscharf am Kern der Fragestellung vorbei.

»Das Spiel beginnt um fünfzehn Uhr und dauert sicher nicht länger als zwei Stunden, das heißt, um fünf wärst du sozusagen erlöst«, sagte ich knochentrocken.

»Fünfzehn bis siebzehn Uhr, das wäre dann ... das ist ...
ja, das ist gut, das ist ... wunderbar«, erwiderte sie, wobei sie
sich beim Wort *wunderbar* der Gefahr der Überdehnung ihrer
Mundwinkel aussetzte.

»Das heißt, du kommst mit?«

»Ja, doch, da komme ich natürlich sehr gerne mit, und wir
feuern Manuel und Machmut gemeinsam an. Danke für die
liebe Einladung«, sagte sie, etwas gefasster.

»Ist vielleicht eine nette Einstimmung für deine abendliche ... Verabredung«, sagte ich in bemüht brüderlichem Ton.
Sie lächelte verschämt, und ihre Wangen färbten sich leider
wieder ein bisschen kaki-orangerot. »Ist es was Ernstes?«, fragte
ich, getrieben von der offenbar ansteckenden Verlockung, an
empfindlichen Nerven zu bohren.

»Ach, ernst, was ist schon ernst?«, fragte sie und bewegte die
Schultern auf und ab. Es war also etwas Ernstes. Klarer Fall.
Mist.

Rebecca im Sinn

Die Sterntalerland-Reportage schrieb sich wie von allein, und
stockte ich, so hatte Manuel immer gleich ein passendes Stichwort parat. Bei der Geschichte über die Linke Hand ging mir
zwischendurch ein paarmal die Luft aus, da war ich am Vorabend einfach zu spät ins Bett gekommen, aber Peter Seibernigg war mit dem Ergebnis letztendlich zufrieden, also werde
ich es wohl halbwegs ordentlich hingekriegt haben.

Am meisten plagte ich mich bei meinen Schilderungen
über den gemeinnützigen Zahnsozialdienst. Erstens hatte ich
thematisch langsam wirklich genug von kaputten Gebissen.
Zweitens kam mir zwischen den Zeilen und manchmal sogar
mehrmals innerhalb einer Zeile Rebecca in den Sinn, wie sie

mit den Schultern zuckte und »Was ist schon ernst?« sagte, und da zerflossen mir alle Buchstaben quasi vor den Augen. Ich verspürte nämlich plötzlich den mir bis dato völlig unvertrauten Hang zum Melodramatischen, weil es einfach eine Gemeinheit war, dass so ein mieser, charakterloser Typ meinen Beziehungsaufbau störte. Der Mann war bestimmt nur auf den Eros ausgerichtet, visierte für seine Dates stets die Samstagabende an, um sich auf diese Weise die Samstagnächte frei zu baggern, und Sonntagmittag wurden die Bettdecken bereits wieder frisch überzogen und die lila Zahnbürsten seiner Opfer, darunter bildhübsche und grenzenlos gutgläubige Dentistinnen, entsorgt. Ja, spätestens nächsten Samstag würde es auch Rebecca erwischen, und es lag leider so gar nicht bei mir, sie zu warnen und die logische Alternative aufzuzeigen. Ich war in meinem Leben ja noch nie richtig eifersüchtig gewesen, aber ich merkte gerade, dass es selbst dafür nie zu spät war und im Fall Rebecca gar keiner großen Anstrengung bedurfte.

Okay, es gab da neben Zahnekel und wirren Sinnen noch ein drittes Problem mit der Zahnsozialreportage: die anonyme Geldspende. Nie zuvor hatte ich auf sie spekuliert. Aber diesmal erwischte ich mich dabei, wie ich es geradezu darauf anlegte, sie herbeizuschreiben, was zu eklig plastikblumigen Formulierungen wie *die rührigen Ärztinnen, das Herz am rechten Fleck* oder *ihr aufopfernder Dienst für die gute Sache* führte. Zwischendurch wurden mir die Finger klamm vor Angst, dass vielleicht eines der beiden anderen vorgestellten Hilfsprojekte mit zehntausend Euro belohnt werden könnte, nicht aber das Engagement von Nora, Rebecca und Co. Und Rebecca würde mit einem knappen und gequälten »danke jedenfalls für die Mühe und Grüße von Nora« darauf reagieren.

»Und was ist mit unserem nächsten Treffen?«, würde ich noch einmal nachhechten.

»Terminvereinbarungen bitte telefonisch zu den Sprechzeiten. Tut mir leid, Gerold«, nein: »Tut mir leid, *Geri*, ich kann da bei dir keine Ausnahme machen.« So, das wären dann also Rebeccas letzte Worte gewesen. Und deshalb begann ich die Reportage nun bereits zum dritten Mal wohltätergerecht zu überarbeiten und hatte dabei ein ziemlich flaues Gefühl.

Geschenk von den Engelbrechts

Die Reportagen erschienen in drei aufeinanderfolgenden Ausgaben der *Neuzeit* – am Montag das Zehnerhaus, am Dienstag das Sterntalerland, am Mittwoch die Linke Hand.

Danach ging es mir noch einmal kurz gut. Am Mittwoch stand ich relativ zeitig auf, holte mein Fahrrad aus dem Keller, fuhr damit auf den fast vierhundert Meter hohen Wilhelminenberg – also nicht mit dem Fahrrad selbst, sondern mit dem Autobus, ich wollte ja kein Hochgebirgsradprofi werden. Aber oben schwang ich mich tatsächlich auf den Sattel und ließ mich die gesamte Johann-Staud-Straße hinunterrollen, das war schwierig, weil man immer wieder scharf bremsen musste, um nicht letztlich in der Donau zu landen. Daheim lagerte ich meine müden Knochen hoch und versuchte, an gar nichts zu denken. Dabei blieb ich leider ungestört, Manuel hatte Schulexkursion. Am Mittwochabend tauchte ich noch kurz in Zoltan's Bar auf, dann ab und schließlich komplett unter.

Am Donnerstag – Manuel war nach dem Training mit Mitschülern verabredet, jetzt fehlte er mir schon ziemlich – verschanzte ich mich daheim, las keine Zeitungen, hörte keine Nachrichten, schaltete kein elektronisches Gerät ein, war nicht ansprechbar und nach den ersten Schneeflocken der Saison, die bei der Straßenlaterne draußen vorbeitanzten, so gut wie von der Außenwelt abgeschnitten.

Am Freitag war ich phasenweise nicht einmal für mich selbst mehr erreichbar. Ich schwor mir jedenfalls, nie wieder eine mit meinem Namen gezeichnete, auf zehntausend Euro dotierte Sozialgeschichte zur Veröffentlichung freizugeben. *Leistung* war die Geißel meiner Gesinnung, *Druck* der Erzfeind meines Gemüts. Wenn sich die beiden zum *Leistungsdruck* verbündeten, war ich nicht mehr der Mensch, mit dem ich es auf Dauer aushalten konnte, das war schon in der Schule so gewesen. Die letzte Schnapsflasche war leider bereits halbleer – nein, nicht halbvoll, sondern eindeutig halbleer. Und ich war sonst eher ein Schönfärber, überhaupt bei Alkohol, da ging es oft bis ins Tiefblaue hinein. Doch diesmal hielt mich nichts davon ab, einmal so richtig schwarz in die Gegenwart, in die Zukunft und über beides nur scheinbar erhaben ins Nichts zu blicken.

Irgendwann am Nachmittag riss mich das Krächzen meiner Türglocke aus der Agonie. Manuel besaß zwar einen Schlüssel, aber vielleicht hatte er ihn verloren oder vergessen. Mit jemand anderem war prinzipiell nicht zu rechnen.

»Guten Tag, Herr Nachbar, ich will nicht stören«, sagte Frau Engelbrecht. Herr Engelbrecht stand Schulter an Schulter neben ihr und tat so, als wollte er ebenfalls nicht stören. Von allen Menschen, mit denen prinzipiell nicht zu rechnen gewesen war, waren die alten Engelbrechts von nebenan diejenigen, mit denen prinzipiell am allereindeutigsten nicht zu rechnen gewesen war.

»Was kann ich für Sie tun?«, wollte ich fragen, aber ich schaffte es nicht. Denn die Engelbrechts hatten mich mehrmals wegen Lärmbelästigung angezeigt, nur weil ich im Stiegenhaus gestolpert war und dieses Stolpern im Nachhinein vielleicht ein bisschen unschön kommentiert hatte – und vermutlich auch nicht extrem leise.

»Ja, bitte?«, fragte ich. Irgendwie sahen sie beide verklärt drein, wie Spätberufene, die einer Marienerscheinung anheimgefallen waren.

»Herr Plassek, ich habe es gerade in den Nachrichten gehört, und da habe ich mir gedacht, ich und mein Mann, wir müssen das jetzt einmal sagen, wir müssen sagen, was wir uns schon länger denken, nämlich wie sehr wir Sie bewundern und wie glücklich und stolz wir sind, dass wir Tür an Tür ...«

»Was haben Sie in den Nachrichten gehört?«, unterbrach ich sie.

»Von den neuen Spenden«, sagte sie. Sie hatte »neue Spenden« gesagt, Plural.

»Zwei neue Spenden?«, fragte ich.

»Drei neue Spenden, dreißigtausend Euro insgesamt, nicht wahr, Oskar? In den Nachrichten haben sie es groß gebracht, es war gleich die erste Meldung, noch vor dem Anschlag in Syrien, und Sie, Herr Plassek, Sie wurden wieder mit Ihrem Namen genannt, sehr lobend, für die Berichte, die wieder zu den Spenden geführt haben«, sagte sie.

»Welche Berichte?«, fragte ich. Jetzt musste ich es natürlich sofort genau wissen.

»Für die kranken Kinder im Burgenland, für die Rauschgiftsüchtigen auf der Straße und ... was war doch schnell das Dritte, Oskar?«

»Vielleicht Zahnärztinnen?«, fragte ich.

»Ja richtig, die freiwilligen Zahnärztinnen waren es«, erwiderte Frau Engelbrecht.

»Sehr schön, das freut mich«, sagte ich. Sie konnten natürlich nicht ahnen, wie sehr und für wen konkret.

»Und da wollten wir Ihnen einfach ...«

»Das ist nett von Ihnen, vielen Dank«, sagte ich, ein wenig verfrüht. Jedenfalls hatte ich ihnen hiermit verziehen. Sie sahen ja plötzlich irgendwie entzückend aus, so eng nebeneinander und so untypisch nachbarschaftlich. Und als sie mich angezeigt hatten, konnten sie ja noch nicht ahnen, dass ich einmal in den Radio-Weltnachrichten erwähnt werden würde, noch dazu lobend, dass sozusagen eine lokale Berühmtheit unmittelbar neben ihnen wohnte – und das in einem stinknormalen Wiener Gemeindebau, wo man sich gegenseitig nur über die Einhaltung der Hausordnung definierte. »Und da wollten wir Ihnen … als kleines Zeichen, weil wir ja immerhin Tür an Tür wohnen …« Herr Engelbrecht zog ein Päckchen aus der Tasche und überreichte es mir. Es sah zuerst bedrohlich nach Mozartkugeln aus, aber als ich es näher betrachtete, handelte es sich um fünf goldene Münzen, Golddukaten sozusagen. »Wir besitzen sie schon seit fast fünfzig Jahren, sie sollten für etwas ganz Besonderes sein, wir haben nie gewusst, wer sie einmal kriegen soll. Wir sind ja leider ohne Kinder geblieben, also auch ohne Enkel. Aber jetzt wissen wir es. Bei Ihnen sind sie in den besten Händen.«

»Nein, das kann ich nicht annehmen«, wehrte ich mich.

»Doch, das müssen Sie. Es ist unsere Spende, unser kleiner Beitrag«, sagte sie.

»Wir haben keine zehntausend Euro, aber wir haben diese Münzen. Bei Ihnen sind sie gut aufgehoben. Vielleicht können Sie mehr daraus machen, mit Ihren Berichten«, sagte er. Ich war zwar jetzt nicht gerade der wundersame Goldmünzen-Vermehrer, und der Messias war ich ebenfalls nicht, aber wenn es ihnen ein gutes Gefühl bereitete, dann wollte ich jetzt nicht kleinlich sein und nahm das Geschenk schließlich an. Wir schüttelten uns dann noch ausgiebig die Hände, wobei Frau Engelbrecht es sich nicht nehmen ließ, mich an ihren Busen zu drücken. Bevor wir noch Blutsbrüderschaft trinken würden, sagte ich: »Vielen Dank, ich werde Ihnen Bescheid geben, wer von Ihrer Spende profitiert, jetzt muss ich aber wieder …«

Ich hatte es nämlich plötzlich ziemlich eilig, die Situation komplett neu zu überdenken. Und ich konnte es kaum mehr erwarten, dass Manuel endlich kam und ich ihm alle guten Nachrichten erzählen durfte.

Mann der Minute

Zuallererst nahm ich mein Telefon wieder in Betrieb. Zweiundvierzig Anrufe in Abwesenheit – so viele bekam ich normalerweise in einem Jahr. Die meisten hatten es sich nicht nehmen lassen, mir auf die Mobilbox zu sprechen. Clara Nemez gratulierte mir, sagte, dass ich die *Neuzeit* quasi im Alleingang aus dem Dornröschenschlaf erweckt hatte und dass ich mich auf schöne Honorare freuen durfte. Sekretärin Angelina gratulierte mir und richtete mir aus, dass mir alle paar Minuten jemand gratulierte, dass sie mir stündlich die neuen Mails weiterleiten werde, dass es Dutzende Anfragen an mich gab, und sie fragte selbst an, wie sie sich bei Anfragen verhalten sollte und ob wir das vielleicht einmal besprechen könnten.

Meine Mama gratulierte mir mit tränenerstickter Stimme, sagte, dass ihr die Nachbarinnen, die mir ebenfalls gratulierten, immer die Zeitungen mit meinen Artikeln brachten, dass sie so stolz auf mich war, wie schade es war, dass der Papa das nicht mehr erleben durfte, und dass ich bitte aufpassen sollte, mich nicht zu überarbeiten. Darauf wollte ich aufpassen.

Florentina gratulierte mir und teilte mir bei dieser Gelegenheit mit, dass sie es daheim nicht länger aushielt. Gudrun gratulierte mir, teilte mir mit, dass mir auch Berthold gratulierte, lud mich auf ein Familienessen ein und bat mich, doch einmal mit Florentina zu reden, die derzeit nämlich komplett durchdrehte.

Einige mir unbekannte Menschen, denen ich hiermit unter

Protest dazu gratuliere, dass sie an meine Telefonnummer gelangt waren, gratulierten mir und sagten, ich sollte mit meiner Arbeit unbedingt so weitermachen wie bisher, einen Schub in Richtung Barmherzigkeit und Solidarität mit den Schwachen hätte unser Land längst gebraucht.

Tante Julia gratulierte mir, richtete mir aus, dass mir auch Alice gratulierte, und freute sich, mich am Samstag beim Basketballspiel zu sehen.

Einige Journalisten, die ich nicht kannte, einige, die ich kannte, und einige, die ich nicht kennen wollte, gratulierten mir und baten mich zurückzurufen, um einen Termin für ein längst überfälliges Exklusiv-Interview oder für eine Talkshow zu vereinbaren. Außerdem sollte ich ihnen endlich verraten, wer der Spender war, selbstverständlich ganz vertraulich. Auch eine Journalistin vom beliebten deutschen Frauenmagazin *Birgit* gratulierte mir, verriet mir eine *tolle Überraschung*, nämlich dass sie vorhatte, mich von der Redaktion zum *Mann des Jahres* wählen zu lassen. Da stand mir ja ein Quantensprung bevor, hatte ich mich doch bisher damit zufriedengegeben, für die wenigen wichtigen Einzelpersonen in meinem Leben gerade einmal ein *Mann der Minute* zu sein, und selbst solche Minuten hatte ich überdies oft genug verpasst. Des Weiteren drohte mir *Birgit* an, nach Wien zu kommen und mit mir eine *Homestory* zu gestalten. Das war so ungefähr das absurdeste Angebot, dass man mir machen konnte. Zum einen wegen des Zustands, in dem sich mein Miniloft befand, zum anderen, weil mir zum Begriff *Homestory* unwillkürlich *Schlüsselloch* einfiel, das war ein Sex-Heftchen aus meiner Kindheit, das wir unter der Schulbank verschämt weitergereicht hatten, um uns durchs Schlüsselloch *Homestorys* reinzuziehen. Aber vielleicht würde ich tatsächlich zurückrufen und einwilligen, unter der Bedingung, dass mir *Birgit* zuvor einen Putztrupp plus Entrümpelung und Spedition nach Hause schickte.

Eine der letzten Nachrichten kam von Rebecca. Ich hätte sie gerne mehrmals abgehört, schon wegen der darin enthaltenen freudigen Aufgeregtheit, ihr versagte fast die Stimme, was ziemlich anziehend klang, wobei es zugegebenermaßen nichts an Rebecca gab, das ich nicht anziehend fand, ich hätte ihre Nachricht also gerne öfter gehört, aber dann hätte ich mir alle vorangegangenen Mitteilungen ebenfalls noch einmal zu Gemüte führen müssen, inklusive der Homestorysache, und so viel Muße hatte ich nun wirklich nicht. Rebecca sagte unter anderem:

Ich bin so glücklich, ich würde am liebsten die ganze Welt umarmen.

Wie wäre es, wenn sie stellvertretend für die ganze Welt erst einmal mich umarmte, dachte ich. Vielleicht sollte ich ihr diesen Vorschlag am Samstag unterbreiten. Denn es war wahrscheinlich mein derzeit dringlichster Wunsch, für Rebecca ein ganz besonders wichtiger Mensch zu sein, für den Anfang vielleicht einmal ein *Mann der Minute*.

Zwei äußerst verdächtige E-Mails

Stellvertretend für Rebecca und da wiederum stellvertretend für die ganze Welt umarmte ich Manuel, dem das als Vierzehnjährigem zwar ein bisschen unangenehm war, aber da konnte ich ihm jetzt auch nicht helfen.

Ich erzählte ihm von den Golddukaten der Engelbrechts und von den drei neuen anonymen Spenden, über die er natürlich bereits besser informiert war als ich selbst, er war ja im Gegensatz zu mir ein Medienmensch, und auch in der Schule waren die Spenden Thema Nummer eins, nicht zuletzt wegen Paul und dem Geldsegen für das Sterntalerland. Ich genoss in seiner Klasse ja bereits den Ruf eines Volkshelden, einer Art

Che Guevara aus Simmering, erfreulicherweise ohne Foto und deshalb auch ohne bedruckte T-Shirts. Die waren dem anonymen Wohltäter vorbehalten.

»Weißt du eigentlich inzwischen, wer es ist?«, fragte Manuel.

»Nein.«

»Hast du eine Idee?«

»Nein.«

»Einen Verdacht?«

»Nein.«

»Eine Ahnung?«

»Nein.«

»Keine Ahnung?«

»Nein.« Nicht einmal keine.

»Hast du schon deine E-Mails genau angeschaut?«

»Nein, warum?«

»Vielleicht hat er oder sie dir geschrieben.«

»Warum sollte er? Oder sie?«

»So ganz geheim bleiben, das muss ja auf Dauer langweilig sein, stelle ich mir vor. Vielleicht will er oder sie, dass du dahinterkommst, wer er oder sie ist, nur du, und sonst niemand.« Das war ein typischer Manuel-Gedanke, also ein kluger. Und deshalb vereinbarten wir ein Tauschgeschäft: Ich machte mich ohne Murren an seine Deutschaufgabe mit dem Titel *Hausarbeit gerecht aufgeteilt*, das war praktisch genau mein Thema. Und er übernahm dafür mein Internet-Postfach, sortierte die Anfragen, beantwortete die Glückwünsche und filterte eventuelle versteckte Botschaften heraus, die Hinweise auf den Wohltäter enthielten.

Als wir fertig waren – ich übrigens in der Hälfte der Zeit – konnte er mir zwei verdächtige Mails vorlegen. Die erste war eine seltsam formulierte Interview-Anfrage der Programmzeitung *Leute heute* mit dem Text:

Sehr geehrter Herr Plassek, ich würde mich gerne mit Ihnen in einem Vier-Augen-Gespräch über den anonymen »Wohltäter« unterhalten. Wenn Sie nicht wollen, ist das natürlich Ihre Sache, es muss auch gar nicht sein. Wir fänden es allerdings fair, auch Sie hier zu Wort kommen zu lassen. Selbstverständlich ist unser Gespräch vertraulich und sollte bis spätestens Montag stattgefunden haben. Wegen Uhrzeit und Ort bin ich flexibel. Freundliche Grüße, Thomas Liebknecht.

»Das klingt so, als weiß der was«, sagte Manuel.

»Oder er tut nur so und will mich aushorchen.«

»Er hat Wohltäter in Anführungszeichen gesetzt. Das klingt so negativ. Und dass er dich nur der Fairness halber zu Wort kommen lassen will – das gefällt mir gar nicht.« Ich erinnerte Manuel daran, dass *Leute heute* in Zusammenhang mit der Spendenaffäre in einen Prozess wegen Verleumdung der Plus-Eigentümer verwickelt war, und dass aus dieser Ecke nichts Angenehmes zu erwarten war.

»Ich werde ihn einfach ignorieren«, sagte ich.

»Ich würde ihn an deiner Stelle treffen, vielleicht weiß er wirklich was, aber wie du meinst …«, erwiderte Manuel.

Die zweite verdächtige Nachricht las sich in meinen Augen wesentlich brisanter. Sie war nämlich anonymisiert und stammte von der gleichen Adresse, von der ich schon vor ein paar Wochen einmal eine kryptische Mitteilung bekommen hatte. Der Text lautete folgendermaßen:

Sehr geehrter Herr Plassek, warum ausgerechnet Sie? Haben Sie schon Zeit gefunden, in sich zu gehen und darüber nachzusinnen? Wie fühlt es sich an, wenn man plötzlich die Mittel in der Hand hat, ein Überbringer des Guten, ein Bote der Nächstenliebe zu sein? Ich stelle mir vor, dass das ein wunderbares Gefühl sein muss. Ich hoffe, Sie können es genießen. Ihr treuer Leser. PS: Was sagt eigentlich Ihre Frau Mama dazu?

Ehrlich gestanden bewegte mich diese Botschaft, vor allem der PS-Satz, da hob es mir sogar ein bisschen die Magengrube aus.

»Weißt du, was ich mir gerade denke?«

»Ja, ungefähr«, sagte Manuel.

»Dass die Spende zwar nichts mit mir selbst zu tun hat, aber dafür vielleicht ...«

»Mit deiner Mutter«, sagte er.

»Ja, das kann ich mir vorstellen. Sie ist nämlich wirklich ein guter Mensch und hat allen immer nur geholfen.«

»Vielleicht kennt er sie«, sagte Manuel.

»Wer, der E-Mail-Schreiber oder der Geldspender?«

»Vielleicht einer von beiden, oder beide oder ein und derselbe«, erwiderte er. Das war mir zwar ein bisschen zu intellektuell, aber er meinte vermutlich, dass der E-Mail-Schreiber tatsächlich auch der Wohltäter sein konnte und dass er mit meiner Mutter in Verbindung stand. Jedenfalls formulierten wir sofort eine Antwortmail und schickten sie ihm:

Sehr geehrter »treuer Leser«, nein, ich weiß nicht, warum ausgerechnet ich der Bote dieses großzügigen Wohltäters und guten Menschen werden durfte. Haben Sie vielleicht einen Anhaltspunkt für mich? Können Sie mir ein Stichwort geben? Und noch eine Frage: Kennen Sie meine Mutter? Darf ich ihr etwas ausrichten? Vielleicht würde sie sich ja freuen. Herzliche Grüße, Gerold Plassek.

»Weißt du, was *ich* mir schon ein paarmal gedacht habe?«, fragte mich Manuel ein bisschen später.

»Nein«, erwiderte ich. Ich war leider kein so begnadeter Mitdenker.

»Aber du darfst mich nicht auslachen«, sagte er.

»Würde ich nie tun«, schwindelte ich.

»Ich hab mir gedacht, dass die Spende zwar nichts mit dir zu tun hat, aber dafür vielleicht ...« Er machte eine extralange

Pause, doch ich kam einfach nicht dahinter. »Sondern mit mir, das heißt, eigentlich mit meiner Mama.«

»Interessant«, sagte ich und meinte es auch ganz genau so.

»Ja, das kann ich mir nämlich auch gut vorstellen. Weil meine Mama ist nämlich auch ein wirklich sehr guter Mensch und hat schon vielen geholfen.«

»Stimmt.«

»Und die Spenden gibt es erst, seit wir beide uns kennen, also seit ich zu dir ins Büro gekommen bin, genau da hat es begonnen.«

»Stimmt eigentlich, Manuel, genau da hat alles begonnen«, sagte ich.

KAPITEL ZWÖLF

Showeinlage in der Sportarena

Ich war an sich der Typ, der eine relativ klar eingegrenzte Vorstellung von den Dingen hatte, die auf ihn zukamen. Oft war die Vorstellung so klar eingegrenzt, dass ich gar nicht groß darüber nachdachte, was sonst noch auf mich zukommen könnte. Das war ein Fehler, wie ich am Samstagnachmittag bemerkte. Da war meine Vorstellung gewesen, dass ich Zuschauer bei einem Jugend-Basketballmatch sein würde, bei dem »mein« Manuel mitspielte und Rebecca hoffentlich neben mir saß. Und dann hatte ich mir noch vorgestellt, dass Manuels Torpedo 15 einen spielentscheidenden Korb warfen, Rebecca und ich würden aufspringen und jubeln, würden uns im Zuge des Jubelns in die Arme fallen, und ich war plötzlich ihr *Mann der Minute*. Das war aber ehrlich gestanden eher eine Phantasie als eine Vorstellung.

Ich hätte jedenfalls niemals in Erwägung gezogen, auf die Idee kommen zu können, mir vorzustellen, dass es mir so ergehen würde, als wäre ich nicht ich, sondern, sagen wir, Elvis Presley, der aus Madame Tussauds Wachsfigurenkabinett heraus wieder ins Leben getreten war und in der Ottakringer Körner-Sporthalle in voller Montur die Zuschauertribüne betrat, und zwar ohne fünfzig Mann stiernackiger und mit Kalaschnikows bewaffneter Security um sich, sondern lediglich flankiert von einer Fitnesstrainerin und einer Zahnärztin. Was ich damit sagen will: Praktisch alle Menschen dort erkannten mich, noch dazu gleichzeitig, verlangten ein Autogramm von mir, wollten mich fotografieren, wollten sich mit mir fotografieren lassen, während ich ihnen ein Autogramm gab, wollten mit mir über die Spendenserie reden, wollten sich mit mir fotografieren lassen, während ich ihnen ein Autogramm gab und mit ihnen über die Spendenserie redete. Und so weiter. Und in der Kantine gab es überdies nur alkoholfreies Bier – diese Sportler und Sportfreunde mussten mit ihrem Gesundheitsdenken immer übers Ziel hinausschießen.

Endlich ging es in Richtung Anpfiff, der Trubel ließ nach, und ich konnte, im Grunde bereits völlig fertig, auf meinen Sitz sinken. Zwischen mich, Rebecca und meine Phantasie quetschte sich übrigens noch Tante Julia. Und am Spielfeldrand musste sich jetzt unbedingt auch noch ein Jugendsportreferent oder sogar Präsident mit Mikrofon ein bisschen wichtig machen.

»Gestatten Sie mir zu diesem besonderen Anlass ein paar einleitende Worte«, sagte er. Dann erzählte er von Machmut Pajew, dass es ein kleines Wunder war, dass er heute hier sein und mitspielen durfte, dass das Asylverfahren neu aufgerollt wurde und die Chancen gut standen, dass die Pajews echte Österreicher werden konnten, dass es an diesem Nachmittag keinen Verlierer geben würde, weil die Menschlichkeit gesiegt hatte, und dass das vor allem vier Personen zu verdanken war, einem großherzigen Paar, das die Familie aufgenommen hatte, einem großzügigen geheimen Wohltäter, der die Mittel zur Verfügung gestellt hatte, und »last but not least ...« O nein, bitte nicht! »... und deshalb freut es uns sehr, Herrn Gerold Plassek hier heute begrüßen zu dürfen, der es sich nicht nehmen hat lassen, diesem besonderen Spiel beizuwohnen. Ich darf ihn nun zu mir herunterbitten und um ein paar kurze Worte ersuchen.« Mein erstes Wort war tatsächlich kurz und lautete »Nein«. Es ging allerdings im Applaus unter. Gleichzeitig beugte sich Rebecca an Julia vorbei zu mir, warf mir einen tief bewundernden, ansatzweise sogar eroberungsfreudigen Blick zu und gab mir damit untrüglich das Zeichen, ihr

Mann der Minute zu sein, der mittels kurzer Ansprache sogar zum *Mann der Stunde* avancieren konnte. Das war schlimm, denn ich verabscheute Öffentlichkeit, und ich hasste Reden. Doch es half nichts, ich musste es tun. Ich musste nun öffentlich reden.

»Ich kann mich wirklich kurz fassen, weil mein Vorredner im Grunde bereits alles Wichtige gesagt hat«, begann ich mit der mir innewohnenden Leidenschaft für Ansprachen.

»Was hier vielleicht noch nicht so bekannt ist, ist mein persönliches Motiv, mich um diese Sache, also um Machmut und seine Familie, ganz besonders zu bemühen.« Dieser Satz hatte sich unaufgefordert und jedenfalls ohne Zutun meines Denkapparats von meiner Zunge gelöst. Danach stockte ich und überlegte, ob dies denn wirklich der richtige Rahmen war und ob ich es Manuel zumuten konnte, hier meine Vater-Sohn-Geschichte auszubreiten. Dann fiel mir auf, dass das ganz und gar nicht ging. Ich musste mir also sehr plötzlich, quasi in der Sekunde, etwas anderes einfallen lassen.

»Ich war als Kind leider ein fürchterlich mieser Basketballspieler«, begann ich. »Selbst wenn man mir eine Leiter zum Korb hingestellt hätte – ich hätte wahrscheinlich danebengetroffen oder den Korb aus seiner Verankerung gerissen.« Einige im Publikum lachten, das motivierte mich. »Vor etwa zwei Monaten habe ich aus den begeisterten Schilderungen meines jungen … Bürogefährten, des Basketballspielers Manuel, erstmals von seinem Freund Machmut erfahren, und zwar dass dieser Teufelskerl, dieser Wirbelwind von Torpedo 15, aus großer Entfernung die irrsten Körbe werfen kann. Und dann erzählte mir Manuel irgendwann, dass dem vierzehnjährigen Buben die österreichische Luft nicht vergönnt sein soll, die er hier atmet, dass er und seine Eltern aus ihrer neuen Heimat vertrieben werden sollen. Da dachte ich: Nein, nein, so geht das nicht, die müssen hierbleiben, denn der Bub muss mir unbedingt zeigen, wie er das macht, wie er diese spektakulären Körbe wirft. So kam es zu der Reportage. Das war quasi mein Motiv.« Das Argument war offenbar stichhaltig, denn im Publikum wurde heftig geklatscht. »Jetzt packe ich die Gelegenheit sozusagen beim Schopf. Machmut, kannst du bitte hierher zu mir kommen, und wir beide treten je einmal zum Wurf an. Und zwar zuerst du, dann sehe ich endlich aus der Nähe, wie es funktioniert. Und anschließend probiere ich es.« Da wurde ziemlich laut gelacht, die Leute liebten ja Brot und Spiele, bei denen es schon im Vorfeld selbsternannte Verlierer wie mich gab. Der aufgeregte Zwerg mit den roten, vermutlich glühend heißen, Segelohren nahm den Ball, stellte sich an die Mittellinie, nahm elegant Schwung und pfefferte die Kugel leider knapp neben das Gehäuse. Das war klar, der Druck war einfach zu groß gewesen.

»Das ist sehr nett von dir, Machmut, du bist wirklich ein extrem höflicher Bub und willst mich hier nicht öffentlich blamieren, da musst du als Österreicher aber noch einiges dazulernen«, sagte ich. Ab jetzt war ganz egal, was ich sagte, sie lachten auf jeden Fall. Ich lud Machmut also zu einem zweiten Versuch ein, da hatte sich seine Anspannung schon gelegt, und er baute den Ball unter frenetischem Jubel exakt in der Mitte des Korbkreises ein.

»Danke, Machmut, ich glaube, jetzt habe ich es begriffen«, sagte ich. Ich übergab also dem Buben kurz das Mikrofon, nahm den Ball, ging theatralisch in die Knie, holte Schwung und warf. Die Kugel verendete unter schadenfrohem Gelächter und Getöse des Publikums etwa auf halber Strecke. »Okay, Machmut, die Technik hast du mir beigebracht. Jetzt fehlen mir nur noch drei Wochen intensives Krafttraining. Danach melde ich mich und fordere Revanche«, sagte ich. Dafür erntete ich noch ein paar hundert Dezibel Abschiedsapplaus, schritt zurück zur Zuschauertribüne und setzte mich, nein, ich quetschte mich zwischen Julia und Rebecca. Das hatte ich mir nämlich redlich verdient, fand ich.

Inniger Jubel mit Rebecca

Ein paar Worte zum Spiel: Es verlief hochdramatisch, sodass ich mein Jahreskontingent an Adrenalin ausschüttete. Und mit den Nerven, die ich zwischenzeitlich verlor, hätte man eine Gebirgsseilbahnanlage errichten können. Nach dem ersten Viertel führte Torpedo 15, nach dem zweiten Union CS, nach dem dritten Torpedo 15, nach dem vierten Union CS – und mehr als vier Viertel gab es leider prinzipiell nicht, zumindest nicht in der Mathematik, nur in der Weinschenke. Somit ging das Spiel zwar mit 105 zu 98 Punkten knapp zu Ungunsten von Manuel und Machi aus, aber das war halb so schlimm, denn Union CS hätte mit elf Punkten Differenz gewinnen müssen, um Meister zu werden. Somit konnte sich Torpedo 15 trotz Niederlage den Herbsttitel sichern, und kein Bub verließ das Feld mit hängendem Kopf.

Mein Sohn hatte, dies sei hier in aller väterlichen Bescheidenheit bemerkt, eine Glanzpartie hingelegt. Zwischendurch dachte man, er hätte sich den Ball um die Hand gebunden, weil er praktisch nicht davon zu trennen war, bis er im Korb landete – der Ball. Manuel selbst blieb immer auf dem Boden. Der kleine Machmut war wieselflink und entschlüpfte seinen Bewachern serienmäßig. Einige Male wurde er ziemlich derb gefoult, als Entschädigung verwandelte er einen Strafwurf nach dem anderen und versenkte das Leder überdies ein paarmal spektakulär und aus großer Distanz im gegnerischen Körbchen.

98 Punkte für Torpedo 15 – das bedeutete für mich gut fünf-

zig Mal Jubel, mehr noch, gemeinsamer Jubel mit Rebecca, wohl auch gemeinsamer Jubel mit Julia, aber gemeinsamer Jubel war nicht gleich gemeinsamer Jubel, das war für mich eine der großen Lehren aus diesem Spiel. Denn wenn man mit einer Frau, die man vorher schon heiß verehrt hatte, gut fünfzig Mal gemeinsam jubelte, dann war man nachher mit ihr emotional praktisch zusammengewachsen und hatte eigentlich bereits ein prächtiges Fundament für eine langjährige Partnerschaft gelegt, fand ich. Nichts ließ sich zu zweit nämlich inniger teilen als Begeisterung.

»Ich muss mich dann leider schon verabschieden«, widersprach Rebecca wenig später. Richtig, ihr stand ja noch dieses völlig unnötige Rendezvous ins Haus, das jetzt wirklich keiner brauchte, und das sie offenbar nicht ganz so gut verdrängt hatte wie ich. Das war für mich wohl ein kleiner Dämpfer, aber ich spürte, dass es der Samstagabend-Mann mit ihr heute schwer haben würde, und damit musste ich mich einstweilen zufriedengeben.

Bedrohlicher Abgang

Auf dem Weg von der Tribüne zum Ausgang sprachen mich alle möglichen Leute an, die meisten wollten zum Glück nur *guten Tag* oder *tolles Spiel* oder *lustige Einlage* oder *jämmerlicher Wurf* sagen, oder sie baten, dass ich mich kurz zu ihnen drehte, weil sie dringend noch ein Bild von mir brauchten. Fotografen sind ja im Grunde extrem bescheiden in ihren Motiv-Ansprüchen, manchmal, wenn sie als Touristen tätig sind, fotografieren sie überhaupt nur Statuen, das heißt, sie bilden Abbildungen von Abbildungen von Einbildungen ab, und dies oft mit atemberaubender Hingabe.

Ein Mann im weißen Sakko war mir schon vorher aufgefallen, weil ich mich von ihm irgendwie beobachtet gefühlt hatte, und weil er das Kunststück zuwege gebracht hatte, in einer dichten Menschenmasse auf zehn Meter Entfernung aufdringlich zu erscheinen. Außerdem, wer trug in seiner Freizeit ein weißes Sakko, beziehungsweise wer trug überhaupt freiwillig ein weißes Sakko, außer er kam gerade aus einem Bordell in Bangkok? Nun strebte der Mann zappeligen Schrittes unmittelbar neben mir dem Ausgang zu, was den Anschein von Aufdringlichkeit noch exponentiell verstärkte.

»Verzeihung, Herr Plassek, darf ich Sie was fragen?«

»Fragen darf man immer, sage ich immer«, sagte ich, weil ich leider oft zum ungünstigsten Zeitpunkt ein höflicher Mensch war.

»Kennen Sie einen gewissen Herrn Berthold Hille?« Das war eine sonderbare und auffallend nicht hierhergehörende Frage, die mich sofort stutzig machte, sodass ich abrupt stehen blieb.

»Ja, den kenne ich. Warum fragen Sie?«

»Stimmt es, dass es zwischen Ihnen und Herrn Hille ein gewisses ... Naheverhältnis gibt?« So, jetzt wurde mir der Mann aber langsam körperlich unangenehm.

»Naheverhältnis? Schwer zu sagen. Was ist Nähe? Was ist ein Verhältnis? Außerdem, warum fragen Sie? Und wer sind Sie überhaupt?«

»Stimmt es, Herr Plassek, dass Herr Hille der zweite Mann Ihrer ehemaligen Gattin ist und dass Sie sich auch öfter privat treffen?«, fragte er weiter.

»Ich glaube nicht, dass das eine Frage ist, die auf einen Basketballplatz gehört. Ich glaube auch nicht, dass Sie das etwas angeht, oder irre ich mich da?«, erwiderte ich. Aber der Mann war nicht mehr zu bremsen.

»Wussten Sie, dass gegen Herrn Hille ein Strafverfahren wegen Scheingeschäften und wegen des Verdachts der Geld-

wäsche läuft und dass er Schwarzgeldkonten in Liechtenstein ...«

»Wer sind Sie, und was wollen Sie von mir?«, fragte ich
derart unfreundlich, dass ich mich an seiner Stelle schon ein
bisschen vor mir gefürchtet hätte. Aber der Mann war nicht
ängstlich, und er erklärte auch gleich, warum nicht.

»Ich bin Journalist bei *Leute heute*. Mein Name ist Thomas
Liebknecht, ich habe Ihnen eine E-Mail geschrieben. Ich recherchiere im Fall Berthold Hille ...« Okay, jetzt wusste ich wenigstens, wo ich diese Figur hintun musste.

»Dann gebe ich Ihnen den kollegialen Tipp, dass Sie im Fall
Hille bei Herrn Hille recherchieren. Und wenn Sie irgendwann einmal im Fall Plassek recherchieren, dann kommen Sie
wieder zu mir, falls ich dann noch am Leben bin, einverstanden?«, sagte ich und wandte mich Julia zu, die mich ziemlich
verunsichert ansah.

»Wie Sie wollen«, rief mir der Mann bedrohlich nach. »Nur
zu Ihrem Verständnis, ich recherchiere nicht nur im Fall Hille,
sondern auch bereits im Fall Plassek. Sie können mich morgen
noch den ganzen Tag erreichen.«

Liebe, hallo, hello, hi

Am Sonntag hatte ich erwartungsgemäß den ganzen Tag keine
Lust, diesen schmierigen Typ im weißen Sakko zu erreichen,
auch wenn er das weiße Sakko bereits durch ein normales er-
setzt haben sollte. Aber ich konnte nicht behaupten, dass mir
egal war, was er da gesagt beziehungsweise gefragt hatte. Ehrlich gestanden hatte dieser Liebknecht mir den kompletten
Schlaf geraubt. Natürlich hätte ich jetzt, da ich mehr oder weniger hellwach war, allerlei Spekulationen anstellen können,
worauf der *Leute-heute*-Widerling eigentlich konkret hinaus-

wollte. Aber es entsprach nicht meinem Naturell, mich mit Dingen zu beschäftigen, bei deren näherer Betrachtung ich Gefahr lief, mich zu grausen. Diesen Liebknecht zum Beispiel hatte ich für mein Leben lang nah genug gesehen, und Berthold war eben ein pseudofamiliärer Sonderfall, der für mich ohnehin nur auf Distanz erträglich war.

Genau gegensätzlich verhielt es sich natürlich mit Rebecca, bei der ich meinem Herzenswunsch, sie zu erreichen, stündlich beim Wachsen zusehen oder zuhören konnte. Immerhin war ich mittlerweile stolzer Besitzer ihrer privaten Telefonnummer, aber ich war nicht der Typ, der Besitz sehr lange nur für sich behalten konnte, also schrieb ich ihr zu Mittag eine SMS. Ich wollte bewusst so schreiben, wie jemand schrieb, dem man nicht anmerken konnte, warum er schrieb, also schrieb ich: *Liebe Rebecca*, aus *Liebe* machte ich *Hallo*, aus *Hallo Hello*, aus *Hello Hi*, aus *Hi* dann wieder *Hello* und aus *Hello* schließlich doch *Hallo*, weil *Hallo* eigentlich genau die Mitte zwischen *Liebe* und *Hi* war. Ich schrieb:

Hallo Rebecca, schön, dass du gestern beim Spiel dabei warst. Manuel hat sich sehr gefreut. Ich hoffe, du hattest noch einen spannenden Abend. Aus *spannend* machte ich *interessant*, aus *interessant anregend*, aus *anregend nett* – nett im Sinne der platonischen Kehrseite von *scheiße* –, aus *nett* schließlich *angenehm*, das klang irgendwie gerade noch positiv und genügte vollkommen. Daran schloss ich an: *Wir hatten es noch sehr lustig.* Das war mein Lieblingssatz, weil *wir* nicht näher bestimmt war und somit Rebeccas Phantasie anregen konnte, und weil sie es außerdem garantiert auch sehr gerne lustig mit *uns* gehabt hätte, lieber jedenfalls, als sich von diesem Samstagabend-Gigolo stundenlang plump anbaggern zu lassen und sich zwischendurch seine öden Angebergeschichten anhören zu müssen. Schließlich schrieb ich noch: *Hab einen schönen Sonntag, und ich hoffe, wir sehen uns bald! Gerold.* Das war noch nicht perfekt, ich korrigierte zu: *Hab einen schönen Sonntag. Hoffe, wir sehen uns bald. Gerold. Hoffe* klang beiläufiger als *und ich hoffe*, es klang nach einer Hoffnung, auf die der Hoffende nicht angewiesen war. So gesehen war *hoffe* eigentlich die Unwahrheit, aber egal.

Manuel prüft Oma auf Herz und Nieren

Sonntagnachmittag besuchten wir Mama. Nicht Rebecca und ich, Manuel und ich. Es war schon eher verwunderlich, dass er mitging, aber vielleicht hatte er unter Einsatz eines tief vergrabenen Urinstinkts gespürt, dass er mir damit eine Riesenfreude machte und dass das für meine Mama eine ganz besondere Begegnung sein würde, auch wenn sie noch nicht erfahren sollte, weshalb, denn das musste ich erst einmal Manuel selbst sagen. Der Dialog, der zu dem Besuch geführt hatte, hörte sich jedenfalls eher lapidar an.

»Was machst du am Sonntag?«

»Was soll ich am Sonntag machen?«, fragte Manuel zurück.

»Was steht zur Auswahl?«, fragte ich wiederum zurück. Ich tappte ihm jetzt nämlich nur noch selten in die Rückfrage-Falle.

»Weiß noch nicht. Was machst du?«

»Ich besuche meine Mama.«

»Aha.«

»Willst du mitkommen?«

»Ja.«

»Ja?«

»Ja.«

»Ehrlich?«

»Ja, ehrlich.«

»Warum?«

»Weil mich interessiert, ob sie auch so ist wie du.«

»Wie, auch so wie ich?«, fragte ich.

»Ob sie auch so viel Bier trinkt.« Er lachte.

Wir brachten ihr einen rosa blühenden Weihnachtsstern mit, ferner zwei Packungen Kaffee und einen Marmorkuchen vom Billa, der im Angebot gewesen war, vermutlich hatte er die Feinstaub-Warnstufe überschritten. Mama liebte trockenen Kuchen. Sie sah gut aus, zumindest machte ich sie sofort darauf aufmerksam, und sie hatte tatsächlich schon einmal weniger Gesichtsfarbe und tiefer eingefallene Wangen gehabt.

»Das ist Manuel«, sagte ich, ohne nähere Angaben zu machen. Meine Mama war eine höfliche, kultivierte Frau, die niemals nachgefragt hätte, aus welchem Ärmel ich plötzlich einen vierzehnjährigen Buben geschüttelt hatte, was er hier wollte und wer er überhaupt war. Letzteres wusste sie übrigens ohnehin.

»Du musst der Bub sein, der so hinreißend über den anderen Buben geschrieben hat, ich habe alles gelesen«, sagte sie und umarmte ihn, ohne dass er sich davon unangenehm berührt gefühlt hätte – trotz schwerer Pubertät. Das war für mich eine ergreifend schöne Szene, ich wollte sie mir fest einprägen, fürs Familienalbum sozusagen.

Mama und ich erzählten uns dann eine Weile gegenseitig, wie phantastisch gut es uns ging, woran ich erst merkte, dass es mir eigentlich wirklich ziemlich gut ging, abgesehen von ein bisschen Liebeskummer – Rebecca hatte meine SMS noch immer nicht beantwortet. Mama blühte so richtig auf, weil sie ihr eigenes Wohlbefinden immer am Wohlbefinden der anderen maß, überhaupt an *meinem* Wohlbefinden, da nahm sie immer gleich doppelt Maß. Und Manuel saß andächtig daneben und beobachtete uns beide mit für mich unerklärlich großem Interesse.

Natürlich kamen wir bald auf die Spendenserie und die mir zugewiesene Schlüsselrolle darin zu sprechen.

»Ist das nicht verrückt?«, fragte ich.

»Nein, das finde ich gar nicht verrückt, Geri. Da hat dir jemand eine Aufgabe zugewiesen«, erwiderte Mama.

»Und warum gerade mir?«

»Wahrscheinlich, weil du sie erfüllen kannst«, sagte sie.

»Das könnten viele.«

»Da bin ich mir nicht so sicher.«

»Wissen Sie, wer es ist?«, mischte sich Manuel ins Gespräch ein. Er hatte plötzlich diesen Hauptkommissar-Blick, und jetzt wusste ich auf einmal, warum er unbedingt hatte mitgehen wollen. Er hatte sich offenbar in den Kopf gesetzt, den Fall aufzuklären.

»Wer es ist? Ist das denn so wichtig?«, fragte Mama und lächelte, wie eine altersweise Frau lächelt, die scheinbar grundlos altersweise lächelt, die aber ganz genau weiß, warum sie altersweise lächelt.

»Onkel Geri hat nämlich eine geheimnisvolle E-Mail gekriegt«, erklärte Manuel. Da war er mir wieder einmal zuvorgekommen, ich hätte das erst später erwähnt.

»Ja, Mama, da hat mir jemand eine E-Mail geschickt, in der er am Ende so eine eigenartige Anspielung macht ...«

»Ich habe sie hier. Ich habe sie ausgedruckt«, unterbrach mich Manuel, holte einen Zettel hervor und überreichte ihn ihr. Es war schon verblüffend, wie extrem gut der Bub immer auf alles vorbereitet war, vielleicht sollte ich doch einen Vaterschaftstest machen. Mama setzte jedenfalls ihre Lesebrille auf und überflog den Text, ohne von ihrem entspannten Lächeln abzurücken. Bruchstückhaft murmelte sie vor sich hin: *Sehr geehrter Herr Plassek ... die Mittel ... ein Überbringer des Guten ... wunderbares Gefühl ... genießen. Ihr treuer Leser. PS: ... Was sagt eigentlich Ihre Frau Mama dazu ...?* Manuel hatte sie mit zugekniffenen Augen beobachtet, aber aus ihrer Reaktion konnte man nicht viel klüger werden, als Manuel ohnehin bereits gewesen war.

»Und, Mama, was sagst du zu dieser Botschaft?«, fragte ich.

»Das ist ein treuer Leser, der es gut mit dir meint und der sich mit dir freut.«

»Und mit dir.«

»Und mit mir.«

»Und wer?«, fragte Manuel.

»Wenn er sich zu erkennen geben will, wird er es schon tun«, erwiderte sie ausweichend.

»Onkel Geri hat ihm zurückgeschrieben und gefragt, ob wir Ihnen Grüße ausrichten sollen, aber er hat noch nicht geantwortet«, berichtete Manuel. Ich mochte es, wenn er »Onkel Geri« sagte.

»Dann will er sich wahrscheinlich nicht zu erkennen geben.«

»Und du weißt wirklich nicht, wer es ist?«, fragte nun auch ich, aber eher stellvertretend für den ungeduldigen Manuel.

»Wenn ich ehrlich bin, will ich es gar nicht wissen«, sagte sie.

»Warum nicht? Es könnte der Spender sein«, bemerkte Manuel.

»Ja, das könnte sein. Ich will aber auch nicht wissen, wer der Spender oder die Spenderin ist.«

»Warum nicht?

»Weil es doch so viel schöner für uns alle ist«, sagte sie.

»Was ist so schöner für uns alle?«

»Wenn wir nicht wissen, wer es ist.«

»Warum ist das schöner?«, fragte Manuel.

»Dann kann es jeder sein«, erwiderte sie.

KAPITEL DREIZEHN

Mutmaßlicher Wohltäter enttarnt

Hallo Gerold, danke für deine nette SMS von gestern. Der Nachmittag mit dir und Julia und Manuel hat mir großen Spaß gemacht. Mit euch wäre es am Abend sicher lustiger gewesen. Na ja, wieder was dazugelernt. Ich hoffe, wir sehen uns bald, vielleicht mal auf einen Kaffee? Herzlich, Rebecca.

Die *Neuzeit* hatte mir leider nur eine knappe Stunde gegönnt, diesen außergewöhnlich erfreulichen Beginn eines Montags mit meinem Handy, dem Übermittler von Rebeccas Nachricht, im Bett zu verbringen, wenn schon nicht mit ihr selbst. Dann rief Clara Nemez an, und ich drückte irrtümlich auf *Annehmen* statt wie üblicherweise an Montagen auf *Ablehnen*, wodurch der Tag unwiderruflich kippte.

»Hallo Gerold, hast du schon *Leute heute* gesehen?«, fragte sie.

»Nein, warum sollte ich?« Das war wirklich eine groteske Idee, da wäre die Wahrscheinlichkeit größer gewesen, dass ich zufällig eine unangekündigte Sonnenfinsternis beobachtet hatte.

»Die präsentieren uns den Spender.«

»Wen?«

»Den anonymen Spender.«

»Ehrlich? Wer ist es?«

»Berthold Hille.«

»Wer?«

»Berthold Hille.«

»Berthold?«

»Hille«, sagte sie. Ich bemühte mich zu lachen, aber diese Pointe war selbst mir zu makaber.

»Berthold Hille war offenbar der anonyme Wohltäter«, wiederholte sie. Dazu fiel mir spontan gar nichts ein, zumindest nichts, was meinem Gehirn zumutbar war. Ich stand also zunächst einmal eine Zeitlang ganz bewusst unter Schock und schwor mir, diesen Zustand frühestens in Zoltan's Bar wieder zu verlassen. Bis zum rettenden Ufer war es allerdings noch ein weiter Weg.

»Kannst du zu uns in die Redaktion kommen?«

»Wann?«, fragte ich.

»Am besten gleich.«

»Muss das sein?«

»Ich glaube, dass es wirklich notwendig wäre«, erwiderte sie.

Die Titelseite erweckte den Anschein, als hätte man eines der größten Rätsel der Kriminalgeschichte gelöst. Die fetteste der Schlagzeilen lautete: *Mutmaßlicher Wohltäter ausgeforscht.* Das war meiner Meinung nach ein grober Widerspruch, denn entweder man mutmaßte, wer der Wohltäter war, oder man hatte ihn ausgeforscht, beides gleichzeitig war nur medial möglich, und zwar in Schmierblättern wie *Leute heute.* Unter der Schlagzeile befand sich dann ein Riesenbild von Berthold mit arrogant verzogenem Mundwinkel und Zigarre in der Hand. Das Foto war naturgemäß extrem unvorteilhaft, unter anderem deshalb, weil man es gar nicht viel vorteilhafter hätte hinkriegen können. Berthold hatte eben eines der wenigen Gesichter, dem mit einem schwarzen Balken über den Augen noch wirklich gedient wäre, was die Sympathie anging. Aber vielleicht war ich da nicht ganz objektiv.

Der Rest der Seite bestand hauptsächlich aus fettgedruckten alarmierenden Wortfetzen:

Leute heute exklusiv: Knalleffekt in der Spendenserie.

Nichts als Schwarzgeld-Geschenke für die Armen.

Ein Lobbyist spielte Weihnachtsmann.

Plus-Gruppe in den Finanzschwindel involviert.

Tag-für-Tag-Journalist fungierte als Geldbote. [Damit meinten sie mich.]

Ausführliche Berichte und Hintergründe zum Spendenskandal, Seiten 2 bis 8.

Ich las mir das jetzt natürlich nicht im Detail durch, und es war auch gar nicht so leicht, die wenigen Fakten aus dieser Sumpflandschaft billiger Effekthaschereien herauszufiltern, aber so viel stand fest: Gegen Berthold Hille lief tatsächlich ein Strafverfahren wegen des Verdachts der Steuerhinterziehung. Die Behörde war bei ihren Ermittlungen auf ein geheimes Konto in Liechtenstein gestoßen, von dem in den vergangenen Monaten immer wieder hohe Geldsummen abgebucht worden waren, mehrmals waren es exakt zehntausend Euro gewesen. Außerdem hatte es Geldflüsse und angeblich dazupassende belastende Telefongespräche zwischen Hille und Axel Mittereiner gegeben, einem Vorstandsmitglied der Handelskette Plus.

Jedenfalls war es laut *Leute heute* für die ermittelnden Beamten *hundert Kilometer gegen den Wind zu riechen*, dass die Wohltäterserie *ein übles Komplott und ein Machwerk aus den schmutzigen Händen von Geschäftemachern und Lobbyisten* war.

Involviert in den Schwindel, so las man, war auch *Gerold Plassek, der erste Ehemann der Industriellengattin*. Dazu hatten sie sich ein schönes Symbolfoto von mir beim Basketballspiel ausgesucht, auf dem ich in Abwehrhaltung alle zehn Finger von mir streckte, scheinbar um mein Gesicht zu verbergen. Bildtext: *Der vermeintliche Glücksbote Plassek – im Gespräch mit Chefreporter Liebknecht gab er sich eher wortkarg.*

Und was sagte eigentlich Berthold zu den Vorwürfen? *Auf*

Anfrage von Leute heute *hieß es, der Industrielle befinde sich auf Dienstreise in Dubai und sei derzeit zu keiner Stellungnahme bereit.*

Zum Abschluss überflog ich noch Liebknechts Kommentar:

ENTZAUBERT. Es war wie im Märchen: Die Ärmsten der Armen erhalten riesige Geldgeschenke von unsichtbarer Hand. 10 000 Euro für die Obdachlosen, 10 000 für die Straßenkinder, 10 000 da, 10 000 dort. Und eine tschetschenische Familie durfte weiter vom Wohlstands-Paradies träumen. Nun ist die Märchenstunde vorbei. Ein Industrieller, dem die Behörden auf der Spur sind, weiß nicht, wohin mit seinem vielen Schwarzgeld. Ein Großhandelsriese will seine angeschlagene Gratiszeitung retten. Was macht man? Man erfindet den Weihnachtsmann neu. Zur Schlüsselfigur in dem Spiel wurde ein Verwandter des Industriellen, ein bis dato unscheinbarer Journalist. Um den Verdacht vom Gratisblatt abzulenken, verlagerte man die großen Geschenk-Aktionen in ein linksalternatives Blatt. Noch sind nicht alle Rätsel gelöst, noch bleiben viele Detailfragen offen. Und vom Gesetz her gilt felsenfest die Unschuldsvermutung. Aber es lässt sich schon jetzt die ernüchternde Bilanz ziehen: Das Gute ist wieder einmal entzaubert. Geld ist schmutzig. Und es regiert die Welt.

Clara ratlos, Neuzeit in Not

»Gerold, was ich dich natürlich zu allererst fragen muss ... Bitte nimm es mir nicht übel, aber das sollten wir ... das muss einfach geklärt sein ...«, druckste Clara herum.

»Du meinst, ob ich ...? Nein, ich hatte keinen blassen Schimmer von alldem, das kannst du mir glauben«, sagte ich.

»Danke«, murmelte sie. Sie wirkte ziemlich zerstört, meiner Meinung nach brauchte sie dringend einen Schnaps, aber darauf musste sie schon selbst kommen. Was ich gerade brauchte, könnte man wahrscheinlich gar nicht mehr in herkömmliche Gläser abfüllen.

»Mit Berthold – da gab es nie Gespräche. Sein Geld, woher er es hat, wie er es vermehrt, wo es liegt, was er damit tut, das hat mich nie interessiert. Geld hat mich nie interessiert. Berthold hat mich nie interessiert. Er lebt in einer anderen Welt, die mich ankotzt. Leider lebt er dort mit meiner Ex. Und mit Florentina. Hab ich dir schon von Florentina erzählt? Das ist meine Kleine. Also so klein ist sie eigentlich gar nicht mehr ...« Ich hörte dann besser auf zu reden, denn ich merkte, dass ich meine Stimme nicht mehr so ganz unter Kontrolle hatte. Ich durfte jetzt nur nicht an Mama denken oder an Manuel oder an die Pajews oder an Rebecca oder auch nur an die Engelbrechts, wie sie an meiner Tür gestanden hatten, mit den Golddukaten in der Hand. »Scheiße«, sagte ich. Clara nickte, sie war ganz meiner Meinung. Wir saßen dann eine Weile einfach nur wortlos da, weil »Scheiße« ohnehin für sich stand und keiner weiteren Erklärung bedurfte.

»Glaubst du, dass an der Sache wirklich was dran ist? Ich meine, traust du Berthold Hille so was zu?«, fragte sie schließlich.

»Ich traue Berthold an sich alles zu«, sagte ich. Obwohl ich mir nicht vorstellen konnte, dass er auf die Idee hatte kommen können, ausgerechnet mich als Glücksengel einzusetzen, es sein denn ... es sei denn ... es sei denn, Gudrun hätte ihn gebeten ... Mir schoss da gerade ein übler Gedanke durch den Kopf. »Ich muss dringend mit Gudrun reden«, wusste ich plötzlich, sprang auf und eilte zur Tür.

»Halt, bevor du gehst, sag mir bitte noch, wie wir reagieren sollen. Was sollen wir schreiben?«

»Am besten die Wahrheit«, fiel mir ein.

»Sehr gut. Und was ist die Wahrheit?«

»Dass wir sie nicht kennen«, sagte ich. Sie sah mich verzweifelt an. Gerüchte als Wahrheiten zu verkaufen, das war ein Kinderspiel. Aber über eine Wahrheit zu schreiben, die man nicht kannte, das ging weit über das hinaus, wozu Journalismus geeignet war. Und das galt leider auch für anständige Blätter wie die *Neuzeit*.

Gudrun trennt
Privates und Geschäftliches

Gudrun schien mit mir gerechnet zu haben, obwohl ich schon dreizehn Jahre nicht mehr unangekündigt vor ihrer Tür beziehungsweise in ihrem Leben aufgetaucht war. Sie hatte verheulte Augen, und die Art unserer Begrüßung erinnerte mich an die grauenhaften Zeiten, als wir mit heftigen Umarmungen gegen das Scheitern unserer Liebesbeziehung angekämpft hatten, wie angeschlagene Boxer, die sich in den Clinch zu retten versuchten, da der K. o. unmittelbar bevorstand.

Jedenfalls war ich sofort beruhigt, weil ich spürte, dass Gudrun nicht imstande gewesen sein konnte, mich zu demütigen, indem sie den Gutsherrn darauf ansetzte, aus mir hinterrücks einen Starjournalisten zu machen und mir unter dem Deckmantel der barmherzigen Großtat sein schmieriges Geld in den Arsch zu schieben, damit ich im Hause Hille nicht mehr als Bittsteller antreten musste, und damit Töchterchen Florentina nicht zeitlebens darunter leiden musste, mit den Genen eines versoffenen Verlierertyps ausgestattet zu sein.

»Magst du einen Whiskey?«, fragte sie, vielleicht weil sie selbst einen gebrauchen konnte.

»Ja gerne, ich hab sowieso noch nicht gefrühstückt«, erwiderte ich. Solche Bemerkungen hatte sie auch in weniger beklemmenden Situationen niemals lustig gefunden, deshalb passten wir eben nicht zusammen, nicht nur deshalb, aber deshalb auch. Nachdem sie mir eine ordentliche Erwachsenen-Portion eingeschenkt hatte, damit ich eine Weile mit mir beschäftigt war, setzte sie zu einem längeren Monolog an.

»Gerold, bitte glaube mir, ich wusste nichts davon, mich trifft das wie ein Blitz aus heiterem Himmel. Ich fühle mich genauso überrumpelt wie du. Papa hat mich heute früh angerufen und mir alles erzählt. Er hat es vom alten Kunz erfahren. Bei denen ist natürlich auch der Teufel los. Ich hab geglaubt, ich drehe durch, wie ich höre, was da in *Leute heute* steht. Ich hab natürlich sofort versucht, Berthold zu erreichen, aber ich komme immer nur auf seine Mobilbox, das macht mich wahnsinnig. Er ist geschäftlich in Dubai, das heißt, ich glaube, er sitzt gerade im Flugzeug nach Frankfurt. Wahrscheinlich weiß er noch gar nicht, was ihn hier erwartet. Ihn wird der Schlag treffen, wenn er erfährt …«

»Also du glaubst nicht, dass er bei der Spendensache seine Finger im Spiel hat?«

»Nein. Das ist unmöglich. Das gibt es nicht. Das kann nicht sein. Berthold ist keiner, der so was macht«, erwiderte sie.

»Und das Konto in Liechtenstein? Und die hohen Summen, die er abgehoben hat? Ist Berthold auch keiner, der *so was* macht?«, fragte ich.

»Das hat bestimmt nichts mit den Spenden zu tun.«

»Ich meine, mich geht es ja nichts an. Aber warum hebt ein einzelner Mensch so viel Geld ab? Wozu braucht er das? Will er eine Insel kaufen? Oder will er sich eine Pyramide bauen lassen?«

»Hör zu, Gerold. Ich hab mich mit diesen Dingen nie beschäftigt. Wir haben das immer strikt getrennt, das Private und das Geschäftliche. Er hat seine beruflichen Transaktionen im Alleingang gemacht und für sich behalten. Er wollte mich und die Familie damit nicht belasten.«

»Sehr feinfühlig von ihm.«

»Er hat mir immer schon gesagt, dass er einen Job hat, bei dem er automatisch mit einem Bein im Ungesetzlichen steht, egal was er tut, es ist alles Auslegungssache.«

»Toller Job«, sagte ich.

»Das ist eben der Preis.«

»Der Preis wofür?« Das war eine riskante Frage, denn ich traute Gudrun zu, mich jetzt zu einer Führung durch die Räumlichkeiten zu nötigen, wo die Trophäen des Wohlstands versammelt waren, vom chinesischen Kleiderschrank über den lebensnotwendigen elektrischen Tellerwärmer bis hin zum mit dem Antwerpener Designpreis ausgezeichneten Klopapierhalter. Nur die Klorollen selbst waren überraschenderweise aus ganz normalem Papier. Aber sie schwieg und schenkte mir noch einen Whiskey ein.

Probleme, Alkohol und Kaffee

Als ich nach Hause kam, war Manuel noch da. Vor seinem Anblick hatte ich mich gefürchtet. Und er hatte tatsächlich schon einmal freundlichere Nasenlöcher gemacht. Zum Glück nahm ich sie nur noch relativ unscharf war.

»Wo warst du?«, fragte er.

»Bei Gudrun, meiner Exfrau.«

»Du bist betrunken.«

»Sag nicht so grausame Dinge, wenn es mir sowieso schon nicht gut geht.«

»Immer wenn du ein Problem hast, trinkst du Alkohol.«

»Was glaubst du, was für Probleme ich hätte, würde ich keinen Alkohol trinken«, sagte ich.

»Ich finde das überhaupt nicht lustig«, sagte er. Jetzt war er wirklich zornig.

»Tut mir leid, Manuel, aber ich hatte keinen guten Tag.«

»Glaubst du, mein Tag war besser? In meiner Klasse glauben jetzt alle, dass du ein Riesenschwindler und Betrüger bist.«

»Und du glaubst das auch?«, fragte ich.

»Nein, natürlich nicht. Aber was hilft mir das, wenn es alle anderen glauben?«

»Was die anderen glauben, kann man nicht ändern«, sagte ich.

»Du kannst sowieso nie was ändern. Du hast noch nie etwas geändert. Dir ist immer alles egal.« Wenn er schrie, kam die hohe Kinderstimme noch manchmal so richtig durch, das hörte sich an, als würden sie gerade einen Hahn abschlachten.

»Nein, das stimmt nicht, dass mir alles egal ist, Manuel, wirklich nicht.«

»Dann tu was, mach was, unternimm was!«

»Was soll ich tun? Es gibt Situation, da kann man nichts tun, da sind einem die Hände gebunden, und das ist jetzt leider so eine Situation«, sagte ich. Da warf er mir einen wirklich hochgiftigen, einen abgrundtief verächtlichen Blick zu, sprang auf, packte seine Schulsachen zusammen, zog Schuhe und Jacke an und knallte hinter sich die Tür zu.

Ich war nicht gerade stolz auf mich, dass mir nichts Besseres als das Übliche einfiel, aber daheim hielt ich es einfach nicht aus, also übersiedelte ich in Zoltan's Bar. Es dauerte eine Weile, bis meine Kumpels der Reihe nach eintrudelten und mir ihr Beileid aussprachen.

»Erinnerst du dich an meine Worte? Hier haben wir gestanden, und ich hab gesagt, Geri, pass auf, das ist jemand aus deinem engsten Kreis, und zwar jemand, der Kohle hat. Das war klar«, sagte Josi, der Konditor.

»Schwarzkohle, deshalb die Geheimniskrämerei«, ergänzte Horst, der Wettbüro-Betreiber. Ich erzählte ihnen von meinem

Gespräch mit Gudrun und dass sie es für ausgeschlossen hielt, dass Berthold Hille etwas mit der Sache zu tun hatte.

»Natürlich wird sie ihn decken«, meinte Josi.

»Andererseits kann man auch nicht unbedingt glauben, was in so einem Schmierblatt steht. Die haben ja überhaupt keine Beweise, das sind nur vage Behauptungen, sonst nichts«, widersprach Franticek, der Kunstschmied.

»Außerdem steht denen das Wasser bis zum Hals, wegen dem Prozess gegen dein Exschmierblatt, Geri. Wenn die den verlieren, können sie wahrscheinlich zusperren. Darum haben sie sich eben eine schöne Geschichte zusammengereimt«, sagte Arik, der Berufsschullehrer.

»Wie auch immer – der Schaden ist angerichtet, so oder so. Die Spendensache ist erledigt, kein Mensch glaubt mehr an den heiligen Samariter«, sagte Josi.

»Soll ich diesem fiesen Schreiberling, dem Liebknecht, ein paar Henker aus der Ukraine nach Hause schicken?«, fragte Horst.

»Heast, sei net scho wieda so deppert«, erwiderte Josi.

Ich erzählte ihnen dann, was mich am meisten belastete, dass nämlich ausgerechnet Manuel mich jetzt für einen Totalversager hielt und dass er stinkwütend auf mich war, weil ich nichts unternahm, aber was sollte ich schon unternehmen?

»Da kannst du ohnehin nur eins machen«, sagte Franticek.

»Was?«, fragte ich. Ich rechnete mit »Abwarten, wie sich die Dinge entwickeln« oder Ähnlichem.

»Schreiben«, erwiderte Franticek.

»Ich schreibe keine Zeile mehr«, verkündete ich, oder vielleicht hatte ich es auch nur extrem laut gedacht, egal.

»Es bleibt dir gar nichts anderes übrig. Du musst so schnell wie möglich über ein Sozialprojekt schreiben und kannst nur hoffen, dass dort noch einmal zehntausend Euro eingehen«, sagte Franticek.

»Er hat recht. Gehen keine zehntausend Euro ein, dann war es der Mann deiner Ex. Gehen welche ein – dann hast du Glück gehabt, du bleibst der Held, der Spender lebt, und die Welt ist doch noch nicht ganz verloren«, sagte Josi.

»Genau. Und dein Bub kann wieder stolz auf dich sein«, ergänzte Arik.

Ich wollte gerade zu meinem Glas greifen, aber irgendwie schien sich selbiges einem sonderbaren Schrumpfungsprozess plus Farbwechsel unterzogen zu haben, oder mir war wirklich schon deutlich zu schwarz vor den Augen.

»Was ist das?«, fragte ich.

»Kaffee«, erwiderte Zoltan.

»Wer hat das bestellt?«

»War nur ein gutgemeinter Vorschlag«, erwiderte der Wirt.

»Der Chef hat recht, du solltest jetzt langsam wieder nüchtern werden. Du hast morgen einen harten Arbeitstag vor dir«, spöttelte Horst. Josi lachte. Man hat eben immer nur die Freunde, die übrig blieben, wenn alle anderen ausgeschieden waren, die man sich nicht verdient hatte.

»Mir noch ein Bier«, sagte Josi.

»Mir auch«, bekräftigte Franticek.

»Mir auch«, ergänzte Horst.

»Mir auch«, vervollständigte Arik.

KAPITEL VIERZEHN

Rain Man in der Donaustadt

Punkt 7.34 Uhr stand ich freiwillig auf, die Zahl wollte ich mir merken – für das Guinnessbuch der Rekorde. Ich war übrigens sogar schon eine Stunde früher wach gewesen, und da war mir eine geniale, zeitsparende und gerechte Methode eingefallen, die Sozialgeschichte zu ermitteln, in die ich mich dann gleich knien wollte, um dem Wohltäter oder der Wohltäterin sozusagen noch eine Chance zu geben, nicht Berthold Hille zu heißen. Angelina von der *Neuzeit* hatte mir nämlich ein Dokument mit gut zwei Dutzend Hilfesuchenden beziehungsweise unterstützungswürdigen Projekten angelegt, die sich entweder selbst gemeldet hatten oder von Lesern für eine Reportage empfohlen worden waren. Noch im Bett hatte ich mich für die Zahl Vierzehn entschieden, das war Manuels Alter, und die an vierzehnter Stelle gelistete Datei wählte ich nun aus und öffnete sie.

Sehr geehrter Herr Plassek, ich bin eine langjährige Leserin der Neuzeit *und möchte Sie auf eine Familie aufmerksam machen, die es wirklich verdienen würde, dass Sie einmal über sie schreiben. Und zwar handelt es sich um Nachbarn von mir, Frau und Herrn Nowotny, die seit vielen Jahren aufopfernd ein autistisches Waisenkind betreuen. Das Mädchen ist heute immerhin schon sechzehn Jahre alt, sie heißt Romana. Romana lebt in ihrer eigenen Welt, kann kaum Gefühle zeigen, hat keine Freunde, wenige Kontakte nach außen, aber ein riesengroßes Talent: Sie malt. Das Besondere daran ist, dass sie immer nur Tiere malt, real und aus der Phantasie. Die Bilder sind erstaunlich, ich durfte sie einmal sehen. Romanas größter Wunsch wäre es, die Kunstakademie oder eine höhere Schule der Malerei zu besuchen, um ihrer Leidenschaft weiter nachgehen zu können. Aber obwohl die Nowotnys jeden Euro zur Seite legen, haben sie selbst für die notwendigen Vorbereitungskurse das Geld noch nicht beisammen, weil sehr viel in die Therapie fließt. Nachbarn und Freunde haben schon gesammelt, aber es reicht noch nicht. Vielleicht geschieht ja ein Wunder …*

Danke, dass Sie meine Nachricht gelesen haben. Romanas Tierbilder sollten Sie sich wirklich ansehen! Alles Liebe und Gute, Christina Kronberger.

Zunächst schrieb ich Manuel eine SMS. Ich fragte ihn, wann er frühestens von der Schule abbiegen konnte, weil wir nämlich schleunigst gemeinsam zur Recherche antreten mussten. Danach rief ich bei Christina Kronberger an, die zum Glück noch nichts von den *Leute-heute*-Enthüllungen mitbekommen hatte, sodass ich mir umständliche Erklärungen sparen konnte. Sie versprach mir, sofort Kontakt mit den Nowotnys aufzunehmen und sie auf meinen Besuch vorzubereiten. Wenig später rief sie zurück und sagte, dass ich zu Mittag kommen könne, Erika Nowotny sei daheim, Romana zwar ebenfalls, aber da dürfe ich nicht zu viel erwarten, vielleicht würde man sie gar nicht zu Gesicht bekommen, denn wenn unbekannte Menschen die Wohnung betraten, versteckte sie sich meistens.

Als ich schon glaubte, Manuel würde mich im Stich lassen, schrieb er mir, dass er wegen eines Französischtests vorübergehend verhindert war – sie mussten die Telefone bei Tests offenbar ausschalten –, dass er nun aber auf dem Weg war und dass ihm Physik und Geometrie ohnehin gestohlen bleiben konnten. Er wollte lieber etwas vom Leben erfahren. Und, ja, er war sehr glücklich, dass ich endlich etwas unternahm.

Unterwegs erklärten wir uns gegenseitig, was Autismus im Grunde war, wobei ich zugeben muss, dass sich Manuel wesentlich besser auskannte, weil er schon Dokumentationen darüber gesehen und sogar Bücher dazu gelesen hatte, während ich eigentlich nur Dustin Hoffman in *Rain Man* damit verband.

Die Trabantensiedlung in Wien-Donaustadt bot quasi die perfekte Einstimmung auf eine düstere Familiengeschichte an einem nasskalten Tag Ende November, der stürmische Wind wirbelte abgerissene Werbeplakat-Gesichtsfetzen von Wohlstand vorgaukelnden Stadtpolitikern übers Pflaster. Allein darin spiegelte sich das ganze Elend einer Großstadt, die sich zwar rühmte, zu den glanzvollsten und reichsten der Welt zu zählen, aber dieser glanzvolle Reichtum ging leider haarscharf an etwa achtzig Prozent der Bevölkerung vorbei. An dieser Wohnsiedlung ging er sogar deutlich mehr als nur haarscharf vorbei. Praktisch an jedem zweiten Haustor lud ein Schild zu psychologischer Betreuung ein. In den Betonklötzen rechts und links der Straße gab es vermutlich täglich entweder einen Amoklauf, einen Suizidversuch, ein Ehedrama oder ein herkömmliches Blutbad.

Erika Nowotny sah man an, dass sie sich die letzten Jahre praktisch durchgehend Sorgen gemacht hatte. Sie erzählte mir auf mehr oder weniger nüchternen Magen, dass ihr eigenes Kind vor dreizehn Jahren bei einem Verkehrsunfall ums Leben gekommen war, dass ihr Mann Ludwig das Auto gelenkt hatte und seit damals Tag für Tag Schuld abbüßte, ohne dass die Schuld deswegen kleiner geworden wäre. Wenig später hatten die Nowotnys ein Waisenkind adoptiert, das ebenfalls bei einem Unfall seine Eltern verloren hatte – Romana. Was man bei der Kleinen anfangs für reine Traumatisierung hielt, entpuppte sich nach und nach als schwere autistische Grundstörung, die sich etwa darin äußerte, dass sie ihre Pflegeeltern auch nach zwölf Jahren intensiver Zuwendung ansah und behandelte, als wären sie wildfremde Personen.

Ungefähr an diesem Punkt musste ich Frau Nowotny unterbrechen und ihr mitteilen, dass ich vor allem an Werktagen ein extrem labil geschichteter Mensch war, der sich solche traurigen Dinge nicht lange anhören konnte, ohne loszuheulen, was ich ihr und mir lieber ersparen würde. Der Grund meines Besuches sei jedenfalls ein äußerst positiver, und darüber würde ich gerne mit ihr reden.

»Ich habe nämlich gehört, dass Romana phantastisch zeichnen kann.« Dieser eine Satz genügte, um Frau Nowotny ein seliges Lächeln ins Gesicht zu zaubern, sodass sie plötzlich wie ein fröhlicher Mensch wirkte, mit dem man jede Menge Spaß haben konnte. Das bestätigte übrigens genau meine persönliche Theorie zum Thema Glück/Unglück. Darüber hatten Manuel und ich erst vor wenigen Tagen vielleicht eines unserer tiefgründigsten Gespräche geführt, in meinem Fall war es sogar das bei weitem tiefgründigste der letzten Jahre gewesen.

Ausflug in die Theorie des Glücks

Manuel fand es total ungerecht, dass es auf der Welt manchen Menschen so extrem gut ging und anderen wiederum so furchtbar schlecht. Ginge es denen, denen es extrem gut ging, etwas schlechter, ginge es ihnen immer noch sehr gut. Aber ginge es denen, denen es furchtbar schlecht ging, auch nur ein bisschen besser, so ginge es ihnen eigentlich gleich deutlich besser, sie hätten jedenfalls ein spürbar glücklicheres Leben. So ähnlich war sein Gedankengang.

Ich hatte zum Thema Glück eine ein bisschen andere Theorie:

Angenommen, zwei Menschen haben je hundert Gedanken zur Verfügung, die sie im nächsten Moment denken könnten. A ist ein richtiger Unglücksrabe, fünfundneunzig seiner möglichen Gedanken wären negativ, nur fünf positiv. Umgekehrt verhält es sich mit B, einem ausgesprochenen Glücksritter. Ihm könnten fünfundneunzig sehr erfreuliche und nur fünf absolut unerfreuliche Gedanken in den Sinn kommen. Und hier meine Behauptung: Wenn Glücksritter B einem seiner nur fünf negativen Gedanken nachhängt, ist er in dieser Situation mindestens genauso unglücklich wie Unglücksrabe A, wenn dieser einen seiner fünfundneunzig negativen Gedanken spinnt. Und andersrum: Ergreift Unglücksrabe A einen seiner nur fünf positiven Gedanken, so fühlt er sich in diesem Moment wenigstens genauso glücklich wie Glücksritter B, wenn diesem einer seiner fünfundneunzig positiven Gedanken in den Sinn kommt.

»Und was willst du damit sagen?«, fragte mich Manuel, als ich meine Ausführungen beendet hatte und ihn erwartungsvoll ansah.

»Dass Menschen, denen es schlecht geht, genauso glücklich sein können, wie Menschen, denen es gut geht.«

»Sie müssen nur an was Gutes denken?«, fragte Manuel nach.

»So ungefähr«, sagte ich.

»Weißt du, was das Problem an deiner Theorie ist?«

»Nein.«

»Man kann es sich leider nicht aussuchen, woran man denkt.«

»Wer sagt das?«, fragte ich.

»Ich sage das. Wenn es einem schlecht geht, fallen einem natürlich viel eher die schlechten Dinge ein, als wenn es einem gut geht. Und wenn man an etwas Schlechtes denkt, dann fällt einem wahrscheinlich gleich das nächste Schlechte ein. Denn wenn man Sorgen hat, dann hat man eben Sorgen, und aus«, sagte er.

»Aber wenn es einem gelingt, trotz Sorgen an etwas Schönes zu denken, dann werden die Sorgen automatisch kleiner, weil sich das Schöne im Kopf ausbreiten kann. Und wenn man an eine schöne Sache denken kann, dann kann man auch gleich an eine zweite schöne Sache denken. Die Sorgen werden dann in irgendein finsteres Eck gedrängt, bis sie schließlich ganz verschwinden«, sagte ich, wobei ich gestehen musste, dass diese Theorie schon dezent utopische Auswüchse hatte und ich sie besser nur für Manuel und mich behielt.

»Sorgen verschwinden aber nicht von allein, schon gar nicht, indem man sie verdrängt. Sie werden dadurch eher noch größer«, behauptete Manuel.

»Bei mir nicht«, erwiderte ich knapp. Die Diskussion hatte mich angestrengt, ich wollte sie dann mal langsam beenden.

»Du bist überhaupt ein Phänomen«, sagte er.

»Wie meinst du das?«

»Du müsstest mindestens hundert Sorgen haben, aber dir ist anscheinend noch gar nicht aufgefallen, dass es Sorgen sind«, sagte er.

»Na also. Bin ich nicht ein beneidenswert glücklicher Mensch?«, fragte ich.

»Aber nur nach deiner Theorie«. Er lachte. Und ich ließ meine Hand auf seine Schulter fallen. Er war nämlich nicht nur ein kluges, sondern sogar *mein* kluges Kind. Bei nächster Gelegenheit würde ich es ihm verraten. Oder spätestens bei übernächster.

Frau Nowotny hatte ich offenbar das ideale Stichwort gegeben, endlich einmal an etwas Erfreuliches zu denken, indem ich sagte:

»Ich habe gehört, dass Romana phantastisch zeichnen kann.«

»Ja, sie zeichnet wunderbar. Vielleicht gelingt es uns, dass sie uns ein paar ihrer Bilder zeigt«, erwiderte sie. Noch während sie diese Worte sprach, fiel mir auf, dass Manuel gar nicht bei uns saß, sondern verschollen war. Frau Nowotny stand auf, steuerte auf Zehenspitzen eine angelehnte Tür an, öffnete sie behutsam, blieb dann einigermaßen überrascht stehen und rief mir im Flüsterton zu: »Schauen Sie sich das an!«

Der Anblick war wirklich pittoresk. In dem kleinen Raum, der hauptsächlich aus einem Bett bestand, lagen überall auf dem Boden Zeichenblätter verstreut, Manuel rutschte auf den Knien herum und begutachtete ein Bild nach dem anderen. Auf dem Bettrand hockte Romana, ein zartes, weißhäutiges Mädchen mit rotblonden Haaren und einer ziemlich eckigen Brille. Sie konnte sich anscheinend nicht entscheiden, ob sie Manuel bei seinem Studium beobachten oder ignorieren sollte. Bei mir konnte sie sich entscheiden, sie ignorierte mich, aber ich nahm das nicht persönlich. Es hatte schon Menschen gegeben, die erschrocken waren, als sie mich zum ersten Mal gesehen hatten, vor allem Kinder.

»Wie hast du das nur geschafft?«, fragte Frau Nowotny Manuel mit süßlich pädagogischer Stimme, an der man erkannte, dass sie früher Kindergärtnerin gewesen war.

»Wie soll ich was geschafft haben?«, erwiderte Manuel erwartungsgemäß.

»Dass dir die Romana ihre Malereien zeigt.«

»Ich hab sie gefragt, ob ich ihre Tierbilder sehen kann.«

»Und sie hat ja gesagt?«

»Nein, sie hat nicht ja gesagt, sie hat aber auch nicht nein gesagt, sie hat gar nichts gesagt, also hab ich mir die Mappe einfach genommen. Wie man sieht, hat sie nichts dagegen.« Ich setzte ein verschämtes väterliches Lächeln auf, im Sinne von *Ja, so sind sie halt, die Kinder, kaum lässt man sie eine Minute allein* ...

»Schau mal, Onkel Geri, das ist cool. Das sind immer so Kreuzungen zwischen ganz kleinen und ganz großen Tieren, halb Spinne, halb Wildschwein zum Beispiel. Oder schau, das ist besonders cool, das hat den Kopf von einem Tiger, die Beine von einem Affen und den Körper von einer ... Was ist das, ist das eine Maus?«, fragte Manuel die mehr oder weniger anwesende Künstlerin persönlich.

»Bisamratte«, sagte Romana. Das war quasi ihr erstes Wort. Ein guter Einstand. So schlecht konnte es um das Mädel jedenfalls nicht bestellt sein, dachte ich.

»Sie hat ein ausgeprägtes fotografisches Gedächtnis, sie sieht Abbildungen von Tieren und merkt sich alles bis ins kleinste Detail. Manchmal kombiniert sie gleich vier, fünf Tiere in einer Zeichnung«, erklärte Frau Nowotny.

Die Bilder waren auf ihre Art wirklich beeindruckend, sie erinnerten mich ein bisschen an die Malerei der Phantastischen Realisten, an Hutter, Hausner, Brauer und diese Leute, vielleicht noch mit einer kräftigen Extraportion LSD als Unterlage. Aber bei aller Wertschätzung – ich würde mir so etwas niemals ins Schlafzimmer hängen, meine Horrorvisionen schuf ich mir selbst, dafür brauchte ich keine Anleitungen von den Wänden.

»Cool, das würde ich auch gerne können«, sagte Manuel, gar nicht an Romana, sondern eher an sich selbst gerichtet. Sie freute sich aber trotzdem, denn nun verließ sie das Bett, bückte sich, kramte ein Bild zwischen den anderen hervor und drückte es Manuel in die Hand.

»Wow, geil, was ist das für ein Monster?«

»Ein Kreuzotterschwertfischpuma.«

»Darf ich ein Foto davon machen? Es kommt in die Zeitung, stimmt's, Onkel Geri? Vielleicht wirst du sogar noch berühmt damit«, meinte der selbsternannte Herr Chefreporter.

»Klar, mach ein Foto, wenn du willst«, murmelte Romana. Begeisterungsfähigkeit war jetzt nicht unbedingt ihre große Stärke. Aber so wahnsinnige Unterschiede zwischen Autist und Nicht-Autist erkannte man beim besten Willen nicht, wenn man die beiden Jugendlichen betrachtete. Natürlich behielt ich diesen Gedanken besser für mich, ich wollte ja nicht medizinisch unkorrekt sein. Hauptsache, wir hatten ein bisschen frischen Wind und vor allem etwas Licht in diese düstere Stube gebracht.

Herzlicher Gruß – und basta

Daheim mussten wir uns leider kurz den unerquicklichen journalistischen Tatsachen stellen. Manuel durchstöberte das Internet und sortierte meine Post. Über mein Notebook gebeugt sagte er, dass einige Leserinnen und Leser wegen mir, dem »Spendenschwindler«, ihr *Neuzeit*-Abonnement gekündigt hatten. Die meisten aber schrieben, dass sie auf mein soziales Gewissen vertrauten und sich sicher waren, dass ich mit der Sache nichts zu tun hatte.

Ich selbst rief Clara Nemez an und ließ mich auf den aktuellen Stand der Berichterstattung bringen. *Leute heute* hatte in der jüngsten Ausgabe noch einmal fleißig den Skandalbrei gerührt, aber keine neuen Fakten hineingestreut. *Tag für Tag* kündigte auf der Titelseite eine weitere Millionenklage der Plus-Eigentümer gegen das Konkurrenzblatt wegen Verleumdung an. Auch Berthold Hilles Anwälte vermeldeten, ein wenig schaumgebremst, sich rechtliche Schritte gegen *Leute heute* zu überlegen. Von Hille selbst gab es weiterhin keine Stellungnahme.

Die seriöseren Medien berichteten distanziert, aber mitunter spöttisch von den Enthüllungen. Was die Rolle der *Neuzeit* und im Speziellen auch meiner Person in der Spendenserie betraf, gab man mehr oder weniger unumwunden zu, keine Ahnung zu haben. »Was wusste Journalist Plassek?«, war quasi die beliebteste Zeile unter den abgedruckten Meuchelfotos von mir. Immerhin gingen sie davon aus, dass ich zu keinem Interview bereit war, und da hatten sie völlig recht.

Ich erzählte Clara von unserer Reise in die Welt der autistischen Zeichnerin Romana und erhielt sofort grünes Licht für die Reportage.

»Du hast recht. Weiter wie bisher, das ist das Einzige, was wir momentan tun können«, sagte sie.

»Wann soll die Geschichte erscheinen?«, fragte ich. Das war ein folgenschwerer Fehler, denn Clara fiel nichts Besseres ein, als »natürlich gleich morgen« zu sagen.

»Das geht nicht, da bleiben mir nur noch zwei Stunden, das schaffe ich nicht«, sagte ich.

»Das schaffst du«, erwiderte Clara, eher im Befehlston.

»Klar schaffen wir das«, plärrte Manuel hinter meinem Rücken. Das waren mindestens zweieinhalb Stimmen gegen eine. Also schafften wir es eben.

Gegen achtzehn Uhr schickten sie uns die fertigen Seiten, auf denen einem gleich einmal ein monströser Kreuzotterschwertfisch auf Pumabeinen ins Auge sprang. Manuel war begeistert und brachte mir zur Belohnung unaufgefordert ein Bier aus dem Kühlschrank. Die Reportage war uns wirklich gut gelungen, Manuel hatte wie gewohnt überschäumend und wortreich den Großteil des Erzählstoffs geliefert, ich hatte verschlankt. Zwei Drittel der Arbeit waren freilich von der *Neuzeit*-Redaktion beigesteuert worden, und zwar wirklich interessante Hintergrundinformationen über Autismus und *Inselbegabungen*, das sogenannte *Savant-Syndrom*. Hier konnte man lesen, dass Menschen mit Behinderungen oder Entwicklungsstörungen in Teilbereichen, also auf ihren kognitiven Inseln, sehr oft außergewöhnliche Leistungen erbringen konnten. Hervorragende Musiker, die blind waren, oder Autisten mit enormen Gedächtnisleistungen und spezifischen künstlerischen Begabungen waren deshalb keine Seltenheit.

»Auch wenn es keine Geldspende mehr gibt – deine Geschichten sind einfach immer total berührend und eine große Bereicherung für unser Blatt«, lobte mich Clara am Telefon.

»Das verdanke ich vor allem meinem aufstrebenden Jungkollegen Manuel«, erwiderte ich laut genug, dass er es hören konnte. Dafür brachte er mir zwar kein weiteres Bier, aber er rümpfte auch nicht die Nase, als ich mir selbst noch eins holte.

»Da sind übrigens noch zwei Überraschungen in deinem Postfach«, sagte er dann.

»Negative Überraschungen? Dann behalte sie bitte für dich.«

»Nein, eher positive«, erwiderte er.

»Und zwar?«

»Der Mann, der *treue Leser*, der in Wirklichkeit vielleicht der echte Wohltäter ist, wenn es der Hille nicht ist, der hat wieder geschrieben«, berichtete er. Dann las er mir den Text vor:

Lieber Herr Plassek, ich habe Ihnen freilich hier keine Ratschläge zu erteilen, aber ich wünschte mir, sie ließen sich durch etwaige absurde Medienberichte nicht von Ihrem Weg abbringen. Und da Sie fragten, ob ich Ihre Mutter kannte und ob Sie ihr wohl eine Botschaft von mir überbringen dürfen, so antworte ich gerne: Ja, ich kannte sie. Und ja, seien Sie doch so gut und nennen Sie ihr bitte nur vier Zahlen, in folgender Reihenfolge: 1, 9, 7, 4. Vielen lieben Dank und herzliche Grüße, Ihr treuer Leser.

»Er meint wahrscheinlich das Jahr 1974«, sagte ich.

»Klar, was denn sonst?«, erwiderte Manuel. Er konnte mich nicht einmal der Klügere sein lassen.

»1974 war ich vier Jahre alt«, bemerkte ich.

»Das wollte er damit aber nicht sagen.«

»Natürlich wollte er das damit nicht sagen.«

»Warum erwähnst du es dann?«

»Darf ich bitte erwähnen, was ich will?«, fragte ich.

»Aber es lenkt nur ab, wenn du immer irgendwas erwähnst, was momentan völlig egal ist«, rügte er mich.

Wir überlegten noch eine Weile hin und her, bis uns klar war, dass wir das Rätsel nur lösen konnten, wenn wir Mama damit konfrontierten. Und zwar lieber heute als morgen, wenn es nach Manuel gegangen wäre. Aber diesmal ging es nach mir.

»Und die zweite Nachricht?«, fragte ich.

»Ach, die ist nicht so wichtig.«

»Von wem ist sie?«

»Willst du's wirklich wissen?«, fragte er gelangweilt.

»Sag schon.«

»Okay, von der Zahnärztin.«

»Von Rebecca?« Ich ließ mir meine Aufgeregtheit natürlich überhaupt nicht anmerken – zumindest beinahe überhaupt nicht. »Zeig her, was schreibt sie?«

»Oje, ich sehe gerade, ich hab die Mail leider schon gelöscht«, sagte er.

»Bist du wahnsinnig?« Sonst war ich ja eher nicht der Typ für spontane Wutausbrüche.

»Tut mir leid, ich dachte, dass interessiert dich ohnehin nicht so sehr.« Jetzt war ich nahe dran, ihm eine spätväterliche Ohrfeige anzutragen. »Kann man das nicht irgendwie aus dem Netz zurückholen?«, fragte ich.

Da erst bemerkte ich, dass er einen hochroten Kopf hatte

und bereits Tränen weinte vor lauter Lachen. Die Mail hatte er natürlich nicht gelöscht.

»Sehr lustig, Manuel! Haha.«

»Dich hat es ja ordentlich erwischt«, quetschte er zwischen seinen Lachanfällen hervor.

»Warte nur ab, bis es dich das erste Mal erwischt!«

»Mich erwischt es sicher nie«, schwor er. Jetzt konnte endlich einmal ich überlegen lächeln, denn wenigstens in diesem Punkt war ich garantiert der Klügere von uns beiden.

Rebeccas Nachricht lautete:

Hallo Gerold, da du deine Mobilbox offenbar nicht abhörst, probiere ich es per E-Mail. Ich wollte nur sagen, dass ich dich so gut kenne, dass ich weiß, dass du bei so einem Schwindel niemals mitmachen würdest. Ich hoffe, dass dich die Sache nicht allzu sehr betrübt. Nora, meine Kollegin vom Zehnerhaus, du kennst sie ja, hat mich gebeten, dich zu fragen, ob wir die zehntausend Euro jetzt wieder zurückgeben müssen. Das wäre schlimm, weil die Geräte zum Teil schon bestellt sind, aber was soll man machen. Bitte melde dich. Über ein Treffen würde ich mich freuen. Ich hab abends meistens Zeit. Liebe Grüße, Rebecca.

Nachdem Manuel aufgebrochen war und ich meinen absoluten Lieblingssatz in der gesamten bisherigen Ära Rebecca – *Ich hab abends meistens Zeit* – lange genug auf mich hatte einwirken lassen, schrieb ich ihr zurück.

Liebe Rebecca … Von *Hallo* hatte ich nämlich langsam genug.

Liebe Rebecca, die zehntausend Euro müsst ihr auf keinen Fall zurückgeben, glaube ich …« Das *glaube ich* löschte ich gleich wieder … *müsst ihr auf keinen Fall zurückgeben, dafür werde ich sorgen. Wenn du morgen, Mittwochabend, noch nicht verplant bist, dann freu ich mich sehr, dich zu sehen …* Aus *sehen* machte ich *treffen*, das klang unverfänglicher, im Übrigen sah man sich sowieso, wenn man sich traf. Über den Zeitpunkt des Treffens grübelte ich länger. Wenn es nach mir gegangen wäre, hätte ich einundzwanzig Uhr vorgeschlagen. Wenn ich auf Nummer sicher hätte gehen wollen, was die Unverfänglichkeit betraf, hätte ich achtzehn Uhr gewählt. Es stellte sich also die Frage, ob ich neunzehn oder zwanzig Uhr schreiben sollte. Weil ich in solchen Dingen ein entscheidungsschwacher Mensch war, schrieb ich: *Als Zeitpunkt schlage ich 19.30 Uhr vor. Du kannst gerne ein stimmungsvolles Lokal aussuchen …* Wegen *stimmungsvoll* löschte ich das wieder und schrieb stattdessen: *Suche gerne du ein Lokal aus, wo du dich wohlfühlst. Herzliche Grüße, Gerold. PS: Ich freue mich!* Nein, das klang zu aufgesetzt. Ich verbesserte: *Herzlicher Gruß, ich freue mich, Gerold.* Basta.

Ohne Geld kein Geschäft

Danach wollte ich mir eigentlich die Sprachbox-Nachricht von Rebecca anhören, genauer gesagt ihre Stimme, aber ich blieb schon bei der ersten Mitteilung hängen, und die klang eher betreten und stammte von Gudrun.

Hallo Gerold, bitte ruf mich an. Berthold ist jetzt wieder zu Hause und möchte dringend mit dir reden. Vielleicht kannst du am Abend auf einen Sprung bei uns vorbeikommen? Bitte melde dich!

Ich rief sofort zurück und sagte, dass ich praktisch schon auf dem Sprung zu ihnen war. Ich sagte das, ohne nachgedacht zu haben, denn hätte ich nachgedacht, hätte ich auf diesen Sprung verzichtet, oder ich hätte ihn zumindest hinausgezögert. Aber manche Sprünge musste man einfach so schnell wie möglich hinter sich bringen. Das sah sogar ich ein, obwohl ich im Prinzip ein rigoroser Befürworter von Sprüngen war, zu denen man erst gar nicht ansetzte, weil sie ohnehin nur Zeit- und Kraftverschwendung waren.

Wir setzten uns in sein Büro, wo man sich beinahe unterhalten konnte, weil es der von Florentinas Zimmer am weitesten entfernte Raum war. Von ebendort ging nämlich ohrenbetäubende Musik aus, die die gesamte dreihundert Quadratmeter große Wohnung beschallte. Meiner Meinung nach hätte man Florentina bitten können, die Lautstärke etwas herunterzufahren, aber ich wollte mich nicht in die pädagogischen Gepflogenheiten der Hilles einmischen.

»Whiskey?«, fragte Berthold.

»Da sage ich nicht nein.«

Er wirkte niedergeschlagen und zündete sich unbeholfen und fahrig eine Zigarre an. Er hatte offenbar nicht einmal mehr die Kraft, arrogant zu wirken, sodass er mir irgendwie fast schon wieder leid tat. Es war immer schlimm, wenn jemand plötzlich nicht mehr der sein konnte, für den er sich hielt, beziehungsweise für den man ihn halten sollte. Zuerst seufzte er ein paarmal tief, dann erst legte er Worte nach. »Ja, wir haben die Steuerfahnder am Hals«, sagte er.

»Wir?«, fragte ich.

»Die Familie. Es hängen alle drin. Wir haben mächtig viel aufgebaut, wir haben mächtig viel zu verlieren«, informierte er mich.

»Hauptsache mächtig«, sagte ich.

»Ja, spotte nur, mein Guter, du kannst es dir ja neuerdings sogar leisten, du bist richtig berühmt geworden. Gratuliere, gratuliere!« Das war eine ideale Überleitung zum Thema, fand ich. »Hast du etwas mit den Spenden zu tun? Hast du das gemacht?«

Jetzt lachte er laut auf oder hustete oder atmete aus oder tat alles gleichzeitig, jedenfalls entwickelte sich dabei Rauch.

»Glaubst du das im Ernst, Gerold?«

»Nein.«

»Hältst du das auch nur im Entferntesten für denkbar?«

»Eigentlich nicht«, erwiderte ich.

»Warum fragst du dann? Willst du mich beleidigen?«

»Ist es eine Beleidigung, wenn man sein Geld ausnahms-weise einmal Menschen gibt, die es brauchen?«, fragte ich.

»Hast du es denn nicht gebraucht all die Jahre?«, erwiderte er. Damit hatte er mich eindeutig auf dem falschen Fuß erwischt. »Doch, und das ist mir auch ziemlich unangenehm. Ich würde es dir lieber heute als morgen zurückgeben, das kannst du mir glauben«, sagte ich.

»Sehr lobenswert, Gerold, vielleicht werde ich es noch bitter benötigen.« Da musste ich lachen. Sein Selbstmitleid war noch um einiges größer als mein Mitleid.

Dann erklärte er mir, was es mit den Millionenbeträgen in Liechtenstein auf sich hatte. Die waren sozusagen das Taschengeld für seine Geschäftspartner, für Politiker und leitende Beamte in Lateinamerika und im Fernen Osten.

»Ich dachte, du vermittelst Aufträge für Stahlkonstruktionen«, sagte ich. Okay, ich spürte schon irgendwie, dass das naiv klang, aber deswegen musste er nicht gleich die Zigarre verschlucken und an seinem geräucherten Husten ersticken.

»Gerold, ich vermittle keine Aufträge, ich *kaufe* Aufträge. Und um Aufträge zu kaufen, benötige ich Geld, sehr viel Geld. Und dieses Geld kann ich mir nicht komplett von der Steuer auffressen lassen, das kann ich mir nicht leisten, das können wir uns alle nicht leisten, verstehst du?« Nein. Das ewige Jammern über zu hohe Steuern hatte ich nämlich noch nie verstanden. Eigentlich müssten doch diejenigen jammern, die fast keine Steuern zu bezahlen hatten, denn die verdienten auch kaum etwas. Aber egal. Seine Rechnungen gingen eben anders.

»Je größer der Kuchen, desto mehr wollen mitnaschen. Je höher die Aufträge, die ich an Land ziehe, desto teurer sind sie erkauft. Ohne Geld kein Geschäft, und ohne Geschäft kein Geld. So einfach ist das. So funktioniert die Wirtschaft. So funktioniert die Welt.« Zum Glück hatte ich mich noch nie dafür interessiert, wie die Welt funktionierte. Mich wunderte höchstens, dass sie schon so lange funktionierte.

»Und dass es immer genau zehntausend Euro waren, die du abgehoben hast? Reiner Zufall?«

»Das ist unsere Einheit. Im Supermarkt ist es ein Euro, den man in den Schlitz des Einkaufwagens schiebt. In der Geschäftswelt sind es zehntausend. Das ist unser Grundpreis.« Schön, jetzt blitzte endlich wieder der alte Bonze in ihm auf. Der anschließende Zug von der Zigarre gelang ihm auch gleich um einiges besser.

»Und deine Gespräche mit den Plus-Eigentümern? Das hatte nichts mit den Spenden zu tun?«

»Nicht das Geringste.«

»Warum schreiben die das dann?«

»Weil es eine gute Skandalstory ist. Weil sie über mich derzeit alles schreiben können, ich bin der Schurke, der Steuerhinterzieher, ich kann mich nicht wehren, ich hab die Schlinge um den Hals. Verstehst du?« Das verstand ich, zumindest klang seine Stimme ganz nach Schlinge um den Hals. »Und das ist es auch, was ich dir sagen wollte«, sagte er.

»Was genau?«

»Dass ich momentan nicht öffentlich dementieren kann, der große Gönner gewesen zu sein, weil ich sonst erklären müsste, wohin das Geld geflossen ist, und das darf ich nicht.« Da blieb mir mal kurz die Luft weg.

»Das heißt, die Menschen sollen also durchaus weiterhin glauben …«

»Ich kann nichts dagegen tun, mein Anwalt hat mich zum Schweigen verpflichtet, tut mir leid.« Ich hatte immer gedacht, man selbst verpflichtete Anwälte, und nicht umgekehrt, aber in dieser perversen Geschäftswelt hielt ich mittlerweile alles für möglich.

»Gerold, es tut mir aufrichtig leid, dass deine an sich gute Sache ...«

»Bemühe dich nicht.«

»Doch, und ich meine das ganz ehrlich, auch im Namen von Gudrun und Florentina – du tust mir insofern leid, als du noch daran glaubst ...«

»Ich brauche dir wirklich nicht leid zu tun, leid musst du dir schon selber tun«, erwiderte ich. Arme Gudrun, sie hatte nach mir wirklich einen Besseren verdient, nicht nach der Not auch noch das Elend.

»Und unser Gespräch bleibt bitte unter uns, das musst du mir versprechen«, schob er halb reumütig, halb demütig nach.

»Okay, aber unter einer Bedingung«, sagte ich.

»Und die wäre?«

Ich hätte ihn gerne noch etwas länger auf die Folter gespannt, doch es war vielleicht wirklich nicht der ideale Zeitpunkt dafür, wenn ich ihn mir so ansah.

»Noch einen Whiskey«, erwiderte ich.

KAPITEL FÜNFZEHN

Von aller Ruhe keine Spur

Am nächsten Tag wachte ich zum Glück erst gegen Mittag auf und las nach dem Zähneputzen genau zwei von ungefähr zwanzig neuen Mails. Wobei ich in die zweite, von Peter Seibernigg, eher unabsichtlich hineingeraten war, weil ich meine Gedanken noch bei der ersten gehabt hatte. Die stammte von Rebecca.

Lieber Gerold, wir sind sehr erleichtert, dass wir die Spende nicht zurückzahlen müssen. Mittwochabend, 19.30 Uhr, passt mir gut! Wie wäre es mit dem José Antonio in der Friedmanngasse? Die haben spanisches Cerveza und hervorragende Tapas. Bis dahin war die Nachricht nahezu perfekt, aber dann kam der Umschwung:

Ich habe übrigens auch Nora gefragt, ob sie mitkommen möchte. Ich hoffe, das stört dich nicht. Es geht ihr momentan nicht so besonders, und da dachte ich, dass ihr ein bisschen Ablenkung bestimmt guttut. Sie findet dich äußerst sympathisch ... ☺ Also dann, bis Mittwochabend! Wir freuen uns, Rebecca.

Das war gewissermaßen niederschmetternd und im Grunde eine echte Gemeinheit, überhaupt in Kombination mit dem auf Nora bezogenen Smiley, sodass ich kurz überlegte, ob ich zur Strafe einen meiner Kumpels mitnehmen und auf Rebecca ansetzen sollte, zum Beispiel Horst oder Josi, aber das erschien mir dann doch zu brutal. Jedenfalls hatte sie mir bereits im Vorfeld jede Freude auf unser erstes richtiges Rendezvous genommen. Sie mochte ja etwas von Zähnen verstehen, aber in der Romantik war sie eine Versagerin. Den Gedanken, dass sie vielleicht doch absolut keinen Gefallen an mir als Mann fand und sich deshalb in ein unverfängliches Dreiertreffen retten wollte, konnte ich wegen zu hohen Grades an Trostlosigkeit nicht länger als ein paar Zehntelsekunden aufrechterhalten.

Also schlitterte ich in Seiberniggs Mail. Er beglückwünschte mich zu der feinfühligen Reportage über die autistische Zeichnerin Romana, zu der bereits zahlreiche positive Rückmeldungen eingegangen waren. Sogar eine angeblich namhafte Wiener Galeristin, deren Name mir natürlich überhaupt nichts sagte, hatte angerufen und eine Vernissage mit der »interessanten jungen Künstlerin« in Aussicht gestellt. Als ich mich aus Seiberniggs E-Mail eigentlich schon wieder ausblenden wollte, las ich:

Noch etwas anderes, ich weiß nicht, ob Clara Nemez schon mit Ihnen darüber geredet hat. Aber wir würden Sie gerne fester an unser Blatt binden. Ihre Sozialreportagen sind bereits ein Markenzeichen, etwas, das der Neuzeit *immer gefehlt hat. Und das hat rein gar nichts mit der Spendenserie zu tun. Vielleicht wollen Sie sich einmal überlegen, ob Sie sich ein festes Dienstverhältnis vorstellen können, im Jänner wird nämlich eine Stelle frei. Sie kriegen dann auch einen Büroplatz, ohne dass regelmäßige Anwesenheit erforderlich wäre. Lassen Sie es sich einmal in aller Ruhe durch den Kopf gehen. Für Fragen stehe ich gerne zur Verfügung. Herzliche Grüße, Peter Seibernigg.*

Das war objektiv gesehen endlich eine erfreuliche Nachricht, wobei ich es hasste, mir neuerdings ständig Dinge in aller Ruhe durch den Kopf gehen lassen zu müssen. Wenn es mehr als zwei Dinge gleichzeitig waren, war mein Kopf nämlich randvoll gefüllt, da ging absolut nichts mehr durch, da blieb alles stecken, und von aller Ruhe fehlte jede Spur.

Außerdem fiel mir auf, dass ich erst an Manuel denken musste, um mich über das Angebot auch wirklich zu freuen, weil »Ich bin dein Vater, und im Übrigen arbeite ich dem-

nächst fest für die *Neuzeit*« deutlich besser klang als: »Ich
liefere ab und zu einen Artikel ab, damit ich gerade genügend Kohle habe, um mir mein tägliches Brot leisten zu können und mein tägliches Bier, und im Übrigen bin ich dein
Vater.«

Just in diesem Augenblick rief Manuel an, erkundigte sich
nach dem bisherigen Echo auf unsere Reportage, fragte, ob
es Neuigkeiten zur Spendenserie gab, was ich verneinte, und
teilte mir mit, dass er heute nicht kommen konnte, weil er mit
Schulfreunden verabredet war. »Aber Tante Julia will dir noch
was sagen. Tschüss!«

»Tante Julia?«

»Ja hallo, hier ist Julia. Du, Gerold, können wir uns unterhalten?«

»Ja klar, unterhalten wir uns. Was gibt es?«

»Ich meine, nicht am Telefon. Können wir uns vielleicht
heute irgendwann …«

»Ja natürlich, du kannst gern zu mir kommen, aber das
müsste noch am Nachmittag sein, weil am Abend bin ich …
da bin ich … Am Abend bin ich … verhindert.« Ja leider, verhindert war wohl der einzig passende Ausdruck für das, was
ich am Abend sein würde.

Der Wodka schmeckte leider fahl

»Die Wohnung ist derzeit leider nicht aufgeräumt«, sagte ich.
Julia nickte, ohne sich umzusehen.

Wir tranken Früchtetee, also sie trank Früchtetee, noch dazu
ohne Zucker, ich trank Bier, und sie warf mir trotzdem keinen
einzigen vorwurfsvollen Blick zu. Wir redeten über Manuel,
was für ein toller Bub er war, wie intelligent und vernünftig, eigentlich schon eher wie ein Sechzehn- oder Siebzehnjähriger.

»Manchmal kommt er mir reifer vor als ich mir selbst«, gestand ich. Peinlicherweise machte Julia keine Anstalten zu widersprechen. Aber ich erntete auch schöne Komplimente von ihr.

»Geri, du tust ihm gut, er blüht so richtig auf. Und Alice ist glücklich, dass du dich so sehr um ihn kümmerst und dass du ihn sogar zu den Reportagen mitnimmst und dass er volles Vertrauen zu dir haben kann und dass das so gut klappt zwischen euch. Für ihn stehst du auf einem Podest«, sagte sie. Das ging mir runter wie, okay, sagen wir, es ging mir runter wie Öl.

»Ich werde ihm bei nächster Gelegenheit verraten, dass ich sein Papa bin«, versprach ich. In diesem Moment hatte ich es mir nämlich wirklich ganz fest vorgenommen.

»Ja«, sagte sie, eher sogar »Ja?«, also mit fragendem Unterton, was mich ein bisschen irritierte.

»Ich hab mir extra ein Fahrrad gekauft und möchte mit ihm einen Ausflug machen, wie das alle echten Väter tun, eigentlich hab ich das schon lange vor, aber leider ist mir irgendwie der blöde Winter dazwischengekommen«, erzählte ich.

Danach entstand eine Pause, in der ich das Gefühl hatte, dass mir Julia etwas Unangenehmes mitteilen wollte.

»Ich bin in ständigem Kontakt zu meiner Schwester. Ich telefoniere viel mit ihr«, sagte sie dann mehr oder weniger ansatzlos.

»Ja? Fein. Afrika ist heute auch nicht mehr aus der Welt, nicht wahr?«

»Zu Weihnachten kommt sie übrigens nach Wien.«

»Schön, da wird sich Manuel freuen«, erwiderte ich.

»Dann nur noch zwei Monate, und sie bleibt fürs Erste hier.«

»Wahnsinn, so schnell vergeht ein halbes Jahr«, sagte ich.

»Ja, wahnsinnig schnell.«

»Irre«, sagte ich. Wir nickten beide vor uns hin.

»Sie hat jetzt übrigens ...«

»Ja?«

»Sie hat jetzt einen festen Freund, einen richtigen Partner, endlich.«

»Tatsächlich? Einen richtigen ... ich meine, aus Somalia?«, fragte ich.

»Nein, aus Braunschweig. Ein Arzt. Ein Kollege von ihr. Jochen.«

»Jochen«, wiederholte ich möglichst wertneutral. Wir in Österreich haben ja doch eine ganz andere Namenskultur. – Walter, Günter, Werner, da kann man sich einen Typ drunter vorstellen. Aber Jochen? Von mir aus Kurti, Karli, Franzi – das sind wenigstens Charaktere. Oder Manuel, eigentlich ein schöner Name, vor allem, wenn man den Menschen dazu kennt, hat mir von Anfang an gut gefallen, also fast von Anfang an. Aber Jochen?

»Die beiden sind gemeinsam ... Sie kannten sich schon vorher. Jochen war auch mit ein Grund, warum sie sich für das Afrika-Projekt entschieden hat. Und das hat sich jetzt vertieft, das hat sich sogar ziemlich vertieft.«

»Schön für die beiden«, sagte ich. Julia nickte und sah dabei relativ säuerlich drein, was garantiert nichts mit dem ungezuckerten Früchtetee zu tun hatte.

»Die beiden wollen heiraten.«

»Heiraten?«

»Ja, sie kommen gemeinsam nach Wien und werden heiraten, wahrscheinlich schon im Mai.«

»Im Mai. Der Mai ist ideal zum Heiraten. Alle heiraten im Mai. Also alle, die heiraten«, sagte ich.

»Genau. Sie werden dann eine größere Wohnung brauchen, für ... äh ... für drei Personen dann eben.«

»Drei Personen? Ist Alice schwanger?«, fragte ich. Sie lachte.

»Nein, nein, noch nicht, dass wären dann ja schon vier Personen. Ich meine … Manuel.«

»Manuel. Ach ja. Natürlich«, sagte ich. Ich spürte ein Kribbeln oder leichtes Brennen, als hätte jemand in meinem Magen gerade eine zu warme Cola-Dose geöffnet. »Weiß er es schon? Kennt er … äh … Jochen schon?«

»Noch nicht, nur aus Erzählungen«, sagte sie. In mir rührte sich etwas, ich wusste nicht ganz genau, was es war, aber es betraf irgendwie vor allem auch Florentina und mich. Und Berthold. Es war so eine Art Déjà-vu, so ein Film von früher, Bilder im Kopf, die man schon hundert Mal gelöscht hat, und immer blendeten sie sich von selbst wieder ein.

»Das wird eine ganz neue Situation für ihn sein«, sagte Julia.

»Ja, vollkommen neu, mit Sicherheit«, erwiderte ich.

»Und schwierig, Alice hat schon ein bisschen Angst davor.«

»Ja klar. Wovor konkret?«, fragte ich. Obwohl ich es natürlich wusste.

»Na ja, Jochen und Manuel, wie das mit den beiden wird. Wie das funktioniert, in ein und derselben Wohnung, die ganze Familie. Verstehst du?«

»Die ganze Familie. Ja, ich verstehe.« Ich sprang auf, verließ fluchtartig den Raum und holte mir ein Bier aus dem Kühlschrank. Julia nutzte die Gelegenheit und rief mir die Schlüsselbotschaft hinterher, zumindest den Beginn davon.

»Und deshalb wäre es wahrscheinlich besser, meint Alice, es wäre besser für Manuel, wenn er … damit er nicht komplett verwirrt und überfordert ist …«

»Du meinst …«

»Alice meint …«

»Alice meint, es ist besser, dass er nicht weiß, dass ich sein Vater bin.«

»Zumindest vielleicht nicht gerade jetzt.«

»Ich verstehe«, sagte ich. Irgendwo musste es auch noch eine halbleere Flasche Wodka geben.

»Sonst hat er plötzlich zwei Väter auf einmal, vorher keinen und auf einmal zwei, und da fühlt er sich dann vielleicht zerrissen, hin und her gerissen. Verstehst du? Das wäre die Befürchtung.« Ich hatte sie gefunden, die Flasche, sie stand beim Glasreiniger hinter der Waschmaschine. »Es wäre nur für den Anfang, bis sich die Sache mit Jochen eingespielt hat.«

»Ja, ich verstehe. Ich hab's verstanden«, sagte ich.

»Was an deinem Kontakt zu Manuel natürlich überhaupt nichts ändern soll. Jochen ist da sicher sehr …«

»Sehr tolerant. Das freut mich. Vielleicht werden wir sogar ganz dicke Freunde. Und dann machen wir gemeinsame Radausflüge. Zu dritt.« Ich lächelte. Der Wodka schmeckte leider ein bisschen fahl.

Weltmeister im Warten

Etwa eine Stunde vor unserem Treffen rief ich Rebecca an, um abzusagen. Ich fühlte mich überhaupt nicht in der Lage, von Nora im Detail zu erfahren, warum es ihr nicht gut ging, oder sie gar abzulenken. Außerdem hatte ich bereits zu viel getrunken, zu viel oder zu wenig, eins von beiden. Wahrscheinlich sogar eher zu wenig. Rebeccas Enttäuschung war jedenfalls größer, als ich erwartet hatte.

»Ehrlich, du kannst nicht kommen? Warum denn nicht? Bist du krank? Ist etwas passiert?«, fragte sie.

»Nein, nein, es ist nichts passiert, es ist nur, es ist einfach nur absolut nicht mein Tag.«

»Aber vielleicht wird es noch dein Tag«, sagte sie.

»Das glaube ich eher nicht. Wenn ein Tag einmal nicht

mein Tag ist, bleibt er auch meistens nicht mein Tag, und dann ist der Abend mit Sicherheit erst recht nicht mein Abend.«

»Ach komm, Gerold. Ich hab mich schon so darauf gefreut.«

»Ja, hast du? Ich eigentlich auch, ursprünglich, eigentlich schon seit Wochen«, sagte ich.

»Außerdem hat Nora abgesagt. Ihr lasst mich also beide hängen, das finde ich gar nicht fein.«

»Nora kommt nicht?«, fragte ich.

»Nein, sie trifft Ronny, das ist … egal. Sie kommt nicht.«

»Und du würdest mich also trotzdem, also du meinst, wir treffen uns zu zweit?«

»Ja, klar, ich hab Hunger. Hast du keinen Hunger?«

»Doch, ein bisschen, eigentlich, merke ich gerade«, log ich.

»Na also, Gerold, dann gib dir einen Ruck, und wir treffen uns wie vereinbart. Okay?«

»Okay.«

»Es wird sicher nett, du wirst sehen, und die haben dort echt tolle Tapas«, sagte sie.

Ich war an sich nicht der Typ, der auf Befehl nüchtern werden konnte, aber nach einer kalten Dusche und in einem frischen, wenn auch ungebügelten weißen Hemd – es war eigentlich mein einziges Ausgehhemd, und mit *Ausgehen* meine ich jetzt nicht unbedingt Zoltan's Bar – jedenfalls fühlte ich mich wieder halbwegs fit, und ich war dankbar, fürs Erste nicht mehr an meine Zukunft mit Manuel beziehungsweise ohne Manuel denken zu müssen, zumindest nicht ununterbrochen.

Zum Glück gab es in diesem extrem kultivierten José Antonio dicht beschriebene, inhaltsstarke Speisekarten, mit denen man sich eine Weile still beschäftigen konnte, denn in den ersten Minuten mit Rebecca brachte ich praktisch überhaupt kein Wort heraus, weil ich von dem mir optisch Dargebotenen quasi paralysiert war. Es war nämlich mehr als beeindruckend, wie eine Frau, die schon im weißen Kittel dringenden Mailänder-Laufsteg-Verdacht aufkommen lassen konnte und selbst mit Mundschutz ein Gesicht für das Titelblatt von *Vogue* aufwärts hatte, wie so eine Frau am Abend aussehen konnte, wo dann praktisch kein einziges blondes Haar mehr dem Zufall überlassen war und auch noch das Kerzenlicht in das ganze Ensemble mit hineinspielte. Und ihr enganliegender schwarzer Pullover hatte vom Halsende abwärts so eine Art feinmaschiges Netz, eine Stickerei oder ein Fliegengitter oder weiß der Kuckuck was – ich konnte dort leider nicht ausreichend lange hinschauen –, wo man dann überhaupt komplett vergaß, damit aufzuhören, den Atem anzuhalten. Irgendwann blickte sie von der Karte auf, sah mir direkt in die Augen, sodass mir schwindlig wurde, und sagte:

»Ich nehme die Fisch-Gemüse-Vorspeisen-Variationen.«

»Das ist eine gute Idee«, erwiderte ich. In Anbetracht meines Zustands war mir da eine wirklich schlagfertige Antwort gelungen.

Rhetorisch kam ich mit ein paar Gläsern Wein in die Gänge. Zuerst klopften wir die naheliegenden Themen ab – das Lokal, das Essen, den Winter, Weihnachten, ein bisschen Job, ein paar Zähne, etwas Journalismus, sehr viele Spenden, sehr viele Rätsel, sehr viele offene Fragen, die Gesellschaft, das Geld, das Ende der Welt und so weiter.

Dann wurde es zunehmend privat. Von Nora ausgehend, die seit ungefähr zehn Jahren unglücklich in Ronny verliebt war, wobei sie nicht aufhören konnte, ihr Unglück statt vielleicht einmal ihre Verliebtheit in Frage zu stellen oder noch besser gleich Ronny selbst, kamen wir dann auf Rebeccas Vorstellung von einem Mann zu sprechen. Der Samstagabend-Mann von unlängst war es jedenfalls nicht gewesen.

»Warum nicht?«

»Weil er verheiratet ist.«

»Das ist ein Argument.«

»Ja, vor allem wenn man es erst am nächsten Morgen erfährt.«

»Also von mir erfährst du es noch am selben Abend – ich bin geschieden und somit frei«, sagte ich. Sie lachte. Das war schön anzusehen, nicht nur, weil sie sich zahntechnisch praktisch als ihr bester Kunde präsentierte.

»Ich mag Männer, die Humor haben, so wie du«, sagte sie.

»So wie dich« wäre mir noch eine Spur lieber gewesen. Außerdem durfte sie dann demnächst beginnen, meinen Humor etwas ernster zu nehmen und mich selbst vielleicht etwas wörtlicher, dachte ich.

»Und ich mag vor allem Männer, bei denen man sich nicht gleich unter Druck gesetzt fühlt«, fuhr sie fort.

»Wie meinst du, unter Druck gesetzt?«

»Na ja, dass sie etwas von mir erwarten. Dass sie auf etwas Bestimmtes hinauswollen. Du weißt schon.«

»Ja, so ungefähr«, sagte ich.

»Es gibt eben wenige Männer, mit denen man ausgehen kann, ohne dass sie das falsch verstehen, ohne dass sie glauben, dass da was ist.«

»Ich verstehe«, sagte ich – wahrheitswidrig. Denn irgendwas war eigentlich immer, und wenn nichts war, dann wünschte man sich natürlich, dass möglichst bald was sein würde, ich sowieso, vor allem in Zusammenhang mit ihr, aber egal.

»Ich möchte einfach so sein können, wie ich bin, ohne jedes Wort auf die Waagschale legen zu müssen.«

»Ja, so geht es mir auch«, erwiderte ich. Am liebsten hätte ich jetzt ihre Hand genommen und auf die Waagschale gelegt, aber das wäre kontraproduktiv gewesen. Außerdem war Rebecca offenbar noch immer nicht ganz am Punkt.

»Bei mir dauert es eben ziemlich lang, bis sich Gefühle entwickeln.« Da hatte sie ja auch den idealen Job gewählt, dachte ich.

»Und es gibt wenige Männer, die geduldig genug sind, die auch warten können, die mir die Zeit geben, die ich brauche«, schloss sie diesen Gedankengang ab.

Na ja, ein Restrisiko bestand schon, wenn man einer Frau, in die man quasi unsterblich verliebt war, die Zeit gab, dass sich ihre Gefühle entwickelten, und Jahre später stellte man vielleicht fest, dass sich diese Gefühle letztendlich doch nicht entwickelt hatten, zumindest nicht in die richtige Richtung. Aber ich schwor mir in diesem Moment, geduldig zu sein. Im Warten war ich ja sowieso Weltmeister. Aushalten konnte ich wie kein anderer. Im Nichtstun war ich der ungekrönte Kaiser.

Ich wollte das Thema zwar nicht anschneiden, sondern eher verdrängen, aber im Wein lag gewissermaßen die Wahrheit, auch die unangenehme, darum trank ich ja sonst auch lieber Bier. Jedenfalls kamen wir schließlich auf Manuel zu sprechen, und da hatte ich einen kurzen Anflug von Depression. Rebecca fragte sofort nach, und ich erzählte ihr die ganze Geschichte von Alice und diesem neu aufgetauchten Jochen aus Braunschweig.

»Ich will ehrlich gestanden nicht schon wieder ein Kind von mir verlieren«, sagte ich.

»Manuel wirst du nicht verlieren, ganz bestimmt nicht«, erwiderte sie.

»Aber gegen eine Familie kommt man als Einzelner nicht an, das kenne ich schon, das war auch bei Florentina so.«

»Der Unterschied ist, dass Florentina damals ein Kleinkind war. Aber Manuel ist bereits fast erwachsen und kann selbst entscheiden, mit wem er Kontakt haben will und mit wem er seine Zeit verbringt. Und da bist und bleibst du für ihn mit Sicherheit eine der allerersten Adressen«, behauptete sie.

»Meinst du?«

»Außerdem wirst du auch mal wieder eine eigene Familie haben, vielleicht schneller, als du glaubst«, sagte sie. Ausgerechnet bei diesen Worten legte sie ihre Hand auf meine, welche ich postwendend umdrehte, von Innenfläche auf Innenfläche, damit ich noch mehr davon spürte.

»So schnell wird das bei mir nicht gehen«, erwiderte ich.

»Wie willst du das wissen?«

»Das weiß ich. Weil ich nämlich die Angewohnheit habe, mich prinzipiell nur in Frauen zu verlieben, die enorm viel Zeit brauchen und bei denen es ewig lange dauern kann, bis sich ihre Gefühle entwickeln«, erwiderte ich.

Rebecca lachte zwar, aber am Kakiorange ihrer Ohren erkannte ich, dass meine Botschaft diesmal ziemlich unmissverständlich angekommen war.

Die Nowotnys im Unglück

Am Donnerstag kam Manuel nach dem Basketballtraining aufgeregt zur Tür hereingestürmt und wollte nur eins wissen: »Hat Romana eine Spende bekommen?« Seit unserem Besuch in der Donaustadt hatte er überhaupt auffallend oft den Namen Romana erwähnt, aber ich verkniff es mir vorerst, ihn darauf anzusprechen.

»Nein, leider, bisher noch nicht, sonst hätte man mich schon verständigt«, erwiderte ich. Daraufhin drängte er mich vehement, bei den Nowotnys anzurufen und nachzufragen, wogegen ich mich ebenso vehement zur Wehr setzte, bis wir schließlich wegen Erschöpfung auf beiden Seiten einen Kompromiss erzielten: Ich würde bei der Nachbarin, bei Christina

Kronberger, anrufen. Und die berichtete mir dann prompt von etwas doppelt Unerfreulichem. Erstens war keine Geldspende eingetroffen, was aber noch das geringere Problem war. Denn zweitens hatte Ludwig Nowotny, vielleicht wegen des Medienrummels, einen Schlaganfall erlitten und lag im Spital. Romana war seither kaum ansprechbar und Erika Nowotny mit den Nerven total am Ende und mit dem Geld sowieso.

Ich wusste genau, wie Manuel darauf reagieren würde, und er tat es dann sogar wortwörtlich. »Da müssen wir was unternehmen.«

Die einzig passende Antwort hatte ich schon auf der Zunge – mein obligatorisches Da-können-wir-nicht-viel-machen –, aber ich schluckte es gerade noch rechtzeitig herunter und sagte: »Ich werde nachdenken, ob mir vielleicht was einfällt.« Damit hatte ich mir zumindest einen zeitlichen Puffer geschaffen. Und Manuel konnte die Tatsache auf sich einwirken lassen, dass Journalismus eben manchmal genau das Gegenteil von dem bewirkte, was er bezweckt hatte.

Den Abend hatte ich eigentlich bereits abgeschrieben und wollte ihm in Zoltan's Bar den Rest geben. Ich hatte sogar schon die Winterjacke in der Hand, warf nur noch rasch einen Blick auf mein Handy und stieß dabei – doch einigermaßen überraschend, schließlich hatte ich mich zurückgehalten und keine der drei SMS, die im Ordner Entwürfe gespeichert waren, abgeschickt – auf eine neue Nachricht von Rebecca.

Lieber Gerold, ich möchte mich noch einmal für den schönen Abend mit dir bedanken. Wenn es nach mir geht, wird es nicht unser letzter gewesen sein. Ich mag, wie du bist, so offen und geradeheraus. Ich hoffe, ich hab nicht zu viel Unsinn geredet, der Wein ist mir ein bisschen zu Kopf gestiegen. Wenn du wieder mal Lust hast, mit mir fortzugehen, melde dich! Herzlich, deine Rebecca.

Ich wusste wohl, dass es auch unter gar nicht allzu engen Bekannten durchaus üblich war, am Ende das Wörtchen *deine* zu schreiben, aber in diesem Fall erlaubte ich mir, Rebeccas *deine Rebecca* komplett persönlich zu nehmen, und genau darüber wollte ich jetzt noch eine Weile nachdenken. Also ließ ich Zoltan's Bar ausnahmsweise Zoltan's Bar sein, machte mir ein Bier auf und blieb daheim, wo ich das Bild »meiner Rebecca« ungestört in all seine faszinierenden Einzelteile zerlegen und wieder zusammensetzen konnte.

Eine ganz private Spendenaktion

Freitagmittag rief mich Angelina von der *Neuzeit* an, um mir mitzuteilen, dass bei den Nowotnys leider kein Spendenkuvert eingegangen war. Für mich war damit klar, dass die Serie der anonymen Wohltaten ihr Ende gefunden hatte, aus welchen Gründen auch immer.

In diesem Zusammenhang wollte Angelina natürlich wissen, was sie den vielen Anrufern und Schreibern ausrichten sollte. Konkret bat sie mich, auf »fünf bis zehn oder höchstens fünfzehn« Fragen der Leserschaft Antworten zu formulieren, die sie den Leuten dann schriftlich oder mündlich zuteilwerden lassen konnte.

»Ungern, aber okay«, sagte ich. Ich hatte ohnehin gerade nichts Besseres zu tun, also setzte ich mich vor den Computer.

Eine der letzten Fragen betraf direkt die Nowotnys und lautete:

Sehr geehrter Herr Plassek, wir haben mit großer Betroffenheit vom Schicksal der Familie mit der autistischen Tochter gelesen. Wäre es in Ihrer Zeitung eventuell möglich, für diese Familie eine kleine Spendenaktion zu starten, damit sie nicht auf die Gunst eines einzelnen edlen – oder auch gar nicht so edlen – »Big Spender« angewiesen ist?

Irgendwie kamen mir da plötzlich die fünf Golddukaten meiner Nachbarn, der Engelbrechts, in den Sinn. Und dann fiel mir sogar noch ein, wo ich sie hin geräumt hatte. Jedenfalls machte ich mich damit sofort auf den Weg zur Bank. Auf meinem Konto hatten sich – mehr oder weniger ohne mein Zutun, sieht man von dem etwa halben Dutzend Sozialreportagen ab – erstaunliche 7685 Euro an Honoraren angesammelt, 35 Euro beließ ich auf der Bank, damit dort weiterhin eine schwarze und nicht eine rote Zahl wie früher aufschien, den Rest hob ich ab. Für die Goldmünzen gab man mir 615 Euro. Somit verfügte ich über 8265 Euro überschüssigen Bargelds, es fehlten also nur noch 1735 Euro auf die magischen zehntausend. Mir blieb eine knappe Stunde Zeit, bis Manuel nach Hause kommen würde, und da wusste ich eigentlich sofort, wen ich am besten anrief.

»Hallo Gudrun, wie geht's dir?«

»Danke, schlecht. Florentina hat sich in ihrem Zimmer eingesperrt, und Berthold ist momentan nicht ansprechbar. Kurz gesagt: Keiner redet mehr mit mir.«

»Doch, ich schon. Ich hab nämlich ein großes Anliegen. Kannst du mir 1800 Euro borgen?« Sie blies eine kräftige Portion Luft ins Telefon.

»Du bist lustig. Wo soll ich so viel Geld hernehmen?«

»Okay, dann halt nur 1735. Bitte. Ich brauche das Geld dringend. Du kriegst es in wenigen Wochen zurück. Spätestens im Jänner, wenn ich bei der *Neuzeit* fest angestellt bin.«

»Du wirst bei der *Neuzeit* angestellt?«

»Ja, fest.«

»Toll«, sagte sie.

»Finde ich auch. Kann ich auf einen Sprung bei dir vorbeikommen, um das Geld abzuholen?

»Jetzt?«

»Ja, wie gesagt, es ist dringend.«

»Wie viel, sagst du? 1800?«

»Ja, 1800. Oder zweitausend, wenn du's nicht kleiner hast. Ganz egal.«

Manuel musste ein paar Minuten vor mir daheim eingetroffen sein.

»Spende?«, fragte er.

»Leider nein«, erwiderte ich. Er wirkte niedergeschlagen und sah mich wie jemanden an, von dem man sich keine Wunderdinge erhoffen durfte. Zwar war ich genau so ungefähr die letzten zwanzig Jahre angesehen worden, aber erst seit Manuel fiel es mir so richtig unangenehm auf.

Umso mehr freute ich mich auf meine Überraschung, die ich natürlich noch ein bisschen zelebrieren musste.

»Hast du viel zu tun?«, fragte ich.

»Geht so.«

»Wollen wir Romana und ihre Mutter besuchen?«

»Wann?«

»Jetzt«, sagte ich.

»Jetzt?«

»Ja, jetzt. Also wollen wir sie besuchen?«

»Ja. Doch. Schon.« Er wirkte zögerlich.

»Aber?«, fragte ich nach.

»Aber was sollen wir dort machen, was sollen wir ihnen sagen?«

»Wir könnten versuchen, sie aufzubauen, wir könnten sie ein bisschen trösten«, sagte ich.

»Aber wie? Indem wir ihnen sagen, dass keine Spende gekommen ist? Das ist nicht sehr aufbauend. Außerdem wissen sie das ohnehin schon.«

»Hast du eine bessere Idee?«, fragte ich.

»Na ja, wir könnten Romana wenigstens eine Zeichnung abkaufen, wenn sie überhaupt eine hergibt. Ich hab zwanzig Euro. Du?«

Das war die perfekte Steilvorlage.

»Ich hab zehntausend Euro«, erwiderte ich. Zugegebenermaßen fand ich mich in dieser Situation, als ich das dicke Geldkuvert hervorzauberte und vor Manuels extrem weit aufgerissenen Augen auf den Tisch fallen ließ, wirklich cool, so ähnlich wie Michael Douglas in *Wall Street*. Wobei der eigentliche Triumph darin bestand, dass mir Manuel in einer Art Glückstaumel spontan in die Arme fiel. Da hatte ich diesem Jochen also schon einiges vorgelegt. Und damit hatten sich die Zehntausend auch bereits gerechnet.

»Ist also doch eine Spende angekommen?«, fragte er.

»Nicht direkt.«

»Wie, nicht direkt?«

»Ich hab ein bisschen nachgeholfen, ich hab … im Freundeskreis gesammelt«, antwortete ich.

»Wow. Ich hab gar nicht gewusst, dass du so reiche Freunde hast.«

»Ich auch nicht, ehrlich gestanden«, erwiderte ich.

Das Wunder vom zweiten Kuvert

Für Manuel verlief der Besuch über weite Strecken insofern enttäuschend, als er Romana nicht zu Gesicht bekam. Wenigstens gab es zwei neue Tierzeichnungen in der Mappe, wobei man nicht behaupten konnte, dass die Künstlerin gerade eine von Wärme und innerer Ruhe geprägte Schaffensperiode hatte. Wen wunderte es.

Ich selbst war zunächst einmal bis zur völligen Erschöpfung damit beschäftigt, mir von Erika Nowotny in allen Details die aktuelle Krankengeschichte ihres Mannes anzuhören, dessen rechter Arm gelähmt war, und der vermutlich monatelang dienstunfähig bleiben würde, denn ein Installateur mit steifem Arm – das ging leider gar nicht. Ich erzählte ihr, dass ich von einem Fall gelesen hatte, wo jemand ein Jahr nach einem Schlaganfall mit halbseitiger Lähmung nicht nur wieder alle Tätigkeiten hatte verrichten können, sondern sogar einen Halbmarathon gewonnen hatte. In Wirklichkeit war es natürlich kein Halbmarathon gewesen, auch kein Viertelmarathon, sondern ein internationales Schachturnier, wenn ich mich recht entsann. Aber ich merkte, wie sehr Frau Nowotny darauf angewiesen war, sich an jeden Strohhalm zu klammern.

Die gute Nachricht, also unser Geschenk, hielten wir so lange wie möglich zurück, damit sich die Freude darüber nach unserem Besuch erst so richtig entfalten konnte.

Als wir bereits im Vorraum standen, um uns zu verabschieden, brachte ich meinen Satz endlich an, oder zumindest Teile davon: »Der anonyme Wohltäter hat zwar diesmal ausgesetzt, aber dafür sind bei uns in der Redaktion und auch im privaten Umfeld viele, viele kleine Spenden eingegangen, und deshalb freut es uns ganz besonders ...« Weiter kam ich nicht, weil Manuel plötzlich dringenden Mitteilungsbedarf hatte und die Sache quasi an sich riss.

»In diesem Kuvert sind genau zehntausend Euro, und das ist dafür, dass Romana einen Kurs für Malerei besuchen kann, weil sie nämlich ganz toll zeichnen kann und coole Bilder macht«, rief er laut genug, dass man es auch im Badezimmer hören musste, wo sich Romana angeblich schon seit ein paar Stunden aufhielt. Obwohl keiner mehr damit gerechnet hatte und Frau Nowotny bei meiner Mitteilung sowieso aus allen Wolken gefallen war und scheinbar noch auf die sanfte Landung wartete, ging mit einer kleinen zeitlichen Verzögerung plötzlich die Tür auf, das blasse Mädchen kam heraus, huschte an uns vorbei in Richtung ihres Zimmers und rief uns dabei die Worte »Halt, noch nicht gehen!« zu.

Und dann spielte sich vor unseren Augen erst die eigentliche Überraschung dieses Tages ab. Romana hatte nämlich Mut gefasst, sich zu uns zu gesellen, und das hing mit dem Ding zusammen, das sie zunächst hinter ihrem Rücken versteckte und uns schließlich stolz unter die Nase hielt. Es handelte sich um ein Briefkuvert, also bereits das zweite, das hier binnen kürzester Zeit sozusagen im Umlauf war, wobei sie sich nicht entscheiden konnte, wem sie es überreichen sollte, bis ihr Manuel beides gleichzeitig abnahm, die Entscheidung und das Kuvert. Im bereits geöffneten Umschlag befanden sich exakt zwanzig Fünfhunderteuroscheine und ein Zeitungsausschnitt, über dem ein Kreuzotterschwertfischpuma prangte.

»Das ist für mich gekommen, das gehört mir«, sagte Romana und deutete auf ihren Namen auf dem Umschlag.

»Die anonyme Spende«, murmelte Manuel. Er war fast genau so perplex wie ich.

»Ja, aber Kind, seit wann holst du denn die Post? Und wieso hast du mir kein Sterbenswort davon erzählt?«, fragte Erika Nowotny. Sie war sichtlich noch nicht dort angelangt, wo sie die rasche Abfolge freudiger Sensationen so richtig bewusst wahrnehmen konnte.

»Das ist für mich gekommen, das gehört mir«, wiederholte Romana.

Als wäre die Situation noch nicht aufwühlend genug gewesen, mussten wir auch noch darüber debattieren, was mit dem von uns mitgebrachten Geldkuvert nun zu geschehen hatte. Erika Nowotny und sogar Romana wehrten sich nämlich mit Händen und Füßen dagegen, das Geschenk zu behalten. Ich wiederum fand es seltsam, eine Spende zurückzuziehen, nur weil eine zweite eingetroffen war.

Bezeichnenderweise war es wieder einmal Manuel, der eine salomonische Lösung herbeiführte, die dann allen irgendwie recht war: Frau Nowotny sollte von nun an die anonyme Spende für ihre Tochter verwalten. Dafür bekam Romana zweitausend Euro Cash aus unserem Kuvert – und zwar als Honorar für den Kreuzotterschwertfischpuma, der hiermit in Manuels Besitz überging. Und die übrig gebliebenen achttausend Euro nahmen wir einfach wieder mit.

KAPITEL SECHZEHN

Erste Hilfe für die Kumpels

Ich persönlich hätte ja kein Problem damit gehabt, das Geheimnis der elften Wohltat für mich zu behalten und darauf zu verzichten, es via *Neuzeit* der Öffentlichkeit preiszugeben. Aber es ging nicht nach mir, sondern nach Manuel, und das war schon gut so. Denn in den nächsten Tagen sollte sich zeigen, wie dankbar und glücklich beinahe jeder Mensch war, der sich von der Nachricht angesprochen fühlte, wobei es den Anschein hatte, dass sich halb Österreich angesprochen fühlte. Nur die Redaktion der Zeitschrift *Leute heute* hielt eisern an der These fest, dass Plus und Berthold Hille hinter der Spendenserie steckten.

Und wieder zeigte sich, dass gute Taten offenbar extrem ansteckende Wirkung hatten: Wie Recherchen der *Neuzeit* ergaben, waren an den Tagen nach der Meldung über das elfte anonyme Zehntausend-Euro-Geschenk bei praktisch allen befragten Hilfsorganisationen überdurchschnittlich viele und hohe Spendenbeiträge eingegangen. Und die Postlawine, die auf mich zugerollt war und die Angelina dankenswerterweise für mich entschärft hatte, bestand zu nicht unbeträchtlichen Teilen aus Anfragen, wie man der Familie Nowotny im Speziellen und autistischen Kindern, Unfall-Waisen, Schlaganfall-Patienten, armen Künstlern et cetera im Allgemeinen helfen könne und an wen man die Spenden adressieren solle.

Sogar ich selbst war in gewisser Weise ein mehr oder weniger anderer Mensch, weil ich schon seit Tagen nicht mehr später als um zehn Uhr oder höchstens halb elf Uhr morgens aufstand und dabei nur noch in absoluten Ausnahmefällen einen schweren Kopf hatte.

Apropos: Am Mittwoch traf ich nach längerer Abstinenz wieder einmal meine Kumpels in Zoltan's Bar. Ich hatte eine für meine Verhältnisse wirklich harte Arbeitsphase hinter mir – Manuel und ich hatten zwei komplette Doppelseiten vorbereitet, die in den nächsten Tagen erscheinen sollten. Dementsprechend war ich natürlich in Feierlaune.

»Seht, wer da ist, unser Heroe persönlich gibt uns die Ehre«, hieß mich Horst, der Wettbüro-Betreiber, willkommen. Auch bei ihm war längst eine gröbere Zahnreparatur fällig, aber ich hatte es bisher einfach noch nicht übers Herz gebracht, ihn an Rebecca zu vermitteln. Über kurz oder lang würde ich es wohl tun müssen, dachte ich, obwohl ich ihr seine Sprüche gern erspart hätte.

»Hallo Geri, altes Haus! Wenigstens einer von uns, der das Lachen noch nicht verlernt hat«, begrüßte mich Josi, der gelernte Konditor. Josi war nach einem halben Jahr Arbeitslosigkeit nun mäßig stolzer Empfänger der Notstandshilfe, und mit siebenhundert Euro im Monat wurde es dann auch für einen Lebenskünstler wie ihn langsam eng. Aber ich wusste, dass er ein wirklich leidenschaftlicher Surfer war, wenn auch gänzlich ohne Surfbrett, sondern nur im Internet. Und da konnte ich mir gut vorstellen, dass er mich und Manuel künftig hin und wieder bei unseren immer aufwendigeren Recherchen unterstützte. Das würde ihm Spaß machen, und etwas Geld käme auch herein, dachte ich.

»Geri, wie wäre es, wenn du zur Abwechslung mal so eine richtige Herz-Schmerz-Geschichte über bedürftige Kunstschmiede tschechischer Abstammung schreibst? Das interessiert bestimmt ein Millionenpublikum – und vielleicht sogar den Wohltäter«, scherzte Franticek. Er war ein begnadeter Handwerker und hielt sich mit Gelegenheitsarbeiten im

Pfusch noch immer recht wacker über Wasser. Sollte ihm dieses einmal bis zum Hals stehen, hatte ich ohnehin schon einen Großauftrag für ihn im Hinterkopf: Er durfte dann aus meiner Unterkunft eine echte Wohnung machen, so mit frisch gestrichenen Wänden und begehbaren Schränken – oder wenigstens begehbaren Zimmern.

Schließlich meldete sich auch Arik, der Berufsschullehrer, zu Wort. »Bei eurem Gejammer kommen mir gleich die Tränen. Stellt euch einmal Morgen für Morgen in eine Klasse mit lauter Halbwahnsinnigen. In Amerika und sonst wo sind es ja seltsamerweise immer nur die Schüler, die irgendwann einmal mit einer Pumpgun im Schulhof auftauchen und das Feuer eröffnen. Ich werde der erste Lehrer sein. Und Tausende Kollegen weltweit werden es mir nachfühlen«, versprach er uns. Okay, ihm war schwer zu helfen, aber die von der *Neuzeit* kannten bestimmt ganz gute, auf Amokläufe spezialisierte Strafverteidiger.

Wenigstens um unseren Wirt musste man sich keine Sorgen machen. Mit Gästen wie uns war eine Bar wie die von Zoltan eine Goldgrube. Obwohl es gegen drei Uhr früh dann wirklich Zeit gewesen wäre, es bei der aktuellen Abschlussrunde zu belassen und nach Hause zu gehen, wenn man mich gefragt hätte. Man hatte mich aber leider nicht gefragt.

Florentina heult sich aus

Den folgenden Donnerstag wollte ich ohne mein nennenswertes Zutun sich selbst überlassen, wie in alten Zeiten. Aber der Tag bäumte sich in den frühen Nachmittagsstunden dagegen auf, indem er etwas Unvorhergesehenes geschehen ließ, das ich, unter anderem aus wohnkomforttechnischen Gründen, jahrelang verhindert beziehungsweise aufgeschoben hatte: Es läutete nicht nur an der Tür, sondern es stand dann auch noch meine Tochter Florentina davor, wobei stehen leicht übertrieben war, weil sie sich kaum noch auf den Beinen halten konnte vor lauter Gram und Verzweiflung. Ihren Augen nach zu schließen musste sie jedenfalls schon einige Liter Tränen verloren haben, und es dauerte eine Weile, bis ich sie in die Küche gelotst und so weit beruhigt hatte, dass sie ihr erstes Wort herausbrachte. Es lautete bedauerlicherweise: »Mike.«

»Was ist mit ihm?«

»Er ist …«

»Ja?«

»Er ist … so ein Arschloch.« Das klang realitätsnah, erfrischend und auch sonst nur halb so erschütternd, wie es Florentinas Zustand hatte vermuten lassen.

»Was ist passiert?«, fragte ich.

»Es ist aus. Er hat Schluss gemacht, das heißt, er meldet sich einfach nicht mehr, er will nichts mehr von mir wissen. Und schuld ist diese … Aleksa.«

»Wer ist Aleksa?«

»Eine Schlampe, eine grindige.« Natürlich, das hätte ich mir denken können.

»Sie hat sich an ihn rangemacht, und jetzt geht er mit ihr, ich hab die beiden gesehen, wie sie …« Weiter kam sie nicht, weil sie einer Heulattacke erlag.

»Kein schöner Anblick, kann ich mir vorstellen«, sagte ich.

Jedenfalls war ausgerechnet ich auserkoren, mit meiner Tochter hier, an dem von Bierkisten flankierten provisorischen Küchentisch, einige emotional extrem aufgeladene Phasen durchzumachen, wobei ich es irgendwie schaffte, den Kardinalfehler vermutlich aller um das Wohl ihrer Kinder besorgten Eltern zu vermeiden, nämlich Florentina zu diesem Schicksalsschlag inbrünstig und auf das Allerherzlichste zu beglückwünschen, ihr zu versichern, dass ihr nichts Besseres hätte passieren können, und ihr zu versprechen, dass ich »Schlampe Aleksa« von nun an in mein tägliches Abendgebet einschließen wollte.

Das genaue Gegenteil musste der Fall sein: Um Florentina den Rücken zu stärken, war es notwendig, mit ihr Pläne zu schmieden, wie sie dieses Cannabis-durchflutete Schattengewächs Mike zurückerobern konnte, und zwar möglichst qualvoll für Aleksa. Und hatte sie Mike wieder fest in der Hand oder sonst wo, und war er ihr so richtig hörig und ergeben, dann würde sie ihn in einer weiteren, gut durchdachten Aktion publikumswirksam zur Hölle fahren lassen. Diese Vorgehensweise war zwar meiner bescheidenen Meinung nach ziemlich umständlich und aufwendig, um nämlich zum gleichen Ziel zu gelangen, das sie ohnehin schon erreicht hatte, aber so lernten es die Teenies wahrscheinlich aus den Kultserien im Fernsehen, wo mit dem ewigen Hin und Her nichts anderes als Sendezeit geschunden wurde. Egal, man spürte so richtig, wie sich Florentinas Selbstwertgefühl bei dem Gedanken an das von ihr gestaltete neue Finale mit Mike wie von selbst wieder aufbaute.

»Du bist der Einzige von meinen Eltern, der mich versteht, der mir überhaupt zuhört«, sagte sie schließlich, drückte sich an mich und schluchzte mir meinen Hemdsärmel nass, was meiner Seele ziemlich guttat – ich nahm an, es war die Seele, vielleicht war es aber auch das Herz.

»Deine Mama und Berthold haben es momentan aber auch nicht gerade leicht«, hielt ich alibimäßig dagegen. Dafür hatte sie wenig Verständnis.

»Und was wird jetzt aus Kuba?«, fragte sie ein bisschen später, als sie sich schon zum Aufbruch bereitmachen wollte, weil mittlerweile die letzte Träne getrocknet war.

»Was soll aus Kuba werden?«, erwiderte ich, um Zeit zu gewinnen.

»Fliegen wir trotzdem in den Winterferien?«, fragte sie. Meine Flugangst verpasste mir spontan einen wuchtigen Schlag in die Magengrube.

»Du meinst, wir zwei?«

»Ja, nur wir zwei«, sagte sie. Und sie hatte dabei diesen charakteristischen Florentina-Blick, bei dem ohnehin kein Mensch nein sagen konnte, außer ihren restlichen Eltern vielleicht.

»Natürlich fliegen wir. Was glaubst denn du? Wir lassen uns doch von Mike nicht unsere Reisepläne durchkreuzen.«

Sie hatte gerade noch einen kleinen Jubelschrei ausgestoßen, da trat eine Situation ein, auf die ich mich gerne etwas länger vorbereitet hätte, denn eigentlich erlebte man so etwas als Vater höchstens einmal im Leben, und in den meisten Fällen genau vierzehn Jahre früher.

Manuel schneite herein, warf seine Basketballtasche wie gewohnt auf eine der Leergutkisten und rief mir mehr oder weniger im Vorbeigehen »Hallo« zu. Doch dann schaute er plötzlich sehr schnell wieder her und entschied sich neuerlich für »Hallo«, wobei sich das zweite Hallo vom ersten im Tonfall klar unterschied und auf deutlich gestiegenes Interesse schließen ließ.

»Hallo«, erwiderte Florentina und versuchte rasch, eventuelle letzte Spuren von Liebeskummer aus dem Gesicht zu bekommen.

»Hallo.« Jetzt musste ich langsam was unternehmen.

»Manuel, das ist Florentina, meine Tochter«, sagte ich zu ihm. Das war eindeutig der einfachere der beiden zu formulierenden Sätze.

»Florentina, das ist Manuel.« Punkt, besser ging es nicht.

»Hallo«, sagte Manuel jetzt das vierte Mal. Zuerst sah Florentina mich verdutzt an, dann ihn, dann wieder mich.

»Und wer ist Manuel?«, fragte sie schließlich uns alle drei, am meisten wohl sich selbst.

»Ich bin der Sohn von einer Freundin von ihm.« Er wollte jetzt ganz besonders lässig sein, deshalb sagte er »von ihm«, schnappte sich zudem ein Glas aus dem Schrank und hielt es unter die Wasserleitung.

»Und was machst du hier?« fragte sie.

»Meine Hausaufgaben.«

»Echt?«

»Ja, und ich helfe Geri bei seinen Reportagen.« Jetzt öffnete er auch noch den Kühlschrank, obwohl er darin im Grunde nichts zu suchen hatte, weil er nämlich ganz genau wusste, dass er darin nichts finden würde.

»Manuels Mama ist Ärztin und arbeitet für ein halbes Jahr in Afrika«, erklärte ich.

»Und deshalb bin ich hier«, vervollständigte Manuel. So weit waren die Dinge recht schlüssig dargelegt. Hoffentlich fragte Florentina jetzt nicht, warum ich ihr nie etwas von ihm erzählt hatte. Aber sie fragte etwas viel Besseres.

»Dann bist du also derjenige, der in der Zeitung über den Flüchtlingsbuben ...«

»Machmut«, half ich nach.

»Der über Machmut geschrieben hat?«

»Ja, der bin ich. Machi ist mein Freund«, erwiderte Manuel, ungefähr einen Meter größer als vorher. Danach entstand eine Pause, in der sich die beiden gegenseitig musterten. »Und du bist also Geris Tochter«, sagte Manuel. Das hatten wir allerdings schon einmal.

»Ja, genau«, erwiderte sie.

»Dich habe ich mir komplett anders vorgestellt«, sagte er, und das klang in Kombination mit seinen bewundernden Blicken ziemlich nach einem Kompliment.

»Wie denn?«, wollte sie natürlich wissen.

»Na ja, eher so wie … Geri.« Die Meldung war ein voller Erfolg, denn beide grinsten jetzt auf meine Kosten, noch dazu sehr ähnlich, was aber wahrscheinlich nur mir auffallen konnte. Okay, das genügte dann. Ende der Familienzusammenführung Teil eins, dachte ich. Mir fiel nämlich kein übergreifendes Thema mehr ein. Beim nächsten Mal musste ich einfach besser vorbereitet sein. Ich begleitete Florentina zur Tür.

»Übrigens, Papa und ich haben gerade beschlossen, dass wir in den Winterferien nach Kuba fliegen«, musste sie Manuel unbedingt noch unter die Nase reiben.

»Kuba? Wow. Ehrlich?«, fragte er und sah mich dabei ziemlich finster an. Nein, finster war es nicht, eigentlich eher melancholisch oder wehmütig, so wie die Menschen, die am Flughafen zurückblieben und den Maschinen nachsahen, die gerade abhoben, und in denen ihre Liebsten saßen.

»Ja, Kuba ist ein Projekt«, sagte ich, um es vor Manuel auf eine eher sachlichere Ebene zu heben. Schon absurd: Da war man vierzig Jahre mehr oder weniger überhaupt kein Vater, und plötzlich war man hin und her gerissen, es seinen zwei Kindern gleichzeitig recht zu machen.

Beim Abschied umarmte mich Florentina heftiger als sonst, bedankte sich für meine Seelenmassage und flüsterte mir noch drei Worte ins Ohr:

»Süß, der Kleine.«

Mama hütet ihr Geheimnis

Auf Manuels Drängen besuchten wir auch wieder meine Mama, was mir nur recht sein konnte. Er sollte sie ruhig noch etwas näher kennenlernen, bei Linzer Torte und Wiener Häferlkaffee, bevor dann möglicherweise eine Braunschweiger

Oma mit original niedersächsischem Eisbein ins Spiel kam. Mama schaffte es wieder einmal, mir ihre Einsamkeit als idyllischen Mußezustand zu verkaufen, der es ihr erst möglich machte, sich über Eindringlinge wie uns so richtig, nämlich über alle Maßen, zu freuen. Manuel hätte bei ihrer minutenlangen Umarmung jedenfalls beinahe der Erstickungstod ereilt.

Die Unterhaltung mit Mama war insofern erbaulich, als sie niemals über ihre zunehmenden Krankheiten, sondern immer nur über ihre noch verbliebenen Gesundheiten sprach, was gerade bei älteren Personen absolut unüblich war. Nebenbei erwähnt: Es ist schon bezeichnend, dass die deutsche Rechtschreibung den Plural Gesundheiten gar nicht kennt – als dürfte den abertausend Krankheiten, an denen die Menschheit tagaus, tagein leidet und für die die Medizin praktisch täglich neue Namen erfindet, nur eine einzige Gesundheit gegenüberstehen – die diesem Druck auf Dauer natürlich niemals standhalten kann, was wiederum die Gesellschaft insgesamt nicht unbedingt gesünder macht, wenn man mich fragt.

Mama war immer für episodenhafte Ausflüge in ihre stets positiv belegte Vergangenheit zu haben, wozu sie von Manuel diesmal besonders herzlich eingeladen wurde. Ich wusste natürlich, warum. Endlich war sie in ihrer Zeitreise ungefähr dort angelangt, wo er sie haben wollte, um seine Millionenquiz-Frage anzubringen.

»Was war bei dir eigentlich ... zum Beispiel ... im Jahr 1974?«

»1974? Damals war ich noch jung«, sagte sie. »Ich war aber schon verheiratet. Und Geri war schon auf der Welt. Ja klar, da war er schon ein paar Jahre alt. Aber in die Schule ist er noch nicht gegangen, glaube ich, da war er noch zu klein ...«

»Und sonst? Was war sonst noch 1974?«

»Was sonst noch, Manuel? Da müsste ich nachdenken. Warum gerade 1974? Warum fragst du?« Das hatte er nun von seiner Ungeduld, jetzt musste er die Karten auf den Tisch legen:

»Weil dieser Mann, der dich kennt, du weißt schon, weil der dem Onkel Geri schon wieder eine E-Mail geschrieben hat, in der er dir etwas ausrichten will.« Er kramte das Blatt aus seiner Jackentasche und las die entsprechende Passage der Mitteilung laut vor.

Seien Sie doch so gut, und nennen Sie ihr bitte nur vier Zahlen, in folgender Reihenfolge: 1, 9, 7, 4. Vielen lieben Dank und herzliche Grüße, Ihr treuer Leser.«

»Neunzehnhundertvierundsiebzig«, sinnierte Mama so vor sich hin und steuerte ihre Pupillen dabei nach oben, wo man Erinnerungen gemeinhin am schärfsten zu sehen vermeint. Und als sie mit dem Kopf zu wippen begann und sich ihre Mundwinkel ganz leicht nach oben wölbten, da war uns klar, dass ihre Gedanken an etwas Besonderem festhielten und dass sie sehr wohl wusste, was 1974 unter anderem passiert war, beziehungsweise *wer* ihr da vielleicht passiert war. Das war nämlich mein spontaner Verdacht.

»Und? Erinnerst du dich? Weißt du, wer es ist?«, bohrte Manuel gleich nach. Jetzt lachte sie.

»Du, Manuel, jetzt frage ich dich einmal etwas«, konterte sie: »Hast du Geheimnisse?«

»Nicht viele«, erwiderte er.

»Ich hab auch nicht viele«, erwiderte Mama.

Eislaufen, nein danke

Bis zu dem Tag, an dem mich Sophie Rambuschek anrief, um mir mitzuteilen, dass sie interessante Neuigkeiten für mich hätte, waren zwei weitere anonyme Geldspenden eingegangen. Ein Zehntausend-Euro-Kuvert war an eine wohltätige christliche Vereinigung von Altenpflegern adressiert worden, das zweite traf bei einer Gruppe gemeinnütziger muslimischer Studentinnen und Studenten ein, die sich in der Soforthilfe bei Naturkatastrophen engagierten und erst vor wenigen Tagen nach einem Hangrutsch in Oberösterreich ein halbes Dorf freigeschaufelt hatten.

Diesen Spenden, Nummer zwölf und dreizehn, waren Reportagen von mir beigelegt worden, die es unter tatkräftiger Unterstützung und vor allem mentaler Betreuung Manuels in die *Neuzeit* geschafft hatten. Die Wohltäterin oder der Wohltäter hielt also nach wie vor bedingungslos an mir und meinen Zeilen fest und belohnte indirekt praktisch jede meiner journalistischen Bemühungen.

Warum? Ich konnte nicht behaupten, dass mich das nicht interessiert hätte, allerdings war ich es müde geworden, mir darüber täglich mein Hirn zu zermartern. Vielleicht handelte es sich bei dem Wohltäter ja tatsächlich um diesen geheimnisumwitterten Bekannten meiner Mama, von dem die kryptischen Mails stammten, aber ich hatte wirklich keine Lust, Türen einzurennen, die nicht offen waren und anscheinend auch niemals freiwillig geöffnet werden sollten.

Was meine Herzensangelegenheit betraf, gab es weitere Fortschritte in den Bemühungen, Rebecca zum Entwickeln ihrer Gefühle für mich zu motivieren. Ich schrieb ihr zu möglichst unterschiedlichen Tages- und Nachtzeiten, also *gelegentlich*, kurze, knapp formulierte, mit Flüchtigkeitsfehlern versehene E-Mails oder SMS, deren Inhalt sich darin erschöpfte, dass ich gerade an sie dachte. Meistens schrieb sie zurück, natürlich nie dann, wenn ich darauf wartete, also gewöhnte ich mir das Warten rasch wieder ab. Für ihre Antworten legte ich mir im Kopf eine Skala von 1 bis 100 an. 1: *Schön für dich, aber musst du mir das ständig mitteilen?* 100: *Ich denke auch Tag und Nacht nur an dich.* Auf so einer Skala pendelte sie sich etwa bei 55 ein, an guten

Tagen schafften wir es bis auf 60. Das klang dann etwa so: *Hallo Gerold, schön, dass du an mich denkst. Es tut immer gut zu wissen, dass da jemand ist, der auf der gleichen Wellenlänge schwingt. Hab noch einen schönen Abend, Rebecca.*

Am vergangenen Sonntag, dem Inbegriff eines ungetrübten Wintertags, wurde sie selbst initiativ und fragte mich per SMS, ob ich vielleicht spontan Lust hätte, mit ihr und Nora auf die zugefrorene Alte Donau Eislaufen zu gehen. Leider sprach eine Dreiviertel-Mehrheit dagegen – *Nora, die zugefrorene Alte Donau* und, allen voran, *Eislaufen*. Ich war nämlich praktisch für nichts im Leben noch weniger geschaffen als für die gehobene Balance-Akrobatik, weil es selbst in herkömmlichen Schuhen ohne Kufen und auch ganz ohne Glatteis nicht immer leicht für mich war, die Bodenhaftung zu behalten. Kurz spielte ich mit dem Gedanken an Rebecca-Umarmungen in Sekundenintervallen, aber dabei hätte ich gerne eine bessere Figur gemacht. Und vielleicht war es ja auch nicht Rebecca, sondern Nora, die eigens dafür abgestellt werden sollte, mich aufzufangen, wenn ich ins Wanken geriet, mich einzusammeln, wo immer ich lag, oder auf der spiegelglatten Weite der Alten Donau nach mir zu fahnden, wenn ich verlustig gegangen war. Das wollte ich lieber nicht riskieren. Also schrieb ich: *Heute bin ich leider verhindert, aber vielleicht können wir zwei nächste Woche wieder einmal einen schönen Abend gemeinsam verbringen.*

Als Antwort erhielt ich: *Schade. Aber gerne ein Abend nächste Woche. Wir könnten wieder nett essen gehen. Oder du besuchst mich daheim, und ich koche uns etwas. Ich koche nämlich leidenschaftlich gerne, aber nicht für mich allein!!* Das klang ungefähr nach 95, mit dem Doppel-Ausrufezeichen sogar nach 96 auf der Hunderter-Gefühle-Entwicklungs-Skala, zumindest auf meiner. Leider gab es keinen Beweis, dass diese deckungsgleich mit ihrer war.

KAPITEL SIEBZEHN

Sophie löst das Spendenrätsel

Den Anruf von Sophie Rambuschek nahm ich eher unabsichtlich entgegen.

»Gerold, ich will nicht lange drum herumreden«, sagte sie, was meiner Meinung nach eine hervorragende Idee war. »Können wir uns treffen?«

»Leider, in nächster Zeit ist es bei mir ein bisschen schwierig«, wehrte ich mich.

»Es wäre sehr wichtig«, sagte sie.

»In nächster Zeit ist es bei mir leider ein bisschen schwierig, weil ...«

»Eine Stunde würde genügen«, sagte sie.

»Schon, aber eine Stunde ist in nächster Zeit leider ein bisschen schwierig, weil ...«

»Gerold, bitte.«

»Worum geht es denn?«, fragte ich.

»Um viel. Unter anderem um mein Gewissen und um meine berufliche Zukunft. Und um deine eigentlich auch«, sagte sie. Mich interessierte ja mehr meine nicht-berufliche Gegenwart.

»Sophie, vielleicht kann ich es verkürzen. Bitte richte Kunz und den anderen aus: Ich habe noch immer nichts mit den Spenden zu tun, und ich weiß auch noch immer nicht, von wem sie stammen.«

»Aber ich«, sagte sie. Das H von ich ließ sie dabei ewig lang nachschwingen, sodass es wie ein Sandsturm in der Wüste klang, zumindest stellte ich mir vor, dass es so klang, ich war nämlich noch nie bei einem Sandsturm in der Wüste gewesen, ich war überhaupt noch nie in der Wüste gewesen.

»Du? Woher willst du das wissen?«

»Ich weiß es. Glaube mir, ich weiß es«, erwiderte sie.

Wir trafen uns im Jahrhundertbeisl in der Florianigasse, wo ich vor ungefähr einem Jahrhundert statt am Unterricht öfter an einem Flipperautomaten gehangen hatte, bei dem man relativ leicht ein Freispiel hatte erzielen können, weil der zusätzliche Schwingerarm auf seiner linken Seite die Kugel ständig im Superbonuspunkte-Loch versenkt hatte. Ich hörte noch immer das Rattern der Zählmaschine und sah das triumphale Aufblinken der bunten Lichter, so etwas vergaß man sein ganzes Leben lang nicht.

Sophie berichtete mir, dass sie im Begriff war, bei *Tag für Tag* zu kündigen, beziehungsweise gefeuert zu werden, weil dort die Zustände sozusagen von Tag zu Tag schlimmer wurden. Außerdem hatte sie einen tollen Job in Deutschland in Aussicht. Ihre Chancen standen gut, beim *Berliner Börsenblatt* die Leitung der Online-Wirtschaftsredaktion zu übernehmen. Sie war jedenfalls eine von drei Bewerberinnen, die für diesen Job noch im Rennen waren, wozu ich ihr schon einmal herzlich gratulierte. Besser mit einer Zehe in der deutschen Wirtschaft als mit beiden Füßen knöcheltief im Morast des österreichischen Boulevards.

»Jetzt brauchst du praktisch nur noch ein bisschen Glück«, sagte ich.

»Ja, und ich muss ihnen vor allem beweisen, dass ich eine seriöse Journalistin bin«, bemerkte sie.

»Wie meinst du seriös?«, fragte ich.

»Gerold, ich weiß, wer hinter der Spendenserie steckt«, sagte sie. Das allein klang noch nicht unseriös, sofern es sich dabei um die Wahrheit handelte, was mein Bauchgefühl allerdings stark in Zweifel zog. »Ich weiß, wer die Wohltäterin ist«, schob sie nach.

»Eine Frau?«

»Ja. Aber das bleibt jetzt bitte wirklich unter uns, das musst du mir versprechen.«

»Und wer ist sie?«, fragte ich.

»Das ist das Problem. Ich darf es nicht sagen. Ich hab es ihr versprochen. Sie will auf keinen Fall, dass es bekannt wird. Sie will anonym bleiben.« Sophie erkannte wohl an meinem Blick, dass ich spontan den Eindruck hatte, hier unnötig meine Zeit zu versitzen. Deshalb bestellte sie aus taktischen Gründen gleich einmal zwei Bier. Und dann erzählte sie mir, nicht gerade übertrieben direkt, mit welcher Leichtigkeit sie angeblich hinter das Geheimnis gekommen war. »Es ist nämlich außer mir offenbar keiner so schlau gewesen, einfach dort zu recherchieren, wo das Geld angekommen ist«, sagte sie.

Konkret hatte sie den Auftrag gehabt, eine Reportage über die Empfänger jener Spenden abzuliefern, die in Verbindung zu *Tag-für-Tag*-Artikeln gestanden hatten, um den Lesern zu veranschaulichen, wie gut es denen allen nun ging – quasi dank der Berichte in der Gratiszeitung. Unter anderem hatte sie Egon Seilstätter getroffen, den Leiter des Obdachlosenheims in Floridsdorf, dem das allererste Zehntausend-Euro-Kuvert zugestellt worden war. Und der habe sich irgendwann im Gespräch verplappert, dass intern ohnehin längst bekannt sei, wer die Wohltäterin war, dass die Frau aber unbedingt anonym bleiben wollte. Unter dem Siegel der Verschwiegenheit war es Sophie schließlich gelungen, ihm den Namen der Spenderin zu entlocken, behauptete sie.

»Und?«, fragte ich.

»Ich hab bei ihr angerufen, und sie hat es zähneknirschend bestätigt«, sagte Sophie.

»Ehrlich?«

»Ja, Gerold, großes Ehrenwort. Sie war total unglücklich, dass Seilstätter ihren Namen verraten hatte. Und ich musste ihr hoch und heilig versprechen, dass ihre Identität in der Öffentlichkeit geschützt bleibt.«

»Okay«, sagte ich, nichtssagender Weise. Ich war nämlich nicht gerade der Typ, der sich innerhalb von Zehntelsekunden blendend auf neue Situationen einstellen konnte, bei denen völlig unklar war, was von ihnen zu halten war. Außerdem wusste ich ehrlich gestanden nicht, was Sophie Rambuschek jetzt eigentlich von mir wollte. »Und dann hab ich leider einen schweren Fehler gemacht, ich habe in der Redaktionskonferenz alles erzählt, ich habe dort blöderweise auch ihren Namen genannt, ich weiß selbst nicht, was mich da geritten hat«, fuhr sie fort.

»Und?«

»Norbert war komplett aus dem Häuschen.«

»Kunz?«

»Ja, Norbert. Zuerst hat er gemeint, wir machen überhaupt gleich eine Sonderausgabe. Dann hab ich gesagt, wir dürfen aber den Namen von ihr nicht nennen. Darauf sagt er: Natürlich werden wir den Namen nennen. Darauf ich: Das geht nicht, sie will anonym bleiben. Darauf er: Wenn ein Name einmal unter Journalisten bekannt ist, ist er nicht mehr anonym. Darauf ich: Das ist unseriös, sie will es nicht. Das können wir nicht machen. Darauf er: Das müssen wir sogar machen, das ist unsere journalistische Pflicht …« Ich unterbrach sie und Kunz ja ungern, aber ich bestellte uns noch rasch zwei Bier.

»Also darauf er: Das ist unsere journalistische Pflicht. Der Eigentümer köpft uns, wenn wir das nicht machen. Darauf ich: Ich habe es ihr aber versprochen. Darauf er: Als Journalistin kannst du so etwas gar nicht versprechen. Natürlich berichten wir darüber. Und zwar groß, in allen Details, mit Biografie, Lebenslauf, ihren Motiven und so weiter.« Sie gönnte sich eine kurze Atempause.

»Und?«, fragte ich.

»Da bin ich dann natürlich vollkommen ausgezuckt und hab gesagt, dass ich das ganz bestimmt nicht mache. Darauf er: Dann macht es halt ein anderer. Darauf ich: Dann kündige ich. Und dann hab ich den Raum verlassen.«

»Bravo. Und darauf er?«, fragte ich.

»Er ist noch mal zu mir gekommen und hat gesagt: Sophie, wir müssen die Story bringen, schon wegen *Leute heute* und der Verleumdungsklage. Wir haben dank dir den Beweis in der Hand. Da geht es um die Existenz unserer ganzen Redaktion. Du kriegst natürlich ein Riesen-Sonderhonorar.«

»Und darauf du?«, fragte ich.

»Darauf bin ich gegangen.«

»Bravo. Und?«

»Und jetzt sitzen wir hier.«

»Aha«, sagte ich. Ich musste kurz nachdenken, bis mir die Schlüsselfrage einfiel. »Und was erwartest du von mir, was soll ich tun?«

»Mich interviewen«, erwiderte sie.

»Interviewen?«

»Ja, genau. Du berichtest darüber in der *Neuzeit*, noch bevor *Tag für Tag* die Bombe platzen lässt, also spätestens in der Freitagsausgabe.« Sie zog einen Zettel heraus und las den vorgefertigten Text vor:

Neuzeit: *Frau Rambuschek, Sie haben sich intensiv mit der Serie anonymer Geldspenden beschäftigt. Sind Sie zu einem Ergebnis gekommen?*

Rambuschek: *Ja, ich weiß definitiv, wer die Person ist, die diese wunderbaren Geschenke an Bedürftige und ihre Helfer verteilt hat – und hoffentlich noch weiter verteilen wird.*

Neuzeit: *Dürfen Sie uns verraten, um wen es sich handelt?*

Rambuschek: *Nein, das darf ich leider nicht. Es ist der dringliche Wunsch dieser Person, weiterhin anonym zu bleiben. Schutz* der Identität von Privatpersonen ist eines der wichtigsten journalistischen Gebote, daran will ich mich unbedingt halten. Die Person hat ja kein Verbrechen begangen, sondern etwas Gutes getan, das schon vielen Menschen geholfen hat.

Neuzeit: *Können Sie uns irgendetwas über das Motiv des Wohltäters oder der Wohltäterin erzählen?*

Rambuschek: Es ist eine Person, die sich selbst einmal in einer schlimmen Notlage befunden hat und die jenen, die sie damals aufgefangen haben, unendlich dankbar ist. Dafür wollte sie sich revanchieren.

Neuzeit: *Diese Person hat bisher mindestens 130 000 Euro verschenkt. Wie konnte sie sich das finanziell leisten?*

Rambuschek: Dazu kann ich versichern, dass es sich um Geld handelt, dass legal in ihrem Besitz gewesen ist. Diese Person hat einen freischaffenden Beruf, in dem sie zuletzt auch international sehr erfolgreich war.

Neuzeit: *Sie sind Redakteurin bei der Gratiszeitung* Tag für Tag. *Was wird man in Ihrer Zeitung darüber lesen?*

Rambuschek: Das ist nicht meine Entscheidung. Ich habe jedenfalls ausdrücklich darum gebeten, dass die Anonymität dieses vorbildlichen Menschen gewahrt bleibt. Ich fühle mich dafür verantwortlich.

Neuzeit: *Und wenn nun aber doch der Name publik gemacht wird?*

Rambuschek: Dann werde ich die entsprechenden Konsequenzen ziehen.

Neuzeit: *Frau Rambuschek, wir danken für das Gespräch.*

Das war so eine Situation, wo man glaubte, noch ungefähr hundert wichtige Fragen zu haben, wo einem aber konkret keine einzige einfiel. Außerdem merkte ich, dass ich drei Bier um die Mittagszeit schon einmal besser vertragen hatte. Irgendwie fühlte ich mich nämlich ziemlich erschlagen. Das

Interview selbst fand ich wirklich sehr okay, vor allem weil es auch bereits fertig ausformuliert war. Und was Sophie betraf, war ich außerordentlich positiv überrascht, sie hatte ja wirklich Rückgrat, und das trotz täglicher *Tag-für-Tag*-Massagen. Ihre Haltung nötigte mir jedenfalls Respekt ab. Zum Glück musste ich in der Sache selbst keine Entscheidungen treffen.

»Ich werde das alles mit Clara Nemez von der *Neuzeit* besprechen und dir dann gleich Bescheid geben«, sagte ich.

Darauf sie: »Ja bitte, tu das.«

Darauf ich: »Mache ich.«

Darauf sie: »Danke, Gerold.«

Darauf ich: »Nichts zu danken.«

Darauf sie: »Doch. Danke!«

Bohrende Zusatzfragen

»Und wer ist die Frau?«, fragte Clara Nemez am Telefon.

»Das weiß ich nicht.«

»Warum weißt du das nicht? Hast du nicht gefragt?«

»Doch, ich glaube schon. Aber Sophie hat es mir irgendwie nicht gesagt. Die Frau will ja anonym bleiben, deshalb, denke ich.«

»Das ist zu respektieren. Aber wir müssen trotzdem wissen, um wen es sich handelt, wenn wir das Interview tatsächlich bringen wollen.«

»Meinst du?«, fragte ich.

»Ja sicher. Was ist, wenn die Sache nicht stimmt, wenn die Kollegin, diese …«

»Sophie Rambuschek.«

»Wenn diese Frau Rambuschek eine ganz andere Strategie verfolgt, wenn sie hier ihr eigenes Süppchen kocht?«

»Das glaube ich irgendwie eher nicht, sie hat ziemlich ehrlich gewirkt«, erwiderte ich.

»Oder wenn sich das Ganze als großer Irrtum herausstellt, wenn die Rambuschek selbst in eine Falle getappt ist?«

»Ich kenne Sophie. Sie ist an sich nicht der Typ, der in eine Falle tappt«, sagte ich. Ich kannte mich da aus, denn ich war eher der gegenteilige Typ.

»Trotzdem sollten wir unbedingt wissen, wer es ist, wenn wir die Geschichte bringen«, erwiderte Clara.

»Du meinst, ich soll Sophie noch einmal fragen …«

»Ja genau, du kannst ja sagen, das wäre die Bedingung für das Interview. Wir müssen uns da einfach absichern. Sonst sind wir am Ende die Blamierten. Da schaut die ganze Öffentlichkeit drauf.«

»Und wer ist die Frau? Wie heißt sie? Woher kennt sie dich? Warum hat sie für die Spenden immer nur deine Zeitungsartikel genommen?«, fragte Manuel wenig später.

»Keine Ahnung.« Langsam nervten sie mich mit ihren ständigen bohrenden Zusatzfragen.

»Hast du nicht gefragt?«

»Ehrlich gestanden, nein.«

»Warum nicht?«

»Weil ich … weil ich einfach nicht gefragt habe. Es waren so viele Dinge … Ich hab einfach nicht gefragt, aus, Schluss, basta.« Manuel schnitt eine Grimasse und machte Gesten, die zum Ausdruck bringen sollten, dass er ernste Bedenken bezüglich meines Geisteszustands anmeldete.

»Aber das ist doch das Allerwichtigste.« Er durfte dann langsam aufhören, ständig den Kopf zu schütteln, auch wenn er im Prinzip natürlich nicht so unrecht hatte, gestand ich mir insgeheim ein, denn natürlich hätte ich an sich gerne gewusst, was diese Frau mit mir zu tun hatte, jetzt, da Manuel mich daran erinnerte. Irgendwie machte ich mir ernsthafte Sorgen über mich, weil ich plötzlich mittags offenbar keine drei Biere mehr vertrug.

»Wie kann man nur so einen Fehler machen!« So, jetzt reichte es. Ich hatte das Gefühl, dringend ein Machtwort sprechen zu müssen.

»Genug. Hör auf zu nerven! Ich rufe Sophie Rambuschek ja schon an.«

»Gute Idee«, sagte er.

Alma Cordula Stein

Ich musste eine ganze Reihe hochkarätiger Verschwiegenheits-Gelübde ablegen, bis ich Sophie endlich so weit hatte, dass sie mir die Identität der großen Gönnerin preisgab. Sie hieß Alma Cordula Stein.

»Alma Cordula Stein?«, fragte Manuel.

»Alma Cordula Stein«, erwiderte ich.

Wie nicht anders erwartet, sagte mir der Name, so gut er klang, rein gar nichts. Dank Manuel und Google erfuhr ich freilich nur ein paar Minuten später alles, was man schon immer über Alma Cordula Stein hätte wissen können, hätte man sich für modernen Tanz interessiert. Ich interessierte mich weder für modernen noch für unmodernen Tanz, ich war also doppelt aus dem Schneider.

Alma Cordula Stein, 1975 in Wiener Neustadt geboren, also fünf Jahre jünger als ich, war früher einmal Tänzerin bei der London Dance Company gewesen und arbeitete heute offenbar mindestens weltweit als Choreografin, unter anderem in New York, Hanoi und Madrid. Außerdem leitete sie ein gewisses Modern Dance Studio Nr. 1 in Warschau, was sie nicht daran hinderte, in Wien und/oder Marseille zu wohnen.

Tänzerinnen galten zwar gemeinhin als extrem beweglich, aber wie sie solche globalen Grätschen schafften, war mir ein Rätsel. Derzeit probte sie übrigens für ein Performance-Theaterprojekt im Wiener Art-Dance-Forum, worüber man einen aktuellen Kurzbericht im *Tagblatt-Online* nachlesen konnte.

»Also du kennst sie nicht?«, fragte Manuel.

»Noch nie etwas von ihr gehört.«

»Und du hast auch keine Ahnung, was sie mit dir zu tun haben könnte?«

»Keine Ahnung«, sagte ich. Tanz konnte es jedenfalls eher nicht sein.

»Dann bleibt uns nur eine Möglichkeit«, meinte er. Ich erkannte genau eine weniger, aber Manuel war diesbezüglich immer für Überraschungen gut.

»Und welche?«

»Wir müssen sie fragen, und zwar am besten gleich heute.« Normalerweise hätte ich laut aufgelacht, zumindest früher, als ich Manuel noch nicht gekannt hatte. Mittlerweile wusste ich, dass bei ihm Sätze, die mit »Wir müssen« eingeleitet wurden, prinzipiell hundertprozentigen Anspruch auf Umsetzung hatten, egal wer davon betroffen war, seit Mitte September meistens ich.

»Wie sollen wir sie fragen? Sie wird nicht unbedingt auf uns warten«, sagte ich.

»Dann müssen wir eben auf sie warten.«

»Und wo?«

»Dreimal darfst du raten«, sagte er.

»In diesem Art-Dance-Forum?«

»Kluger Onkel Geri«, erwiderte er.

Der Plan war an sich gut, obwohl er nicht von mir stammte – kleiner Scherz. Im Gewirr von etwa fünfzig Wühlmäusen würde man eine Wühlmaus, die sich dreimal schneller bewegte als alle anderen, vielleicht eine außerordentlich flotte Wühlmaus nennen. Unter Menschen bei einer Theaterprobe bezeichnete man so jemanden gemeinhin als Regieassistentin, deshalb erkannten wir die entsprechende Person auch sofort. Manuel steuerte direkt auf sie zu und fragte, ob er in einer Probenpause fünf Minuten mit Alma Cordula Stein sprechen könnte, es wäre wichtig, denn er hatte sich für sein quasi über Sein oder Nichtsein entscheidendes Schulreferat *Prominente Künstler und ihre Arbeit* das Thema *Tanz-Choreografie* und eben Alma Cordula Stein persönlich ausgesucht. Ich fungierte diesmal hochoffiziell als sein Vater, der ihn begleitete. Es war schon ein ganz eigenes, ziemlich erhebendes Gefühl, als er mich sozusagen vor Zeugen zum ersten Mal »Papa« nannte.

Wir durften in einem kleinen Backstage-Salon warten, in dem sogar ein Kühlschrank stand, dessen Inhalt mich sehr interessiert hätte, aber ich ließ höflichkeitshalber die Finger davon. Manuel war deutlich aufgeregter als ich, wobei er meinte, dass mich Frau Stein entweder schon am Aussehen erkennen würde oder spätestens dann, wenn ich meinen Namen nannte. Sie würde uns unseren Schwindel auch ganz bestimmt nicht übelnehmen, weil ich bei Frau Stein sicher einige Dutzend Steine im Brett hatte, sonst hätte sie mich nicht indirekt an ihren großen geheimen Spendenaktionen beteiligt.

Die drahtige junge Frau mit kurzem, blauweißem oder zumindest blauweiß gefärbtem Haar, die dann zu uns hereinkam und sich ziemlich anstrengte, leutselig zu wirken, wozu sie gleich einmal in einem Zug eine halbe Zigarette in Rauch auflösen musste, war von den Proben sichtlich gezeichnet, von den Proben oder vom Leben, oder von beiden.

»Was kann ich für dich tun, junger Mann?«, sagte sie zu Manuel, dem sie fahrig ihre Nicht-Zigaretten-Hand entgegenstreckte. Bis die Antwort eintraf, hatte sie mich ebenfalls bereits begrüßt, wobei man nicht behaupten konnte, dass mein Anblick sie besonders in den Bann geschlagen hätte.

»Frau Stein, ich heiße Manuel, und das ist mein ... mein Onkel Gerold. Gerold Plassek. Der Journalist. Von der *Neuzeit*.«

»Aha«, sagte sie, und sie sagte es so, dass man annehmen konnte, dass sie allerhöchstens das Gefühl hatte, den Namen vielleicht schon einmal gehört oder gelesen zu haben. Somit war sozusagen der Worst Case eingetreten, weil die Frau offensichtlich überhaupt nichts mit mir anzufangen wusste und ich im Grunde auch nicht viel mit ihr, obwohl sie mir vom Typ her sympathisch war und man mit ihr sicher das eine oder andere Bier zwitschern konnte, so wie sie aussah.

Ich an Manuels Stelle hätte eingesehen, dass da nichts zu holen war, hätte alibimäßig meine fünf Schulfragen heruntergebetet, hätte mir artig die Antworten notiert und wäre wieder verschwunden. Aber er musste in dieser Hinsicht mehr nach Alice geraten sein, denn er sagte: »Frau Stein, warum wir in Wirklichkeit hier sind, ist, weil wir wissen wollen, ob es stimmt, dass Sie die anonyme Spenderin sind. Wir wollen es wirklich nur für uns wissen, wir erzählen niemandem davon, großes Ehrenwort.«

Alma Cordula Steins Miene verfinsterte sich, was dieser schon an sich düsteren Miene gar nicht gut stand, fand ich. Wenn man bereits mehrmals Menschen gesehen hatte, die sich kurz vor einem Tobsuchtsanfall befanden, dann konnte man sich lebhaft vorstellen, dass es in diesem Fall nicht mehr lange dauern würde, bis es so weit war. Ihr Blick hetzte dabei aufgeregt von Manuel zu mir und wieder zurück, bis sie sich dann doch für mich entschied, wahrscheinlich weil ich eindeutig der Volljährige von uns beiden war.

»Woher haben Sie das? Wer hat Ihnen das erzählt? Ich habe diese Frau ... diese Journalistin ausdrücklich ersucht, dass das geheim bleibt. Ich bin Künstlerin, und ich stehe in der Öffentlichkeit. Was ich privat spende, geht niemanden was an.«

»Entschuldigung, wir wollten wirklich nicht, dass Sie jetzt böse auf uns sind, wir wollten nur wissen, warum Sie so viel Geld gespendet haben«, sagte Manuel, und das war gar keine hohe Schauspielkunst, sondern seine echte, erbärmlich klingende Stimme, die die Worte sozusagen direkt vom Herzen abgeholt und die Kehle hinauf gegurgelt hatte. Sein Gesicht war dabei hochrot angelaufen, er genierte sich in Grund und Parkettboden. Nervös trippelte er herum und zappelte wie ein kleiner Bub, der dringend die Toilette aufsuchen sollte. Er tat mir so leid, dass ich unwillkürlich meine Hand auf seine Schulter legte, und diese Choreografie stimmte Alma Cordula Stein wieder ein bisschen versöhnlich.

»Nein, nein, ich bin überhaupt nicht böse auf euch«, sagte sie milde.

Das war meiner Meinung nach ein gutes Schlusswort, aber Manuel, der Kämpfer, witterte offenbar seine Chance und ließ seinen ganzen kindlichen Charme spielen.

»Vielleicht können Sie uns doch verraten, warum Sie so viel Geld gespendet haben, wir behalten es auch wirklich für uns, niemand wird es erfahren, großes Ehrenwort.« Sie musterte den Buben lange und sah dann auch mir tief in die Augen, was mir gar nicht angenehm war. Schließlich bot sie uns an, uns zu setzen. Und dann erzählte sie.

Sie hatte bereits als ganz kleines Mädchen davon geträumt, eine berühmte Tänzerin zu werden. Beziehungsweise hatten es ihre Eltern geträumt, und sie hatte den Traum schließlich in die Realität umgesetzt. Dafür musste sie leider ihre gesamte Kindheit und Jugend opfern. Im Alter von achtundzwanzig hatte sie tatsächlich alle wichtigen europäischen Bühnen erobert, und plötzlich war kein Ziel mehr vor ihren Augen, keines mehr in Reichweite, und auch am Horizont tat sich keines auf. Von da an ging es steil bergab mit ihr: Streit und Bruch mit Eltern und Freunden, innere Leere, Isolation, Depressionen, Tabletten, Alkohol, das volle Programm. Manuel warf mir zwar einen strafenden Seitenblick zu, aber ich konnte mir zugutehalten, niemals Drogen gebraucht zu haben, um Alkohol zu konsumieren. Außerdem war es mit mir nie so wirklich bergab gegangen, weil ich von relativ niedrigem Niveau weg gestartet war, das war praktisch mein Vorteil gegenüber Frau Stein.

Drei Jahre später war sie in Wien dann endgültig in der Gosse gelandet, und waren es früher Tanzbühnen gewesen, so führten ihre Tourneen sie nun von einer Entgiftungsstation zur nächsten – und dann wieder auf die Straße zurück, wo sich natürlich niemand um sie scherte, weil dort jeder mit seinem eigenen Absturz beschäftigt war.

In einer eisigen Februarnacht war im Wiener Stadtpark ein Obdachloser, der neben ihr eingeschlafen war, an Unterkühlung gestorben, das hatte ihr selbst praktisch das Leben gerettet, denn irgendein barmherziger Samariter musste sie dort aufgelesen und in die Schlafstätte nach Floridsdorf gebracht haben. Dort wurde sie dann quasi Zeugin ihrer eigenen Wiedergeburt, weil sie nach und nach erfuhr, was Mitmenschlichkeit ausmachte, nämlich dass diejenigen, die etwas hatten, es denen gaben, denen es fehlte, egal ob Quartier, Verpflegung, Wärme oder Zuwendung.

Nach weiteren drei Jahren, in denen sie unter anderem selbst als Pflegerin gearbeitet hatte, fühlte sie sich wieder kräftig und mutig genug, in die Tanzszene zurückzukehren, wo sich alle sogenannten Freunde von früher so verhielten, als wäre sie nie weg gewesen. Was sie in den sechs Jahren ihrer Bühnenabstinenz erlebt hatte, wollte keiner so genau wissen.

Bereits mit ihren ersten choreografischen Arbeiten für eher kleinere Tanztheaterbühnen gelang es ihr, Aufmerksamkeit zu erregen, bis ihr schließlich bei einem Modern-Dance-Festival in Marseille zum zweiten Mal der internationale Durchbruch gelang. Seit einigen Jahren eilte sie sozusagen von Erfolg zu Erfolg, wobei sie sich und uns und der gesamten Welt schwor, den wiedergewonnenen Halt nie mehr zu verlieren. Wenn man sah, wie krampfhaft sie sich bei diesen Worten an ihre Zigarette klammerte, konnte man ihr dafür nur alles Gute wünschen.

Als sie jedenfalls im September nach langer Zeit wieder einmal in Wien gelandet war, blätterte sie in einer Zeitung – es handelte sich offensichtlich um *Tag für Tag* – und stieß auf die Notiz von der heillos überfüllten Obdachlosen-Schlafstätte in Floridsdorf, der die Subventionen gekürzt worden waren. Sie schnitt die Zeitungsmeldung aus, zweigte von ihren Ersparnissen zehntausend Euro ab, besorgte sich ein Kuvert, legte Geld und Artikel hinein und schickte es ohne Absender an Egon Seilstätter, den Leiter des Heims, der ihr trotzdem bald auf die Schliche kam – so lange, wie sie sich nun schon kannten.

»So habe ich endlich ein bisschen etwas von dem zurückgeben können, was ich bekommen habe«, sagte sie und lehnte sich zurück, als wäre die Geschichte damit bereits zu Ende erzählt.

»Und dann?«, fragte Manuel.

»Was dann? Nichts dann«, sagte sie.

»Und die anderen Spenden?«

»Die anderen Spenden?«

»Ja, die anderen Spenden«, wiederholte Manuel.

»Du meinst ... diese anonyme Serie?«

»Ja, die zwölf anderen Geldkuverts.«

»Ich habe einmal im Flugzeug darüber gelesen. Zwölf sind es schon? Donnerwetter«, sagte sie.

»Heißt das, dass die gar nicht von Ihnen sind?« Jetzt lachte sie erstmals. Als ich ihre Zähne sah, musste ich unweigerlich an Rebecca denken. Ich musste übrigens sowieso andauernd an Rebecca denken – während Manuel die wichtigen Fragen stellte.

Immerhin dämmerte mir, dass hier gerade eine völlig neue Wahrheit im Begriff war, ans Licht zu kommen, die mich vermutlich längere Zeit beschäftigen würde, mich und Manuel sowieso.

»Kind, wer behauptet denn so einen Unsinn? Mit den anderen Geldspenden habe ich rein gar nichts zu tun«, sagte sie kopfschüttelnd.

»Jetzt verstehe ich. Und deshalb kennen Sie auch meinen Onkel Gerold nicht«, dachte Manuel. Unnötigerweise dachte er es laut, denn nun sah sich Alma Cordula Stein genötigt, mich von oben bis unten zu mustern, um schließlich gelangweilt bis abweisend den Kopf zu schütteln.

»So, ich glaube, wir haben Ihre Aufmerksamkeit lange genug strapaziert«, sagte ich und gab mir und Manuel jeweils einen Ruck, unseren überfallartigen Besuch zu beenden. Und als Belohnung, weil wir endlich von ihr abließen, trugen wir schließlich sogar noch zwei Freikarten für die Premiere davon.

»Magst du mit Tante Julia?«, fragte ich Manuel.

»Nein danke, du kannst gern mit der Zahnärztin gehen«, erwiderte er.

»Oder Rebecca und Tante Julia gehen«, fiel mir ein. Tanz war eben nicht so ganz unseres.

KAPITEL ACHTZEHN

Superstar Geri darf weiterschreiben

Die mitternächtlichen Chefanalytiker in Zoltan's Bar brachten die jüngsten Entwicklungen in der Causa folgendermaßen auf den Punkt:

»Also eins steht fest, es gibt zwei verschiedene Spender«, sagte Horst.

»Oder dreizehn«, bemerkte Josi. Das meinte er zwar natürlich nicht im Ernst, aber lustig fand es trotzdem keiner.

»Wahrscheinlich war es so, dass diese Tänzerin die Zehntausend gespendet hat, so, wie du es erzählt hast, Geri. Dann hat das jemand in der Zeitung gelesen oder hat sonst wo davon gehört und sich gedacht – gute Idee, das mache ich auch, Geld spielt bei mir ohnehin keine Rolle, da mache ich gleich eine ganze Serie draus«, meinte Arik.

»Wobei es die Tänzerin konkret für das Obdachlosenheim gemacht hat. Während es der anderen Spenderin, wenn es eine Frau ist, ziemlich egal ist, für welche gute Sache sie spendet. Hauptsache, der Zeitungsartikel ist von dir, Geri«, meinte Franticek.

»Nicht nur wenn es eine Frau ist, auch wenn es ein Mann ist«, ergänzte Arik.

»Klugscheißer«, erwiderte Horst.

»Also könnte es dann doch der Alte von deiner Ex sein, damit er dem Finanzamt die Arschkarte zeigen kann«, meinte Josi.

»Nein, Berthold Hille war es auf keinen Fall, den können wir abhaken«, sagte ich.

»Aber er ist der Einzige, der ein Motiv hat, dich in die Sache mit hineinzuziehen«, erwiderte Josi.

»Der Einzige, den wir kennen«, schränkte Arik ein.

»Wie auch immer, Hauptsache, unser Superstar Geri darf weiterschreiben, und es fließt weiter Spendengeld, dann haben wir hier wenigstens was, worüber wir reden können, und Österreich schadet es auch nicht«, sagte Franticek.

»Richtig, und deshalb geht die nächste Runde meiner Meinung nach auf Geri«, sagte Horst. Dem widersprach natürlich keiner.

»Meister Zoltan, fünf Einheiten«, vervollständigte Josi.

Zum Glück wurde Alma Cordula Steins Geheimnis weder in der *Neuzeit* noch sonst wo gelüftet. Sophie Rambuschek schwor mir ewige Dankbarkeit, obwohl ich wahrscheinlich nicht der Typ war, der mit ewigen Dankbarkeiten auf Dauer etwas anzufangen wüsste. Ihr auf einem kapitalen Trugschluss aufgebautes Interview verschwand jedenfalls im elektronischen Nirvana, wodurch ihr möglicherweise ein frühzeitiges Ende ihrer journalistischen Karriere erspart blieb. *Tag für Tag* war die Geschichte nun zu unbedeutend, also beließ man es bei einer Kurzmeldung darüber, dass zwar eine der dreizehn geheimen Spenden von der tüchtigen Chefreporterin des Hauses aufgeklärt und die Urheberin ermittelt werden konnte, dass sich der Serienwohltäter aber noch immer auf freiem Fuß befand und jederzeit wieder zuschlagen konnte.

Manuels Draht nach Quebec

Für Donnerstag, 19.30 Uhr – diese Uhrzeit hatte sich beim letzten Mal bewährt –, war ich bei Rebecca daheim zum Essen eingeladen. Mein Hauptproblem bestand darin, dass es erst Dienstagvormittag war und dass ich nicht wusste, womit ich die Zeit bis dahin totschlagen konnte, während es draußen in dicken, schweren Flocken von links oben nach rechts unten schneite.

Normalerweise freute ich mich um elf Uhr bereits auf Manuel, der immer ein bisschen Leben in die Bude brachte, und das war sogar noch stark untertrieben, denn im Grunde lebte meine Bude ausschließlich vom Leben, das Manuel hereinbrachte. Ohne ihn stand hier mehr oder weniger alles still, einschließlich der Zeit. Seit dem Beginn meines Gedankens daran war zum Beispiel nicht mehr als eine Minute vergangen, und ich musste noch dazu schnell an etwas anderes denken, damit ich nicht vollständig trübsinnig wurde, denn heute Nachmittag war Manuel verhindert. Er und Tante Julia mussten nämlich unbedingt schon erste Weihnachtseinkäufe erledigen. Okay, so konnte ich nun ungestört über die demnächst hereinbrechenden Weihnachtsfeiertage sinnieren, aber das hielt ich auch nicht länger als eine halbe Minute aus.

Andere knieten sich in solchen Situationen vermutlich in ihre Arbeit, aber dafür war ich weiterhin nicht gerade der Prototyp, nicht nur, weil ich prinzipiell nur im äußersten Notfall kniete, das war schon vor gut dreißig Jahren bei der Kommunion so gewesen, die ich nicht als einen Knie-Notfall hatte akzeptieren können. Außerdem hatten wir erst am Vortag unsere jüngste Reportagen-Doppelseite über ein neu gegründetes Betreuungszentrum für blinde und sehschwache Kinder fertiggestellt, die am Mittwoch erscheinen sollte. Ich konnte ja nicht ununterbrochen nur arbeiten.

Apropos: Angelina von der *Neuzeit* sorgte liebevoll für dauerhafte Beschäftigung für mich, indem sie meine Mailbox alle paar Stunden mit neuer Post zupflasterte. Weil ich dort schon länger nicht hineingesehen hatte, überflog ich sie jetzt einmal routinemäßig, mit dem Wunsch, nirgendwo länger hängenbleiben zu müssen und den Schreibern keine mühseligen Antworten schuldig zu sein.

Interessanterweise stieß ich dabei auf eine relativ neue Mitteilung des mysteriösen Bekannten meiner Mutter, die mir zunächst komplett aus dem Zusammenhang gerissen erschien. Sie lautete:

Lieber Herr Plassek, aber nein, der Verdacht allein ehrt mich zwar, aber dahingehend muss ich Sie enttäuschen, denn zu so großen Ersparnissen habe ich es leider nicht gebracht. Ich bin nur ein kleiner pensionierter Lehrer, der an einer Privatschule in Quebec Deutsch unterrichtet hat. Ja, ich bin 1975 ein wenig fluchtartig nach Kanada übersiedelt, eine Entscheidung, an der Ihre geschätzte Frau Mama nicht unwesentlich beteiligt war. Sie hätte ihre Familie niemals im Stich gelassen, und auch dafür bewundere ich sie. Nun lebe ich also 6200 Kilometer entfernt – und lese noch immer täglich meine geliebten Nachrichten von daheim, das World Wide Web macht es möglich. Es erfüllt mich mit Freude, dass mich Ihre Mutter wenigstens in angenehmer Erinnerung behalten hat. Und was Sie betrifft: Bitte schreiben Sie weiter und helfen Sie den Armen und Schwachen. Erfüllen Sie Ihre Mission als Bote der Nächstenliebe! Ich beneide Sie um diese wundervolle Gabe. Ihr treuer Leser aus Quebec.

Abgesehen davon, dass der pastorale Schreibstil dieses Mannes irgendwie überhaupt nicht mein Ding war und dass ich mir absolut nicht ausmalen wollte, wie nahe er meiner Mama jemals gestanden oder sogar gelegen hatte, also ganz abgesehen davon fragte ich mich, worauf er mir da eigentlich geantwortet hatte. Als ich weiter runter scrollte, stieß ich tatsächlich auf eine vor drei Tagen von mir verfasste Mail, die ich, offenbar in geistiger Umnachtung, an mir selbst vorbei geschrieben haben musste. Sie lautete:

Sehr geehrter treuer Leser, ich habe meiner Mama die Zahlen 1, 9, 7, 4 ausgerichtet. Und sie hat sich sofort an Sie erinnert. Es ist eine schöne Erinnerung, hat sie gesagt. Sie hofft, dass es Ihnen gut geht. Sie möchte auch sehr gerne wissen, ob Sie vielleicht der große ano-

nyme Wohltäter sind?! Sie traut Ihnen nämlich zu, dass Sie es sind. Und ich auch. Sind Sie es? Herzliche Grüße, Gerold Plassek.

»Manuel?«, rief ich ziemlich laut, als ich ihn endlich in einer Unterrichtspause am Telefon hatte. »Manuel, hast du mir etwas zu beichten?«

»Warum soll ich dir etwas zu beichten haben?«

»Die Frage kannst du dir gleich selbst beantworten. Also?«

»Ich habe dir nichts zu beichten«, beschloss er.

»Warst du in meiner Mailbox?«

»Kann schon sein. Einer muss ja deine Post lesen, wenn du es schon nicht tust.«

»Hast du in meinem Namen eine E-Mail geschrieben?« Jetzt entstand eine Pause, in der ich nur leises Rauschen vernahm. Da konnte ich seinem schlechten Gewissen sozusagen bei der Arbeit zuhören.

»Ah so, *die* meinst du«, sagte er kleinlaut.

»Bist du wahnsinnig? Was ist dir denn da eingefallen?« Ich war überrascht, wie wütend ich sein konnte, das musste mit der Vaterrolle zu tun haben, in die ich gerade hineinwuchs.

»Entschuldige, ich wollte es dir eh sagen, ich bin nur noch nicht dazu gekommen.«

»Und meine Mama hast du da auch noch mit hineingezogen.«

»Ist doch egal. Der Mann lebt sowieso in Kanada, und er ist eh nicht der Spender.«

»Das ist überhaupt nicht egal. Und wieso weißt du das eigentlich schon wieder?«

»Weil ich lesen kann«, erwiderte er. Jetzt ging er offensichtlich zum Angriff über. Aber ich dachte gar nicht daran, hier klein beizugeben.

»Manuel, ich will nicht, dass du meine Mails liest, ohne mich zu fragen. Verstehst du mich?«

»Klar verstehe ich dich, wenn du so schreist.«

»Und du schreibst nie wieder eine E-Mail unter meinem Namen. Verstanden?«, setzte ich nach.

»Ja, aber ...«

»Was aber?«

»Ich hab es tun müssen.«

»Warum?«

»Weil, weil ... weil ich es endlich wissen will. Weil es alle wissen wollen – Machi, Paul, meine ganze Klasse, alle Lehrer und alle. Überhaupt alle normalen Menschen. Alle außer dir.«

»Was?«

»Na was wohl?«, fragte er zurück.

»Keine Ahnung.«

»WER ES IST.«

»Schrei nicht so, ich bin nicht taub«, erwiderte ich.

Achtungserfolg für mein Bauchgefühl

Keine drei Minuten später tat mir unser Wortgefecht schon wieder leid, und ich beschloss, sofort an was Schönes zu denken – an Rebecca, woran sonst, sehr viel Auswahl hatte ich ja nicht. Mit der Lektüre ihrer letzten E-Mails wollte ich die Lesestunde am Computer an sich beenden. Dabei stolperte ich über eine noch ungeöffnete Mitteilung, die nicht von Angelina weitergeleitet worden, sondern direkt an mich gerichtet war. Der Text lautete folgendermaßen:

Herr plassek, ihre adresse habe ich von der redaktion. Ich will ihnen nur mitteilen, ich habe leider nur noch 19 000. Beim nächsten mal kommen 9000, dann wissen sie, dass ich es bin. Dann schreib ich ihnen noch einmal. Niemandem weitererzählen, bitte! Auch nicht ... also wirklich niemandem!

Darauf musste ich praktisch noch im selben Augenblick

ganz dringend ein Bier trinken. Denn mein Bauchgefühl sagte mir, dass die Chancen extrem gut standen, dass sich hinter dieser schnörkellosen, etwas hektisch formulierten Botschaft tatsächlich die wahre Wohltäterin oder der Wohltäter verbarg. Und ein im linken Finger spürbarer Ausläufer meines Bauchgefühls sagte mir obendrein, dass Manuel besser nichts davon erfahren sollte. Noch nicht. Also schob ich die Mail sicherheitshalber in meinen privaten Ordner und wünschte mir, dass ich recht behalten und Manuel vielleicht schon bald mit einer tollen Neuigkeit überraschen würde.

Ich würde diese Überraschung vielleicht gleich mit der zweiten, noch viel größeren, verbinden – ohne Rücksicht auf alle Jochens und sonstigen Neo-Pseudo-Familienoberhäupter dieser Welt, dachte ich weiter. Ich würde auf einen ganz besonderen Moment warten, auf die beste aller passenden Gelegenheiten, und dann würde ich ungefähr zu ihm sagen: »Manuel, ich verrate dir jetzt zwei Geheimnisse. Die erste Botschaft würde ich am liebsten gleich via Satellit in die Erdumlaufbahn schicken, damit das gesamte Universum davon erfährt: Ich bin dein Vater, und ich bin sehr stolz darauf.« Nein, so pathetisch würde ich das natürlich niemals formulieren, obwohl es im Grunde genommen die absolute Wahrheit war. Aber egal, ich würde dann fortfahren und sagen: »Die zweite Sache bleibt unter uns beiden, niemand anderer soll davon erfahren. Ich sage es dir, und nur dir, weil du mein Sohn bist und ich dir vertraue. Es bleibt auf ewig unser beider Geheimnis: Ich bin nämlich dahintergekommen, wer die vielen anonymen Geldkuverts verteilt hat. Das heißt, die Person hat es mir unter dem Siegel der Verschwiegenheit verraten. Eigentlich darf ich es nicht weitererzählen. Aber dir sage ich es, nur dir: Es ist …« In dieser Sekunde brannte sogar ich darauf, es endlich zu wissen.

Am Mittwoch erschien unsere Reportage über das neu geschaffene gemeinnützige Betreuungszentrum für blinde und sehschwache Kinder in Königstetten. Am Donnerstagmittag rief mich Clara Nemez an und nahm mir nachhaltig die komplette Aufregung auf mein Date mit Rebecca.

»Hallo Gerold, soeben habe ich mit einer begeisterten Frau Binder aus Königstetten telefoniert. Was glaubst du wohl, was sie mir erzählt hat?«

»Ist eine Spende gekommen?«

»Du hast es erfasst.«

»Schön«, sagte ich.

»Ja, das finde ich auch. Die haben es verdient. Also alle haben es verdient, aber die ganz besonders.« Alle hatten es ganz besonders verdient, fand ich.

»Aber weißt du, was diesmal anders war?«

»Nein?« Doch.

»Im Kuvert waren nur neuntausend Euro«, sagte sie.

»Ehrlich?« Ich hatte es gewusst. Ich hatte es gespürt. Ich war eben ein Bauchgefühlsmensch. Auf meinen Bauch war Verlass. Wenn auf irgendetwas an beziehungsweise in mir Verlass war, dann auf meinen Bauch, zumindest manchmal, zumindest diesmal.

»Ja, ehrlich, achtzehn Fünfhunderterscheine, also neuntausend Euro. Sie haben es hundertmal nachgeprüft.«

»Vielleicht hat sich unsere wohltätige Person verzählt«, sagte ich.

»Oder ihr geht langsam das Geld aus«, sagte Clara.

»Auch das könnte natürlich sein«, erwiderte ich.

Obwohl ich an sich nicht der Typ war, der lange überlegte, was auf ihn zukam, überlegte ich diesmal extrem lange, nämlich während des gesamten Wegs nach Penzing, was heute Abend auf mich zukommen würde, beziehungsweise worauf ich selbst gerade zukam. Auf Rebecca zweifellos. Aber auf welche Rebecca? Besser gefragt: auf eine worauf eingestellte Rebecca? Warum hat sie mich zu sich nach Hause eingeladen? Was wollte sie von mir? Noch spannender: Was wollte sie nicht von mir? Und am allerspannendsten: Was blieb übrig, wenn man das, was sie nicht von mir wollte, von dem abzog, was sie von mir wollte? Das war ja überhaupt die Schlüsselfrage, die quer durch alle Beziehungen ging, die in irgendeiner Weise etwas mit Liebe zu tun hatten beziehungsweise zu tun haben wollten.

Ich erkannte anfangs gerade so viel, dass sie jedenfalls nicht die Frau war, die einen daheim mit Filzpatschen, braunen Leggings und XX-Large-Rollkragenpullover empfing. Wir küssten uns beide flüchtig auf die rechte Wange, leider gleichzeitig, sodass nicht viel dabei herauskam. Ich überreichte ihr eine Flasche chilenischen Rotwein und eine weiß blühende Grünpflanze.

»Schön hast du es hier«, sagte ich.

»Ach Gerold, das ist ja nur das Vorzimmer«, erwiderte sie bescheiden und lächelte.

»Schon, aber da hast du *mein* Vorzimmer noch nicht gesehen«, antwortete ich.

Sie drückte mir relativ bald unaufgefordert ein Bier in die Hand, und wir machten einen kleinen Rundgang durch die hohen Räume ihrer farblich und auch temperaturmäßig extrem freundlichen Altbauwohnung, in der ein altmodischer weißgelber Kachelofen mit dem hellen Parkettboden um die

Wette wärmte, was im Winter im Grunde schon die halbe Miete war.

Als wir am Eingang zum Schlafzimmer stehen blieben, das über ein ziemlich breites Bett verfügte, in dem etwa dreißig Rebeccas nebeneinander untergebracht werden konnten, wenn sie sorgsam geschlichtet waren, kam mir ein absurder Gedanke. Ich fragte mich, ob es wohl Männer gab, die in meiner Situation geradewegs auf das Bett zugesteuert wären und mit der Hand einen kleinen Matratzen-Härtetest durchgeführt hätten, um Rebecca anschließend frivol und zufrieden zuzunicken oder ihr auf zwei- bis eindeutige Weise auffordernd zuzuzwinkern. Wie hätte sie darauf wohl reagiert? Ich würde es nie erfahren, denn ich setzte mehr oder weniger ein Pokerface auf und sagte: »Und hier schläfst du also.« Daraufhin war es nämlich sie, die nickte, wenn auch nicht unbedingt frivol.

Es gab mehrere wirklich wundervoll zubereitete Miniaturspeisen, also Gänge hintereinander, wodurch immer neuer Stoff für in intimem Flüsterton gehaltene Gespräche entstand – über Rezepte, biologischen Anbau und gesunde Ernährung, die deshalb nicht zwangsläufig schlecht schmecken musste. Stimmungsvolle Musik im Hintergrund gab es ebenfalls, wahrscheinlich war es Bach. Ich hatte nämlich die Erfahrung gemacht, dass Sonaten für Klavier und/oder Violine in so einer Situation fast immer Bach waren, aber wehe, man wagte zu sagen: »Ah, schön, Bach«, dann hieß es postwendend: »Nein, das ist Vivaldi.« Umgekehrt war die Gefahr leider genauso groß, also schwieg ich besser. Klassische Musik war nicht so ganz mein Fach.

Nach der Hauptspeise entstand eine Art Verschnaufpause, die Rebecca dazu nutzte, ein paar Kerzen anzuzünden und das Licht zu dimmen. Hätte ich das gemacht, wäre der Fall klar gewesen, aber bei Frauen wusste man nie wirklich, was an sich eindeutige Gesten tatsächlich zu bedeuten hatten. So wartete ich lieber auf ein geeignetes Stichwort, wobei mir auffiel, dass ich Rotwein besser vertrug, als er mir schmeckte, und dass mein Wunsch, Rebecca nahe zu sein, also noch näher, von Schluck zu Schluck anwuchs. Solche Effekte konnten Bier und Schnaps übrigens nicht immer erzielen, aber egal.

»Ich finde es einfach angenehm und immer sehr kurzweilig mit dir«, sagte Rebecca wenig später. Am Telefon wäre das schon ein schönes Kompliment gewesen, aber wir saßen nun bereits relativ eng nebeneinander auf der Couch vis-à-vis vom Kamin, und da war verbal doch noch Spielraum nach oben, dachte ich.

Mein Arm machte bereits Anstalten, sich auf ihre Schultern zu legen, da fragte sie: »Weißt du, was das ganz Besondere an dir ist, Gerold?« Nein, aber das hätte ich ehrlich gestanden immer schon gerne gewusst, dachte ich.

»Du hast eine unendliche Ruhe und Geduld. Du nimmst und lässt die Dinge so, wie sie sind. Nicht nur die Dinge, auch die Menschen. Auch mich.« Das hatten wir schon beim letzten Mal, »Lassen« musste wirklich meine Königsdisziplin sein.

»Du verfolgst keine Taktik, hast noch nie etwas von mir verlangt, hast mich noch nie gedrängt, hast mich keine Sekunde unter Druck gesetzt oder versucht, mich zu überrumpeln, und du bist einer der ganz wenigen Männer, die so sind, das kannst du mir glauben.« Das war quasi der letzte Beweis, dass der Matratzen-Härtetest im Schlafzimmer bei ihr nicht optimal angekommen wäre.

»Ach, ich würde dich schon ganz gerne unter Druck setzen und überrumpeln, aber mir fehlen leider die Mittel dazu«, sagte ich. Das kam ziemlich gut an, denn dafür knallte sie mir tatsächlich einen Kuss auf die Wange, der mich eine kurze Weile ziemlich benommen machte.

»Und du bist überhaupt der uneitelste Mann, den ich kenne.

Das ist so wohltuend. Alle wollen mir ständig nur beweisen, was für tolle Hechte sie sind. Du bist ganz anders, du bist echt, du zeigst auch deine Schwächen.« Kein Wunder, davon hatte ich ja ein reichhaltiges Sortiment anzubieten.

»So, darf ich jetzt auch einmal was Nettes über dich sagen?«, fragte ich schließlich in einer Art Notwehrreaktion, weil ich bereits vollständig in Watte gepackt worden war. Sie lächelte einigermaßen erwartungsvoll. Ich überlegte kurz, ob ich irgendeinen Körper- oder Gesichtsteil von ihr erwähnen sollte, zum Beispiel die kakiorangen Ohren, die kein mir bekannter Maler jemals so hinbekommen hätte, weder Vermeer noch Gauguin – und schon gar nicht Van Gogh. Ich wählte dann aber etwas eher Allgemeines, das zwar vielleicht schwärmerisch klang, das ich aber todernst meinte: »Du bist die perfekte Frau, von der jeder Mann sein Leben lang träumt. Und ausgerechnet ich darf hier neben dir sitzen, obwohl du schon rein optisch in einer ganz anderen Liga spielst als ich. Das ist ein irrer Glücksgriff für mich.« Kurz überlegte ich, ob Glücksgriff wirklich das ideale Wort war, ob nicht zum Beispiel Glücksfall eleganter gewesen wäre, aber in dieser Sekunde dürfte Glücksgriff gepasst haben, denn Rebecca überwand das letzte Stück Distanz zwischen unseren Köpfen, und ich wusste zu hundert Prozent, dass es okay war, dass ich sie jetzt umarmte und küsste, was ich mir natürlich nicht nehmen lassen konnte. Schon mittendrin merkte ich an der Grandiosität dieses Kussgefühls, dass ich damit gedanklich locker über Weihnachten kommen konnte. Es war jetzt nur noch interessant, ob es bei dieser Szene bleiben oder sogar noch zu einer Fortsetzung kommen würde. Um meiner Rolle als Geduldsengel nicht untreu zu werden, überließ ich die Entscheidung voll und ganz Rebecca. Und sie sagte schließlich, als ihre Lippen wieder zum Sprechen freigegeben waren:

»Was hältst du eigentlich von einer kleinen Nachspeise?«

Sie war keine Frau zweideutiger Formulierungen, deshalb war klar, dass ihr Vorschlag im Bereich der Küche angesiedelt war und auch dort bleiben sollte.

»Selbstgemachter Schokokuchen«, legte sie dann auch nach.

»Hervorragende Idee«, sagte ich. Auf diese Worte war ich mächtig stolz, denn sie bewiesen echte Körperbeherrschung. Das mussten mir andere Männer tatsächlich erst einmal nachmachen. Außerdem war Schokokuchen für mich eigentlich schon immer eine Alternative zu beinahe allem gewesen. Und mit dem *beinahe* würde ich in diesem spezifischen Fall hoffentlich noch einige Zeit ganz gut leben können, dachte ich.

Ein gnadenloser letzter Wille

Ein Liebestaumel hat den Vorteil, dass man Alltagsabläufe, bei denen es einen normalerweise einiges an Überwindung kostet, bis man sie dazu bringt, dass sie endlich ablaufen, plötzlich einfach wie in Trance vollzieht. Zum Beispiel stand ich am Freitag so früh auf, dass es draußen sogar noch finster war, spülte Geschirr, zumindest spülte ich eine Tasse und einen Kaffeelöffel, machte mir einen Kaffee, setzte mich vor den Bildschirm und öffnete mein Postfach mit der Absicht, Rebecca ein paar Zeilen zu schreiben. Da offenbar unter anderem auch Angelina noch schlief, hatte ich nur eine einzige neue Nachricht im Ordner. Die aber hatte es in sich und stellte in ihrer Wirkung den doppelten Espresso quasi in den Schatten. Sie lautete:

Herr plassek, wie angekündigt, melde ich mich wieder. Es ist also so, dass ich noch 10 000 euro habe, die ich hergeben kann. Ganz wichtig: Ich möchte für immer unerkannt bleiben. Warum ich ihnen trotzdem schreibe: Weil es meine letzte geldgabe ist, hab ich einen wunsch, wer sie kriegen soll. Das heißt, ich sage ihnen, worüber sie bitte berichten sollen. Dann berichten sie. Und wenn der beitrag erschienen ist, dann schicke ich dorthin das geld. Ich warte jetzt auf ihr okay, und dann sag ich ihnen, für wen die letzte geldgabe sein soll. Bitte wirklich niemandem weitererzählen!

Es wäre gar nicht uninteressiert gewesen, welches Wohltäterprofil ein guter Psychologe hieraus vielleicht erstellt hätte. Mir gefiel jedenfalls die direkte Art dieser Person, die nicht lange drum herumredete, sondern gleich zur Sache kam. Und deshalb schrieb ich auch sofort zurück:

Sehr geehrte Frau oder Herr X, ich finde, es steht Ihnen wirklich mehr als zu, dass Sie bestimmen, wer die letzte Spende bekommt. Wenn es organisatorisch zu bewerkstelligen und nicht gerade mit einer Reise nach China oder Mekka verbunden ist, werde ich die Reportage gerne schreiben.

Ich selbst habe auch noch ein paar Fragen an Sie, die mich schon länger beschäftigen: Warum spenden Sie immer nur nach Erscheinen meiner Artikel? Wie kommen Sie ausgerechnet auf mich? Wer sind Sie? Ich respektiere natürlich, dass Sie anonym bleiben wollen. Ihre Antworten bleiben also unter uns. Herzliche Grüße, Gerold Plassek. PS: Vielen Dank im Namen aller Beschenkten! Und mein eigenes Leben hat sich dadurch übrigens auch ganz schön verändert.

Keine zehn Minuten später kam bereits die Antwort. Und diese traf einen wunden Punkt, von dem ich gar nicht vermutet hätte, dass er wirklich so wund war, wie ich ihn nach der Lektüre dieses Textes empfand. Frau oder Herr Wohltäter schrieb nämlich Folgendes:

Herr plassek, ich wünsche mir, dass sie über 0,0 promille berichten. 0,0 promille ist eine stationäre betreuungsstelle für alkoholkranke und dazu noch eine selbsthilfegruppe für familien, wo jemand alkoholkrank geworden oder daran gestorben ist. Die haben ihr zentrum in der simmeringer hauptstraße. Die kann man sicher besuchen und darüber schreiben. Das wäre mein wunsch. Danach kommt es zu meiner letzten geldgabe.

Und auf ihre frage, wer ich bin und warum gerade sie: das ist gar nicht so wichtig. Auch ich bedanke mich, dass sie ihre artikel geschrieben haben, auch wenn es nicht immer leicht war.

Das musste ich erst einmal setzenlassen. Denn damit war erstens klar, dass mich dieser barmherzige Mensch nicht wirklich kennen konnte oder es zumindest nicht gut mit mir meinte, sonst hätte er mich nicht in diese beschissene Lage gebracht. Ich hatte nämlich ehrlich gestanden absolut keine Lust, mich mit Alkoholkranken zu unterhalten und mir ihre Schicksale oder, noch schlimmer, die ihrer Angehörigen anzuhören. Da war ich sozusagen ein doppelt gebranntes Kind, weil mir unweigerlich mein Vater einfiel oder eigentlich meine Mutter, die das über viele Jahre mit ihm hatte durchstehen müssen.

Außerdem war Alkohol für mich selbst quasi das Tabuthema schlechthin, und zwar ganz bewusst, weil ich nämlich der Meinung war, dass jeder Mensch das Recht hatte, eine kleine Schwachstelle zu besitzen, die er nicht ausmerzen konnte oder wollte, und dass es eigentlich viel klüger und rationeller war, rund um diese Schwachstelle eine Festung zu errichten, anstatt sie zu beheben. Bei mir war diese nach außen abgesicherte, mir zugebilligte und tabuisierte kleine Schwachstelle eben einwandfrei der Alkohol, also wollte ich nichts davon hören, und ich hasste es, wenn das jemand überdramatisierte.

Ich hatte aber noch ein zweites Problem mit diesem Himmelfahrtskommando per Mail: Wie sollte ich vor Manuel und allen anderen, die mich gut kannten, so eine Reportage rechtfertigen? Man würde mir zu Recht vorwerfen, dass ich nun auch so ein Moralapostel war, der Wasser predigte, aber Wein trank, beziehungsweise Bier in sich hineinschüttete. Meine Kumpels würden mich ächten, und in Zoltan's Bar hätte ich vermutlich überhaupt auf Lebenszeit Lokalverbot.

Am meisten ärgerte mich aber, dass ich gerade empfindlich

dabei gestört worden war, an Rebecca zu denken und mich detailgetreu dem Nachempfinden der spektakulärsten Szenen dieses Weltklasse-Abends bei ihr hinzugeben. Ich beschloss, ihr eine SMS zu schicken, um ihr wenigstens eine Stichprobe eines Bruchteils meiner Gefühle für sie zuteilwerden zu lassen. An sich hätte die Botschaft hieb- und stichfest »Ich liebe dich« lauten müssen. Aber ich war der Typ, der so etwas lieber etwas verklausulierter zum Ausdruck brachte. Also schrieb ich:

Liebe Rebecca, allein für den Schokokuchen würde ich jederzeit wieder bei dir aufkreuzen. Aber jetzt bin ich an der Reihe! Ich feile bereits an meinem Menüplan. ☺. Den Smiley löschte ich gleich wieder, sie würde die Ironie schon erkennen. Ich schrieb also: *Ich feile bereits an meinem Menüplan ... Dein Gerold. Noch was: Du bist wundervoll!* Den Schlusssatz modifizierte ich: *Noch was: Es war wundervoll mit dir!* Die ersten und letzten beiden Wörter strich ich: *Es war wundervoll!* Aber war *wundervoll* wirklich der richtige Ausdruck? Das klang eher nach einem einmaligen Wunder, das sich nie wiederholen oder gar übertreffen ließ. *Wunderschön* war vielleicht besser, denn *wunderschön* hieß, dass es zwar schön wie ein Wunder war, was aber nicht bedeutete, dass es zwangsläufig bereits selbst ein Wunder war. Außerdem gab es mit *wunderwunderschön* eine natürliche Steigerung fürs nächste Mal, während es *wunderwundervoll* nicht gab. Also schrieb ich: *Es war wunderschön.* Plus zwei Ausrufezeichen.

Manuels Zukunftssorge

Ich hatte bezüglich des anonymen Auftrags noch immer weder einen Plan A noch B oder C, als Manuel von der Schule heimkam. Er wirkte auf mich irgendwie ein bisschen gedämpft, und da fragte ich ihn einfach, ob etwas nicht in Ordnung war.

»Doch, doch, alles in Ordnung«, sagte er. Es war also etwas nicht in Ordnung.

»Bedrückt dich was?«

»Warum soll mich was bedrücken?«

»Die Frage ist unter deinem Niveau, mein liebes Kind. Keiner hat behauptet, dass dich was bedrücken soll. Ich hab dich nur gefragt, ob dich was bedrückt.« Er lachte. Ich war nämlich bereits Weltmeister im Zurückschmettern seiner doofen Kausal-Gegenfragen.

»Zu Weihnachten kommt meine Mama«, sagte er.

»Schön«, erwiderte ich.

»Ja.«

»Freust du dich nicht schon riesig auf sie?«

»Doch, auf sie schon«, erwiderte er. Ich wartete, ob noch etwas Bestimmtes nachfolgen würde – und es folgte. »Aber sie hat jetzt einen neuen Freund, der kommt auch mit.«

»Ja, ich weiß«, sagte ich.

»Du weißt das? Woher weißt du das?«

»Von Tante Julia.«

»Aha.«

»Ja. Und was ist das Problem?«, fragte ich.

»Das Problem ist, dass ich ihn nicht kenne.«

»Das Problem lässt sich lösen, du wirst ihn kennenlernen«, sagte ich.

»Und wenn er mich nicht mag?«

»Er wird dich mögen. Dich kann man gar nicht nicht mögen. Aber frag mich jetzt bitte nur ja nicht, warum man dich nicht nicht mögen können soll.« Er lachte.

»Und wenn ich ihn nicht mag?« Darauf hatte ich spontan keine Antwort parat, aber es war jedenfalls ein lustvoller Gedanke. »Meine Mama will ihn nämlich sogar wahrscheinlich heiraten, und wir sollen zusammenwohnen. Was ist, wenn ich nicht mit ihm wohnen will?«

»Das kann ich mir nicht vorstellen«, log ich.

»Darf ich dann bei dir wohnen?« Das war insgeheim exakt meine Wunschfrage gewesen. Ich reagierte taktisch entsetzt.

»Was? Hier willst du wohnen? Schau dich mal um. Hier holst du dir vom Schnupfen über Typhus bis zur Cholera sämtliche Krankheiten.«

»Na und? Meine Mama ist eh Ärztin. Und ihr neuer Mann auch. Die können mich dann hier besuchen kommen.« Jetzt war er wieder deutlich besser aufgelegt, und ich fuhr ihm durch die Haare, und zwar relativ ruppig, damit er sich mit seinen vierzehneinhalb nicht genierte.

»Was machst du eigentlich zu Weihnachten?«, fragte er schließlich.

»Ich? Keine Ahnung. Wahrscheinlich das Übliche.«

»Was ist das Übliche?«

»Ich lasse mich überraschen, was Weihnachten mit mir macht«, sagte ich. Jetzt grinste er von einem Ohr zum anderen. Die Antwort gefiel ihm. Ich glaube, er hatte doch einige Gene von mir erwischt.

»Du kannst ja mit uns feiern, dann ist es nicht so langweilig«, sagte er. Das war quasi Schokokuchen, Marke Rebecca. Ich spürte, dass so eine Art Rührung in mir hochstieg, und ich musste verhindern, dass sie die Augen erreichte.

»Eine Frau und drei Männer? Ich glaube, da wird deine Mama eher nicht begeistert sein«, sagte ich.

»Du kannst ja deine …« Er brach ab.

»Deine was?«

»Ach nichts«, sagte er. Er zappelte ein wenig verlegen herum.

»Sag schon.«

»Du kannst ja Florentina mitbringen.«

»Ah, jetzt weiß ich, woher der Wind weht«, erwiderte ich. Ich brachte es möglichst übertrieben belustigt rüber, aber mir war gar nicht so wohl bei diesen Worten.

»Nein, nicht das, was du glaubst«, gab er sofort Entwarnung, ohne sich ein Kichern verkneifen zu können.

»Was ich glaube? Also ich glaube, du findest sie einfach sympathisch, weil sie so eine offene, lockere Art hat und weil sie einfach ein guter Typ ist.«

»Ja, genau«, erwiderte er erleichtert. Ich war es ebenfalls.

Unser vertraulicher Plauderton hatte mich ermutigt, in die Offensive zu gehen, und deshalb fasste ich spontan Plan D und sagte zu Manuel: »Stell dir vor, was die von der *Neuzeit* von mir verlangen, wo sie mich hinschicken wollen.«

»Wohin?«

»Zu den schweren Alkoholikern.«

»Echt? Musst du so einen, so einen, wie heißt das … so einen Entzug machen?« Das Bestürzende daran war, dass er das todernst gemeint hatte und sich offensichtlich sehr um mich sorgte. Ich reagierte empört.

»Bist du wahnsinnig? Ich doch nicht! Auf welche Ideen du kommst! Ich soll eine Reportage über ein Zentrum schreiben, wo Alkoholkranke betreut werden und wo man ihren Angehörigen hilft, 0,0 Promille heißen die. Dort sind die wirklich schweren Fälle, nicht nur so Hobby-Biertrinker wie ich.« Ich erzählte ihm anschließend die wenigen Details, die ich bereits kannte.

»Und du machst das wirklich?«, fragte er.

»Ich weiß noch nicht.«

»Doch.«

»Was doch?«

»Mach es. Ich finde es super, wenn du das machst«, sagte er.

»Ehrlich? Wieso?«

»Einfach so, ich finde es super. Und ich komme natürlich mit.«

»Du kommst natürlich nicht mit«, widersprach ich vehement. Ich wollte nicht, dass mein Sohn ausgerechnet diese Sorte von Extremschicksalen zu Gesicht bekommen würde, dafür war er einfach noch zu jung. Aber in der Folge zeigte sich wieder einmal, dass sich bei uns beiden letztendlich immer diejenige Meinung durchsetzte, die nicht von mir stammte. Dafür versprach er mir seine volle Unterstützung bei den Recherchen. Außerdem wusste ich ja, dass dies quasi unser letztes gemeinsames Spenden-Abenteuer sein würde, also durfte er unter Protest mitkommen, was gleichbedeutend damit war, dass ich mich entschieden hatte, den Auftrag anzunehmen – ebenfalls unter Protest.

KAPITEL NEUNZEHN

Im Dialog mit dem Wohltäter

Für Sonntagnachmittag waren wir bei 0,0 Promille angemeldet. Am Vormittag hatte ich einerseits einen schweren Schädel von einem dieser selten gewordenen Samstagabende, die erst Sonntagfrüh zu Ende gegangen beziehungsweise im Dämmerschlaf versickert waren, andererseits hielt sich mein Interesse in Grenzen, mich in irgendeiner Weise auf den Termin vorzubereiten oder einzustimmen, sieht man von einer Brausetablette gegen meinen Kater ab.

Stattdessen schrieb ich der Person, die mir das Ganze eingebrockt hatte und die mir auch sonst nicht mehr aus dem Kopf gehen wollte, eine E-Mail.

Sehr geehrte Frau oder Herr X, ich werde heute am Nachmittag mit der von Ihnen gewünschten Reportage beginnen. Die Geschichte wird wahrscheinlich am Dienstag erscheinen. Wenn danach Ihre Spende eingetroffen ist, wofür ich mich jetzt schon bedanke, sollen wir dann in der Neuzeit *verraten, dass uns anonym mitgeteilt wurde, dass es sich um die letzte Spende in der Serie gehandelt hat?*

Und dann noch zu Ihnen: Sie haben mir geschrieben, dass es nicht so wichtig sei, wer Sie sind und warum Sie mich in Ihre bewundernswerte Geschenkserie einbezogen haben. Das mag sein, ich würde es aber trotzdem gerne wissen. Herzliche Grüße, Gerold Plassek.

Die Antwort kam postwendend.

Herr plassek, mir wäre lieber, wenn nicht in der zeitung steht, dass es die letzte geldgabe ist. Sonst bohrt sicher wieder wer weiter, und ich habe keine ruhe. Für mich ist aber mein einsatz zu ende, so

304

leid es mir tut, denn es waren sehr aufregende wochen, und ich habe immer das gefühl gehabt, mir schenkt gerade jemand was, und nicht umgekehrt. Vielleicht löst mich ja irgendwer ab.

Ich verstehe schon, dass sie wissen wollen, wer ich bin und warum ich nur ihre artikel ausgeschnitten und mitgeschickt habe. Das habe ich vielleicht auch deshalb gemacht, weil ich sie so einschätze, dass sie einfach sagen: so ist es, und aus. Wenn er geheim bleiben will, dann will er eben geheim bleiben. Man muss nicht immer alles auf-decken. Also fragen sie mich am besten gar nicht weiter.

Ein bisschen etwas hatte ich ihm ja doch entlocken können. Also nahm ich noch einen zweiten Anlauf.

Sehr geehrter Herr X, wenigstens haben sie mir mit der Formu-lierung »Wenn er geheim bleiben will . . .« verraten, dass Sie offen-bar ein Mann sind, außer Sie legen es darauf an, mich zu täuschen. Sie haben recht, ich bin nicht der Typ, der um jeden Preis etwas aus jemandem herausquetschen möchte. Wieso wissen Sie das eigent-lich? Haben Sie sich über mich erkundigt? Bei Tag für Tag? Ich will auch wirklich nicht aufdringlich sein, aber ich habe einen triftigen Grund, warum ich gerne wissen würde, wem ich das alles zu ver-danken habe. Also wenn es Ihnen nicht allzu viel ausmacht, wäre es wirklich freundlich von Ihnen, sich mir gegenüber zu outen. Es än-dert sich dadurch nichts für Sie, und Sie haben weiterhin Ihre Ruhe, das verspricht einer, dem seine Ruhe ebenfalls heilig ist. Herzlich, Gerold Plassek.

Leider ließ er sich nicht erweichen. Seine Antwort lautete:

Herr plassek, genau das wollte ich verhindern, dass sie mich jetzt ausfragen. Es bringt wirklich nicht viel, wenn sie wissen, wer ich bin. Sie werden vielleicht sogar enttäuscht sein, weil sie sich da ganz ei-nen anderen menschen vorgestellt haben. Ich könnte wahrschein-lich stundenlang neben ihnen stehen, und sie würden nie auf die idee kommen, dass ich der große geldgeber bin. Es soll also im nach-hinein lieber so sein, dass das besondere diese anonymen geldgaben selbst gewesen sind, weil sie konkret geholfen haben. Jetzt wissen die

leute, dass man so was machen und trotzdem geheim bleiben kann.
Das finde ich gut. Ich als person, oder sie, wir beide sind uninteres-
sant. Das ist alles austauschbar. Ich hoffe, sie verstehen mich in dem,
was ich meine. Guten tag noch.

Besuch bei 0,0 Promille

Es fiel mir verdammt schwer, Manuel gegenüber noch immer
Stillschweigen zu bewahren, denn je öfter dieser Mann betonte, wie unscheinbar und austauschbar er doch war, desto
brennender interessierte mich auf einmal, was für eine Persön-
lichkeit tatsächlich hinter dem Ganzen steckte.

Auf dem Weg zum 0,0-Promille-Haus in Simmering, das
übrigens nur fünf Ecken von der Gasse entfernt war, in der ich
meine Kindheit verbracht hatte, überlegte ich kurz, warum
er mich wohl am Ende ausgerechnet zu den Alkoholikern
schickte, und dazu fielen mir spontan zwei simple logische
Erklärungen ein. Entweder er war selbst einmal schwer alkoholkrank gewesen beziehungsweise war es noch immer, oder
es verband ihn sonst irgendetwas mit diesem Haus – vielleicht
arbeitete er ja als Arzt dort, vielleicht würden wir ihm sogar be-
gegnen, ich würde jedenfalls meine Augen offen halten, so gut
das in meinem etwas angeschlagenen Zustand möglich war.

»Ist es das erste Mal, oder waren Sie schon einmal bei uns?«,
fragte mich die ansonsten kompetent wirkende junge Frau
beim Empfang. Ich klärte das Missverständnis auf, und sie entschuldigte sich tausendmal.

»Kannst du mir erklären, was daran so lustig sein soll?«,
fragte ich Manuel. Er konnte es mir zwar nicht erklären, aber
er grinste weiter. In manchen Situationen war er eben doch
noch ein kleines Kind.

Schließlich holte uns eine Frau Barbara Drössler, wie auf ihrem Namensschild zu lesen war, ab und führte uns durch eine auf Sanatorium gestylte Pflegestation. Sie bemühte sich, uns zu zeigen, was 0,0 Promille an therapeutischen und sonstigen Möglichkeiten zu bieten hatte. Manuel machte sich erfreulicherweise ausgiebig Notizen. Ich sah mir vor allem das Personal etwas genauer an, aber nichts deutete auf den anonymen Wohltäter hin. So wie er schrieb, passte er hier auch gar nicht her, außer er war vielleicht selbst Patient.

»Wollen Sie noch einen Blick in die Notaufnahme oder in die Akutstation werfen?«, fragte Frau Drössler.

»Nein danke«, sagte ich. Ich wusste ja nur zu gut, wie sie aussahen, wenn sie mit ihren Köpfen wippten oder von nervösen Zuckungen befallen waren, wenn sie ständig mit der Zunge ihre Lippen befeuchteten und sich ihre verquollenen Augen rieben, wenn sie stumpf in einer Ecke kauerten und aus ihren aufgedunsenen, knollennasigen, geröteten Gesichtern heraus ins Leere starrten. Irgendwann war es mir gelungen, einfach nicht mehr hinzusehen, beziehungsweise durch meinen Vater hindurchzuschauen. Leider hatte das die unangenehme Begleiterscheinung, dass die Bilder dann plötzlich in meinen Träumen auftauchten, noch dazu gestochen scharf. Ich hatte also wirklich genug davon gesehen.

Endlich waren wir im Beratungszentrum angelangt, wo schon ein eigens für uns abgestellter Doktor Günter Uland wartete, der vermutlich gerade einem Fernsehkanal entstiegen war, wo er sich im Werbeblock für Rasierschaum, Deodorant oder Pro-Aktiv-Vital-Anti-Aging-Produkte starkgemacht hatte. Er kannte Alkohol wahrscheinlich nur vom Hörensagen, fühlte sich aber bemüßigt, ein Schulkind, das natürlich sofort große Augen machte, mit aktuellen Horrormeldungen zu schockieren: jährlich 40 000 Alkoholtote in Deutschland, 350 000 Alkoholkranke in Österreich, 3,3 Millionen Alkoholabhängige in Deutschland, eine um zwanzig Jahre herabgesetzte Lebenserwartung, Alkoholismus als Auslöser für sechzig andere Krankheiten, die Leber, die Bauchspeicheldrüse, das Gehirn, der volkswirtschaftliche Schaden und so weiter und so fort.

»Wann genau ist man eigentlich alkoholkrank?«, wollte Manuel wissen. Der Herr Experte zählte dann schulmäßig ein paar Punkte auf, zu denen ich mir meinen Teil dachte.

»Wenn man nach dem Konsum einer kleinen Menge das dringende Bedürfnis nach mehr hat.« Na ja, wenn der Körper nach mehr verlangte, dann verlangte er eben nach mehr. Das war nach einem Bissen Wiener Schnitzel auch nicht anders, und keiner würde jemanden als *wienerschnitzelkrank* bezeichnen. Außerdem musste man mir den Menschen erst einmal zeigen, der nach einem halben Glas Bier nicht das Bedürfnis nach der zweiten Hälfte hatte.

»Wenn man weitertrinkt, obwohl man weiß, dass man aufhören soll.« Das beruhigte mich, denn das wusste ich in der jeweiligen Situation praktisch nie.

»Wenn man immer mehr Alkohol braucht, um die gleiche Wirkung zu erzielen.« Also mir ging es eigentlich nie darum, eine bestimmte Wirkung zu erzielen, die erzielte sich ab einer gewissen Menge quasi von selbst.

»Wenn man heimlich und auch allein trinkt.« Heimlich trank ich nie und allein nur, wenn niemand da war.

»Wenn man durch seinen Alkoholkonsum Organschäden in Kauf nimmt.« Meiner Meinung nach nahm man Organschäden praktisch bereits mit seiner Geburt in Kauf. Ich würde sogar behaupten: Sowie man lebte, nahm man den Tod in Kauf, aber das war vielleicht eine Grundsatzfrage.

»Wenn man durch sein Trinkverhalten die Beziehung zu seinen Mitmenschen stört.« Da war ich eher der gesunde Typ, der durch sein Trinkverhalten Beziehungen aufbauen wollte. Zugegeben, jene, die zum Beispiel gar nichts tranken, wie sicher dieser Doktor Uland, machten es einem nicht immer leicht.

»Und wenn man mit seinen Gedanken bereits so sehr beim Alkohol ist, dass man dadurch andere Interessen vernachlässigt«, schloss er seine Expertise. Also ich musste nicht zwangsläufig an Alkohol denken, selbst wenn ich gerade Bier trank. Und vernachlässigte Interessen interessierten einen eben nicht mehr, das würde ich nicht unbedingt als krank bezeichnen, dachte ich.

»Aber wissen Sie, was das größte Problem nahezu aller alkoholkranken Menschen ist?«, fragte er mich, obwohl ich mich bisher erfolgreich herausgehalten hatte.

»Sie glauben, dass ihnen der Alkohol nichts anhaben kann. Sie finden hundert Ausreden, um ihren Konsum zu bagatellisieren. Sie wollen einfach nicht zur Kenntnis nehmen, dass sie krank sind.« Zuerst nickte ich, weil neunmalkluge Theoretiker ohnehin immer recht behalten mussten. Aber dann fiel mir doch noch etwas ein.

»Ist es nicht besser, man ist krank und fühlt sich gesund, als man ist gesund und fühlt sich krank – einmal ganz abgesehen von diesem beschissenen volkswirtschaftlichen Schaden, den Sie vorhin angesprochen haben und nach dem der Wert unseres Lebens zunehmend gemessen wird?«, schob ich ihm möglichst lässig hinüber. Denn ich hatte keine gesteigerte Lust, mir hier in Gegenwart meines Sohnes noch länger die Weisheiten von einem Mister Sauberleber anhören zu müssen. Er blieb ruhig und lächelte süffisant.

»Das Problem daran ist, dass einer, der seine Krankheit verleugnet, nicht in der Lage ist, etwas zu unternehmen, um den Suchtprozess zu stoppen. Und ab einem gewissen Punkt kann er sich beim besten Willen nicht mehr gesund fühlen, aber dann ist bereits alles zu spät.«

Okay, wenn solche Schreckensszenarien gezeichnet wurden,

fiel mir nun wirklich nichts mehr ein: Sieg für den Doktor, sympathisch war er mir trotzdem nicht.

Ich merkte schon länger, dass mich Manuel, dem diese Ausführungen offenbar zugesetzt hatten, von der Seite her ziemlich mitleidig ansah, was mir extrem unangenehm war. Schließlich beugte er sich zu mir und flüsterte mir mit flehentlichem Unterton etwas ins Ohr, sodass Mister Uland es nicht hören konnte, was ich Manuel im Nachhinein hoch anrechnete.

»Kannst du nicht wenigstens ein Bier am Tag weniger trinken?« Ich musste diese schräge Aussage erst einmal auf mich wirken lassen.

»Ich?«, fragte ich dann.

Ja, es half nichts, er meinte mich und machte dabei ein furchtbar trauriges Gesicht. Und schuld war der Doktor. Und eigentlich auch der Wohltäter.

Perfekte Teamarbeit

Am Montag überraschte ich Manuel damit, dass ich bereits im Alleingang zwei Kurztexte für unsere Doppelseite fertiggestellt hatte, als er nach Hause kam. In einer Geschichte ging es um den Alkohol-Pro-Kopf-Verbrauch innerhalb der europäischen Länder – im Schnitt nahm jeder Bürger knapp dreizehn Liter reinen Alkohol zu sich, was mir jetzt auf das ganze Jahr verteilt nicht so dramatisch viel vorkam, weil da ja auch der hochprozentige Schnaps mit eingerechnet war.

Im zweiten Text ließ ich ein paar Experten etwas über die Auswirkungen von Alkohol im Straßenverkehr zum Besten geben. Übrigens hatte ich am Vorabend mindestens ein Bier weniger getrunken, indem ich später angefangen und früher aufgehört hatte, das war eine an sich ganz brauchbare Taktik.

Außerdem hatte ich den Eindruck, dass ich ohnehin von Tag zu Tag weniger vertrug und deshalb auch weniger zu mir nehmen musste, um die gleiche Wirkung zu erzielen, was ich mir von Gesundheitsguru Doktor Uland gerne schriftlich geben und auf keinen Fall wieder schlechtreden lassen würde.

Die große Reportage über 0,0 Promille erarbeiteten wir dann in bewährter Manier: Manuel lieferte mir aufgrund seiner Unterlagen die Langversion, die ich wortwörtlich eintippte. Danach strich ich ungefähr jeden zweiten Satz. Was übrig blieb, übersetzte ich anschließend vom Schulaufsatzdeutsch ins Journalistendeutsch. Außerdem nötigte mich Manuel zu einem Informationsteil über die gesundheitlichen Auswirkungen, also über den beschissenen *volkswirtschaftlichen Schaden*, und zu einer Analyse über Alkoholmissbrauch unter Jugendlichen, okay, das sah ich schon ein, dass das wichtig war.

So wenig ich mit dem Grundthema insgesamt anzufangen wusste, so kurzweilig war unsere Zusammenarbeit. Mir gefiel es einfach, mit welcher Begeisterung Manuel bei der Sache war, wie gerne er Seiten konzipierte, Fotos und Grafiken auswählte und mit mir über Titel und Bildtexte tüftelte, da bewies er sich im Grunde als der geborene Journalist. Um mit ihm mitzuhalten, musste ich mich stilistisch voll ins Zeug legen und mir meinen gesamten noch vorhandenen Sprachschatz aus der Großhirnrinde winden. Mit dem Ergebnis waren wir beide dann wieder ziemlich zufrieden.

Ich durfte nur nicht vergessen, mir bei Clara Nemez die Erlaubnis einzuholen, Manuel weiterhin als Koautor einzubinden, wenn ich dann meinen festen Büroplatz hatte. Wir brauchten ja nicht eigens einen zweiten Computer, ein zusätzlicher Stuhl würde genügen. Und für seine Honorare würde ich selbstverständlich persönlich aufkommen, sodass er erst gar nicht auf Taschengeld oder sonstige Zuwendungen von Jochen angewiesen sein würde. Ehrlich gestanden konnte ich mir meine Arbeit ohne Manuel gar nicht mehr vorstellen. Oder besser gesagt, konnte ich mir meine Arbeit überhaupt erst vorstellen, seit es Manuel in meinem Leben gab.

Nur einmal kurz begegnen

Abends verzichtete ich gleich auf mein erstes Bier, damit ich es hinter mir hatte, und schrieb dem anonymen Wohltäter folgende E-Mail:

Sehr geehrter Herr X, unsere Reportage über 0,0 Promille ist fertig und wird morgen erscheinen. Unsere Reportage *sage ich deshalb, weil mir mein Sohn Manuel wie immer geholfen hat. Er war an allen Artikeln in der* Neuzeit, *die Sie ausgeschnitten und mit dem Geld ins Kuvert gesteckt haben, maßgeblich beteiligt. Er hat mit den von uns beschriebenen Schicksalen mitgebangt und mitgefiebert – und er hat Freudensprünge gemacht, wenn sie und ihre Helfer dann tatsächlich wieder von Ihnen beschenkt wurden. Was glauben Sie, was das für einen Vierzehnjährigen bedeutet, was für ein Weltbild da entsteht und welche Werte er sich für seine Zukunft mitnimmt? So was kann die beste Pädagogik nicht leisten.* Diese Passage war zwar vielleicht ein bisschen klischeehaft sozialromantisch und nicht ganz frei von Pathos, aber mich rührte sie jedenfalls, und deshalb holte ich mir jetzt das zweite Bier, also mein erstes insgesamt. Dann fuhr ich fort: *Jetzt verrate ich Ihnen noch etwas, das für Sie vielleicht absurd klingen mag: Manuel weiß nicht, dass ich sein Vater bin, weil ich es auch erst vor ein paar Monaten erfahren habe und bisher noch nicht die richtige Gelegenheit gefunden habe, es ihm zu sagen. Die vierzehn Jahre, die ich mit ihm versäumt habe, werde ich nicht nachholen können. Aber in der kurzen Zeit, seit wir uns kennen, ist viel passiert, wir sind eng zusammengewachsen, und auch das verdanke ich nicht zuletzt Ihnen. Diese intensive Phase geht jetzt leider zu Ende, weil seine Mutter aus Afrika zu-*

rückkommt und ihm eine richtige Familie bieten kann, was bei mir wahrscheinlich nie der Fall sein wird, wie ich mich kenne, aber egal. An dieser Stelle machte ich eine Zwangspause und musste länger nachdenken, wie ich die Schlüsselpassage formulieren sollte. Ich entschied mich schließlich dafür, noch einmal so richtig dick aufzutragen, und schrieb: *Ich habe aber noch einen wirklich großen Wunsch zum Abschluss, ich würde gerne etwas ganz Besonderes mit Manuel teilen, etwas, das (nur) uns beide verbindet und uns ewig an diese Monate erinnern wird. Und dieses Besondere, unser großes gemeinsames und verbindendes Geheimnis, tut mir leid, das sind eindeutig Sie! Manuel brennt darauf zu wissen, wer der anonyme Wohltäter ist, der zum Beispiel seinem Freund Machi aus der Patsche geholfen hat. Ja, ich möchte Manuel gerne sagen dürfen, wer Sie sind, wer so etwas macht, vielleicht auch, warum, und wie Sie ausgerechnet auf mich gekommen sind.* So, das Schwierigste hatte ich hinter mir, jetzt ging es nur noch um die technischen Details.

Dazu möchte ich Sie einmal kurz gesehen und ein paar Worte mit Ihnen gewechselt haben, mehr muss es gar nicht sein. Es wäre schön, wenn es an einem der nächsten Tage mit einem Treffen klappen würde, am besten also noch vor Weihnachten. Und ich verspreche Ihnen noch einmal, dass ich Sie dann für immer in Ruhe lasse. Mit freundlichen Grüßen, Gerold Plassek.

Seltsame weibliche Reaktionen

Wie befürchtet, ließ die Antwort des Wohltäters auf sich warten. Wenigstens hatte er nicht sofort abgesagt. Am Dienstagvormittag rief mich Clara Nemez an, um mir ein Kompliment auszusprechen, nämlich wie mutig es war, das Thema Alkohol aufzugreifen, wobei ich ehrlich gestanden nicht ganz nachvollziehen konnte, was daran mutig gewesen sein sollte, aber bitte.

Jedenfalls sei mir die Doppelseite in der Vielfalt der Aspekte wirklich gut gelungen, meinte sie. In der Redaktion der *Neuzeit* hätte man sich freilich bereits darauf eingestellt, dass nach den neuntausend Euro für Königstetten nun keine oder vielleicht nur eine kleine Restspende kommen würde, was aber meine Leistung keinesfalls schmälern sollte. Dazu schwieg ich besser, um nur ja keinen Verdacht auf Mitwisserschaft aufkommen zu lassen.

Schließlich fragte mich Clara, ob ich um Weihnachten herum Zeit hätte, in die Redaktion zu kommen. Sie wollten mir zu Ehren eine kleine Feier veranstalten. Die nächsten Quartalszahlen der *Neuzeit* würden nämlich so gut wie nie zuvor in der Geschichte dieser Zeitung ausfallen, und das verdankte man hauptsächlich mir, als quasi verlängertem Arm des anonymen Wohltäters.

»Klar, wenn es irgendwo eine Feier gibt, bin ich dabei«, sagte ich eher reflexartig. In Wahrheit war ich der Typ, der gerne am Rand stand, aber nicht unbedingt selbst befeiert werden musste, ganz abgesehen davon, dass mir das in den vergangenen dreißig Jahren ohnehin praktisch nicht mehr passiert war.

Kurz darauf erhielt ich den nächsten Anruf, der mich blitzartig in einen Zustand versetzte, als hätte jemand bei mir die Turbotaste eines frisch eingesetzten Herzschrittmachers bedient.

»Hallo Gerold, ich habe gerade deine Reportage gelesen, und da dachte ich, ich muss dich jetzt einfach anrufen«, sagte Rebecca.

Das fand ich schön, dass sie das gedacht hatte, und deshalb erwiderte ich:

»Schön, dass du das gedacht hast.«

»Ich muss dir nämlich einfach sagen, wie bewundernswert ich es finde, dass du dich diesem ... heiklen und ... sicher auch schwierigen Thema gestellt hast, ich meine, dem Thema Alkohol …«

»Das Thema hat sich eigentlich eher mir gestellt«, unterbrach ich sie kurz.

»Dass du das alles einmal offen aussprichst.«

»Was?«

»Die Gefahren, den Schaden, die Sucht, was Alkohol aus einem Menschen machen kann, du weißt schon«, sagte sie.

»Ah so, ja, klar.«

»Und dieser Doktor, der Arzt, den du interviewt hast, wie heißt er?«

»Uland.«

»Genau, dieser Doktor Uland, das ist ein kluger Mann, der bringt das ja wirklich exakt auf den Punkt.«

»Ja, der ist irre klug«, sagte ich. Ein richtig irrer Klugscheißer sozusagen. Also das mit der Menschenkenntnis hatte Rebecca leider nicht so gut drauf.

»Jedenfalls wollte ich dir sagen, dass ich das ganz toll von dir finde, dass du … dass du jetzt … dass du daran arbeiten willst.«

»Danke«, sagte ich, wobei offenblieb, woran genau ich arbeiten wollte, Hauptsache, das Thema war beendet.

»Und sonst?«, fragte ich.

»Sonst? Ach, sonst gibt es nicht viel Neues bei mir.«

»Hast du meine Mail bekommen?«, fragte ich und wunderte mich gleichzeitig, wie jemand etwas derart Blödsinniges fragen konnte.

»Ja, Gerold, die Mail habe ich natürlich bekommen. Sooooo lieb! Danke, danke. Ich wollte dir ohnehin schon zurückschreiben, aber …«

»Na ja, jetzt telefonieren wir ja.«

»Ja, genau«, sagte sie. Danach entstand eine Pause, in der wir vermutlich beide nachdachten, worüber wir noch telefonieren konnten, wenn wir schon einmal telefonierten.

»Wir wäre es eigentlich wieder einmal mit einem Treffen?«, fragte dann leider doch wieder einmal ich.

»Ja, unbedingt, das machen wir«, sagte sie, relativ aufgeregt, zumindest bemühte sie sich, dass es so klang. »Zu Weihnachten bin ich bei meinen Eltern in Salzburg, aber gleich danach«, schloss sie feurig an.

»Ja, gleich nach Weihnachten ist gut.«

»Schön«, sagte sie.

»Ja, sehr«, bestätigte ich.

»Also dann, auf bald«, sagte sie.

»Ja, auf gleich nach Weihnachten gewissermaßen.«

»Ja, ich melde mich«, sagte sie.

»Ich mich auch«, erwiderte ich. Nur zur Sicherheit.

Eine kleine familiäre Weihnachtsjause

Am Abend erhielt ich dann den dritten Frauen-Anruf in Serie, mit diesem hier hätte ich am allerwenigsten gerechnet. Es war Alice, live aus Mogadischu. Wenn man im tiefsten Winter quasi mit Afrika telefonierte, musste man sich natürlich zunächst einmal ausführlich über Gluthitze versus Schneegestöber austauschen. Danach kamen wir bald auf Manuel zu sprechen.

»Geri, ich bin dir so dankbar, und ich bin so glücklich, wie super du das alles hingekriegt hast mit ihm und dass du dich so sehr um ihn kümmerst«, sagte sie ergriffen, sofern es nicht irgendwelche Dritte-Welt-Handymasten waren, die ihre Stimme derart zum Zittern brachten.

»Nichts zu danken. Eigentlich kümmert ja eher er sich um mich«, erwiderte ich.

»Er ist jedenfalls komplett vernarrt in dich, und er sagt, dass das bestimmt die aufregendsten Monate seines Lebens sind.

Mit dem Buben ist dir wirklich was Großes gelungen, Geri«, sagte sie.

»Dir auch«, erwiderte ich. Meine Bescheidenheit war aber diesmal nicht ganz echt. Denn am liebsten hätte ich Alice gebeten, den Satz mit dem Großen, das mir gelungen war, noch einmal wortwörtlich zu wiederholen, und zwar ganz langsam und zum Mitschreiben. Ich konnte mich nämlich nicht erinnern, dass etwas ähnlich Erfreuliches über mich schon einmal behauptet worden war, noch dazu von einem anderen Kontinent aus.

»Du weißt ja, dass wir ... dass ich in ein paar Tagen nach Wien komme, über Weihnachten. Ich und ... äh ... Jochen. Julia wird dir davon erzählt haben.«

»Ja, Julia hat mir davon erzählt, Julia und Manuel auch.«

»Und da wollte ich dich einfach fragen, also Jochen und ich wollen dich fragen, ob du vielleicht Zeit und Lust hast, am ersten Weihnachtsfeiertag, falls du nicht schon verplant bist, am Nachmittag zu uns zu kommen, zu einer kleinen familiären Weihnachtsjause.«

»Zu einer kleinen familiären Weihnachtsjause?« Dieses Angebot traf mich extrem unvorbereitet und erzeugte spontan sogar eine Art Weihnachtsgänsehaut. Ich war nämlich schon Ewigkeiten zu keiner kleinen familiären Weihnachtsjause mehr eingeladen gewesen, das letzte Mal, als ich schätzungsweise acht Jahre alt war.

»Ja, das wäre schön. Das wünscht sich nämlich Manuel.«

»Das wünscht sich Manuel?« Meine Weihnachtsgänsehaut begann sich jetzt auch noch kräftig zu erwärmen.

»Ja. Und dann lernst du auch gleich Jochen kennen.« Jetzt kühlte sie sich wieder ein bisschen ab. »Ihr werdet euch mögen, das weiß ich«, sagte sie.

»Ja, glaubst du?« Ich musste unweigerlich an Doktor Uland denken.

»Bestimmt. Also willst du kommen? Das wäre eine tolle Überraschung für Manuel.«

»Wenn es eine Überraschung für Manuel ist, dann denke ich gar nicht lange nach und sage natürlich sofort bitte, danke, gerne, ich komme«, erwiderte ich.

»Ja? Sehr fein, Geri.«

»Sehr fein, finde ich auch«, sagte ich.

»Also dann bis Sonntag.«

»Ja, bis Sonntag.«

»Wenn ich in Wien bin, ruf ich dich noch einmal an, wegen der Uhrzeit.«

»Ja richtig, die Uhrzeit«, sagte ich. In Europa hatte man Uhren, in Afrika hatte man Zeit, fiel mir dazu spontan ein. Keine Ahnung, woher der Spruch stammte, aber ich fand ihn irgendwie gut.

Danach saß ich ungefähr eine Stunde vor der ersten noch ungeöffneten Bierflasche, ehe ich sie zurück in den Kühlschrank stellte und mir die zweite holte. Ich hatte plötzlich das Gefühl, dass das Schicksal es momentan extrem gut mit mir meinen musste. Sofern das Schicksal überhaupt eine eigene Meinung über mich hatte.

Rendezvous mit dem Wohltäter

Mein Glückslauf setzte sich am Mittwochvormittag fort. Dabei hatte ich die Hoffnung auf eine positive Reaktion des anonymen Wohltäters auf meine Anfrage bereits aufgegeben, und das war auch gut so, denn oft traten die Dinge bei mir genau dann ein, wenn ich sie im Geiste abgehakt hatte.

In meinem Postfach war soeben die kurze und bündige Nachricht eingetroffen:

Herr plassek, also meinetwegen, treffen wir uns am samstag am späten abend in wien in einem lokal.

Samstag war der 24. Dezember. Sofern es sich bei ihm nicht um Santa Claus höchstpersönlich handelte, war er also entweder frauenlos oder familienlos oder zumindest kinderfrei. Da auch ich nicht der Typ war, der am Heiligen Abend Gefahr lief, in unmittelbarer Nähe eines festlich geschmückten Weihnachtsbaumes zu stehen und im internen *Stille-Nacht*-Karaoke anzutreten, erwiderte ich: *Okay, passt. Und in welchem Lokal? Haben Sie einen Wunsch? Ein Lieblingslokal?*

Die Antwort ließ nicht lange auf sich warten:

Das können sie aussuchen. Wo sie gerne hingehen.

Wo ich gerne hinging? Ob das wirklich so eine gute Idee war? Jedenfalls wusste ich, dass das Lokal auch am 24. Dezember abends geöffnet hatte und trotzdem kein Bordell war. Also schrieb ich: *Mein Stammlokal heißt Zoltan's Bar. Aber ich weiß nicht, ob ich Sie dort wirklich hinschicken kann. Es handelt sich eher um so eine richtig urige Wirtsstube, in der der Alkohol in Strömen fließt, was vielleicht nicht so Ihr Ding ist, wegen 0,0 Promille und so weiter. Wir können uns gerne auch woanders treffen.*

Keine fünf Minuten später kam die Antwort: *Einverstanden. Nehmen wir dieses lokal.*

Ich bedankte mich und erhielt noch eine letzte kurze Mitteilung: *Aber ich werde sie nicht ansprechen. Das müssen schon sie tun, herr plassek!*

Und ich erwiderte: *Ich glaube nicht, dass das ein Problem sein wird. Ich werde Sie schon erkennen, da bin ich mir sicher! Schönen Tag noch, G. P.*

KAPITEL ZWANZIG

Das barmherzige Weihnachtsvirus

Am Donnerstag, den 22. Dezember, kamen bei 0,0 Promille sozusagen programmgemäß die vermutlich letzten zehntausend Euro Spendengeld an. Im Umschlag befand sich außerdem der Zeitungsausschnitt meiner aktuellen *Neuzeit*-Reportage, wie mir Peter Seibernigg brühwarm und unermüdlich hocherfreut mitteilte.

Kein Geringerer als Doktor »oo« Uland schrieb mir dazu eine sogar einigermaßen herzliche Dankes-Mail. Am Ende konnte er sich freilich die Bemerkung nicht verkneifen, dass ich mich jederzeit gerne an ihn wenden durfte, wenn ich einmal persönlich »eine Frage hätte«, er würde mir mit Rat und Tat zur Seite stehen. Am liebsten hätte ich mich gleich dafür bedankt und geschrieben: Ich komme gerne auf Ihr Angebot zurück und frage Sie, welche selbstbräunende Gesichtscreme Sie mir empfehlen würden.

Aber ich ließ es und widmete mich lieber den Unmengen an Post, die mir Angelina weitergeleitet hatte. Offenbar waren sämtliche Elfeinhalbmonats-Ignoranten zu Weihnachten plötzlich wild entschlossen, ihr soziales Gewissen zu entdecken. Medial aufgestachelt, verspürte man jedenfalls landesweit das dringende Bedürfnis, etwas Gutes zu tun oder zumindest das Gute anderer gutzuheißen. Weil man dabei an das große zeitgenössische Vorbild, den anonymen Wohltäter, nicht herankam, war ich quasi die auserkorene erste Adresse, bei der man seine komplette saisonal begrenzte Großherzigkeit abladen konnte. Da ich ein eher labil geschichteter Mensch war, wurde ich relativ bald selbst vom barmherzigen Weihnachtsvirus ergriffen und kippte in eine Stimmungslage, in der religiösere Personen in Erwägung zogen, sich zur Papstwahl zu stellen, in die Fußstapfen von Gandhi zu treten, oder – für Besitzer kleinerer Füße – wenigstens den Jakobsweg zu beschreiten.

Für die Anfrage einer Leserin musste ich schließlich mein Google-Lexikon bemühen, und dabei machte ich eine überraschende Entdeckung. Im Suchverlauf bildete sich gleich auf den ersten Blick ein massiver inhaltlicher Schwerpunkt namens Kuba heraus: *Kuba Reisezeit*, *Kuba Klima*, *Kuba Wetter Februar*, *Kuba Essen*, *Kuba Preise*, *Kuba Land und Leute*, *Kuba Sehenswürdigkeiten*, *Kuba Tourismus*, *Kuba Unterkünfte*, *Kuba Kultur Musik* und mehrere weitere Kuba-Kombinationen.

Da ich selbst Kuba niemals in den Computer eingegeben hatte, weil ich mir über Kuba ehrlich gestanden noch keine Gedanken gemacht hatte, weil Kuba für mich in einer Zukunft angesiedelt war, die mir noch immer irreal fern erschien, konnte es nur Manuel gewesen sein.

Als er von der Schule kam, wollte ich ihn darauf ansprechen. Ich hatte die Frage praktisch bereits auf der Zunge, holte sie mir aber klugerweise noch einmal ins Gehirn zurück und erkannte plötzlich, dass ich sie mir eigentlich komplett sparen und Manuel damit verschonen konnte. Sie hätte gelautet: »Warum interessierst du dich so sehr für Kuba?« Die Antwort konnte ich mir nämlich gleich selbst geben: »Warum wohl?« Oder in Manuels Jargon: »Warum sollte ich mich nicht so sehr für Kuba interessieren?«

Gudrun in der Kuba-Krise

In der Nacht plagte mich eine Art schlechtes Gewissen. Erstens hatte ich am Vorabend vergessen, ein Bier weniger zu trinken. Nein, ich hatte es nicht vergessen, sondern ich hatte einfach keine Lust gehabt, mich daran zu erinnern. Zweitens war ich im Grunde ein doppelt mieser Vater, weil ich weder für Florentina noch für Manuel ein Weihnachtsgeschenk besorgt hatte – das Besorgen von Weihnachtsgeschenken hatte bei mir eben absolut keine Tradition, weil jahrelang kein Mensch ein Weihnachtsgeschenk von mir erwartet hatte, und das natürlich völlig zu Recht. Aber mitten in der Nacht spürte ich plötzlich, dass es in diesem Jahr so weit war, dass ich sozusagen reif für Weihnachtsgeschenke an meine Kinder war, wobei das Problem darin bestand, dass ich es sozusagen zum letztmöglichen Zeitpunkt spürte.

In der Früh kam mir dann eine wirklich grandiose Idee, es war wahrscheinlich die grandioseste dieses Jahres, in den Medien hätte man vermutlich sogar von einer Jahrhundertidee gesprochen, analog zum Jahrhunderthochwasser, das sich nur alle paar Jahre ereignete. Die Idee war zwar in der Umsetzung mit einigen Schwierigkeiten verbunden, aber die ersten Hürden nahm ich relativ souverän: Ich ging zur Bank, wo man mich von Mal zu Mal freundlicher begrüßte und wo neuerdings tatsächlich Geld auf mich wartete, welches in diesem Fall locker ausreichte, um meine grandiose Idee mit Leben zu füllen. Alsdann begab ich mich in das Reisebüro Winter, an dem ich bestimmt schon tausendmal vorbeigegangen war und mir jedes Mal die Frage gestellt hatte, ob Winter wirklich ein guter Name für ein Reisebüro war, oder ob es vielleicht irgendwo noch eine rettende zweite Filiale gab, die Reisebüro Sommer hieß, wobei man, wenn es gut liefe, sogar einmal in Richtung Frühling oder Herbst würde expandieren können.

Jedenfalls ging im Büro Winter alles reibungslos über die Bühne, sodass ich nun bei Gudrun anrufen konnte, um ihr den für sie relevanten Teil meiner Jahrhundertidee schonungslos darzulegen:

»Ich hab ein tolles Weihnachtsgeschenk für Florentina«,
sagte ich.

»Du? Ein Weihnachtsgeschenk?

»Ja, für Florentina.«

»Und zwar?«, fragte Gudrun.

»Und zwar fliege ich mit ihr zwei Wochen nach Kuba.«

»Was? Du fliegst? Mit deiner Flugangst?«

»Ja. Nach Kuba. Mit Florentina. Zwei Wochen. Ich habe die
Tickets bereits in der Hand.« Es entstand eine der Wucht der
Neuigkeit angemessene kognitive Einsickerungspause.

»Kein Witz?«, fragte sie.

»Kein Witz.«

»Wahnsinn«, sagte sie.

»Ja.«

»Und wann? Im Sommer?«

»Im Winter«, erwiderte ich.

»Nächsten Winter?«

»Diesen Winter.«

»Was? Jetzt, im Winter?«

»Ja, genau, in den Ferien, die ersten zwei Februarwochen.«

»Aber die Ferien dauern nur eine Woche«, sagte sie in dem
von mir gefürchteten Gudrun'schen Klageton, der quasi die
erste größere Hürde meiner Geschenkidee darstellte.

»Ja, ich weiß.«

»Geri, wie stellst du dir das vor?«

»Ich stelle mir das so vor, dass sie sich eine Woche schulfrei
nimmt.«

»Geri, man kann sich nicht einfach schulfrei nehmen. Das
geht heute nicht mehr. Das kann sich Florentina auch gar
nicht leisten, bei ihren Noten.«

»Sie wird es sich leisten müssen«, sagte ich.

»Wieso?«

»Weil ich die Kuba-Tickets bereits gekauft habe.«

»Geri! Wie kannst du das machen?«, jammerte sie.

»Ich musste es tun. Es war mein dringlicher Wunsch. Und es ist ihr Geschenk. Es ist eigentlich sogar mein Geschenk, mein erstes richtiges Geschenk für sie und mich. Eine Kubareise mit ihrem Papa.« Ich konnte ihr ja schlecht sagen, dass mir Kuba relativ egal war, dass es aber für ihre Tochter höchste Zeit war, einmal aus ihrem Nest herauszukommen.

»Schön, aber nicht während der Schulzeit. Das ist verantwortungslos, das kann ich nicht zulassen.« Mit »verantwortungslos« meinte sie vermutlich eher mich persönlich, aber das würde ich ihr in diesem Leben auch nicht mehr ausreden können.

»Fünfzehn Jahre hast du mir vorgeworfen, dass ich nichts für mein Kind tue. Jetzt habe ich etwas getan, und jetzt wirfst du mir vor, dass ich etwas getan habe«, konterte ich. Die Aufregung war zwar eher künstlich, aber wirksam.

»Ach Geri«, sagte sie. Die Hürde war quasi so gut wie genommen.

»Ich regle das mit der Schule«, versprach ich.

»Was regelst du mit der Schule?«

»Ich rede mit ihrer Lehrerin.«

»Sie hat viele Lehrerinnen.«

»Mit der wichtigsten.«

»Ach Geri«, sagte sie.

Das perfekte Familienabenteuer

Am späten Nachmittag traf ich Florentina im Treiblos. Mein Vorschlag war das dem Anlass eher angemessene Café Mozart in der Argentinierstraße gewesen, aber ich hatte mich irgendwie nicht durchsetzen können. Sie sah zwar extrem zerknittert und abgerissen aus, ein bisschen so, als wäre sie soeben einem

Container der Altkleidersammlung entstiegen, und die Haare standen ihr in alle Richtungen, aber ihr Gesicht war relativ unbeschichtet und wirkte lebendiger als zuletzt, und die Augen waren erfreulich weit offen, fast schon »aufgeweckt«, was darauf hindeutete, dass sie wieder freie Sicht auf andere Dinge hatte, weil die Beziehung zu Mike, dem Schattengewächs, überwunden war.

»Ich hab ihn endgültig aus meinem Leben gestrichen«, sagte sie.

»Wie ist dir das gelungen?«, fragte ich.

»Ich bin draufgekommen, dass er der volle Loser ist.« Das gefiel mir, darüber wollte ich mehr hören.

»Wie bist du da draufgekommen?«, fragte ich weiter.

»Aleksa hat ihn sitzenlassen.«

»Aha. Und dann?«

»Nichts dann. Einer, den sogar Aleksa sitzenlässt, der muss der volle Loser sein«, sagte sie. Okay, das war zwar eher eine Milchmädchenrechnung, aber Hauptsache, sie wollte nichts mehr von ihm wissen.

Ich kam dann bald zur Sache, legte unsere beiden Flugtickets auf den Tisch und verkündete: »Frohe Weihnachten, die Reise ist durch, deine Mama hat sie bereits abgesegnet.« Sie schrie so laut auf, dass die Gläser beinahe Paso doble zu tanzen begannen. Dann beugte sie sich zu mir und schmuste mich minutenlang ab. Sogar ein paar Tränen liefen ihr über die Wangen. »Wir fliegen wirklich«, murmelte sie vor sich hin und ballte dabei die Fäuste.

»Natürlich, das haben wir doch ausgemacht«, sagte ich lässig.

»Schon, aber ich hab nicht gedacht, dass du das ernst meinst, dass es wirklich dazu kommt.«

»Ehrensache«, sagte ich, aber zugegebenermaßen hatte ich diese Art von Ehre soeben erst entdeckt. So, und nun stand ich mit meiner Jahrhundert-Geschenkidee praktisch vor der entscheidenden Hürde und nahm vorsichtig Anlauf. »Du, Florentina, hättest du was dagegen, wenn ... wenn wir ... wenn wir noch jemanden mitnehmen?«

»Nach Kuba?«

»Ja.«

»Wen?« Okay, klar, die Frage war berechtigt, darauf lief die gesamte Angelegenheit ja eigentlich hinaus.

»Manuel«, sagte ich.

»Manuel? Der Kleine, der bei dir Hausaufgaben macht?« In ihren grün-kupfer-bernstein-gelben Augen hatten sich winzige Solarzellen aktiviert.

»Ja, genau dieser Manuel.« Jetzt schmunzelte sie, sah mich dabei aber irgendwie ziemlich prüfend an.

»Aber wieso soll er mitkommen?«

»Ach, einfach so, weil er ein ... wirklich netter Bursche ist und weil er sich wahnsinnig freuen würde und weil das ... weil das sicher gut zusammenpasst, weil wir drei ein gutes ... ein gutes Reiseteam wären«, stotterte ich herum.

»Willst du mich mit ihm verkuppeln?«, fragte sie.

Verkuppeln? Was für ein absurder Gedanke, er war ja noch ein Kind und sie im Grunde ebenfalls. Jedenfalls musste ich sofort eine den schrillenden Alarmglocken angemessene Notbremsung einleiten und sagte: »Das schlag dir bitte am besten gleich für immer und ewig aus dem Kopf.«

»Warum?«, fragte sie, wobei mir ihr kokettes Lächeln gar nicht mehr kindlich, sondern so richtig unheimlich erwachsen und ausgefuchst vorkam.

»Weil ...«

»Ja?«

»Weil er dein Bruder ist.« Ich hatte es nicht vorgehabt, sie hatte mich vielmehr dazu gezwungen, aber jetzt war es wenigstens heraußen.

»Mein bitte was?«

»Dein Bruder.«

»Mein Bruder?«

»Dein Halbbruder.«

»Mein Halbbruder?«

»Mein Sohn.«

»Dein was?«

»Mein Sohn.«

»Nein.«

»Doch.«

»Du machst Witze.«

»Ich mache keine Witze.«

»Ich hab einen Halbbruder?

»Ja.«

»Nein.«

»Doch. Und zwar Manuel.«

»Manuel?«

So ging das noch eine Weile hin und her, bis sie langsam aus dem allergrößten Staunen herausgekommen war. Dann erzählte ich ihr die ganze Geschichte. Dazwischen kamen mir ein paarmal die Tränen, weil ich ein rührseliger Typ bin, was zur Folge hatte, dass Florentina ebenfalls die Tränen kamen, weil sie wiederum der Typ ist, der mitweinen muss, wenn jemand anderer weint, das hatte sie von mir.

Danach legte ich das dritte Kuba-Ticket auf den Tisch. Damit war das Familienabenteuer Plassek auf die Schiene beziehungsweise die Flugbahn gelegt. Und wir bestellten uns zwei Glühwein, einen mit und einen ohne Alkohol, um auf Florentinas Bruder anzustoßen.

Am Samstag wurde es relativ bald Abend, nicht nur, weil die Tage um diese Jahreszeit traditionsgemäß nicht lange brauchten, um alt zu werden. Ich war auch ziemlich beschäftigt. Am Vormittag räumte ich zum Beispiel meine Wohnung auf, zumindest sorgte ich gewissenhaft dafür, dass man wieder überall schön durchkam.

Zu Mittag wünschte ich Clara Nemez und der gesamten *Neuzeit* telefonisch Frohe Weihnachten, und wir besprachen die Details der mir gewidmeten internen Feier und meines offiziellen Jobantritts. Bei dieser Gelegenheit fragte ich sicherheitshalber nach, ob es für sie in Ordnung war, dass ich mir die ersten beiden Februarwochen freinahm.

»Drei Wochen Arbeit und danach zwei Wochen Urlaub? Du bist lustig«, sagte sie. Ich musste ihr jedenfalls hoch und heilig versprechen, dass es mit mir und der *Neuzeit* nicht in diesem Rhythmus weitergehen würde.

Am Nachmittag besuchte ich, wie praktisch immer am 24., meine Mama. Unsere Geschenke waren, abgesehen von Blumen, Kaffee und Kuchen, eher verbaler Natur, weil wir uns gegenseitig durchaus glaubhaft und ausdauernd versicherten, die beste Mutter beziehungsweise den besten Sohn erwischt zu haben, wobei dann jeder von uns selbstkritisch die Frage stellte, ob man es wirklich war. Also sie war es tatsächlich, bei mir war ich mir ehrlich gestanden nicht so sicher, aber wir konnten es uns ohnehin nicht aussuchen.

Als es finster wurde, begann ich überraschenderweise mit einer gewissen Nervosität zu kämpfen, was meine bevorstehende Begegnung mit Mister Wohltäter betraf. Der Mann hatte mich jetzt immerhin durchgehend vier Monate lang unterschwellig beschäftigt und dabei unabsichtlich sogar mein Leben neu strukturiert. Was mich besonders nervös machte:

Wir hatten für unser Treffen zwar den späten Abend anvisiert, aber vergessen, eine konkrete Uhrzeit zu vereinbaren. Und auf meine diesbezügliche Mail vom Vormittag hatte ich keine Antwort erhalten. Hoffentlich hatte er es sich nicht anders überlegt.

Gegen halb neun tauchte ich in Zoltan's Bar auf, das erschien mir für ein Blind Date am späten Heiligen Abend früh genug. Ich positionierte mich auf dem zum Glück noch unbesetzten Hocker am hinteren Ende der Theke, mit dem nicht zu spaßen war, weil ihm die Rückenlehne fehlte und er mich schon einige Male in den Morgenstunden brutal abgeworfen hatte. Von dort aus genoss man jedenfalls einen idealen Ausblick auf das gesamte Lokal.

Einige Weihnachtsverweigerer hatten bereits ihre Plätze bezogen. Von einer Tarock-Runde am Fenstertisch ging die vergleichsweise größte Dynamik aus, die meisten anderen wirkten eher lethargisch beziehungsweise besinnlich, um es weihnachtlich auszudrücken, und waren entweder in ein Gespräch oder in sich selbst versunken – oder in ihr Handy vertieft. Seit diese Geräte in Umlauf waren und gesellschaftlich den Ton und auch das Bild angaben, wirkten die Menschen ja sogar in der absoluten Einsamkeit und Leere noch immer irgendwie vollzeitbeschäftigt.

Ich konnte mich in meiner Wohltätersucher-Rolle jedenfalls ausschließlich auf alleinstehende oder -sitzende männliche Gäste konzentrieren, und da war keiner darunter, der wenigstens die Spur eines Anscheins erweckte, er könnte der große anonyme Wohltäter sein, wobei ich mir bald die Frage zu stellen begann, wie ich mir so jemanden tatsächlich vorzustellen hatte. Also er musste jetzt nicht unbedingt einen weißen Anzug mit schwarzer Krawatte und dunkler Sonnenbrille tragen und einen Sombrero oder eine Baskenmütze, aber auch wenn er mir schriftlich versichert hatte, absolut unauffällig zu sein, so rechnete ich instinktiv doch mit jemandem, der mir auf irgendeine Weise fremd, exotisch, nicht hierhergehörig erscheinen würde, und jene, die anwesend waren, gehörten allesamt eindeutig hierher und nirgendwo anders hin zu dieser Stunde.

»Frohe Weihnachten, Geri, schön, dich zu sehen, du hast heute Abend anscheinend auch nichts Besseres zu tun«, begrüßte mich Zoltan, der Chef des Hauses. Wir wechselten ein paar belanglose Worte, bei denen es mir meiner Meinung nach hervorragend gelang, zu vertuschen, dass ich hier auf jemanden wartete, ehe ich, mit deutlicher Verspätung, meine erste Bierbestellung aufgab, der dann zugegebenermaßen rasch eine zweite und dritte folgten. Ich musste nur aufpassen, dass ich rechtzeitig aufhörte, damit ich Manuel am nächsten Tag ausführlich über mein Erlebnis würde berichten können. Außerdem stand mir ja die erste Feier mit meiner durch Jochen bereicherten neuen Kleinfamilie samt Kuba-Bescherung für meinen Sohn ins Haus. Ich schlitterte derzeit sozusagen von einem Spektakel ins nächste.

Mein Blick war nun schon die längste Zeit schwerpunktmäßig auf den Eingang gerichtet, wobei ich natürlich entsprechend angespannt war, wann immer die Tür aufging, aber wenn die eintretende Person Gestalt annahm, schied sie praktisch sofort wieder aus, weil ihr das Besondere fehlte, das sie von allen anderen nicht anonymen Nichtwohltätern unterschieden hätte.

Bei einem einzigen Gast, einem Mann um die fünfzig mit Vollbart und Glatze, schöpfte ich kurz Verdacht, weil er lange Zeit suchend beim Eingang stand und herumschaute, als rechnete er damit, von jemandem angesprochen zu werden. Doch als ich auf ihn zuging und gerade unverbindlich guten Abend sagen wollte, drehte er sich um und verließ das Lokal.

Es fehlte nur noch eine knappe Stunde auf Mitternacht, als das Handy in meiner Hosentasche einmal kurz vibrierte. Die SMS war genau das richtige Mittel gegen meine rapide fortschreitende Müdigkeit, denn sie stammte von Rebecca und lautete:

Lieber Gerold, ich hoffe, du hattest einen schönen Weihnachtsabend. Bei mir war es im Kreise meiner Familie und meiner engsten Freunde in Salzburg sehr lustig, aber ich freue mich schon wieder auf Wien, wo wir beide uns dann hoffentlich bald sehen werden. Bis dahin noch angenehme Festtage, deine Rebecca.

Man konnte das jetzt so oder so interpretieren, ich war jedenfalls exakt in der richtigen Stimmung, davon auszugehen, dass es sich hierbei um eine verkappte Liebeserklärung oder zumindest um eine wilde weihnachtliche Sehnsuchtsattacke ihrerseits handelte. Und deshalb nahm ich mir vor, etwas besonders Inniges zu erwidern, sowie wir hier fertig waren.

Spenden macht unheimlich viel Spaß

Ab Mitternacht begann ich mich langsam damit abzufinden, dass mich Mister Wohltäter hier auf meinem ledernen Barhocker beinhart hatte sitzenlassen. Noch einmal ging ich alle Gesichter der anwesenden und teilweise bereits schwer illuminierten Gäste durch, die auch ich freilich nicht mehr extrem konturenscharf sah, aber es genügte, um zu erkennen, dass sich der von mir gesuchte Mann bestimmt nicht unter ihnen befand, so viel Menschenkenntnis besaß ich, selbst in etwas eingetrübtem Zustand.

Vielleicht hatte er mir ja bereits geschrieben und erklärt, warum er nicht hatte kommen können oder wollen. Also kramte ich wieder mein Handy hervor, öffnete die Mailbox – und hatte tatsächlich eine neue, erst vor wenigen Minuten gesendete Nachricht von ihm im Posteingang.

Herr plassek, tut mir leid, dass es nicht geklappt hat, ich habe aber damit gerechnet, und deshalb einen text vorbereitet, den ich ihnen jetzt schicke. Dann können sie ihrem sohn wenigstens ein bisschen etwas über den anonymen geldgeber sagen.

Ich bin ein normaler mensch, einer wie sie, herr plassek. Ich habe einen job, der zwar hart ist, aber der mir großen spaß macht. Leider bleibt momentan keine zeit für eine eigene familie, aber man kann nicht alles haben. Ich bin kein millionär, aber ich habe ersparnisse (gehabt), weil ich gar nicht dazu komme, mein geld auszugeben. Ich hab mir immer alles leisten können, was ich wollte, bei mir müssen es keine flugzeuge sein. Ich kaufe mir auch keine aktien oder goldbarren, so ein mensch bin ich nicht, ich bin kein dagobert duck. Für mich ist geld zum ausgeben da und nicht zum aufheben. Was ich für die zukunft brauche, werde ich wieder verdienen, da habe ich keine angst. So denke ich eben. Und sie werden das am besten verstehen, weil sie so ähnlich denken, das weiß ich.

Wie es dann im september zur ersten geldgabe von 10 000 euro an die obdachlosen gekommen ist, und sich alle gefreut haben, habe ich mir gedacht, das mache ich jetzt auch, das ist eine sinnvolle aktion, weil es eben viele gibt, die das geld wirklich dringend brauchen. Es war für mich spannend wie ein krimi, vielleicht mein größtes abenteuer überhaupt.

Und sie als person haben dabei für mich immer eine große rolle gespielt, ohne sie wäre das alles gar nicht so glatt abgelaufen. Wenn sie das ihrem buben so erzählen, dann freut es mich, aber sonst bitte niemandem. Versprochen?

Zum schluss sage ich ihnen auch noch, warum ich wollte, dass die letzte geldgabe den alkoholikern zugutekommt: Damit mein schlechtes gewissen beruhigt wird, und ein bisschen auch wegen ihnen, herr plassek, lieber geri. Frohe weihnachten.

»Und ein bisschen auch wegen Ihnen, Herr Plassek, lieber Geri.« In solchen Situationen wünschte man sich, dass man einen etwas kühleren oder, besser gesagt, klareren Kopf behalten hätte, aber wenn ich die Botschaft richtig verstanden hatte, dann musste mich der Mann wirklich ziemlich gut kennen, und seine Worte waren mir auf seltsame Weise doch irgendwie sehr vertraut. Außerdem wurde ich plötzlich den Verdacht nicht los, dass er an diesem Abend tatsächlich hier im Lokal gewesen war, weil er sonst nicht geschrieben hätte, dass er damit gerechnet hatte, dass es mit unserem Gespräch nicht klappen würde. Hatte er vielleicht stundenlang darauf gewartet, von mir angesprochen zu werden, und ich hatte ihn einfach übersehen?

Sperrstunde

Keine Ahnung, wie viele Biere ich noch bestellt und wie oft ich diese Mail in alle Richtungen zerpflückt und immer wieder neu gelesen hatte, jedenfalls verschwammen mir irgendwann die Buchstaben vor den Augen.

Mittlerweile hatten auch die letzten Stimmen den Gastraum verlassen, und ich hörte hinter mir nur noch das Rücken von Tischen und das Klirren von Gläsern, die weggeräumt wurden. Zoltan's Bar stand unmittelbar vor seiner gefürchteten Sperrstunde.

»Na Geri, schlägst du heute wieder einmal Wurzeln bei mir?«, fragte der Chef und stellte uns beiden je einen Schnaps zur Verabschiedung auf die Theke.

»Entschuldige, aber ich habe auf jemanden gewartet.« Die Erklärung brachte ich relativ problemlos über die Lippen, obwohl »entschuldige« wirklich ein extrem schwieriges Wort für diese Uhrzeit war.

»Und?«

»Er ist nicht gekommen.«

»Sieht ganz danach aus«, sagte er.

»Oder er ist da gewesen, und ich hab ihn nicht erkannt.«

»Aha«, sagte er. Danach vergingen ein paar Minuten oder Sekunden. »Wer soll es denn gewesen sein?«

»Das ... darf ich leider nicht verraten«, erwiderte ich.

»Ah so.«

»Ich hab es ihm nämlich versprochen.«

»Aha.« Zoltan war noch nie ein Mann vieler Worte gewesen.

»Ich darf es nur meinem Sohn Manuel sagen.«

»Schön«, erwiderte er.

»Aber weißt du, was das Problem ist, Zoltan?«

»Nein.«

»Ich kann es ihm gar nicht sagen, denn ich weiß es nicht.«

»Aha.« Es entstand eine Pause, die ich dazu nutzte, ein paar abschließende Gedankenrunden zu drehen. Außerdem beschloss ich, dass das hier bis auf weiteres mein letzter Rausch war, und zwar wirklich mein allerletzter, das war ich Manuel schuldig, Manuel und Florentina und Rebecca und wie sie alle hießen.

»Zoltan?«, fragte ich.

»Ja, Geri?«

»Geht noch ein Schnaps?«

»Geri, ich glaube, es genügt. Ich sperre dann wirklich zu.«

»Wenn ich noch einen Schnaps kriege, verrate ich dir, verrate ich dir ...«

»Was verrätst du mir?

»Dann verrate ich dir, auf wen ich gewartet habe.«

»Aber wirklich der letzte für heute«, erwiderte er streng.

»Willst du es wissen?«

»Muss nicht sein, Geri.«

»Ich sag es dir trotzdem, nur damit du es weißt.«

»Okay.«

»Ich habe auf den anonymen Wohltäter gewartet.«

»Aha.«

»Auf den Wohltäter, weißt du, wen ich meine, Zoltan?«

»Diesen anonymen Geldgeber?«

»Geldgeber, richtig, das hat er auch immer geschrieben.«

»Tatsächlich?«, fragte Zoltan.

»Ja, tatsächlich, Geldgeber, das war praktisch genau sein Wort, alle anderen sagen Wohltäter, aber er sagt Geldgeber, wie du.«

»So ein Zufall«, sagte Zoltan.

»Ja«, bestätigte ich.

»Das kannst du morgen deinem Buben erzählen«, meinte er.

»Ja, das erzähle ich Manuel.«

»Wenn du dich noch daran erinnerst.«

»Doch, ich erinnere mich, ganz bestimmt.«

ENDE